CRITICAL PRAISE FOR JOSE...

Comp...

"At long last someone has done for exec......................did for lawyers: create fictional ones sufficiently three-dimensional to care about. . . . The book doesn't slow down for a second."
—*Fortune*

"Compelling . . . *Company Man* confirms what *Paranoia* made clear: [Finder] has unusually keen instincts for backstabbing in the business world. . . . As much a novel about the chicanery of the business world as it is a mystery story . . . Finder weaves these prospects menacingly throughout the story."
—*The New York Times*

"Sharply created characters. . . . Makes the workplaces as duplicitous a world as any in the Cold War. *Company Man* resonates with anyone who has seen corporate politics at its worst."
—*Orlando Sun-Sentinel*

"Finder skillfully places his story of corporate intrigue (who is trying to sell the company, and why?) in counterpoint to the unraveling of a family's secrets (why is Nick's son Lucas so disturbed?), and the plot, which also features rogue cops and at least one homicide, accelerates to a headlong finish." —*The New Yorker*

"It's everything a thriller should be: suspenseful, entertaining—and, above all, thrilling."
—*Chicago Sun-Times*

"Finder expertly keeps the pages turning as he ups the stakes chapter after chapter in Conover's professional and personal life. He is equally confident in portraying the small stuff involving family conflicts, marriages in turmoil, and especially the telling details of corporate life. . . . It more than achieves its main goal of entertaining the reader—as a good thriller is supposed to do."
—*The Baltimore Sun*

"Once again, Finder has produced a page-turning corporate thriller with enough twists and turns for any reader."
—*The Denver Post*

"Not only fast-paced excitement but also sympathetic characters with authentic back stories and realistic situations. Highly recommended."
—*Library Journal* (starred review)

"Finder has become a master of the modern thriller. There are twists and deceptions packed in here. . . . Once again, Finder has managed to update the claustrophobic thriller into something that resonates with our times. . . . Joseph Finder has secured his niche as a master of the contemporary corporate thriller, a smart plotter in touch with our new century's soft spots." —*Boston Globe*

"Propulsive . . . should cement Finder's reputation as a reliable chronicler of the perils lurking in e-mail and the executive suite." —*Entertainment Weekly*

"A solid, engrossing thriller . . . the novel's pacing is strong, with steady suspense. . . . There are few thriller fans who won't stay up to finish this assured tale." —*Publishers Weekly*

"Finder expertly doles out the suspense and comes up with a climactic twist. . . . A highly efficient thriller combining state-of-the-art corporate malfeasance with the old-fashioned kind." —*Kirkus Reviews*

"The business thriller is rejuvenated by Joseph Finder with *Company Man*. That's because Finder puts the emphasis on sharply created characters instead of potentially eye-glazing business minutiae." —*Chicago Tribune*

Paranoia

"The most entertaining thriller of the year." —*Publishers Weekly*

"Jet-propelled. . . . This twisting, stealthily plotted story . . . weaves a tangled and ingeniously enveloping web . . . [with a] killer twist for the end."
—*The New York Times*

"Last year brought Dan Brown's *The Da Vinci Code* . . . this year's first contender for Page Turner of the Year is Joseph Finder's *Paranoia*." —*USA Today*

"Riveting. . . . Perhaps the finest of the contemporary thriller novelists, Finder is reminiscent of Michael Crichton, only with more character development and less slavish attention to detail. . . . In the case of *Paranoia*, he's an expert on suspenseful storytelling that is at once slick and substantive. . . . You may think you've read one mystery too many. Find Finder and you'll think again."
—*Pittsburgh Post-Gazette*

"Kudos to Joseph Finder. . . . In Finder's lively prose, even his thumbnail sketches come alive. . . . It may go without saying that in a thriller of this quality, just about everyone has a story that's other than it first appears. What sets *Paranoia* apart from others of its genre is not only Finder's fun, chatty pose, but also his command of the setting. A former Sovietologist, the author knows his spy stuff—

and has researched well the ins and outs of post-Enron corporate security. . . .
In a way, it's an intellectual puzzle that he has shaped into a thriller."
—*The Boston Globe*

"Combining nail-biting suspense with state-of-the-art technology, it's sure to
become one of the hotter books this year. . . . Finder excels in keeping the reader
guessing until the last sentence, literally."　　　　—*Dallas Morning News*

"*Paranoia* is a cleverly nuanced suspense story. It builds slowly and relentlessly,
developing character and plot, creating intrigue. . . . Fresh, original, and without cliché, this is a cerebral, contemporary thriller that ends with a wrenching
twist followed by a supple extra turn."　　　　　　—*Boston Herald*

"Page-turning perfection . . . dead-on dialogue . . . palpable tension. . . . Finder
has that rare knack for instantly pulling the reader into the story and then tops
that with surprises within surprises."　　　　　—*Cleveland Plain Dealer*

"Terrific . . . riveting. . . . Practically redefines the high-stakes, high-tech thriller.
It's the best novel of its kind since Michael Crichton's *Disclosure*."
—*Providence Journal-Bulletin*

"A terrific thriller . . . expertly paced and full of suspense and surprises."
—*San Jose Mercury News*

ALSO BY JOSEPH FINDER

FICTION

The Moscow Club

Extraordinary Powers

The Zero Hour

High Crimes

Killer Instinct

NONFICTION

*Red Carpet: The Connection Between the Kremlin
and America's Most Powerful Businessmen*

JOSEPH FINDER

PARANOIA

COMPANY MAN

St. Martin's Griffin
New York

www.stmartins.com

ISBN-13: 978-0-312-36688-9
ISBN-10: 0-312-36688-4

Paranoia was originally published by St. Martin's Press in 2004.

Company Man was originally published by St. Martin's Press in 2005.

First St. Martin's Griffin Edition: September 2006

10 9 8 7 6 5 4 3 2 1

PARANOIA

*This one's for Henry: brother and consigliere
and, as always, for the two girls in my life:
my wife, Michele, and my daughter, Emma.*

PART ONE

THE FIX

Fix: A CIA term, of Cold War origin, that refers to a person who is to be compromised or blackmailed so that he will do the Agency's bidding.

—*The Dictionary of Espionage*

1

Until the whole thing happened, I never believed the old line about how you should be careful what you wish for, because you might get it.

I believe it now.

I believe in all those cautionary proverbs now. I believe that pride goeth before a fall. I believe the apple doesn't fall far from the tree, that misfortune seldom comes alone, that all that glitters isn't gold, that lies walk on short legs. Man, you name it. I believe it.

I could try to tell you that what started it all was an act of generosity, but that wouldn't be quite accurate. It was more like an act of stupidity. Call it a cry for help. Maybe more like a raised middle finger. Whatever, it was my bad. I half thought I'd get away with it, half expected to be fired. I've got to say, when I look back on how it all began, I marvel at what an arrogant prick I was. I'm not going to deny that I got what I deserved. It just wasn't what I expected—but who'd ever expect something like this?

All I did was make a couple of phone calls. Impersonated the VP for Corporate Events and called the fancy outside caterer that did all of Wyatt Telecom's parties. I told them to just make it exactly like the bash they'd done the week before for the Top Salesman of the Year award. (Of course, I had no idea how lavish that was.) I gave them all the right disbursement numbers, authorized the transfer of funds in advance. The whole thing was surprisingly easy.

The owner of Meals of Splendor told me he'd never done a function on a company loading dock, that it presented "décor challenges," but I knew he wasn't going to turn away a big check from Wyatt Telecom.

Somehow I doubt Meals of Splendor had ever done a retirement party for an assistant foreman either.

I think that's what really pissed Wyatt off. Paying for Jonesie's retirement party—a *loading dock guy, for Christ's sake!*—was a violation of the natural order. If instead I'd used the money as a down payment on a Ferrari 360 Modena convertible, Nicholas Wyatt might have almost understood. He would have recognized my greed as evidence of our shared humanity, like a weakness for booze, or "broads," as he called women.

If I'd known how it would all end up, would I have done it all over again? Hell, no.

Still, I have to say, it was pretty cool. I was into the fact that Jonesie's party was being paid for out of a fund earmarked for, among other things, an "offsite" for the CEO and his senior vice presidents at the Guanahani resort on the island of St. Barthélemy.

I also loved seeing the loading dock guys finally getting a taste of how the execs lived. Most of the guys and their wives, whose idea of a splurge was the Shrimp Feast at the Red Lobster or Ribs On The Barbie at Outback Steakhouse, didn't know what to make of some of the weird food, the osetra caviar and saddle of veal Provençal, but they devoured the filet of beef en croûte, the rack of lamb, the roasted lobster with ravioli. The ice sculptures were a big hit. The Dom Perignon flowed, though not as fast as the Budweiser. (This I called right, since I used to hang out on the loading dock on Friday afternoons, smoking, when someone, usually Jonesie or Jimmy Connolly, the foreman, brought in an Igloo of cold ones to celebrate the end of another week.)

Jonesie, an old guy with one of those weathered, hangdog faces that make people like him instantly, was lit the whole night. His wife of forty-two years, Esther, at first seemed standoffish, but she turned out to be an amazing dancer. I'd hired an excellent Jamaican reggae group, and everyone got into it, even the guys you'd never expect to dance.

This was after the big tech meltdown, of course, and companies everywhere were laying people off and instituting "frugality" policies, meaning you had to pay for the lousy coffee, and no more free Cokes in the break room, and like that. Jonesie was slated to just stop work one Friday, spend a few hours at HR signing forms, and go home for the rest of his life, no party, no nothing. Meanwhile, the Wyatt Telecom E-staff was planning to head down to St. Bart's in their Learjets, boink their wives or girlfriends in their private villas, slather coconut oil on their love handles, and discuss company-wide frugality policies over obscene buffet breakfasts of papayas and hummingbird tongues. Jonesie and his friends didn't really question too closely who was paying for it all. But it did give me some kind of twisted secret pleasure.

Until around one-thirty in the morning, when the sound of electric guitars and the screams of a couple of the younger guys, blotto out of their minds, must have attracted the curiosity of a security guard, a fairly new hire (the pay's lousy, turnover is unbelievable) who didn't know any of us and wasn't inclined to cut anyone any slack.

He was a pudgy guy with a flushed, sort of Porky Pig face, barely thirty. He just gripped his walkie-talkie as if it were a Glock and said, "What the hell?"

And my life as I knew it was over.

2

The voice mail was waiting for me when I got in to work, late as usual.

Even later than usual, actually. I felt queasy and my head thudded and my heart was going too fast from the giant cup of cheap coffee I'd gulped down on the subway. A wave of acid splashed over my stomach. I'd considered calling in sick, but that little voice of sanity in my head told me that after the events of last night the wiser thing to do was to show up at work and face the music.

Thing is, I fully expected to get fired—almost looked forward to it, the way you might both dread and look forward to having an aching tooth drilled. When I came out of the elevator and walked the half-mile through the lower forty of the cubicle farm to my workstation, I could see heads popping up, prairie-dog style, to catch a glimpse of me. I was a celebrity; the word was out. E-mail was no doubt flying.

My eyes were bloodshot, my hair was a mess, I looked like a walking JUST SAY NO public service spot.

The little LCD screen display on my IP phone said, "You have eleven voice mails." I put it on speaker and zipped through them. Just listening to the messages, frantic and sincere and wheedling, increased the pressure behind my eyeballs. I got out the Advil bottle from the bottom desk drawer and dry-swallowed two. That made six Advils already this morning, which exceeded the recommended maximum. So what could happen to me? Die from an ibuprofen overdose just moments before being fired?

I was a junior product line manager for routers in our Enterprise Division. You don't want the English translation, it's too mind-numbingly boring. I spent my days hearing phrases like "dynamic bandwidth circuit emulation service" and "integrated access device" and "ATM backbones" and "IP security tunneling protocol," and I swear I didn't know what half the shit meant.

A message from a guy in Sales named Griffin, calling me "big guy," boasting of how he'd just sold a couple dozen of the routers I was managing by assuring the customer that they'd have a particular feature—extra multicast protocols for live video streaming—that he knew damned well it didn't have. But it sure would be nice if the feature was added to the product, like maybe in the next two weeks, before the product was supposed to ship. Yeah, dream on.

A follow-up call five minutes later from Griffin's manager just "checking on the progress of the multicast protocol work we heard you're doing," as if I actually did the technical work myself.

And the clipped, important voice of a man named Arnold Meacham, who identified himself as Director of Corporate Security and asked me to please "come by" his office the moment I got in.

I had no idea who Arnold Meacham was, beyond his title. I'd never heard his name before. I didn't even know where Corporate Security was located.

It's funny: when I heard the message, my heart didn't start racing like you might expect. It actually slowed, as if my body knew the gig was up. There was actually something Zen going on, the inner serenity of realizing there's nothing you can do anyway. I almost luxuriated in the moment.

For a few minutes I stared at my cubicle walls, the nubby charcoal Avora fabric that looked like the wall-to-wall in my dad's apartment. I kept the panel walls free of any evidence of human habitation—no photos of the wife and kids (easy, since I didn't have any), no Dilbert cartoons, nothing clever or ironic that said I was here under protest, because I was way beyond that. I had one bookshelf, holding a routing protocol reference guide and four thick black binders containing the "feature library" for the MG-50K router. I would not miss this cubicle.

Besides, it wasn't like I was about to get shot; I'd *already* been shot, I figured. Now it was just a matter of disposing of the body and swabbing up the blood. I remember once in college reading about the guillotine in French history, and how one executioner, a medical doctor, tried this gruesome experiment (you get your kicks wherever you can, I guess). A few seconds after the head was lopped off he watched the eyes and lips twitch and spasm until the eyelids closed and everything stopped. Then he called out the dead man's name, and the eyes on the decapitated head popped open and stared right at the executioner. A few seconds more and the eyes closed, then the doctor called the man's name again, and the eyes came open again, staring. Cute. So thirty seconds after being separated from the body, the head's still reacting. This was how I felt. The blade had already dropped, and they're calling my name.

I picked up the phone and called Arnold Meacham's office, told his assistant that I was on my way, and asked how to get there.

My throat was dry, so I stopped at the break room to get one of the formerly-free-but-now-fifty-cent sodas. The break room was all the way back in the middle of the floor near the bank of elevators, and as I walked, in a weird sort of fugue state, a couple more colleagues caught sight of me and turned away quickly, embarrassed.

I surveyed the sweaty glass case of sodas, decided against my usual Diet Pepsi—I really didn't need more caffeine right now—and pulled out a Sprite. Just to be a rebel I didn't leave any money in the jar. Whoa, that'll show *them*. I popped it open and headed for the elevator.

I hated my job, truly despised it, so the thought of losing it wasn't exactly bumming me out. On the other hand, it wasn't as if I had a trust fund, and I sure did need the money. That was the whole point, wasn't it? I had moved back here essentially to help with my dad's medical care—my dad, who considered me a fuckup. In Manhattan, bartending, I made half the money but lived better. We're talking Manhattan! Here I was living in a ratty street-level studio apartment on Pearl Street that reeked of traffic exhaust, and whose windows rattled when the trucks rumbled by at five in the morning. Granted, I was able to go out a couple of nights a week with friends, but I usually ended up dipping into my checking account's credit line a week or so before my paycheck magically appeared on the fifteenth of the month.

Not that I was exactly busting my ass either. I coasted. I put in the minimum required hours, got in late and left early, but I got my work done. My performance review numbers weren't so good—I was a "core contributor," a two band, just one step up from "lowest contributor," when you should start packing your stuff.

I got into the elevator, looked down at what I was wearing—black jeans and a gray polo shirt, sneakers—and wished I'd put on a tie.

3

When you work at a big corporation, you never know what to believe. There's always a lot of tough, scary macho talk. They're always telling you about "killing the competition," putting a "stake in their heart." They tell you to "kill or be killed," "eat or be eaten," to "eat their lunch" and "eat your own dog food" and "eat your young."

You're a software engineer or a product manager or a sales associate, but after a while you start to think that somehow you got mixed up with one of those aboriginal tribes in Papua New Guinea that wear boar's tusks through their noses and gourds on their dicks. When the reality is that if you e-mail an off-color, politically incorrect joke to your buddy in IT, who then cc's it to a guy a few cubicles over, you can end up locked in a sweaty HR conference room for a grueling week of Diversity Training. Filch paper clips and you get slapped with the splintered ruler of life.

Thing is, of course, I'd done something a little more serious than raiding the office-supply cabinet.

They kept me waiting in an outer office for half an hour, forty-five minutes, but it seemed longer. There was nothing to read—just *Security Management*, stuff like that. The receptionist wore her ash-blond hair in a helmet, yellow smoker's circles under her eyes. She answered the phone, tapped away at a keyboard, glanced over at me furtively from time to time, the way you might try to catch a glimpse of a grisly car accident while you're trying to keep your eyes on the road.

I sat there so long my confidence began to waver. That might have been the point. The monthly paycheck thing was beginning to look like a good idea. Maybe defiance wasn't the best approach. Maybe I should eat shit. Maybe it was way past that.

Arnold Meacham didn't get up when the receptionist brought me in. He sat behind a giant black desk that looked like polished granite. He was around forty, thin and broad, a Gumby build, with a long square head, long thin nose, no lips. Graying brown hair that was receding. He wore a double-breasted blue blazer and a blue striped tie, like the president of a yacht club. He glared at me through oversized steel aviator glasses. You could tell he was totally humorless. In a chair to the right of his desk sat a woman a few years older than me who seemed to be taking notes. His office was big and spare, lots of framed diplomas on the wall. At one end, a half-opened door let onto a darkened conference room.

"So you're Adam Cassidy," he said. He had a prissy, precise way of speaking. "Party down, dude?" He pressed his lips into a smirk.

Oh, God. This was not going to go well. "What can I do for you?" I said. I tried to look perplexed, concerned.

"What can you *do* for me? How about start with telling the truth? *That's* what you can do for me." He had the slightest trace of a Southern accent.

Generally people like me. I'm pretty good at winning them over—the pissed-off math teacher, the enterprise customer whose order is six weeks overdue, you name it. But I could see at once this wasn't a Dale Carnegie moment. The odds of salvaging my odious job were dwindling by the second.

"Sure," I said. "The truth about what?"

He snorted with amusement. "How about last night's catered event?"

I paused, considered. "You're talking about the little retirement party?" I said. I didn't know how much they knew, since I'd been pretty careful about the money trail. I had to watch what I said. The woman with the notebook, a slight woman with frizzy red hair and big green eyes, was probably there as a witness. "It was a much-needed morale boost," I added. "Believe me, sir, it'll do wonders for departmental productivity."

His lipless mouth curled. " 'Morale boost.' Your fingerprints are all over the funding for that 'morale boost.' "

"Funding?"

"Oh, cut the crap, Cassidy."

"I'm not sure I'm understanding you, sir."

"Do you think I'm *stupid?*" Six feet of fake granite between him and me and I could feel droplets of his spittle.

"I'm guessing . . . no, sir." The trace of a smile appeared at the corner of my mouth. I couldn't help it: pride of workmanship. Big mistake.

Meacham's pasty face flushed. "You think it's funny, hacking into proprietary company databases to obtain confidential disbursement numbers? You think it's recreation, it's *clever?* It doesn't *count?*"

"No, sir—"

"You lying sack of shit, you *prick*, it's no better than stealing an old lady's purse on the fucking subway!"

I tried to look chastened, but I could see where this conversation was going and it seemed pointless.

"You stole *seventy-eight thousand dollars* from the Corporate Events account for a goddamned party for your buddies on the *loading dock?*"

I swallowed hard. Shit. Seventy-eight thousand dollars? I knew it was pretty high-end, but I had no idea how high-end.

"This guy in on it with you?"

"Who do you mean? I think maybe you're confused about—"

" 'Jonesie'? The old guy, the name on the cake?"

"Jonesie had nothing to do with it," I shot back.

Meacham leaned back, looking triumphant because he'd finally found a toehold.

"If you want to fire me, go ahead, but Jonesie was totally innocent."

"Fire you?" Meacham looked as if I'd said something in Serbo-Croatian. "You think I'm talking about *firing* you? You're a smart guy, you're good at computers and math, you can add, right? So maybe you can add up these numbers. Embezzling funds, that gets you five years of imprisonment and a two-hundred-fifty-thousand-dollar fine. Wire fraud and mail fraud, that's another five years in prison, but wait—if the fraud affects a financial institution—and lucky you, you fucked with our bank *and* the recipient bank, your lucky day, you little shit—that brings it up to thirty years in prison and a one-million-dollar fine. You tracking? What's that, thirty-five years in prison? And we haven't even got into forgery and computer crimes, gathering information in a protected computer to steal data, that'll get you anywhere from one year to twenty years in prison and more fines. So what have we got so far, forty, fifty, *fifty-five* years in prison? You're twenty-six now, you'll be, let's see, *eighty-one* when you get out."

Now I was sweating through my polo shirt, I felt cold and clammy. My legs were trembling. "But," I began, my voice hoarse, then cleared my throat. "Seventy-eight thousand dollars is a rounding error in a thirty-billion-dollar corporation."

"I suggest you shut your fucking mouth," Meacham said quietly. "We've consulted our lawyers, and they're confident they can get a charge of embezzlement in a court of law. Furthermore, you were clearly in a position to do more, and we believe that was just one installment in an ongoing scheme to defraud Wyatt Telecommunications, part of a pattern of multiple withdrawals and diversions. It's just the tip of the iceberg." For the first time he turned to the mousy woman taking notes. "We're off the record now." He turned back to me. "The U.S. Attorney was a college roommate of our house counsel, Mr. Cassidy, and we have every assurance he intends to throw the book at you. Plus, the district attorney's office, you may not have noticed, is on a white-collar crime campaign, and they're looking to make an example out of someone. They want a poster child, Cassidy."

I stared at him. My headache was back. I felt a trickle of sweat run down the inside of my shirt from my armpit to my waist.

"We've got both the state and the feds in our corner. We've *got* you, pure and simple. Now it's just a matter of how hard we're going to hit you, how much destruction we want to do. And don't imagine you're going to some country club, either. Cute young guy like you, you're going to be bent over the bunk someplace in Marion Federal Penitentiary. You're going to come out a toothless old man. And in case you're not current on our criminal justice system, there's no longer any parole at the federal level. Your life just changed as of this moment. You're fucked, pal." He looked at the woman with the notebook. "We're back on the record now. Let's hear what you have to say, and you'd better make it good."

I swallowed, but my saliva had stopped flowing. I saw flashes of white around the edges of my vision. He was dead serious.

In my high school and college years I got stopped fairly often for speeding, and I developed a reputation as a virtuoso at getting out of tickets. The trick is to make the cop feel your pain. It's psychological warfare. That's why they wear mirrored sunglasses, so you can't look into their eyes while you're pleading. They're human beings too, even cops. I used to keep a couple of law-enforcement textbooks on the front seat and tell them I was studying to be a police officer and I sure hoped this ticket wouldn't hurt my chances. Or I'd show them a prescription bottle and tell them I was in a rush because I needed to get mom her epilepsy medication as quickly as possible. Basically I learned that if you're going to start, you have to go all the way; you have to totally put your heart into it.

We were way beyond salvaging my job. I couldn't shake the image of that bunk at Marion Federal Penitentiary. I was scared shitless.

So I'm not proud of what I had to do, but you see, I had no choice. Either I reached deep inside and spun my very best tale for this security creep, or I was going to be someone's prison bitch.

I took a deep breath. "Look," I said, "I'm going to level with you."

"About time."

"Here's the thing. Jonesie—well, Jonesie has cancer."

Meacham smirked and leaned back in his chair, like, Entertain me.

I sighed, chewed the inside of my cheek like I was spilling something I really didn't want to. "Pancreatic cancer. Inoperable."

Meacham stared at me, stonefaced.

"He got the diagnosis three weeks ago. I mean, there's nothing they can do about it—the guy's dying. And so Jonesie, you know—well, you don't know him, but he's always putting on a brave front. He says to the oncologist, 'You mean I can stop flossing?' " I gave a sad smile. "That's Jonesie."

The note-taking woman stopped for a moment, actually looked stricken, then went back to her notes.

Meacham licked his lips. Was I getting to him? I couldn't really tell. I had to amp it up, really go for it.

"There's no reason you should know any of this," I went on. "I mean, Jonesie's not exactly an important guy around here. He's not a VP or anything, he's just a loading dock guy. But he's important to me, because . . ." I closed my eyes for a few seconds, inhaled deeply. "The thing is—I never wanted to tell anyone this, it was like our secret, but Jonesie's my father."

Meacham's chair slowly came forward. Now he was paying attention.

"Different last name and all—my mom changed my name to hers when she left him like twenty years ago, took me with her. I was a kid, I didn't know any better. But Dad, he . . ." I bit my lower lip. I had tears in my eyes now. "He kept on supporting us, worked two, sometimes three jobs. Never asked for anything. Mom didn't want him to see me at all, but on Christmas . . ." A sharp intake of breath, almost a hiccup. "Dad came by the house every Christmas, sometimes he'd ring the doorbell for an hour out in the freezing cold before Mom let him come in. Always had a present for me, some big expensive thing he couldn't afford. Later on, when Mom said she couldn't afford to send me to college, not on a nurse's salary, Dad started sending money. He—he said he wanted me to have the life he never had. Mom never gave him any respect, and she'd sort of poisoned me against him, you know? So I never even thanked the guy. I didn't even invite him to graduation, 'cause I knew Mom wouldn't feel comfortable with him around, but he showed up anyway, I saw him sort of hanging around, wearing some ugly old suit—I never saw him wear a suit or a tie before, he must have got it at the Salvation Army, because he really wanted to see me graduate from college, and he didn't want to embarrass me."

Meacham's eyes actually seemed to be getting moist. The woman had stopped taking notes, and was just watching me, blinking back tears.

I was on a roll. Meacham deserved my best, and he was getting it. "When I started working here at Wyatt, I never expected to find Dad working on the fucking *loading* dock. It was like the greatest accident. Mom died a couple of years ago, and here I am, connecting up with my father, this sweet wonderful guy who never ever asked anything from me, never demanded anything, working his fucking fingers to the bone, supporting a goddamned ungrateful son he never got to see. It's like fate, you know? And then when he gets this news, he's got inoperable pancreatic cancer, and he starts talking about killing himself before the cancer gets him, I mean . . ."

The note-taking woman reached for a Kleenex and blew her nose. She was glowering at Arnold Meacham now. Meacham winced.

I whispered, "I just had to show him what he meant to me—what he meant to all of us. I guess like it was my own sort of Make-a-Wish Foundation. I told him—I told him I'd hit the trifecta at the track, I didn't want him to know or to worry or anything. I mean, believe me, what I did was wrong, totally wrong. It was wrong in a hundred different ways, I'm not going to bullshit you. But maybe in just one small way it was right." The woman reached for another Kleenex and looked at Meacham as if he were the scum of the earth. Meacham was looking down, flushed and unable to meet my gaze. I was giving *myself* chills.

Then from the shadowed far end of the office I heard a door open and what sounded like clapping. Slow, loud clapping.

It was Nicholas Wyatt, the founder and CEO of Wyatt Telecommunications. He approached as he clapped, smiling broadly. "Brilliant performance," he said. "Absolutely brilliant."

I looked up, startled, then shook my head sorrowfully. Wyatt was a tall man, around six foot six, with a wrestler's build. He just got bigger and bigger as he got closer until, standing a few feet away from me, he seemed larger than life. Wyatt was known as a sharp dresser, and sure enough, he was wearing some kind of Armani-looking gray suit with a subtle pinstripe. He wasn't just powerful, he *looked* powerful.

"Mr. Cassidy, let me ask you a question."

I didn't know what to do, so I stood up, extended my hand to shake.

Wyatt didn't shake my hand. "What's Jonesie's first name?"

I hesitated, a beat too long. "Al," I finally said.

"Al? As in—what?"

"Al—Alan," I said. "Albert. Shit."

Meacham stared at me.

"Details, Cassidy," Wyatt said. "They'll fuck you over every time. But I have to say, you moved me—you really did. The part about the Salvation Army suit really got me right here." He tapped his chest with a fist. "Extraordinary."

I grinned sheepishly, really feeling like a tool. "The guy here said to make it good."

Wyatt smiled. "You're a supremely gifted young man, Cassidy. A goddamned Scheherazade. And I think we should have a talk."

4

Nicholas Wyatt was one scary dude. I had never met him before, but I'd seen him on TV, on CNBC, and on the corporate Web site, the video messages he'd recorded. I'd even caught a few glimpses of him, live, in my three years working for the company he founded. Up close he was even more intimidating. He had a deep tan, shoe polish–black hair that was gelled and combed straight back. His teeth were perfectly even and Vegas-white.

He was fifty-six but didn't look it, whatever fifty-six is supposed to look like. Anyway, he sure didn't look like my dad at fifty-six, a paunchy, balding old man even in his so-called prime. This was some other fifty-six.

I had no idea why he was here. What could the CEO of the company threaten me with that Meacham hadn't already pulled out? Death by a thousand paper cuts? Being eaten alive by wild boar?

Secretly I had this fleeting fantasy that he was going to high-five me, congratulate me for pulling off a good one, say he liked my spirit, my moxie. But that sad little daydream shriveled as quickly as it popped into my desperate mind. Nicholas Wyatt wasn't some basketball-playing priest. He was a vindictive son of a bitch.

I'd heard stories. I knew that if you had any brains you made a point of avoiding him. You kept your head down, tried not to attract his attention. He was famous for his rages, his tantrums and shouting matches. He was known to fire people on the spot, have Security pack up their desks, have them escorted out of the building. At his executive staff meetings he always picked one person to humiliate the whole time. You didn't go to him with bad news, and you didn't waste a split second of his time. If you were unlucky enough to have to make some PowerPoint presentation to him, you'd rehearse it and rehearse it until it was perfect, but if there was a single glitch in your presentation, he'd interrupt you, shouting, "I don't *believe* this!"

People said he'd mellowed a lot since the early years, but from what? He was viciously competitive, a weightlifter and triathlete. Guys who worked out in the company gym said he was always challenging the serious jocks to chin-up competitions. He never lost, and when the other guy gave up he'd taunt, "Want me to keep going?" They said he had the body of Arnold Schwarzenegger, like a brown condom stuffed with walnuts.

Not only was he insane about winning, for him it wasn't sweet unless he also got to ridicule the loser. At a companywide Christmas party he once wrote the name of his chief competitor, Trion Systems, on a wine bottle, and smashed it against the wall, to a lot of drunken cheering and catcalls.

He ran a high-testosterone shop. His top guys all dressed like he did, in seven-thousand-dollar suits by Armani or Prada or Brioni or Kiton or other designers I hadn't even heard of. And they put up with his shit because they were disgustingly well compensated for it. The joke about him that everybody's heard by now: What's the difference between God and Nicholas Wyatt? God doesn't think he's Nicholas Wyatt.

Nick Wyatt slept three hours a night, seemed to eat nothing but Power Bars for breakfast and lunch, was a nuclear reactor of nervous energy, perspired heavily. People called him "The Exterminator." He managed by fear and never forgot a slight. When an ex-friend of his got fired as CEO of some big tech company, he sent a wreath of black roses—his assistants always knew where to get black roses. The quote he's famous for, the one thing he repeated so often it should have been carved in granite above the main entrance, made into a screen saver on everyone's desktop, was "Of course I'm paranoid. I want everyone who works for me to be paranoid. Success *demands* paranoia."

I followed Wyatt down the hall from Corporate Security to his executive suite, and it was hard to keep up with him—he was a power-walker. I had to

almost run. Behind me followed Meacham, swinging a black leather portfolio like a baton. As we approached the executive area, the walls went from
white plasterboard to mahogany; the carpeting became soft and deep-pile.
We were at his office, his lair.

His matched set of admins looked up and beamed at him as we caravaned
through. One blonde, one black. He said, "Linda, Yvette," as if captioning
them. I wasn't surprised they were both fashion-model beautiful — everything
here was high-end, like the walls and the carpeting and the furniture. I wondered if their job description included nonclerical responsibilities, like
blowjobs. That was the rumor, anyway.

Wyatt's office was vast. An entire Bosnian village could live there. Two of
the walls were glass, floor to ceiling, and the views of the city were unbelievable. The other walls were fancy dark wood, covered with framed things,
magazine covers with his mug on them, *Fortune, Forbes, Business Week.* I
looked, goggle-eyed, as I half walked, half ran by. A photo of him and some
other guys with the late Princess Diana. Him with both George Bushes.

He led us to a "conversation group" of tufted black leather chairs and
sofa that looked like they belonged in MOMA. He sank down at one end of
the enormous sofa.

My head was spinning. I was disoriented, in another world. I couldn't
imagine why I was here, in Nicholas Wyatt's office. Maybe he'd been one of
those boys who liked to pull the legs off insects one by one with tweezers,
then burn them to death with a magnifying glass.

"So this is some pretty elaborate scam you pulled off," he said. "Very
impressive."

I smiled, ducked my head modestly. Denial wasn't even an option. *Thank
God,* I thought. It looked like we were going the high-five, moxie route.

"But no one kicks me in the balls and walks away, you should know that
by now. I mean fucking *nobody.*"

He'd gotten out the tweezers and the magnifying glass.

"So what's your deal, you've been a PLM here for three years, your performance reviews suck, you haven't gotten a raise or a promotion the whole
time you've been here; you're going through the motions, phoning it in. Not
exactly an ambitious guy, are you?" He talked fast, which made me even
more nervous.

I smiled again. "I guess not. I sort of have other priorities."

"Like?"

I hesitated. He'd got me. I shrugged.

"Everyone's got to be passionate about *something,* or they're not worth shit. You're obviously not passionate about your work, so what *are* you passionate about?"

I'm almost never speechless, but this time I couldn't think of anything clever to say. Meacham was watching me too, a nasty, sadistic little smile on his knife-blade face. I was thinking that I knew guys in the company, in my business unit, who were always scheming how to get thirty seconds with Wyatt, in an elevator or at a product launch or whatever. They'd even prepared an "elevator pitch." Here I was in the big guy's office and I was silent as a mannequin.

"You an actor or something in your spare time?"

I shook my head.

"Well, you're good, anyway. A regular Marlon fucking Brando. You may suck at marketing routers to enterprise customers, but you are a fucking *Olympic*-level bullshit artist."

"If that's a compliment, sir, thank you."

"I hear you do a damned good Nick Wyatt—that true? Let's see it."

I blushed, shook my head.

"Anyway, bottom line, you ripped me off and you seem to think you're going to get away with it."

I looked appalled. "No, sir, I *don't* think I'm going to 'get away with it.' "

"Spare me. I don't need another demonstration. You had me at hello." He flicked his hand like a Roman emperor, and Meacham handed him a folder. He glanced at it. "Your aptitude scores are in the top percentile. You were an engineering major in college, what kind?"

"Electrical."

"You wanted to be an engineer when you grew up?"

"My dad wanted me to major in something I could get a real job with. I wanted to play lead guitar with Pearl Jam."

"Any good?"

"No," I admitted.

He half-smiled. "You did college on the five-year-plan. What happened?"

"I got kicked out for a year."

"I appreciate your honesty. At least you're not trying that 'junior year abroad' shit. What happened?"

"I pulled a stupid prank. I had a bad semester, so I hacked into the college computer system and changed my transcript. My roommate's too."

"So it's an old trick." He looked at his watch, glanced at Meacham, then back at me. "I've got an idea for you, Adam." I didn't like the way he said my first name; it was creepy. "A very good idea. An extremely generous offer, in fact."

"Thank you, sir." I had no idea what he was talking about, but I knew it couldn't be good or generous.

"What I'm about to say to you I'm going to deny I ever said. In fact, I won't just deny it, I'll fucking sue you for defamation if you ever repeat it, are we clear? I will fucking crush you." Whatever he was talking about, he had the resources. He was a billionaire, like the third or fourth richest man in America, but he had once been number two before our share price collapsed. He wanted to be the richest—he was gunning for Bill Gates—but that didn't seem likely.

My heart thudded. "Sure."

"Are you clear on your situation? Behind door number one you've got the certainty—the fucking *certainty*—of at least twenty years in prison. So it's that, or else whatever's behind the curtain. You want to play Let's Make a Deal?"

I swallowed. "Sure."

"Let me tell you what's behind the curtain, Adam. It's a very nice future for a smart engineering major like you, only you have to play by the rules. My rules."

My face was prickly-hot.

"I want you to take on a special project for me."

I nodded.

"I want you to take a job at Trion."

"At . . . Trion Systems?" I didn't understand.

"In new product marketing. They've got a couple of openings in strategic places in the company."

"They'd never hire me."

"No, you're right, they'd never hire *you*. Not a lazy fuckup like you. But a

Wyatt superstar, a young hotshot who's on the verge of going supernova, they'd hire you in a nanosecond."

"I don't follow."

"Street-smart guy like you? You just lost a couple of IQ points. Come on, dipshit. The Lucid—that was your baby, right?"

He was talking about Wyatt Telecom's flagship product, this all-in-one PDA, sort of a Palm Pilot on steroids. An incredible toy. I had nothing to do with it. I didn't even own one.

"They'd never believe it," I said.

"Listen to me, Adam. I make my biggest business decisions on gut instinct, and my gut tells me you've got the brass balls and the smarts and the talent to do it. You in or out?"

"You want me to report back to you, is that it?"

His eyes bore down on me, steely. "More than that. I want you to get information."

"Like being a spy. A mole or whatever."

He turned his palms open, like, are you a moron or what? "Whatever you want to call it. There's some valuable, uh, *intellectual property* I want to get my hands on inside Trion, and their security is damned near impenetrable. Only a Trion insider can get what I want, and not just any insider. A major player. Either you recruit one, buy one, or you get one in the front door. Here we got a smart, personable young guy, comes highly recommended—I think we got a pretty decent shot."

"And what if I'm caught?"

"You won't be," Wyatt said.

"But if I am . . . ?"

"If you do the job right," Meacham said, "you won't be caught. And if somehow you screw up and you *are* caught—well, we'll be here to protect you."

Somehow I doubted that. "They'll be totally suspicious."

"Of what?" Wyatt said. "In this business people jump from company to company all the time. The top talent gets poached. Low-hanging fruit. You're fresh off a big win at Wyatt, you maybe don't have the juice you think you should, you're looking for more responsibility, a better opportunity, more money—the usual bullshit."

"They'll see right through me."

"Not if you do your job right," said Wyatt. "You're going to have to learn product marketing, you're going to have to be fucking brilliant, you're going to have to work harder than you've ever worked in your whole sorry life. Really bust your ass. Only a major player's going to get what I want. Try your phone-it-in shit at Trion, you'll either get shot or shoved aside, and then our little experiment is over. And you get door number one."

"I thought new product guys all have to have MBAs."

"Nah, Goddard thinks MBAs are bullshit—one of the few things we agree on. He doesn't have one. Thinks it's limiting. Speaking of limiting." He snapped his fingers, and Meacham handed him something, a small metal box, familiar looking. An Altoids box. He popped it open. Inside were a few white pills that looked like aspirin but weren't. Definitely familiar. "You're going to have to cut out this shit, this Ecstasy or whatever you call it." I kept the Altoids box on my coffee table at home; I wondered when and how they got it, but I was too dazed to be pissed off. He dropped the box into a little black leather trash can next to the couch. It made a *thunk* sound. "Same with pot, booze, all that shit. You're going to have to straighten up and fly right, guy."

That seemed like the least of my problems. "And what if I don't get hired?"

"Door number one." He gave an ugly smile. "And don't pack your golf shoes. Pack your K-Y."

"Even if I give it my best shot?"

"Your job is not to blow it. With the quals we're giving you, and with a coach like me, you won't have any excuse."

"What kind of money are we talking about?"

"What kind of *money*? The fuck do I know? Believe me, it'll be a hell of a lot more than you get here. Six figures anyway." I tried not to gulp visibly.

"Plus my salary here."

He turned his tight face over to me and gave me a dead stare. He didn't have any expression in his eyes. *Botox?* I wondered. "You're shitting me."

"I'm taking an enormous risk."

"Excuse me? *I'm* the one taking the risk. You're a total fucking black box, a big fat question mark."

"If you really thought so, you wouldn't ask me to do it."

He turned to Meacham. "I don't believe this shit."

Meacham looked like he'd swallowed a turd. "You little prick," he said. "I ought to pick up the phone right now—"

Wyatt held up an imperial hand. "That's okay. He's ballsy. I like ballsy. You get hired, you do your job right, you get to double-dip. But if you fuck up—"

"I know," I said. "Door number one. Let me think it over, get back to you tomorrow."

Wyatt's jaw dropped, his eyes blank. He paused, then said, all icy: "I'll give you till nine A.M. When the U.S. Attorney gets into his office."

"I advise you not to say a word about this to any of your buddies, your father, anybody," Meacham put in. "Or you won't know what hit you."

"I understand," I replied. "No need to threaten me."

"Oh, that's not a threat," said Nicholas Wyatt. "That's a promise."

5

There didn't seem to be any reason to go back to work, so I went home. It felt strange to be on the subway at one in the afternoon, with the old people and the students, the moms and kids. My head was still spinning, and I felt queasy.

My apartment was a good ten-minute walk from the subway stop. It was a bright day, ridiculously cheerful.

My shirt was still damp and gave off a funky sweat smell. A couple of young girls in overalls and multiple piercings were tugging a bunch of little kids around on a long rope. The kids squealed. Some black guys were playing basketball with their shirts off, on an asphalt playground behind a chain-link fence. The bricks on the sidewalk were uneven, and I almost tripped, then I felt that sickening slickness underfoot as I stepped in dog shit. Perfect symbolism.

The entrance to my apartment smelled strongly of urine, either from a cat or a bum. The mail hadn't come yet. My keys jingled as I unlocked the three locks on my apartment door. The old lady in the unit across the hall opened her door a crack, the length of her security chain, then slammed it; she was too short to reach the peephole. I gave her a friendly wave.

The room was dark even though the blinds were wide open. The air was stifling, smelled of stale cigarettes. Since the apartment was street level, I couldn't leave the windows open during the day to air it out.

My furnishings were pretty pathetic: the one room was dominated by a greenish tartan-plaid sleeper sofa, high-backed, beer-encrusted, gold threads woven throughout. It faced a Sanyo nineteen-inch TV that was missing the remote. A tall narrow unfinished-pine bookcase stood lonely in one corner. I sat down on the sofa, and a cloud of dust rose in the air. The steel bar underneath the cushion hurt my ass. I thought of Nicholas Wyatt's black leather sofa and wondered if he'd ever lived in such a dump. The story was that he came up from nothing, but I didn't believe it; I couldn't see him ever living in such a rat hole. I found the Bic lighter under the glass coffee table, lighted a cigarette, looked over at the pile of bills on the table. I didn't even open the envelopes anymore. I had two MasterCards and three Visas, and they all had whopping balances, and I could barely even make the minimum payments.

I had already made up my mind, of course.

6

"You get busted?"

Seth Marcus, my best buddy since junior high school, bartended three nights a week at a sort of yuppie dive called Alley Cat. During the days he was a paralegal at a downtown law firm. He said he needed the money, but I was convinced that secretly he was bartending in order to maintain some vestige of coolness, to keep from turning into the sort of corporate dweeb we both liked to make fun of.

"Busted for what?" How much had I told him? Did I tell him about the call from Meacham, the security director? I hoped not. Now I couldn't tell him a goddamned thing about the vise they'd got me in.

"Your big party." It was loud, I couldn't hear him well, and someone down at the other end of the bar was whistling, two fingers in his mouth, loud and shrill. "That guy whistling at *me?* Like I'm a fucking *dog?*" He ignored the whistler.

I shook my head.

"You got away with it, huh? You actually pulled it off, amazing. What can I get you to celebrate?"

"Brooklyn Brown?"

He shook his head. "Nah."

"Newcastle? Guinness?"

"How about a draft? They don't keep track of those."

I shrugged. "Sure."

He pulled me a draft, yellow and soapy: he was clearly new at this. It sloshed on the scarred wooden bar top. He was a tall, dark-haired, good-looking guy—a veritable chick magnet—with a ridiculous goatee and an earring. He was half-Jewish but wanted to be black. He played and sang in a band called Slither, which I'd heard a couple of times; they weren't very good, but he talked a lot about "signing a deal." He had a dozen scams going at once just so he wouldn't have to admit he was a working stiff.

Seth was the only guy I knew who was more cynical than me. That was probably why we were friends. That plus the fact that he didn't give me shit about my father, even though he used to play on the high school football team coached (and tyrannized) by Frank Cassidy. In seventh grade we were in the same homeroom, liked each other instantly because we were both singled out for ridicule by the math teacher, Mr. Pasquale. In ninth grade I left the public school and went to Bartholomew Browning & Knightley, the fancy prep school where my dad had just been hired as the football and hockey coach and I now got free tuition. For two years I rarely saw Seth, until Dad got fired for breaking two bones in a kid's right forearm and one bone in his left forearm. The kid's mother was head of the board of overseers of Bartholomew Browning. So the free tuition tap got shut off, and I went back to the public school. Dad got hired there too, after Bartholomew Browning.

We both worked at the same Gulf station in high school, until Seth got tired of the holdups and went to Dunkin' Donuts to make donuts on the overnight. For a couple of summers he and I worked cleaning windows for a company that did a lot of downtown skyscrapers, until we decided that dangling from ropes on the twenty-seventh floor sounded cooler than it actually was. Not only was it boring, but it was scary as hell, a lousy combination. Maybe some people consider hanging off the side of a building hundreds of feet up some kind of extreme sport, but to me it seemed more like a slow-motion suicide attempt.

The whistling grew louder. People were looking at the whistler, a chubby balding guy in a suit, and some people were giggling.

"I'm going to fucking lose it," Seth said.

"Don't," I said, but it was too late, he was already headed to the other end of the bar. I took out a cigarette and lighted it as I watched him lean over the bar, glowering at the whistler, looking like he was going to grab the guy's lapel but stopping short. He said something. There was some laughter from the whistler's general vicinity. Looking cool and relaxed, Seth headed back this way. He stopped to talk to a pair of beautiful women, a blonde and a brunette, and flashed them a smile.

"There. I don't believe you're still smoking," he said to me. "Fucking stupid, with your dad." He took a cigarette from my pack, lighted it, took a drag and set it down in the ashtray.

"Thank you for not thanking me for not smoking," I said. "So what's *your* excuse?"

He exhaled through his nostrils. "Dude, I like to multitask. Also, cancer doesn't run in my family. Just insanity."

"He doesn't have cancer."

"Emphysema. Whatever the fuck. How is the old man?"

"Fine." I shrugged. I didn't want to go there, and neither did Seth.

"Man, one of those babes wants a Cosmopolitan, the other wants a *frozen drink.* I hate that."

"Why?"

"Too labor-intensive, then they'll tip me a quarter. Women never tip, I've learned this. Jesus, you crack two Buds, you make a couple of bucks. Frozen drinks!" He shook his head. "Man."

He went off for a couple of minutes, banging things around, the blender screaming. Served the girls their drinks with one of his killer smiles. They weren't going to tip him a quarter. They both turned to look at me and smiled.

When he came back, he said, "What are you doing later?"

"Later?" It was already close to ten, and I had to meet with a Wyatt engineer at seven-thirty in the morning. A couple days training with him, some big shot on the Lucid project, then a couple more days with a new-products marketing manager, and regular sessions with an "executive coach." They'd lined up a vicious schedule. Boot camp for bootlickers, was how I thought of it. No more fucking off, getting in at nine or ten. But I couldn't tell Seth; I couldn't tell anyone.

"I'm done at one," he said. "Those two chicks asked if I wanted to go to Nightcrawler with them after. I told them I had a friend. They just checked you out, they're into it."

"Can't," I said.

"Huh?"

"Got to get to work early. On time, really."

Seth looked alarmed, disbelieving. "What? What's going on?"

"Work's getting serious. Early day tomorrow. Big project."

"This is a joke, right?"

"Unfortunately no. Don't you have to work in the morning too?"

"You becoming one of Them? One of the pod people?"

I grinned. "Time to grow up. No more kid stuff."

Seth looked disgusted. "Dude, it's *never* too late to have a happy childhood."

7

After ten grueling days of tutoring and indoctrination by engineers and product marketing types who'd been involved with the Lucid handheld, my head was stuffed with all kinds of useless information. I was given a tiny "office" in the executive suite that used to be a supply room, though I was almost never there. I showed up dutifully, didn't give anyone any trouble. I didn't know how long I'd be able to keep this up without flipping out, but the image of the prison bunk bed at Marion kept me motivated.

Then one morning I was summoned to an office two doors down the executive corridor from Nicholas Wyatt's. The name on the brass plate on the door said JUDITH BOLTON. The office was all white—white rug, white-upholstered furniture, white marble slab for a desk, even white flowers.

On a white leather sofa, Nicholas Wyatt sat next to an attractive, fortyish woman who was chatting away familiarly with him, touching his arm, laughing. Coppery red hair, long legs crossed at the knee, a slender body she obviously worked hard at, dressed in a navy suit. She had blue eyes, glossy heart-shaped lips, brows arched provocatively. She'd obviously once been a knockout, but she'd gotten a little hard.

I realized I'd seen her before, over the last week or so, at Wyatt's side, when he paid his quick visits to my training sessions with marketing guys and engineers. She always seemed to be whispering in his ear, watching me, but we were never introduced, and I'd always wondered who she was.

Without getting up from the couch, she extended a hand as I

approached—long fingers, red nail polish—and gave me a firm, no-nonsense shake.

"Judith Bolton."

"Adam Cassidy."

"You're late," she said.

"I got lost," I said, trying to lighten things up.

She shook her head, smiled, pursed her lips. "You have a problem with punctuality. I don't ever want you to be late again, are we clear?"

I smiled back, the same smile I give cops when they ask if I know how fast I was going. The lady was tough. "Absolutely." I sat down in a chair facing her.

Wyatt was watching the exchange with amusement. "Judith is one of my most valuable players," he said. "My 'executive coach.' My *consigliere*, and your Svengali. I suggest you listen to every fucking word she says. I do." He stood up, excused himself. She gave him a little wave as he left.

You wouldn't have recognized me anymore. I was a changed man. No more Bondomobile: now I drove a silver Audi A6, leased by the company. I had a new wardrobe, too. One of Wyatt's admins, the black one, who turned out to be a former model from the British West Indies, took me clothes shopping one afternoon at a very expensive place I had only seen from the outside, where she said she bought clothes for Nick Wyatt. She picked out some suits, shirts, ties, and shoes, and put it all on a company Amex card. She even bought what she called "hose," meaning socks. And this wasn't the Structure crap I usually wore, it was Armani, Ermenegildo Zegna. They had this aura: you could tell they were handstitched by Italian widows listening to Verdi.

The sideburns—"bugger's grips," she called them—had to go, she decided. Also no more of the scraggly bed-head look. She took me to a fancy salon, and I came out looking like a Ralph Lauren model, only not as fruity. I dreaded next time Seth and I got together; I knew I'd never hear the end of it.

A cover story was devised. My co-workers and managers in the Enterprise Division/Routers were informed that I had been "reassigned." Rumors circulated that I was being sent to Siberia because the manager of my division was tired of my attitude. Another rumor had it that one of Wyatt's senior VPs had admired a memo I'd written and "liked my attitude" and I was being given more responsibility, not less. No one knew the truth. All anyone knew was that one day I was suddenly gone from my cubicle.

If anyone had bothered to look closely at the org chart on the corporate Web site, they'd have noticed my title was now Director of Special Projects, Office of the CEO.

An electronic and paper trail was being created.

Judith turned back to me, continued as if Wyatt had never been there. "*If you're hired by Trion, you're to arrive at your cube forty-five minutes early.* Under no circumstances will you have a drink at lunch or after work. No happy hours, no cocktail parties, no 'hanging out' with 'friends' from work. No partying. If you have to attend a work-related party, drink club soda."

"You make it sound like I'm in AA."

"Getting drunk is a sign of weakness."

"Then I assume smoking's out of the question."

"Wrong," she said. "It's a filthy, disgusting habit, and it indicates a lack of self-control, but there are other considerations. Standing around in the smoking area is an excellent way to cross-pollinate, connect with people in different units, obtain useful intelligence. Now, about your handshake." She shook her head. "You blew it. Hiring decisions are made in the first five seconds—at the handshake. Anyone who tells you anything else is lying to you. You get the job with the handshake, and then the rest of the job interview you fight to keep it, to not lose it. Since I'm a woman, you went easy on me. Don't. Be firm, do it hard, and hold—"

I smiled impishly, cut in: "The last woman who told me that . . ." I noticed she'd frozen in midsentence. "Sorry."

Now, head cocked kittenishly to one side, she smiled. "Thanks." A pause. "Hold the shake a second or two longer. Look me in the eye, and smile. Aim your heart at me. Let's do it again."

I stood up, shook Judith Bolton's hand again.

"Better," she said. "You're a natural. People meet you and think, there's something about this guy I like, I don't know what it is. You've got the chops." She looked at me appraisingly. "You broke your nose once?"

I nodded.

"Let me guess: playing football."

"Hockey, actually."

"It's cute. Are you an athlete, Adam?"

"I was." I sat down again.

She leaned forward toward me, her chin resting in a cupped hand, checking me out. "I can tell. It's in the way you walk, the way you carry your body. I like it. But you're not synchronizing."

"Excuse me?"

"You've got to synchronize. *Mirror.* I'm leaning forward, so you do the same. I lean back, you lean back. I cross my legs, you cross your legs. Watch the tilt of my head, and mimic me. Even synchronize your *breathing* with mine. Just be subtle, don't be blatant about it. This is how you connect with people on a subconscious level, make them feel comfortable with you. *People like people who are like themselves.* Are we clear?"

I grinned disarmingly, or what I thought was disarmingly, anyway.

"And another thing." She leaned in even closer until her face was a few inches away from mine. She whispered, "You're wearing too much aftershave."

My face burned with embarrassment.

"Let me guess: Drakkar Noir." She didn't wait for my answer, because she knew she was right. "Very high school stud. Bet it made the cheerleaders weak at the knees."

Later, I learned who Judith Bolton was. She was a senior VP who'd been brought into Wyatt Telecom a few years earlier as a powerhouse consultant with McKinsey & Company to advise Nicholas Wyatt personally on sensitive personnel issues, "conflict resolution" in the uppermost echelons of the company, certain psy-ops aspects of deals, negotiations, and acquisitions. She had a Ph.D. in behavioral psychology, so she was called Dr. Bolton. Whether you called her an "executive coach" or a "leadership mastery strategist," she was kind of like Wyatt's private Olympic trainer. She advised him on who was executive material and who wasn't, who should be fired, who was plotting behind his back. She had an x-ray eye for disloyalty. No doubt he'd hired her away from McKinsey at some ridiculous salary. She was powerful enough and secure enough here to contradict him to his face, say shit to him he wouldn't take from anybody else.

"Now, our first assignment is to learn how to do a job interview," she said.

"I got hired here," I said, feebly.

"We're playing in a whole new league, Adam," she said, smiling. "You're a hotshot, and you have to interview like a hotshot, someone Trion's going to fall all over themselves to steal away from us. How do you like working at Wyatt?"

I looked at her, feeling stupid. "Well, I'm trying to leave there, aren't I?"

She rolled her eyes, inhaled sharply. "No. You keep it positive." She turned her head to one side and then did an amazing imitation of my voice: "I *love* it! It's totally *inspiring!* My co-workers are *great!*" The mimicry was so good, it weirded me out; it was like hearing your voice on an answering machine tape.

"So why am I interviewing at Trion?"

"*Opportunities*, Adam. There's *nothing* wrong with your job at Wyatt. You're *not* disgruntled. You're just taking the logical next step in your career, and there are more opportunities at Trion to do *even bigger, better things*. What's your greatest weakness, Adam?"

I thought for a second. "Nothing, really," I said. "Never admit to a weakness."

She scowled. "Oh, for Christ's sake. They'll think you're either delusional or stupid."

"It's a trick question."

"Of *course* it's a trick question. Job interviews are *minefields*, my friend. You *have* to 'admit' to weaknesses, but you must *never* tell them anything derogatory. So you confess to being *too faithful a husband, too loving a father*." She did the Adam-voice again: "Sometimes I get so comfortable with one software application that I don't explore others. Or: sometimes when little things bother me, I don't always speak up, because I figure most things tend to blow over. *You don't complain enough!* Or how about this: I tend to get *really absorbed in a project*, so I sometimes put in long hours, too long, because I love doing them, doing them right. Maybe I work on things more than is necessary. Get it? They'll be salivating, Adam."

I smiled, nodded. Man, oh man, what had I gotten myself into?

"What's the biggest mistake you ever made on the job?"

"Obviously I have to admit something," I said nervously.

"You're a fast study," she said dryly.

"Maybe I took on too much once, and I—"

"—And you fucked it up? So you don't know the depths of your own incompetence? I don't think so. You say, 'Oh, nothing really big. Once I was working on a big report for my boss and I forgot to back up, and my *computer crashed*, I lost everything. I had to stay up till three in the morning, completely re-create the work I'd lost. Boy, did *I* learn my lesson—always back up.' Get it? The biggest mistake you ever made was *not your fault*, plus you made everything right."

"I get it." My shirt collar felt too tight, and I wanted to get out of there.

"You're a natural, Adam," she said. "You're going to do just fine."

8

The night before my first interview at Trion I went over to see my dad. I did this at least once a week, sometimes more, depending on if he called and asked me to come over. He called a lot, partly because he was lonely (Mom had died six years earlier) and partly because he was paranoid from the steroids he took and convinced his caregivers were trying to kill him. So his calls were never friendly, never chatty; they were complaints, rants, accusations. Some of his painkillers were missing, he'd say, and he was convinced Caryn the nurse was pilfering them. The oxygen supplied by the oxygen company was of shitty quality. Rhonda the nurse kept tripping over his air hose and yanking the little tubes, the cannulas, out of his nose, nearly ripping his ears off.

To say that it was hard to retain people to take care of him was a comic understatement. Rarely did they last more than a few weeks. Francis X. Cassidy was a bad-tempered man, had been as long as I could remember, and had only grown angrier as he grew older and sicker. He'd always smoked a couple of packs a day and had a loud hacking cough, was always getting bronchitis. So it came as no surprise when he was diagnosed with emphysema. What did he expect? He hadn't been able to blow out the candles on his birthday cake for years. Now his emphysema was what they called end-stage, meaning that he could die in a couple of weeks, or months, or maybe ten years. No one knew.

Unfortunately, it fell to me, his only offspring, to arrange his care. He still lived in the first-floor-and-basement apartment in a triple-decker I'd grown up in, and he hadn't changed a thing since Mom died—the same harvest-gold refrigerator that never worked right, the couch that sagged on one side, the lace window curtains that had gone yellow with age. He hadn't saved any money, and his pension was pitiful; he barely had enough to cover his medical expenses. That meant part of my paycheck went to his rent, the home health aide's salary, whatever. I never expected any thanks, and never got any. Never in a million years would he ask me for money. We both sort of pretended that he was living off a trust fund or something.

When I arrived, he was sitting in his favorite Barcalounger, in front of the huge TV, his main occupation. It allowed him to complain about something in real time. Tubes in his nose (he got oxygen round the clock now), he was watching some infomercial on cable.

"Hey, Dad," I said.

He didn't look up for a minute or so—he was hypnotized by the infomercial, like it was the shower scene in *Psycho*. He'd gotten thin, though he still had a barrel chest, and his crew cut was white. When he looked up at me, he said, "The bitch is quitting, you know that?"

The "bitch" in question was his latest home healthcare aide, a pinched-faced, moody Irish woman in her fifties named Maureen with blazing fake red hair. She limped through the living room, as if on cue—she had a bad hip—with a plastic laundry basket heaped with neatly folded white T-shirts and boxer shorts, my dad's extensive wardrobe. The only surprise about her quitting was that it had taken her so long. He had a little Radio Shack wireless doorbell on the end table next to his Barcalounger that he'd press to call her whenever he needed something, which seemed to be constantly. His oxygen wasn't working, or the nose-tube thingies were drying out his nose, or he needed help getting to the bathroom to take a pee. Once in a while she'd take him out for "walks" in his motorized go-cart so he could cruise around the shopping mall and complain about "punks" and abuse her some more. He accused her of trying to poison him. It would drive a normal person crazy, and Maureen already seemed pretty high-strung.

"Why don't you tell him what you called me?" she said, setting the laundry down on the couch.

"Oh, for Christ's sake," he said. He spoke in short, clipped sentences, since he was always short of breath. "You've been putting antifreeze in my coffee. I can taste it. They call this eldercide, you know. Gray murders."

"If I wanted to kill you I'd use something better than antifreeze," she snapped back. Her Irish accent was still strong even after living here for twenty-some years. He inevitably accused his caretakers of trying to kill him. If they did, who could blame them? "He called me a—a word I won't even repeat."

"Jesus fucking Christ, I called her a cunt. That's a polite word for what she is. She assaulted me. I sit here hooked up to fucking air tubes, and this bitch is slapping me around."

"I grabbed a cigarette out of his hands," Maureen said. "He was trying to sneak a smoke when I was downstairs doing the laundry. As if I can't smell it throughout the house." She looked at me. One of her eyes wandered. "He's not allowed to smoke! I don't even know where he hides the cigarettes—he's hiding them somewhere, I *know* it!"

My father smiled triumphantly but said nothing.

"Anyway, what do I care?" she said bitterly. "This is my last day. I can't *take* it anymore."

The paid studio audience in the infomercial gasped and applauded wildly.

"Like I'm going to notice," Dad said. "She doesn't do shit. Look at the dust in this place. What the hell does the bitch *do?*"

Maureen picked up the laundry basket. "I should have left a month ago. I should never have taken this job." She left the room in her strange lame-pony canter.

"I should have fired her the minute I met her," he grumbled. "I could tell she was one of those gray-murderers." He breathed with pursed lips as if he were inhaling through a straw.

I didn't know what I was going to do now. The guy couldn't be alone—he couldn't get to the bathroom without help. He refused to go into a nursing home; he said he'd kill himself first.

I put my hand on his left hand, the one with an index finger hooked up to a glowing red indicator, the pulse oximeter, I think it was called. The digital numbers on the monitor read 88 percent. I said, "We'll get someone, Dad, don't worry about it."

He lifted his hand, flung mine away. "What the hell kind of nurse is she anyway?" he said. "She doesn't give a shit about anyone else." He went into a long coughing fit, hawked and spit into a balled-up handkerchief he pulled out from somewhere in his chair. "I don't know why the hell you don't move back in. The hell you got to do anyway? You got some go-nowhere job."

I shook my head, said gently, "I can't, Dad. I got student loans to pay off." I didn't want to mention that someone had to make money to pay for the help that was always quitting.

"Fat lot of good college did you," he said. "Huge waste of money, all it was. Spent your time carousing with all your fancy friends, I didn't need to spend twenty thousand bucks a year so you could fuck off. You coulda done that here."

I smiled to let him know I wasn't offended. I didn't know whether it was the steroids, the prednisone he took to keep his airways open, that was making him such an asshole, or just his natural sweet nature. "Your mother, rest in peace, spoiled you rotten. Made you into a big fat pussy." He sucked in some air. "You're wasting your life. When the fuck you gonna get a real job, anyway?"

Dad was skilled at pushing the right buttons. I let a wave of annoyance pass over me. You couldn't take the guy seriously, you'd go whacko. He had the temper of a junkyard dog. I always thought his anger was like rabies—he wasn't really in control, so you couldn't blame him. He'd never been able to control his temper. When I was a kid, small enough not to fight back, he'd whip off his leather belt at the slightest provocation, whomp the shit out of me. As soon as he finished the beating, he'd invariably mutter, "See what you made me do?"

"I'm working on that," I said.

"They can smell a loser a mile off, you know."

"Who?"

"These companies. Nobody wants a loser. Everyone wants winners. Go get me a Coke, would you?"

This was his mantra, and it came from his coaching days—that I was a "loser," that the only thing that counted was winning, that coming in second was losing. There was a time when that sort of talk used to piss me off. But I was used to it by now; I barely even heard it.

I went to the kitchen, thinking about what we were going to do now. He needed round-the-clock help, no question about that. But none of the agencies would send anyone anymore. At first we had real hospital nurses, doing outside shifts for money. When he'd chewed through those, we managed to find a series of marginally qualified people who'd done two weeks' training to get their nursing-assistant certificate. Then it was whoever the hell we could find through ads in the paper.

Maureen had organized the harvest-gold Kenmore refrigerator so that it could have belonged in a government lab. A row of Cokes stood, one behind the other, on a wire shelf that she'd adjusted so it was just the right height. Even the glasses in the cabinet, usually cloudy and smeared, sparkled. I filled two glasses with ice, poured the contents of a can into each. I'd have to sit Maureen down, apologize on Dad's behalf, beg and plead, bribe her if necessary. At least she could stay until I found a replacement. Maybe I could appeal to her sense of responsibility to the elderly, though I figured that had been pretty much eroded by Dad's bile. The truth was, I was desperate. If I blew the interviews tomorrow, I'd have all the time in the world, but I'd be behind bars somewhere in Illinois. That wouldn't help.

I came back out holding the glasses, the ice tinkling as I walked. The infomercial was still going. How long did these things go on for? Who watched them anyway? Besides my father, I mean.

"Dad, don't worry about anything," I said, but he'd passed out.

I stood before him for a few seconds, watching to see if he was still breathing. He was. His chin was on his chest, his head at a funny angle. The oxygen made a quiet whooshing sound. Somewhere in the basement Maureen was banging stuff around, probably mentally rehearsing her exit line. I set down the Cokes on his little end table, which was crowded with meds and remote controls.

Then I leaned over and kissed the old man's blotchy red forehead. "We'll get someone," I said quietly.

9

The headquarters of Trion Systems looked like a brushed-chrome Pentagon. Each of the five sides was a seven-story "wing." It had been designed by some famous architect. Underneath was a parking garage filled with BMWs and Range Rovers and a lot of VW bugs and you name it, but no reserved spaces, so far as I could see.

I gave my name to the B Wing "lobby ambassador," which was their fancy name for the receptionist. She printed out an ID sticker that said VISI-TOR. I pasted it onto the breast pocket of my gray Armani suit and waited in the lobby for a woman named Stephanie to come get me.

She was the assistant to the hiring VP, Tom Lundgren. I tried to zone out, meditate, relax. I reminded myself that I couldn't ask for a better setup. Trion was looking to fill a product marketing manager slot—a guy had left suddenly, and I'd been custom-tooled for the job, genetically engineered, digitally remastered. In the last few weeks a few selected headhunters had been told about this amazing young guy at Wyatt who was just ripe for the picking. Low-hanging fruit. The word was spread, casually, at an industry convention, on the grapevine. I began to get all sorts of calls from recruiters on my voice mail.

Plus I'd done my homework on Trion Systems. I'd learned it was a consumer-electronics giant founded in the early 1970s by the legendary Augustine Goddard, whose nickname was not Gus but Jock. He was almost a cult figure. He graduated from Cal Tech, served in the navy, went to work for

Fairchild Semiconductor and then Lockheed, and invented some kind of breakthrough technology for manufacturing color TV picture tubes. He was generally considered to be a genius, but unlike some of the tyrant geniuses who found huge multinational corporations, he apparently wasn't an asshole. People liked him, were fiercely loyal to him. He was kind of a distant, paternal presence. The rare glimpses of Jock Goddard were called "sightings," as if he were a UFO.

Even though Trion didn't make color TV tubes anymore, the Goddard tube had been licensed to Sony and Mitsubishi and all the other Japanese companies that make America's TVs. Later Trion moved into electronic communications—catapulted by the famous Goddard modem. These days Trion made cell phones and pagers, computer components, color laser printers, personal digital assistants, all that kind of stuff.

A wiry woman with frizzy brown hair emerged from a door into the lobby. "You must be Adam."

I gave her a nice firm handshake. "Nice to meet you."

"I'm Stephanie," she said. "I'm Tom Lundgren's assistant." She took me to the elevator and up to the sixth floor. We made small talk. I was trying to sound enthusiastic but not geeky, and she seemed distracted. The sixth floor was your typical cube farm, cubicles spread out as far as the eye could see, high as an elephant's eye. The route she led me down was a maze; I couldn't retrace my steps to the elevator bank if I dropped bread crumbs. Everything here was standard-issue corporate, except for the computer monitor I passed by whose screen saver was a 3-D image of Jock Goddard's head grinning and spinning like Linda Blair's in *The Exorcist*. Do that at Wyatt—with Nick Wyatt's head, I mean—and Wyatt's corporate goons would probably break your knees.

We came to a conference room with a plaque on the door that said STUDEBAKER.

"Studebaker, huh?" I said.

"Yeah, all the conference rooms are named after classic American cars. Mustang, Thunderbird, Corvette, Camaro. Jock loves American cars." She said Jock with a little twist, almost with quotation marks around it, seemingly indicating that she wasn't really on a first-name basis with the CEO but that's what everyone called him. "Can I get you something to drink?"

Judith Bolton had told me to always say yes, because people like doing favors, and everyone, even the admins, would be giving feedback on what they thought of me. "Coke, Pepsi, whatever," I said. I didn't want to sound too fussy. "Thanks."

I sat down at one side of the table, the side facing the door, not at the head of the table. A couple of minutes later a compact guy wearing khakis and a navy-blue golf shirt with the Trion logo on it came bounding into the room. Tom Lundgren: I recognized him instantly from the dossier that Dr. Bolton had prepared for me. The VP of the Personal Communications Sector business unit. Forty-three, five kids, an avid golfer. Right behind him followed Stephanie, holding a can of Coke and a bottle of Aquafina water.

He gave me a crusher handshake. "Adam, I'm Tom Lundgren."

"Nice to meet you."

"Nice to meet *you.* I hear great things about you."

I smiled, shrugged modestly. Lundgren wasn't even wearing a tie, I thought, and I looked like a funeral director. Judith Bolton warned me that might happen, but said it was better for me to overdress for the interviews than to go too casual. Sign of respect and all that.

He sat down next to me, turned to face me. Stephanie shut the door behind her quietly as she left.

"So working at Wyatt's pretty intense, I bet." He had thin, thin lips and a quick smile that clicked on and off. His face was chafed, reddened, like either he played too much golf or had rosacea or something. His right leg pistoned up and down. He was a bundle of nervous energy, a ganglion; he seemed overcaffeinated, and he made me talk fast. Then I remembered he was a Mormon and didn't drink caffeine. I'd hate to see him after a pot of coffee. He'd probably go into intergalactic orbit.

"Intense is how I like it," I said.

"Good to hear it. So do we." His smile clicked on, then off. "I think there's more type A people here than anywhere else. Everyone's got a faster clock speed." He unscrewed the top of his water bottle and took a sip. "I always say Trion's a great place to work—when you're on vacation. You can return e-mails, voice mails, get all kinds of stuff done, but man, you pay a price for taking off time. You come back, your voice mailbox is full, you get crushed like a grape."

I nodded, smiled conspiratorially. Even marketing guys at high-tech corporations like to talk like engineers, so I gave some back. "Sounds familiar," I said. "You only have so many cycles, you've got to decide what to spend your cycles on." I was mirroring his body language, almost aping him, but he didn't seem to notice.

"Absolutely. Now, we're not really in a hiring mode these days—no one is. But one of our new-product managers got transferred suddenly."

I nodded again.

"The Lucid is genius—really saved Wyatt's bacon in an otherwise dismal quarter. That's your baby, huh?"

"My team, anyway. I was just part of the team. Wasn't running the show."

He seemed to like that. "Well, you were a pretty key player, from what I've heard."

"I don't know about that. I work hard and I love what I do, and I found myself in the right place at the right time."

"You're too modest."

"Maybe." I smiled. He got it, really gobbled up the fake modesty and the directness.

"How'd you do it? What's the secret?"

I blew out a puff of air through pursed lips, as if recalling running a marathon. I shook my head. "No secret. Teamwork. Driving consensus, motivating people."

"Be specific."

"The basic idea started as a Palm-killer, to be honest." I was talking about Wyatt's wireless PDA, the one that buried the Palm Pilot. "At the early concept-planning sessions, we got together a cross-functional group—engineering, marketing, our internal ID folks, an external ID firm." ID is the jargon for industrial design. I was jamming; I knew this answer by heart. "We looked at the market research, what the flaws were in the Trion product, in Palm, Handspring, Blackberry."

"And what was the flaw in our product?"

"Speed. The wireless sucks, but you know that." This was a carefully planned dig: Judith had downloaded for me some candid remarks Lundgren had made at industry conferences, in which he confessed as much. He was blisteringly critical of Trion's efforts whenever they fell short. My bluntness was a calculated risk on Judith's part. Based on her assessment of his manage-ment style, she'd concluded he despised toadyism, grooved on straight talk.

"Correct," he said. He flashed a millisecond of a smile.

"Anyway, we went through a whole range of scenarios. What would a soccer mom really want, a company exec, a construction foreman. We talked feature set, form factor, all that. The discussions were pretty free-form. My big thing was elegance of design married to simplicity."

"I wonder if maybe you erred too much on the side of design, sacrificing functionality," Lundgren put in.

"How do you mean?"

"Lack of a flash slot. The only serious weakness in the product, far as I can see."

A big fat pitch, and I swung at it. "I absolutely agree." Hey, I was totally prepped with stories of "my" successes, and pseudofailures I managed so well they might as well have been battlefield victories. "A big screwup. That was definitely the biggest feature that got jettisoned—it was in the original prod-uct definition, but it grew the form factor outside of the bounds we wanted, so it got scrapped midway through the cycle." Take *that*.

"Doing anything about it in the next generation?"

I shook my head. "Sorry, I can't say. That's proprietary to Wyatt Telecom. This isn't just a legal nicety, it's a moral thing with me—when you give your word, it's got to mean something. If that's a problem . . ."

He gave what looked like a genuine, appreciative smile. Slam dunk. "Not a problem at all. I respect that. Anyone who leaks proprietary information from their last employer would do the same to me."

I noted the words "last employer": Lundgren had already signed on, he'd just given it away.

He pulled out his pager and quickly checked it. He'd gotten several pages while we were talking, on the silent vibrate mode. "I don't need to take any more of your time, Adam. I want you to meet Nora."

10

Nora Sommers was blond, around fifty, with wide-set staring eyes. She had the carnivore look of a wild pack animal. Maybe I was biased by her dossier, which described her as ruthless, tyrannical. She was a director, the team leader of the Maestro project, a sort of scaled-down Blackberry knockoff that was circling the drain. She was notorious for calling seven A.M. staff meetings. No one wanted to be on her team, which was why they were having a hard time filling the job internally.

"So Nick Wyatt must be no fun to work for, huh?" she began.

I didn't need Judith Bolton to tell me you're never supposed to complain about your previous employer. "Actually," I said, "he's demanding, but he brought out the best in me. He's a perfectionist. I have nothing but admiration for him."

She nodded wisely, smiled as if I'd selected the right multiple-choice answer. "Keeps the drive alive, hmm?"

What did she expect me to say, the truth about Nick Wyatt? That he's a boor and an asshole? I don't think so. I riffed a bit longer: "Working at Wyatt is like getting ten years of experience in one year—instead of one year of experience ten times."

"Nice answer," she said. "I like my marketing people to try to snow me. It's a key component of the skill-set. If you can snow me, you can snow the *Journal*."

Danger, Will Robinson. I wasn't going there. I could see the teeth of that jaw trap. So I just looked at her blankly.

"Well," she went on, "the word has certainly spread about you. What was the hardest battle you had to wage on the Lucid project?"

I rehashed the story I'd just given Tom Lundgren, but she sounded underwhelmed. "Doesn't sound like much of a battle to me," she countered. "I'd call that a trade-off."

"Maybe you had to be there," I said. Lame. I scrolled through my mental CD-ROM of anecdotes about the development of the Lucid. "Also, there was a pretty big tussle over the design of the joy pad. That's a five-way directional pad with the speaker built into it."

"I'm familiar with it. What was the controversy?"

"Well, our ID people really keyed in on that as a focal point of the product—it really drew your eye to it. But I was getting major pushback on that from the engineers, who said it was near impossible, way too tricky; they wanted to separate the speaker from the directional pad. The ID guys were convinced that if you separated them, the design would get cluttered, asymmetric. That was tense. So I had to put my foot down. I said this was cornerstone. The design not only made a visual statement, but it also made a major technology statement—told the market we could do something our competitors couldn't."

She was lasering in on me with her wide-set eyes like I was a crippled chicken. "Engineers," she said with a shudder. "They can really be impossible. No business sense at all."

The metal teeth of the jaw trap were glistening with blood. "Actually, I never have problems with engineers," I said. "I think they're really the heart of the enterprise. I never confront them; I *inspire* them, or try, anyway. Thought leadership and mindshare, those are the keys. That's one of the things that most appeals to me about Trion—engineers reign supreme here, which is as it should be. It's a real culture of innovation."

All right, so I was pretty much parroting an interview Jock Goddard once gave to *Fast Company*, but I thought it worked. Trion's engineers were famous for loving Goddard, because he was one of them. They considered it a cool place to work, since so much of Trion's funding went into R&D.

She was speechless for a second. Then she said, "At the end of the day, innovation is mission-critical." Jesus, I thought I was bad, but this woman spoke business cliché as a second language. It was as if she'd learned it from a Berlitz book.

"Absolutely," I agreed.

"So tell me, Adam—what's your greatest weakness?"

I smiled, nodded, and mentally uttered a prayer of gratitude to Judith Bolton.

Score.

Man, it all seemed almost too easy.

1 1

I got the news from Nick Wyatt himself. When I was shown into his office by Yvette, I found him on his Precor elliptical trainer in a corner of his office. He was wearing a sweat-soaked tank top and red gym shorts and looked buff. I wondered if he did steroids. He had a wireless phone headset on and was barking orders.

More than a week had gone by since the Trion interviews, and nothing but radio silence. I knew they'd gone well, and I had no doubt that my references were spectacular, but who knows, anything could happen.

I figured, wrongly, that once I'd done my interviews I'd be given time off from KGB school, but no such luck. The training went on, including what they called "tradecraft"—how to steal stuff without getting caught, copy documents and computer files, how to search the Trion databases, how to contact them if something came up that couldn't wait for a scheduled rendezvous. Meacham and another veteran of Wyatt's corporate security staff, who'd spent two decades in the FBI, taught me how to contact them by e-mail, using an "anonymizer," a remailer based in Finland that buries your real name and address; how to encrypt my e-mail with this super-strong 1,024-bit software developed, against U.S. law, somewhere offshore. They taught me about traditional spy stuff like dead drops and signals, how to let them know I had documents to pass to them. They taught me how to make copies of the ID badges most corporations use these days, the ones that unlock a door when you wave them at a sensor. Some of this stuff was pretty cool. I was beginning to feel like a real spy. At the time, anyway, I was into it. I didn't know any better.

But after a few days of waiting and waiting for some word from Trion, I was scared shitless. Meacham and Wyatt had been pretty clear about what would happen if I didn't land the job.

Nick Wyatt didn't even look at me.

"Congratulations," he said. "I got the word from the headhunter. You just got parole."

"I got an offer?"

"A hundred seventy-five thousand to start, stock options, the whole deal. You're being hired in as an individual contributor at the manager level but without any direct reports, grade ten."

I was relieved, and amazed by the amount. That was about three times what I was making now. Adding in my Wyatt salary took me to two hundred and thirty-five thousand. Jesus.

"Sweet," I said. "Now what do we do, negotiate?"

"The fuck you talking about? They interviewed eight other guys for the job. Who knows who's got a favorite candidate, a crony, whatever. Don't risk it, not yet. Get in the door, show 'em your stuff."

"My stuff—"

"Show 'em how amazing you are. You've already whetted their appetites with a few hors d'oeuvres. Now you blow 'em away. If you can't blow 'em away after graduating our little charm school here, and with me and Judith whispering in your ear, then you're an even bigger fucking loser than I thought."

"Right." I realized I was mentally rehearsing this sick fantasy of telling Wyatt off as I walked out the door to go work for Trion, until I remembered that not only was Wyatt still my boss, he pretty much had me by the balls.

Wyatt stepped off the machine, drenched with sweat, grabbed a white towel off the handlebars, and blotted his face, his arms, his armpits. He stood so close to me I could smell the musk of his perspiration, his sour breath. "Now, listen carefully," he said with an unmistakable note of menace. "About sixteen months ago Trion's board of directors approved an extraordinary expenditure of almost five hundred million dollars to fund some kind of skunkworks."

"A what?"

He snorted. "A top-secret in-house project. Anyway, it's highly unusual for a board to approve an expenditure that large without a lot of information. In this case they approved it blind, based solely on assurances from the CEO. Goddard's the founder, so they trust him. Also, he assured them the technology they were developing, whatever the hell it is, was a monumental breakthrough. I mean huge, paradigm-shifting, a quantum leap. Disruptive beyond disruptive. He assured them that it's the biggest thing since the transistor, and anyone who's not a part of this gets left behind."

"What is it?"

"If I knew, you wouldn't be here, idiot. My sources assure me that it's going to transform the telecommunications industry, turn everything upside down. And I don't intend to get left behind, you follow me?"

I didn't, but I nodded.

"I've invested far too much in this firm to let it go the way of the mastodon and the dodo. So your assignment, my friend, is to find out everything you can about this skunkworks, what it's up to, what they're developing. I don't care whether they're developing some fucking electronic pogo stick, point is, I'm not taking any chances. Clear?"

"How?"

"That's your job." He turned, walked across the vast expanse of office toward an exit I hadn't noticed before. He opened the door, revealing a gleaming marble bathroom with a shower. I stood there awkwardly, not sure whether I was supposed to wait for him, or leave, or what.

"You'll get the call later on this morning," Wyatt said without turning around. "Act surprised."

PART TWO

BACKSTOPPING

Backstopping: An array of bogus cover identifications issued to an operative that will stand up to fairly rigorous investigation.

—*The Dictionary of Espionage*

1 2

I'd placed an ad in three local papers looking for a home healthcare aide for my dad. The ad made it clear anyone was welcome, the requirements weren't exactly strict. I doubted there was anyone left out there—I'd already been to the well too many times.

Exactly seven responses came in. Three of them were from people who somehow misunderstood the ad, were themselves looking to hire someone. Another two phone messages were in foreign accents so thick I couldn't even be sure they were trying to speak English. One was from a perfectly reasonable-sounding, pleasant-voiced man who said his name was Antwoine Leonard.

Not that I had much free time, but I arranged to meet this guy Antwoine for coffee. I wasn't going to have him meet my father until he had to—I wanted to hire him first, before he could see what he was going to have to deal with, so he couldn't back out so easily.

Antwoine turned out to be a huge, scary-looking black dude with prison tats and dreadlocks. My guess was right: just as soon as he could, he told me he'd just got out of prison for auto theft, and it wasn't his first stint in the slammer. He gave me the name of his parole officer as a reference. I liked the fact that he was so open about it, didn't try to hide it. In fact, I just liked the guy. He had a gentle voice, a surprisingly sweet smile, a low-key manner. Granted, I was desperate, but I also figured that if anyone could handle my dad, he could, and I hired him on the spot.

"Listen, Antwoine," I said as I got up to leave. "About the prison thing?"

"It's a problem for you, isn't it?" He looked at me directly.

"No, it's not that. I like you being so straight with me about it."

He shrugged. "Yeah, well—"

"I just think you don't need to be so totally honest with my dad."

The night before I started at Trion, I got to bed early. Seth had left a phone message inviting me to go out with him and some friends of ours, since he wasn't working that night, but I said no.

The alarm clock went off at five-thirty, and it was like something was wrong with the clock: it was still nighttime. When I remembered, I felt a jolt of adrenaline, a weird combination of terror and excitement. I was going into the big game, this was it, practice time was over. I showered and shaved with a brand-new blade, went slow so I didn't cut myself. I'd actually laid out my clothes before I went to sleep, picked out my suit and tie, gave my shoes a glossy shine. I figured I'd better show up on the first day in a suit no matter how out-of-it I looked; I could always take off the jacket and tie.

It was bizarre—for the first time in my life I was making a six-figure salary, even though I hadn't actually gotten any of the paychecks yet, and I was still living in the rat hole. Well, that would change soon enough.

When I got into the silver Audi A6, which still had that new-car smell, I felt more high-end, and to celebrate my new station in life I stopped at a Starbucks and got a triple grande latte. Almost four dollars for a goddamned cup of coffee, but hey, I was making the big bucks now. I cranked up the volume on Rage Against the Machine all the way to the Trion campus so that by the time I got there Zack de la Rocha was screaming "Bullet in the Head" and I was screaming, "No escape from the mass mind rape!" along with him, wearing my perfect corporate Zegna suit and tie and Cole-Haan shoes. I was pumped.

Amazingly, there were a fair number of cars in the underground garage, even at seven-thirty. I parked two levels down.

The lobby ambassador in B Wing couldn't find my name on any list of visitors or new employees. I was a nobody. I asked her to call Stephanie, Tom

Lundgren's admin, but Stephanie wasn't in yet. Finally she reached someone in HR, who told her to send me up to the third floor of E Wing, a long walk.

For the next two hours I sat in the Human Resources reception area with a clipboard, filling out form after form: W-4, W-9, credit union account, insurance, automatic deposit to my bank account, stock options, retirement accounts, nondisclosure agreements. . . . They took my picture and gave me an ID badge and a couple of other little plastic cards that attached to my badge holder. They said things like TRION—CHANGE YOUR WORLD and OPEN COMMUNICATION and FUN and FRUGALITY. It was kind of Soviet, but it didn't really bother me.

One of the HR people took me on a quickie tour of Trion, which was pretty impressive. A great fitness center, ATM cash machines, a place to drop off your laundry and dry cleaning, break rooms with free sodas, bottles of water, popcorn, cappuccino machines.

In the break rooms they had big glossy color posters up that showed a group of square-shouldered men and women (Asian, black, white) posed triumphantly on top of planet Earth under the words DRINK RESPONSIBLY! DRINK FRUGALLY! "The typical Trion employee consumes five beverages a day," it said. "Simply by taking one less cold beverage per day, Trion could save $2.4 million a year!"

You could get your car washed and detailed; you could get discount tickets to movies, concerts, and baseball games; they had a baby gift program ("one gift per household, per occurrence"). I noticed that the elevator in D Wing didn't stop on the fifth floor—"Special Projects," she explained. "No access." I tried not to register any particular interest. I wondered if this was the "skunkworks" Wyatt was so interested in.

Finally, Stephanie came by to take me up to the sixth floor of B Wing. Tom was on the phone but waved me in. His office was lined with photos of his kids—five boys, I noticed—individually and in groups, and drawings they'd done, stuff like that. The books on the shelf behind him were all the usual suspects—*Who Moved My Cheese?*; *First, Break All the Rules*; *How to Be a CEO*. His legs were pistoning away like crazy, and his face looked like it had been scrubbed raw with a Brillo pad. "Steph," he said, "can you ask Nora to come by?"

A few minutes later he slammed down the phone and sprang to his feet, shook my hand. His wedding band was wide and shiny.

"Hey, Adam, welcome to the team!" he said. "Man, am I glad we bagged you! Sit down, sit down." I did. "We need you, buddy. Bad. We're all stretched thin here, really raked. We're covering twenty-three products, we've lost some key staff, and we're stretched way thin. The gal you're replacing got trans-ferred. You're going to be joining Nora's team, working on the refresh of the Maestro line which, as you'll find out, is running into some heavy weather. There are some serious fires to put out, and—here she is!"

Nora Sommers was standing at the doorway, one hand on the doorjamb, posing like a diva. She extended the other hand coyly. "Hi, Adam, welcome! So glad you're with us."

"Nice to be here."

"It was not an easy hire, I'll tell you frankly. We had a lot of really strong candidates. But as they say, cream rises to the top. Well, shall we get right to it?"

Her voice, which had almost had a girlish lilt to it, seemed to deepen instantly as soon as we walked away from Tom Lundgren's office. She spoke faster, almost spitting out her words. "Your cubicle's right over here," she said, jabbing the air with her index finger. "We use Web phones here—I assume you know how?"

"No worries."

"Computer, phone—you should be all set. Anything else, just call Facil-ity Services. All right, Adam, I should warn you, we don't hold hands around here. It's a pretty steep learning curve, but I have no doubt you're up to it. We throw you right in the pool, sink or swim." She looked at me challengingly.

"I'd rather swim," I said with a sly smile.

"Good to hear it," she said. "I like your attitude."

1 3

I had a bad feeling about Nora. She was the type who'd put cement boots on me, bundle me into the trunk of a Cadillac, and throw me in the East River. Sink or swim, tell me about it.

She left me at my new cube to finish reading orientation stuff, learn code names for all the projects. Every high-tech company gives their products code names; Trion's were types of storms—Tornado, Typhoon, Tsunami, and so on. Maestro was codenamed Vortex. It was confusing, all the different names, and on top of it I was trying to get the lay of the land for Wyatt. Around noon, when I was starting to get really hungry, a stocky guy in his forties, graying black hair in a ponytail, wearing a vintage Hawaiian shirt and round black heavy-framed glasses, appeared at my cube.

"You must be the latest victim," he said. "The fresh meat hurled into the lion cage."

"And you all seem so friendly," I said. "I'm Adam Cassidy."

"I know. I'm Noah Mordden. Trion Distinguished Engineer. It's your first day, you don't know who to trust, who to align yourself with. Who wants to play with you, and who wants you to fall flat on your face. Well, I'm here to answer all your questions. How would you like to grab some lunch in the subsidized employee cafeteria?"

Strange guy, but I was intrigued. As we walked to the elevator, he said, "So, they gave you the job no one else wanted, huh?"

"That right?" Oh, great.

"Nora wanted to fill the slot internally, but no one qualified wanted to work for her. Alana, the woman whose job you're filling, actually begged to get out from under her thumb, so they moved her somewhere else in-house. Word on the street is, Maestro's on the bubble." I could barely hear him; he was muttering quietly as he strode toward the elevator bank. "They're always quick to pull the plug when something's failing. Around here, you catch a cold and they're measuring you for a coffin."

I nodded. "The product's redundant."

"A piece of crap. Also doomed. Trion's also coming out with an all-in-one cell phone that has the exact same wireless text-messaging packet, so what's the point? Put the thing out of its misery. Plus, it doesn't help that Nora's a bitch on wheels."

"Is she?"

"If you didn't figure that out within ten seconds of meeting her, you're not as bright as your advance billing. But do not underestimate her: she's got a black belt in corporate politics, and she has her lieutenants, so beware."

"Thank you."

"Goddard's into classic American cars, so she's into them too. Owns a couple of restored muscle cars, though I've never seen her drive any of them. I think the point is for Jock Goddard to know she's cut from the same cloth. She's slick, that Nora."

The elevator was crowded with other employees going down to the third-floor cafeteria. A lot of them wore Trion-logo golf or polo shirts. The elevator stopped on every floor. Someone behind me joked, "Looks like we got the local." I think someone cracks that joke in every single corporate elevator around the world every single day.

The cafeteria, or employee dining room as it was called, was immense, buzzing with the electricity of hundreds, maybe thousands, of Trion employees. It was like a food court in a fancy shopping mall—a sushi bar, with two sushi chefs; a gourmet choose-your-own-topping pizza counter; a burrito bar; Chinese food; steaks and burgers; an amazing salad bar; even a vegetarian/vegan counter.

"Jesus," I said.

"Give the people bread and circuses," Noah said. "Juvenal. Keep the peasants well fed and they won't notice their enslavement."

"I guess."

"Contented cows give better milk."

"Whatever works," I said, looking around. "So much for frugality, huh?"

"Ah. Take a look at the vending machines in the break rooms—twenty-five cents for peanut satay chicken, but a buck for a Klondike bar. Fluids and caffeinated substances are free. Last year the CFO, a man named Paul Camilletti, tried to eliminate the weekly beer bashes, but then managers started spending their own pocket money to buy beer, and someone circulated an e-mail that set out a business case for keeping the beer bashes. Beer costs X per year, whereas it costs Y to hire and train new employees, so given the morale-boosting and employee-retaining costs, the return on investment, ya de ya de ya, you get it. Camilletti, who's all about making the numbers, gave in. Still, his frugality campaign rules the day."

"Same way at Wyatt," I said.

"Even on overseas flights, employees are required to fly economy. Camilletti himself stays at Motel 6 when he travels in the U.S. Trion doesn't have a corporate jet—I mean, let's be clear, Jock Goddard's wife bought one for him for his birthday, so we don't have to feel sorry for him."

I got a burger and Diet Pepsi and he got some kind of mysterious Asian stir-fry thing. It was ridiculously cheap. We looked around the room, holding our trays, but Mordden didn't find anyone he wanted to sit with, so we sat at a table by ourselves. I had that first-day-of-school feeling, when you don't know anyone. It reminded me of when I started Bartholomew Browning.

"Goddard doesn't stay at Motel 6s too, does he?"

"I doubt it. But he's not too in-your-face about his money. He won't take limos. He drives his own car—though granted he has a dozen or so, all antiques he's restored himself. Also, he gives his top fifty execs the luxury car of their choice, and they all make a shitload of money—really obscene. Goddard's smart—he knows you've got to pay the top talent well in order to retain them."

"What about you Distinguished Engineers?"

"Oh, I've made an obscene amount of money here myself. I could in theory tell everyone to go fuck themselves and still have trust funds for my kids, if I had any kids."

"But you're still working."

He sighed. "When I struck gold, just a few years after I started here, I quit and sailed around the world, packing only my clothes and several heavy suitcases containing the Western canon."

"The western cannon?"

He smiled. "The greatest hits of Western literature."

"Like Louis L'Amour?"

"More like Herodotus, Thucydides, Sophocles, Shakespeare, Cervantes, Montaigne, Kafka, Freud, Dante, Milton, Burke—"

"Man, I slept through that class in college," I said.

He smiled again. Obviously he thought I was a moron.

"Anyway," he said, "once I'd read everything, I realized that I'm constitutionally unable not to work, and I returned to Trion. Have you read Étienne de la Boétie's *Discourse on Voluntary Servitude*?"

"Will that be on the final?"

"The only power tyrants have is that relinquished by their victims."

"That and the power to hand out free Pepsis," I said, tipping my can toward him. "So you're an engineer."

He gave a polite smile that was more of a grimace. "Not just any engineer, take note, but, as I said, a Distinguished Engineer. That means I have a low employee number and I can pretty much do whatever I want. If that means being a thorn in Nora Sommers's side, so be it. Now, as for the cast of characters on the marketing side of your business unit. Let's see, you've already met the toxic Nora. And Tom Lundgren, your exalted VP, who's basically a straight shooter who lives for the church, his family, and golf. And Phil Bohjalian, old as Methuselah and just about as technologically up-to-date, who started at Lockheed Martin when it was called something else and computers were as big as houses and ran on IBM punch cards. His days are surely numbered. And—lo and behold, it's Elvis himself, venturing into our midst!"

I turned to where he was looking. Standing by the salad bar was a white-haired, stoop-shouldered guy with a heavily lined face, heavy white eyebrows, large ears, and a sort of pixieish expression. He was wearing a black turtleneck. You could sense the energy in the room change, rippling around him in waves, as people turned to look, whispered, everyone trying to be blasé and subtle.

Augustine Goddard, Trion's founder and chief executive officer, in the flesh.

He looked older than in the pictures I'd seen. A much younger and taller guy was standing next to him, saying something. The younger guy, around forty, was lean and really fit, black hair run through with gray. Italian-looking, movie-star handsome like an action hero who was aging really well, but with deeply pitted cheeks. Except for the bad skin, he reminded me of Al Pacino in the first couple of *Godfather* movies. He was wearing a great charcoal-gray suit.

"That Camilletti?" I asked.

"Cutthroat Camilletti," Mordden said, digging into his stir-fry with chop-sticks. "Our chief financial officer. The czar of frugality. They're together a lot, those two." He spoke through a mouthful of food. "You see his face, those *acne vulgaris* scars? Rumor has it they say 'eat shit and die' in Braille. Anyway, Goddard considers Camilletti the second coming of Jesus Christ, the man who's going to slash operating costs, increase profit margins, launch Trion stock back into the stratosphere. Some say Camilletti is Jock Goddard's id, the bad Jock. His Iago. The devil on his shoulder. I say he's the bad cop who lets Jock be the good cop."

I finished my burger. The CEO and his CFO were in line, paying for their salads, I noticed. Couldn't they just walk out without paying? Or butt to the front of the line or something?

"It's also very Camilletti to get lunch in the employee dining room," Mordden continued, "to demonstrate to the masses his commitment to slash-ing costs. He doesn't cut costs, he 'slashes' them. No executive dining room at Trion. No personal executive chef. No catered lunches brought in, not for them, oh no. Break bread with the peasants." He took a swallow of Dr Pepper. "Where were we in my little *Playbill*, my Who's Who in the Cast? Ah, yes. There's Chad Pierson, Nora's golden-haired boy and protégé, boy wonder and professional suckup. MBA from Tuck, moved from B school right into product marketing at Trion, recently did a stint in Marketing Boot Camp, and no doubt he's going to consider you a threat to be eliminated. And there's Audrey Bethune, the only black woman in . . ."

Noah fell silent suddenly, poked more stir-fry into his mouth. I saw a handsome blond guy around my age gliding quickly up to our table, a shark through water. Button-down blue shirt, preppy-looking, a jock. One of those white-blond guys you see in multipage magazine ad spreads, consorting with other specimens of the master race at a cocktail party on the lawn of their baronial estate.

Noah Mordden took a hasty swig of his Dr Pepper and stood up. He had brown stir-fry stains on the front of his Aloha shirt. "Pardon me," he said uncomfortably. "I have a one-on-one." He left his dishes spread out on the table and bolted just as the white-blond guy got there, hand outstretched.

"Hey, man, how you doing?" the guy said. "Chad Pierson."

I went to shake his hand, but he did one of those hip-hop too-cool-to-shake-hands-the-normal-way hand-slide things. His fingernails looked manicured. "Man," he said, "I've heard so much about you, you stud!"

"All bullshit," I said. "Marketing, you know."

He laughed conspiratorially. "Nah, you're supposed to be the *man*. I'm hangin' with you, learn a trick or two."

"I'm going to need all the help I can get. They tell me it's sink-or-swim around here, and it definitely looks like the deep end."

"So, Mordden give you his cynical egghead shit?"

I smiled neutrally. "Gave me his take."

"All negative. He thinks he's in some kind of soap opera, some Machiavelli-type deal. Maybe *he* is, but I wouldn't pay him much attention."

I realized that I'd just sat with the unpopular kid on the first day of school, but that just made me want to defend Mordden. "I like him," I said.

"He's an engineer. They're all weird. You play hoops?"

"Some, sure."

"Every Tuesday and Thursday lunchtime in the gym there's always a pick-up game, we gotta get you on the court. Plus maybe you and me can go out for a drink some time, catch a game, whatever."

"Sounds great," I said.

"Anyone tell you about the Corporate Games beer bash yet?"

"Not yet."

"I guess that's not exactly Mordden's thing. Anyway, it's a blast." He was hyper, torquing his body from side to side like a basketball player looking for a lane to make a monster dunk. "So, bud, you're going to be at the two o'clock, right?"

"Wouldn't miss it."

"Cool. Nice having you on the team, bud. We're gonna do some damage, you and me." He gave me a big smile.

14

Chad Pierson was standing at a whiteboard, writing up a meeting agenda with red and blue markers, when I walked into Corvette. This was a conference room like every other conference room I'd ever seen—the big table (only high-tech-designer black instead of walnut), the Polycom speakerphone console sitting in the middle of the table like a geometric black widow spider, a basket of fruit and ice bucket of soft drinks and juice boxes.

He gave me a quick wink as I sat down on one of the long sides of the table. There were a couple of other people already there. Nora Sommers was sitting at the head of the table, wearing black reading glasses on a chain around her neck, reading through a file and occasionally muttering something to Chad, her scribe. She didn't seem to notice me.

Next to me sat a gray-haired guy in a blue Trion polo shirt tapping away on a Maestro, probably doing e-mail. He was thin but had a potbelly, skinny arms and knobby elbows poking out of his short-sleeved shirt, a fringe of gray hair and unexpectedly long gray sideburns, big red ears. He wore bifocals. If he'd had a different kind of shirt on, he'd probably be wearing a plastic shirt-pocket protector. He looked like an old-style nerd engineer from the Hewlett-Packard-calculator days. His teeth were small and brown, like he chewed tobacco.

This had to be Phil Bohjalian, the old-timer, though from the way Mordden talked about him, I half expected him to be using a quill and parchment. He kept sneaking nervous, furtive glances at me.

Noah Mordden slipped quietly into the room, didn't acknowledge me or anyone else for that matter, and opened his notebook computer at the far end of the conference table. More people filed in, laughing and talking. There were maybe a dozen people in the room now. Chad finished at the white-board and put his stuff down in the empty seat next to me. He clapped a hand on my shoulder. "Glad you're with us," he said.

Nora Sommers cleared her throat, stood up, walked over to the white-board. "Well, why don't we get started? All right, I'd like to introduce our newest team member, to those of you who haven't yet had the privilege of meeting him. Adam Cassidy, welcome."

She fluttered her red fingernails at me, and all heads turned. I smiled modestly, ducked my head.

"We were very fortunate in being able to steal Adam away from Wyatt, where he was one of the key players on Lucid. We're hoping he'll apply some of his magic to Maestro." She smiled beatifically.

Chad spoke up, looking from side to side as if he were sharing a secret. "This bad boy's a genius, I've talked to him, so everything you've heard is true." He turned to me, his baby-blues wide, and shook my hand.

Nora went on, "As we all know far too well, we're getting some serious pushback on Maestro. The knives are out throughout Trion, and I don't have to name names." There was some low chortling. "We have a rather large, looming deadline—a presentation before Mr. Goddard himself, where we will make the case for maintaining the Maestro product line. This is far more than a functional staff update, more than a checkpoint meeting. This is life or death. Our enemies want to put us in the electric chair; we're pleading for a stay of execution. Are we clear about that?"

She looked around menacingly, saw obedient nods. Then she turned around and slashed through the first item in the agenda with a purple marker, a little too violently. Whipping back around, she handed a sheaf of stapled papers to Chad, who began passing them around to his right and left. They looked like some kind of specs, a product definition or product protocol or whatever, but the name of the product, presumably on the top sheet, had been removed.

"Now," she said, "I'd like us to do an exercise—a demonstration, if you will. Some of you may recognize this product protocol, and if so, keep it to yourselves. As we work to refresh the Maestro, I want us all to think outside the box for a couple of moments, and I'd like to ask our newest star to look this over and give us his thoughts."

She was looking right at me.

I touched my chest and said stupidly, "Me?"

She smiled. "You."

"My . . . thoughts?"

"That's right. Go/no-go. Greenlight this project or no. You, Adam, are the gatekeeper on this proposed product. Tell us what you think. Do we go for it, or not?"

My stomach dropped. My heart started thudding. I tried to control my breathing, but I could feel my face flushing as I thumbed through it. It was all but inscrutable. I really didn't know what the hell it was for. I could hear little nervous noises in the silence—Nora clicking the top of the Expo marker off and on, twisting it with a scrunchy noise. Someone was playing with the little plastic flex-straw on his Minute Maid apple juice box, pushing it in and pulling it out, making it squeak.

I nodded slowly, wisely as I scanned it, trying not to look like a deer caught in the headlights, which was how I felt. There was some gobbledygook there about "market segment analysis" and "rough estimate of size of market opportunity." Man oh man. The nerve-wracking music from *Jeopardy* was playing in my head.

Scrunch, scrunch. Squeak, squeak.

"Well, Adam? Go or no-go?"

I nodded again, trying to look fascinated and amused at the same time. "I like it," I said. "It's clever."

"Hmm," she said. There was some low chuckling. Something was up. Wrong answer, I guessed, but I could hardly change it now.

"Look," I said, "based solely on the product definition, of course, it's hard to say much more than—"

"That's all we have to go on at this point," she interrupted. "Right? Go or no-go?"

I riffed. "I've always believed in being bold," I said. "I'm intrigued. I like the form factor, the handwriting recognition specs. . . . Given the usage model, the market opportunity, I'd certainly pursue this further, at least to the next checkpoint."

"Aha," she said. One side of her mouth turned up in an evil smile. "And to think our friends in Cupertino didn't even need Adam's wisdom to green-light this stink bomb. Adam, these are the specs for the Apple Newton. One of the biggest bombs Cupertino ever dropped. Cost them over five hundred million dollars to develop, and *then*, when it came out, they lost sixty million bucks a *year* on it." More chuckles. "But it sure gave *Doonesbury* and Jay Leno plenty of material back in 1993."

People were looking away from me. Chad was biting the inside of his cheek, looking grave. Mordden seemed to be in another world. I wanted to rip Nora Sommers's face off, but I did the good-loser thing.

Nora looked around the table, from one face to the next, her eyebrows arched. "There's a lesson here. You've always got to drill down, look beyond the marketing hype, get under the hood. And believe me, when we present to Jock Goddard in two weeks, he's going to be getting under the hood. Let's keep that at top of mind."

Polite smiles all around: everyone knew Goddard was a gearhead, a car nut.

"All right," she said. "I think I've made my point. Let's move on."

Yeah, I thought. Let's move on. Welcome to Trion. You've made your point. I felt a hollowness in the pit of my stomach.

What the hell had I gotten myself into?

15

The meeting between my dad and Antwoine Leonard did not go smoothly. Well, actually, it was a total, unmitigated disaster. Put it this way: Antwoine encountered significant pushback. No synergy. Not a strategic fit.

I arrived at Dad's apartment right after I finished my first day at Trion. I parked the Audi down the block, because I knew Dad was always looking out of his window, when he wasn't watching his thirty-six-inch TV screen, and I didn't want to get grief from him about my new car. Even if I told him I'd gotten a big raise or something, he'd find a way to put some nasty spin on it.

I got there just in time to see Maureen wheeling a big black nylon suitcase up to a cab. She was tight-lipped, wearing her "dressy" outfit, a lime green pantsuit with a riot of tropical flowers and fruits all over it, and a perfectly white pair of sneakers. I managed to intercept her just as she was yelling at the driver to put her suitcase in the trunk and handed her a final check (including a generous bonus for pain and suffering), thanked her profusely for her loyal service, and even tried to give her a ceremonial peck on the cheek, but she turned her head away. Then she slammed the door, and the cab took off.

Poor woman. I never liked her, but I couldn't help but feel sorry for the torture my father had put her through.

Dad was watching Dan Rather, really mostly yelling at Rather, when I arrived. He despised all the network anchormen equally, and you didn't want to get him started on the "losers" on cable. The only cable shows he liked were the ones where opinionated right-wing hosts bait their guests, try to piss them off, froth at the mouth. That was his kind of sport these days.

He was wearing one of those sleeveless white undershirts that are sometimes called "wifebeaters." They always gave me the willies. I had bad associations with them—whenever he "disciplined" me as a kid, he seemed to be wearing one. I could still remember, clear as a snapshot, the time when, eight years old, I accidentally spilled Kool-Aid on his Barcalounger, and he took the strap to me, standing over me—stained ribbed undershirt, red sweating face—roaring, "See what you made me do?" Not the most pleasant memory.

"When's this new guy getting here?" he said. "He's already late, isn't he?"

"Not yet." Maureen refused to spend a minute showing him the ropes, so unfortunately there'd be no overlap.

"What're you all dressed up for? You look like an undertaker—you're making me nervous."

"I told you, I started a new job today."

He turned back to Rather, shaking his head in disgust. "You got fired, didn't you?"

"From Wyatt? No, I left."

"You tried to coast like you always do, and they fired you. I know how these things work. They can smell a loser a mile off." He took a couple of heavy breaths. "Your mother always spoiled you. Like hockey—you coulda gone pro if you applied yourself."

"I wasn't that good, Dad."

"Easy to say that, isn't it? Makes it easier if you just say that. That's where I really fucked you up—I put you through that high-priced college so you could spend all your time partying with your fancy friends." He was only partly right, of course: I did work-study to put myself through college. But let him remember what he wanted to remember. He turned to look at me, his eyes bloodshot, beady. "So where are all your fancy friends now, huh?"

"I'm okay, Dad," I said. He was on one of his jags, but fortunately the doorbell rang, and I almost ran to answer it.

Antwoine was right on time. He was dressed in pale blue hospital scrubs, which made him look like an orderly or a male nurse. I wondered where he picked them up, since he'd never worked in a hospital, as far as I knew.

"Who's that?" Dad shouted hoarsely.

"It's Antwoine," I said.

"*Antwoine?* What the hell kinda name is Antwoine? You hired some French faggot?" But Dad had already turned to see Antwoine standing at the front door, and his face had gone purple. He was squinting, his mouth open in horror. "Jesus—Christ!" he said, puffing hard.

"How's it going?" Antwoine said, giving me a bone-crushing handshake. "So this must be the famous Francis Cassidy," he said, approaching the Barcalounger. "I'm Antwoine Leonard. Pleasure to meet you, sir." He spoke in a deep, pleasant baritone.

Dad kept staring, puffing in and out. Finally he said, "Adam, I wanna talk to you, right now."

"Sure, Dad."

"No—you tell *An-twoine* or whatever the hell his name is to get outta here, let you and me talk."

Antwoine looked at me, puzzled, wondering what he should do.

"Why don't you bring your stuff to your room?" I said. "It's the second door on the right. You can start unpacking."

He carried two nylon duffel bags down the hall. Dad didn't even wait for him to get out of the room before he said, "Number one, I don't want a *man* taking care of me, you understand? Find me a woman. Number two, I don't want a *black* man here. They're unreliable. What were you thinking? You were gonna leave me alone with Leroy? I mean, look at your *homeboy* here, the tattoos, the braids. I don't want that in my house. Is this so damned much to ask?" He was puffing harder than ever. "How can you bring a black guy in here, after all the trouble I have with those goddamned kids from the projects breaking into my apartment?"

"Yeah, and they always turn right around when they figure out there's nothing here worth stealing." I kept my voice down, but I was pissed. "Number one, Dad, we don't really have a choice here, because the agencies won't even *deal* with us anymore, because you've made so many people quit, okay? Number two, I can't stay with you, because I've got a day job, remember? And number three, you haven't even given the guy a chance."

Antwoine came back down the hall toward us. He approached my father, almost menacingly close, but he spoke in a soft, gentle voice. "Mr. Cassidy, you want me to leave, I'll leave. Hell, I'll leave right now, I don't got no problem with that. I don't stay where I'm not wanted. I don't need a job *that* bad. As long as my parole officer knows I made a serious attempt to get a job, I'm cool."

Dad was staring at the TV, an ad for Depends, a vein twitching under his left eye. I'd seen that face before, usually when he was chewing someone out, and it could scare the shit out of you. He used to make his football players run till someone puked, and if anyone refused to keep going, they got the Face. But he'd used it so many times on me that it had lost its power. Now he pivoted around and turned it on Antwoine, who'd no doubt seen a hell of a lot worse in the joint.

"Did you say *parole officer?*"

"You heard me right."

"You're a fucking *convict?*"

"*Ex*-con."

"The *hell* you trying to do to me?" he said, staring at me. "You trying to kill me before the disease does? Look at me, I can't hardly move, and you put me alone in the house with a fucking *convict?*"

Antwoine didn't even seem to be annoyed. "Like your son says, you ain't got nothing worth stealing, even if I wanted to," he said calmly, through sleepy eyes. "At least give me a little credit, if I wanted to pull off some kinda scam, I wouldn't take a job *here.*"

"You hear *that?*" Dad puffed, enraged. "You hear *that?*"

"Plus, if I'm going to stay, we gotta come to agreement on a couple of things, you and me." Antwoine sniffed the air. "I can smell the smokes, and you're going to have to cut that shit out right now. That's the shit that got you here." He reached out one huge hand and tapped the arm of the Barcalounger. A compartment popped open, which I'd never seen before, and a red-and-white pack of Marlboros popped up like a jack-in-the-box. "Thought so. That's where my dad always hid his."

"Hey!" my dad yelled. "I don't believe this!"

"And you're gonna start a workout routine. Your muscles are wasting away. Your problem isn't your lungs, it's your muscles."

"Are you out of your fuckin' mind?" Dad said.

"You got the respiratory disease, you gotta exercise. Can't do anything about the lungs, those are gone, but the muscles we can do something about.

We're gonna start with some leg lifts in your chair, get your leg muscles working again, and then we're going to walk for one minute. My old man had the
emphysema, and me and my brother—"

"You tell this big—tattooed nigger," Dad said between puffs, "to get his
stuff—out of that room—and get the hell out of my house!"

I almost lost it. I'd just had a supremely lousy day, and my temper was
short, and for months and months I'd been busting my ass trying to find
someone who'd put up with the old guy, replacing each one as he made them
leave, a whole long parade, a huge waste of time. And here he was, summar-
ily dismissing the latest who, granted, may not have been an ideal candidate,
but was the only one we had. I wanted to let into him, let fly, but I couldn't. I
couldn't scream at my father, this pathetic dying old man with end-stage
emphysema. So I held it in, at the risk of exploding.

Before I could say anything, Antwoine turned to me. "I believe your son
hired me, so he's the only one who can fire me."

I shook my head. "No such luck, Antwoine. You're not getting out of
here—not so easy. Why don't you get started?"

16

I needed to blow off steam. It was everything—the way Nora Sommers had rubbed my face in it, being unable to tell her to go fuck herself, the impossibility of my surviving at Trion long enough to steal even a coffee mug, the general feeling of being in way over my head. And then, the cherry on the cake: my dad. Keeping the anger in, stopping myself from telling him off— *you fucking ungrateful bigot, die already!*—was corroding my insides.

So I just showed up at Alley Cat, knowing that Seth would be working that night. I just wanted to sit at the bar and get shitfaced on free booze.

"Hey, homey," Seth said, delighted to see me, "your first day at the new place, huh?"

"Yeah."

"That bad, huh?"

"I don't want to talk about it."

"Seriously bad. Wow." He poured me a Scotch like I was some old drunk, a regular. "*Love* the haircut, dude. Don't tell me you got drunk and woke up with that haircut."

I ignored him. The Scotch went immediately to my head. I hadn't eaten any supper, and I was tired. It felt great.

"How bad could it be, bud? It's your first day, they like show you where the bathroom is, right?" He looked up at the basketball game on TV, then back at me.

I told him about Nora Sommers and her cute little Apple Newton trick.

"What a bitch, huh? What'd she come down on you so hard for? What'd she expect—you're new, you don't know anything, right?"

I shook my head. "No, she—" Suddenly I realized that I'd left out a key part of the story, the part about my allegedly being a superstar at Wyatt Telecom. Shit. The anecdote only made sense if you knew the dragon lady was trying to take me down a peg. My brain was fried. Trying to extricate myself from this minor slip seemed an insurmountable goal, like climbing Mount Everest or swimming across the Atlantic. Already I'd gotten caught in a lie. I felt gooey inside and very tired. Fortunately someone caught Seth's eye, signaled to him. "Sorry, man, it's half-price hamburger night," he announced as he went to fetch someone a couple of beers.

I found myself thinking about the people I'd met today, the "cast of characters" as the bizarro Noah Mordden had referred to them, who were now parading through my head, getting more and more grotesque. I wanted to debrief with somebody, but I couldn't. Mostly I wanted to *download*, talk about Chad and Phil Whatever, the old-timer. I wanted to tell someone about Trion and what it was like and about my sighting of Jock Goddard in the cafeteria. But I couldn't, because I didn't trust myself to remember where the Great Wall ran, which part no one was supposed to know about.

The Scotch buzz began to fade, and this humming low note of anxiety, a pedal note, was slowly growing louder, gradually getting higher-pitched, like microphone feedback, high and ear-splitting. By the time Seth came back, he'd forgotten what we were talking about. Seth, like most guys, tends to focus more on his own stuff than on anyone else's. Saved by male narcissism.

"God, women love bartenders," he said. "Why is that?"

"I don't know, Seth. Maybe it's you." I tipped my empty glass toward him.

"No doubt. No doubt." He glugged another few ounces of Scotch in there, refreshed the ice. In a low, confiding voice, barely audible over the din of whooping voices and the blaring ballgame, he said, "My manager says he doesn't like my pour. Keeps making me use a pour tester, practice all the time. Plus he's always testing me now. 'Pour for me! Too much! You're giving away the store!' "

"I think your pour's perfectly fine," I said.

"I'm really supposed to write up a ticket, you know."

"Go ahead. I'm making the big bucks now."

"Na-ah, they let us comp four drinks a night, don't worry about it. So, you think you've got it bad at work. My boss at the firm is always giving me shit if I'm like ten minutes late."

I shook my head.

"I mean, Shapiro doesn't know how to use the copier. He doesn't know how to send a fax. He doesn't even know how to do a Lexis-Nexis search. He'd be totally sunk without me."

"Maybe he wants someone else to do the shitwork."

Seth didn't seem to hear me. "So did I tell you about my latest scam?"

"Tell me."

"Get this—jingles!"

"Huh?"

"*Jingles!* There—like that!" He pointed up at the TV, some cheesy low-production-value ad for a mattress company with a stupid, annoying song they were always playing. "I met this guy at the law firm who works for an ad agency, he told me all about it. Told me he could get me an audition with one of those jingle companies like Megamusic or Crushing or Rocket. He said the easiest way to break in is by writing one of them."

"You can't even read music, Seth."

"Neither can Stevie Wonder. Look, a lot of the really talented guys can't read music. I mean, how long does it take to learn a thirty-second piece of music? This girl who does all those JCPenney ads, he said she can barely read music, but she's got the *voice!*"

A woman next to me at the bar called out to Seth, "What kind of wine do you have?"

"Red, white, and pink," he said. "What can I get you?"

She said white, and he poured some into a water glass.

He circled back to me. "The big bucks is in the singing, though. I just got to put a reel together, a CD, and pretty soon I'll be on the A list—it's all who you know. You following me? No work, mucho bucks!"

"Sounds great," I said with not enough enthusiasm.

"You're not into this?"

"No, it sounds great, it really does," I said, mustering a little more enthusiasm. "Great scam." In the last couple of years, Seth and I talked a lot about scamming by, about how to do the least work possible. He loved hearing my stories of how I used to goof off at Wyatt, how I used to spend hours on the Internet looking at *The Onion* or Web sites like BoredAtWork.com or ILove-Bacon.com or FuckedCompany.com. I especially liked the sites that had a "manager" button you could click when your manager passed by, that killed the funny stuff and put back up whatever boring Excel spreadsheet you were working on. We both took pride in how little work we could get away with. That's why Seth loved being a paralegal—because it allowed him to be marginal, mostly unsupervised, cynical, and uncommitted to the working world.

I got up to take a leak and on the way back bought a pack of Camel straights from the vending machine.

"Again with this shit?" Seth said when he spied me tearing the plastic off the cigarette pack.

"Yeah, yeah," I said in a leave-me-alone tone.

"Don't come to me for help wheeling your oxygen tank around." He pulled a chilled martini glass out of the freezer, poured in a little vermouth. "Watch this." He tossed the vermouth out, over his shoulder, then poured in some Bombay Sapphire. "Now *that's* a perfect martini."

I took a long swig of the Scotch as he went to ring up the martini and deliver it, enjoyed the burn at the back of my throat. Now it was really starting to kick in. I felt a little unsteady on the bar stool. I was drinking like your proverbial coal miner with a paycheck in his pocket. Nora Sommers and Chad Pierson and all the others had begun to recede, to shrink, to take on a harmless, antic, cartoon-character aura. So I had a shitty first day, what was so unusual about that? Everyone felt a little out-of-their-element on the first day in a new job. I was *good*, I had to keep this in mind. If I weren't so good, Wyatt would never have chosen me for his mission. Obviously he and his *consigliere* Judith wouldn't be wasting their time on me if they didn't think I could pull it off. They'd have just fired me and tossed me into the legal system to fend for myself. I'd be bent over that bunk in Marion.

I began to feel a pleasant, alcohol-fueled surge of confidence bordering on megalomania. I'd been parachuted into Nazi Germany, with little more than K rations and a shortwave radio, and the success of the allies was riding entirely on me, nothing less than the fate of Western civilization.

"I saw Elliot Krause today downtown," Seth said.

I looked at him, uncomprehending.

"Elliot Krause? Remember? Elliot Port-O-San?"

My reaction time had slowed; it took me a few seconds, but then I burst out laughing. I hadn't heard Elliot Krause's name in years.

"He's a partner in some law firm, of course."

"Specializing in . . . environmental law, right?" I said, choking with laughter, spitting out a mouthful of Scotch.

"Do you remember his face?"

"Forget his face, remember his *pants*?"

This was why I liked spending time with Seth. We talked in Morse code; we got each other's references, all the inside jokes. Our shared history gave us a secret language, the way twins talk to each other when they're babies. One summer in high school when Seth was working at a snooty tennis club doing grounds maintenance during a big international tennis match, he let me sneak in without paying. They'd brought in some of those rented "portable restroom facilities" for the influx of spectators—Handy Houses or Port-O-Sans or Johnny On the Job, whatever cute name they had, I don't remember—those things that look like big old refrigerators. By the second or third day they'd gotten full, the Handy House crew hadn't bothered to come by and pump them out, and they reeked.

There was this preppy kid named Elliot Krause we both hated, partly because he'd stolen Seth's girlfriend, and partly because he looked down on us as working-class kids. He showed up at the tournament, dressed in a faggoty tennis sweater and white duck pants, Seth's girlfriend on his arm, and he made the mistake of going into one of the Handy Houses to relieve himself. Seth, who was spearing trash at the moment, saw this and gave me an evil smile. He ran over to the booth, jammed the wooden handle of his trash-picker-upper thing through the latch, and me and a friend of ours, Flash Flaherty, started rocking the Porta Potti back and forth. You could hear Elliot inside shouting, "Hey! Hey! What the hell's going on?" and you could hear the sloshing of the unspeakable contents, and finally we got the thing flipped over, with Elliot trapped inside. I don't want to think about what the poor guy was floating in. Seth lost his job but he insisted that it was worth it—he'd have paid good money just for the privilege of seeing Elliot Krause emerge in his no-longer-white tennis whites, retching, covered in shit.

By this point, recalling Elliot Krause putting his shit-splashed glasses back on his shit-covered face as he stumbled out of the Handy House, I was laughing so hard I lost my balance and sprawled onto the floor. For a couple of seconds I lay there, unable to get up. People crowded around me, giant heads leaning in, asking if I was okay. I was definitely looped. Everything had gotten smeary. For some reason I flashed on an image of my father and Antwoine Leonard, and the thought struck me as screamingly hilarious, and I couldn't stop laughing.

I felt someone grab me by the shoulder, someone else grab me by the elbow. Seth and another guy were helping me out of the bar. Everyone seemed to be watching me.

"Sorry, man," I said, feeling a wave of embarrassment wash over me. "Thanks. My car's right here."

"You're not driving, bud."

"It's right *here*," I insisted feebly.

"That's not your car. That's an Audi or something."

"It's mine," I said firmly, punctuating the statement with a vigorous nod. "Audi—A6, I think."

"What happened to Bondo?"

I shook my head. "New car."

"Man, this new job, they paying you a lot more?"

"Yeah," I said, then I added, my words slurred, "not that much more."

He whistled for a cab, and he and the other guy hustled me into it. "You remember where you live?" Seth said.

"Come on," I said. "Of course I remember."

"You want a coffee for the ride home, sober you up a little?"

"Nah," I said. "I got to get to sleep. Work tomorrow."

Seth laughed. "I don't envy you, man," he said.

17

In the middle of the night my cell phone rang, ear-splittingly loud, only it wasn't the middle of the night. I could see a shaft of light behind the shades. The clock said five-thirty—A.M.? P.M.? I was so disoriented I had no idea. I grabbed the phone, wished I hadn't left it on.

"Yeah?"

"You're still asleep?" a voice said, incredulous.

"Who is this?"

"You left the Audi in a tow zone." Arnold Meacham, I realized at once: Wyatt's security Nazi. "It's not *your* car, it's leased by Wyatt Telecommunications, and the least you can do is take decent care of it—not leave it lying around like a discarded *condom*."

It came back to me: last night, getting wasted at Alley Cat, somehow getting home, forgetting to set the alarm . . . Trion!

"Oh, shit," I said, jolting upright, my stomach doing a flip. My head throbbed, felt enormous, like one of those aliens on *Star Trek*.

"We set out the rules quite clearly," Meacham said. "No more carousing. No partying. You're expected to function at peak capacity." Was he talking faster and louder than normal? He sure seemed to be. I could barely keep up.

"I know," I croaked lamely.

"This is not an auspicious start."

"It was real—real busy yesterday. My first day, and my father—"

"I really don't give a shit. We have an explicit agreement, which you're expected to abide by. And what have you turned up on the skunkworks?"

"Skunkworks?" I flung my legs around to the floor, sat on the edge of the bed, massaged my temples with my free hand.

"Classified, codeword projects. What the hell do you think you're there for?"

"No, it's too early," I said. "Too soon, I mean." Slowly my brain was starting to function. "I was escorted everywhere yesterday. There wasn't a minute when I was left alone. It would have been far too risky for me to do anything sneaky. You don't want me blowing this assignment on the first day."

Meacham was silent for a few seconds. "Fair enough," he said. "But you should have an opportunity quite soon, and I expect you to take advantage of it. I want a report by close of business *today*, are we clear?"

18

By lunchtime I began to feel less like the walking wounded, and I decided to go up to the gym—the "fitness center," excuse me—to get in a quick workout. The fitness center was on the roof of E Wing, in a sort of bubble, with tennis courts, all sorts of cardio equipment, treadmills and StairMasters and elliptical trainers all outfitted with individual TV/video screens. The locker room had a steam room and sauna and was as spacious as any high-end sports club I'd ever seen.

I'd changed and was about to hit the machines and the weights when Chad Pierson sauntered into the locker room.

"There he is," Chad said. "How's it going, big guy?" He opened a locker near mine. "You here for B-ball?"

"Actually, I was going to—"

"There's probably a game on, you wanna play?"

I hesitated a second. "Sure."

There was no one else on the basketball court, so we waited around for a couple of minutes, dribbling and taking shots. Finally, Chad said, "How about a little one-on-one?"

"Sure."

"To eleven. Winners out?"

"Okay."

"Listen, how 'bout we put a little wager on the game, huh? I'm not really a competitive guy—maybe that'll juice it up a little."

Yeah, right, I thought. *You're* not competitive. "Like a six-pack or something?"

"Come on, man. A C-note. Hundred bucks."

A *C-note?* What, were we in Vegas with the Rat Pack? Reluctantly, I said, "Okay, sure, whatever."

A mistake. Chad was good, played aggressively, and I was hungover. He went to the top of the three-point line, shot, and sank it. Then, looking pleased with himself, he made a pistol with his finger and thumb, blew the smoke off the barrel, and said, "Smokin'!"

Backing me in, he hit a few fadeaway jumpers and immediately took the lead. From time to time he'd do this little Alonzo Mourning move where he waggled both hands back and forth like a sharpshooter slinging his guns around at a shootout. It was supremely annoying. "Looks like you didn't bring your A game, huh?" he said. His expression seemed benevolent, even concerned, but his eyes gleamed with condescension.

"Guess not," I said. I was trying to be a nice guy, enjoy the game, not go after him like a dick, but he was beginning to piss me off. When I drove, I wasn't in sync, didn't have a feel yet. I missed a few shots, and he blocked a couple. But then I scored a few points off him, and before long it was six to three. I began to notice he kept driving right.

He pumped his fist, did his stupid finger-pistol thing. He drove right, hit another jumper. "Money!" he crowed.

It was at that point that I sort of hit a mental toggle switch and let the competitive juices flow. Chad kept driving to the right and shooting right, I noticed. It was obvious he couldn't go left, didn't have a decent left hand. So I started taking away his right, forcing him left, then I hit a layup.

I'd guessed right. He had no left hand. He missed shots going left, and a couple of times I easily picked off the ball as his dribble crossed over. I got in front of him, then suddenly jumped back and to the right, forcing him to switch directions quickly. Mostly, as I got into the rhythm of the game, I'd been driving, so Chad must have figured I didn't have a jump shot. He looked stunned when my jump shot started dropping.

"You've been holding out on me," he said through gritted teeth. "You *do* have a jump shot—but I'm going to shut it down."

I started playing with his mind a little. I faked going for a jump shot, forcing him up in the air, then blew right by him. This worked so well that I tried it again; Chad was so unnerved that it worked even better the second time. Pretty soon the score was even.

I was getting under his skin. I'd do a little stutter step, just a little movement, fake to the left, and he'd jump left, giving me space to drive right. With each score you could see he was getting more and more rattled.

I drove in and shot a layup, then hit my fadeaway. I was ahead now, and Chad was getting red-faced, short of breath. No more cocky repartee.

I was ahead, ten to nine, when I drove hard and then suddenly stopped short. Chad reeled back and fell on his ass. I took my time, got my feet set, and put up my shot—all net. I made a little pistol with my thumb and forefinger, blew off the smoke, and, with a nice big smile, said, "Smokin'."

Half backing up, half collapsing against the padded gym wall, Chad gasped, "Well, you surprised me, big guy. You've got more game than I thought." He took a deep gulp of air. "This was good. Lot of fun. But I'm going to kick your ass next time, buddy—I know your game now." He grinned, like he was only kidding, reached out and put a clammy, sweaty hand on my shoulder. "I owe you a Benjamin."

"Forget about it. I don't like playing for money anyway."

"No, really. I insist. Buy yourself a new tie or something."

"No way, Chad. Won't take it."

"I owe you—"

"You don't owe me anything, man." I thought for a moment. There's nothing people love to part with more than advice. "Except maybe a Nora tip or two."

His eyes lit up; I was playing on his field now. "Aw, she does that to all the newbies. It's her own form of hazing, doesn't mean anything more than that. It's nothing personal, believe me—I got the same treatment when I started here."

I noticed the unstated, *And now look at me.* He was careful not to criticize Nora; he knew to be wary of me, not to open up. "I'm a big boy," I said. "I can take it."

"I'm saying you won't have to, bud. She made her point—just stay on your toes—and now she'll move on. She wouldn't have done that if she didn't consider you a high-po." High-potential, he meant. "She likes you. She wouldn't have fought to get you on her team if she didn't."

"Okay." I couldn't tell if he was holding out on me or not.

"I mean, if you wanna . . . like, this afternoon's meeting—Tom Lundgren's going to be there, reviewing the product specs, right? And we've been spinning our wheels for weeks already, stuck in some dumbass debate over whether to add GoldDust functionality." He rolled his eyes. "Like, give me a break. Don't even get Nora started on that crap. Anyway, it's probably a good idea if you have *some* opinion on GoldDust—you don't have to agree with Nora that it's complete and total bullshit and a huge waste of money. The important thing is to just have an opinion on it. She likes informed debate."

GoldDust, I knew, was the latest big thing in electronic consumer products. It was some engineering industry committee's fancy marketing name for low-power, short-range wireless transmission technology that's supposed to let you connect your Palm or Blackberry or Lucid to a phone or a laptop or a printer, whatever. Anything within twenty feet or so. Your computer can talk to your printer, everything talks to everything else, and no unsightly cables to trip over. It was going to free us all from our chains, from wires and cables and tethers. Of course, what the industry geeks who invented Gold-Dust didn't figure on was the explosion in WiFi, 802.11 wireless. Hey, even before Wyatt put me through the Bataan Death March, I had to know about WiFi. GoldDust I learned about from Wyatt's engineers, who ridiculed it up and down.

"Yeah, there was always someone at Wyatt trying to push that on us, but we held the line."

He shook his head. "Engineers want to pack everything into everything, no matter what it costs. What do they care if it pushes our price point up over five hundred bucks? Anyway, that'll come up for sure—I'll bet you can really whale on it."

"All I know is what I read, you know?"

"I'll tee it up for you at the meeting, you can whomp it. Earn a couple of strategic brownie points with the boss, can't hurt, right?"

Chad was like tracing paper: he was translucent; you could see his motives. He was a snake and I knew I could never trust him, but he was obviously trying to establish an alliance with me, probably on the theory that it was better for him to be aligned with the hot new talent, be my buddy, than to appear to be threatened by me, which of course he was.

"All right, man, thanks," I said.

"Least I can do."

By the time I got back to my cube there was half an hour before the meeting, so I got on the Internet and did some quick-and-dirty research on GoldDust so at least I could sound like I knew what I was talking about. I was whipping through dozens of Web sites of varying quality, some industry-promo types, and some (like GoldDustGeek.com) run by geeks obsessed with this shit, when I noticed someone standing over my shoulder, watching me. It was Phil Bohjalian.

"Eager beaver, huh?" he said. He introduced himself. "Only your second day, and look at you." He shook his head in wonderment. "Don't work too hard, you'll burn out. Plus you'll make us all look bad." He made a sort of chortle, like this was a line out of *The Producers* or something, and he exited stage left.

19

The Maestro marketing group met once again in Corvette, everyone sitting pretty much in the same place, as if we had assigned seats.

But this time Tom Lundgren was in the room, sitting in a chair against the wall in the back, not at the conference table. Then, just before Nora called the meeting to order, in walked Paul Camilletti, Trion's CFO, looking spiffy, like a matinee idol out of *Love Italian Style*, wearing a nubby dark-gray houndstooth jacket over a black mock turtleneck. He took a seat next to Tom Lundgren, and you could feel the entire room go still, electrically charged, as if someone had flipped a power switch.

Even Nora looked a little rattled. "Well," she said, "why don't we get started? I'm pleased to welcome Paul Camilletti, our chief financial officer—welcome, Paul."

He ducked his head, the kind of acknowledgment that said, *Don't pay any attention to me—I'm just going to sit here incognito, anonymous, like an elephant in the room.*

"Who else is with us today? Who's teleconning in?"

A voice came over the intercom speaker: "Ken Hsiao, Singapore."

Then: "Mike Matera, Brussels."

"All right," she said, "so the gang's all here." She looked excited, jazzed, but it was hard to tell how much of that was a show of enthusiasm she was putting on for Tom Lundgren and Paul Camilletti. "This seems as good a time as any to take a look at forecasts, drill down, get a sense of where we stand. None of us wants to hear that old cliché, 'dying brand,' am I right? Maestro is no dying brand. We are not going to torpedo the brand equity that Trion has built up in this product line just for the sake of novelty. I think we're all on board on that."

"Nora, this is Ken in Singapore."

"Yes, Ken?"

"Uh, we're feeling some pressure here, I have to say, from Palm and Sony and Blackberry, especially in the Enterprise space. Advance orders for Maestro Gold in Asia Pacific are looking a little soft."

"Thank you, Ken," she said hastily, cutting him off. "Kimberly, what's your sense of the channel community?"

Kimberly Ziegler, wan and nervous-looking with a head of wild curls and horn-rimmed glasses, looked up. "My take is quite different from Ken's, I have to say."

"Really? In what way?"

"I'm seeing product differentiation that's benefiting us, actually. We've got a better price point than either Blackberry or Sony's advanced text-paging devices. It's true there's a little wear-and-tear on the brand, but the upgrade in the processor and the flash memory are really going to add value. So I think we're hanging in there, especially in the vertical markets."

Suckup, I thought.

"Excellent," Nora beamed. "Good to hear. I'd also be quite interested to hear whatever feedback that's come in on GoldDust—" She saw Chad holding his index finger in the air. "Yes, Chad?"

"I thought maybe Adam might have a thought or two about GoldDust."

She turned to me. "Terrific, let's hear it," she said as if I'd just volunteered to sit down and play the piano.

"GoldDust?" I said with a knowing smirk. "Like, how 1999 is that? The Betamax of wireless. It's up there with New Coke, cold fusion, XFL football, and the Yugo."

There were some appreciative titters. Nora was watching me closely.

I went on, "The compatibility problems are so massive, we don't even want to go there—I mean, the way GoldDust-enabled devices work only with devices from the same manufacturer, the lack of any standardized code. Philips keeps saying they're going to come out with a new, standardized version of GoldDust—yeah, right, maybe when we're all speaking Esperanto."

Some more laughter, though I noticed in passing that maybe half the people in the room were stone-faced. Tom Lundgren was looking at me with a funny crooked smile, his right leg jackhammering.

I was really grooving now, getting into it. "I mean, the transfer rate is, what, less than one megabit per second? Really pathetic. Less than a tenth of WiFi. This is horse-and-buggy stuff. And let's not even talk about how easy it is to intercept—no security whatsoever."

"Right on," someone said in a low voice, though I didn't catch who it was. Mordden was downright beaming. Phil Bohjalian was watching me through narrowed eyes, his expression cryptic, unreadable. Then I looked over and saw Nora. Her face was flushing. I mean, you could see a wave of red rising from her neck to her wide-set eyes.

"Are you finished?" she snapped.

I felt queasy all of a sudden. This was not the reaction I expected. What, had I gone on too long? "Sure," I said warily.

An Indian-looking guy sitting across from me said, "Why are we revisiting this? I thought you made a final decision on this last week, Nora. You seemed to feel very strongly that the added functionality was worth the cost. So why are you marketing people going back to this old debate? Isn't the matter settled?"

Chad, who'd been studying the table, said, "Hey, come on, guys, give the newbie a break, huh? You can't expect him to know everything—the guy doesn't even know where the cappuccino machine is yet, come on."

"I think we don't need to waste any more time here," said Nora. "The matter's decided. We're adding GoldDust." She gave me a look of the darkest fury.

When the meeting ended, a stomach-churning twenty minutes later, and people began filing out of the room, Mordden gave my shoulder a quick, furtive pat, which should have told me everything. I'd fucked up, big time. People were giving me all sorts of curious looks.

"Uh, Nora," said Paul Camilletti, holding up a finger, "you mind staying behind a sec? I want to go over a few things."

As I walked out, Chad came up to me and spoke in a low voice. "Sounds like she didn't take it well," he said, "but that was really valuable input, guy."

Yeah right, motherfucker.

20

Maybe fifteen minutes after the meeting broke up, Mordden stopped by my cubicle.

"Well, I'm impressed," he said.

"Really," I said without much enthusiasm.

"Absolutely. You've got more spine than I'd have given you credit for. Taking on your manager, the dread Nora, on her pet project. . . ." He shook his head. "Talk about creative tension. But you should be made aware of the consequences of your actions. Nora does not forget slights. Bear in mind that the most ruthless of the guards in the Nazi concentration camps were women."

"Thanks for the advice," I said.

"You should be on the alert for subtle signs of Nora's displeasure. For instance, empty boxes stacked up next to your cubicle. Or suddenly being unable to log on to your computer. Or HR demanding your badge back. But fear not, they'll give you a strong recommendation, and Trion outplacement services are provided *gratis*."

"I see. Thanks."

I noticed that I had a voice mail. When Mordden left, I picked up the phone.

It was a message from Nora Sommers, asking me—no, *ordering* me—to come to her office at once.

She was tapping away at her keyboard when I got there. She gave a quick, sidelong, lizardlike glance and went back to her computer. She ignored me like that for a good two minutes. I stood there awkwardly. Her face had started flushing again—I felt sort of bad that her own skin gave her away so easily.

Finally she looked up again, wheeled around in her chair to face me. Her eyes glistened, but not with sadness. Something different, something almost feral.

"Listen, Nora," I said gently. "I want to apologize for my—"

She spoke so quietly I could barely hear her. "I suggest *you* listen, Adam. You've done quite enough talking today."

"I was an idiot—" I began.

"And to make such a remark in the presence of Camilletti, Mister Bottom Line, Mister Profit Margin. . . . I've got some serious damage control to do with him, thanks to you."

"I should have kept my mouth—"

"You try to undermine me," she said, "you don't know what you've taken on."

"If I'd known—" I tried to get in.

"Don't even go there. Phil Bohjalian told me he passed by your cube and saw you feverishly doing research on GoldDust before the meeting, before your 'casual,' 'offhand' dismissal of this vital technology. Let me assure you of this, Mr. Cassidy. You may think you're some hot shit because of your track record at Wyatt, but I wouldn't get too comfortable here at Trion. If you don't get on the bus, you're going to get run over. And mark my words: I'm going to be behind the wheel."

I stood there for a few seconds while she bore down on me with those wide-set predator eyes. I looked down at the floor, then back up again. "I blew it big-time," I said, "and I really owe you a huge apology. Obviously I misjudged the situation, and I probably brought with me my old Wyatt Telecom biases, but that's no excuse. It won't happen again."

"There won't be an opportunity for it to happen again," she said quietly. She was tougher than any jackbooted state trooper who'd ever flagged me over to the side of the road.

"I understand," I said. "And if anyone had told me the decision had been made, I certainly would have kept my big mouth shut. I guess I was going on the assumption that folks here at Trion had heard about Sony, that's all. My bad."

"Sony?" she said. "What do you mean, 'heard about Sony?' "

Wyatt's competitive-intelligence people had sold him this tidbit, which he'd given me to use at a strategic moment. I figured that saving my ass counted as a strategic moment. "You know, just that they're scrapping their plans to incorporate GoldDust in all their new handhelds."

"Why?" she asked suspiciously.

"The latest release of Microsoft Office isn't going to support it. Sony figures if they incorporate GoldDust, they lose out on millions of dollars of enterprise sales, so they're going with BlackHawk, the local-wireless protocol that Office *will* support."

"It will?"

"Absolutely."

"And you're sure about this? Your sources are completely reliable?"

"Completely, one hundred percent. I'd stake my life on it."

"You'd stake your career on it as well?" Her eyes drilled into me.

"I think I just did."

"Very interesting," she said. "*Extremely* interesting, Adam. Thank you."

21

I stayed late that evening.

By seven-thirty, eight, the place was empty. Even the diehard workaholics worked from home at night, logging back on to the Trion network, so there was no need to stay late at the office anymore. By nine o'clock, there was no one in sight. The overhead fluorescent lights stayed on, faintly flickering. The floor-to-ceiling windows looked black from some angles; from other angles you could see the city spread out before you, lights twinkling, headlights streaking by noiselessly.

I sat at my cubicle and started poking around the Trion internal Web site.

If Wyatt wanted to know who'd been hired in to some kind of "skunk-works" that had been started some time in the last two years, I figured I should try to find out who Trion had *hired* in the last two years or so. That was as good a start as any. There were all sorts of ways to search the employee database, but the problem was, I didn't really know exactly who or what I was looking for.

After a while, I figured it out: the employee number. Every Trion employee gets a number. A lower number means you were hired earlier on. So after looking at a bunch of different, random employee bios, I began to see the range of numbers of people who'd started working here two years ago. Luckily (for my purposes anyway), Trion had been in a real slow period, so there weren't that many. I came up with a list of a few hundred new hires—

new being within the last two years—and downloaded all the names and their bios to a CD. So that was a start at least.

Trion had its own, proprietary instant-messaging service called InstaMail. It worked just like Yahoo Messenger or America Online's Instant Messenger—you could keep a "buddy list" that told you when colleagues were online and when they weren't. I noticed that Nora Sommers was logged in. She wasn't here, but she was online, which meant she was working from home.

Which was good, because that meant I could now attempt to break into her office without the risk of her showing up unannounced.

The thought of doing it made my guts clench like a fist, but I knew I had no choice. Arnold Meacham wanted tangible results, like yesterday. Nora Sommers, I knew, was on several Trion new product–marketing committees. Maybe she'd have information on any new products or new technology Trion was secretly developing. At the very least it was worth a close look.

The most likely place where she'd keep this information would be on her computer, in her office.

The plaque on the door said N. SOMMERS. I summoned up the nerve to try the doorknob. It was locked. That didn't entirely surprise me, since she kept sensitive HR records there. I could see right through the plate glass into her darkened office, all of ten feet by ten feet. There was not much in it, and it was, of course, fanatically neat.

I knew there had to be a key somewhere in her admin's desk. Strictly speaking, her administrative assistant—a large, broad-beamed, tough woman of around thirty named Lisa McAuliffe—wasn't only *hers*. Nominally, Lisa worked for all of Nora's unit, including me. Only VPs got their own admins; that was Trion policy. But that was just a formality. I'd already figured out that Lisa McAuliffe worked for Nora and resented anybody who got in the way.

Lisa wore her hair really short, almost in a crew cut, and wore overalls or painters' pants. You wouldn't think Nora, who always dressed fashionably and femme, would have an admin like Lisa McAuliffe. But Lisa was fiercely loyal to Nora; she reserved her few smiles for Nora and scared the bejesus out of everyone else.

Lisa was a cat person. Her cubicle was cluttered with dozens of cat things: Garfield dolls, Catbert figurines, that sort of thing. I looked around, saw no one, and began to pull open her desk drawers. After a few minutes I found the key ring hidden on the soil of her fluorescent light–compatible plant, inside a plastic paper clip holder. I took a deep breath, took the key ring—it must have had twenty keys on it—and began trying the keys, one by one. The sixth key opened Nora's door.

I flipped on the lights, sat down at Nora's desk, and powered up her computer.

In case anyone happened to come by unexpectedly, I was prepared. Arnold Meacham had pumped me full of strategies—go on the offensive, ask *them* questions—but what were the odds that a cleaning person, who spoke Portuguese or Spanish and no English, was going to figure out that I was in somebody else's office? So I focused on the task at hand.

The task at hand, unfortunately, wasn't so easy. USER NAME/PASSWORD blinked on the screen. Shit. Password-protected: I should have expected it. I typed in NSOMMERS; that was standard. Then I typed NSOMMERS in the password space. Seventy percent of people, I'd been taught, make their password the same as their user name.

But not Nora.

I had a feeling that Nora wasn't the sort of person who wrote down her passwords on a Post-it note in a desk drawer or something, but I had to make sure. I checked the usual places—under the mouse pad, under the keyboard, in back of the computer, in the desk drawers, but nothing. So I'd have to wing it.

I tried just SOMMERS; I tried her birth date, tried the first and last seven digits of her Social Security number, her employee number. A whole range of combinations. DENIED. After the tenth try, I stopped. Each attempt was logged, I had to assume. Ten attempts was already too many. People generally didn't fumble more than two or three times.

This was not good.

But there were other ways to crack the password. I'd gone through hours of training on that, and they'd supplied me with some equipment that was almost idiotproof. I wasn't a computer hacker or anything, but I was decent at computers—enough to get into a world of trouble back at Wyatt, right?—and the stuff they gave me was ridiculously easy to install.

Basically, it was a device called a "keystroke logger." These things secretly record every keystroke a computer's user makes.

They can be software, like computer programs, or actual hardware devices. But you had to be careful about installing the software versions, because you never knew how closely the corporation's network systems were being monitored; they might be able to detect it. So Arnold Meacham urged me to use the equipment.

He'd given me an assortment of little toys. One was a tiny cable connector that got plugged in between a computer keyboard and the PC. You'd never notice it. It had a chip embedded in it that recorded and stored up to two million keystrokes. You just came back later and took it off the target's computer, and you had a record of everything the person had typed in.

In a total of about ten seconds, I unplugged Nora's keyboard, attached it to the little Keyghost thing, and then plugged that into her computer. She'd never see it, and in a couple of days I'd come back and get it.

But I wasn't going to leave her office empty-handed. I looked through some of the stuff on her desk. Not much here. I found a draft of an e-mail to the Maestro team, which she hadn't yet sent. "My most recent market research," she wrote, "indicates that, though GoldDust is undoubtedly superior, Microsoft Office will instead be supporting BlackHawk wireless technology. Though this may be a disruption to our fine engineers, I'm sure we all agree it's best not to swim against the Microsoft tide. . . ."

Fast work, Nora, I thought. I hoped to hell Wyatt was right.

There were also the file cabinets to go through. Even in a high-tech place like Trion, important files almost always exist on paper, whether originals or hard-copy backups. This is the great truth of the so-called paperless office: the more we all use computers, the more reams of copy paper we seem to go through. I opened the first cabinet I came to, which turned out to be not a file cabinet at all but an enclosed bookcase. Why were some books kept in here, out of sight, I wondered? Then I looked closely at the titles and I whooped out loud.

She had rows and rows of books with titles like *Women Who Run with the Wolves* and *Hardball for Women* and *Play Like a Man, Win Like a Woman.* Titles like *Why Good Girls Don't Get Ahead . . . but Gutsy Girls Do* and *Seven Secrets of Successful Women* and *The Eleven Commandments of Wildly Successful Women.*

Nora, Nora, I found myself thinking. You go, girl.

Four of her file cabinets were unlocked, and I went for those first, thumbed through the stultifyingly dull contents: ops reviews, product specs, product development files, financial. . . . She documented seemingly everything, probably printed out a copy of every e-mail she sent or received. The good stuff, I knew, had to be in the locked cabinets. Why else would they be locked?

Pretty quickly I located the small file-cabinet key on Lisa's key ring. In the locked drawers I found a lot of HR files on her subordinates, which might have made for interesting reading if I had the time. Her personal financial records indicated that she'd been at Trion a long time, a lot of her options had vested, and she traded actively, so her net worth was in seven figures. I found my file, which was thin and contained nothing scary. Nothing of interest.

Then I looked closer and came across a few pieces of paper, printouts of e-mails Nora had received from someone high up at Trion. From what I could tell, the woman named Alana Jennings, who'd had my job before me, had abruptly been transferred somewhere else inside the company. And Nora was pissed—so pissed, in fact, that she escalated her complaint all the way up the food chain to the senior vice president level, a pretty bold move:

```
SUBJ: Re: Reassignment of Alana Jennings
DATE: Tuesday, April 8, 8:42:19 AM
FROM: GAllred
TO:   NSommers


Nora,
I am in receipt of your several e-mails protesting the
transfer of ALANA JENNINGS to another division of the
company. I understand your upset, since Alana is your
highest-ranked employee as well as a valued player on
your team.
Regretfully, however, your objections have been overruled
on the highest authority. Alana's skill set is urgently
needed in Project AURORA.
Let me assure you that you will not lose your head count.
You have been granted a backfill requisition, so that you
```

may fill Alana's position with any interested and qualified
employee within the company.
Please let me know if I can do anything further to help.

Best,
Greg Allred
Senior VP, Advanced Research Business Unit
Trion Systems
Helping You Change the Future

And then, two days later, another e-mail:

SUBJ: Re: Re: Reassignment of Alana Jennings
DATE: Thursday, April 10, 2:13:07 PM
FROM: GAllred
TO: NSommers

Nora,
Regarding AURORA, my deepest apologies, but I am not at
liberty to disclose the exact nature of this project
except to say that it is mission-critical to the future
of Trion. Since AURORA is a classified R&D project of the
utmost sensitivity, I would respectfully ask you not to
pursue the matter further.
That said, I appreciate your difficulty in filling Alana's
position internally with someone appropriately qualified.
Therefore I am happy to tell you that you are, in this
instance, permitted to disregard the general companywide
ban on hiring from outside. This slot may be designated a
"silver bullet" position, enabling you to hire from outside Trion. I trust and hope this will allay your concerns.
Don't hesitate to call or write with any questions.

Best,

Greg Allred
Senior VP, Advanced Research Business Unit
Trion Systems
Helping You Change the Future

Whoa. Suddenly things were starting to make a little sense. I'd been hired to replace this Alana woman, who'd been moved into something called Project AURORA.

Project AURORA was clearly a top-secret undertaking—a skunkworks. I'd found it.

It didn't seem like a good idea to pull out the e-mails and take them out to the copy machine, so I took a yellow legal pad from a tall stack in Nora's supply closet and began taking notes.

I don't know how long I'd been sitting there on the carpeted floor of her office, writing, but it must have been a good four or five minutes. And suddenly I became aware of something in my peripheral vision. I glanced up, saw a security guard standing in the open doorway watching me.

Trion didn't do rent-a-cops; they had their own security personnel, who wore navy blazers and white shirts and looked sort of like policemen, or church ushers. This guy was a tall, beefy black man with gray hair and a lot of moles, like freckles, on his cheeks. He had large, heavy-lidded, basset-hound eyes and wore wire-rimmed glasses. He was standing there, watching me.

For all the time I'd spent mentally rehearsing what I'd say if I was caught, I went blank.

"I see what you got there," the guard said. He wasn't looking at me; he was staring right toward Nora's desk. At the computer—the Keyghost? No, God, please, *no*.

"Excuse me?" I said.

"I see what you got there. Hell, yeah. I *know* it."

I freaked, heart racing. Jesus Christ almighty, I thought: I'm hosed.

22

He blinked, kept staring. Had he seen me install the device? And then I was suddenly seized by another, equally sickening thought: had he noticed Nora's name on the door? Wouldn't he wonder why a man was in a woman's office, thumbing through her files?

I glanced over at the name plaque on the open door, right behind the guard. It said N. SOMMERS. N. SOMMERS could be anyone, male *or* female. Then again, for all I knew he'd been patrolling the halls forever, and he and Nora went way back.

The guard was still standing in the doorway, blocking the exit. What the hell was I supposed to do now? I could try to bolt, but I'd first have to get by the man, which meant I'd have to take a dive at him, tackle him to the ground, get him out of the way. He was big, but old, probably not fast; it might work. So what were we talking about here, assault and battery? On an old guy? *Christ.*

I thought quickly. Should I say I was new? I ran though a series of explanations in my head: I was Nora Sommers's new assistant. I was her direct report—well, I *was*—working late at her behest. What the hell did this guy know? He was a goddamned *security guy.*

He took a few steps into the office, shook his head. "Man, I thought I'd seen everything."

"Look, we've got a huge project due tomorrow morning—" I started to say, indignantly.

"You got a Bullitt there. That's a genuine Bullitt."

Then I saw what he was staring at, moving toward. It was a large color photograph in a silver frame hanging on the wall. A picture of a beautifully restored, vintage muscle car. He was moving toward it in a daze, as if he were approaching the Ark of the Covenant. "Shit, man, that's a genuine 1968 Mustang GT three-ninety," he breathed like he'd just seen the face of God.

The adrenaline kicked in and the relief seeped out of my pores. Jesus.

"Yep," I said proudly. "Very good."

"Man, look at that 'Stang. That pony a factory GT?"

What the hell did I know? I couldn't tell a Mustang from a Dodge Dart. For all I knew that could have been a picture of an AMC Gremlin. "Sure," I said.

"Lotta fakes out there, you know. You ever check under the rear seat, see if it got those extra metal plates, those reinforcements for the dual exhaust?"

"Oh yeah," I said airily. I stood up, extended my hand. "Nick Sommers."

His handshake was dry, his hand large, engulfing mine. "Luther Stafford," he said. "I haven't seen you 'round here before."

"Yeah, I'm never here at night. This damned project—it's always, 'We need it at nine A.M., big rush,' hurry up and wait." I tried to sound casual. "Glad to see I'm not the only one working late."

But he wouldn't drop the car. "Man, I don't think I've ever seen a fastback pony in Highland Green. Outside the movies, I mean. That looks like the exact same one Steve McQueen used to chase the evil black Dodge Charger off the road and into the gas station. Hubcaps flying all over the place." He gave a low, mellow, cigarette-and-whiskey chuckle. "*Bullitt*. My favorite movie. I must've seen it a thousand times."

"Yep," I said. "Same one."

He moved in closer. Suddenly I realized that there was a huge gold statuette on the shelf right next to the silver-framed photo. Engraved on the statuette's base, in huge black letters, was WOMAN OF THE YEAR, 1999. PRESENTED TO NORA SOMMERS. Quickly I walked over behind the desk, blocking the security guard's view of the award with my body, as if I too were inspecting the photograph closely.

"Got the rear spoiler and everything," he went on. "Dual exhaust tips, right?"

"Oh, yeah."

"With the rolled edges and everything?"

"Absolutely."

He shook his head again. "Man. You restore it yourself?"

"Nah, I wish I had the time."

He laughed again, a low, rumbling laugh. "I know what you mean."

"Got it from a guy who'd been keeping it in his barn."

"Three-twenty horsepower on that pony?"

"Right," I said, like I knew.

"Look at the turn-signal hood on that baby. I once had a '68 hardtop but I had to get rid of it. My wife made me, after we had the first kid. I've been lusting after it ever since. But I won't even look at that new GT Bullitt Mustang, no sir."

I shook my head. "No way." I didn't know what the hell he was talking about. Was everyone in this company obsessed with cars?

"Correct me if I'm wrong, but it looks like you got GR-seventy–size tires on fifteen-by-seven American Torque Thrust rims, that right?"

Jesus, could we move off this topic? "Truth is, Luther, I don't know shit about Mustangs. I don't even deserve to own one. My wife just got it for me for my birthday. 'Course, it's going to be *me* paying off the loan for the next seventy-five years."

He chuckled a little more. "I hear you. I've been there." I noticed him looking down at the desk, and then I realized what he was looking at.

It was a big manila envelope with Nora's name on it in big, bold capital letters in red Sharpie marker. NORA SOMMERS. I looked around the desk for something to slide over it, to cover it up, just in case he hadn't yet read the name, but Nora kept her desk immaculate. Trying to act casual, I yanked at a page of the legal pad and ripped it out quietly, let it drop to the surface of the desk and slid it over the envelope with my left hand. Real cool, Adam. The yellow paper had a few notes on it in my handwriting, but nothing that would make any sense to anyone.

"Who's *Nora* Sommers?" he said.

"Ah, that's my wife."

"Nick and Nora, huh?" he chortled.

"Yeah, we get that all the time." I smiled broadly. "It's why I married her. Well, I'd better get back to the files, or I'm going to be here all night. Nice to meet you, Luther."

"Same here, Nick."

By the time the security guy left I was so nervous I couldn't do much more than finish copying the e-mails, then turn off the light and relock Nora's office door. As I turned to return the key ring to Lisa McAuliffe's cubicle, I noticed someone walking not too far away. Luther again, I figured. What did the guy want, more Mustang talk? All I wanted was to drop off the keys unseen, and I was out of here.

But it wasn't Luther; it was a paunchy guy with horn-rim glasses and a ponytail.

The last person I expected to see in the office at ten o'clock at night, but then again, engineers worked strange hours.

Noah Mordden.

Had he seen me locking up Nora's office, or maybe even *in* it? Or was his eyesight not that good? Maybe he wasn't even paying attention; maybe he was in his own world—but what was he *doing* here?

He didn't say anything, didn't acknowledge me. I wasn't even sure he noticed me at all. But I was the only other person in the vicinity, and he wasn't blind.

He turned into the next aisle down and left a folder in someone's cubicle. Fake-casually, I strolled past Lisa's cubicle and deposited the key ring in the plant, right in the soil where I'd found it, one swift movement, then I kept moving.

I was halfway to the elevators when I heard, "Cassidy."

I turned back.

"And I thought only engineers were nocturnal creatures."

"Just trying to get caught up," I said lamely.

"*I* see," he said. The way he said it sent a chill up my spine. Then he asked, "In what?"

"Sorry?"

"What are you caught up in?"

"I'm not sure I understand," I said, my heart pounding.

"Try to remember that."

"Come again?"

But Mordden was already on his way to the elevator, and he didn't answer.

PART THREE

PLUMBING

Plumbing: Tradecraft jargon for various support assets such as safehouses, dead drops, et al. of a clandestine intelligence agency.

—*The International Dictionary of Espionage*

23

By the time I got home, I was a wreck, even worse than before. I wasn't cut out for this line of work. I wanted to go out and get smashed again, but I had to get to bed, get some sleep.

My apartment seemed even smaller and more squalid than ever. I was making a six-figure salary, so I should have been able to afford one of those apartments in the new tall buildings on the wharf. There was no reason for me to stay in this hellhole except that it was *my* hellhole, my reminder of the low-life underachieving bum I really was, not the well-dressed, slick poseur I'd become. Plus I didn't have the time to look for a new place.

I hit the light switch by the door and the room stayed dark. Damn. That meant the bulb in the big ugly lamp by the sofa, the main light source in the room, had burned out. I always kept the lamp switched on so I could turn it on and off at the door. Now I had to stumble through the dark apartment to the little closet where I kept the spare bulbs and stuff. Fortunately I knew every inch of the tiny apartment, literally with my eyes closed. I felt around in the corrugated cardboard box for a new bulb, hoping it was a hundred-watt and not a twenty-five or something, and then navigated through the room to the sofa table, unscrewed the thing that keeps the shade on, unscrewed the bulb, put in the new one. Still no light came on. Shit: a fitting end to a lousy day. I found the little switch on the lamp's base and turned it, and the room lit up.

I was halfway to the bathroom when the thought hit me: How'd the lamp get switched off? I never turned it off there—never. Was I losing my mind?

Had someone been in the apartment?

It was a creepy feeling, some flicker of paranoia. Someone *had* been here. How else could the lamp have been switched off at its base?

I had no roommates, no girlfriend, and no one else had the key. The sleazy management company that ran the building for the sleazy absentee slumlord never accessed the units. Not even if you begged them to send someone over to fix the radiators. No one was *ever* in here but me.

Looking over at the phone directly beneath the lamp, this old black Panasonic telephone/answering-machine combo whose answering machine part I never used anymore, now that I had voice mail through the phone company, I saw something else was off. The black phone cord lay across the phone's keypad, on top of it, instead of coiled to one side of the phone the way it always was. Granted, these were dumb little details, but you do notice these things when you live alone. I tried to remember when I'd last made a phone call, where I'd been, what I'd been doing. Was I so distracted that I hung up the phone wrong? But I was sure the phone hadn't been like this when I left this morning.

Someone had *definitely* been in here.

I looked back at the phone/answering-machine thing and realized something else was wrong, and this wasn't even subtle. The answering machine that I never used had one of those dual-tape systems, one microcassette for the outgoing message, another to record incoming messages.

But the cassette that recorded incoming messages was gone. *Someone had removed it.*

Someone, presumably, who wanted a copy of my phone messages.

Or—the idea suddenly hit me—who wanted to make sure I hadn't used the answering machine to *record* any phone calls I'd received. That had to be it. I got up, started searching for the only other tape recorder I had, a small microcassette thing I'd bought in college for some reason I no longer remembered. I vaguely remembered seeing it in my bottom desk drawer some weeks ago when I'd been searching for a cigarette lighter. Pulling open the desk drawer, I rummaged through it, but it wasn't there. Nor was it in any of the other desk drawers. The more I looked, the more certain I was that I'd seen the tape recorder in the bottom drawer. When I looked again, I found the AC power adapter that went with it, confirming my suspicion. That recorder was gone too.

Now I was certain: whoever had searched my apartment had been looking for any tape recordings I might have made. The question was, who had searched my apartment? If it was Wyatt and Meacham's people, that was totally infuriating, outrageous.

But what if it wasn't them? What if it was *Trion?* That was so scary I didn't even want to think about it. I remembered Mordden's blank-faced question: *What are you caught up in?*

24

Nick Wyatt's house was in the poshest suburb, a place everyone's heard of, so rich that they make jokes about it. It was easily the biggest, fanciest, most outrageously high-end place in a town known for big, fancy, and outrageously high-end estates. No doubt it was important to Wyatt to live in the house that everyone talked about, that *Architectural Digest* put on its cover, that the local journalists were always trying to find excuses to get into and write about. They loved doing awestruck, jaw-dropping takes on this Silicon San Simeon. They loved the Japanese thing—the fake Zen serenity and spareness and simplicity clashing so grotesquely with Wyatt's fleet of Bentley convertibles and his totally un-Zen stridency.

In Wyatt Telecommunications's PR department one guy's entire job was handling Nick Wyatt's personal publicity, planting items in *People* and *USA Today* or wherever. From time to time he put out stories about the Wyatt estate, which was how I knew it had cost fifty million dollars, that it was way bigger and fancier than Bill Gates's lake house near Seattle, that it was a replica of a fourteenth-century Japanese palace that Wyatt had had built in Osaka and shipped in pieces to the U.S. It was surrounded by forty acres of Japanese gardens full of rare species of flowers, rock gardens, a man-made waterfall, a man-made pond, antique wooden bridges flown in from Japan. Even the irregularly cut stones paving the driveway had been shipped from Japan.

Of course I didn't see any of this as I drove up the endless stone driveway. I saw a stone guardhouse and a tall iron gate that swung open auto-matically, seemingly miles of bamboo, a carport with six different-colored Bentley convertibles like a roll of Lifesavers (no American muscle cars for this guy), and a huge low-slung wooden house surrounded by a tall stone wall.

I'd gotten the order to report for this meeting from Meacham by secure e-mail—a message to my Hushmail account from "Arthur," sent through the Finnish anonymizer, the remailer that made it untraceable. There was a whole vocabulary of code language that made it look like a confirmation of an order I'd placed with some online merchant, but actually told me when and where and so on.

Meacham had given me precise instructions on where and how to drive. I had to drive to a Denny's parking lot and wait for a dark blue Lincoln, which I then followed to Wyatt's house. I guess the point was to make sure *I* wasn't being followed there. They were being a little paranoid about it, I thought, but who was I to argue? After all, I was the guy on the hot seat.

As soon as I got out of the car, the Lincoln pulled away. A Filipino man answered the door, told me to take off my shoes. He led me into a waiting room furnished with shoji screens, tatami mats, a low black lacquered table, a low futon-looking squarish white couch. Not very comfortable. I thumbed through the magazines arrayed artistically on the black coffee table—*The Robb Report, Architectural Digest* (including, naturally, the issue with Wyatt's house on the cover), a catalog from Sotheby's.

Finally, the houseman or whatever you call him reappeared and nodded at me. I followed him down a long hallway and walked toward another almost-empty room where I could see Wyatt seated at the head of a long, low black dining table.

As we approached the entrance to the dining room I suddenly heard a high-pitched alarm go off, incredibly loud. I looked around in bewilderment but before I could figure out what was going on I was grabbed by the Filipino man and another guy who appeared out of nowhere, and the two of them wrestled me to the ground. I said, "What the fuck?" and struggled a little, but these guys were as powerful as sumo wrestlers. The second guy then held me while the Filipino patted me down. What were they looking for, weapons? The Filipino guy found my iPod MP3 music player, yanked it out of my workbag. He looked at it, said something in whatever they speak in the Philippines, handed it to the other guy, who looked at it, turned it over, said something gruff and indecipherable.

I sat up. "This how you welcome all Mr. Wyatt's guests?" I said. The houseman took the iPod and, entering the dining room, handed it to Wyatt, who was watching the action. Wyatt handed it right back to the Filipino without even looking at it.

I got to my feet. "Your guys never seen one of those before? Or is outside music not allowed in here?"

"They're just being thorough," Wyatt said. He was wearing a tight black long-sleeved shirt that looked like it was made of linen, and probably cost more than I made in a month, even now at Trion. He seemed to be more tanned than normal. He must sleep in a tanning bed, I thought.

"Afraid I might be packing?" I said.

"I'm not 'afraid' of anything, Cassidy. I like everyone to play by the rules. If you're smart and don't try to get tricky, everything will go fine. Don't even think about trying to take out an 'insurance policy,' because we're way ahead of you." Funny, the idea had never occurred to me until he mentioned it.

"I don't follow."

"I'm saying that if you plan to do something foolish like try to tape-record our meetings or any phone calls you get from me or anyone else associated with me, things will not go well for you. You don't need insurance, Adam. *I'm* your insurance."

A beautiful Japanese woman in a kimono appeared with a tray and handed him a rolled hot towel with silver tongs. He wiped his hands and handed it back to her. Up close you could tell that he'd had a facelift. The skin was too tight, gave his eyes an almost Eskimo cast.

"Your home phone isn't secure," he continued. "Neither is your home voice mail or computer or your cell phone. You're to initiate contact with us only in case of emergency, except in response to a request from us. All other times you'll be contacted by secure, encrypted e-mail. Now, may I see what you have?"

I gave him the CD of all recent Trion hires I'd downloaded from the Web site, and a couple of sheets of paper, covered with typed notes. While he was reading through my notes, the Japanese woman came back with another tray and began to set before Wyatt an array of tiny, perfect, sculptural pieces of sushi and sashimi on lacquered mahogany boxes, with little mounds of white rice and pale-green wasabi and pink slices of pickled ginger. Wyatt didn't look up; he was too absorbed in the notes I'd brought him. After a few minutes he picked up a small black phone on the table, which I hadn't noticed before, and said something in a low voice. I thought I heard the word "fax."

Finally he looked at me. "Good job," he said. "Very interesting."

Another woman appeared, a prim middle-aged woman, lined face, gray hair, reading glasses on a chain around her neck. She smiled, took the sheaf of papers from him, left without saying a word. Did he keep a secretary on call all night?

Wyatt picked up a pair of chopsticks and lifted a morsel of raw fish to his mouth, chewed thoughtfully while he stared at me. "Do you understand the superiority of the Japanese diet?" he said.

I shrugged. "I like tempura and stuff."

He scoffed, shook his head. "I'm not talking about tempura. Why do you think Japan leads the world in life expectancy? A low-fat, high-protein diet, rich in plant foods, high in antioxidants. They eat forty times more soy than we do. For centuries they refused to eat four-legged creatures."

"Okay," I said, thinking: And your point is . . . ?

He took another mouthful of fish. "You really ought to get serious about enhancing the quality of your life. You're, what, twenty-five?"

"Twenty-six."

"You've got decades ahead of you. Take care of your body. The smoking, the drinking, the Big Macs and all that crap—that shit's got to stop. I sleep three hours a night. Don't need more than that. Are you having fun, Adam?"

"No."

"Good. You're not there to have fun. Are you comfortable at Trion in your new role?"

"I'm learning the ins and outs. My boss is a serious bitch—"

"I'm not talking about your cover. I'm talking about your *real* job—the penetration."

"Comfortable? No, not yet."

"It's pretty high-stakes. I feel your pain. You still see your old friends?"

"Sure."

"I don't expect you to dump them. That might raise suspicions. But you better make goddamned sure you keep your mouth shut, or you'll be in a world of shit."

"Understood."

"I assume I don't need to remind you of the consequences of failure."

"I don't need to be reminded."

"Good. Your job's difficult, but failure is far worse."

"Actually, I sort of like being at Trion." I was being truthful, but I also knew he'd take it as a jab.

He looked up, smirked as he chewed. "I'm delighted to hear that."

"My team is making a presentation before Augustine Goddard pretty soon."

"Good old Jock Goddard, huh. Well, you'll see quickly he's a pretentious, sententious old gasbag. I think he actually believes all the ass-kissing profiles, that 'conscience of high-tech' bullshit you always see in *Fortune*. Really believes his shit doesn't stink."

I nodded; what was I supposed to say? I didn't know Goddard, so I couldn't agree or disagree, but Wyatt's envy was pretty transparent.

"When are you presenting to the old fart?"

"Couple weeks."

"Maybe I can be of some assistance."

"I'll take whatever help I can get."

The phone rang, and he picked it right up. "Yes?" He listened for a minute. "All right," he said, then hung up. "You hit something. In a week or two you'll be receiving a complete backgrounder on this Alana Jennings."

"Sure, like I got on Lundgren and Sommers."

"No, this is of another magnitude of detail."

"Why?"

"Because you'll want to follow up. She's your way in. And now that you have a code name, I want the names of everyone connected in any way with AURORA. Everyone, from project director all the way down to janitor."

"How?" As soon as I said it, I regretted it.

"Figure it out. That's your job, man. And I want it tomorrow."

"*Tomorrow?*"

"That's right."

"All right," I said, with just a little defiance creeping into my voice. "But then you'll have what you need, right? And we'll be done."

"Oh, no," he said. He smiled, flashing his big white chompers. "This is only the beginning, guy. We've barely scratched the surface."

25

By now I was working insane hours, and I was constantly zonked. In addition to my normal work hours at Trion, I was spending long hours, late into the night, every night, doing Internet research or going over the competitive-intelligence files that Meacham and Wyatt sent over, the ones that made me sound so smart. A couple of times, on the long, traffic-constipated drive home, I almost fell asleep at the wheel. I'd suddenly open my eyes, jolt awake, stop myself at the last second from veering into the lane of oncoming traffic or slamming into the car in front of me. After lunch I'd usually start to fade, and it took massive infusions of caffeine to keep me from folding my arms and passing out in my cubicle. I would fantasize about going home early and getting under the covers in my dark hovel and falling deep asleep in the middle of the afternoon. I was living on coffee and Diet Pepsi and Red Bull. You could see dark circles under my eyes. At least workaholics get some kind of sick buzz out of it; I was just whipped, like a flogged horse in some Russian novel.

But running on fumes wasn't even my biggest problem. The thing was, I was losing track of what my "real" job was and what my "cover" job was. I was so busy just getting by from meeting to meeting, trying to stay on top of things enough that Nora wouldn't smell blood in the water and go after me, that I barely had time to skulk around and gather information on AURORA.

Every once in a while I'd see Mordden, at Maestro meetings or in the employee dining room, and he'd stop to chat. But he never mentioned that night when he either did or didn't see me coming out of Nora's office. Maybe he hadn't seen me in her office. Or maybe he had and he was for some reason not saying anything about it.

And then every couple of nights I'd get an e-mail from "Arthur" asking me where I was with the investigation, how things were going, what the hell was taking me so long.

I stayed late almost every night, and I was hardly ever at home. Seth left a bunch of phone messages for me and after a week or so gave up. Most of my other friends had given up on me, too. I'd try to squeeze in half an hour here or there to drop by Dad's apartment and check in on him, but whenever I'd show up, he was so pissed off at me for avoiding him that he barely looked at me. A sort of truce had settled in between Dad and Antwoine, some kind of a Cold War. At least Atwoine wasn't threatening to quit. Yet.

One night I got back into Nora's office and removed the little key logger thing, quickly and uneventfully. My Mustang-loving-guard friend usually came by on his rounds at between ten o'clock and ten-twenty, so I did it before he showed up. It took less than a minute, and Noah Mordden was nowhere in sight.

That tiny cable now stored hundreds of thousands of Nora's keystrokes, including all her passwords. It was just a matter of plugging the device into my computer and downloading the text. But I didn't dare do it right there at my cubicle. Who knew what kind of detection programs they had running on the Trion network? Not a risk worth taking.

Instead, I logged on to the corporate Web site. In the search box I typed in AURORA, but nothing came up. Surprise, surprise. But I had another thought, and I typed in Alana Jennings's name and pulled up her page. There was no photo there—most people had their pictures up, though some didn't—but there was some basic information like her telephone extension, her job title (Marketing Director, Disruptive Technologies Research Unit), her department number, which was the same as her mailstop.

This little number, I knew, was extremely useful information. At Trion, just like at Wyatt, you were given the same department number as everyone else who worked in your part of the company. All I had to do was to punch that number into the corporate database and I had a list of everyone who worked directly with Alana Jennings—which meant that they all worked in the AURORA Project.

That didn't mean I had the *complete* list of AURORA employees, who might be in separate departments on the same floor, but at least I had a good chunk of them: forty-seven names. I printed out each person's Web page and slipped the sheets into a folder in my workbag. That, I figured, should keep Wyatt's people happy for a while.

When I got home that night, around ten, intending to sit down at my computer and download all the keystrokes from Nora's computer, something else grabbed my attention. Sitting in the middle of my "kitchen" table—a Formica-topped thing I'd bought at a used furniture place for forty-five bucks—was a crisp-looking, thick, sealed manila envelope.

It hadn't been there in the morning. Once again, someone from Wyatt had slipped into my apartment, almost as if they were trying to make the point that they could get in anywhere. Okay, point made. Maybe they figured this was the safest way to get something to me without being observed. But to me it seemed almost like a threat.

The envelope contained a fat dossier on Alana Jennings, just as Nick Wyatt had promised. I opened it, saw a whole bunch of photos of the woman, and suddenly lost interest in Nora Sommers's keystrokes. This Alana Jennings was, not to put too fine a point on it, a real hottie.

I sat down in my reading chair and pored over the file.

It was obvious that a lot of time and effort and money had gone into it. P.I.s had followed her around, taken close note of her comings and goings, her habits, the errands she ran. There were photos of her entering the Trion building, at a restaurant with a couple of female friends, at some kind of tennis club, working out at one of those all-women health clubs, getting out of her blue Mazda Miata. She had glossy black hair and blue eyes, a slim body (that was fairly evident from the Lycra workout togs). Sometimes she wore heavy-framed black glasses, the kind that beautiful women wear to signal that they're smart and serious and yet so beautiful that they can wear ugly glasses. They actually made her look sexier. Maybe that was the point.

After an hour of reading the file, I knew more about her than I ever knew about any girlfriend. She wasn't just beautiful, she was rich — a double threat. She'd grown up in Darien, Connecticut, went to Miss Porter's School in Farmington, and then went to Yale, where she'd majored in English, specializing in American literature. She also took some classes in computer science and electrical engineering. According to her college transcript she got mostly As and A minuses and was elected to Phi Beta Kappa in her junior year. Okay, so she was smart, too; make that a triple threat.

Meacham's staff had pulled up all kinds of financial background on her and her family. She had a trust fund of several million dollars, but her father, a CEO of a small manufacturing company in Stamford, had a portfolio worth a whole lot more than that. She had two younger sisters, one still in college, at Wesleyan, the other working at Sotheby's in Manhattan.

Since she called her parents almost every day, it was a fair guess that she was close with them. (A year's worth of phone bills were included, but fortunately someone had predigested them for me, summarized who she called most often.) She was single, didn't seem to be seeing anyone regularly, and owned her own condo in a very upper-crust town not far from Trion headquarters.

She shopped for groceries every Sunday at a whole-foods supermarket and seemed to be a vegetarian, because she never bought meat or even chicken or fish. She ate like a bird, a bird from the tropical rainforest — lots of fruits, berries, nuts. She didn't do bars or happy hours, but she did get the occasional delivery from a liquor store in her neighborhood, so she had at least one vice. Her house vodka seemed to be Grey Goose; her house gin was Tanqueray Malacca. She went out to restaurants once or twice a week, and not Denny's or Applebee's or Hooters; she seemed to like high-end, "chef-y" places with names like Chakra and Alto and Buzz and Om. Also she went to Thai restaurants a lot.

She went out to movies at least once a week, and usually bought her tickets ahead of time on Fandango; she occasionally saw your typical chick flick but mostly foreign films. Apparently this was a woman who'd rather watch *The Tree of Wooden Clogs* than *Porky's*. Oh, well. She bought a lot of books online, from Amazon and Barnes and Noble, mostly trendy serious fiction, some Latin American stuff, and a fair number of books about movies. Also, recently, some books on Buddhism and Eastern wisdom and crap like that. She'd also bought some movies on DVD, including the whole *Godfather* boxed set as well as some forties noir classics like *Double Indemnity*. In fact, she'd bought *Double Indemnity* twice, once in video a few years earlier, and once, more recently, on DVD. Obviously she'd only gotten a DVD player within the last two years; and obviously that old Fred MacMurray/Barbara Stanwyck flick was a favorite of hers. She seemed to have bought every record ever made by Ani DiFranco and Alanis Morissette.

I stored these facts away. I was beginning to get a picture of Alana Jennings. And I was beginning to come up with a plan.

2 6

Saturday afternoon, dressed in tennis whites (which I'd bought that morning—normally I play tennis in ragged cutoffs and a T-shirt) and wearing a ridiculously expensive Italian diver's watch I'd recently splurged on, I arrived at a very hoity-toity, very exclusive place called the Tennis and Racquet Club. Alana Jennings was a member, and according to the dossier she played here most Saturdays. I confirmed her court time by calling the day before, saying I was supposed to play her tomorrow and forgot the time, couldn't reach her, when was that again? Easy. She had a four-thirty doubles game.

Half an hour before her scheduled game I had a meeting with the club's membership director to get a quick tour of the place. That took a little doing, because it was a private club; you couldn't just walk in off the street. I had Arnold Meacham ask Wyatt to arrange to have some rich guy, a club member—a friend of a friend of a friend, a couple of degrees removed from Wyatt—contact the club about sponsoring me. The guy was on the membership committee, and his name obviously pulled some weight at the club, because the membership director, Josh, seemed thrilled to take me around. He even gave me a guest pass for the day so I could check out the courts (clay, indoor and out), maybe pick up a game.

The place was a sprawling Shingle Style mansion that looked like one of those Newport "cottages." It sat in the middle of an emerald-green sea of perfectly manicured lawn. I finally shook Josh at the café by pretending to wave at someone I knew. He offered to arrange a game for me, but I told him I was cool, I knew people here, I'd be fine.

A couple of minutes later I saw her. You couldn't miss this babe. She was wearing a Fred Perry shirt and she had (for some reason the surveillance photos didn't really show this) bodacious ta-tas. Her blue eyes were dazzling. She came into the cafe with another woman around her age, and both of them ordered Pellegrinos. I found a table close to hers, but not too close, and behind her, out of her line of sight. The point was to observe, watch, listen, and most of all not be seen. If she noticed me, I'd have a major problem next time I tried to loiter nearby. It's not like I'm Brad Pitt, but I'm not exactly butt-ugly either; women do tend to notice me. I'd have to be careful.

I couldn't tell if the woman Alana Jennings was with was a neighbor or a college friend or what, but they clearly weren't talking business. It was a fair guess that they didn't work together on the AURORA team. This was unfortunate—I wasn't going to overhear anything juicy.

But then her cell phone rang. "This is Alana," she said. She had a velvety-smooth, private-school voice, cultured without being too affected.

"You did?" she said. "Well, it sounds like you've solved it."

My ears pricked up.

"Keith, you've just slashed the time to fab in half, that's *incredible*."

She was definitely talking business. I moved a little closer toward her so I could hear more clearly. There was a lot of laughter and the clinking of dishes and the *thop thop* of tennis balls, which was making it hard to hear much of what she was saying. Someone squeezed by my table, a big guy with a huge gut that jostled my Coke glass. He was laughing loudly, obliterating Alana's conversation. *Move*, asshole.

He waddled by, and I heard another snatch of her conversation. She was now talking in a hushed voice, and only random bits floated my way. I heard her say: ". . . Well, that's the sixty-four-*billion*-dollar question, isn't it? I wish I knew." Then, a little louder: "Thanks for letting me know—great stuff." A little beep tone, and she ended the call. "Work," she said apologetically to the other woman. "Sorry. I wish I could keep this thing off, but these days I'm supposed to be on call 'round the clock. There's Drew!" A tall, studly guy came up to her—early thirties, bronzed, the broad and flat body of a rower—and gave her a kiss on the cheek. I noticed he didn't kiss the other woman.

"Hey, babe," he said.

Great, I thought. So Wyatt's goons didn't pick up on the fact that she was seeing someone after all.

"Hey, Drew," she said. "Where's George?"

"He didn't call you?" Drew said. "That space shot. He forgot he's got his daughter for the weekend."

"So we don't have a fourth?" the other woman said.

"We can pick someone up," said Drew. "I can't believe he didn't call you. What a wuss."

A lightbulb went on over my head. Jettisoning suddenly my carefully worked-out plan of anonymous observation, I made a bold split-second decision. I stood up and said, "Excuse me."

They looked over at me.

"You guys need a fourth?" I said.

I introduced myself by my real name, told them I was checking the place out, didn't mention Trion. They seemed relieved I was there. I think they assumed from my Yonex titanium pro racquet that I was really good, though I assured them I was just okay, that I hadn't played in a long time. Basically true.

We had one of the outdoor courts. It was sunny and warm and a little windy. The teams were Alana and Drew versus me and the other woman, whose name was Jody. Jody and Alana were about evenly matched, but Alana was by far the more graceful player. She wasn't particularly aggressive, but she had a nice backhand slice, she always returned serves, always got the ball, no wasted movements. Her serve was simple and accurate: she almost always got it in. Her game was as natural as breathing.

Unfortunately, I'd underestimated Pretty Boy. He was a serious player. I started out shaky, pretty rusty, and I double-faulted my first serve, to Jody's visible annoyance. Soon, though, my game came back. Meanwhile, Drew was playing like he was at Wimbledon. The more my game returned, the more aggressive he got, until it was ridiculous. He started poaching at the net, crossing over the court to get shots that were meant for Alana, really hogging the ball. You could see her grimace at him. I began to sense some kind of history between the two of them—some serious tension here.

There was this whole other thing going here—the battle of the Alpha Males. Drew started serving right at me, hitting them really hard, sometimes too long. Though his serves were viciously fast, he didn't have much control, and so he and Alana started losing. Also, I got onto him after a while, anticipating that he was going to poach, disguising my shots, hitting the ball behind him. Pretty Boy had pressed that same old competition button in me. I wanted to put him in his place. Me want other caveman's woman. Pretty soon I was working up a sweat. I realized I was working way too hard at it, being too aggressive for this mostly social game; it didn't look right. So I dialed back and played a more patient point, keeping the ball in play, letting Drew make his mistakes.

Drew came up to the net and shook my hand at the end. Then he patted me on the back. "You're a good fundamental player," he said in this fake-chummy way.

"You too," I said.

He shrugged. "I had to cover a lot of court."

Alana heard that, and her blue eyes flashed with annoyance. She turned to me. "Do you have time for a drink?"

It was just Alana and me, on the "porch," as they called it—this mammoth wooden deck overlooking the courts. Jody had excused herself, sensing through some kind of female windtalking that Alana didn't want a group, saying that she had to get going. Then Drew saw what was happening, and he excused himself too, though not as graciously.

The waitress came around, and Alana told me to go first, she hadn't decided what she wanted. I asked for a Tanqueray Malacca G & T. She gave me a startled glance, just a split second, before she regained her composure.

"I'll second that," Alana said.

"Let me go check and see if we have that," the waitress, a horsy blond high-school student, said. A few minutes later she came back with the drinks.

We talked for a while, about the club, the members ("snotty," she said), the courts ("best ones around by *far*"), but she was too sophisticated to do the whole boring what-do-*you*-do? thing. She didn't mention Trion, so neither did I. I began to dread that part of the conversation, wasn't sure how I'd smooth over the bizarre coincidence that we both worked at Trion, and hey, *you* used to have *my* very exact job! I couldn't believe I'd volunteered to join their game, vaulted myself right into her orbit instead of keeping a low profile. It was a good thing we'd never seen each other at work. I wondered whether the AURORA people used a separate entrance. Still, the gin went to my head pretty quickly, and it was this beautiful sunny day, and the conversation really flowed.

"I'm sorry about Drew being so out of control," she said.

"He's good."

"He can be an asshole. You were a threat. Must be a male thing. Combat with racquets."

I smiled. "It's like that Ani DiFranco line, you know? ' 'Cause every tool is a weapon if you hold it right.' "

Her eyes lit up. "Exactly! Are you into Ani?"

I shrugged. " 'Science chases money, and money chases its tail—' "

" 'And the best minds of my generation can't make bail,' " she finished. "Not many men are into Ani."

"I'm a sensitive guy, I guess," I deadpanned.

"I *guess*. We should go out some time," she said.

Was I hearing right? Had she just asked *me* out?

"Good idea," I said. "So, do you like Thai food?"

27

I got to my dad's apartment so exhilarated from my mini-date with Alana Jennings that I felt like I was wearing a suit of armor. Nothing he did or said could get to me now.

As I climbed the splintery wooden-deck front steps I could hear them arguing—my dad's high-pitched, nasal squawk, sounding more and more like a bird, and Antwoine's rumbling reply, deep and resonant. I found them in the first-floor bathroom, which was filled with steam billowing out of a vaporizer. Dad was lying facedown on a bench, a bunch of pillows under his head and chest propping him up. Antwoine, his pale-blue scrubs soaking wet, was thumping on Dad's naked back with his huge hands. He looked up when I opened the door.

"Yo, Adam."

"This son of a bitch is trying to kill me," Dad screeched.

"This is how you loosen the phlegm in the lungs," Antwoine said. "That shit get all gunked up in there 'cause of all the damaged cilias." He went back to it, making a hollow thump. Dad's back was sickly pale, paper-white, droopy and saggy. It seemed to have no muscle tone. I remembered what my father's back used to look like, when I was a kid: ropy, sinewy, almost frightening. This was old-man skin, and I wished I hadn't seen it.

"The bastard lied to me," Dad said, his voice muffled by the pillows. "He told me I was just going to breathe in steam. He didn't say he was going to crack my goddamned *ribs*. Jesus Christ, I'm on *steroids*, my bones are fragile, you goddamned nigger!"

"Hey, Dad," I yelled, "enough!"

"I'm not your *prison bitch*, nigger!" he said.

Antwoine showed no reaction. He kept clapping on Dad's back, steadily, rhythmically.

"Dad," I said, "this man is a whole lot bigger and stronger than you. I don't think it's a good idea to alienate him."

Antwoine looked up at me with sleepy, amused eyes. "Hey, man, I had to deal with Aryan Nation every day I was jammed up. Believe me, a mouthy old cripple's no big deal."

I winced.

"You *god*damned son of a *bitch!*" Dad shrieked. I noticed he didn't use the N-word.

Later Dad was parked in front of the TV, hooked up to the bubbler, the tube in his nose.

"This arrangement is not working out," he said, scowling at the TV. "Have you seen the kind of rabbit-food shit he tries to give me?"

"It's called fruits and vegetables," Antwoine said. He was sitting in the chair a few feet away. "I know what he likes—I can see what's in the pantry. Dinty Moore beef stew in the big can, Vienna sausages, and liverwurst. Well, not as long as I'm here. You need the healthy stuff, Frank, build up your immunity. You catch a cold, you end up with pneumonia, in the hospital, and then what am I going to do? You're not going to need me when you're in the hospital."

"Christ."

"Plus no more Cokes, that shit is over. You need fluids, thin your mucus, nothing with the caffeine in it. You need potassium, you need calcium 'cause of the steroids." He was jabbing his index finger into his palm like he was a trainer for the world heavyweight champion.

"Make whatever rabbit-food crap you want, I won't eat it," Dad said.

"Then you're just killing yourself. Takes you ten times more energy to breathe than a normal guy, so you need to eat, build up your strength, your muscle mass, all that. You expire on my watch, I'm not taking the rap."

"Like you really give a shit," Dad said.

"You think I'm here to help you die?"

"Looks that way to me."

"If I wanted to kill you, why would I do it the slow way?" Antwoine said. "Unless you think this is fun for me. Like maybe I *enjoy* this shit."

"This is a blast, isn't it?" I said.

"Hey, wouldja check out the watch on that man?" Antwoine suddenly said. I'd forgotten to take off the Panerai. Maybe subconsciously I thought it wouldn't even register with him or my dad. "Let me see that." He came up to me, inspected it, marveling. "Man, that's gotta be a five-thousand-dollar watch." He was pretty close. I was embarrassed—it was more than he made in two months. "That one of those Italian diving watches?"

"Yep," I said hastily.

"Oh, you gotta be shittin' me," Dad said, his voice like a rusty hinge. "I don't fucking *believe* this." Now he was staring at my watch too. "You spent five thousand dollars on a goddamned *watch?* What a loser! Do you have any idea how I used to bust my hump for five thousand bucks when I was putting you through school? You spent that on a fucking *watch?*"

"It's my money, Dad." Then I added, feebly, "It's an investment."

"Oh, for Christ's sakes, you think I'm an *idiot?* An *investment?*"

"Dad, look, I just got a huge promotion. I'm working at Trion Systems for, like, twice the salary I was getting at Wyatt, okay?"

He looked at me shrewdly. "What kinda money they paying you, you can throw away five *thousand*—Jesus, I can't even say it."

"They're paying me a lot, Dad. And if I want to throw my money away, I'll throw it away. I've earned it."

"You've earned it," he repeated with thick sarcasm. "Any time you want to pay me back for"—he took a breath—"I don't know *how* many tens of thousands of dollars I dumped on you, be my guest."

I came this close to telling him then how much money I threw his way, but I pulled back just in time. The momentary victory wouldn't be worth it. Instead I told myself over and over, this is not your dad. It's an evil cartoon version of Dad, animated by Hanna-Barbera, distorted out of recognition by prednisone and a dozen other mind-altering substances. But of course I knew that wasn't quite true, that this really was the same old asshole, just with the dial turned up a couple of notches.

"You're living in a fantasy world," Dad went on, then took a loud breath. "You think just 'cause you buy the two-thousand-dollar suits and the five-hundred-dollar shoes and the five-thousand-dollar watches you're going to become one of *them*, don't you?" He took a breath. "Well, let me tell you something. You're wearing a fucking Halloween costume, that's all. You're dressing up. I tell you this 'cause you're my son and no one else is going to give it to you straight. You're nothing more than an ape in a fucking tuxedo."

"What's that supposed to mean?" I mumbled. I noticed Antwoine tactfully walking out of the room. My face went all red.

He's a sick man, I told myself. He has end-stage emphysema. He's dying. He doesn't know what he's saying.

"You think you're ever gonna be one of them? Boy, you'd like to think that, wouldn't you? You think they're gonna take you in and let you join their private clubs and screw their daughters and play fucking *polo* with them." He sucked in a tiny lungful of air. "But *they* know who you are, son, and where you come from. Maybe they'll let you play in their sandbox for a while, but as soon as you start to forget who you really are, someone's going to fucking remind you."

I couldn't restrain myself any longer. He was driving me crazy. "It doesn't work that way in the business world, Dad," I said patiently. "It's not like a club. It's about making money. If you help them make money, you fulfill a need. I'm where I am because they need me."

"Oh, they *need* you," Dad repeated, drawing out the word, nodding. "That's a good one. They need you like a guy taking a shit needs a piece of toilet paper, you unnerstand me? Then when they're done wiping away their shit, they flush. Lemme tell you, all they care about is winners, and they know you're a loser and they're not going to let you forget it."

I rolled my eyes, shook my head, didn't say anything. A vein throbbed at my temple.

A breath. "And you're too stupid and full of yourself to know it. You're living in a goddamned fantasy world, just like your mother. She always thought she was too good for me, but she wasn't shit. She was dreaming. And you ain't shit. You went to a fancy prep school for a couple of years, and you got a high-priced do-nothing college degree, but you still ain't shit."

He took a deep breath, and his voice seemed to soften a little. "I tell you this because I don't want you to be fucked over the way they fucked me over, son. Like that fucking candy-ass prep school, the way all the rich parents looked down on me, like I wasn't one of them. Well, guess what. Took me a while to figure it out, but they were right. I wasn't one of them. Neither are you, and the sooner you figure it out, the better off you'll be."

"Better off, like you," I said. It just slipped out.

He stared at me, his eyes beady. "At least I know who I am," he said. "You don't fucking know who you are."

28

The next morning was Sunday, my only chance to sleep late, so of course Arnold Meacham insisted on meeting me early. I'd replied to his daily e-mail using the name "Donnie," which told him I had something to deliver. He e-mailed right back, told me to be at the parking lot of a particular Home Depot at nine A.M. sharp.

There were a lot of people here already—not everyone slept late on Sunday—buying lumber and tile and power tools and bags of grass seed and fertilizer. I waited in the Audi for a good half hour.

Then a black BMW 745i pulled into the space next to mine, looking a little out of place among the pickup trucks and SUVs. Arnold Meacham was wearing a baby-blue cardigan sweater and looked like he was on his way to play golf somewhere. He signaled for me to get into his car, which I did, and I handed him a CD and a file folder.

"And what do we have here?" he asked.

"List of AURORA Project employees," I said.

"All of them?"

"I don't know. At least some."

"Why not all?"

"It's forty-seven names there," I said. "It's a decent start."

"We need the complete list."

I sighed. "I'll see what I can do." I paused for a second, torn between not wanting to tell the guy anything I didn't have to—the more I told him, the more he'd push me—and wanting to brag about how much progress I'd been making. "I have my boss's passwords," I finally said.

"Which boss? Lundgren?"

"Nora Sommers."

He nodded. "You use the software?"

"No, the Keyghost."

"What'll you do with them?"

"Search her archived e-mail. Maybe go into her MeetingMaker and find out who she meets with."

"That's penny-ante shit," Meacham said. "I think it's time to penetrate AURORA."

"Too risky right now," I said, shaking my head.

"Why?"

A guy rolled a shopping cart stacked with green bags of Scott's starter fertilizer by Meacham's window. Four or five little kids ran around behind him. Meacham looked over, electrically rolled up his window, turned back to me. "Why?" he repeated.

"The badge access is separate."

"For Christ's sake, follow someone in, steal a badge, whatever. Do I need to put you back in basic training?"

"They log all entries, and every entrance has a turnstile, so you can't just sneak in."

"What about the cleaning crew?"

"There's also closed-circuit TV cameras trained on every entry point. It's not so easy. You don't want me to get caught, not now."

He seemed to back down. "Jesus, the place is well defended."

"You could probably learn a trick or two."

"Fuck you," he snapped. "What about HR files?"

"HR's pretty well protected too," I said.

"Not like AURORA. That ought to be relatively easy. Get us the personnel files on everyone you can who's associated in any way with AURORA. At least the people on this list." He held up the CD.

"I can try for it next week."

"Do it tonight. Sunday night's a good time to do it."

"I've got a big day tomorrow. We're making a presentation to Goddard."

He looked disgusted. "What, you're too busy with your cover job? I hope you haven't forgotten who you really work for."

"I've got to be up to speed. It's important."

"All the more reason why you'd be in the office working tonight," he said, and he turned the key in the ignition.

29

Early that evening I drove to Trion headquarters. The parking garage was almost entirely empty, the only people there probably security, the people who manned the twenty-four-hour ops centers, and the random work-crazed employee, like I was pretending to be. I didn't recognize the lobby ambassador, a Hispanic woman who didn't look happy to be there. She barely looked at me as I let myself in, but I made a point of saying hi, looking harried or sheepish or something. I went up to my cubicle and did a little real work, some spreadsheets on Maestro sales in the region of the world they call EMEA, for Europe/Middle East/Asia. The trend lines weren't good, but Nora wanted me to massage the numbers to bring out whatever encouraging data points I could.

Most of the floor was dark. I even had to switch on the lights in my area. It was unnerving.

Meacham and Wyatt wanted the personnel files on everyone in AURORA. They wanted to find out each person's employment history, which would tell them what companies they were all hired from and what they did at their last jobs. It was a good way to suss out what AURORA was all about.

But it wasn't as if I could just saunter into Human Resources, pull open some file cabinets, and pluck out whatever files I wanted. The HR department at Trion, unlike most other parts of the company, actually took security precautions. For one thing, their computers weren't accessible through the main corporate database; it was a whole separate network. I guess that made sense—personnel records contained all sorts of private information like people's performance appraisals, the value of their 401(k)s and stock options, all that. Maybe HR was afraid that the rank-and-file would find out how much more the top Trion execs got paid than everyone else and there'd be riots down in the cube farms.

HR was located on the third floor of E Wing, a long hike from New Product Marketing. There were a lot of locked doors along the way, but my badge would probably open each one of them.

Then I remembered that somewhere it was recorded who entered which checkpoints and at what time. The information was stored, which didn't necessarily mean that anybody looked at it or did anything about it. But if there were ever trouble later, it wouldn't look good that on a Sunday night for some reason I walked from New Products to Personnel, leaving digital bread crumbs along the way.

So I left the building, just took the elevator down and took one of the back entrances. The thing about these security systems was that they only kept track of entrances, not exits. When you walked out, you didn't use your badge. This might have been some fire-department code thing, I didn't know. But that meant that I could leave the building without anyone knowing I'd left.

It was dark outside by now. The Trion building was lit up, its brushed-chrome skin gleaming, the glass windows a midnight blue. It was relatively quiet out here at night, just the *shush* of the occasional car passing by on the highway.

I walked around to E Wing, where a lot of the administrative functions seemed to be housed—Central Purchasing, Systems Management, that sort of thing—and saw someone coming out of a service entrance.

"Hey, can you hold the door?" I shouted. I waved my Trion badge at the guy, who looked like he was on the cleaning crew or something. "Damned badge isn't working right."

The man held the door open for me, didn't give me a glance, and I walked right in. Nothing recorded. As far as the central system was concerned, I was still upstairs at my cubicle.

I took the stairs to the third floor. The door to the third floor was unlocked. This, too, was a fire department law of some kind: in buildings above a certain height you had to be able to go from floor to floor by the stairs, in case of emergency. Probably some floors had a badge-reader station just inside the stair exit. But the third floor didn't. I walked right into the reception area outside Human Resources.

The waiting area had just the right kind of HR look—a lot of dignified mahogany, to say we're serious and this is about your career, and colorful, welcoming, cushy-looking chairs. Which told you that whenever you came to HR you were going to sit there on your butt for an ungodly long time.

I looked around for closed-circuit TV cameras and didn't see any. Not that I was expecting any; this wasn't a bank—or the skunkworks—but I just wanted to make sure. Or as sure as I could be, anyway.

The lights were on low, which made the place look even more stately. Or spooky, I couldn't decide.

For a few seconds I stood there, thinking. There weren't any cleaning people around to let me in; they probably came late at night or early in the morning. That would have been the best way in. Instead, I'd have to try the same old my-badge-won't-work trick, which had gotten me this far. I went back downstairs and headed into the lobby through the back way, where a female lobby ambassador with big brassy red hair was watching a rerun of *The Bachelor* on one of the security monitors.

"And I thought I was the only one who had to work on Sunday," I said to her. She looked up, laughed politely, turned back to her show. I looked like I belonged, I had a badge clipped to my belt, and I was coming from the inside, so I was supposed to be there, right? She wasn't the talkative type, but that was a good thing—she just wanted to be left alone to watch *The Bachelor*. She'd do anything to get rid of me.

"Hey, listen," I said, "sorry to bother you, but do you have that machine to fix badges? It's not like I *want* to get into my office or anything, but I have to or I'm out of a job, and the damned badge-reader won't let me in. It's like it *knows* I should be home watching football, you know?"

She smiled. She probably wasn't used to Trion employees even noticing her. "I know what you mean," she said. "But sorry, the lady who does that won't be in till tomorrow."

"Oh, man. How am I supposed to get in? I can't wait till tomorrow. I'm totally screwed."

She nodded, picked up her phone. "Stan," she said, "can you help us out here?"

Stan, the security guard, showed up a couple minutes later. He was a small, wiry, swarthy guy in his fifties with an obvious toupee that was jet black while the fringe of real hair all around it was going gray. I could never understand why you would bother to wear a hairpiece if you weren't going to update it once in a while to make it look halfway convincing. We took the elevator up to the third floor. I gave him some complicated blather about how HR was on a hierarchically separate badging system, but he wasn't too interested. He wanted to talk sports, and that I could do, no problem. He was bummed out about the Denver Broncos, and I pretended I was too. When we got to HR, he took out his badge, which probably let him in anywhere he worked in this part of the building. He waved it at the card reader. "Don't work too hard," he said.

"Thanks, brother," I said.

He turned to look at me. "You better get that badge fixed," he said.

And I was in.

30

Once you got past the reception area, HR looked like every other damned office at Trion, the same generic cube-farm layout. Only the emergency lights were on, not the overhead fluorescents. From what I could see walking around, all of the cubicles were empty, as were all the offices. It didn't take long to figure out where the records were kept. In the center of the floor was a huge grid made up of long aisles of beige horizontal files.

I'd thought about trying to do my espionage totally online, but that wouldn't work without an HR password. While I was here, though, I figured I'd leave one of those key logger devices. Later on I could come back and get it. Wyatt Telecom was paying for these little toys, not me. I found a cubicle and installed the thing.

For now, though, I had to root around through the file drawers, find the AURORA people. And I'd have to move fast—the longer I stayed here, the greater the chance I'd be caught.

The question was, how were they organized? Alphabetically, by name? In order of employee number? The more I looked over the file drawer labels, the more discouraged I got. What, did I think I was just going to waltz in and slide open a door and pluck out a few choice files? There were rows of drawers titled BENEFITS ADMINISTRATION and PENSION/ANNUITY/RETIREMENT and SICK, ANNUAL AND OTHER LEAVE RECORDS; drawers labeled CLAIMS, WORKMEN'S COMPENSATION and CLAIMS, LITIGATED; one area called IMMIGRATION AND NATURALIZATION RECORDS . . . and on and on. Mind-numbing.

For some reason some sappy golden-oldie song was playing in my head—"Band on the Run," by Paul McCartney in his unfortunate Wings period. A song I really detest, worse even than anything by Celine Dion. The tune is annoying but catchy, like pinkeye, and the words make no sense. "A bell was ringing in the village square for the *rabbits on the run!*" Um, okay.

I tried one of the file drawers, and of course it was locked; they all were. Each file cabinet had a lock at the top, and they had to be all keyed alike. I looked for an admin's desk, and meanwhile that damned song was circling around in my head. . . . "*The county judge . . . held a grudge*" . . . as I looked for an admin's desk, and sure enough, a key to the files was there, on a ring in an unlocked top center drawer. Boy, Meacham was right; the key's always easy to find.

I went for the alphabetized employee files.

Choosing one name from the AURORA list—Yonah Oren—I looked under O. Nothing there. I looked for another name—Sanjay Kumar—and found nothing there either. I tried Peter Daut: nothing. Strange. Just to be thorough, I checked under those names in the INSURANCE POLICIES, ACCIDENT drawers. Nothing. Same with the pension files. In fact, nothing in any of the files, so far as I could see.

"*The jailer man and Sailor Sam. . . .*" This was like Chinese water torture—what did those insipid lyrics mean anyway? Did anyone know?

What was strange was that in the places where the records *should* have been, there sometimes seemed to be little gaps, little loose places, as if the files had been removed. Or was I just imagining this? Just when I was about to give up, I took one more circuit around the rows of file cabinets, and then I noticed an alcove—a separate, open room next to the grid of file drawers. A sign posted on the entrance to the alcove said:

CLASSIFIED PERSONNEL RECORDS—
ACCESS ONLY BY DIRECT AUTHORIZATION
OF JAMES SPERLING OR LUCY CELANO.

I entered the alcove and was relieved to see that things were simple here: the drawers were organized by department number. James Sperling was the director of HR, and Lucy Celano, I knew, was his administrative assistant. It took me a couple of minutes to find Lucy Celano's desk, and maybe thirty seconds to find her key ring (bottom right drawer).

Then I returned to the restricted file cabinets and found the drawer that held the department numbers, including the AURORA project. I unlocked the cabinet, and pulled it open. It made a kind of metallic *thunk* sound, as if some caster at the back of the drawer had somehow dropped. I wondered how often anyone actually went into these drawers. Did they work with online records mostly, keeping the hard copies just for legal and audit reasons?

And then I saw something truly bizarre: *all* of the files for the AURORA department were gone. I mean, there was a gap of a foot and a half, maybe two feet, between the number before and the number after. The drawer was half empty.

The AURORA files had been removed.

For a second it felt as if my heart had stopped. I felt light-headed.

Out of the corner of my eye, I saw a bright light start to flash. It was one of those xenon emergency strobe lights mounted high on the wall, near the ceiling, just outside the file alcove. What the hell was that for? And a few seconds later there came the unbelievably loud, throaty *hoo-ah, hoo-ah* of a siren.

Somehow I'd triggered an intrusion-detection system, no doubt protecting the classified files.

The siren was so loud you could probably hear it throughout the whole wing.

3 1

Any second Security would be here. Maybe the only reason they hadn't shown up yet was that it was a weekend and there were fewer of them around.

I raced to the door, slammed my side against the crash bar, and the door didn't move. The impact hurt like hell.

I tried again; the door was bolted shut. Oh, Jesus. I tried another door, and that too was locked from inside.

Now I realized what that funny metallic thunking sound had been a minute or two earlier—by opening the file drawer I must have set off some kind of mechanism that auto-locked all the exit doors in the area. I ran to the other side of the floor, where there was another set of exit doors, but they wouldn't open either. Even the emergency fire-escape door to a small back stairwell was locked, and that *had* to be against code.

I was trapped like a rat in a maze. Security would be here any second now, and they'd search the place.

My mind raced. Could I try to pull something over on them? Stan, the security guard, had let me in—maybe I could convince him I'd just accidentally stepped into the wrong area, pulled open the wrong drawer. He seemed to like me, that might work. But then, what if he actually did his job right, asked to look at my badge, saw that I didn't belong anywhere remotely near here?

No, I couldn't chance it. I had no choice, I had to hide.

I was stuck inside here.

"Stuck inside these four walls," Wings wailed sickeningly at me. *Christ!*

The xenon strobe was pulsing, blindingly bright, and the alarm was going *hoo-ah*, *hoo-ah*, as if this were a nuclear reactor during a core melt.

But *where* could I hide? I figured the first thing I should do was create some sort of a diversion, some plausible, innocent explanation for why the alarm had gone off. Shit, there was no time!

If I was caught here, it was over. Everything. I wouldn't just lose my job at Trion. Far worse. It was a disaster, a total nightmare.

I grabbed the nearest metal trash can. It was empty, so I grabbed a piece of paper off a nearby desk, crumpled it up, took my lighter and lit it. Running back toward the classified-records alcove, I set it against the wall. Then I took out a cigarette from my pack and tossed it into the can too. The paper burned, flamed out, sending up a big cloud of smoke. Maybe, if part of the cigarette were found, they'd blame the old smoldering butt. Maybe.

I heard loud footsteps, voices that seemed to be coming from the back stairwell.

No, please, God. It's all over. It's all over.

I saw what looked like a closet door. It was unlocked. Behind was a supply closet, not very wide, but maybe twelve feet deep, crowded with tall rows of shelves stacked with reams of paper and the like.

I didn't dare put the light on, so it was hard to see, but I could make out a space between two shelves in the rear where I might be able to squeeze myself in.

Just as I pulled the door shut behind me I heard another door open, and then muffled shouts.

I froze. The alarm kept whooping. People were running back and forth, shouting louder, closer.

"Over here!" someone bellowed.

My heart was thundering. I held my breath. When I moved even slightly, the shelf in back of me squeaked. I shifted, and my shoulder brushed against a box, making a rustling sound. I doubted anyone passing by could hear the small noises I was making, not with all that racket out there, the shouting and the sirens and all. But I forced myself to remain totally still.

"—fucking *cigarette!*" I heard, to my relief.

"—extinguisher!—" someone replied.

For a long, long time—it could have been ten minutes, it could have been half an hour, I had no idea, I couldn't move my arm to check my wrist-watch—I stood there squirming uncomfortably, hot and sweaty, in a state of suspended animation, my feet going numb because of the funny position I was in.

I waited for the closet door to swing open, the light to cascade in, the jig to be up.

I didn't know what the hell I could say then. Nothing, really. I would be caught, and I had no idea how I could possibly explain my way out of it. I'd be *lucky* just to be fired. I'd likely face legal action at Trion—there was simply no good explanation for my being here. I didn't want to *think* about what Wyatt would do to me.

And for all my trouble, what had I turned up here? Nothing. All the AURORA records were gone anyway.

I could hear some kind of hosing, squirting sound, obviously a fire extinguisher going off, and by now the shouts had diminished. I wondered whether Security had called in-house firefighters, or the local fire department. And whether the wastebasket fire had explained away the alarm. Or would they keep searching the place?

So I stood there, my feet turning into tingling blocks of ice while sweat ran down my face, and my shoulders and back seized up with cramps.

And I waited.

Once in a while I heard voices, but they seemed calmer, more matter-of-fact. Footsteps, but no longer frantic.

After an endless stretch of time, everything went quiet. I tried to raise my left arm to check the time, but my arm had fallen asleep. I wriggled it, moved my right arm around to pinch at the dead left one until I was able to move it up toward my face and check the illuminated dial. It was a few minutes after ten, though I'd been in there so long I was sure it was after midnight.

Slowly I extricated myself from my contortionist's position, moved noise-lessly toward the door of the closet. There I stood for a few moments, listening intently. I couldn't hear a sound. It seemed a safe bet that they'd gone—they'd put out the fire, satisfied themselves that there hadn't been a break-in after all. Human beings, especially security guards who must on some level resent all those computers that have all but put them out of a job, don't trust machines anyway. They'd be quick to blame it on some alarm-system glitch. Maybe, if I were really lucky, no one would wonder why the *intrusion*-detection alarm had gone off before the *smoke* alarm had.

Then I took a breath and slowly opened the door.

I looked to either side and straight ahead, and the area seemed to be empty. No one there. I took a few steps, paused, looked around again.

No one.

The place smelled pretty strongly of smoke, and also some kind of chemical, probably from the fire extinguisher stuff.

Quietly, I made my way along the wall, away from any outside windows or glass-paneled doors, until I reached one of the sets of exit doors. Not the main reception doors, and not the rear stairwell doors through which the security guys had entered.

And they were locked.

Still locked.

Christ, no.

They hadn't deactivated the auto-lock. Moving a little more quickly now, the adrenaline surging again, I went to the reception-area doors and pushed against the crash bars, and those too were locked.

I was still locked inside.

Now what?

I had no choice. There was no way to unlock the doors from inside, at least no way that I'd been taught. And I couldn't exactly call Security for help, especially not after what had just happened.

No. I'd just have to stay inside here until someone let me out. Which might not be until the morning, when the cleaning crew came in. Or worse, when the first HR staff arrived. And then I'd have some serious explaining to do.

I was also exhausted. I found a cubicle far from any door or window, and sat down. I was totally fried. I needed sleep badly. So I folded my arms and, like a frazzled student at the college library, passed right out.

32

Around five in the morning I was awakened by a clattering noise. I bolted upright. The cleaning crew had arrived, wheeling big yellow plastic buckets and mops and the kind of vacuum cleaners you strap to your shoulder. There were two men and a woman, speaking rapidly to each other in Portuguese. I knew a little: a lot of our neighbors growing up were Brazilians.

I'd drooled a little puddle of saliva onto whoever's desk this was. I mopped it up with my sleeve, then got up and sauntered over to the exit doors, which they'd propped open with a rubber doorstop.

"*Bom dia, como vai?*" I said. I shook my head, looking embarrassed, glanced ostentatiously at my watch.

"*Bem, obrigado e o senhor?*" the woman replied. She grinned, exposing a couple of gold teeth. She seemed to get it—poor office guy, working all night, or maybe in here ridiculously early, she didn't know or care.

One of the men was looking at the scorched metal waste can and saying something to the other guy. Like, what the hell happened here?

"*Cançado,*" I said to the lady: I'm tired, that's how I am. "*Bom, até logo.*" See you later.

"*Até logo, senhor,*" the woman said as I walked out the door.

I thought for a second about driving home, changing clothes, turning right back around. But that was more than I could handle, so instead I left E Wing—by now people were starting to come in—and re-entered B Wing and went up to my cubicle. Okay, so if anyone checked the entrance records, they'd see that I'd come in to the building Sunday night around seven, then came back around five-thirty in the morning on Monday. Eager beaver. I just hoped I didn't run into anyone I knew, looking the way I did, like I'd slept in my clothes, which of course I had. Fortunately I didn't see anyone. I grabbed a Diet Vanilla Coke from the break room and took a deep swig. It tasted nasty this early in the morning, so I made a pot of coffee in the Bunn-O-Matic, and went to the men's room to wash up. My shirt was a little wrinkled, but overall I looked presentable, even if I felt like shit. Today was a big day, and I had to be at my best.

An hour before the big meeting with Augustine Goddard, we gathered in Packard, one of the bigger conference rooms, for a dress rehearsal. Nora was wearing a beautiful blue suit and she looked like she'd had her hair done specially for the occasion. She was totally on edge; she crackled with nervous energy. She was smiling, her eyes wide.

She and Chad were rehearsing in the room while the rest of us gathered. Chad was playing Jock. They were doing this back-and-forth like an old married couple going through the paces of a long-familiar argument, when suddenly Chad's cell phone rang. He had one of those Motorola flip phones, which I was convinced he favored so he could end a call by snapping it shut.

"This is Chad," he said. His tone abruptly warmed. "Hey, Tony." He held an index finger in the air to tell Nora to wait, and he went off into a corner of the room.

"Chad," Nora called after him with annoyance. He turned back, nodded at her, held up his finger again. A minute or so later I heard him snap the phone closed, and then he came up to Nora, speaking fast in a low voice. We were all watching, listening in; they were in the center ring.

"That's a buddy of mine in the controller's office," he said quietly, grim-faced. "The decision on Maestro has already been made."

"How do you know?" Nora said.

"The controller just put through the order to do a one-time write-off of fifty million bucks for Maestro. The decision's been made at the top. This meeting with Goddard is just a formality."

Nora flushed deep crimson and turned away. She walked over to the window and looked out, and for a full minute she didn't say anything.

3 3

The Executive Briefing Center was on the seventh floor of A Wing, just down the hall from Goddard's office. We trooped over there in a group, the mood pretty low. Nora said she'd join us in a few minutes.

"Dead men walking!" Chad sang out to me as we walked. "Dead men walking!"

I nodded. Mordden glanced at Chad walking beside me, and he kept his distance, no doubt thinking all kinds of evil thoughts about me, trying to figure out why I wasn't giving Chad the cold shoulder, what I was up to. He hadn't been stopping by my cubicle as often since the night I'd sneaked into Nora's office. It was hard to tell if he was acting strangely, since strange was his default mode. Also, I didn't want to succumb to the situational paranoia — was he looking at me funny, that sort of thing. But I couldn't help wondering whether I had blown the whole mission with one single act of carelessness, whether Mordden was going to cause me serious trouble.

"Now, seating's crucial, big guy," Chad muttered to me. "Goddard always takes the center seat on the side of the table near the door. If you want to be invisible, you sit on his right. If you want him to pay attention to you, either sit to his left or directly across the table from him."

"Do I *want* him to pay attention to me?"

"I can't answer that. He *is* the boss."

"Have you been in a lot of meetings with him?"

"Not that many," he shrugged. "A couple."

I made a mental note to sit anywhere Chad recommended against, like to Goddard's right. Fool me once, shame on you, and all that.

The EBC was a truly impressive sight. There was a huge wooden conference table made of some kind of tropical-looking wood that took up most of the room. One entire end of the room was a screen for presentations. There were heavy acoustic blinds that you could tell were supposed to slide down electrically from the ceiling, probably not only to block out light but to keep anyone outside from hearing what went on inside the room. Built into the table were speakerphones and little screens in front of each chair that slid up when a button was pushed somewhere.

There was a lot of whispering, nervous laughter, muttered wisecracks. I was sort of looking forward to seeing the famous Jock Goddard up close and personal, even if I never got to shake his hand. I didn't have to speak or make any part of the presentation, but I was a little nervous anyway.

By five minutes before ten, Nora still hadn't shown up. Had she jumped out of a window? Was she calling around, trying to lobby, making a last-ditch effort to save her precious product, pulling whatever strings she had?

"Think she got lost?" Phil joked.

Two minutes before ten, Nora entered the room, looking calm, radiant, somehow more attractive. She looked like she'd put on fresh makeup, lip-liner and all that stuff. Maybe she'd even been meditating or something, because she looked transformed.

Then, at exactly ten o'clock, Jock Goddard and Paul Camilletti entered the room, and everyone went quiet. "Cutthroat" Camilletti, in a black blazer and an olive silk T-shirt, had slicked his hair back and looked like Gordon Gekko in *Wall Street*. He took a seat way off at a corner of the immense table. Goddard, in his customary black mock turtleneck under a tweedy brown sport coat, walked up to Nora and whispered something that made her laugh. He put his hand on her shoulder; she put her hand on top of his hand for a few seconds. She was acting girlish, sort of flirtatious; it was a side of Nora I'd never seen before.

Goddard then sat down right at the head of the table, facing the screen. Thanks, Chad. I was across the table and to his right. I could see him just fine and I sure didn't *feel* invisible. He had round shoulders, a little stooped. His white hair, parted on one side, was unruly. His eyebrows were bushy, white,

each one looked like a snow-capped mountaintop. His forehead was deeply
creased, and he had an impish look in his eyes.

There were an awkward few seconds of silence, and he looked around
the big table. "You all look so nervous," he said. "Relax! I don't bite." His
voice was pleasant and sort of crackly, a mellow baritone. He glanced at Nora,
winked. "Not often, anyway." She laughed; a couple of other people chuckled politely. I smiled, mostly to say, I appreciate that you're trying to put us all
at ease.

"Only when you're threatened," she said. He smiled, his lips forming a V.
"Jock, do you mind if I start off here?"

"Please."

"Jock, we've all been working so incredibly hard on the refresh of Maestro that I think sometimes it's just hard to get outside ourselves, get any real
perspective. I've spent the last thirty-six hours thinking about pretty much
nothing else. And it's clear to me that there are several important ways in
which we can update, improve Maestro, make it more appealing, increase
market share, maybe even significantly."

Goddard nodded, made a steeple with his fingers, looked down at his
notes.

She tapped the laminated bound presentation notebook. "We've come
up with a strategy, quite a good one, adding twelve new functionalities, bringing Maestro up to date. But I have to tell you quite honestly that if I were sitting where you're sitting, I'd pull the plug."

Goddard turned suddenly to look at her, his great white eyebrows aloft.
We all stared at her, shocked. I couldn't believe I was hearing this. She was
burning her entire team.

"Jock," she went on, "if there's one thing you've taught me, it's that sometimes a true leader has to sacrifice the thing he loves most. It kills me to say it.
But I simply can't ignore the facts. Maestro was great for its time. But its time
has come—and gone. It's Goddard's Rule—if your product doesn't have the
potential to be number one or number two in the market, you get out."

Goddard was silent for a few moments. He looked surprised, impressed,
and after a few seconds he nodded with a shrewd I-like-what-I-see smile. "Are
we—is everyone in agreement on this?" he drawled.

Gradually people started nodding their heads, jumping on the moving train as it pulled out of the station. Chad was nodding, biting his lip the way Bill Clinton used to; Mordden was nodding vigorously, like he was finally able to express his true opinion. The other engineers grunted, "Yes" and "I agree."

"I must say, I'm surprised to hear this," Goddard said. "This is certainly not what I expected to hear this morning. I was expecting the Battle of Gettysburg. I'm impressed."

"What's good for any of us as individuals in the short term," Nora added, "isn't necessarily what's best for Trion."

I couldn't believe the way Nora was leading this immolation, but I had to admire her cunning, her Machiavellian skill.

"Well," Goddard said, "before we pull the trigger, hang on for a minute. You—I didn't see you nodding."

He seemed to be looking directly at me.

I glanced around, then back at him. He was definitely looking at me.

"You," he said. "Young man, I didn't see you nodding your head with the rest."

"He's new," Nora put in hastily. "Just started."

"What's your name, young man?"

"Adam," I said. "Adam Cassidy." My heart started hammering. Oh, shit. It was like being called on in school. I felt like a second-grader.

"You got some kind of problem with the decision we're making here, uh, Adam?" said Goddard.

"Huh? No."

"So you're in agreement on pulling the plug."

I shrugged.

"You are, you're not—what?"

"I certainly see where Nora's coming from," I said.

"And if you were sitting where I'm sitting?" Goddard prompted.

I took a deep breath. "If I were sitting where you're sitting, I wouldn't pull the plug."

"No?"

"And I wouldn't add those twelve new features, either."

"You wouldn't?"

"No. Just one."

"And what might that be?"

I caught a quick glimpse of Nora's face, and it was beet red. She was staring at me as if an alien were bursting out of my chest. I turned back toward Goddard. "A secure-data protocol."

Goddard's brows sunk all the way down. "Secure data? Why the hell would that attract consumers?"

Chad cleared his throat and said, "Come on, Adam, look at the market research. Secure data's like what? Number seventy-five on the list of features consumers are looking for." He smirked. "Unless you think the average consumer is Austin Powers, International Man of Mystery."

There was some snickering from the far reaches of the table.

I smiled good-naturedly. "No, Chad, you're right—the average consumer has no interest in secure data. But I'm not talking about the average consumer. I'm talking about the military."

"The military." Goddard cocked one eyebrow.

"Adam—" Nora interrupted in a flat, warning sort of voice.

Goddard fluttered a hand toward Nora. "No, I want to hear this. The military, you say?"

I took a deep breath, tried not to look as panicked as I felt. "Look, the army, the air force, the Canadians, the British—the whole defense establishment in the U.S., the U.K., and Canada—recently overhauled their global communications system, right?" I pulled out some clippings from *Defense News, Federal Computer Week*—magazines I always happen to have hanging around the apartment, of course—and held them up. I could feel my hand shaking a little and hoped no one else noticed. Wyatt had prepared me for this, and I hoped I had the details right. "It's called the Defense Message System, the DMS—the secure messaging system for millions of defense personnel around the world. It's all done via desktop PCs, and the Pentagon is desperate to go wireless. Imagine what a difference that could make—secure wireless remote access to classified data and communications, with authentication of senders and receivers, end-to-end secure encryption, data protection, message integrity. Nobody owns this market!"

Goddard tilted his head, listening intently.

"And Maestro's the perfect product for this space. It's small, sturdy—practically indestructible—and totally reliable. This way, we turn a negative into a positive: the fact that Maestro is dated, legacy technology, is a *plus* for the military, since it's totally compatible with their five-year-old wireless transfer protocols. All we need to add is secure data. The cost is minimal, and the potential market is huge—I mean, *huge!*"

Goddard was staring at me, though I couldn't tell if he was impressed or he thought I'd lost my mind.

I went on: "So instead of trying to tart up this old, frankly inferior product, we remarket it. Throw on a hardened plastic shell, pop in secure encryption, and we're golden. We'll *own* this niche market, if we move fast. Forget about writing off fifty mil—now we're talking about hundreds of millions in added revenue per year."

"Jesus," Camilletti said from his end of the table. He was scrawling notes on a pad.

Goddard started nodding, slowly at first, then more vigorously. "Most intriguing," he said. He turned toward Nora. "What's his name again—Elijah?"

"Adam," Nora said crisply.

"Thank you, Adam," he said. "That's not bad at all."

Don't thank me, I thought; thank Nick Wyatt.

And then I caught Nora looking at me with an expression of pure and undisguised hatred.

34

The official word came down by e-mail before lunch: Goddard had ordered a stay of execution for Maestro. The Maestro team was ordered to crash a proposal for minor retooling and repackaging to meet the military's requirements. Meanwhile, Trion's Government Affairs staff would start negotiating a contract with the Pentagon's Defense Information Systems Agency Department of Acquisition and Logistics.

Translation: slam dunk. Not only had the old product been taken off life support, but it had gotten a heart transplant and a massive blood transfusion.

And the shit had hit the fan.

I was in the men's room, standing in front of the urinal and unzipping my fly, when Chad came sauntering in. Chad, I'd noticed, seemed to have a sixth sense that I was pee-shy. He was always following me into the men's room to talk work or sports and effectively shut off my spigot. This time he came right up to the next urinal, his face all lit up like he was thrilled to see me. I could hear him unzip. My bladder clamped down. I went back to staring at the tile grout above the urinal.

"Hey," he said. "Nice job, big guy. *That's* the way to 'manage up'!" He shook his head slowly, made a sort of spitting sound. His urine splashed noisily against the little lozenge at the bottom of the urinal. "Christ." He oozed sarcasm. He'd crossed some invisible line—he wasn't even pretending anymore.

I thought, Could you please go now so I can relieve myself? "I saved the product," I pointed out.

"Yeah, and you burned Nora in the process. Was it worth it, just so you could score some points with the CEO, get yourself a little face time? That's not how it works around here, bud. You just made a huge fucking mistake." He shook dry, zipped up, and walked out of the rest room without washing his hands.

A voice mail from Nora was waiting for me when I returned to my cubicle.

"Nora," I said as I entered her office.

"Adam," she said softly. "Sit down, please." She was smiling, a sad, gentle smile. This was ominous.

"Nora, can I say—"

"Adam, as you know, one of the things we pride ourselves on at Trion is always striving to fit the employee to the job—to make sure our most high-potential people are given responsibilities that best suit them." She smiled again, and her eyes glittered. "That's why I've just put through an employee transfer request form and asked Tom to expedite it."

"Transfer?"

"We're all awfully impressed with your talents, your resourcefulness, the depth of your knowledge. This morning's meeting illustrated that just so well. We feel that someone of your caliber could do a world of good at our RTP facility. The supply-chain management unit down there could really use a strong team player like you."

"RTP?"

"Our Research Triangle Park satellite office. In Raleigh-Durham, North Carolina."

"North *Carolina*?" Was I hearing her right? "You're talking about transferring me down to North Carolina?"

"Adam, you make it sound like it's Siberia. Have you ever been to Raleigh-Durham? It's really such a lovely area."

"I—but I can't move, I've got responsibilities here, I've got—"

"Employee Relocation will coordinate the whole thing for you. They cover all your moving expenses—everything within reason, of course. I've already started the ball rolling with HR. Any move can be a little disruptive, obviously, but they make it surprisingly painless." Her smile broadened. "You're going to love it there, and they're going to love *you!*"

"Nora," I said, "Goddard asked me for my honest thoughts, and I'm a big fan of everything you've done with the Maestro line, I wasn't going to deny it. The last thing I intended to do was to piss you off."

"Piss me off?" she said. "Adam, on the contrary—I was grateful for your input. I only wish you'd shared your thoughts with me *before* the meeting. But that's water under the bridge. We're on to bigger and better things. And so are *you!*"

The transfer was to take place within the next three weeks. I was completely freaked out. The North Carolina site was for strictly back-office stuff. A million miles away from R&D. I'd be useless to Wyatt there. And he'd blame me for screwing up. I could practically hear the guillotine blade rushing down on its tracks.

It's funny: not until I walked out of her office did I think about my dad, and then it really hit me. I *couldn't* move. I couldn't leave the old man here. Yet how could I refuse to go where Nora was sending me? Short of escalating—going over her head, or at least trying to, which would surely backfire on me—what choice did I have? If I refused to go to North Carolina, I'd have to resign from Trion, and then all hell would break loose.

It felt as if the whole building were revolving slowly; I had to sit down, had to think. As I passed by Noah Mordden's office he waggled his finger at me to summon me in.

"Ah, Cassidy," he said. "Trion's very own Julien Sorel. Do be nice to the Madame de Renal."

"Excuse me?" I said. I didn't know what the hell he was talking about.

In his signature Alòha shirt and his big round black glasses he was looking more and more like a caricature of himself. His IP phone rang, but naturally it wasn't any ordinary ring tone. It was a sound file clipped from David Bowie's "Suffragette City": "Oh *wham* bam thank you *ma'am!*"

"I suspect you impressed Goddard," he said. "But at the same time, you must also take care not to unduly antagonize your immediate superior. Forget Stendahl. You might want to read Sun Tzu." He scowled. "The ass you save could be your own."

Mordden's office was decorated with all sorts of strange things. There was a chessboard painstakingly laid out in midgame, an H.P. Lovecraft poster, a large doll with curly blond hair. I pointed to the chessboard questioningly.

"Tal-Botvinnik, 1960," he said, as if that meant anything to me. "One of the great chess moves of all time. In any case, my point is, one does not besiege walled cities if it can be avoided. Moreover, and this is wisdom not from Sun Tzu but from the Roman emperor Domitian, if you strike at a king, you must kill him. Instead, you waged an attack on Nora without arranging air support in advance."

"I didn't intend to wage an attack."

"Whatever you intended to accomplish, it was a serious miscalculation, my friend. She will surely destroy you. Remember, Adam. Power corrupts. PowerPoint corrupts absolutely."

"She's transferring me to Research Triangle."

He cocked an eyebrow. "Could have been much worse, you know. Have you ever been to Jackson, Mississippi?"

I had, and I liked the place, but I was bummed and didn't feel like engaging in a long conversation with this strange dude. He made me nervous. I pointed to the ugly doll on the shelf and said, "That yours?"

"Love Me Lucille," he said. "A huge flop and one that, I'm proud to say, was my initiative."

"You engineered . . . *dolls?*"

He reached over and squeezed the doll's hand, and it came to life, its scary-realistic eyes opening and then actually squinting with the animation of a human being. Its cupid's bow mouth opened and turned down into a frightening scowl.

"You've never seen a doll do that."

"And I don't think I ever want to again," I said.

Mordden allowed a glint of a smile. "Lucille has a full range of human facial expressions. She's fully robotic, and actually quite impressive. She whines, she gets fussy and annoying, just like a real baby. She requires burping. She gurgles, coos, even tinkles in her diaper. She exhibits alarming signs of colic. She does everything but get diaper rash. She has speech-localization, which means she looks at whoever's talking to her. You teach her to speak."

"I didn't know you did dolls."

"Hey, I can do anything I want here. I'm a Trion Distinguished Engineer. I invented it for my little niece, who refused to play with it. She thought it was creepy."

"It *is* kind of homely," I said.

"The sculpt was bad." He turned to the doll and spoke slowly. "Lucille? Say hello to our CEO."

Lucille turned her head slowly to Mordden. I could hear a faint mechanical whir. She blinked, scowled again, and began speaking in the deep voice of James Earl Jones, her lips forming the words: "Eat my shorts, Goddard."

"*Jesus*," I blurted out.

Lucille turned slowly to me, blinked again, and smiled sweetly.

"The technological guts inside this butt-ugly troll were way ahead of its time," Mordden said. "I developed a full multithreaded operating system that runs on an eight-bit processor. State-of-the-art artificial intelligence on some really tightly compiled code. The architecture's quite clever. Three separate ASICs in her fat tummy, which I designed."

An ASIC, I knew, was geek-speak for a fancy custom-designed computer chip that does a bunch of different things.

"Lucille?" Mordden said, and the doll turned to look at him, blinking. "Fuck you, Lucille." Lucille's eyes slowly squinted, her mouth turned down, and she emitted an anguished-sounding *wa-a-h*. A single tear rolled down her cheek. He pulled up her frilly pink pajama top, exposing a small rectangular LCD screen. "Mommy and Daddy can program her and see the settings on this little proprietary Trion LCD here. One of the ASICs drives this LCD, another drives the motors, another drives the speech."

"Incredible," I said. "All this for a doll."

"Correct. And then the toy company we partnered with fucked up the launch. Let this be a lesson to you. The packaging was terrible. They didn't ship until the last week in November, which is about eight weeks too late—Mommy and Daddy have already made up their Christmas lists by then. Moreover, the price point sucked—in this economy, Mommy and Daddy don't like spending over a hundred bucks for a fucking toy. Of course, the marketing geniuses in Trion Consumer and Educational thought I'd invented the next Beanie Baby, so we stockpiled several hundred thousand of these custom chips, manufactured for us in China at enormous expense and good for nothing else. Which means Trion got stuck with almost half a million ugly dolls that no one wanted, along with three hundred thousand extra doll parts waiting to be assembled, sitting to this day in a warehouse in Van Nuys."

"Ouch."

"It's okay. Nobody can touch me. I've got kryptonite."

He didn't explain what he meant, but this was Mordden, borderline crazy, so I didn't pursue it. I returned to my cubicle, where I found that I had several voice messages. When I played the second one, I recognized the voice with a jolt even before he identified himself.

"Mr. Cassidy," the scratchy voice said, "I really. . . . Oh, this is Jock Goddard. I was very much taken by your remarks at the meeting today, and I wonder if you might be able to stop by my office. Do you think you could call my assistant Flo and set something up?"

PART FOUR

COMPROMISE

Compromise: The detection of an agent, a safe house, or an intelligence technique by someone from the other side.

— *The Dictionary of Espionage*

3 5

Jock Goddard's office was no bigger than Tom Lundgren's or Nora Sommers's. This realization blew me away. The goddamned CEO's office was maybe a few feet bigger than my own pathetic cubicle. I walked right by it once, sure I was in the wrong place. But the name was there—AUGUSTINE GODDARD—on a brass plaque on his door, and he was in fact standing right outside his office, talking to his admin. He had on one of his black mock turtlenecks, no jacket, and wore a pair of black reading glasses. The woman he was talking to, who I assumed was Florence, was a large black woman in a magnificent silver-gray suit. She had skunk stripes of gray running through her hair on either side of her head and looked formidable.

They both looked up as I approached. She had no idea who I was, and it took Goddard a minute, but then he recognized me—it was the day after the big meeting—and said, "Oh, Mr. Cassidy, great, thanks for coming. Can I get you something to drink?"

"I'm all set, thanks," I said. I remembered Dr. Bolton's advice, then said, "Well, maybe some water." Up close he seemed even smaller, more stoop-shouldered. His famous pixie face, the thin lips, the twinkling eyes—it looked exactly like the Halloween masks of Jock Goddard that one of the business units had had made for last year's companywide Halloween party. I'd seen one hanging from a pushpin on someone's cubicle wall. Everyone in the unit wore one and did some kind of skit or something.

Flo handed him a manila file—I could see it was my HR file—and he told her to hold all calls and showed me into his office. I had no idea what he wanted, so my guilty conscience went into full swing. I mean, here I'd been skulking around the guy's corporation, doing spy-versus-spy stuff. I'd been careful, sure, but there'd been a couple of goofs.

Still, could it really be anything bad? The CEO never swings the axe himself, he always has his henchmen do it. But I couldn't help but wonder. I was ridiculously nervous, and I wasn't doing much of a job of hiding it.

He opened a small refrigerator concealed in a cabinet and handed me a bottle of Aquafina. Then he sat down behind his desk and immediately leaned back in his high leather chair. I took one of two chairs on the other side of the desk. I looked around, saw a photograph of an unglamorous-looking woman who I assumed was his wife, since she was around the same age. She was white-haired, plain, and amazingly wrinkled (Mordden had called her the shar-pei) and she wore a Barbara Bush–style three-strand pearl necklace, probably to conceal the wattles under her chin. I wondered if Nick Wyatt, so consumed with bilious envy toward Jock Goddard, had any idea who Augustine Goddard came home to every night. Wyatt's bimbos were changed, or rotated, every couple of nights and they all had tits like a centerfold; that was a job requirement.

One entire shelf was taken up with old-fashioned tin models of cars, convertibles with big tail fins and swooping lines, a few old Divco milk trucks. They were models from the forties and fifties, probably when Jock Goddard was a kid, a young man.

He saw me looking at them and said, "What do you drive?"

"Drive?" For a moment I didn't get what he was talking about. "Oh, an Audi A6."

"Audi," he repeated as if it were a foreign word. Okay, so maybe it is. "You like it?"

"It's okay."

"I would have thought you'd drive a Porsche 911, or at least a Boxster, or something of that sort. Fella like you."

"I'm not really a gearhead," I said. It was a calculated response, I'll admit, deliberately contrarian. Wyatt's *consigliere*, Judith Bolton, had even devoted part of a session to talking about cars so I could fit in with the Trion corporate culture. But my gut now told me that one-on-one I wasn't going to pull it off. Better to avoid the subject entirely.

"I thought everyone at Trion was into cars," Goddard said. I could see he was being arch. He was making a jab at the slavishness of his cult following. I liked that.

"The ambitious ones, anyway," I said, grinning.

"Well, you know, cars are my only extravagance, and there's a reason for that. Back in the early seventies, after Trion went public and I started making more money than I knew what to do with, I went out one day and bought a boat, a sixty-one-footer. I was so damned pleased with this boat until I saw a seventy-footer in the marina. Nine damned feet longer. And I felt this twinge, you understand. My competitive instincts were aroused. Suddenly I'm feel-ing—oh, I know it's childish, but I can't help it, I need to get me a bigger boat. So you know what I did?"

"Bought a bigger boat."

"Nope. Could have bought a bigger boat no sweat, but then there'd always be some other jackass with a bigger boat. Then who's really the jack-ass? Me. Can't win that way."

I nodded.

"So I sold the damned thing. I mean the next day. Only thing keeping that craft afloat was fiberglass and jealousy." He chuckled. "That's why this small office. I figured if the boss's office is the same as every other manager's, at least we're not going to have much office-envy in the company. People are always going to compete to see whose is bigger—let 'em focus on something else. So, Elijah, you're a new hire."

"It's Adam, actually."

"Damn, I keep doing that. I'm sorry. Adam, Adam. Got it." He leaned forward in his chair, put on his reading glasses, and scanned my HR file. "We hired you away from Wyatt, where you saved the Lucid."

"I didn't 'save' the Lucid, sir."

"No need for false modesty here."

"I'm not being modest. I'm being accurate."

He smiled as if I amused him. "How does Trion compare to Wyatt? Oh, forget I asked that. I wouldn't want you to answer it anyway."

"That's okay, I'm happy to answer it," I said, all forthrightness. "I like it here. It's exciting. I like the people." I thought for a split second, realizing how kiss-ass this sounded, such complete bullshit. "Well, most of them."

His pixie eyes crinkled. "You took the first salary package we offered you," he said. "Young fellow with your credentials, your track record, you could have negotiated for a good bit more."

I shrugged. "The opportunity interested me."

"Maybe, but it tells me you were eager to get the hell out of there."

This was making me nervous, and anyway, I knew Goddard would want me to be discreet. "Trion's more my kind of place, I think."

"You getting the opportunity you hoped for?"

"Sure."

"Paul, my CFO, mentioned to me your intervention on GoldDust. You've obviously got sources."

"I stay in touch with friends."

"Adam, I like your idea for retooling the Maestro, but I worry about the ramp-up time of adding the secure encryption protocol. The Pentagon's going to want working prototypes yesterday."

"Not a problem," I said. The details were still fresh in my head like I'd crammed for an organic chemistry final. "Kasten Chase has already developed the RASP secure access data security protocol. They've got their Fortezza crypto card, Palladium secure modem—the hardware and software solutions have already been developed. It might add two months to incorporate into the Maestro. Long before we're awarded the contract, we'd be good to go."

Goddard shook his head, looked befuddled. "The whole goddamned market has changed. Everything is e-this and i-that, and all the technology's converging. It's the age of all-in-one. Consumers don't want a TV and a VCR and a fax and computer and stereo and phone and you-name-it." He looked at me out of the corner of his eye. He was obviously floating the idea to see what I thought. "Convergence is the future. Don't you think?"

I looked skeptical, took a deep breath and said, "The long answer is . . . No."

After a few seconds of silence, he smiled. I'd done my homework. I'd read a transcript of some informal remarks Goddard had made at one of those future-of-technology conferences, in Palo Alto a year ago. He'd gone on a rant against "creeping featurism," as he called it, and I'd committed it to memory, figuring I could pull it out at a Trion meeting some time.

"How come?"

"That's just featuritis. Loading on the chrome at the expense of ease of use, simplicity, elegance. I think we're all getting fed up with having to press thirty-six buttons in sequence on twenty-two remote controls just to watch the evening news. I think it already pisses a lot of people off to have the CHECK ENGINE light go on in your car, and you can't just pop the hood and check it out—you've got to take it in to some specialty mechanic with a diagnostic computer and an engineering degree from MIT."

"Even if you're a gearhead," Goddard said with a sardonic smile.

"Even if. Plus, this whole convergence thing is a myth anyway, a buzzword that's dangerous if you take it seriously. Bad for business. Canon's faxphone was a flop—a mediocre fax and an even lousier phone. You don't see the washing machine converging with the dryer, or the microwave converging with the gas oven. I don't want a combination microwave-refrigerator-electric range-television if I just want something to keep my Cokes cold. Fifty years after the computer was invented, it's converged with—what? Nothing. The way I see it, this convergence bullshit is just the jackalope all over again."

"The what?"

"The jackalope—a mythical creation of some nutty taxidermist, made up out of a jackrabbit and an antelope. You see 'em on postcards all over the West."

"You don't mince words, do you?"

"Not when I'm convinced I'm right, sir."

He put down the HR file, leaned back in his chair again. "What about the ten-thousand-foot view?"

"Sir?"

"Trion as a whole. Any other strong opinions?"

"Some, sure."

"Let's hear 'em."

Wyatt was always commissioning competitive analyses of Trion, and I'd committed them to memory. "Well, Trion Medical Systems is a pretty robust portfolio, real best-in-class technologies in magnetic resonance, nuclear medicine, and ultrasound, but a little weak in the service stuff like patient information management and asset management."

He smiled, nodded. "Agreed. Go on."

"Trion's Business Solutions unit obviously sucks—I don't have to tell *you* that—but you've got most of the pieces in place there for some serious market penetration, especially in IP-based and circuit-switched voice and ethernet data services. Yeah, I know fiber optic's in the toilet right now, but broadband services are the future, so we've gotta hang tough. The Aerospace division has had a rough couple of years, but it's still a terrific portfolio of embedded computing products."

"But what about Consumer Electronics?"

"Obviously it's our core competency, which is why I moved here. I mean, our high-end DVD players beat Sony's hands down. Cordless phones are strong, always have been. Our mobile phones are killer—we rule the market. We've got the marquee name—we're able to charge up to thirty percent more for our products, just because they say Trion on the label. But there are just way too many soft spots."

"Such as?"

"Well, it's crazy that we don't have a real Blackberry-killer. Wireless communications devices should be our playground. Instead, it's like we're just ceding the ground to RIM and Handspring and Palm. We need some serious hip-top wireless devices."

"We're working on that. We've got a pretty interesting product in the pipeline."

"Good to hear," I said. "I do think we're really missing the boat on technology and products for transmitting digital music and video over the Internet. We really should focus on R&D there, maybe partnering. *Huge* potential for revenue generation."

"I think you're right."

"And, forgive me for saying it, but I think it's sort of pathetic that we don't have a serious kid-targeted product line. Look at Sony—their PlayStation game console can make the difference between red ink and black ink some years. The demand for computers and home electronics seems to slump every couple of years, right? We're fighting electronics makers in South Korea and Taiwan, we're waging price wars over LCD monitors and digital video

decks and cell phones—this is a fact of life. So we should be selling to kids—
'cause children don't care about recessions. Sony's got their PlayStations,
Microsoft's got its Xbox, Nintendo has GameCube, but what do we have for
television video games? Diddly squat. It's a *major* weakness in a consumer-
oriented product line."

I'd noticed he was sitting upright again, looking at me with a cryptic
smile on his crinkly face. "How would you feel about priming the retooling of
the Maestro?"

"Nora owns that. I wouldn't feel comfortable about it, frankly."

"You'd report to her."

"I'm not sure she'd like that."

His grin got crooked. "She'd get over it. Nora knows what side her bread's
buttered on."

"Obviously I won't fight you on it, sir, but I think it might be bad for
morale."

"Well, then, how would you like to come work for me?"

"Don't I already?"

"I mean here, on the seventh floor. Special assistant to the chairman for
new-product strategy. Dotted line responsibility to the Advanced Technology
unit. I'd give you an office, just down the hall. But no bigger than mine, you
understand. Interested?"

I couldn't believe what I was hearing. I felt like bursting from excitement
and nerves.

"Well, sure. Reporting directly to you?"

"That's right. So, do we have a deal?"

I gave a slow smile. In for a penny, I thought, and all that. "I think more
responsibility calls for more money, sir, don't you?"

He laughed. "Oh, does it?"

"I'd like the additional fifty thousand I should have asked for when I
started here. And I'd like forty thousand more in stock options."

He laughed again, a robust, almost Santa Claus–y ho-ho. "You've got
balls, young man."

"Thank you."

"I'll tell you what. I'm not going to give you fifty thousand more. I don't
believe in incrementalism. I'm going to *double* your salary. *Plus* your forty

thousand options. That way you'll feel all sorts of pressure to bust your ass for me."

To keep from gasping, I bit the inside of my lip. *Jesus.*

"Where do you live?" he asked.

I told him.

He shook his head. "Not quite appropriate for someone of your level. Also, the hours you're going to be working, I don't want you driving forty-five minutes in the morning and another forty-five minutes at night. You're going to be working late nights, so I want you living close by. Why don't you get yourself one of those condos in the Harbor Suites? You can afford it now. We've got a lady who works with the Trion E-staff, specializes in corporate housing. She'll set you up with something nice."

I swallowed. "Sounds okay," I said, trying to suppress the little nervous chuckle.

"Now, I know you've said you're not a gearhead, but this Audi . . . I'm sure it's perfectly nice, but why don't you get yourself something fun? I think a man should love his car. Give it a chance, why don't you? I mean, don't go overboard or anything, but something *fun*. Flo can make the arrangements."

Was he saying they were going to give me a *car*? Good God.

He stood up. "So, are you on board?" He stuck out his hand.

I shook. "I'm not an idiot," I said good-naturedly.

"No, that's obvious. Well, welcome to the team, Adam. I look forward to working with you."

I stumbled out of his office and toward the bank of elevators, my head in a cloud. I could barely walk right.

And then I caught myself, remembered why I was here, what my real job was—how I'd gotten here, into Goddard's office, even. I'd just been promoted way, way above my ability.

Not that I even knew what my ability *was* anymore.

36

I didn't have to break the news to anyone: the miracle of e-mail and instant messaging had already taken care of that for me. By the time I got back to my cube, the word was all over the department. Obviously Goddard was a man of immediate action.

No sooner had I reached the men's room for a much-needed pee than Chad burst in and unzipped at the urinal next to me. "So, are the rumors true, dude?"

I looked impatiently at the wall tile. I really needed to go. "Which rumors?"

"I take it congratulations are in order."

"Oh, that. No, congratulations would be premature. But thanks, anyway." I stared at the little automatic-flush thing that was attached to the American Standard urinal. I wondered who invented that, whether they got rich and their family made cute jokes about the family fortune being in the toilet. I wanted Chad to just leave already.

"I underestimated you," he said, letting loose a powerful stream. Meanwhile my own internal Colorado River was threatening the Hoover Dam.

"Oh, yeah?"

"Oh, yeah. I knew you were good, but I didn't know how good. I didn't give you credit."

"I'm lucky," I said. "Or maybe I just have a big mouth, and for some reason Goddard likes that."

"No, I don't think so. You've got some kind of Vulcan mind-meld going with the old guy. You, like, know all the right buttons to push. I'll bet you two don't even need to talk. That's how good you are. I'm impressed, big guy. I don't know how you did it, but I'm seriously impressed."

He zipped up, clapped me on the shoulder.

"Let me in on the secret, will ya?" he said, but he didn't wait for a reply.

When I got back to my cubicle, Noah Mordden was standing at my cubicle inspecting the books on top of the file cabinet. He was holding a gift-wrapped package, which looked like a book.

"Cassidy," he said. "Our too-cool-for-school Widmerpool."

"Excuse me?" Man, was the guy into cryptic references.

"I want you to have this," he said.

I thanked him and unwrapped the package. It was a book, an old one that smelled of mildew. *Sun Tzu on The Art of War* was stamped on the cloth front cover.

"It's the 1910 Lionel Giles translation," he said. "The best, I think. Not a first edition, which is impossible to come by, but an early printing at least."

I was touched. "When did you have time to buy this?"

"Last week, online, actually. I didn't intend it to be a departure gift, but there you are. At least now you'll have no excuse."

"Thank you," I said. "I'll read it."

"Please do. I suspect you'll need it all the more. Recall the Japanese *kotowaza*, 'the nail that sticks up gets hammered down.' You're fortunate that you're being moved out of Nora's orbit, but there are great perils in rising too quickly in any organization. Hawks may soar, but chipmunks don't get sucked into jet engines."

I nodded. "I'll keep that in mind," I said.

"Ambition is a useful quality, but you must always cover your tracks," he said.

He was definitely hinting at something—he *had* to have seen me coming out of Nora's office—and it scared the shit out of me. He was toying with me, sadistically, like a cat with a mouse.

Nora summoned me to her office by e-mail, and I braced myself for a shitstorm. "Adam," she called out as I approached. "I just heard the news."

She was smiling. "Sit down, sit down. I am *so* happy for you. And maybe

I shouldn't reveal this, but I'm *delighted* that they took my enthusiasm about you seriously. Because, you know, they don't always listen."

"I know."

"But I assured them, if you do this, you won't be sorry. Adam's got the right stuff, I told them, he's going to go the extra mile. You've got my word on it. I *know* him."

Yeah, I thought, you think you know me. You have no idea.

"I could see you were concerned about relocating, so I made a few calls," she said. "I'm so happy things are turning out right for you."

I didn't reply. I was too busy thinking about what Wyatt would say when he heard.

3 7

"Holy shit," Nicholas Wyatt said.

For a split second his polished, self-contained, deep-tanned shell of arrogance had cracked open. He gave me a look that almost seemed to border on respect. Almost. Anyway, this was a whole new Wyatt, and I enjoyed seeing it.

"You are fucking kidding me." He continued staring. "This better not be a joke." Finally he looked away, and it was a relief. "This is un-fucking-believable."

We were sitting on his private plane, but it wasn't moving anywhere. We were waiting for his latest bimbo girlfriend to show up so the two of them could take off for the Big Island of Hawaii, where he had a house in the Hualalai resort. It was me, Wyatt, and Arnold Meacham. I'd never been in a private jet before, and this one was sweet, a Gulfstream G-IV, interior cabin twelve feet wide, sixty-something feet long. I'd never seen all this empty space in an airplane. You could practically play football in here. No more than ten seats, a separate conference room, two huge bathrooms with showers.

Believe me, I wasn't flying to the Big Island. This was just a tease. Meacham and I would get off before the plane went anywhere. Wyatt was wearing some kind of black silk shirt. I hoped he got skin cancer.

Meacham smiled at Wyatt and said quietly, "Brilliant idea, Nick."

"I gotta give credit to Judith," Wyatt said. "She came up with the idea in the first place." He shook his head slowly. "But I doubt even she could have seen this coming." He picked up his cell, hit two keys.

"Judith," he said. "Our boy is now working directly for Mister Big himself. The Big Kahuna. Special executive assistant to the CEO." He paused, smiled at Meacham. "I kid you not." Another pause. "Judith, sweetheart, I want you to do a crash course with our young man here." Pause. "Right, well, obviously this is top priority. I want Adam to know that guy inside and out. I want him to be the best fucking special assistant the guy's ever hired. Right." And he ended the call with a beep. Looking back at me, he said, "You just saved your own ass, my friend. Arnie?"

Meacham looked like he'd been waiting for this cue. "We ran all the AURORA names you gave us," he said darkly. "Not a single fucking one of them popped up with anything."

"What does that mean?" I asked. God, did I hate the guy.

"No Social Security numbers, no nothing. Don't fuck with us, buddy."

"What are you talking about? I downloaded them directly from the Trion directory on the Web site."

"Yeah, well, they're not real names, asshole. The admin names are real, but the research-division names are obviously cover names. That's how deep they're buried—they don't even list their real names on the Web site. Never heard of such a thing."

"That doesn't sound right," I said, shaking my head.

"Are you being straight with us?" Meacham said. "Because if you aren't, so help me, we will fucking crush you." He looked at Wyatt. "He totally fucked up the personnel records—got diddly-squat."

"The records were *gone*, Arnold," I shot back. "Removed. They're being super-careful."

"What do you have on the broad?" Wyatt broke in.

I smiled. "I'm seeing 'the broad' next week."

"Like boyfriend-girlfriend stuff?"

I shrugged. "The woman's interested in me. She's on AURORA. She's a direct link into the skunkworks."

To my surprise, Wyatt just nodded. "Nice."

Meacham seemed to sense which way the wind was blowing now. He'd been stuck on how I'd blown the HR operation, and how the AURORA names on the Trion Web site were for some reason fake, but his boss was focusing on what was going *right*, on the amazing turn of events, and

Meacham didn't want to be out of lockstep. "You're going to have access to Goddard's office now," he said. "There's any number of devices you can plant."

"This is so fucking incredible," Wyatt said.

"I don't think we need to be paying him his old Wyatt salary," Meacham said. "Not with what he's making at Trion now. Christ, this goddamned kite's making more than *me*."

Wyatt seemed amused. "Nah, we made a deal."

"What'd you call me?" I asked Meacham.

"There's a security risk in having us transfer corporate funds into an account for this kid, no matter how many shells it goes through," Meacham said to Wyatt.

"You called me a 'kite,' " I persisted. "What's that supposed to mean?"

"I thought it's untraceable," Wyatt said to Meacham.

"What's a 'kite'?" I said. I was a dog with a bone; I wasn't letting this drop, no matter how much I annoyed Meacham.

Meacham wasn't even listening, but Wyatt looked at me and muttered, "It's corporate-spy talk. A kite's a 'special consultant' who goes out there and gathers the intel by whatever means necessary, does the work."

"Kite?" I said.

"You fly a kite, and if it gets caught in a tree, you just cut the string," Wyatt said. "Plausible deniability, you ever hear of that?"

"Cut the string," I repeated dully. On one level I wouldn't mind that at all, because that string was really a leash. But I knew when they talked about cutting the string, they meant leaving me high and dry.

"If things go bad," Wyatt said. "Just don't let things go bad, and no one has to cut the string. Now, where the hell is this bitch? If she's not here in two minutes, I'm taking off without her."

38

So I did something then that was totally insane but felt great. I went out and got myself a ninety-thousand-dollar Porsche.

There was a time when I would have celebrated some great piece of news by getting hammered, maybe splurging on champagne or a couple of CDs. But this was a whole new league. I liked the idea of cutting my Wyatt apron strings by exchanging the Audi for a Porsche, lease courtesy of Trion.

Ever been in a Porsche dealership? It's not like buying a Honda Accord, okay? You don't just walk in off the street and ask for a test drive. You have to go through a lot of foreplay. You've got to fill out a form, they want to talk about why you're here, what do you do, what's your sign.

Also, there's so many options you could go out of your mind. You want bi-xenon headlights? Arctic Silver instrument panel? You want leather or *supple* leather? You want Sport Design wheels or Sport Classic II wheels or Turbo-Look I wheels?

What I wanted was a Porsche, and I didn't want to wait four to six months for it to be custom built in Stuttgart-Zuffenhausen. I wanted to drive it off the lot. I wanted it *now*. They had only two 911 Carrera coupes on the lot, one in Guards Red and one in metallic Basalt Black. It came down to the stitching on the leather. The red car had black leather that felt like leatherette and, worst of all, had red stitching on it, which looked cowboy-western and gross. Whereas the Basalt Black model had a terrific Natural Brown supple leather interior, with a leather gearshift and steering wheel. I came right back from the test drive and said let's do it. Maybe he'd sized me up as the kind of guy who was just looking, or wouldn't in the end be able to pull the trigger, but I did it, and he assured me I was making a smart move. He even offered to have someone return the leased Audi to the Audi dealership—totally zipless.

It was like flying a jet; when you floored it, it even *sounded* like a 767. Three hundred twenty horsepower, zero to sixty in five-point-zero seconds, unbelievably powerful. It throbbed and roared. I popped in my latest favorite burned CD and blasted the Clash, Pearl Jam, and Guns N' Roses while redlining it to work. It made me feel like everything was happening right.

Even before I moved into my new office, Goddard wanted me to find a new place to live, more convenient to the Trion building. I wasn't exactly going to argue; it was long past time.

His people made it easy for me to abandon the dump I'd lived in for so long and move into a new apartment on the twenty-ninth floor of the south tower of the Harbor Suites. Each of the two towers had like a hundred and fifty condos, on thirty-eight floors, ranging from studios to three-bedrooms. The towers were built on top of the swankiest hotel in the area, whose restaurant was top-rated in Zagat's.

The apartment looked like something out of an *In Style* photo shoot. It was around two thousand square feet, with twelve-foot ceilings, hardwood parquet and stone floors. There was a "master suite" and a "library" that could also be used as a spare bedroom, a formal dining room, and a giant living room.

There were floor-to-ceiling windows with the most staggering views I'd ever seen. The living room itself looked over the city, spread out below, in one direction, and over the water in another.

The eat-in kitchen looked like a showroom display at a high-end kitchen-design firm, with all the right names: Sub-Zero refrigerator, Miele dishwasher, Viking duel-fuel oven/range, cabinets by Poggenpohl, granite countertops, even a built-in wine "grotto."

Not that I'd ever need the kitchen. If you wanted "in-room dining," all you had to do was pick up the wall phone in the kitchen and press a button, and you could get a room service meal from the hotel, even have a cook from the hotel restaurant come up on short notice and make dinner for you and your guests.

There was an immense, state-of-the-art health club, a hundred thousand square feet, where a lot of rich people who didn't live here worked out or played squash or did Taoist yoga, followed by saunas and protein smoothies at the café.

You didn't even park your own car. You drove it up to the front of the building, and the valet would whisk it away somewhere and park it for you, and you called down to get it back.

The elevators zoomed at such supersonic speed that your ears popped. They had mahogany walls and marble floors and were about the same size as my old apartment.

The security here was a whole hell of a lot better too. Wyatt's goons wouldn't be able to break in here so easily and search my stuff. I liked that.

None of the Harbor Suites apartments cost less than a million, and this baby was over two million, but it was all free—furnishings included—courtesy of Trion Systems, as a perk.

Moving in was painless, since I kept almost nothing from my old apartment. Goodwill and the Salvation Army came and took away the big ugly plaid couch, the Formica kitchen table, the box spring and mattress, all the assorted junk, even the cruddy old desk. Crap fell out of the couch as they dragged it away—Zig-Zag papers, roaches, assorted druggie paraphernalia. I kept my computer, my clothes, and my mother's black cast-iron frying pan (for sentimental reasons—not that I ever used it). I packed all my stuff into the Porsche, which tells you how little there was, because there's almost zero luggage space in a Porsche. All the furniture I ordered from that fancy furniture store Domicile (the agent's suggestion)—big, puffy, overstuffed couches you could get swallowed up in, matching chairs, a dining table and chairs that looked like they came out of Versailles, a huge bed with iron railing, Persian area rugs. Super-expensive Dux mattress. Everything. A shitload of money, but hey—I wasn't paying for any of it.

In fact, Domicile was delivering all the furniture when the doorman, Carlos, called up to me to tell me that I had a visitor downstairs, a Mister Seth Marcus. I told him to send Seth right up.

The front door was already open for the delivery people, but Seth rang the doorbell and stood there in the hall. He was wearing a Sonic Youth T-shirt and ripped Diesel jeans. His normally lively, even manic, brown eyes looked dead. He was subdued—I couldn't tell if he was intimidated, or jealous, or pissed off that I'd disappeared from his radar screen, or some combination of all three.

"Hey, man," he said. "I tracked you down."

"Hey, man," I said, and gave him a hug. "Welcome to my humble abode." I didn't know what else to say. For some reason I was embarrassed. I didn't want him to see the place.

He stayed where he was in the hall. "You weren't going to tell me you were moving?"

"It kind of happened suddenly," I said. "I was going to call you."

He pulled a bottle of cheap New York State champagne from his canvas bicycle-courier bag, handed it to me. "I'm here to celebrate. I figured you were too good for a case of beer anymore."

"Excellent!" I said, taking the bottle and ignoring the dig. "Come on in."

"You dog. This is great," he said in a flat, unenthusiastic voice. "Huge, huh?"

"Two thousand square feet. Check it out." I gave him the tour. He said funny-cutting stuff like "If that's a library, don't you need to have books?" and "Now all you need to furnish the bedroom is a babe." He said my apartment was "sick" and "ill," which was his pseudogangsta way of saying he liked it.

He helped me take the plastic wrap and tape off one of the enormous couches so we could sit on it. The couch had been placed in the middle of the living room, sort of floating there, facing the ocean.

"Nice," he said, sinking in. He looked like he wanted to put his feet up on something, but they hadn't brought in the coffee table yet, which was a good thing, because I didn't want him putting his mud-crusted Doc Martens on it.

"You getting manicures now?" he said suspiciously.

"Once in a while," I admitted in a small voice. I couldn't believe he noticed a little detail like my fingernails. Jesus. "Gotta look like an executive, you know."

"What's with the haircut? Seriously."

"What about it?"

"Don't you think it's, I don't know, sort of fruity?"

"Fruity?"

"Like all fancy looking. You putting shit in your hair, like gel or mousse or something?"

"A little gel," I said defensively. "What about it?"

He squinted, shook his head. "You got cologne on?"

I wanted to change the subject. "I thought you worked tonight," I said.

"Oh, you mean the bartending gig? Nah, I quit that. It turned out to be totally bogus."

"Seemed like a cool place."

"Not if you work there, man. They treat you like you're a fucking *waiter*."

I almost burst out laughing.

"I got a much better gig," he said. "I'm on the 'mobile energy team' for Red Bull. They give you this cool car to drive around in, and you basically hand out samples and talk to people and shit. Hours are totally flexible. I can do it after the paralegal gig."

"Sounds perfect."

"Totally. Gives me plenty of free time to work on my corporate anthem."

"Corporate anthem?"

"Every big company's got one—like, cheesy rock or rap or something." He sang, badly: "*Trion!—Change your world!* Like that. If Trion doesn't have one, maybe you could put in a word for me with the right guy. I bet I'd get royalties every time you guys sing it at a corporate picnic or whatever."

"I'll look into it," I said. "Hey, I don't have any glasses. I'm expecting a delivery, but it hasn't come yet. They say the glass is mouth-blown in Italy— wonder if you can still smell the garlic."

"Don't worry about it. The champagne's probably shit anyway."

"You still working at the law firm too?"

He looked embarrassed. "It's my only steady paycheck."

"Hey, that's important."

"Believe me, man, I do as little as possible. I do just enough to keep Shapiro off my back—faxes, copies, searches, whatever—and I still have plenty of time to surf the Web."

"Cool."

"I get like twenty bucks an hour for playing Web games and burning music CDs and pretending to work."

"Great," I said. "You're really getting one over on them." It was pathetic, actually.

"You got it."

And then I don't know why I came out with it, but I said, "So, who do you think you're cheating the most, them or yourself?"

Seth looked at me funny. "What are you talking about?"

"I mean, you fuck around at work, you scam by, doing as little as possible—you ever ask yourself what you're doing it for? Like, what's the point?"

Seth's eyes narrowed in hostility. "What's up with you?"

"At some point you got to commit to something, you know?"

He paused. "Whatever. Hey, you want to get out of here, go somewhere? This is sort of too grown-up for me, it's giving me hives."

"Sure." I'd been debating calling down to the hotel to send up a cook to make us dinner, because I thought Seth might be impressed, but then I came to my senses. It would not have been a good idea. It would have sent Seth over the edge. Relieved, I called down to the valet and asked them to bring my car around.

It was waiting for me by the time we got down there.

"That's *yours?*" he gasped. "No fucking way."

"Way," I said.

His cynical, aloof composure had finally cracked. "This baby must cost like a hundred grand!"

"Less than that," I said. "Way less. Anyway, the company leases it for me."

He approached the Porsche slowly, awestricken, the way the apes approached the monolith in *2001: A Space Odyssey,* and he stroked the gleaming Basalt Black door.

"All right, buddy," he demanded, "what's your scam? I want a piece of this."

"Not a scam," I said uncomfortably as we got in. "I sort of fell into this."

"Oh, come on, man. This is *me* you're talking to—Seth. Remember me? Are you selling drugs or something? Because if you are, you better cut me in."

I laughed hollowly. As we roared away, I saw a stupid-looking car parked on the street that had to be his. A huge blue-silver-and-red can of Red Bull was mounted on top of a dinky car. A joke.

"That yours?"

"Yep. Cool, huh?" He didn't sound so enthusiastic.

"Nice," I said. It was ridiculous.

"You know what it cost me? Nada. I just gotta drive it around."

"Good deal."

He leaned back in the supple leather seat. "Sweet ride," he said. He took a deep breath of the new-car smell. "Man, this is great. I think I want your life. Wanna trade?"

39

It was totally out of the question, of course, for me to meet again with Dr. Judith Bolton at Wyatt headquarters, where I might be seen coming or going. But now that I was hunting with the big cats, I needed an in-depth session. Wyatt insisted, and I didn't disagree.

So I met her at a Marriott the next Saturday, in a suite set up for business meetings. They'd e-mailed me the room number to go to. She was already there when I arrived, her laptop hooked up to a video monitor. It's funny, the lady still made me nervous. On the way I stopped for another hundred-dollar haircut, and I wore decent clothes, not my usual weekend junk.

I'd forgotten how intense she was—the ice-blue eyes, the coppery red hair, the glossy red lips and red nail polish—and how hard-looking at the same time. I gave her a firm handshake.

"You're right on time," she said, smiling.

I shrugged, half-smiled back to say I got it but I wasn't really amused.

"You look good. Success seems to agree with you."

We sat at a fancy conference table that looked like it belonged in someone's dining room—mine, maybe—and she asked me how it was going. I filled her in, the good stuff and the bad, including about Chad and Nora.

"You're going to have enemies," she said. "That's to be expected. But these are threats—you've left a cigarette butt smoldering in the woods, and if you don't put them out you may have a forest fire on your hands."

"How do I put them out?"

"We'll talk about that. But right now I want to focus on Jock Goddard. And if you take away nothing else today, I want you to remember this: he's *pathologically honest.*"

I couldn't help smiling. This from the chief consigliere to Nick Wyatt, a guy so crooked he'd cheat on a prostate exam.

Her eyes flashed in annoyance, and she leaned in toward me. "I'm not making a joke. He's singled you out not just because he likes your mind, your ideas—which of course aren't your ideas at all—but because he finds your honesty refreshing. You speak your mind. He likes that."

"That's 'pathological'?"

"Honest is practically a fetish with him. The blunter you are, the less calculating you seem, the better you'll play." I wondered briefly if Judith saw the irony in what she was doing—counseling me in how to pull the wool over Jock Goddard's eyes by feigning honesty. One hundred percent synthetic honesty, no natural fibers. "If he starts to detect anything shifty or obsequious or calculating in your manner—if he thinks you're trying to suck up or game him—he'll cool on you fast. And once you lose that trust, you may never regain it."

"Got it," I said impatiently. "So from now on, no gaming the guy."

"Sweetheart, what planet are you living on?" she shot back. "Of *course* we game the old geezer. That's lesson two in the art of 'managing up,' come on. You'll mess with his head, but you have to be supremely artful about it. Nothing obvious, nothing he'll sniff out. The way dogs can smell fear, Goddard can smell bullshit. So you've got to come across as the ultimate straight shooter. You tell him the bad news other people try to sugarcoat. You show him a plan he likes—then you be the one to point out the flaws. Integrity's a pretty scarce commodity in our world—once you figure out how to fake it, you'll be on the good ship *Lollipop.*"

"Where I want to be," I said dryly.

She had no time for my sarcasm. "People always *say* that nobody likes a suckup, but the truth is, the vast majority of senior managers *adore* suckups, even when they know they're being sucked up to. It makes them feel powerful, reassures them, bolsters their fragile egos. Jock Goddard, on the other hand, has no need for it. Believe me, he thinks quite highly of himself already. He's not blinded by need, by vanity. He's not a Mussolini who needs to be surrounded by yes-men." Like anyone we know? I wanted to say. "Look who he surrounds himself with—bright, quick-witted people who can be abrasive and outspoken."

I nodded. "You're saying he doesn't like flattery."

"No, I'm not saying that. Everyone likes flattery. But it's got to feel real to him. A little story: Napoleon once went hunting in the Bois de Boulogne with Talleyrand, who desperately wanted to impress the great general. The woods were teeming with rabbits, and Napoleon was delighted when he killed fifty of them. But when he found out later that these weren't wild rabbits—that Talleyrand had sent one of his servants to the market to buy dozens of rabbits and then set them loose in the woods—well, Napoleon was enraged. He never trusted Talleyrand again."

"I'll keep that in mind next time Goddard invites me rabbit hunting."

"The point is," she snapped, "that when you flatter, do so indirectly."

"Well, I'm not running with rabbits, Judith. More like wolves."

"There you go. Know much about wolves?"

I sighed. "Bring it on."

"It's all laid bare. There's always an Alpha male, of course, but what's interesting to keep in mind is that the hierarchy's always being tested. It's highly unstable. Sometimes you'll see the Alpha male wolf drop a fresh piece of meat on the ground right in front of the others and then move away a couple of feet and just watch. He's outright daring the other ones to even sniff at it."

"And if they do, they're supper."

"Wrong. The Alpha usually doesn't have to do anything more than glare. Maybe posture a bit. Raise his tail and ears, snarl, make himself look big and fierce. And if a fight does break out, the Alpha will attack the least vulnerable parts of the transgressor's body. He doesn't want to seriously maim a member of his own pack, and certainly not kill anyone. You see, the Alpha wolf needs the others. Wolves are small animals, and no individual wolf is going to bring down a moose, a deer, a caribou, without help from a pack. Point is, they're always testing."

"Meaning that I'm always going to be tested." Yeah, I didn't need an MBA to work for Goddard. I needed a veterinary degree.

She gave me a sidelong glance. "The point, Adam, is that the testing is always subtle. But at the same time, the leader of a wolf pack wants strength on his team. That's why occasional displays of aggression are acceptable— they demonstrate the stamina, the strength, the vitality of the entire pack. This is the importance of honesty, of *strategic candor*. When you flatter, do it subtly and indirectly, and make sure that Goddard thinks he can always get the unvarnished truth from you. Jock Goddard realizes what a lot of other CEOs don't—that candor from his aides is vital if he's going to know what's going on inside his company. Because if he's out of touch with what's really happening, he's history. And let me tell you something else you need to know. In every male mentor-protégé relationship there's a father-son element, but I suspect it's even more germane in this case. You likely remind him of his son, Elijah."

Goddard had called me that a couple of times by mistake, I recalled. "My age?"

"Would have been. He died a couple of years ago at the age of twenty-one. Some people think that since the tragedy Goddard has never been the same, that he got a little too soft. The point is, just as you may come to ideal-ize Goddard as the father you wish you had"—she smiled, she *knew* about my Dad somehow—"you may well remind him of the son he wishes *he* still had. You should be aware of this, because it's something you may be able to use. And it's something to watch out for—he may cut you some undeserved slack at times, yet at other times he may be unreasonably demanding."

She turned to her laptop and tapped at a few keys. "Now, I want your undivided attention. We're going to watch some television interviews God-dard has given over the years—an early one from *Wall Street Week with Louis Rukeyser*, several from CNBC, one he did with Katie Couric on *The Today Show*."

A video image of a much younger Jock Goddard, though still impish, pixielike—was frozen on the screen. Judith whirled around in her chair to face me. "Adam, this is an extraordinary opportunity you've been handed. But it's also a far more dangerous situation than you've been in at Trion, because you'll be far more constrained, far less able to move about the com-pany unnoticed or just 'hang out' with regular people and network with them. Paradoxically, your intelligence-gathering assignment has just become *hugely* more difficult. You're going to need all the ammunition you can collect. So before we finish today, I want you to know this fellow *inside and out*, are you with me?"

"I'm with you."

"Good," she said, and gave me her scary little smile. "I *know* you are." Then she lowered her voice almost to a whisper. "Listen, Adam, I have to tell you—for your own sake—that Nick is getting very impatient for results. You've been at Trion for how many weeks?—and he has yet to know what's going on in the skunkworks."

"There's a limit," I began, "to how aggressive—"

"Adam," she said quietly, but with an unmistakable note of menace. "This is *not* someone you want to fuck with."

40

Alana Jennings lived in a duplex apartment in a redbrick town house not far from Trion headquarters. I recognized it immediately from the photograph.

You know how when you just start going out with a girl and you notice everything, where she lives and how she dresses and her perfume, and everything seems so different and new? Well, the strange thing was how I knew so much about her, more than some husbands know about their wives, and yet I'd spent no more than an hour or two with her.

I pulled up to the town house in my Porsche—isn't that part of what Porsches are for, to impress chicks?—and climbed the steps and rang the doorbell. Her voice chirped over the speaker, said she'd be right down.

She was wearing a white embroidered peasant blouse and black leggings and her hair was up, and she wasn't wearing the scary black glasses. I wondered whether peasants ever actually wore peasant blouses, and whether there really were peasants in the world anymore, and if there were, whether they thought of themselves as peasants. She looked too spectacularly beautiful. She smelled great, different from most of the girls I usually went out with. A floral fragrance called Fleurissimo; I remembered reading that she'd pick it up at a place called the House of Creed whenever she went to Paris.

"Hey," I said.

"Hi, Adam." She had glossy red lipstick on and was carrying a tiny square black handbag over one shoulder.

"My car's right here," I said, trying to be subtle about the brand-new shiny black Porsche ticking away right in front of us. She gave it an appraising glance but didn't say anything. She was probably putting it together in her mind with my Zegna jacket and pants and open-collar black casual shirt, maybe the five-thousand-dollar Italian navy watch too. And thinking I was either a show-off or trying too hard. She wore a peasant blouse; I wore Ermenegildo Zegna. Perfect. She was pretending to be poor, and I was trying to look rich and probably overdoing it.

I opened the passenger's side door for her. I'd moved the seat back before I got here so there'd be plenty of legroom. Inside, the air was heavy with the aroma of new leather. There was a Trion parking sticker on the left rear side of the car, which she hadn't yet noticed. She wouldn't see it from inside the car either, but soon enough she would, when we were getting out at the restaurant, and that was just as well. She was going to find out soon enough, one way or another, that I worked at Trion too, and that I'd been hired to fill the job she used to have. It was going to be a little weird, the coincidence, given that we hadn't met at work, and the sooner it came up the better. In fact, I was ready with a dumb line of patter. Like: "You're kidding me. You do? So do I! How bizarre!"

There were a few moments of awkward silence as I drove toward her favorite Thai restaurant. She glanced up at the speedometer, then back at the road. "You should probably watch it around here," she said. "This is a speed trap. The cops are just waiting for you to go over fifty, and they really sock you."

I smiled, nodded, then remembered a riff from one of her favorite movies, *Double Indemnity*, which I'd rented the night before. "How fast was I going, officer?" I said in that sort of flat-affect film-noir Fred MacMurray voice.

She got it immediately. Smart girl. She grinned. "I'd say around ninety." She had the vampish Barbara Stanwyck voice down perfectly.

"Suppose you get down off your motorcycle and give me a ticket."

"Suppose I let you off with a warning this time," she came back, playing the game, her eyes alive with mischief.

I faltered for only a few seconds until the line came to me. "Suppose it doesn't take."

"Suppose I have to whack you over the knuckles."

I smiled. She was good, and she was into it. "Suppose I bust out crying and put my head on your shoulder."

"Suppose you try putting it on my husband's shoulder."

"That tears it," I said. End of scene. Cut, print, that's a take.

She laughed delightedly. "How do you *know* that?"

"Too much wasted time watching old black-and-white movies."

"Me too! And *Double Indemnity* is probably my favorite."

"It's right up there with *Sunset Boulevard*." Another favorite of hers.

"Exactly! 'I *am* big. It's the pictures that got small.' "

I wanted to quit while I was ahead, because I'd pretty much exhausted my supply of memorized noir trivia. I moved the conversation into tennis, which was safe. I pulled up in front of the restaurant, and her eyes lit up again. "You know about this place? It's the best!"

"For Thai food, it's the only place, as far as I'm concerned." A valet parked the car—I couldn't believe I was handing the keys to my brand-new Porsche to an eighteen-year-old kid who was probably going to take it out on a joyride when business got slow—and so she never saw the Trion sticker.

It was actually a great date for a while. That *Double Indemnity* stuff seemed to have set her at ease, made her feel that she was with a kindred spirit. Plus a guy who was into Ani DiFranco, what more could she ask for? Maybe a little depth—women always seemed to like depth in a guy, or at least the occasional fleeting moment of self-reflection, but I was all over that.

We ordered green papaya salad and vegetarian spring rolls. I considered telling her I was a vegetarian, like she was, but then I decided that would be too much, and besides, I didn't know if I could stand to keep up the ruse for more than one meal. So I ordered Masaman curry chicken and she ordered a vegetarian curry without coconut milk—I remembered reading that she was allergic to shrimp—and we both drank Thai beer.

We moved from tennis to the Tennis and Racquet Club, but I quickly steered us away from those dangerous shoals, which would raise the question of how and why I was there that day, and then to golf, and then to summer vacations. She used "summer" as a verb. She figured out pretty quickly that we came from different sides of the tracks, but that was okay. She wasn't going to marry me or introduce me to her father, and I didn't want to have to fake my family background too, which would be a lot of work. And besides, it

didn't seem necessary—she seemed to be into me anyway. I told her some stories about working at the tennis club, and doing the night shift at the gas station. Actually, she must have felt a little uncomfortable about her privileged upbringing, because she told a little white lie about how her parents forced her to spend part of her summers doing scutwork "at the company where my dad works," neglecting to mention that her dad was the CEO. Also, I happened to know she had never worked at her father's company. Her summers were spent on a dude ranch in Wyoming, on safari in Tanzania, living with a couple of other women in an apartment paid for by Daddy in the Sixth in Paris, interning at the Peggy Guggenheim on the Grand Canal in Venice. She wasn't pumping gas.

When she mentioned the company where her father "worked," I braced myself for the inevitable subject of what-do-you-do, where-do-you-work. But it never happened, until much later. I was surprised when she brought it up in a strange way, kind of making a game of it. She sighed. "Well, I suppose now we have to talk about our jobs, right?"

"Well . . ."

"So we can talk endlessly about what we do during the day, right? I'm in high-tech, okay? And you—wait, I know, don't tell me."

My stomach tightened.

"You're a chicken farmer."

I laughed. "How'd you guess?"

"Yep. A chicken farmer who drives a Porsche and wears Fendi."

"Zegna, actually."

"Whatever. I'm sorry, you're a guy, so work is probably all you want to talk about."

"Actually, no." I modulated my voice into a tone of bashful sincerity. "I really prefer to live in the present moment, to be as mindful as I can. You know, there's this Vietnamese Buddhist monk who lives in France, named Thich Nhat Nanh, and he says—"

"Oh, my God," she said, "this is so uncanny! I can't believe you know Thich Nhat Nanh!"

I hadn't actually read anything this monk had written, but after I saw how many books of his she'd ordered from Amazon I did look him up on a couple of Buddhist Web sites.

"Sure," I said as if everyone had read the complete works of Thich Nhat Nanh. " 'The miracle is not to walk on water, the miracle is to walk on the green earth.' " I was pretty sure I had that right, but just then my cell phone vibrated in my jacket pocket. "Excuse me," I said, taking it out and glancing at the caller ID.

"One quick second," I apologized, and answered the phone.

"Adam," came Antwoine's deep voice. "You better get over here. It's your dad."

41

Our dinners were barely half eaten. I drove her home, apologizing profusely all the while. She could not have been more sympathetic. She even offered to come to the hospital with me, but I couldn't expose her to my father, not this early on: that would be too gruesome.

Once I'd dropped her off, I took the Porsche up to eighty miles an hour and made it to the hospital in fifteen minutes—luckily, without being pulled over. I raced into the emergency room in an altered state of consciousness: hyper-alert, scared, with tunnel vision. I just wanted to get to Dad and see him before he died. Every damned second I had to wait at the ER desk, I was convinced, might be the moment Dad died, and I'd never get a chance to say good-bye. I pretty much shouted out his name at the triage nurse, and when she told me where he was, I took off running. I remember thinking that if he was already dead she'd have said something to that effect, so he must still be alive.

I saw Antwoine first, standing outside the green curtains. His face was for some reason scratched and bloodied, and he looked scared.

"What's up?" I called out. "Where is he?"

Antwoine pointed to the green curtains, behind which I could hear voices. "All of a sudden his breathing got all labored. Then he started turning kind of dark in the face, kind of bluish. His fingers started getting blue. That's when I called the ambulance." He sounded defensive.

"Is he—?"

"Yeah, he's alive. Man, for an old cripple he's got a lot of fight left in him."

"He did that to you?" I asked, indicating his face.

Antwoine nodded, smiling sheepishly. "He refused to get into the ambulance. He said he was fine. I spent like half an hour fighting with him, when I should have just picked him up and threw him in the car. I hope I didn't wait too long to call the ambulance."

A small, dark-skinned young guy in green scrubs came up to me. "Are you his son?"

"Yeah?" I said.

"I'm Dr. Patel," the man said. He was maybe my age, a resident or an intern or whatever.

"Oh. Hi." I paused. "Um, is he going to make it?"

"Looks like it. Your father has a cold, that's all. But he doesn't have any respiratory reserve. So a minor cold, for him, is life-threatening."

"Can I see him?"

"Of course," he said, stepping to the curtain and pulling it back. A nurse was hooking up an IV bag to Dad's arm. He had a clear plastic mask on over his mouth and nose, and he stared at me. He looked basically the same, just smaller, his face paler than normal. He was connected to a bunch of monitors.

He reached down and pulled the mask off his face. "Look at all this fuss," he said. His voice was weak.

"How're you doing, Mr. Cassidy?" Dr. Patel said.

"Oh, great," Dad said, heavy on the sarcasm. "Can't you tell?"

"I think you're doing better than your caregiver."

Antwoine was sidling up to take a look. Dad looked suddenly guilty. "Oh, that. Sorry about your face, there, Antwoine."

Antwoine, who must have realized this was as elaborate an apology as he was ever going to get from my father, looked relieved. "I learned my lesson. Next time I fight back harder."

Dad smiled like a heavyweight champ.

"This gentleman saved your life," Dr. Patel said.

"Did he," Dad said.

"He sure did."

Dad shifted his head slightly to stare at Antwoine. "What'd you have to go and do that for?" he said.

"Didn't want to have to look for another job so quick," Antwoine said right back.

Dr. Patel spoke softly to me. "His chest X ray was normal, for him, and his white count is eight point five, which is also normal. His blood gasses came back indicating he was in impending respiratory failure, but he appears to be stable now. We've got him on a course of IV antibiotics, some oxygen, and IV steroids."

"What's the mask?" I said. "Oxygen?"

"It's a nebulizer. Albuteral and Atrovent, which are bronchodilators." He leaned over my father and put the mask back in place. "You're a real fighter, Mr. Cassidy."

Dad just blinked.

"*That's* an understatement," Antwoine said, laughing huskily.

"Excuse us." Dr. Patel pulled back the curtain and took a few steps. I followed him, while Antwoine hung back with Dad.

"Does he still smoke?" Dr. Patel asked sharply.

I shrugged.

"There are nicotine stains on his fingers. That's completely insane, you know."

"I know."

"He's killing himself."

"He's dying one way or the other."

"Well, he's hastening the process."

"Maybe he wants to," I said.

42

I started my first official day of working for Jock Goddard having been up all night.

I'd gone from the hospital to my new apartment around four in the morning, considered trying to grab an hour of sleep, then rejected the idea because I knew I'd oversleep. That might not be the best way to start off with Goddard. So I took a shower, shaved, and spent some time on the Internet reading about Trion's competitors, poring over News.com and Slashdot for the latest tech news. I dressed, in a lightweight black pullover (the closest thing I had to one of Jock Goddard's trademark black mock turtlenecks), a pair of dress khakis, and a brown houndstooth jacket, one of the few "casual" items of clothing Wyatt's exotic admin had picked out for me. Now I looked like a full-fledged member of Goddard's inner posse. Then I called down to the valet and asked them to have my Porsche brought around.

The doorman who seemed to be on in the early morning and evening, when I most often came and went, was a Hispanic guy in his mid-forties named Carlos Avila. He had a strange, strangled voice as if he'd swallowed a sharp object and couldn't get it all the way down. He liked me—mostly, I think, because I didn't ignore him like everybody else who lived there.

"Workin' hard, Carlos?" I said as I passed by. Normally this was the line he used on me, when I came home ridiculously late, looking wiped out.

"Hardly workin', Mr. Cassidy," he said with a grin and turned back to the TV news.

I drove it a couple of blocks away to the Starbucks, which was just opening, and bought a triple grande latte, and while I was waiting for the Seattle-
grunge-wannabe multiple-piercing-victim kid to steam a quart of two-percent
milk, I picked up a *Wall Street Journal*, and my stomach seized up.

There, right on the front page, was an article about Trion. Or, as they put
it, "Trion's woes." There was an engraved-looking, stippled drawing of Goddard, looking inappropriately chipper, as if he were totally out of it, didn't get
it. One of the smaller headlines said, "Are Founder Augustine Goddard's
Days Numbered?" I had to read that twice. My brain wasn't functioning at
peak capacity, and I needed my triple grande latte, which the grunge kid
seemed to be struggling over. The article was a hard-hitting and smart piece
of reporting by a *Journal* regular named William Bulkeley, who obviously
had good contacts at Trion. The gist of it seemed to be that Trion's stock price
was slipping, its products were long in the tooth, the company ("generally
deemed the leader in telecommunications-based consumer electronics") was
in trouble, and Jock Goddard, Trion's founder, seemed to be out of touch.
His heart wasn't in it anymore. There was a whole riff about the "long tradition" of founders of high-technology companies who got replaced when their
company reached a certain size. It asked whether he was the wrong person to
preside over the period of stability that followed a period of explosive growth.
There was a lot of stuff in there about Goddard's philanthropy, his charitable
efforts, his hobby of collecting and repairing vintage American cars, how he'd
completely rebuilt his prize 1949 Buick Roadmaster convertible. Goddard,
the article said, seemed to be headed for a fall.

Great, I thought. If Goddard falls, guess who falls with him.

Then I remembered: Wait a second, Goddard's not my real employer.
He's the *target*. My real employer is Nick Wyatt. It was easy to forget where
my true loyalties were supposed to lie, with the excitement of the first day
and all.

Finally my latte was ready, and I stirred in a couple of Turbinado sugar
packets, took a big gulp, which scalded the back of my throat, and pressed on
the plastic top. I sat down at a table to finish the rest of the article. The jour-
nalist seemed to have the goods on Goddard. Trion people were talking to
him. The knives were out for the old guy.

On the drive in, I tried to listen to an Ani DiFranco CD I'd picked up at

Tower as part of my Alana research project, but after a few cuts I ejected the thing. I couldn't stand it. A couple of songs weren't songs at all but just spoken pieces. If I wanted that, I'd listen to Jay-Z or Eminem. No thanks.

I thought about the *Journal* piece and tried to come up with a spin in case anyone asked me about it. Should I say it was a piece of crap planted by one of our competitors to undermine us? Should I say the reporter had missed the real story (whatever that was)? Or that he'd raised some good questions that had to be dealt with? I decided to go with a modified version of this last one—that whatever the truth of the allegations, what counted was what our shareholders thought, and they almost all read the *Wall Street Journal*, so we'd have to take the piece seriously, truth or not.

And privately I wondered who Goddard's enemies were who might be stirring up trouble—whether Jock Goddard really was in trouble, and I was boarding a sinking ship. Or, to be accurate about it, whether Nick Wyatt had *put* me on a sinking ship. I thought: The guy *must* be in bad shape—he hired me, didn't he?

I took a sip of coffee, and the lid wasn't quite on tight, and the warm milky brown liquid doused my lap. It looked like I'd had an "accident." What a way to start the new job. I should have taken it as a warning.

43

On my way out of the lobby men's room, where I did my best to blot up the coffee spill, leaving my khakis damp and wrinkled, I passed the small newsstand in the lobby of A Wing, the main building, which sold the local papers plus *USA Today*, the *New York Times*, the salmon-colored *Financial Times*, and the *Journal*. The normally towering pile of *Wall Street Journals* was already half gone and it was barely seven in the morning. Obviously everyone at Trion was reading it. I figured copies of the piece from the *Journal*'s Web site were in everyone's e-mail by now. I said hi to the lobby ambassador and took the elevator to the seventh floor.

Goddard's chief admin, Flo, had already e-mailed me the details of my new office. That's right, not cubicle, but a real office, the same size as Jock Goddard's (and, for that matter, the same size as Nora's and Tom Lundgren's). It was down the hall from Goddard's office, which was dark like all the other offices on the executive corridor. Mine, however, was lit up.

Sitting at her desk outside my office was my new administrative assistant, Jocelyn Chang, a fortyish, imperious-looking Chinese-American woman in an immaculate blue suit. She had perfectly arched eyebrows, short black hair, and a tiny bow-shaped mouth decorated with wet-looking peach-colored lipstick. She was labeling a sorter for correspondence. As I approached, she looked up with pursed lips and stuck out her hand. "You must be Mr. Cassidy."

"Adam," I said. I didn't know, was that my first mistake? Was I supposed to maintain a distance, be formal? It seemed ridiculous and unnecessary. After all, almost everyone here seemed to call the CEO "Jock." And I was about half her age.

"I'm Jocelyn," she said. She had some kind of a flat, nasal Boston-area accent, which I hadn't expected. "Nice to meet you."

"You too. Flo said you've been here forever, which I'm glad to hear." Oops. Women don't like being told that.

"Fifteen years," she said warily. "The last three for Michael Gilmore, your immediate predecessor. He was reassigned a couple of weeks ago, so I've been floating."

"Fifteen years. Excellent. I'll need all the help I can get."

She nodded, no smile, nothing. Then she seemed to notice the *Journal* under my arm. "You're not going to mention that to Mr. Goddard, are you?"

"Actually, I was going to ask you to have it mounted and framed as a gift to him. For his office."

She gave me a long, terrified stare. Then a slow smile. "That's a joke," she said. "Right?"

"Right."

"Sorry. Mr. Gilmore wasn't really known for his sense of humor."

"That's okay. I'm not either."

She nodded, not sure how to react. "Right." She glanced at her watch. "You've got a seven-thirty with Mr. Goddard."

"He's not in yet."

She looked at her watch again. "He will be. In fact, I'll bet he just got in. He keeps a very regular schedule. Oh, hold on." She handed me a very fancy-looking document, easily a hundred pages long, bound in some kind of blue leatherette, that said BAIN & COMPANY on the front. "Flo said Mr. Goddard wanted you to read this before the meeting."

"The meeting . . . in two and a half minutes."

She shrugged.

Was this my first test? There was no way I could read even a page of this incomprehensible gibberish before the meeting, and I sure wasn't going to be late. Bain & Company is a high-priced global management-consulting firm that takes guys around my age, guys that know even less than I do, and works them until they're drooling idiots, making them visit companies and write reports and bill hundreds of thousands of dollars for their bogus wisdom. This one was stamped TRION SECRET. I skimmed it quickly, and all the clichés and buzzwords jumped right out at me—"streamlined knowledge management," "competitive advantage," "operations excellence," "cost inefficiencies," "diseconomies of scale," "minimizing non–value-adding work," blah blah blah—and I knew I didn't even have to read the thing to know what was up.

Layoffs. Head-harvesting on the cubicle farm.

Groovy, I thought. Welcome to life at the top.

44

Goddard was already sitting at a round table in his back office with Paul Camilletti and another guy when Flo escorted me in. The third guy was in his mid- to late fifties, bald with a gray fringe, wearing an unfashionable gray plaid suit, shirt, and tie right out of a shopping mall men's store, a big bulky class ring on his right hand. I recognized him: Jim Colvin, Trion's chief operations officer.

The room was the same size as Goddard's front office, ten by ten, and with only four guys here and the big round table it felt crowded. I wondered why we weren't meeting in some conference room, someplace a little bigger, more fitting for such high-powered executives. I said hi, smiled nervously, sat in a chair near Goddard, and put down my Bain document and the Trion mug of coffee Flo had given me. I took out a yellow pad and pen and got ready to take notes. Goddard and Camilletti were in shirtsleeves, no jackets — and no black turtlenecks. Goddard looked even older and more tired than last time I'd seen him. He had on a pair of black half-glasses on a string around his neck. Spread out on the table were several copies of the *Wall Street Journal* article, one of them marked up with yellow and green highlighter.

Camilletti scowled at me as I sat down. "Who's this?" he said. Not exactly 'Nice to have you aboard.'

"You remember Mr. Cassidy, don't you?"

"No."

"From the Maestro meeting? The military thing?"

"Your new assistant," he said without enthusiasm. "Right. Welcome to damage control central, Cassidy."

"Jim, this is Adam Cassidy," Goddard said. "Adam, Jim Colvin, our COO."

Colvin nodded. "Adam."

"We were just talking about this darned *Journal* piece," Goddard said, "and how to handle it."

"Well," I said sagely, "it's just one article. It'll blow over in a couple of days, no doubt."

"Bullshit," Camilletti snapped, glaring at me with an expression so scary I thought I was going to turn to stone. "It's the *Journal*. It's front-page. Everyone reads it. Board members, institutional investors, analysts, everyone. This is a friggin' train wreck."

"It's not good," I agreed. I told myself to keep my mouth shut from now on.

Goddard exhaled noisily.

"The worst thing to do is to over-rotate," Colvin said. "We don't want to send up panic smoke signals to the industry." I liked "over-rotate." Jim Colvin was obviously a golfer.

"I want to get Investor Relations in here now, Corporate Communications, and draft a response, a letter to the editor," Camilletti said.

"Forget the *Journal*," Goddard said. "I think I'd like to offer a face-to-face exclusive to the *New York Times*. An opportunity to address issues of broad concern to the whole industry, I'll say. They'll get it."

"Whatever," said Camilletti. "In any case, let's not protest too loudly. We don't want to force the *Journal* to do a follow-up, stir up the mud even more."

"Sounds to me like the *Journal* reporter must have talked to insiders here," I said, forgetting the part about keeping my mouth shut. "Do we have any idea who might have leaked?"

"I did get a voice mail from the reporter a couple of days ago, but I was out of the country," Goddard said. "So I'm 'unavailable for comment.' "

"The guy may have called me—I don't know, I can check my voice mail—but I surely didn't return his call," said Camilletti.

"I can't imagine anyone at Trion would knowingly have any part in this," Goddard said.

"One of our competitors," Camilletti said. "Wyatt, maybe."

No one looked at me. I wondered if the other two knew I came from Wyatt.

Camilletti went on, "There's a lot of stuff here quoting some of our resellers—British Tel, Vodafone, DoCoMo—about how the new cell phones aren't moving. The dogs aren't eating the dog food. So how does a reporter with a New York byline even *know* to call DoCoMo in Japan? It's got to be Motorola or Wyatt or Nokia who dropped a dime."

"Anyway," Goddard said, "it's all water under the bridge. My job isn't to manage the media, it's to manage the darned company. And this asinine piece, however skewed and unfair it might be—well, how terrible is it, really? Apart from the grim-reaper headline, what's in here that's all that new? We used to hit our numbers on the dot each quarter, never missed, maybe beat 'em by a penny or two. We were Wall Street's darling. Okay, revenue growth is flat, but good Lord, the entire industry is suffering! I can't help but detect a little Schadenfreude in this piece. Mighty Homer has nodded."

"Homer?" said Colvin, confused.

"But all this tripe about how we may be facing our first quarterly loss in fifteen years," said Goddard, "that's pure invention—"

Camilletti shook his head. "No," he said quietly. "It's even worse than that."

"What are you talking about?" Goddard said. "I just came from our sales conference in Japan, where everything was hunky-dory!"

"Last night when I got the e-mail alert about this article," Camilletti said, "I fired off e-mails to the VP/Finance for Europe and for Asia/Pacific telling them I wanted to see all the revenue numbers as of this week, the QTD sales revenue numbers broken down by customer."

"And?" prompted Goddard.

"Covington in Brussels just got back to me an hour ago, Brody in Singapore in the middle of the night, and the numbers look like crap. The sell-in was strong, but the sell-through has been terrible. Between Asia/Pacific and EMEA, that's sixty percent of our revenue, and we're falling off a cliff.

The fact is, Jock, we're going to miss this quarter, and miss big. It's a flat-out disaster."

Goddard glanced at me. "You're obviously hearing some privileged, non-public information, Adam, let's be clear about that, not a word—"

"Of course."

"We've got," Goddard began, faltered, then said, "for God's sake, we've got AURORA—"

"The revenue from AURORA is several quarters off," said Camilletti. "We've got to manage for *now*. For current operations. And let me tell you, when these numbers come out, the stock's going to take a *huge* hit," Camilletti went on. He spoke in a low voice. "Our revenues for the fourth quarter are going to be off by *twenty-five percent*. We're going to have to take a significant charge for excess inventory."

Camilletti paused, gave Goddard a significant look. "I'm estimating a pretax loss of close to half a *billion* dollars."

Goddard winced. "My God."

Camilletti went on, "I happen to know that CS First Boston is *already* about to downgrade us from 'overweight' to 'market weight.' That's from a 'buy' to a 'hold.' And that's *before* any of this comes out."

"Good Lord," Goddard said, groaning and shaking his head. "It's so absurd, given what we *know* we have in the pipeline."

"That's why we need to take another look at this," Camilletti said, jabbing his copy of the blue Bain document with his index finger.

Goddard's fingers drummed on the Bain study. His fingers, I noticed, were chubby, the back of his hands liver-spotted. "And quite the handsomely bound report it is, too," he said. "You never told me what it cost us."

"You don't want to know," Camilletti said.

"I don't, do I?" He grimaced, as if he'd made his point. "Paul, I swore I would never do this. I gave my word."

"Christ, Jock, if this is about your ego, your vanity—"

"This is about keeping my word. It's also about my credibility."

"Well, you should never have made such a promise. Never say never. In any case, you were talking in a different economy—prehistoric times. The Mesozoic Era, for God's sake. Rocketship Trion, growing at warp speed. We're one of the few high-tech companies that *hasn't* gone through layoffs yet."

"Adam," Goddard said, turning to me and looking over his glasses, "have you had a chance to plow through all this gobbledygook?"

I shook my head. "Just got it a few minutes ago. I've skimmed it."

"I want you to look closely at the projections for consumer electronics. Page eighty-something. You have some familiarity with that."

"Right now?" I asked.

"Right now. And tell me if they look realistic to you."

"Jock," said Jim Colvin, "it's just about impossible to get honest projections from any of the division heads. They're all protecting their head count, guarding their turf."

"That's why Adam's here," Goddard replied. "He doesn't have turf to protect."

I frantically thumbed through the Bain report, trying to look like I knew what I was doing.

"Paul," Goddard said, "we've gone through all this before. You're going to tell me we have to slash eight thousand jobs if we want to be lean and mean."

"No, Jock, if we want to remain *solvent*. And it's more like ten thousand jobs."

"Right. So tell me something. Nowhere in this darned treatise does it say that a company that downsizes or rightsizes or whatever the hell you want to call it is ever better off in the long run. All you hear about is the short term." Camilletti looked like he was about to respond, but Goddard kept going. "Oh, I know, everyone does it. It's a knee-jerk response. Business stinks? Get rid of some people. Throw the ballast overboard. But do layoffs ever really lead to a *sustained* increase in share price, or market share? Hell, Paul, you know as well as I do that as soon as the skies clear up again we just end up hiring most of 'em back. Is it really worth all the goddamned *turmoil*?"

"Jock," Jim Colvin said, "it's what they call the Eighty-Twenty Rule — twenty percent of the people do eighty percent of the work. We're just cutting the fat."

"The 'fat' is dedicated Trion employees," Goddard shot back. "To whom we issue those little culture badges that talk about loyalty and dedication. Well, it's a two-way street, isn't it? We expect loyalty from them, but they don't get it back from us? Far as I'm concerned, you go down this road, you lose more than head count. You lose a fundamental sense of trust. If our employees have upheld their half of the contract, how come we don't have to? It's a damned breach of trust."

"Jock," Colvin said, "the fact is, you've made a lot of Trion employees very rich in the last ten years."

Meanwhile I was racing through the charts of projected earnings, trying to compare them to the numbers I'd seen over the last couple of weeks.

"This is no time to be high-minded, Jock," Camilletti said. "We don't have that luxury."

"Oh, I'm not being high-minded," Goddard said, drumming his fingers some more on the tabletop. "I'm being brutally practical. I don't have a problem with getting rid of the slackers, the coasters, the rest-'n-vesters. Screw 'em. But layoffs on this scale just lead to increased absenteeism, sick leaves, people standing around the water cooler asking each other about the latest rumor. Paralysis. Put it in a way you can understand, Paul, that's called a decrease in productivity."

"Jock—" Colvin began.

"*I'll* give you an eighty-twenty rule," Goddard said. "If we do this, eighty percent of my remaining employees are going to be able to focus no more than about twenty percent of their mental abilities on their work. Adam, how do the forecasts look to you?"

"Mr. Goddard—"

"I fired the last guy who called me that."

I smiled. "Jock. Look, I'm not going to dance around here. I don't *know* most of the numbers, and I'm not going to shoot from the hip. Not on something this important. But I do know the Maestro numbers, and I can tell you these look overly optimistic, frankly. Until we start shipping to the Pentagon—assuming we land that deal—these numbers are way high."

"Meaning the situation could be even worse than our hundred-thousand-dollar consultants tell us."

"Yes, sir. At least, if the Maestro numbers are any indication."

He nodded.

Camilletti said, "Jock, let me put it to you in human terms. My father was a goddamned schoolteacher, okay? Sent six kids through college on a school-teacher's salary, don't ask me how, but he did. Now he and my mom are living off his measly life's savings, most of which is tied up in Trion stock, because I told him this was a great company. This is not a lot of money, by our standards, but he's already lost twenty-six percent of his nest egg, and he's about to lose a whole hell of a lot more. Forget about Fidelity and TIAA-CREF. The vast majority of our shareholders are Tony Camillettis, and what are we supposed to tell *them?*"

I had the distinct feeling that Camilletti was making this up, that in reality his investment-banker father lived in a gated community in Boca and played a lot of golf, but Goddard's eyes seemed to glisten.

"Adam," Goddard said, "*you* see my point, don't you?"

For a moment I felt like a deer frozen in the headlights. It was obvious what Goddard wanted to hear from me. But after a few seconds I shook my head. "To me," I said slowly, "it looks like if you don't do it now, you'll probably have to cut even more jobs a year from now. So I have to say I'm with Mr.—with Paul."

Camilletti reached out a hand and patted me on the shoulder. I recoiled a little. I didn't want it to look like I was choosing sides—against my boss. Not a good way to start off the new job.

"What sort of terms are you proposing?" Goddard said with a sigh.

Camilletti smiled. "Four weeks of severance pay."

"No matter how long they've been with us? No. Two weeks of severance pay for every year they've been with us, plus an additional two weeks for every year beyond ten years."

"That's *insane*, Jock! In some cases, we'll be paying out a year's severance pay, maybe more."

"That's not severance," muttered Jim Colvin, "that's welfare."

Goddard shrugged. "Either we lay off on those terms, or we don't lay off at all." He gave me a mournful look. "Adam, if you ever go out to dinner with Paul, don't let him choose the wine." Then he turned back to his CFO. "You want the layoffs effective June 1, is that right?"

Camilletti nodded warily.

"Somewhere in the back of my mind," Goddard said, "I have this vague recollection that we signed a one-year severance contract with the CableSign division we acquired last year that expires on May thirty-first. Day before."

Camilletti shrugged.

"Well, Paul, that's almost a thousand workers who'd get a month's salary plus a month's pay for each year served — if we lay them off one day earlier. A decent severance package. That one day'll make a huge difference to those folks. Now they'll get a lousy two weeks."

"June first is the beginning of the quarter—"

"I won't do that. Sorry. Make it May thirtieth. And as for those employees whose stock options are underwater, we'll give 'em twelve months to exercise them. And I'm taking a voluntary pay cut myself—to a dollar. How about you, Paul?"

Camilletti smiled nervously. "You get a lot more stock options than I do."

"We're doing this once," Goddard said. "Doing it once and doing it right. I'm not slicing twice."

"Understood," Camilletti said.

"All right," Goddard said with a sigh. "As I'm always telling you, sometimes you just gotta get in the car, get with the program. But first I want to run this by the entire management team, conference in as many of them as we can get together. I also want to get on the horn to our investment bankers. If it flies, as I fear it will, I'll tape a Webcast announcement to the company," Goddard said, "and we'll release it tomorrow, after the close of trading. And make the public announcement at the same time. I don't want a word of this leaking out before then—it's demoralizing."

"If you'd prefer, I'll make the announcement," Camilletti said. "That way you keep your hands clean."

Goddard glared at Camilletti. "I'm not hanging this on you. I refuse. This is my decision—I get the credit, the glory, the magazine covers, and I get the blame too. It's only right."

"I only say it because you've made so many pronouncements in the past. You'll get skewered—"

Goddard shrugged, but he looked miserable. "Now I suppose they're all going to be calling me Chainsaw Goddard or something."

"I think 'Neutron Jock' has a better ring to it," I said, and for the first time, Goddard actually smiled.

4 5

I left Goddard's office feeling both relieved and weighted down.

I'd survived my first meeting with the guy, didn't make too big a fool of myself. But I was also in possession of a serious company secret, real inside information that was going to change a lot of people's lives.

Here's the thing: I'd made up my mind that I wasn't going to pass this on to Wyatt and company. It wasn't part of my assignment, wasn't in my job description. It had nothing to do with the skunkworks. I wasn't required to tell my handlers. They didn't know I knew, anyway. Let them find out about the Trion layoffs when everyone else did.

Preoccupied, I stepped off the elevator on the third floor of A Wing to grab a late lunch in the dining room when I saw a familiar face coming at me. A tall, skinny young guy, late twenties, bad haircut, called out, "Hey, Adam!" as he got into the elevator.

Even in that fraction of a second before I could put a name to the face, my stomach clenched. My animal hindbrain had sensed the danger before my cerebrum figured it out.

I nodded, kept on walking. My face was burning.

His name was Kevin Griffin, an affable if goofy-looking guy, and a decent basketball player. I used to shoot hoops with him at Wyatt Telecommunications. He was in sales in the Enterprise Division, in routers. I remembered him as very sharp, very ambitious behind that laid-back demeanor. He always beat his numbers, and he used to joke with me, in a good-natured sort of way, about my casual attitude toward work.

In other words, he knew who I really was.

"Adam!" he persisted. "Adam Cassidy! Hey, what are *you* doing here?"

I couldn't exactly ignore him anymore, so I turned back. He had one hand on the elevator doors to keep them from closing.

"Oh, hey, Kevin," I said. "You work here now?"

"Yeah, in sales." He seemed thrilled, like this was a high-school reunion or something. He lowered his voice. "Didn't they kick you out of Wyatt because of that party?" He made a sort of sniggering sound, not nasty or anything, just kind of conspiratorial.

"Nah," I said, faltering for a second, trying to sound lighthearted and amused. "It was all a big misunderstanding."

"Yeah," he said dubiously. "Where're you working here?"

"Same old same old," I said. "Hey, nice to see you, guy. Sorry, I've got to run."

He looked back at me curiously as the elevator doors closed.

This was not good.

PART FIVE

BLOWN

Blown: Exposure of personnel, installation (such as a safe house) or other elements of a clandestine activity or organization. A blown agent is one whose identity is known to the opposition.

—*Spy Book: The Encyclopedia of Espionage*

46

I was screwed.

Kevin Griffin knew I wasn't on the Lucid project back at Wyatt, knew I wasn't any superstar either. He knew the real story. He was probably already back at his cubicle looking me up on the Trion intranet, amazed to see me listed as executive assistant to the president and CEO. How long would it be before he started talking, telling stories, asking around? Five minutes? Five *seconds?*

How the hell could this have happened, after all the careful planning, the laying of the groundwork by Wyatt's people? How could they have *let* Trion hire someone who could sabotage the whole scheme?

I looked around, dazed, at the cafeteria's deli counter. Suddenly I didn't have any appetite. I took a ham-and-cheese sandwich anyway, because I needed the protein, and a Diet Pepsi, and went back to my new office.

Jock Goddard was standing in the hall near my office talking to some other executive type. He caught my eye, held up an index finger to let me know he wanted to talk to me, so I stood there awkwardly at a distance while he finished his conversation.

After a couple of minutes Jock put a hand on the other man's shoulder, looking solemn, then led the way into my office.

"You," he said as he sat down in the visitor's chair. The only other place to sit was behind my desk, which felt all wrong—he was the goddamned

CEO!—but I had no choice. I sat down, smiled at him hesitantly, didn't know what to expect.

"I'd say you passed with flying colors," Goddard said. "Congratulations."

"Really? I thought I blew it," I said. "I didn't exactly feel comfortable taking someone else's side."

"That's why I hired you. Oh, not to take sides against me. But to speak truth to power, as it were."

"It wasn't truth," I said. "It was just one guy's opinion." Maybe that was going a little too far.

Goddard rubbed his eyes with a stubby hand. "The easiest thing in the world for a CEO—and the most dangerous—is to be out of touch. No one ever really wants to give me the unvarnished truth. They want to spin me. They've all got their own agenda. Do you like history?"

I'd never thought of history as something you could "like." I shrugged. "Some."

"During the Second World War, Winston Churchill set up an office outside of the chain of command whose job was to give him the straight, blunt truth. I think he called it the Statistical Office or something. Anyway, the point was, no one liked to give him bad news, but he knew he had to hear it or he couldn't do his job."

I nodded.

"You start a company, have fortune smile upon you a few times, and you can get to be almost a cult figure among folks who don't know any better," Goddard continued. "But I don't need my, er, ring kissed. I need candor. Now more than ever. There's an axiom in this business that technology companies inevitably outgrow their founders. Happened with Rod Canion at Compaq, Al Shugart at Seagate. Apple Computer even kicked out Steve Jobs, remember, until he came riding back in on his white horse and saved the place. Point is, there are no old, bold founders. My board has always had deep wells of faith in me, but I suspect those wells are starting to run dry."

"Why do you say that, sir?"

"The 'sir' stuff has got to stop," Goddard snapped. "The *Journal* piece was a shot across the bow. It wouldn't surprise me if it came from disgruntled board members, some of whom think it's time for me to step down, retire to my country house, and tinker with my cars full-time."

"You don't want to do that, do you?"

He scowled. "I'll do whatever's best for Trion. This damned company is my whole life. Anyway, cars are just a hobby—you do a hobby full-time and it's no fun anymore." He handed me a thick manila folder. "There's an Adobe PDF copy of this in your e-mail. Our strategic plan for the next eighteen months—new products, upgrades, the whole kit and caboodle. I want you to give me your blunt, unvarnished take—a presentation, whatever you want to call it, an overview, a helicopter ride."

"When would you like it?"

"Soon as you possibly can. And if there's any particular project you think you'd like to get involved in, as my emissary, be my guest. You'll see there are all kinds of interesting things in the pipeline. Some of which are quite closely held. My God, there's one thing in the works, codenamed Project AURORA, which may reverse our fortunes entirely."

"AURORA?" I said, swallowing hard. "I think you mentioned that in the meeting, right?"

"I've given it to Paul to manage. Truly mind-blowing stuff. A few kinks in the prototype that still need to be ironed out, but it's just about ready to be unveiled."

"Sounds intriguing," I said, trying to sound casual. "I'd love to help out on that."

"Oh, you will, no doubt about that. But all in good time. I don't want to distract you just yet from some of the housecleaning issues, because once you get caught up in AURORA . . . well, I don't want to send you in too many directions at once, spread you too thin." He stood up, clasped his hands together. "Now I've got to head over to the studio to tape the Webcast, which is *not* something I'm looking forward to, let me tell you."

I smiled sympathetically.

"Anyway," Goddard said, "sorry to plunge you in that way, but I have a feeling you're going to do just fine."

47

I arrived at Wyatt's house at the same time as Meacham, who made some crack about my Porsche. We were shown in to Wyatt's elaborate gym, in the basement level but, because of the landscaping, it wasn't below ground. Wyatt was lifting weights at a reclining bench—a hundred fifty pounds. He wore only a skimpy pair of gym shorts, no shirt, and looked more bulked-up than ever. This guy was Quadzilla.

He finished his set before he said a word, then got up and toweled himself off.

"So you get fired yet?" he said.

"Not yet."

"No, Goddard's got things on his mind. Like the fact that his company's falling apart." He looked at Meacham, and the two men chortled. "What'd Saint Augustine have to say about that?"

The question wasn't unexpected, but it came so abruptly I wasn't quite prepared. "Not that much," I said.

"Bullshit," Wyatt said, coming closer to me and staring, trying to intimidate me with his physical presence. Hot damp air rose from his body, smelling unpleasantly like ammonia: the odor of weight lifters who ingest too much protein.

"Not that much that I was around for," I amended. "I mean, I think the article really spooked them—there was a flurry of activity. Crazier than usual."

"What do you know about 'usual'?" said Meacham. "It's your first day on the seventh floor."

"Just my perception," I said lamely.

"How much of the article's true?" said Wyatt.

"You mean, you didn't plant it?" I said.

Wyatt gave me a look. "Are they going to miss the quarter or not?"

"I have no idea," I lied. "It's not like I was in Goddard's office all day." I don't know why I was so stubborn about not revealing the disastrous quarter numbers, or the news about the impending layoffs. Maybe I felt like I'd been entrusted with a secret by Goddard, and it would be wrong to break that confidence. Christ, I was a goddamned mole, a spy—where did I get off being so high and mighty? Why was I suddenly drawing lines: this much I'll tell you, this much I won't? When the news about the layoffs came out tomorrow, Wyatt would go medieval on me for holding back. He wouldn't believe I hadn't heard. So I fudged a little. "But there's something going on," I said. "Something big. Some kind of announcement coming."

I handed Wyatt a folder containing a copy of the strategic plan Goddard had given me to review.

"What's this?" Wyatt said. He set it down on the weight bench, pulled a tank top over his head, and then started leafing through the document.

"Trion's strategic plan for the next eighteen months. Including detailed descriptions of all the new products in the pipeline."

"Including AURORA?"

I shook my head. "Goddard did mention it, though."

"How?"

"He just said there was this big project codenamed AURORA that would turn the company around. Said he'd given it to Camilletti to run."

"Huh. Camilletti's in charge of all acquisitions, and my sources say Project AURORA was put together from a collection of companies Trion's secretly bought over the last few years. Did Goddard say what it was?"

"No."

"You didn't *ask*?"

"Of course I asked. I told him I'd be interested in taking part in something so significant."

Wyatt, paging through the strategic plan, was silent. His eyes were scanning the pages rapidly, excitedly.

Meanwhile, I handed Meacham a scrap of paper. "Jock's personal cell number."

"*Jock?*" said Meacham in disgust.

"Everyone calls him that. It doesn't mean we're asshole buddies. Anyway, this should help you trace a lot of his most important calls."

Meacham took it without thanks.

"One more thing," I said to Meacham as Wyatt continued reading, fascinated. "There's a problem."

Meacham stared at me. "Don't fuck with us."

"There's a new hire at Trion, a kid named Kevin Griffin, in Sales. They hired him away from you—from Wyatt."

"So?"

"We were sort of friends."

"*Friends?*"

"Sort of. We played hoops together."

"He knew you at the company?"

"Yep."

"Shit," Meacham said. "That *is* a problem."

Wyatt looked up from the document. "Nuke him," he said.

Meacham nodded.

"What does that mean?" I said.

"It means we'll take care of him," Meacham said.

"This is valuable information," Wyatt said at last. "Very, *very* useful. What does he want you to do with it?"

"He wants my overall take on the product portfolio. What's promising, what isn't, what might run into trouble. Whatever."

"That's not very specific."

"He told me he wants a helicopter ride over the terrain."

"Piloted by Adam Cassidy, marketing genius," Wyatt said, amused. "Well, get out a notepad and a pen and start taking notes. I'm going to make you a star."

48

I was up most of the night: unfortunately, I was starting to get used to this.

The odious Nick Wyatt had spent more than an hour giving me his whole take on the Trion product line, including all sorts of inside information, stuff very few other people would know. It was like getting Rommel's take on Montgomery. Obviously he knew a hell of a lot about the market, since he was one of Trion's principal competitors, and he had all sorts of valuable information, which he was willing to give up for the sole purpose of making Goddard impressed with me. His short-term strategic loss would be his long-term strategic gain.

I raced back to the Harbor Suites by midnight and got to work on Power-Point, putting the slides together for my presentation to Goddard. To be honest, I was pretty amped up about it. I knew I couldn't coast; I had to keep performing at peak. As long as I had the benefit of inside information from Wyatt, I'd impress Goddard, but what would happen when I didn't? What if he asked my opinion on something, and I revealed my true, ignorant self? Then what?

When I couldn't work on the presentation anymore, I took a break and checked my personal e-mail on Yahoo and Hotmail and Hushmail. The usual junk-mail spam—"Viagra Online BUY IT HERE VIAGRA NO PRE-SCRIPTION" and "BEST XXX SITE!" and "Mortgage Approval!" Nothing more from "Arthur." Then I signed on to the Trion Web site.

One e-mail leaped out at me: It was from KGriffin@trionsystems.com. I
clicked on it.

```
SUBJ: You
FROM: KGriffin
TO:   ACassidy


Dude! Great seeing you! Nice to see you looking so slick
& doing so well—way to go! Very impressed by your career
here. Is it something in the water? Give ME some!
I'm getting to know people around Trion & would love to
take you to lunch or whatever. Let me know!


Kev
```

I didn't reply—I had to figure out how to handle it. The guy had obviously looked me up, saw my new title, couldn't figure it out. Whether he
wanted to get together out of curiosity, or to brownnose, this was big trouble.
Meacham and Wyatt had said they'd "nuke" him, whatever that meant, but
until they did whatever they were going to do, I'd have to be extra careful.
Kevin Griffin was a loaded gun lying around, waiting to go off. I didn't want
to go near it.

Then I signed off, and signed back on using Nora's user ID and password. It was two in the morning, and I figured she had to be offline. It would
be a good time to try to get into her archived e-mail, go through it all, download anything that had to do with AURORA, if there was anything.

All I got was INVALID PASSWORD, PLEASE RE-ENTER.

I re-entered her password, this time more carefully, and got INVALID PASS-
WORD again. This time I was certain I hadn't made a mistake.

Her password had been changed.

Why?

When I finally crashed for the night, my mind was racing, running
through all the possibilities as to why Nora had changed her password.
Maybe the security guard, Luther, had come by one night when Nora happened to be staying a little later than usual, and he was expecting to see me,

engage in a conversation about Mustangs or whatever, but he saw Nora instead. He might wonder what she was doing there in that office, might even—it wasn't totally unlikely—confront her. And then he'd give her a description and she'd figure it out; it wouldn't take her long at all.

But if that's what had happened, she wouldn't just change her password, would she? She'd do more than that. She'd want to know why I was in her office, when she hadn't given me permission to be there. Where that could lead, I didn't want to think about. . . .

Or maybe it was all innocent. Maybe she'd just changed her password routinely, the way every Trion employee was supposed to do every sixty days.

Probably that's all it was.

I didn't sleep well at all, and after a couple of hours of tossing and turning I decided to just get up, take a shower and get dressed, and head into work. My Goddard work was done; it was my *Wyatt* work, my espionage, that was way behind. If I got into work early enough, maybe I could try to find out something about AURORA.

I glanced in the mirror as I walked out. I looked—like shit.

"You up already?" Carlos the concierge said as my Porsche pulled up to the front curb. "Man, you can't keep hours like this, Mr. Cassidy. You get sick."

"Nah," I said. "Keeps me honest."

49

At a little after five in the morning the Trion garage was just about empty. It felt strange being there when it was all but deserted. The fluorescent lights buzzed and washed everything in a kind of greenish haze, and the place smelled of gasoline and motor oil and whatever else dripped from cars: brake fluid and coolant and probably spilled Mountain Dew. My footsteps echoed.

I took the back elevator to the seventh floor, which was also deserted, and walked down the dark executive corridor to my office, past Colvin's office, Camilletti's office, other offices of people I hadn't met yet, until I came to mine. All the offices were dark and closed; no one was in yet.

My office was all potential—not much more than a bare desk and chairs and a computer, a Trion-logo mousepad, a filing cabinet with nothing in it, a credenza with a couple of books. It looked like the office of an itinerant, a drifter, someone who could up and leave in the middle of the night. It was badly in need of some personality—framed photographs, some sporting-goods collectibles, something jokey and funny, something serious and inspirational. It needed an imprint. Maybe, once I caught up on my sleep, I'd do something about it.

I entered my password, logged in, checked my e-mail again. Sometime in the last few post-midnight hours a companywide e-mail had gone out to all Trion employees worldwide asking them to watch the company Web site later on today, at five o'clock Eastern Standard Time, for "an important announcement from CEO Augustine Goddard." That should set off the rumor mills.

The e-mails would be flying. I wondered how many people at the top—
a group that now included me, bizarrely enough—knew the truth. Not many,
I bet.

Goddard had mentioned that AURORA, the mind-blowing project he
wouldn't talk about, was Paul Camilletti's turf. I wondered if there was anything in Camilletti's official bio that might shed some light on AURORA, so
I entered his name in the company directory.

His photo was there, stern and forbidding and yet more handsome than
in person. A thumbnail biography: born in Geneseo, New York, educated in
public schools in upstate New York—translation, probably didn't grow up
with money—Swarthmore, Harvard Business School, meteoric rise in some
consumer-electronics company that was once a big rival to Trion but was
later acquired by Trion. Senior VP at Trion for less than a year before being
named CFO. A man on the move. I clicked on the hyperlinks for his reporting chain, and a little tree chart popped up, showing all the divisions and
units that were under him.

One of the units was the Disruptive Technologies Research Unit, which
reported directly to him. Alana Jennings was marketing director.

Paul Camilletti *directly oversaw* the AURORA project. Suddenly, he was
very, very important.

I walked by his office, my heart hammering away, and saw, of course, no sign
of him. Not at quarter after five in the morning. I also noticed that the cleaning crew had already been by: there was a fresh liner in his admin's trash can,
you could see the undisturbed vacuuming lines on the carpet, and the place
still smelled like cleaning fluid.

And there was no one in the corridor, likely no one on the entire floor.

I was about to cross a line, do something risky at a whole new level.

I wasn't worried so much about a security guard coming by. I'd say I was
Camilletti's new assistant—what the hell did they know?

But what if Camilletti's admin came in really early, to get a jump on the
day? Or, more likely, what if Camilletti *himself* wanted to get an early start?
Given the big announcement, he might well have to start placing calls, writing e-mails, making faxes to Trion's European offices, which were six or

seven hours ahead. At five-thirty in the morning, it was noon in Europe. Sure, he could e-mail from home, but I couldn't put it past him to get in to his office unusually early today.

So to break into his office today, I realized, was insanely risky.

But for some reason I decided to do it anyway.

50

Yet the key to Camilletti's office was nowhere to be found.

I checked all the usual places—every drawer in his admin's desk, inside the plants and paper-clip holder, even the filing cabinets. Her desk was open to the hallway, totally exposed, and I began to feel nervous poking around there, where I so clearly didn't belong. I looked behind the phone. Under the keyboard, under her computer. Was it hidden on the underside of the desk drawers? No. Underneath the desk? Also no. There was a small waiting-room area next to her desk—really just a couch, coffee table, and a couple of chairs. I looked around there, but nothing. There was no key.

So maybe it wasn't exactly unreasonable that the company's chief financial officer might actually take a security precaution or two, make it hard for someone to break into his office. You had to admire that, right?

After a nerve-wracking ten minutes of looking everywhere, I decided it wasn't meant to be, when suddenly I remembered an odd little detail about my own new office. Like all the offices on the executive floor, it was equipped with a motion detector, which is not as high-security as it sounds. It's actually a common safety feature in the higher-end offices—a way to make sure that no one ever gets locked inside his own office. As long as there's motion inside an office, the doors won't lock. (More proof that the offices on the seventh floor really were a little more equal.)

If I moved quickly I could take advantage of this. . . .

The door to Camilletti's office was solid mahogany, highly polished, heavy. There was no gap between the door and the deep pile carpet; I couldn't even slide a piece of paper under it. That would make things a bit more complicated—but not impossible.

I needed a chair to stand on, not his admin's chair, which rolled on casters and wouldn't be steady. I found a ladderback chair in the sitting area and brought it next to the glass wall of Camilletti's office. Then I went back to the sitting area. Fanned out on the coffee table were all of the usual magazines and newspapers—the *Financial Times, Institutional Investor, CFO, Forbes, Fortune, Business 2.0, Barron's*. . . .

Barron's. Yes. That would do. It was the size and shape and heft of a tabloid newspaper. I grabbed it, then—looking around once again to make sure I wasn't caught doing something I couldn't even *begin* to explain—I climbed up on the chair and pushed up one of the square acoustic ceiling panels.

I reached up into the empty space above the suspended ceiling, into that dark dusty place choked with wires and cables and stuff, felt for the next ceiling panel, the one directly over Camilletti's office, and lifted that one too, propped it up on the metal grid thing.

Taking the *Barron's*, I reached over, lowered it slowly, waving it around. I lowered it as far as I could reach, waved it around some more—but nothing happened. Maybe the motion detectors didn't reach high enough. Finally I stood up on tiptoe, crooked my elbow as sharply as I could, and managed to lower the newspaper another foot or so, waving it around wildly until I really began to strain some muscles.

And I heard a click.

A faint, unmistakable click.

Pulling the *Barron's* back through, I put the acoustic ceiling panel back, sat it snugly in place. Then I got down from the chair, moved it back where it belonged.

And tried Camilletti's doorknob.

The door came open.

In my workbag I'd brought a couple of tools, including a Mag-Lite flashlight. I immediately drew the Venetian blinds, closed the door, then switched on the powerful beam.

Camilletti's office was as devoid of personality as everyone else's—the generic collection of framed family photos, the plaques and awards, the same old lineup of business books they all pretended to read. Actually, this office was pretty disappointing. This wasn't a corner office, didn't have floor-to-ceiling windows like at Wyatt Telecomm. There was no view at all. I wondered whether Camilletti disliked having important guests visit such a humble office. This might be Goddard's style, but it sure didn't seem to be Camilletti's. Cheapskate or no, he seemed grandiose. I'd heard that there was a fancy visitors' reception suite on the penthouse of the executive building, A Wing, but no one I knew had ever seen it. Maybe that's where Camilletti received bigwigs.

His computer had been left on, but when I clicked the space bar on the modernistic black keyboard, and the monitor lit up, I could see the ENTER PASSWORD screen, the cursor blinking. Without his password, of course, I couldn't get into his computer files.

If he'd written down his password somewhere, I sure as hell couldn't find it—in drawers, under the keyboard, taped to the back of the big flat-panel monitor. Nowhere. Just for kicks I entered his user name (PCamilletti@trion-systems.com) and then the same password, PCamilletti.

Nope. He was more cautious than that, and after a few attempts I gave up.

I'd have to get his password the old-fashioned way: by stealth. I figured he probably wouldn't notice if I swapped out the cable between his keyboard and CPU with a Keyghost. So I did.

I admit I was even more nervous being inside Camilletti's office than I'd been inside Nora's. You'd think by now I'd be an old pro about breaking into offices, but I wasn't, and there was a vibe in Camilletti's office that scared the shit out of me. The guy himself was terrifying, and the consequences of being caught didn't bear thinking about. Plus I had to assume that the security precautions in the executive-level offices were more elaborate than in the rest of Trion. They *had* to be. Sure, I'd been trained to defeat most standard security measures. But there were always invisible detection systems that didn't set off any alarm bells or lights. That possibility scared me most of all.

I looked around, groping for inspiration. For some reason the office seemed somehow neater, more spacious than others I'd been in at Trion. Then I realized why: there were no filing cabinets in here. *That's* why it seemed so uncluttered. Well, so where *were* all his files?

When I finally figured out where they had to be, I felt like an idiot. Of course. They weren't in here, because there wasn't any room, and they weren't in his admin's area, because that was too open to the public, not secure enough.

They had to be in the back room. Like Goddard, every top-level Trion executive had a double office, a back conference room the same size as the front. That was the way Trion got around the equality-of-office-space problem. Hey, everyone's office is the same size; the top guys just get *two* of them.

The door to the conference room was unlocked. I shined the Mag-Lite around the room, saw a small copying machine, noticed that each wall was lined with mahogany file cabinets. In the middle was a round table, like Goddard's but smaller. Each drawer was meticulously labeled in what looked like an architect's hand. Most of them seemed to contain financial and accounting records, which probably had good stuff in them if only I knew where to look.

But when I saw the drawers labeled TRION CORPORATE DEVELOPMENT, I lost all interest in anything else. Corporate development is just a biz buzz-word for mergers and acquisitions. Trion was known for gobbling up startups or small and midsize companies. More in the go-go years of the late nineteen-nineties than now, but they still acquired several companies a year. I guessed that the files were here because Camilletti oversaw acquisitions, focusing mainly on cost issues, how good an investment, all that.

And if Wyatt was right that Project AURORA was made up of a bunch of companies Trion had secretly acquired, then the solution to the mystery of AURORA had to be here.

These cabinets were unlocked, too, another stroke of luck. I guess the idea was that if you couldn't get into Camilletti's back office, you weren't going to even get near the file cabinets, so to lock them would be a pointless annoyance.

There were a bunch of files here, on companies Trion had either acquired outright or bought a chunk of or looked at closely and decided not to get involved. Some of the company names I recognized, but most I didn't. I dipped into a folder on each company to try to figure out what it did. This was pretty slow work, and I didn't even know what I was looking for, really. How the hell was I supposed to know if some small startup was part of

AURORA, when I didn't even know what AURORA *was?* It seemed totally impossible.

But then my problems were solved.

One of the corporate development drawers was labeled PROJECT AURORA.

And there it was. Simple as that.

51

Breathing shallowly, I pulled the drawer open. I half expected the drawer to be empty, like the AURORA files in HR. But it wasn't. It was jam-packed with folders, all color-coded in some way I didn't understand, each stamped TRION CONFIDENTIAL. This was clearly the good stuff.

From what I could tell, these files were on several small startups—two in Silicon Valley, California, and another couple in Cambridge, Massachusetts—that had recently been acquired by Trion in conditions of strictest secrecy. "Stealth mode," the files said.

I knew this was something big, something important, and my pulse really started pounding. Each *page* was stamped SECRET or CONFIDENTIAL. Even in these top-secret files kept in the CFO's locked office, the language was obscure, veiled. There were sentences, phrases, like "Recommend acquire soonest" and "Must be kept below the radar."

So the secret of AURORA was here.

I didn't really get it, much as I pored over the files. One company seemed to have developed a way to combine electronic and optical components in one integrated circuit. I didn't know what this meant. A note said that the company had solved the problem of "the low yield of the wafers."

Another company had figured out a way to mass-produce photonic circuits. Okay, but what did that *mean*? A couple more were software firms, and I had no idea what they did.

One company called Delphos Inc.—this one actually seemed interesting—had come up with a process for refining and manufacturing some chemical compound called indium phosphide, made of "binary crystals from metallic and nonmetallic elements," whatever that meant. This stuff had "unique optical absorption and transmission properties," its disclosure statement said. Apparently it was used for building a certain kind of laser. From what I could tell, Delphos Inc. had effectively cornered the market on indium phosphide. I was sure that better minds than mine could figure out what massive quantities of indium phosphide were good for. I mean, how many lasers could anyone need?

But here was the interesting part: the Delphos file was stamped ACQUISI-TION PENDING. So Trion was in negotiations to buy the company. The file was thick with financials, which were just a blur before my eyes. There was a document of ten or twelve pages, a term sheet for the acquisition of Delphos by Trion. The bottom line seemed to be that Trion was offering *five hundred million dollars* to buy the company. It looked like the company's officers, a bunch of research scientists from Palo Alto, as well as a venture-capital firm based in London that owned most of the company, had agreed to the terms. Yeah, half a billion dollars sure can grease the skids. They were just dotting the *i*'s. An announcement was tentatively scheduled for a week from now.

But how was I supposed to copy these files? It would take forever—hours of standing at a copy machine. By now it was six o'clock in the morning, and if Jock Goddard got in at seven-thirty, you'd better believe Paul Camilletti got in before that. So I really had to get the hell out of here. I didn't have *time* to make copies.

I couldn't think of any other way but to take them. Maybe move some files from somewhere else to fill up the empty space, and then . . .

And then raise all kinds of alarms the second Camilletti or his assistant tried to access the AURORA files.

No. Bad idea.

Instead, I took a key page or two from each of the eight company files, switched on the copying machine, and photocopied them. In less than five minutes I replaced the pages into the file folders and put the copies into my bag.

I was done, and it was time to get the hell out of here. Lifting a single slat in the front office window blinds, I peered out to make sure no one was coming.

By quarter after six in the morning I was back in my own office. For the rest of the day I was going to have to carry around these top-secret AURORA files, but that was better than leaving them in a desk drawer and risk having Jocelyn discover them. I know it sounds paranoid, but I had to operate on the assumption that she might go through my desk drawers. Maybe she was "my" administrative assistant, but her paycheck came from Trion Systems, not me.

Exactly at seven, Jocelyn arrived. She stuck her head in my office, eyebrows up, and said, "Good morning," with a surprised, meaningful lilt.

"Morning, Jocelyn."

"You're here early."

"Yeah," I grunted.

Then she squinted at me. "You—you been here a while?"

I blew out a lungful of air. "You don't want to know," I said.

52

My big presentation to Goddard kept getting postponed and postponed. It was supposed to be at eight-thirty, but ten minutes before, I got an InstaMail message from Flo telling me that Jock's E-staff meeting was running over, let's make it nine. Then another instant message from Flo: the meeting shows no sign of breaking up, let's push it back to nine-thirty.

I figured all the top managers were duking it out over who'd get the brunt of the cuts. They were probably all in favor of layoffs, in some general sense, but not in their own division. Trion was no different from any other corporation: the more people under you on the org chart, the more power you had. Nobody wanted to lose bodies.

I was starving, so I scarfed down a protein bar. I was exhausted also, but too wired to do anything but work some more on my PowerPoint presentation, make it even slicker. I put in an animated fade between slides. I stuck in that stick-figure drawing of the head-scratching guy with the question mark over his head, just for comic relief. I kept paring down the text: I'd read somewhere about the Rule of Seven—no more than seven words per line and seven lines or bullets per page. Or was it the Rule of Five? You heard that, too. I figured Jock might be a little short of patience and attention, given what he was going through, so I kept making it shorter, punchier.

The more I waited, the more nervous I got, and the more minimalist my PowerPoint slides became. But the special effects grew cooler and cooler. I'd figured out how to make 'the bar graphs shrink and grow before your eyes. Goddard would be impressed.

Finally, at eleven-thirty I got a message from Flo saying I could head over to the Executive Briefing Center now, since the meeting was just wrapping up.

People were leaving as I got there. Some I recognized—Jim Colvin, the COO; Tom Lundgren; Jim Sperling, the head of HR; a couple of powerful-looking women. None of them looked very happy. Goddard was surrounded by a gaggle of people who were all taller than him. It hadn't really sunk in before how small the guy was. He also looked terrible—red-rimmed, blood-shot eyes, the pouches under his eyes even bigger than normal. Camilletti stood next to him, and they seemed to be arguing. I heard only snatches.

". . . Need to raise the metabolism of this place," Camilletti was saying.

". . . All kinds of resistance, demoralization," Goddard muttered.

"The best way to deal with resistance is with a bloody ax," said Camilletti.

"I usually prefer plain old persuasion," Goddard said wearily. The others standing in a circle around them were watching the two go at it.

"It's like Al Capone said, you get a lot more done with a kind word and a gun than with a kind word alone," said Camilletti. He smiled.

"I suppose next you're going to tell me you've got to break eggs to make an omelet."

"You're always one step ahead of me," Camilletti said, patting Goddard on the back as he walked off.

Meanwhile I busied myself hooking up my laptop to the projector built into the conference table. I pushed the button that lowered the blinds electrically.

Now it was just Goddard and me in the darkened room. "What do we have here—a matinee?"

"Sorry, just a slide show," I said.

"I'm not so sure it's a good idea to turn off the lights. I'm liable to fall fast asleep," said Goddard. "I was up most of the night, agonizing over all this bushwa. I consider these layoffs a personal failure."

"They're not," I said, then cringed inwardly. Who the hell was I to try to reassure the CEO? "Anyway," I added quickly, "I'll keep it brief."

I started with a very cool animated graphic of the Trion Maestro, all the pieces flying in from offscreen and fitting perfectly together. This was followed by the head-scratching guy with the question mark floating above his head.

I said, "The only thing more dangerous than being in today's consumer-electronics market is not to be in the market at all." Now we were in a Formula One–type racecar moving at warp speed. "Because if you're not driving the car, you're liable to get run over." Then a slide came up that said TRION CONSUMER ELECTRONICS — THE GOOD, THE BAD, AND THE UGLY.

"Adam."

I turned around. "Sir?"

"What the hell is this?"

Sweat broke out at the back of my neck. "That was just intro," I said. Obviously too much of it. "Now we get down to business."

"Did you tell Flo you were planning to do, what the hell is this called, Power—PowerPoint?"

"No. . . ."

He stood up, walked over to the light switch, and put the lights on. "She would have told you—I hate that crap."

My face burned. "I'm sorry, no one said anything."

"Good Lord, Adam, you're a smart, creative, original-thinking young man. You think I want you wasting your time trying to decide whether to go with Arial eighteen point or Times Roman twenty-four point, for God's sake? How about you just tell me what you think? I'm not a child. I don't need to be spoon-fed this darned cream of wheat."

"I'm sorry—" I began again.

"No, I'm sorry. I shouldn't have snapped at you. Low blood sugar, maybe. It's lunchtime, and I'm starved."

"I can go down and get us some sandwiches."

"I have a better idea," Goddard said.

53

Goddard's car was a perfectly restored 1949 Buick Roadmaster convertible, sort of a custardy ivory, beautifully streamlined, with a chrome grille that looked like a crocodile's mouth. It had whitewall tires and a magnificent red leather interior and it gleamed like something you'd see in a movie. He powered down the cloth top before we emerged from the garage into the sunshine.

"This thing really moves," I said, surprised, as we accelerated onto the highway.

"Three-twenty cubic inch, straight eight," Goddard said.

"Man, it's a beauty."

"I call it my Ship of Theseus."

"Huh," I said, chuckling like I knew what he was talking about.

"You should have seen it when I bought it—it was a real junk heap, my goodness. My wife thought I'd taken leave of my senses. I must have spent five years of weekends and evenings rebuilding this thing from the ground up—I mean, I replaced everything. Completely authentic, of course, but I don't think there's a single part left from the original car."

I smiled, leaned back. The car's leather was buttery-smooth and smelled pleasantly old. The sun was on my face, the wind rushing by. Here I was sitting in this beautiful old convertible with the chief executive officer of the company I was spying on—I couldn't decide if it felt great, like I'd reached the mountaintop, or creepy and sleazy and dishonest. Maybe both.

Goddard wasn't some deep-pockets collector like Wyatt, with his planes

, and boats and Bentleys. Or like Nora, with her Mustang, or any of the Goddard clones at Trion who bought collectible cars at auction. He was a genuine old-fashioned gearhead who really got engine grease on his fingers.

He said, "You ever read *Plutarch's Lives?*"

"I don't think I even finished *To Kill a Mockingbird*," I admitted.

"You don't know what the devil I'm talking about when I call this my Ship of Theseus, do you?"

"No, sir, I don't."

"Well, there's a famous riddle of identity the ancient Greeks loved to argue over. It first comes up in Plutarch. You may recognize the name Theseus, the great hero who slew the Minotaur in the Labyrinth."

"Sure." I remembered something about a labyrinth.

"The Athenians decided to preserve Theseus's ship as a monument. Over the years, of course, it began to decay, and they found themselves replacing each rotting timber with a new one, and then another, and another. Until every single plank on the ship had been replaced. And the question the Greeks asked—it was sort of a philosophers' conundrum—was: Is this really the Ship of Theseus anymore?"

"Or just an upgrade," I said.

But Goddard wasn't joking around. He seemed to be in a serious frame of mind. "I'll bet you know people who are just like that ship, don't you, Adam?" He glanced at me, then back at the road. "People who move up in life and start changing everything about themselves until you can't recognize the original anymore?"

My insides clutched. Jesus. We weren't talking Buicks anymore.

"You know, you go from wearing jeans and sneakers to wearing suits and fancy shoes. You become more refined, more socially adept, you've got more polished manners. You change the way you talk. You acquire new friends. You used to drink Budweiser, now you're sipping some first-growth Pauillac. You used to buy Big Macs at the drive-through, now you're ordering the . . . salt-crusted sea bass. The way you see things has changed, even the way you *think*." He was speaking with a terrifying intensity, staring at the highway, and when he turned to look at me from time to time his eyes flashed. "And at a certain point, Adam, you've got to ask yourself: are you the same person or not? Your costume has changed, your trappings have changed, you're driving

a fancy car, you're living in a big fancy house, you go to fancy parties, you
have fancy friends. But if you have *integrity*, you know deep down that you're
the same ship you always were."

My stomach felt tied up in knots. He was talking about *me*; I felt this
queasy sense of shame, embarrassment, as if I'd been caught doing something
embarrassing. He saw right through me. Or did he? How much *did* he see?
How much did he *know*?

"A man has to respect the person he's been. Your past—you can't be a
captive to it, but you can't discard it, either. It's part of you."

I was trying to figure out how to respond when he announced breezily,
"Well, here we are."

It was an old-fashioned, streamlined, stainless steel dining car from a passenger train, with a blue neon sign in script that said THE BLUE SPOON.
Beneath that, red neon letters said AIR CONDITIONING. Another red neon sign
said OPEN and BREAKFAST ALL DAY.

He parked the car and we got out.

"You've never been here before?"

"No, I haven't."

"Oh, you'll love it. It's the real thing. Not one of those phony retro-repro
things." The door slammed with a satisfying thunk. "It hasn't changed since
1952."

We sat at a booth that was upholstered in red Naugahyde. The table was gray
fake-marble Formica with a stainless steel edge, and there was a tabletop
jukebox. There was a long counter with swiveling stools bolted to the floor,
cakes and pies in glass domes. No 1950s memorabilia, fortunately; no Sha-
Na-Na playing on the jukeboxes. There was a cigarette vending machine, the
kind where you pull on the handles to make the pack drop down. They served
breakfast all day (Country Breakfast—two eggs, home fries, sausage or bacon
or ham, and hotcakes, for $4.85), but Goddard ordered a sloppy joe on a bun
from a waitress who knew him, called him Jock. I ordered a cheeseburger
and fries and a Diet Coke.

The food was a little greasy, but decent. I'd had better, though I made all
the right ecstatic sounds. Next to me on the Naugahyde seat was my workbag

with the pilfered files in it from Paul Camilletti's office. Just their presence made me nervous, as if they were emanating gamma waves through the leather.

"So let's hear your thoughts," Goddard said through a mouthful of food. "Don't tell me you can't think without a computer and an overhead projector."

I smiled, took a gulp of Coke. "Well, to begin with, I think we're shipping way too few of the large flat-screen TVs," I said.

"Too *few?* In *this* economy?"

"A buddy of mine works for Sony, and he tells me they're having serious problems. Basically, NEC, which makes the plasma display panels for Sony, is having some kind of production glitch. We've got a sizeable lead on them. Six to eight months easy."

He put down his sloppy joe and gave me his complete attention. "You trust this buddy of yours?"

"Totally."

"I won't make a major production decision on rumor."

"Can't blame you," I said. "Though the news'll be public in a week or so. But we might want to secure a deal with another OEM before the price on those plasma display panels jumps. And it sure will."

His eyebrows shot up.

"Also," I continued, "Guru looks huge to me."

He shook his head, turned his attention back to his sloppy joe. "Ah, well, we're not the only ones coming out with a hot new communicator. Nokia's planning to wipe the floor with us."

"Forget Nokia," I said. "That's all smoke and mirrors. Their device is so tangled up in turf battles—we won't see anything new from them for eighteen months or more, if they're lucky."

"And you know this—from this same buddy of yours? Or a different buddy?" He looked skeptical.

"Competitive intelligence," I lied. Nick Wyatt, where else? But he'd given me cover: "I can show you the report, if you want."

"Not now. You should know that Guru's run into a production problem so serious the thing might not even ship."

"What kind of problem?"

He sighed. "Too complicated to go into right now. Though you might want to start going to some of the Guru team meetings, see if you can help."

"Sure." I thought about volunteering again for AURORA, but decided against it—too suspicious.

"Oh, and listen. Saturday's my annual barbecue at the lake house. It's not the whole company, obviously—just seventy-five, a hundred people tops. In the old days we used to have everyone out to the lake, but we can't do that any-more. So we have some of the old-timers, the top officers and their spouses. Think you can spare some time away from your competitive intelligence?"

"Love to." I tried to act blasé, but this was a big deal. Goddard's barbecue was really the inner circle. Given how few got invited, the Goddard lake-house party was the subject of major one-upsmanship around the company, I'd heard: "Gosh, Fred, sorry, I can't make it Saturday, I've got a . . . sort of barbecue thing that day. You know."

"No salt-crusted sea bass or Pauillac, alas," Goddard said. "More like burgers, hot dogs, macaroni salad—nothing fancy. Bring your swim trunks. Now, on to more important matters. They have the best raisin pie here you've ever tasted. Their apple is great, too. It's all homemade. Though my favorite is the chocolate meringue pie." He caught the eye of the waitress, who'd been hovering nearby. "Debby," he said, "bring this young man a slice of the apple, and I'll have the usual."

He turned to me. "If you don't mind, don't tell your friends about this place. It'll be our little secret." He arched a brow. "You can keep a secret, can't you?"

54

I got back to Trion on a high, wired from my lunch with Goddard, and it wasn't the mediocre food. It wasn't even that my ideas flew so well. No, it was the plain fact that I'd had the big guy's undivided attention, maybe even admiration. Okay, maybe that was overstating it a little. He took me seriously. Nick Wyatt's contempt for me seemed bottomless. He made me feel like a squirrel. With Goddard I felt as if his decision to single me out as his executive assistant might actually have been justified, and it made me want to work my ass off for the guy. It was weird.

Camilletti was in his office, door closed, meeting with someone important-looking. I caught a glimpse of him through the window, leaning forward, intent. I wondered whether he'd type up notes on his meeting after his visitor left. Whatever he entered into his computer I'd soon have, passwords and all. Including anything on Project AURORA.

And then I felt my first real twinge of—of what? Of guilt, maybe. The legendary Jock Goddard, a truly decent human being, had just taken me out to his shitty little greasy-spoon diner and actually listened to my ideas (they weren't Wyatt's anymore, not in my mind), and here I was skulking around his executive suites and planting surveillance devices for the benefit of that sleazeball Nick Wyatt.

Something was seriously wrong with this picture.

Jocelyn looked up from whatever she was doing. "Good lunch?" she asked. No doubt the admin gossip network knew I'd just had lunch with the CEO.

I nodded. "Thanks. You?"

"Just a sandwich at my desk. Lots to do."

I was heading into my office when she said, "Oh, some guy stopped by to see you."

"He leave a name?"

"No. He said he was a friend of yours. Actually, he said he was a 'buddy' of yours. Blond hair, cute?"

"I think I know who you're talking about." What could Chad possibly want?

"He said you left something for him on your desk, but I wouldn't let him into your office—you never said anything about that. Hope that's okay. He seemed a little offended."

"That's great, Jocelyn. Thank you." Definitely Chad, but why was he trying to snoop around my office?

I logged into my computer, pulled up my e-mail. One item jumped out at me—a notice from Corporate Security sent to "Trion C-Level and Staff":

SECURITY ALERT
Late last week, following a fire in Trion's Department of Human Resources, a routine investigation uncovered the presence of an illegally planted surveillance device.
Such a security breach in a sensitive area is, of course, of great concern to all of us at Trion. Therefore, Security has initiated a prophylactic sweep of all sensitive areas of the corporation, including offices and workstations, for any signs of intrusion or placement of devices. You will be contacted soon. We appreciate your cooperation in this vital security effort.

Sweat immediately broke out on my forehead, under my arms.

They'd found the device I'd stupidly planted during my aborted break-in at HR.

Oh, Christ. Now Security would be searching offices and computers in all the "sensitive" areas of the company, which for sure included the seventh floor.

And how long before they found the thing I'd attached to Camilletti's computer?

In fact—what if there were surveillance cameras in the hallway outside Camilletti's office that had recorded my break-in?

But something didn't seem right. How could Security have found the key logger?

No "routine investigation" would have uncovered the tricked-up cable. Some fact was missing; some link in the chain hadn't been made public.

I stepped out of my office and said to Jocelyn, "Hey, you see that e-mail from Security?"

"Mmm?" She looked up from her computer.

"Are we going to have to start locking everything up? I mean, what's the real story here?"

She shook her head, not very interested.

"I figured you might know someone in Security. No?"

"Honey," she said, "I know someone in just about every department in this company."

"Hmph," I said, shrugged, and went to the rest room.

When I came back, Jocelyn was talking into her telephone headset. She caught my eye, smiled and nodded as if she wanted to tell me something. "I think it's time for Greg to go bye-bye," she said into the phone. "Sweetie, I've got to go. Nice catching up with you."

She looked at me. "Typical Security nonsense," she said with a knowing scowl. "I'm telling you, they'd claim credit for the sun and the rain if they could get away with it. It's like I thought—they're taking credit for a piece of dumb luck. One of the computers down in HR wasn't working right after the fire, so they called in Tech Support, and one of the techs saw something funny attached to the keyboard or something, some kind of extra wiring, I don't know. Believe me, the guys in Security aren't the sharpest knives in the drawer."

"So this 'security breach' is bogus?"

"Well, my girlfriend Caitlin says they really did find some kind of spy thingy, but it's not like those Sherlock Holmeses in Security would've ever found it if they didn't catch a lucky break."

I snorted amusement, went back to my office. My insides had just turned to ice. At least my suspicions were correct—Security got "lucky"—but the bottom line was, they'd discovered the Keyghost. I'd have to get back into Camilletti's office as soon as possible and retrieve the little Keyghost cable before it was discovered.

On my computer screen an instant message box had popped up while I was gone.

```
To:   Adam Cassidy
From: ChadP
Yo Adam - I had a very interesting lunch
with an old friend of yours from WyattTel.
You might want to give me a call
- C
```

Now I felt like the walls were closing in. Trion Security was doing a sweep of the building—and then there was Chad.

Chad, whose tone was definitely threatening, as if he'd learned just what I didn't want him to learn. The "very interesting" part was bad, as was the "old friend" part, but worst of all was "You might want to give me a call," which seemed to say, I've got you now, asshole. He wasn't going to call; no, he wanted me to squirm, to sweat, to call him in a panic . . . and yet how could I not call him? Wouldn't I naturally call him out of simple curiosity about an "old friend"? I had to call.

But right now I really needed to work out. It wasn't as if I could exactly spare the time, but I needed a clear head to deal with the latest developments. On my way out of the office, Jocelyn said, "You wanted me to remind you about the Goddard Webcast at five o'clock."

"Oh, right. Thanks." I glanced at my watch. That was in twenty minutes. I didn't want to miss it, but I could watch it while I was working out, on the little monitors on the cardio equipment. Kill two birds and all that.

Then I remembered my workbag and its radioactive contents. It was just sitting on the floor of my office next to my desk, unlocked. Anyone could open it and see the documents I'd stolen from Camilletti's office. Now what? Lock them in one of my desk drawers? But Jocelyn had a key to my desk. In fact, there wasn't a place I could lock it where she couldn't get in if she wanted.

Returning quickly to my office, I sat down at my desk, retrieved the Camilletti documents from my briefcase, put them in a manila folder, and took them with me to the gym. I'd have to carry these damned files around with me until I got home, when I could secure-fax them, and then destroy them. I didn't tell Jocelyn where I was off to, and since she had access to my MeetingMaker, she knew I had no meeting scheduled.

But she was too polite to ask where I was going.

5 5

At a few minutes before five, the company gym still hadn't gotten crowded. I grabbed an elliptical trainer and plugged in the headphones. While I warmed up, I surfed the cable channels—MSNBC, CSPAN, CNN, CNBC—and caught up on the market close. Both the NASDAQ and the Dow were down: another lousy day. Right at five I switched to the Trion channel, which normally broadcast tedious stuff like presentations, Trion ads, whatever.

The Trion logo came up, then a freeze-frame of Goddard in the Trion studio—wearing a dark blue open-necked shirt, his normally unruly fringe of white hair neatly combed. The background was black with blue dots and looked sort of like Larry King's set on CNN except for the Trion logo prominently positioned over Goddard's right shoulder. I found myself actually getting kind of nervous, but why? This wasn't live, he'd taped it yesterday, and I knew exactly what he was going to say. But I wanted him to do it well. I wanted him to make a case for the layoffs that was persuasive and powerful, because I knew that a lot of people around the company would be pissed off.

I didn't have to worry. He was not only good, he was amazing. In the whole of the five-minute speech there wasn't a phony note. He opened simply: "Hello, I'm Augustine Goddard, president and chief executive officer of Trion Systems, and today I have the unpleasant job of delivering some difficult news." He talked about the industry, about Trion's recent problems. He said, "I'm not going to mince words. I'm not going to call these layoffs 'involuntary attrition' or 'voluntary termination.' " He said, "In our business, no one likes to admit when things aren't going well, when the leadership of a company has misjudged, goofed, made mistakes. Well, I'm here to tell you that we've goofed. We've made mistakes. As the CEO of the company, *I've* made mistakes." He said, "I consider the loss of valuable employees, members of our family, to be a sign of grievous failure." He said, "Layoffs are like a terrible flesh wound—they hurt the entire body." You wanted to give the guy a hug and tell him it's okay, it's not your fault, we forgive you. He said, "I want to assure you that I take full responsibility for this setback, and I will do everything in my power to put this company back on a strong footing." He said that sometimes he thought of the company as one big dogsled, but he was only the lead dog, not the guy on the sled with the whip. He said he'd been opposed to layoffs for years, as everyone knew, but, well, sometimes you have to make the hard decision, just get in the car. He pledged that his management team was going to take good care of every single person affected by the layoffs; he said that he believed the severance packages they were offering were the best in the industry—and the very least they could do to help out loyal employees. He ended by talking about how Trion was founded, how industry veterans had predicted its demise time and time again, yet it had emerged from every crisis stronger than ever. By the time he was done I had tears in my eyes and I'd forgotten all about moving my feet. I was standing there on the elliptical trainer watching the tiny screen like a zombie. I heard loud voices nearby, looked around and saw knots of people gathered, talking animatedly, looking stunned. Then I pulled off the headphones and went back to my workout as the place started filling up.

A few minutes later someone got on the machine next to mine, a woman in Lycra exercise togs, a great butt. She plugged her headphones into the monitor, fooled with it for a while, and then tapped me on the shoulder. "Do you have any volume on your set?" she asked. I recognized the voice even before I saw Alana's face. Her eyes widened. "What are *you* doing here?" she said, part shocked, part accusing.

"Oh, my God," I said. I was truly startled; I didn't need to fake it. "I work here."

"You do? So do I. This is so *amazing*."

"Wow."

"You didn't tell me you—well, then again, I didn't ask, did I?"

"This is incredible," I said. Now I was faking it, and maybe not enthusiastically enough. She'd caught me off guard, even though I knew this might happen, and ironically I was too rattled to sound plausibly surprised.

"What a coincidence," she said. "Unbelievable."

5 6

"How long—how long have you worked here?" she said, getting down off the machine. I couldn't quite read her expression. She seemed sort of dryly amused.

"I just started. Like a couple of weeks ago. How about you?"

"Years—five years. Where do you work?"

I didn't think my stomach could sink any lower, but it did. "Uh, I was hired by Consumer Products Division—new products marketing?"

"You're *kidding*." She stared in amazement.

"Don't tell me you're in the same division as me or something. That I'd *know*—I'd have seen you."

"I used to be."

"*Used* to—? Where are you now?"

"I do marketing for something called Disruptive Technologies," she said reluctantly.

"Really? Cool. What's that?"

"It's boring," she said, but she didn't sound convincing. "Complicated, sort of speculative stuff."

"Hmm." I didn't want to seem too interested. "You catch Goddard's speech?"

She nodded. "Pretty heavy. I had no idea we were in such bad shape. I mean, *layoffs*—you sort of figure layoffs are for everyone else, not for Trion."

"How do you think he did?" I wanted to prepare her for the inevitable moment when she looked me up on the intranet and discovered what I really did now. At least later I'd be able to say I wasn't really holding back; I was sort of polling on my boss's behalf—as if I had anything to do with Goddard's speech.

"I was shocked, of course. But it made sense, the way he presented it. Of course, that's easy for me to say, since I probably have some job security. You, on the other hand, as a recent hire—"

"I should be okay, but who knows." I really wanted to get off the subject of what exactly I did. "He was pretty blunt."

"That's his way. The guy's great."

"He's a natural." I paused. "Hey, I'm sorry about the way our date ended."

"Sorry? Nothing to be sorry about." Her voice softened. "How is he, your dad?" I'd left her a voice message in the morning just to say that Dad had made it.

"Hanging in there. In the hospital he has a fresh cast of characters to bully and intimidate, so he has a whole new reason for living."

She smiled politely, not wanting to laugh at the expense of a dying man.

"But if you're up for it, I'd love to have another chance."

"I'd like that too." She got back on the machine and started moving her feet as she punched numbers into the console. "You still have my number?" Then she smiled, genuinely, and her face was transformed. She was beautiful. Really amazing. "What am I saying? You can look me up on the Trion Web site."

Even after seven o'clock Camilletti was still in his office. Obviously it was a busy time, but I wanted the guy to just go home so I could get into his office before Security did. I also wanted to get home and get some sleep, because I was crashing and burning.

I was trying to figure out how I could get Camilletti on my "buddy list" without his permission so I could know when he was online and when he'd signed off, when suddenly an instant-message box from Chad popped up on my computer screen.

> ChadP: You never call, you never write.☹
> Don't tell me you're too important now for
> your old friends?

I wrote: **Sorry, Chad, it's been crazy.**

There was a pause of about half a minute, then he came back:

You probably knew about these layoffs in advance, huh? Lucky for you you're immune.

I wasn't sure how to answer, so for a minute or two I didn't, and then the phone rang. Jocelyn had gone home, so the calls were routed right to me. The caller ID came up on the screen, but it was a name I didn't recognize. I picked it up. "Cassidy."

"I know *that*," came Chad's voice, heavy with sarcasm. "I just didn't know if you were at home or in your office. I should have figured an ambitious guy like you gets in early and stays late, just like all the self-help books tell you to do."

"How're you doing, Chad?"

"I'm filled with admiration, Adam. For you. More than ever, in fact."

"That's nice."

"Especially after my lunch with your old friend Kevin Griffin."

"Actually, I barely knew the guy."

"Not exactly what he said. You know, it's interesting—he was less than impressed with your track record at Wyatt. He said you were a big party-hearty dude."

"When I was young and irresponsible, I was young and irresponsible," I said, doing my best George Bush the Younger.

"He also had no recollection of your being on the Lucid."

"He's in—what, in *sales*, isn't he?" I said, figuring that if I was going to imply that Kevin was out of the loop it was at least better to be subtle.

"He *was*. Today was his last day. In case you didn't hear."

"Didn't work out?" There was a little tremor in my voice, which I disguised by clearing my throat, then coughing.

"Three whole days at Trion. Then Security got a call from someone at Wyatt saying that poor Kevin had a nasty habit of cheating on his T&E

expense sheets. They had the evidence and everything, faxed it right over. Thought Trion should know. Of course, Trion dropped him like a hot potato. He denied it up and down, but you know how these things work—it's not exactly a court of law, right?"

"Jesus," I said. "Unbelievable. I had no idea."

"No idea they were going to make this call?"

"No idea about Kevin. I mean, like I said, I hardly knew him at all, but he seemed nice enough. Man. Well, I guess you can't do that kind of stuff too often and hope to get away with it."

He laughed so loud I had to pull my ear away from the receiver. "Oh, that's good. You're really good, big guy." He laughed some more, a big hearty laugh, as if I were the best stand-up act he'd ever seen. "You are so right. You can't do that kind of stuff too often and hope to get away with it." Then he hung up.

Five minutes earlier I'd wanted to lean back in my chair and doze off, but now I couldn't, I was way too freaked out. My mouth was dry, so I went to the break room and got an Aquafina. I took the long way, past Camilletti's office. He was gone, his office was dark, but his admin was still there. When I came by half an hour later, both of them were gone.

It was a little after eight. I got into Camilletti's office quickly and easily this time, now that I had the technique down. No one seemed to be around. I pulled the blinds closed, retrieved the little Keyghost cable, and lifted one slat to look around. I didn't see anyone, although I suppose I really wasn't as careful as I should have been. I raised the blinds and then opened the door slowly, looking first right, then left.

Standing against the wall of Camilletti's reception area, his arms folded, was a stocky man in a Hawaiian shirt and horn-rimmed glasses.

Noah Mordden.

He had a peculiar smile on his face. "Cassidy," he said. "Our thirty-four-pin Phinneas Finn."

"Oh, hi, Noah," I said. Panic flooded my body, but I kept my expression blasé. I had no idea what he was talking about, except that I figured it was probably some kind of obscure literary dig. "What are you up to?"

"I could ask you the same thing."

"Come by to visit?"

"I must have gone to the wrong office. I went to the one that said 'Adam Cassidy' on it. Silly me."

"They've got me working for everyone here," I said. It was the best I could think of, and it sucked. Did I really think he'd believe I was *supposed* to be in Camilletti's office? At eight o'clock at night? Mordden was too smart, and too suspicious, for that.

"You have many masters," he said. "You must lose track of whom you really work for."

My smile was tight. Inside I was dying. He knew. He'd seen me in Nora's office, now in Camilletti's office, and he *knew*.

It was over. Mordden had found me out. So now what? Who would he tell? Once Camilletti learned I'd been in his office, he'd fire me in an instant, and Goddard wouldn't stand in his way.

"Noah," I said. I took a deep breath, but my mind stayed blank.

"I've been meaning to compliment you on your attire," he said. "You're looking particularly upwardly mobile these days."

"Thanks. I guess."

"The black knit shirt and the tweed jacket—very Goddard. You're looking more and more like our fearless leader. A faster, sleeker Beta version. With lots of new features that don't quite work yet." He smiled. "I notice you have a new Porsche."

"Yeah."

"It's hard to escape the car culture in this place, isn't it? But as you speed along the highway of life, Adam, you might pause and consider. When everything's coming your way, maybe you're driving in the wrong lane."

"I'll keep that in mind."

"Interesting news about the layoffs."

"Well, you're safe, though."

"Is that a question or a proposition?" Something about me seemed to amuse him. "Never mind. I have kryptonite."

"What does that mean?"

"Let's just say I wasn't named Distinguished Engineer simply because of my distinguished career."

"What kind of kryptonite are we talking about? Gold? Green? Red?"

"At last a subject you know something about. But if I showed it to you, Cassidy, it would lose its potency, wouldn't it?"

"Would it?"

"Just cover your trail and watch your back, Cassidy," he said, and he disappeared down the hall.

PART SIX

DEAD DROP

Dead Drop: Drop; hiding place. Tradecraft jargon for a concealed physical location used as a communications cutout between an agent and a courier, case officer or another agent in an agent operation or network.

—*The International Dictionary of Intelligence*

57

An early night for me—I got home by nine-thirty, a nervous wreck, needing three days of uninterrupted sleep. Driving away from Trion, I kept replaying that scene with Mordden in my head, trying to figure it all out. I wondered whether he was planning to tell someone, to turn me in. And if not, why not? Would he hold it over my head somehow? I didn't know how to handle it; that was the worst part.

And I found myself fantasizing about my great new bed with the Dux mattress and how I was going to collapse onto it the second I got home. What had my life come to? I was fantasizing about sleep. Pathetic.

Anyway, I couldn't go right to sleep, because I still had work to do. I had to get those Camilletti files out of my hot little hands and over to Meacham and Wyatt. I didn't want to keep these documents around a minute longer than I had to.

So I used the scanner Meacham had provided me, turned them into PDF documents, encrypted them, and secure–e-mailed them through the anonymizer service.

Once I'd done that, I got out the Keyghost manual, hooked it up to my computer, and started downloading. When I opened the first document, I felt a spasm of irritation—it was a solid block of gibberish. Obviously I'd screwed this up. I looked at it more closely and saw that there actually was a pattern here; maybe I hadn't botched it after all. I could make out Camilletti's name, a series of numbers and letters, and then whole sentences.

Pages and pages of text. Everything the guy had tapped out on his computer that day, and there was a lot.

First things first: I'd captured his password. Six numbers, ending in 82 — maybe it was the birth date of one of his kids. Or the date of his marriage. Something like that.

But far more interesting were all the e-mails. Lots of them, full of confidential information about the company, about the acquisition of a company he was overseeing. That company, Delphos, I'd seen in his files. The one that they were preparing to pay a shitload of money in cash and stock for.

There was an exchange of e-mails, marked TRION CONFIDENTIAL, about a secret new method of inventory control they'd put in place a few months ago to combat forgery and piracy, particularly in Asia. Some part of every Trion device, whether it was a phone or a handheld or a medical scanner, was now laser-etched with the Trion logo and a serial number. These micromachined identification marks could only be seen under a microscope: They couldn't be faked, and they proved that the thing was actually made by Trion.

There was a lot of information about chip-fabrication manufacturers in Singapore that Trion had either acquired or had invested heavily in. Interesting — Trion was going into the chip-making business, or at least buying up a stake in it.

I felt weird reading all this stuff. It was like going through someone's diary. I also felt really guilty — not because of any loyalty to Camilletti, obviously, but because of Goddard. I could almost see Goddard's gnomelike head floating in a bubble in the air, disapprovingly watching me go through Camilletti's e-mails and correspondence and notes to himself. Maybe it was because I was so wiped out, but I felt lousy about what I was doing. It sounds strange, I know — it was okay to steal stuff about the AURORA project and pass it to Wyatt, but giving them stuff I hadn't been assigned to get felt like an outright betrayal of my new employers.

The letters WSJ jumped out at me. They had to stand for the *Wall Street Journal*. I wanted to see what his reaction to the *Journal* piece was, so I zoomed in on the string of words, and I almost fell out of my seat.

From what I could tell, Camilletti used a number of different e-mail accounts outside of Trion—Hotmail, Yahoo, and some local Internet-access company. These other ones seemed to be for personal business, like dealing with his stockbroker, notes to his brother and sister and father, stuff like that.

But it was the Hotmail e-mails that grabbed my attention. One of them was addressed to BulkeleyW@WSJ.com. It said:

```
Bill—
Shit has hit the fan around here. Will be lot of pressure
on you to give up your source—hang tough. Call me at home
tonite 9:30.
—Paul
```

So there it was. Paul Camilletti was—he *had* to be—the leaker. He was the guy who had fed the damaging information on Trion, on Goddard, to the *Journal*.

Now it all made a creepy kind of sense. Camilletti was helping the *Wall Street Journal* wreak serious damage on Jock Goddard, portraying the old man as out of it, over-the-hill. Goddard had to go. Trion's board of directors, as well as every analyst and investment banker, would see this in the pages of the *Journal*. And who would the board appoint to take Goddard's place?

It was obvious, wasn't it?

Exhausted though I was, it took me a long time, tossing and turning, before I finally fell asleep. And my sleep was fitful, tormented. I kept thinking of little round-shouldered old Augustine Goddard at his sad little diner chowing down on pie, or looking haggard and beaten as his E-staff filed past him out of the conference room. I dreamed of Wyatt and Meacham, bullying me, threatening me with all their talk of prison time; in my dreams I confronted them, told them off, went off on them, really lost it. I dreamed of breaking into Camilletti's office and being caught by Chad and Nora together.

And when my alarm clock finally went off at six in the morning and I raised my throbbing head off the pillow, I knew I had to tell Goddard about Camilletti.

And then I realized I was stuck. How the hell could I tell Goddard about Camilletti when I'd gotten my evidence by breaking into Camilletti's office?

Now what?

5 8

The fact that Cutthroat Camilletti—the jerk who pretended to be so pissed off about the *Wall Street Journal* piece—was actually behind it really chafed my ass. The guy was more than an asshole: he was disloyal to Goddard.

Maybe it was a relief to actually have a moral conviction about something after weeks of being a low-down lying scumbag. Maybe feeling so protective of Goddard made me feel a little better about myself. Maybe by being pissed off about Camilletti's disloyalty I could conveniently ignore my own. Or maybe I was just grateful to Goddard for singling me out, recognizing me as somehow special, better than everyone else. It's hard to know how much of my anger toward Camilletti was really selfless. At times I was struck with this terrible knife-jab of anguish that I really wasn't any better than Camilletti. I mean, there I was at Trion, a fraud who pretended he could walk on water, when all the time I was breaking into offices and stealing documents and trying to rip the heart out of Jock Goddard's corporation while I rode around in his antique Buick. . . .

It was all too much. These four-in-the-morning flop-sweat sessions were wearing me down. They were hazardous to my mental health. Better for me not to think, to operate on cruise control.

So maybe I really did have all the conscience of a boa constrictor. I still wanted to catch that bastard Paul Camilletti.

At least *I* didn't have any choice about what I was doing. I'd been cornered into it. Whereas Camilletti's treachery was of a whole different order. He was actively plotting against Goddard, the guy who brought him into the company, put his trust in him. And who knew what else Camilletti was doing?

Goddard needed to know. But I had to have cover—a plausible way I might have found out that didn't involve breaking into Camilletti's office.

All the way into work, while I enjoyed the jet-engine thrust and roar of the Porsche, my mind was working on solving this problem, and by the time I got to my office, I had a decent idea.

Working in the office of the CEO gave me serious clout. If I called someone I didn't know and identified myself as just plain-vanilla Adam Cassidy, the odds were I wouldn't get my call returned. But Adam Cassidy, "calling from the CEO's office" or "Jock Goddard's office"—as if I were sitting in the office next to the old guy and not a hundred feet down the hall—got all his calls returned, at lightning speed.

So when I called Trion's Information Technology department and told them that "we" wanted copies of all archived e-mails to and from the office of the chief financial officer in the last thirty days, I got instant cooperation. I didn't want to point a finger at Camilletti, so I made it appear that Goddard was concerned about leaks from the CFO's *office*.

One intriguing thing I'd learned was that Camilletti made a habit of deleting copies of certain sensitive e-mails, whether he sent them or received them. Obviously he didn't want to have those e-mails stored on his computer. He must have known, since he was a sharp guy, that copies of all e-mails were stored somewhere in the company's data banks. That's why he preferred to use outside e-mail for some of the more sensitive correspondence— including the *Wall Street Journal.* I wondered whether he knew that Trion's computers captured *all* e-mail that went through the company's fiber-optic cables, whether Yahoo or Hotmail or anything else.

My new friend in IT, who seemed to think he was doing a personal favor for Goddard himself, also got me the phone records of all calls in and out of the CFO's office. No problem, he said. The company obviously didn't tape conversations, but of course they kept track of all phone numbers out and in; that was standard corporate practice. He could even get me copies of anyone's voice mails, he said. But that might take some time.

The results came back within an hour. It was all there. Camilletti had received a number of calls from the *Journal* guy in the last ten days. But far more incriminatingly, he'd placed a bunch of calls to the guy. One or two he might be able to explain away as an attempt to return the reporter's calls—even though he'd insisted he never talked to the guy.

But twelve calls, some of them lasting five, seven minutes? That didn't look good.

And then came copies of the e-mails. "From now on," Camilletti wrote, "call me only on my home number. Do not repeat do NOT call me at Trion anymore. E-mails should go only to this Hotmail address."

Explain *that* away, Cutthroat.

Man, I could barely wait to show my little dossier to Goddard, but he was in meeting after meeting from midmorning to late afternoon—meetings, I noted, that he hadn't asked me to.

It wasn't until I saw Camilletti coming out of Goddard's office that I had my chance.

59

Camilletti saw me as he walked away but didn't seem to notice me; I could have been a piece of office furniture. Goddard caught my eye and his brows shot up questioningly. Flo began talking to him, and I did the index-finger-in-the-air thing that Goddard always did, indicating I just needed a minute of his time. He did a quick signal to Flo, then beckoned me in.

"How'd I do?" he asked.

"Excuse me?"

"My little speech to the company."

He actually cared about what *I* thought? "You were terrific," I said.

He smiled, looked relieved. "I always credit my old college drama coach. Helped me enormously in my career, interviews, public speaking, all that. You ever do any acting, Adam?"

My face went hot. *Yeah, like everyday.* Jesus, what was he hinting at? "No, actually."

"Really puts you at ease. Oh, heavens, not that I'm Cicero or anything, but . . . anyway, you had something on your mind?"

"It's about that *Wall Street Journal* article," I said.

"Okay . . . ?" he said, puzzled.

"I've discovered who the leaker was."

He looked at me as if he didn't understand, so I went on: "Remember, we thought it had to be someone inside the company who was leaking information to the *Journal* report—"

"Yes, yes," he said impatiently.

"It's—well, it's Paul. Camilletti."

"What are you talking about?"

"I know it's hard to believe. But it's all here, and it's pretty unambiguous." I slid the printouts across his desk. "Check out the e-mail on top."

He took his reading glasses from the chain around his neck and put them on. Scowling, he inspected the papers. When he looked up his face was dark. "Where's this from?"

I smiled. "IT." I fudged just a bit and said, "I asked IT for phone records of all calls from anyone at Trion to the *Wall Street Journal*. Then when I saw all those calls from Paul's phone, I thought it might be an admin or something, so I requested copies of his e-mails."

Goddard didn't look at all happy, which was understandable. In fact, he looked fairly upset, so I added, "I'm sorry. I know this must come as a shock." The cliché just came barreling out of my mouth. "I don't really understand it, myself."

"Well, I hope you're pleased with yourself," Goddard said.

I shook my head. "Pleased? No, I just want to get to the bottom of—"

"Because I'm disgusted," he said. His voice shook. "What the hell do you think you're doing? What do you think this is, the goddamned *Nixon White House?*" Now he was almost shouting, and spittle flew from his mouth.

The room collapsed around me: it was just me and him, across a four-foot expanse of desk. Blood roared in my ears. I was too stunned to say anything.

"Invading people's privacy, digging up dirt, getting private phone records and private e-mails and for all I know steaming open envelopes! I find that kind of underhandedness reprehensible, and I don't ever want you doing that again. Now get the hell out of here."

I got up unsteadily, light-headed, shocked. At the doorway I stopped, turned back. "I want to apologize," I said hoarsely. "I thought I was helping out. I'll—I'll go clear out my office."

"Oh, for Christ's sake, sit back down." The storm seemed to have passed. "You don't have *time* to clear out your office. I've got far too much for you to do." His voice was now gentler. "I understand you were trying to protect me. I get it, Adam, and I appreciate it. And I won't deny I'm flabbergasted about

Paul. But there's a right way and a wrong way to do things, and I prefer the right way. You start monitoring e-mails and phone records and then you find yourself tapping phones, and next thing you know you've got yourself a police state, not a corporation. And a company can't function that way. I don't know how they did things at Wyatt, but we don't do 'em that way here."

I nodded. "I understand. I'm sorry."

He put up his palms. "It never happened. Forget about it. And I'll tell you something else—at the end of the day, no company ever failed because one of its executives mouthed off to the press. For whatever unfathomable reason. Now, I'll figure out some way of handling it. My way."

He pressed his palms together as if signifying the talk was over. "I don't need any kind of unpleasantness right now. We've got something far more important going on. Now, I'm going to need your input on a matter of the utmost secrecy." He settled himself behind his desk, put on his reading glasses, and took out his worn little black leather address book. He looked at me sternly over his reading glasses. "Don't ever tell anyone that the founder and chief executive officer of Trion Systems can't remember his own computer passwords. And *certainly* don't tell anyone about the specific type of handheld device I use to store them." Looking closely at the little black book, he tapped at his keyboard.

In a minute his printer hummed to life and spit out a few pages. He reached over, removed the pages, and handed them to me. "We're in the final stages of a major, major acquisition," he said. "Probably the most costly acquisition in Trion history. But it's probably also going to be the best investment we've ever made. I can't give you the details just yet, but assuming Paul's negotiations continue successfully, we should have a deal ready to announce by the end of next week."

I nodded.

"I want everything to go perfectly smoothly. These are the basic specs on the new company—number of employees, space requirements, and so on. It's going to be integrated into Trion immediately, and located right here in this building. Obviously that means that something here has to go. Some existing division's going to have to be moved out of headquarters and onto our Yarborough campus, or Research Triangle. I need you to figure out which division, or divisions, can be moved with the least disruption, to make room for . . . for the new acquisition. Okay? Look over these pages, and when you're done, please shred them. And let me know your thoughts as soon as possible."

"Okay."

"Adam, I know I'm dumping a whole lot on you, but it can't be helped. I need you to call it as you see it. I'm counting on your strategic savvy." He reached over and gave me a reassuring shoulder squeeze. "And your honesty."

60

Jocelyn, thank God, seemed to be taking more and more coffee- and little-girls'-room breaks the longer she worked for me. The next time she left her desk, I took the papers on Delphos that Goddard had given me—I knew it had to be Delphos, even though the company's name wasn't anywhere on the sheets—and made a quick photocopy at the machine behind her desk. Then I slipped the copies into a manila envelope.

I fired off an e-mail to "Arthur" telling him, in coded language, that I had some new stuff to pass on—that I wanted to "return" the "clothing" I'd bought online.

Sending an e-mail from work was, I knew, a risk. Even using Hushmail, which encrypted it. But I was short on time. I didn't want to have to wait until I got home, then maybe have to go back out. . . .

Meacham's reply came back almost instantly. He told me not to send the item to the post-office box but the street address instead. Translation: he didn't want me to scan the documents and e-mail them, he wanted to see the actual hard copies, though he didn't say why. Did he want to make sure they were originals? Did that mean they didn't trust me?

He also wanted them immediately, and for some reason he didn't want to set up a face-to-face. Why? I wondered. Was he nervous about my being tailed or something? Whatever his logic, he wanted me to leave the documents for him using one of the dead drops we'd worked out weeks before.

At a little after six, I left work, drove over to a McDonald's about two miles from Trion headquarters. The men's room here was small, one-guy-at-a-time, and you could lock the door. I locked it, found the paper towel dispenser and popped it open, put the rolled-up manila envelope inside and closed the dispenser. Until the paper towel roll needed changing, no one would look inside — except Meacham.

On the way out I bought a Quarter Pounder — not that I wanted one, but for cover, like I'd been taught. About a mile down the road was a 7-Eleven with a low concrete wall around the parking lot in front. I parked in the lot, went in and bought a Diet Pepsi, then drank as much of it as I could. The rest I poured down a drain in the parking lot. I put a lead fishing weight inside the can from the stash in my glove compartment, placed the empty can on the top of the concrete wall.

The Pepsi can was a signal to Meacham, who drove by this 7-Eleven regularly, that I'd loaded dead drop number three, the McDonald's. This simple bit of spy tradecraft would enable Meacham to pick up the documents without being seen with me.

The handover went smoothly, as far as I could tell. I had no reason to think otherwise.

Okay, so what I was doing made me feel sleazy. But at the same time, I couldn't help feeling a little proud: I was getting good at this spy stuff.

By the time I got home there was an e-mail on my Hushmail account from "Arthur." Meacham wanted me to drive to a restaurant in the middle of nowhere, more than half an hour away, immediately. Obviously they considered this urgent.

The place turned out to be a lavish restaurant-spa, a famous foodie mecca called the Auberge. The lobby's walls were decorated with articles about the place in *Gourmet* and magazines like that.

I could see why Wyatt wanted to meet me here, and it wasn't just the food. The restaurant was set up for maximum discretion—for private meetings, for extramarital affairs, whatever. In addition to the main dining room, there were these small, separate alcoves for private dining, which you could enter and leave directly from the parking lot without having to go through the main part of the restaurant. It reminded me of a high-class motel.

Wyatt was sitting at a table in a private alcove with Judith Bolton. Judith was cordial, and even Wyatt seemed a little less hostile than usual. Maybe that was because I'd been so successful in getting him what he wanted. Maybe he was on his second glass of wine, or maybe it was Judith, who seemed to exert a mysterious sway over him. I was pretty sure there was nothing going on between Judith and Wyatt, at least based on their body language. But they were obviously close, and he deferred to her in a way he didn't defer to anyone else.

A waiter brought me a glass of sauvignon blanc. Wyatt told him to leave, come back in fifteen minutes when he was ready to order. Now we were alone in here: me, Wyatt, and Judith Bolton.

"Adam," said Wyatt as he gnawed on a piece of focaccia, "those files you got from the CFO's office—they were very helpful."

"Good," I said. Now I was Adam? And an actual compliment? It gave me the heebie-jeebies.

"Especially that term sheet on this company Delphos," he went on. "Obviously it's a linchpin, a crucial acquisition for Trion. No wonder they're willing to pay five hundred million bucks in stock for it. Anyway, that finally solved the mystery. That put the last piece of the puzzle into place. We've figured out AURORA."

I gave him a blank look, like I really didn't care, and nodded.

"This whole business was worth it, worth every penny," he said. "The enormous trouble we went to to get you inside Trion, the training, the security measures. The expense, the huge risks—they were *all worth it*." He tipped his wineglass toward Judith, who smiled proudly. "I owe you big-time," he said to her.

I thought: And what am I, chopped liver?

"Now, I want you to listen to me very closely," Wyatt said. "Because the stakes are immense, and I want you to understand the urgency. Trion Systems appears to have developed the most important technological breakthrough since the integrated circuit. They've solved a problem that a lot of us have been working on for decades. They've just changed history."

"Are you sure you want to be telling me this?"

"Oh, I want you taking notes. You're a smart boy. Pay close attention. The age of the silicon chip is over. Somehow Trion's managed to develop an optical chip."

"So?"

He stared at me with boundless contempt. Judith spoke earnestly, quickly, as if to cover over my gaffe. "Intel's spent billions trying to crack this without success. The Pentagon's been working on it for over a decade. They know it'll revolutionize their aircraft and missile navigation systems, so they'll pay almost anything to get their hands on a working optical chip."

"The opto-chip," Wyatt said, "handles optical signals—light—instead of electronic ones, using a substance called indium phosphide."

I remember reading something about indium phosphide in Camilletti's files. "That's the stuff that's used for building lasers."

"Trion's cornered the market on the shit. That was the tip-off. They need indium phosphide for the semiconductor in the chip—it can handle much higher data-transfer speeds than gallium arsenide."

"You've lost me," I said. "What's so special about it?"

"The opto-chip has a modulator capable of switching signals at a hundred gigabytes a second."

I blinked. This was all Urdu to me. Judith was watching him, rapt. I wondered if she got this.

"It's the goddamned fucking *Holy Grail.* Let me put it to you in simple terms. A *single particle* of opto-chip one-*hundredth* the diameter of a human hair will now be able to handle all of a corporation's telephone, computer, satellite, and television traffic at once. Or maybe you can wrap your mind around this, guy: with the optical chip, you can download a two-hour movie in digital format in *one-twentieth of a second,* you get it? This is a fucking quantum leap in the industry, in computers and handhelds and satellites and cable TV transmission, you name it. The opto-chip's going to enable things like this"—he held up his Wyatt Lucid handheld—"to receive flicker-free TV images. It is so vastly superior to any existing technology—it's capable of higher speeds, requiring far lower voltage, lower signal loss, lower heat levels. . . . It's amazing. It's the real deal."

"Excellent," I said quietly. The import of what I'd done was beginning to sink in, and now I felt like a damned traitor to Trion—Jock Goddard's own Benedict Arnold. I had just given the hideous Nick Wyatt the most valuable, paradigm-shifting technology since color TV or whatever. "I'm glad I could be of service."

"I want every fucking last spec," Wyatt said. "I want their prototype. I want the patent applications, the lab notes, everything they've got."

"I don't know how much more I can get," I said. "I mean, short of breaking into the fifth floor—"

"Oh, that too, guy. That too. I've put you in the fucking catbird seat. You're working directly for Goddard, you're one of his chief lieutenants, you've got access to just about anything you want to get."

"It's not that simple. You know that."

"You're in a unique position of trust, Adam," put in Judith. "You can gain access to a whole range of projects."

Wyatt interrupted: "I don't want you holding back a single fucking thing."

"I'm not holding back—"

"The layoffs came as a surprise to you, is that it?"

"I told you there was some kind of big announcement coming. I really didn't know anything more than that at the time."

" 'At the time,' " he repeated nastily. "You knew about the layoffs before CNN did, asshole. Where was *that* intelligence? I have to watch CNBC to find out about the layoffs at Trion when I've got a mole in the fucking *CEO's* office?"

"I didn't—"

"You put a bug in the CFO's office. What happened with that?" His overly tanned face was darker than usual, his eyes bloodshot. I could feel the spray of his spittle.

"I had to pull it."

"*Pull* it?" he said in disbelief. "Why?"

"Corporate Security found the thing I put in the HR department, and they've started searching everywhere, so I had to be careful. I could have jeopardized everything."

"How long was the bug in the CFO's office before you pulled it?" he shot back.

"Not much longer than a day."

"A day would get you a shitload."

"No, it—well, the thing must have malfunctioned," I lied. "I don't know what happened."

Frankly, I wasn't sure why I was holding back. I guess it was the fact that the bug revealed that Camilletti had been the one who'd leaked to the *Wall Street Journal*, and I didn't want Wyatt knowing all of Goddard's private business. I hadn't really thought it through.

"Malfunctioned? Somehow I'm dubious. I want that bug in Arnie Meacham's hand by the end of the day tomorrow for his techs to examine.

And believe me, those guys can tell right away if you've tampered with it. Or if you never put it in the CFO's office in the first place. And if you're lying to me, you fuck, you're *dead*."

"Adam," said Judith, "it's crucial that we're totally open and honest with each other. Don't withhold. Far too many things can go wrong. You're not able to see the big picture."

I shook my head. "I don't *have* it. I had to get rid of it."

"Get *rid* of it?" Wyatt said.

"I was—I was in a tight spot, the security guys were searching offices, and I figured I'd better take the thing out and throw it in a Dumpster a couple of blocks away. I didn't want to blow the whole operation over a single busted bug."

He stared at me for a few seconds. "Don't ever hold anything back from us, do you understand? *Ever*. Now, listen up. We've got excellent sources telling us that Goddard's people are putting on a major press conference at Trion headquarters in two weeks. Some major press conference, some big news. The e-mail traffic you handed me suggests they're on the verge of going public with this optical chip."

"They're not going to announce it if they haven't locked down all the patents, right?" I said. I'd done a little late-night Internet research myself. "I'm sure you've had your minions checking all Trion filings at the U.S. Patent Office."

"Attending law school in your spare time?" Wyatt said with a thin smile. "You file with the Patent Office at the last possible second, asshole, to avoid premature disclosure or infringement. They won't file until just before the announcement. Until then, the intellectual property is kept a trade secret. Which means, until it's filed—which may be any time in the next two weeks—it's open season on the design specs. The clock's ticking. I don't want you to sleep, to rest for a goddamned minute until you have every last fucking detail on the optical chip, are we clear?"

I nodded sullenly.

"Now, if you'll excuse us, we'd like to order dinner." I got up from the table and went out to use the men's room before I drove off. As I came out of the private dining room, a guy walking past glanced at me.

I panicked.

I spun around and went back through the private room to the parking lot.

I wasn't one hundred percent sure at the time, but the guy in the hall looked a whole lot like Paul Camilletti.

62

There were people in my office.

When I got into work next morning, I saw them from a distance—two men, one young, one older—and I froze. It was seven-thirty in the morning, and for some reason Jocelyn wasn't at her desk. In an instant my mind ran through a menu of possibilities, one worse than the next: Security had somehow found something in my office. Or I'd been fired and they were clearing out my desk. Or I was being arrested.

Approaching my office, I tried to hide my nervousness. I said jovially, as if these were buddies of mine who'd dropped by for a visit, "What's going on?"

The older one was taking notes on a clipboard, and the younger one was now bent over my computer. The older one, gray hair and walrus mustache, rimless glasses, said, "Security, sir. Your secretary, Miss Chang, let us in."

"What's up?"

"We're doing an inspection of all the offices on the seventh floor, sir. I don't know if you got the notice about the security violation in Human Resources."

Was that all this was about? I was relieved. But only for a few seconds. What if they'd found something in my desk? Had I left any of my spycraft equipment locked in any of the desk or file cabinet drawers? I made it a habit never to leave anything there. But what if I'd slipped? I was stretched so thin I could easily have left something there by mistake.

"Great," I said. "I'm glad you're here. You haven't found anything, have you?"

There was a moment of silence. The younger one looked up from my computer and didn't reply. The older one said, "Not yet, sir, no."

"I wasn't thinking *I* was a target, necessarily," I added. "Gosh, I'm not that important. I mean anything on this floor, in any of the big guys' offices?"

"We're not supposed to discuss that, but no, sir, we haven't found anything. Doesn't mean we won't, though."

"My computer check out okay?" I addressed the young guy.

"No devices or anything like that have turned up so far," he replied. "But we're going to have to run some diagnostics on it. Can you log in for us?"

"Sure." I hadn't sent any incriminating e-mails from this computer, had I?

Well, yes, I had. I'd e-mailed Meacham on my Hushmail account. But even if the message hadn't been encrypted, it wouldn't have told them anything. I was sure I hadn't saved any files on my computer I wasn't supposed to have. That I was sure of. I stepped over behind my desk and typed in my password. Both security guys tactfully looked away until I was logged in.

"Who has access to your office?" the older man asked.

"Just me. And Jocelyn."

"And the cleaning crew," he persisted.

"I guess so, but I never see them."

"You've never seen them?" he repeated skeptically. "But you work late hours, right?"

"They work even later hours."

"What about interoffice mail? Any delivery person ever come in here when you're out, that you know of?"

I shook my head. "All that stuff goes to Jocelyn's desk. They never deliver to me directly."

"Has anyone from IT ever serviced your computer or phone?"

"Not that I know of."

The younger guy asked, "Gotten any strange e-mails?"

"Strange . . . ?"

"From people you don't know, with attachments or whatever."

"Not that I can recall."

"But you use other e-mail services, right? I mean, other than Trion."

"Sure."

"Ever accessed them from this computer?"

"Yeah, I suppose I have."

"And on any of those e-mail accounts did you ever get any funny-looking e-mail?"

"Well, I get spam all the time, like everyone else. You know, Viagra or 'Add Three Inches' or the ones about farm girls." Neither one of them seemed to have a sense of humor. "But I just delete all those."

"This'll just be five or ten minutes, sir," the younger one said, inserting a disk into my CD-ROM drive. "Maybe you can get a cup of coffee or something."

Actually, I had a meeting, so I left the security guys in my office, not feeling so good about it, and headed over to Plymouth, one of the smaller conference rooms.

I didn't like the fact that they'd asked about outside e-mail accounts. That was bad. In fact, it scared the shit out of me. What if they decided to dig up all my e-mails? I'd seen how easy it was to do. What if they found out I'd ordered copies of Camilletti's e-mail traffic? Would that make me a suspect somehow?

As I passed Goddard's office, I saw that both he and Flo were gone—Jock to the meeting, I knew. Then I passed Jocelyn carrying a mug of coffee. Printed on it was GONE OUT OF MY MIND—BACK IN FIVE MINUTES.

"Are those security goons still at my desk?" she asked.

"They're in my office now," I said and kept going.

She gave me a little wave.

63

Goddard and Camilletti were seated around a small round table along with the COO, Jim Colvin, and another Jim, the director of Human Resources, Jim Sperling, plus a couple of women I didn't recognize. Sperling, a black man with a close-cropped beard and oversize wire-rim glasses, was talking about "targets of opportunity," by which I assume he meant staff they could lop off. Jim Sperling didn't do the Jock Goddard mock turtleneck thing, but he was close enough—a sports-jacket-and-dark-polo-shirt. Only Jim Colvin wore a conventional business suit and tie.

Sperling's young blond assistant slid me some papers listing departments and individual poor suckers that were candidates for the axe. I scanned it quickly, saw that the Maestro team wasn't on there. So I'd saved their jobs after all.

Then I noticed a roster of New Product Marketing names, among them Phil Bohjalian. The old-timer was going to get laid off. Neither Chad nor Nora was on the list, but Phil had been targeted. By Nora, it had to be. Each VP and director had been asked to stack-rank their subordinates and lose at least one out of ten. Nora had obviously singled out Phil for execution.

This seemed to be more or less a rubber-stamp session. Sperling was presenting the list, making a "business case" for those "positions" he wanted to eliminate, and there was little discussion. Goddard looked glum; Camilletti looked intent, even a little jazzed.

When Sperling got to New Product Marketing, Goddard turned to me, silently soliciting my opinion. "Can I say something?" I put in.

"Uh, sure," said Sperling.

"There's a name on here, Phil Bohjalian. He's been with the company something like twenty, twenty-one years."

"He's also ranked lowest," said Camilletti. I wondered whether Goddard had said anything to him about the *Wall Street Journal* leak. I couldn't tell from Camilletti's manner, since he was no more, or less, abrasive to me than usual. "Plus given his tenure with the company, his benefits cost us an arm and a leg."

"Well, I'd question his ranking," I said. "I'm familiar with his work, and I think his numbers may be more of a matter of interpersonal style."

"Style," said Camilletti.

"Nora Sommers doesn't like his personality." Granted, Phil wasn't exactly a buddy of mine, but he couldn't do me any harm, and I felt bad for the guy.

"Well, if this is just about a personality clash, that's an abuse of the ranking system," said Jim Sperling. "Are you telling me Nora Sommers is abusing the system?"

I saw clearly where this could go. I could save Phil Bohjalian's job and jettison Nora, all at the same time. It was hugely tempting to just speak up and slash Nora's throat. No one in this room particularly cared one way or another. The word would go down to Tom Lundgren, who wasn't likely to battle to save her. In fact, if Goddard hadn't plucked me out of Nora's clutches, it would surely have been my name on the list, not Phil's.

Goddard was watching me keenly, as was Sperling. The others around the table were taking notes.

"No," I said at last. "I don't think she's abusing the system. It's just a chemistry thing. I think both of them pull their weight."

"Fine," Sperling said. "Can we move on?"

"Look," said Camilletti, "we're cutting four thousand employees. We can't possibly go over them one by one."

I nodded. "Of course."

"Adam," Goddard said. "Do me a favor. I gave Flo the morning off—would you mind getting my, uh, handheld from my office? Seem to have forgotten it." His eyes seemed to twinkle. He meant his little black datebook, and I guess the joke was for my enjoyment.

"Sure," I said, and I swallowed hard. "Be right back."

Goddard's office door was closed but unlocked. The little black book was on his bare, neat desk, next to his computer.

I sat down at his desk chair and looked around at his stuff, the framed photographs of his white-haired, grandmotherly-looking wife, Margaret; a picture of his lake house. No pictures of his son, Elijah, I noticed: probably too painful a reminder.

I was alone in Jock Goddard's office, and Flo had the morning off. How long could I stay here without Goddard becoming suspicious? Was there time to try to get into his computer? What if Flo showed up while I was there . . . ?

No. Insanely risky. This was the CEO's office, and people were probably coming by here all the time. And I couldn't risk taking more than two or three minutes on this errand: Goddard would wonder where I'd been. Maybe I took a quick pee break before I got his book: that might explain five minutes, no more.

But I'd probably never have this opportunity again.

Quickly I flipped the worn little book open and saw phone numbers, pencil scrawlings on calendar entries . . . and on the page inside the back cover was printed, in a neat hand, "GODDARD" and below that "62858."

It had to be his password.

Above those five numbers, crossed out, was "JUN2858." I looked at the two series of numbers and figured out that they were both dates, and they were both the *same* date: June 28, 1958. Obviously a date of some importance to Goddard. I didn't know what. Maybe his wedding date. And both variants were obviously passwords.

I grabbed a pen and a scrap of paper and copied down the ID and password.

But why not copy the whole book? There might well be other important information here.

Closing Goddard's office door behind me, I went up to the photocopier behind Flo's desk.

"You trying to do my job, Adam?" came Flo's voice.

I whipped around, saw Flo carrying a Saks Fifth Avenue bag. She was staring at me with a fierce expression.

"Morning, Flo," I said offhandedly. "No, fear not. I was just getting something for Jock."

"That's good. Because I've been here longer, and I'd hate to have to pull rank on you." Her stare softened, and a sweet smile broke out on her face.

64

As the meeting broke up, Goddard sidled up to me and put his arm around my shoulder. "I like what you did in here," he said in a low voice.

"What do you mean?"

We walked down the hall to his office. "I'm referring to your restraint in the case of Nora Sommers. I know how you feel about her. I know how she feels about *you*. It would have been the easiest thing in the world for you to get rid of her. And frankly, I wouldn't have put up much of a struggle."

I felt a little uncomfortable about Goddard's affection, but I smiled, ducked my head. "It seemed like the right thing to do," I said.

" 'They that have power to hurt and will do none,' " Goddard said, " 'They rightly do inherit heaven's graces.' Shakespeare. In modern English: When you have the power to screw people over and you don't—well, that's when you get to show who you really are."

"I suppose."

"And who's that older fellow whose job you saved?"

"Just a guy in marketing."

"Buddy of yours?"

"No. I don't think he particularly likes me either. I just think he's a loyal employee."

"Good for you." Goddard squeezed my shoulder, hard. He led me to his office, stopped for a moment before Flo's desk. "Morning, sweetheart," he said. "I want to see the confirmation dress."

Flo beamed, opened the Saks bag, pulled out a small white silk girl's dress, and held it up proudly.

"Marvelous," he said. "Just marvelous."

Then we went into his office and he closed the door.

"I haven't said a word to Paul yet," Goddard said, settling behind his desk, "and I haven't decided whether I will. You haven't told anyone else, right? About the *Journal* business?"

"Right."

"Keep it that way. Look, Paul and I have some differences of opinion, and maybe this was his way of lighting a fire under me. Maybe he thought he was helping the company. I just don't know." A long sigh. "If I do raise it with him—well, I don't want word of it getting around. I don't want any unpleasantness. We have far, far more important things going on these days."

"Okay."

He gave me a sidelong glance. "I've never been out to the Auberge, but I hear it's terrific. What'd you think?"

I felt a lurch in my gut. My face grew hot. That *had* been Camilletti there last night, of all the lousy luck.

"I just—I only had a glass of wine, actually."

"You'll never guess who happened to be having dinner there the same night," Goddard said. His expression was unreadable. "Nicholas Wyatt."

Camilletti had obviously done some asking around. To even try to deny that I was with Wyatt would be suicide. "Oh, that," I said, trying to sound weary. "Ever since I took the job at Trion, Wyatt's been after me for—"

"Oh, is that right?" Goddard interrupted. "So of course you had no choice but to accept his invitation to dinner, hmm?"

"No, sir, it's not like that," I said, swallowing hard.

"Just because you change jobs doesn't mean you give up your old friends, I suppose," he said.

I shook my head, frowned. My face felt like it was getting as red as Nora's. "It's not a matter of friendship, actually—"

"Oh, I know how it goes," Goddard said. "The other guy guilts you into taking a meeting with him, just for old times' sake, and you don't want to be rude to him, and then he lays it on nice and thick. . . ."

"You know I had no intention of—"

"Of course not, of course not," Goddard muttered. "You're not that kind of person. Please. I *know* people. Like to think that's one of my strengths."

When I got back to my office, I sat down at my desk, shaken.

The fact that Camilletti had reported to Goddard that he'd seen me at the Auberge at the same time as Wyatt meant that Camilletti, at least, was suspicious of my motives. He must have thought that I was, at the very least, allowing myself to be wooed, courted, by my old boss. But being Camilletti, he probably had darker thoughts than that.

This was a fucking disaster. I wondered, too, whether Goddard really did think the whole thing was innocent. "I *know* people," he'd said. Was he that naïve? I didn't know what to think. But it was clear that I was going to have to watch my ass very carefully from now on.

I took a deep breath, pressed my fingertips hard against my closed eyes. No matter what, I still had to keep plugging away.

After a few minutes, I did a quick search on the Trion Web site and found the name of the guy in charge of the Trion Legal Department's Intellectual Property Division. He was Bob Frankenheimer, fifty-four, been with Trion for eight years. Before that he'd been general counsel at Oracle, and before that he was at Wilson, Sonsini, a big Silicon Valley law firm. From his photo he looked seriously overweight, with dark curly hair, a five o'clock shadow, thick glasses. Looked like your quintessential nerd.

I called him from my desk, because I wanted him to see my caller ID, see I was calling from the office of the CEO. He answered his own phone, with a surprisingly mellow voice, like a late-night radio DJ on a soft rock station.

"Mr. Frankenheimer, this is Adam Cassidy in the CEO's office."

"What can I do for you?" he said, sounding genuinely cooperative.

"We'd like to review all the patent applications for department three twenty-two."

It was bold, and definitely risky. What if he happened to mention it to Goddard? That would be just about impossible to explain.

A long pause. "The AURORA project."

"Right," I said casually. "I know we're supposed to have all the copies on file here, but I've just spent the last two hours looking all over the place, and I just can't find them, and Jock's really in a snit about this." I lowered my voice. "I'm new here—I just started—and I don't want to fuck this up."

Another pause. Frankenheimer's voice suddenly seemed cooler, less cooperative, like I'd pressed the wrong button. "Why are you calling me?"

I didn't know what he meant, but it was clear I'd just stepped in it. "Because I figure you're the one guy who can save my job," I said with a little mordant chuckle.

"You think I have copies here?" he said tightly.

"Well, do you know where the copies of the filings are, then?"

"Mr. Cassidy, I've got a team of six top-notch intellectual-property attorneys here in house who can handle just about anything that's thrown at them. But the AURORA filings? Oh, no. Those have to be handled by outside counsel. Why? Allegedly for reasons of 'corporate security.' " His voice got steadily louder, and he sounded really pissed off. " 'Corporate security.' Because presumably outside counsel practice better security than Trion's own people. So I ask you: What kind of message is that supposed to send?" He wasn't sounding so mellow anymore.

"That's not right," I said. "So who *is* handling the filings?"

Frankenheimer exhaled. He was a bitter, angry man, a prime heart-attack candidate. "I wish I could tell you. But obviously we can't be trusted with that information either. What's that our culture badges say, 'Open Communication'? I love that. I think I'm going to have that printed on our T-shirts for the Corporate Games."

When I hung up, I passed by Camilletti's office on the way to the men's room, and then I did a double take.

Sitting in Paul Camilletti's office, a grave look on his face, was my old buddy.

Chad Pierson.

I quickened my stride, not wanting to be seen by either of them through the glass walls of Camilletti's office. Though *why* I didn't want to be seen, I had no idea. I was running on instinct by now.

Jesus, did Chad even *know* Camilletti? He'd never said he did, and given

Chad's modest and unassuming demeanor, it seemed just the sort of thing he'd have gloated about to me. I couldn't think of any legitimate—or at least innocent—reason why the two of them might be talking. And it sure as hell wasn't social: Camilletti wouldn't waste his time on a worm like Chad.

The only plausible explanation was the one I most dreaded: that Chad had taken his suspicions about me right to the top, or as close to the top as he could get. But why Camilletti?

No doubt Chad had it in for me, and once he'd heard about a new hire from Wyatt Telecom, he'd probably flushed Kevin Griffin out in an effort to gather dirt on me. And he'd got lucky.

But had he really?

I mean, how much did Kevin Griffin really know about me? He knew rumors, gossip; he might claim to know something about my past history at Wyatt. Yet here was a guy whose own reputation was in question. Whatever Wyatt Security had told Trion, clearly the folks at Trion believed it—or they wouldn't have gotten rid of him so fast.

So would Camilletti really believe secondhand accusations coming from a questionable source, a possible sleazebag, like Kevin Griffin?

On the other hand . . . now that he'd seen me out at dinner with Wyatt, in a secluded restaurant, maybe he would.

My stomach was starting to ache. I wondered if I was getting an ulcer.

Even if I was, that would be the least of my problems.

65

The next day, Saturday, was Goddard's barbecue. It took me an hour and a half to get to Goddard's lake house, a lot of it on narrow back roads. On the way I called Dad from my cell, which was a mistake. I talked a little to Antwoine, and then Dad got on, huffing and puffing, his usual charming self, and demanded I come over now.

"Can't, Dad," I said. "I've got a business thing I have to do." I didn't want to say I had to go to a barbecue at the CEO's country house. My mind spun through Dad's possible responses and hit overload. There was his corrupt-CEO rant, the Adam-as-pathetic-brownnoser rant, the you-don't-know-who-you-are rant, the rich-people-rub-your-face-in-their-wealth rant, the whassa-matter-you-don't-want-to-spend-time-with-your-dying-father rant. . . .

"You need something?" I added, knowing he'd never admit he needed anything.

"I don't need anything," he said testily. "Not if you're too busy."

"Let me come by tomorrow morning, okay?"

Dad was silent, letting me know I'd pissed him off, and then put Antwoine on the phone. The old man was back to being his usual asshole self.

I ended the call when I reached the house. The place was marked with a simple wooden sign on a post, just GODDARD and a number. Then a long, rutted dirt path through dense woods that suddenly broadened out into a big circular drive crunchy with crushed clamshells. A kid in a green shirt was serving temporary valet duty. Reluctantly I handed him the keys to the Porsche.

The house was a sprawling, gray-shingled, comfortable-looking place that looked like it had been built in the late nineteenth century or so. It was set on a bluff overlooking the lake, with four fat stone chimneys and ivy climbing on the shingles. In front was a huge, rolling lawn that smelled like it had just been mowed and, here and there, massive old oak trees and gnarled pines.

Twenty or thirty people were standing around on the lawn in shorts and T-shirts, holding drinks. A bunch of kids were running back and forth, shouting and tossing balls, playing games. A pretty blond girl was sitting at a card table in front of the veranda. She smiled and found my name tag and handed it to me.

The main action seemed to be on the other side of the house, the back lawn that sloped gently down to a wooden dock on the water. There the crowd was thicker. I looked around for a familiar face, didn't see anyone. A stout woman of about sixty in a burgundy caftan, with a very wrinkled face and snow-white hair, came up to me.

"You look lost," she said kindly. Her voice was deep and hoarse, and her face was as weathered and picturesque as the house.

I knew right away she had to be Goddard's wife. She was every bit as homely as advertised. Mordden was right: she really did look kind of like a shar-pei puppy.

"I'm Margaret Goddard. And you must be Adam."

I extended my hand, flattered that she'd somehow recognized me until I remembered that my name was on the front of my shirt. "Nice to meet you, Mrs. Goddard," I said.

She didn't correct me, tell me to call her Margaret. "Jock's told me quite a bit about you." She held on to my hand for a long time and nodded, her small brown eyes widening. She looked impressed, unless I was imagining it. She drew closer. "My husband's a cynical old codger, and he's not easily impressed. So you *must* be good."

A screened-in porch wrapped around the back of the house. I passed a couple of large black Cajun grills with plumes of smoke rising from the glowing charcoal. A couple of girls in white uniforms were tending sizzling burgers and steaks and chicken. A long bar had been set up nearby, covered in a white linen tablecloth, where a couple of college-age guys were pouring mixed drinks and soft drinks and beers into clear plastic cups. At another table a guy was opening oysters and laying them out on a bed of ice.

As I approached the veranda, I began to recognize people, most of them fairly high-ranking Trion executives and spouses and kids. Nancy Schwartz, senior vice president of the Business Solutions Unit, a small, dark-haired, worried-looking woman wearing a Day-Glo orange Trion T-shirt from last year's Corporate Games, was playing a game of croquet with Rick Durant, the chief marketing officer, tall and slim and tanned with blow-dried black hair. They both looked gloomy. Goddard's admin, Flo, in a silk Hawaiian muumuu, floral and dramatic, was swanning around as if she were the real hostess.

Then I caught sight of Alana, long legs tan against white shorts. She saw me at the same instant, and her eyes seemed to light up. She looked surprised. She gave me a quick furtive wave and a smile, and she turned away. I had no idea what that was supposed to mean, if anything. Maybe she wanted to be discreet about our relationship, the old don't-fish-off-the-company-pier thing.

I passed my old boss, Tom Lundgren, who was dressed in one of those hideous golf shirts with gray and bright pink stripes. He was clutching a bottle of water and nervously stripping off the label in a long perfect ribbon as he listened with a fixed grin to an attractive black woman who was probably Audrey Bethune, a vice president and the head of the Guru team. Standing slightly behind him was a woman I took to be Lundgren's wife, dressed in an identical golfing outfit, her face almost as red and chafed as his. A gangly little boy was grabbing at her elbow and pleading about something in a squeaky voice.

Fifty feet away or so, Goddard was laughing with a small knot of guys who looked familiar. He was drinking from a bottle of beer and wearing a blue button-down shirt rolled up at the sleeves, a pair of neatly creased, cuffed khakis, a navy-blue cloth belt with whales on it, and battered brown moccasins. The ultimate prepster country baron. A little girl ran up to him, and he leaned over and magically extracted a coin from her ear. She squealed in surprise. He handed her the coin, and she ran off, shrieking with excitement.

He said something else, and his audience laughed as if he were Jay Leno and Eddie Murphy and Rodney Dangerfield all rolled into one. To one side of him was Paul Camilletti, in neatly pressed, faded jeans and a white button-down shirt, also with the sleeves rolled up. *He'd* gotten the appropriate-dress memo, even if I hadn't—I had on a pair of khaki shorts and a polo shirt.

Facing him was Jim Colvin, the COO, his sandpiper legs pasty-white under plain gray Bermuda shorts. A real fashion show this was. Goddard looked up, caught my eye, and beckoned me over.

As I started toward him, someone came out of nowhere and clutched my arm. Nora Sommers, in a pink knit shirt with the collar standing up and over-sized khaki shorts, looked thrilled to see me. "Adam!" she exclaimed. "How nice to see you here! Isn't this a *marvelous* place?"

I nodded, smiled politely. "Is your daughter here?"

She looked suddenly uncomfortable. "Megan's going through a difficult stage, poor thing. She never wants to spend time with me." Funny, I thought, I'm going through the exact same stage. "She'd rather ride horses with her father than waste an afternoon with her mother and her mother's boring work friends."

I nodded. "Excuse me—"

"Have you had a chance to see Jock's car collection? It's in the garage over there." She pointed toward a barnlike building a few hundred feet across the lawn. "You *have* to see the cars. They're *glorious!*"

"I will, thanks," I said, and took a step toward Goddard's little gang.

Nora's clutch on my arm tightened. "Adam, I've been meaning to tell you, I am *so* happy for your success. It really says something about Jock that he was willing to take a chance on you, doesn't it? Place his confidence in you? I'm just so *happy* for you!" I thanked her warmly and extricated my arm from her claw.

I reached Goddard and stood politely off to one side until he saw me and waved me over. He introduced me to Stuart Lurie, the exec in charge of Enterprise Solutions, who said, "How's it going, guy?" and gave me a soul clasp. He was a very good-looking guy of around forty, prematurely bald and shaved short on the sides so it all looked sort of deliberate and cool.

"Adam's the future of Trion," Goddard said.

"Well, hey, nice to meet the future!" said Lurie with just the slightest hint of sarcasm. "You're not going to pull a coin from *his* ear, Jock, are you?"

"No need to," Jock said. "Adam's always pulling rabbits out of hats, right, Adam?" Goddard put his arm around my shoulder, an awkward gesture since I was so much taller than him. "Come with me," he said quietly.

He guided me toward the screened porch. "In a little while I'm going to be doing my traditional little ceremony," he said as we climbed the wooden steps. I held the screen door open for him. "I give out little gifts, silly little things—gag gifts, really." I smiled, wondering why he was telling me this.

We passed through the screened porch, with its old wicker furniture, into a mudroom and then into the main part of the house. The floors were old wide-board pine, and they squeaked as we walked over them. The walls were all painted creamy white, and everything seemed bright and cheery and homey. It had that indescribable old-house smell. Everything seemed comfortable and lived-in and real. This was the house of a rich man with no pretensions, I thought. We went down a wide hallway past a sitting room with a big stone fireplace, then turned a corner into a narrow hall with a tile floor. Trophies and stuff were on shelves on either side of the hall. Then we entered a small book-lined room with a long library table in the center, a computer and printer on it and several huge cardboard boxes. This was obviously Goddard's study.

"The old bursitis is acting up," he apologized, indicating the big cartons on the library table, which were heaped with what looked like wrapped gifts. "You're a strapping young man. If you wouldn't mind carrying these out to where the podium's set up, near the bar. . . ."

"Not at all," I said, disappointed, but not showing it. I lifted one of the enormous boxes, which was not only heavy but unwieldy, unevenly weighted and so bulky that I could barely see in front of me as I walked.

"I'll guide you out of here," Goddard said. I followed him into the narrow corridor. The box scraped against the shelves on both sides, and I had to turn it sort of sideways and up to maneuver it through. I could feel the box nudge something. There was a loud crash, the sound of glass shattering.

"Oh, shit," I blurted out.

I twisted the box so I could see what had just happened. I stared: I must have knocked one of the trophies off a shelf. It lay in a dozen golden shards all over the tile floor. It was the kind of trophy that looked like solid gold but was actually some kind of gilt-painted ceramic or something.

"Oh, God, I'm sorry," I said, setting down the box and crouching down to pick up the pieces. I'd been so careful with the box, but somehow I must have knocked against it, I didn't know how.

Goddard glanced around and he turned white. "Forget it," he said in a strained voice.

I collected as many of the shards as I could. It was—it had been—a golden statuette of a running football player. There was a fragment of a helmet, a fist, a little football. The base was wood with a brass plaque that said 1995 CHAMPIONS—LAKEWOOD SCHOOL—ELIJAH GODDARD—QUARTERBACK.

Elijah Goddard, according to Judith Bolton, was Goddard's dead son.

"Jock," I said, "I'm so sorry." One of the jagged pieces sliced painfully into my palm.

"I said, forget about it," Goddard said, his voice steely. "It's nothing. Now come on, let's get going."

I didn't know what to do, I felt so shitty about destroying this artifact of his dead son. I wanted to clean the mess up, but I also didn't want to piss him off further. So much for all the goodwill I'd built up with the old guy. The cut in my palm was now oozing blood.

"Mrs. Walsh will clean this up," he said, a hard edge to his voice. "Come on, please take these gifts outside." He went down the hall and disappeared somewhere. Meanwhile, I lifted the box and carried it, with extreme caution, down the narrow corridor and then out of the house. I left a smeary handprint of blood on the cardboard.

When I returned for the second box, I saw Goddard sitting in a chair in a corner of his study. He was hunched over, his head in shadow, and he was holding the wooden trophy base in both hands. I hesitated, not sure what I should do, whether I should get out of here, leave him alone, or whether I should keep moving the boxes and pretend I didn't see him.

"He was a sweet kid," Goddard suddenly said, so quietly that at first I thought I'd imagined it. I stopped moving. His voice was low and hoarse and faint, not much louder than a whisper. "An athlete, tall and broad in the chest, like you. And he had a . . . gift for happiness. When he walked into a room, you just felt the mood lifting. He made people feel good. He was beautiful, and he was kind, and there was this—this *spark* in his eyes." He slowly raised his head and stared into the middle distance. "Even when he was a baby, he almost never cried or fussed or . . ."

Goddard's voice trailed off, and I stood there in the middle of the room, frozen in place, just listening. I'd balled up a napkin in my hand to soak up the blood, and I could feel it getting wet. "You would have liked him," Goddard said. He was looking toward me but somehow not *at* me, as if he were seeing his son where I was standing. "It's true. You boys would have been friends."

"I'm sorry I never met him."

"Everybody loved him. This was a kid who was put on the earth to make everybody happy—he had a spark, he had the best sm—" His voice cracked. "The best—smile. . . ." Goddard lowered his head, and his shoulders shook. After a minute he said, "One day I got a call at the office from Margaret. She was screaming. . . . She'd found him in his bedroom. I drove home, I couldn't think straight. . . . Elijah had dropped out of Haverford his junior year— really, they kicked him out, his grades had gone to shit, he stopped going to classes. But I couldn't get him to talk about it. I had a good idea he was on drugs, of course, and I tried to talk to him, but it was like talking to a stone wall. He moved back in, spent most of his time in his room or going out with kids I didn't know. Later I heard from one of his friends that he'd gotten into heroin at the beginning of junior year. This wasn't some juvenile delinquent, this was a gifted, sweet-natured fellow, a good kid. . . . But at some point he started . . . what's the expression, shooting up? And it changed him. The light in his eyes was gone. He started to lie all the time. It was as if he was trying to erase everything he was. Do you know what I mean?" Goddard looked up again. Tears were now running down his face.

I nodded.

A few slow seconds ticked by before he went on. "He was searching for something, I guess. He needed something the world couldn't give him. Or maybe he cared too much, and he decided he needed to kill that part of him." His voice thickened again. "And then the rest of him."

"Jock," I began, wanting him to stop.

"The medical examiner ruled it an overdose. He said there was no question it was deliberate, that Elijah knew what he was doing." He covered his eyes with a pudgy hand. "You ask yourself, what should I have done differently? How did I screw him up? I even threatened to have him arrested once. We tried to get him to go into rehab. I was on the verge of packing him off there, *making* him go, but I never got the chance. And I asked myself over and over again: Was I too hard on him, too stern? Or not hard enough? Was I too involved in my own work?—I think I was. I was far too driven in those days. I was too goddamned busy building Trion to be a real father to him."

Now he looked directly at me, and I could see the anguish in his eyes. It felt like a dagger in my gut. My own eyes got moist.

"You go off to work and you build your little kingdom," he said, "and you lose track of what matters." He blinked hard. "I don't want you to lose track, Adam. Not ever."

Goddard looked smaller, and wizened, and a hundred years old. "He was lying on his bed covered in drool and piss like an infant, and I cradled him in my arms just like he was a baby. Do you know what it's like seeing your child in a coffin?" he whispered. I felt goose bumps, and I had to look away from him. "I thought I'd never go back to work. I thought I'd never get over it. Margaret says I never have. For almost two months I stayed home. I couldn't figure out the reason I was alive anymore. Something like this happens and you—you question the value of everything."

He seemed to remember he had a handkerchief in his pocket, and he pulled it out, mopped his face. "Ah, look at me," he said with a deep sigh, and unexpectedly he sort of chuckled. "Look at the old fool. When I was your age I imagined that when I got to be as old as I am now I'd have discovered the meaning of life." He smiled sadly. "And I'm no closer now to knowing the meaning of life than I ever was. Oh, I know what it's *not* about. By process of elimination. I had to lose a son to learn that. You get your big house and your fancy car, and maybe they put you on the cover of *Fortune* magazine, and you think you've got it all figured out, right? Until God sends you a little telegram saying, 'Oh, forgot to mention, none of that means a thing. And everyone you love on this earth—they're really just on loan, you see. And you'd better love 'em while you can.' " A tear rolled slowly down his cheek. "To this day I ask myself, did I ever know Elijah? Maybe not. I thought I did. I do know I loved him, more than I ever thought I could love someone. But did I really *know* my boy? I couldn't tell you." He shook his head slowly, and I could see him begin to take hold of himself. "Your dad's goddamned lucky, whoever he is, so goddamned lucky, and he'll never know it. He's got a son like you, a son who's still with him. I know he's got to be proud of you."

"I'm not so sure of that," I said softly.

"Oh, I am," Goddard said. "Because I know *I'd* be."

PART SEVEN
CONTROL

Control: Power exerted over an agent or double agent to prevent his defection or redoubling (so-called "tripling").

—*The International Dictionary of Intelligence*

66

The next morning I checked my e-mail at home and found a message from "Arthur":

```
Boss very impressed by your presentation & wants to see
more right away.
```

I stared at it for a minute, and I decided not to reply.

A little while later I showed up, unannounced, at my dad's apartment, with a box of Krispy Kreme donuts. I parked in a space right in front of his triple-decker. I knew Dad spent all his time staring out the window, when he wasn't watching TV. He didn't miss anything that was going on outside.

I'd just come from the car wash, and the Porsche was a gleaming hunk of obsidian, a thing of beauty. I was stoked. Dad hadn't seen it yet. His "loser" son, a loser no more, was arriving in style—in a chariot of 450 horsepower.

My father was stationed in his usual spot in front of the TV, watching some kind of low-rent investigative show about corporate scandals. Antwoine was sitting next to him in the less comfortable chair, reading one of those color supermarket tabloids that all look alike; I think it was the *Star*.

Dad glanced up, saw the donut carton I was waving at him, and he shook his head. "Nah," he said.

"I'm pretty sure there's a chocolate frosted in here. Your favorite."

"I can't eat that shit anymore. Mandingo here's got a gun to my head. Why don't you offer him one?"

Antwoine shook his head too. "No thanks, I'm trying to lose a few pounds. You're the devil."

"What is this, Jenny Craig headquarters?" I set down the box of donuts on the maple-veneer coffee table next to Antwoine. Dad still hadn't said anything about the car, but I figured he'd probably been too absorbed in his TV show. Plus his vision wasn't all that great.

"Soon as you leave this guy's going to start crackin' the whip, making me do laps around the room," Dad said.

"He doesn't stop, does he?" I said to Dad.

Dad's face was more amused than angry. "Whatever floats his boat," he said. "Though nothing seems to get him off like keeping me off my smokes."

The tension between the two of them seemed to have ebbed into some kind of a resigned stalemate. "Hey, you look a lot better, Dad," I lied.

"Bullshit," he said, his eyes riveted on the pseudo-investigative TV story. "You still working at that new place?"

"Yeah," I said. I smiled bashfully, figured it was time to tell him the big news. "In fact—"

"Let me tell you something," he said, finally turning his gaze away from the TV and giving me a rheumy stare. He pointed back at the TV without looking at it. "These S.O.B.s—these bastards—they'll cheat you out of every last fucking nickel if you let them."

"Who, the corporations?"

"The corporations, the CEOs, with their stock options and their big fat pensions and their sweetheart deals. They're all out for themselves, every last one of them, and don't you forget it."

I looked down at the carpet. "Well," I said quietly, "not all of them."

"Oh, don't kid yourself."

"Listen to your father," Antwoine said, not looking up from the *Star.* There almost seemed to be a little affection in his voice. "The man's a fount of wisdom."

"Actually, Dad, I happen to know a little something about CEOs. I just got a huge promotion—I was just made executive assistant to the CEO of Trion."

There was just silence. I thought he hadn't been listening. He was staring at the TV. I thought that might have sounded a little arrogant, so I softened it a bit: "It's really a big deal, Dad."

More silence.

I was about to repeat it when he said, "Executive assistant? What's that, like a secretary?"

"No, no. It's, like, high-level stuff. Brainstorming and everything."

"So what exactly do you do all day?"

The guy had emphysema, but he knew just how to take the wind out of me. "Never mind, Dad," I said. "I'm sorry I brought it up." I was, too. Why the hell did I care what he thought?

"No, really. I'm curious what you did to get that slick new set of wheels out there."

So he had noticed, after all. I smiled. "Pretty nice, huh?"

"How much that vehicle cost you?"

"Well, actually—"

"Per month, I'm talking." He took a long suck of oxygen.

"Nothing."

"Nothing," he repeated, as if he didn't get it.

"Nada. Trion covers the lease totally. It's a perk of my new job."

He breathed in again. "A perk."

"Same with my new apartment."

"You moved?"

"I thought I told you. Two thousand square feet in that new Harbor Suites building. And Trion pays for it."

Another intake of breath. "You proud?" he said.

I was stunned. I'd never heard him say that word before, I didn't think. "Yeah," I said, blushing.

"Proud of the fact that they own you now?"

I should have seen the razor blade in the apple. "Nobody owns me, Dad," I said curtly. "I believe it's called 'making it.' Look it up. You'll find it in the thesaurus next to 'life at the top,' 'executive suite,' and 'high net-worth individuals.' " I couldn't believe what was coming out of my mouth. And all this time I'd been railing about being a monkey on a stick. Now I was actually boasting about the bling bling. *See what you made me do?*

Antwoine put down his newspaper and excused himself, tactfully, pretending to do something in the kitchen.

Dad laughed harshly, turned to look at me. "So lemme get this straight." He sucked in some more oxygen. "You don't own the car *or* the apartment, that right? You call that a perk?" A breath. "I'll tell you what that means. Everything they give you they can take away, and they will, too. You drive a goddamn company car, you live in company housing, you wear a company uniform, and none of it's yours. Your whole life ain't yours."

I bit my lip. It wasn't going to do me any good to let loose. The old guy was dying, I told myself for the millionth time. He's on steroids. He's an unhappy, caustic guy. But it just came out: "You know, Dad, some fathers would actually be proud of their son's success, you know?"

He sucked in, his tiny eyes glittering. "Success, that what you call it, huh? See, Adam, you remind me of your mother more and more."

"Oh, yeah?" I told myself: keep it in, keep the anger in check, don't lose it, or else he's won.

"That's right. You look like her. Got the same social-type personality—everyone liked her, she fit in anywhere, she coulda married a richer guy, she coulda done a lot better. And don't think she didn't let me know it. All those parent nights at Bartholomew Browning, you could see her, getting all friendly with those rich bastards, getting all dressed up, practically pushing her tits in their faces. Think I didn't notice?"

"Oh, that's good, Dad. That's real good. Too bad I'm not more like *you*, you know?"

He just looked at me.

"You know—bitter, nasty. Pissed off at the world. You want me to grow up to be just like you, that it?"

He puffed, his face growing redder.

I kept going. My heart was going a hundred beats a minute, my voice growing louder and louder, and I was almost shouting. "When I was broke and partying all the time you considered me a fuckup. Okay, so now I'm a success by just about anyone's definition, and you've got nothing but contempt. Maybe there's a reason you can't be proud of me no matter what I do, Dad."

He glared and puffed, said, "Oh yeah?"

"Look at you. Look at your life." There was like this runaway freight train inside me, unstoppable, out of control. "You're always saying the world's divided up into winners and losers. So let me ask you something, Dad. What are you, Dad? What are you?"

He sucked in oxygen, his eyes bloodshot and looking like they were going to pop out of his head. He seemed to be muttering to himself. I heard "Goddamn" and "fuck" and "shit."

"Yeah, Dad," I said, turning away from him. "I want to be just like you." I headed for the door in a slipstream of my own pent-up anger. The words were out and couldn't be unsaid, and I felt more miserable than ever. I left his apartment before I could wreak any more destruction. The last thing I saw, my parting image of the guy, was his big red face, puffing and muttering, his eyes glassy and staring in disbelief or fury or pain, I didn't know which.

6 7

"So you really work for Jock Goddard himself, huh?" Alana said. "God, I hope I didn't ever say anything negative to you about Goddard. Did I?"

We were riding the elevator up to my apartment. She'd stopped at her own place after work to change, and she looked great—black boat-neck top, black leggings, chunky black shoes. She also had on that same delicious floral scent she wore on our last date. Her black hair was long and glossy, and it contrasted nicely with her brilliant blue eyes.

"Yeah, you really trashed him, which I immediately reported."

She smiled, a glint of perfect teeth. "This elevator is about the same size as my apartment."

I knew that wasn't true, but I laughed anyway. "The elevator really is bigger than my last place," I said. When I'd mentioned that I'd just moved into the Harbor Suites she said she'd heard about the condos there and seemed intrigued, so I'd invited her to stop by to check it out. We could have dinner at the hotel restaurant downstairs, where I hadn't had a chance to eat.

"Boy, quite the view," she said as soon as she entered the apartment. An Alanis Morissette CD was playing softly. "This is fantastic." She looked around, saw the plastic wrap still on one of the couches and a chair, said archly, "So when do you move in?"

"As soon as I have a spare hour or two. Can I get you a drink?"

"Hmm. Sure, that would be nice."

"Cosmopolitan? I also do a terrific gin-and-tonic."

"Gin-and-tonic sounds perfect, thanks. So you've just started working for him, right?"

She'd looked me up, of course. I went over to the newly stocked liquor cabinet, in the alcove next to the kitchen, and reached for a bottle of Tanqueray Malacca gin.

"Just this week." She followed me into the kitchen. I grabbed a handful of limes from the almost-empty refrigerator and began cutting them in half.

"But you've been at Trion for like a month." She cocked her head to one side, trying to make sense of my sudden promotion. "Nice kitchen. Do you cook?"

"The appliances are just for show," I said. I began pressing the lime halves into the electric juicer. "Anyway, right, I was hired into new-products marketing, but then Goddard was sort of involved in a project I was working on, and I guess he liked my approach, my ideas, whatever."

"Talk about a lucky break," she said, raising her voice above the electric whine of the juicer.

I shrugged. "We'll see if it's lucky." I filled two French bistro–style tumblers with ice, a shot of gin, a good splash of cold tonic water from the refrigerator, and a healthy helping of lime juice. I handed her her drink.

"So Tom Lundgren must have hired you for Nora Sommers's team. Hey, this is delicious. All that lime makes a difference."

"Thank you. That's right, Tom Lundgren hired me," I said, pretending to be surprised she knew.

"Do you know you were hired to fill my position?"

"What do you mean?"

"The position that opened up when I was moved to AURORA."

"Is that right?" I looked amazed.

She nodded. "Unbelievable."

"Wow, small world. But what's 'Aurora'?"

"Oh, I figured you knew." She glanced at me over the rim of her glass, a look that seemed just a bit too casual.

I shook my head innocently. "No . . . ?"

"I figured you probably looked me up too. I got assigned to marketing for the Disruptive Technologies group."

"That's called AURORA?"

"No, AURORA's the specific project I'm assigned to." She hesitated a second. "I guess I thought that working for Goddard you'd sort of have your fingers into everything."

A tactical slip on my part. I wanted her to think we could talk freely about whatever she did. "Theoretically I have access to everything. But I'm still figuring out where the copying machine is."

She nodded. "You like Goddard?"

What was I going to say, no? "He's an impressive guy."

"At his barbecue you two seemed to be pretty close. I saw he called you over to meet his buddies, and you were like carrying things for him and all that."

"Yeah, real close," I said, sarcastic. "I'm his gofer. I'm his muscle. You enjoy the barbecue?"

"It was a little strange, hanging with all the powers, but after a couple of beers it got easier. That was my first time there." Because she'd been assigned to his pet project, AURORA, I thought. But I wanted to be subtle about it, so I let it drop for the time being. "Let me call down to the restaurant and have them get our table ready."

"You know, I thought Trion wasn't really hiring from outside," she said, looking over the menu. "They must have really wanted you, to bend the rules like that."

"I think they thought they were stealing me away. I was nothing special." We'd switched from gin-and-tonics to Sancerre, which I'd ordered because I saw from her liquor bills that that was her favorite wine. She looked surprised and pleased when I'd asked for it. It was a reaction I was getting used to.

"I doubt that," she said. "What'd you do at Wyatt?"

I gave her the job-interview version I'd memorized, but that wasn't enough for her. She wanted details about the Lucid project. "I'm really not supposed to talk about what I did at Wyatt, if you don't mind," I said. I tried not to sound too priggish about it.

She looked embarrassed. "Oh, God, sure, I totally understand," she said.

The waiter appeared. "Are you ready to order?"

Alana said, "You go first," and studied the menu some more while I ordered the paella.

"I was thinking of getting that," she said. Okay, so she wasn't a vegetarian.

"We're allowed to get the same thing, you know," I said.

"I'll have the paella, too," she told the waiter. "But if there's any meat in it, like sausage, can you leave it out?"

"Of course," the waiter said, making a note.

"I love paella," she said. "I almost never have fish or seafood at home. This is a treat."

"Wanna stick with the Sancerre?" I said to her.

"Sure."

As the waiter turned to go, I suddenly remembered Alana was allergic to shrimp and said, "Wait a second, is there shrimp in the paella?"

"Uh, yes, there is," said the waiter.

"That could be a problem," I said.

Alana stared at me. "How did you know . . . ?" she began, her eyes narrowing.

There was this long, long moment of excruciating tension while I wracked my brain. I couldn't believe I'd screwed up like this. I swallowed hard, and the blood drained from my face. Finally I said, "You mean, you're allergic to it, too?"

A pause. "I am. Sorry. How funny." The cloud of suspicion seemed to have lifted. We both switched to the seared scallops.

"Anyway," I said, "enough talking about me. I want to hear about AURORA."

"Well, it's supposed to be kept under wraps," she apologized.

I grinned at her.

"No, this isn't tit-for-tat, I swear," she protested. "Really!"

"Okay," I said skeptically. "But now that you've aroused my curiosity, are you really going to make me poke around and find out on my own?"

"It's not *that* interesting."

"I don't believe it. Can't you at least give me the thumbnail?"

She looked skyward, heaved a sigh. "Well, it's like this. You ever hear of the Haloid Company?"

"No," I said slowly.

"Of course not. No reason you should have heard of it. But the Haloid Company was this small photographic-paper company that, in the late nineteen-forties, bought the rights to this new technology that had been turned down by all the big companies—IBM, RCA, GE. The invention was something called xerography, okay? So in ten, fifteen years the Haloid Company became the Xerox Corporation, and it went from a small family-run company to a gigantic corporation. All because they took a chance on a technology that no one else was interested in."

"Okay."

"Or the way the Galvin Manufacturing Corporation in Chicago, which made Motorola brand car radios, eventually got into semiconductors and cell phones. Or a small oil exploration company called Geophysical Service started branching out and getting into transistors and then the integrated circuit and became Texas Instruments. So you get my point. The history of technology is filled with examples of companies that transformed themselves by grabbing hold of the right technology at the right time, and leaving their competitors in the dust. That's what Jock Goddard is trying to do with AURORA. He thinks AURORA is going to change the world, and the face of American business, the way transistors or semiconductors or photocopying technology once did."

"Disruptive technology."

"Exactly."

"But the *Wall Street Journal* seems to think Jock's washed up."

"We both know better than that. He's just way ahead of the curve. Look at the history of the company. There were three or four points when everyone thought Trion was on the ropes, on the verge of bankruptcy, and then all of a sudden it surprised everyone and came back stronger than ever."

"You think this is one of those turning points, huh?"

"When AURORA's ready to announce, he'll announce it. And then let's see what the *Wall Street Journal* says. AURORA makes all these latest problems practically irrelevant."

"Amazing." I peered into my wineglass and said oh-so-casually, "So what's the technology?"

She smiled, shook her head. "I probably shouldn't have said even this much." Tilting her head to one side she said playfully, "Are you doing some sort of security check on me?"

68

I knew from the moment she said she wanted to eat at the restaurant at the Harbor Suites that we'd sleep together that night. I've had dates with women where an erotic charge came from "will she or won't she?" This was different, of course, but the charge was even stronger. It was there all along, that invisible line that we both knew we were going to cross, the line that separated us from friends and something more intimate; the question was when, and how, we were going to cross it, who'd make the first move, what crossing it would feel like. We came back up to my apartment after dinner, both a little unsteady from too much white wine and G & Ts. I had my arm around her narrow waist. I wanted to feel the soft skin on her tummy, underneath her breasts, on her upper buttocks. I wanted to see her most private areas. I wanted to witness the moment when the hard shell around Alana, the impossibly beautiful, sophisticated woman cracked; when she shuddered, gave way, when those clear blue eyes became lost in pleasure.

We sort of careened around the apartment, enjoying the views of the water, and I made us both martinis, which we definitely didn't need. She said, "I can't believe I have to go to Palo Alto tomorrow morning."

"What's up in Palo Alto?"

She shook her head. "Nothing interesting." She had her arm around my waist too, but she accidentally-on-purpose let her hand slip down to my butt, squeezing rhythmically, and she made a joke about whether I'd finished unpacking the bed.

The next minute I had my lips on hers, my groping fingertips gently stroking her tits, and she snaked a very warm hand down to my groin. Both of us were quickly aroused, and we stumbled over to the couch, the one that didn't have plastic wrap still on it. We kissed and ground our hips together. She moaned. She fished me greedily out of my pants. She was wearing a white silk teddy under her black shirt. Her breasts were ample, round, perfect.

She came loudly, with surprising abandon.

I knocked over my martini glass. We made our way down the long corridor to my bedroom and did it again, this time more slowly.

"Alana," I said when we were snuggling.

"Hmm?"

"Alana," I repeated. "That means 'beautiful' in Gaelic or something, right?"

"Celtic, I think." She was scratching my chest. I was stroking one of her breasts.

"Alana, I have to confess something."

She groaned. "You're married."

"No—"

She turned to me, a flash of annoyance in her eyes. "You're involved with someone."

"No, definitely not. I have to confess—I hate Ani DiFranco."

"But didn't you—you quoted her. . . ." She looked puzzled.

"I had an old girlfriend who used to listen to her a lot, and now it's got bad associations."

"So why do you have one of her CDs out?"

She'd seen the damned thing next to the CD player. "I was trying to make myself like her."

"Why?"

"For you."

She thought for a moment, furrowed her dark brow. "You don't have to like everything I like. I don't like Porsches."

"You don't?" I turned to her, surprised.

"They're dicks on wheels."

"That's true."

"Maybe some guys need that, but you definitely don't."

"No one 'needs' a Porsche. I just thought it was cool."

"I'm surprised you didn't get a red one."

"Nah. Red's cop bait—cops see red Porsches and they switch on their radar."

"Did your dad have a Porsche? My dad had one." She rolled her eyes. "Ridiculous. Like, his male-menopause, midlife-crisis car."

"Actually, for most of my childhood we didn't even *have* a car."

"You didn't have a *car?*"

"We took public transportation."

"Oh." Now she looked uncomfortable. After a minute she said, "So all this must be pretty heady stuff." She waved her hand around to indicate the apartment and everything.

"Yeah."

"Hmm."

Another minute went by. "Can I visit you at work some time?" I said.

"You can't. Access to the fifth floor is pretty restricted. Anyway, I think it's better if people at work don't know, don't you agree?"

"Yeah, you're right."

I was surprised when she curled up next to me and drifted off to sleep: I thought she was going to take right off, go home, wake up in her own bed, but she seemed to want to spend the night.

The bedside clock said three thirty-five when I got up. She remained asleep, buzzing softly. I walked across the carpet and noiselessly closed the bedroom door behind me.

I signed on to my e-mail and saw the usual assortment of spam and junk, some work stuff that didn't look urgent, and one on Hushmail from "Arthur" whose subject line said, "re: consumer devices." Meacham sounded royally pissed off:

```
Boss extremely disappointed by your failure to reply.
Wants additional presentation materials by 6 pm tomorrow
or deal is endangered.
```

I hit "reply" and typed, "unable to locate additional materials, sorry" and signed it "Donnie." Then I read through it and deleted my message. Nope. I wasn't going to reply at all. That was simpler. I'd done enough for them.

I noticed that Alana's little square black handbag was still on the granite bar where she'd left it. She hadn't brought her computer or her workbag, since she'd stopped at home to change.

In her handbag were her badge, a lipstick, some breath mints, a key ring, and her Trion Maestro. The keys were probably for her apartment and car and maybe her home mailbox and such. The Maestro likely held phone numbers and addresses, but also specific datebook appointments. That could be very useful to Wyatt and Meacham.

But was I still working for them?

Maybe not.

What would happen if I just quit? I'd upheld my side of the bargain, got them just about everything they wanted on AURORA—well, most of it, anyway. Odds were they'd calculate that it wasn't worth hassling me further. It wasn't in their interests to blow my cover, not so long as I could potentially be useful to them. And they weren't going to feed the FBI an anonymous tip, because that would just lead the authorities back to them.

What could they do to me?

Then I realized: I'd already quit working for them. I'd made the decision that afternoon in the study at Jock Goddard's lake house. I wasn't going to keep betraying the guy. Meacham and Wyatt could go screw themselves.

It would have been really easy at that moment for me to slip Alana's handheld into the recharging cradle attached to my desktop computer and hot-link it. Sure, there was a risk of her getting up, since she was in a strange bed, finding me gone, and wandering around the apartment to see where I'd gone. In which case she might see me downloading the contents of her Maestro to my computer. Maybe she wouldn't notice. But she was smart and quick, and she was likely to figure out the truth.

And no matter how fast I thought, no matter how cleverly I handled it, she'd know what I was up to. And I'd be caught, and the relationship would be over, and all of a sudden that mattered to me. I was smitten with Alana, and after only a couple of dates and one night together. I was just beginning

to discover her earthy, expansive, sort of wild side. I loved her loopy, unrestrained laugh, her boldness, her dry sense of humor. I didn't want to lose her
because of something the loathsome Nick Wyatt was forcing me to do.

Already I'd handed over to Wyatt all kinds of valuable information on the
AURORA project. I'd done my job. I was finished with those assholes.

And I couldn't stop seeing Jock Goddard hunched over in that dark corner of his study, his shoulders shaking. That moment of revelation. The trust
he'd put in me. And I was going to violate that trust for Nick Fucking Wyatt?

No, I didn't think so. Not anymore.

So I put Alana's Maestro back into her pocketbook. I poured myself a
glass of cold water from the drinking-water dispenser on the Sub Zero door,
gulped it down, and climbed back into my warm bed with Alana. She muttered something in her sleep, and I snuggled right up next to her and, for the
first time in weeks, actually felt good about myself.

69

Goddard was scurrying down the hall to the Executive Briefing Center, and I struggled to keep up with him without breaking into a run. Man, the old guy moved fast, like a tortoise on methamphetamine. "This darned meeting is going to be a circus," he muttered. "I called the Guru team here for a status update as soon as I heard they're going to slip their Christmas ship date. They know I'm royally pissed off, and they're going to be pirouetting like a troupe of Russian ballerinas doing the 'Dance of the Sugar Plum Fairies.' You're going to see a side of me here that's not so attractive."

I didn't say anything—what could I say? I'd seen his flashes of anger, and they didn't even compare to what I'd seen in the only other CEO I'd ever met. Next to Nick Wyatt he was Mister Rogers. And in fact I was still shaken, moved by that intimate little scene in his lake house study—I'd never really seen another human being lay himself so bare. Until that moment there'd been a part of me that was sort of baffled as to why Goddard had singled me out, why he'd been drawn to me. Now I got it, and it rocked my world. I didn't just want to impress the old man anymore, I wanted his approval, maybe something deeper.

Why, I agonized, did Goddard have to fuck it all up by being such a decent guy? It was unpleasant enough working for Nick Wyatt without this complication. Now I was working against the dad I never had, and it was messing with my head.

"Guru's prime is a very smart young woman named Audrey Bethune, a real comer," Goddard muttered. "But this disaster may derail her career. I really have no patience for screwups on this scale." As we approached the room, he slowed. "Now, if you have any thoughts, don't hesitate to speak. But be warned—this is a high-powered and very opinionated group, and they're not going to show you any deference just because I brung you to the dance."

The Guru team was assembled around the big conference table, waiting nervously. They looked up as we entered. Some of them smiled, said, "Hi, Jock," or "Hello, Mr. Goddard." They looked like scared rabbits. I remembered sitting around that table not so long ago. There were a few puzzled glances at me, some whispers. Goddard sat down at the head of the table. Next to him was a black woman in her late thirties, the same woman I'd seen talking to Tom Lundgren and his wife at the barbecue. He patted the table next to him to tell me to sit by his side. My cell phone had been vibrating in my pocket for the last ten minutes, so I furtively fished it out and glanced at the caller ID screen. A bunch of calls from a number I didn't recognize. I switched the phone off.

"Afternoon," Goddard said. "This is my assistant, Adam Cassidy." A number of polite smiles, and then I saw that one of the faces belonged to my old friend Nora Sommers. Shit, she was on Guru, too? She wore a black-and-white striped suit and she had her power makeup on. She caught my eye, beamed like I was some long-lost childhood playmate. I smiled back politely, savoring the moment.

Audrey Bethune, the program manager, was beautifully dressed in a navy suit with a white blouse and small gold stud earrings. She had dark skin and wore her hair in a perfectly coifed and shellacked bubble. I'd done some quick background research on her and knew that she came from an upper-middle-class family. Her father was a doctor, as was her grandfather, and she'd spent every summer at the family compound in Oak Bluffs on Martha's Vineyard. She smiled at me, revealing a gap between her front teeth. She reached behind Jock's back to shake my hand. Her palm was dry and cool. I was impressed. Her career was on the line.

Guru—the project was code-named TSUNAMI—was a supercharged handheld digital assistant, really killer technology and Trion's only convergence device. It was a PDA, a communicator, a mobile phone. It had the power of a laptop in an eight-ounce package. It did e-mail, instant messages, spreadsheets, had a full HTML Internet browser and a great TFT active-matrix color screen.

Goddard cleared his throat. "So I understand we have a little challenge," he said.

"That's one way of putting it, Jock," Audrey said smoothly. "Yesterday we got the results of the in-house audit, which indicated that we've got a faulty component. The LCD is totally dead."

"Ah hah," Goddard said with what I knew was forced calm. "Bad LCD, is it?"

Audrey shook her head. "Apparently the LCD *driver* is defective."

"In every single one?" asked Goddard.

"That's right."

"A quarter of a million units have a bad LCD driver," Goddard said. "I see. The ship date is in—what is it, now?—three weeks. Hmm. Now, as I recall—and correct me if I'm wrong—your plan was to ship these before the end of the quarter, thus bolstering earnings for the third quarter and giving us all thirteen weeks of the Christmas quarter to rake in some badly needed revenue."

She nodded.

"Audrey, I believe we agreed that Guru is the division's big kahuna. And as we all know, Trion is experiencing some difficulties in the market. Which means that it's all the more crucial that Guru ship on schedule." I noticed that Goddard was speaking in an overly deliberate manner, and I knew he was trying to hold back his great annoyance.

The chief marketing officer, the slick-looking Rick Durant, put in mournfully, "This is a huge embarrassment. We've already launched a huge teaser campaign, placed ads all over the place. 'The digital assistant for the next generation.' " He rolled his eyes.

"Yeah," muttered Goddard. "And it sounds like it won't *ship* until the next generation." He turned to the lead engineer, Eddie Cabral, a round-faced, swarthy guy with a dated flattop. "Is it a problem with the mask?"

"I wish," Cabral replied. "No, the whole damned chip is going to have to be respun, sir."

"The contract manufacturer's in Malaysia?" said Goddard.

"We've always had good luck with them," said Cabral. "The tolerances and quality have always been pretty good. But this is a complicated ASIC. It's got to drive our own, proprietary Trion LCD screen, and the cookies just aren't coming out of the oven right—"

"What about replacing the LCD?" Goddard interrupted.

"No, sir," said Cabral. "Not without retooling the whole casing, which is another six months easy."

I suddenly sat up. The buzzwords jumped out at me. *ASIC . . . proprietary Trion LCD . . .*

"That's the nature of ASICs," Goddard said. "There are always some cookies that get burnt. What's the yield like, forty, fifty percent?"

Cabral looked miserable. "Zero. Some kind of assembly-line flaw."

Goddard tightened his mouth. He looked like he was about to lose it. "How long will it take to respin the ASIC?"

Cabral hesitated. "Three months. If we're lucky."

"If we're *lucky*," Goddard repeated. "Yep, if we're *lucky*." His voice was getting steadily louder. "Three months puts the ship date into December. That won't work at all, will it?"

"No, sir," said Cabral.

I tapped Goddard on the arm, but he ignored me. "Mexico can't manufacture this for us quicker?"

The head of manufacturing, a woman named Kathy Gornick, said, "Maybe a week or two faster, which won't help us at all. And then the quality will be substandard at best."

"This is a goddamned mess," Goddard said. I'd never really heard him curse before.

I picked up a product spec sheet, then tapped Goddard's arm again. "Will you please excuse me for a moment?" I said.

I rushed out of the room, stepped into the lounge area, flipped open my phone.

Noah Mordden wasn't at his desk, so I tried his cell phone, and he answered on the first ring: "What?"

"It's me, Adam."

"I answered the phone, didn't I?"

"You know that ugly doll you've got in your office? The one that says 'Eat my shorts, Goddard'?"

"Love Me Lucille. You can't have her. Buy your own."

"Doesn't it have an LCD screen on its stomach?"

"What are you up to, Cassidy?"

"Listen, I need to ask you about the LCD driver. The ASIC."

When I returned to the conference room a few minutes later, the head of engineering and the head of manufacturing were engaged in a heated debate about whether another LCD screen could be squeezed into the tiny Guru case. I sat down quietly and waited for a break in the argument. Finally I got my chance.

"Excuse me," I said, but no one paid any attention.

"You see," Eddie Cabral was saying, "this is *exactly* why we have to post-pone the launch."

"Well, we can't *afford* to slip the launch of Guru," Goddard shot back.

I cleared my throat. "Excuse me for a second."

"Adam," said Goddard.

"I know this is going to sound crazy," I said, "but remember that robotic doll Love Me Lucille?"

"What are we doing," grumbled Rick Durant, "taking a swim in Lake Fuckup? Don't remind me. We shipped half a million of those hideous dolls and got 'em all back."

"Right," I said. "That's why we have three hundred thousand ASICs, custom-fabricated for the proprietary Trion LCD, sitting in a warehouse in Van Nuys."

A few chuckles, some outright guffaws. One of the engineers said to another, loud enough for everyone to hear, "Does he know about connec-tors?"

Someone else said, "That's hilarious."

Nora looked at me, wincing with fake sympathy, and shrugged.

Eddie Cabral said, "I wish it were that easy, uh, Adam. But ASICs aren't interchangeable. They've got to be pin-compatible."

I nodded. "Lucille's ASIC is an SOLC-68 pin array. Isn't that the same pin layout that's in the Guru?"

Goddard stared at me.

There was another beat of silence, and the rustling of papers.

"SOLC-68 pin," said one of the engineers. "Yeah, that should work."

Goddard looked around the room, then slapped the table. "All right, then," he said. "What are we waiting for?"

Nora beamed moistly at me and gave me the thumbs-up.

On the way back to my office I pulled out my cell phone again. Five messages, all from the same number, and one marked "Private." I dialed my voice mail and heard Meacham's unmistakable smarmy voice. "This is Arthur. I have not heard from you in over three days. This is not acceptable. E-mail me by noon today or face the consequences."

I felt a jolt. The fact that he'd actually *called* me, which was a security risk no matter how the call was routed, showed how serious he was.

He was right: I had been out of touch. But I had no plans to get back in touch. Sorry, buddy.

The next one was Antwoine, his voice high and strained. "Adam, you need to get over to the hospital," he said in his first message. The second, the third, the fourth, the fifth—they were all Antwoine. His tone was increasingly desperate. "Adam, where the hell are you? Come *on*, man. Get over here *now*."

I stopped by Goddard's office—he was still schmoozing with some of the Guru team—and said to Flo, "Can you tell Jock I've got an emergency? It's my dad."

70

I knew what it was even before I got there, of course, but I still drove like a lunatic. Every red light, every left-turning vehicle, every twenty-miles-an-hour-while-school-is-in-session sign—everything was conspiring to delay me, keep me from getting to the hospital to see Dad before he died.

I parked illegally because I couldn't take the time to cruise the hospital parking garage for a space, and I ran into the emergency room entrance, banging the doors open the way the EMTs did when they were pushing a gurney, and rushed up to the triage desk. The sullen attendant was on the phone, talking and laughing, obviously a personal call.

"Frank Cassidy?" I said.

She gave me a look and kept chattering.

"Francis Cassidy!" I shouted. "Where is he?"

Resentfully she put down the phone and glanced at her computer screen. "Room three."

I raced through the waiting area, pulled open the heavy double doors into the ward, and saw Antwoine sitting on a chair next to a green curtain. When he saw me he just looked blank, didn't say anything, and I could see that his eyes were bloodshot. Then he shook his head slowly as I approached and said, "I'm sorry, Adam."

I yanked the curtain open and there was my dad sitting up in the bed, his eyes open, and I thought, *You see, you're wrong, Antwoine, he's still with us, the bastard,* until it sank in that the skin of his face was the wrong color, with sort of a yellow waxy tinge to it, and his mouth was open, that was the horrible thing. For some reason that was what I fixated on; his mouth was open in a way it never is when you're alive, frozen in an agonized gasp, a last desperate breath, furious, almost a snarl.

"Oh, no," I moaned.

Antwoine was standing behind me with his hand on my shoulder. "They pronounced him ten minutes ago."

I touched Dad's face, his waxy cheek, and it was cool. Not cold, not warm. A few degrees cooler than it should be, a temperature you never feel in the living. The skin felt like modeling clay, inanimate.

My breath left me. I couldn't breathe; I felt like I was in a vacuum. The lights seemed to flicker. Suddenly I cried out, "Dad. No."

I stared at Dad through blurry tear-filled eyes, touched his forehead, his cheek, the coarse red skin of his nose with little black hairs coming out of the pores, and I leaned over and kissed his angry face. For years I'd kissed Dad's forehead, or the side of his face, and he'd barely respond, but I was always sure I could see a tiny glint of secret pleasure in his eyes. Now he really wasn't responding, of course, and it turned me numb.

"I wanted you to have a chance to say good-bye to him," Antwoine said. I could hear his voice, feel the rumble, but I couldn't turn around and look. "He went into that respiratry distress again and this time I didn't even waste time arguing with him, I just called the ambulance. He was really gasping bad. They said he had pneumonia, probably had it for a while. They kept arguing about whether to put the tube in him but they never had the chance. I kept calling and calling."

"I know," I said.

"There was some time . . . I wanted you to say good-bye to him."

"I know. It's okay." I swallowed. I didn't want to look at Antwoine, didn't want to see his face, because it sounded like he was crying, and I couldn't deal with that. And I didn't want him to see me crying, which I knew was stupid. I mean, if you don't cry when your father dies, something's wrong with you. "Did he . . . say anything?"

"He was mostly cursing."

"I mean, did he—"

"No," Antwoine said, really slowly. "He didn't ask after you. But you know, he wasn't really saying anything, he—"

"I know." I wanted him to stop now.

"He was mostly cursing the doctors, and me. . . ."

"Yeah," I said, staring at Dad's face. "Not surprised." His forehead was all wrinkled, furrowed angrily, frozen that way. I reached up and touched the wrinkles, tried to smooth them out but I couldn't. "Dad," I said. "I'm sorry."

I don't know what I meant by that. What was I sorry for? It was long past time for him to die, and he was better off dead than living in a state of constant agony.

The curtain on the other side of the bed pulled back. A dark-skinned guy in scrubs with a stethoscope. I recognized him as Dr. Patel, from the last time.

"Adam," he said. "I'm so sorry." He looked genuinely sad.

I nodded.

"He developed full-blown pneumonia," Dr. Patel said. "It must have been underlying for a while, although in his last hospitalization his white count didn't show anything abnormal."

"Sure," I said.

"It was too much for him, in his condition. Finally, he had an MI, before we could even decide whether to intubate him. His body couldn't tolerate the assault."

I nodded again. I didn't want the details; what was the point?

"It's really for the best. He could have been on a vent for months. You wouldn't have wanted that."

"I know. Thanks. I know you did everything you could."

"There's just—just him, is that right? He was your only surviving parent? You have no brothers or sisters?"

"Right."

"You two must have been very close."

Really? I thought. And you know this . . . how? Is that your professional medical opinion? But I just nodded.

"Adam, do you have any particular funeral home you'd like us to call?"

I tried to remember the name of the funeral home from when Mom died. After a few seconds it came to me.

"Let us know if there's anything we can do for you," Dr. Patel said.

I looked at Dad's body, at his curled fists, his furious expression, his staring beady eyes, his gaping mouth. Then I looked up at Dr. Patel and said, "Do you think you could close his eyes?"

71

The guys from the funeral home came within an hour and zipped his body up in a body bag and took it away on a stretcher. They were a couple of pleasant, thickset guys with short haircuts, and both of them said, "I'm sorry for your loss." I called the funeral-home director from my cell and numbly talked through what would happen next. He too said, "I'm sorry for your loss." He wanted to know if there would be any elderly relatives coming from out of town, when I wanted to schedule the funeral, whether my father worshipped at a particular church where I'd like to have the service. He asked if there was a family burial plot. I told him where my mom was buried, that I was pretty sure Dad had bought two plots, one for Mom and one for him. He said he'd check with the cemetery. He asked when I wanted to come in and make the final arrangements.

I sat down in the ER waiting area and called my office. Jocelyn had already heard there was some emergency with my father, and she said, "How's your dad?"

"He just passed," I said. That was the way my dad talked: people "passed," they didn't die.

"Oh," Jocelyn gasped. "Adam, I'm sorry."

I asked her to cancel my appointments for the next couple of days, then asked her to connect me with Goddard. Flo picked up and said, "Hey there. The boss is out of the office—he's about to fly to Tokyo tonight." In a hushed voice, she asked, "How's your father?"

"He just passed." I went on quickly, "Obviously I'm going to be out of it for a couple of days and I wanted you to give Jock my apologies in advance—"

"Of *course*," she said. "Of *course*. My condolences. I'm sure he'll check in before he gets on the plane, but I know he'll understand, don't worry about it."

Antwoine came into the waiting area, looking out of place, lost. "What do you want me to do now?" he asked gently.

"Nothing, Antwoine," I said.

He hesitated. "You want me to clear my stuff out?"

"No, come on. You take your time."

"It's just that this came on suddenlike, and I don't have any other place—"

"Stay in the apartment as long as you want," I said.

He shifted his weight from one foot to the other. "You know, he did talk about you," he said.

"Oh, sure," I said. He was obviously feeling guilty about telling me that Dad hadn't asked for me at the end. "I know that."

A low, mellow chuckle. "Not always the most positive shit, but I think that's how he showed his love, you know?"

"I know."

"He was a tough old bastard, your father."

"Yeah."

"It took us some time to kind of work things out, you know."

"He was pretty nasty to you."

"That was just his way, you know. I didn't let it get to me."

"You took care of him," I said. "That meant a lot to him even though he wasn't able to say it."

"I know, I know. Toward the end we kind of had a relationship."

"He liked you."

"I don't know about that, but we had a relationship."

"No, I think he liked you. I know he did."

He paused. "He was a good man, you know."

I didn't know what to say in response to that. "You were really great with him, Antwoine," I finally said. "I know that meant a lot to him."

It's funny: after that first time I broke out crying at my dad's hospital bed, something in me shut down. I didn't cry again, not for a long while. I felt like an arm that's gone to sleep, gone all limp and prickly after having been lain on all night.

On the drive out to the funeral home I called Alana at work and got her voice mail, a message saying she was "out of the office" but would be checking her messages frequently. I remembered she was in Palo Alto. I called her cell, and she answered on the first ring.

"This is Alana." I loved her voice: it was velvety smooth with a hint of huskiness.

"It's Adam."

"Hey, jerk."

"What'd I do?"

"Aren't you supposed to call a girl up the morning after you sleep with her, to make her feel less guilty about putting out?"

"God, Alana, I—"

"Some guys even send flowers," she went on, businesslike. "Not that this has ever happened to me personally, but I've read about it in *Cosmo*."

She was right, of course: I hadn't called her, which was truly rude. But what was I supposed to tell her, the truth? That I hadn't called her because I was frozen like some insect in amber and I didn't know what to do? That I couldn't believe how lucky I was to find a woman like her—she was an itch I couldn't stop scratching—and yet I felt like a complete and total evil fraud? Yeah, I thought, you've read in *Cosmo* about how men are users, baby, but you have no idea.

"How's Palo Alto?"

"Pretty, but you're not changing the subject so easily."

"Alana," I said, "listen. I wanted to tell you—I got some bad news. My dad just died."

"Oh, Adam. Oh, I'm so sorry. Oh God. I wish I were there."

"Me, too."

"What can I do?"

"Don't worry about it, nothing."

"Do you know . . . when the funeral's going to be?"

"Couple of days."

"I'll be out here till Thursday. Adam, I'm so sorry."

I called Seth next, who said pretty much the same thing: "Oh, man, buddy, I'm so sorry. What can I do?" People always say that, and it's nice, but you do begin to wonder, what is there to do, right? It wasn't like I wanted a casserole. I didn't know what I wanted.

"Nothing, really."

"Come on, I can get out of work at the law firm. No worries."

"No, it's okay, thanks, man."

"There going to be a funeral and everything?"

"Yeah, probably. I'll let you know."

"Take care, buddy, huh?"

Then the cell phone rang in my hand. Meacham didn't say hello or anything. His first words were, "Where the *fuck* have you been?"

"My father just died. About an hour ago."

A long silence. "Jesus," he said. Then he added stiffly, as if it were an afterthought: "Sorry to hear it."

"Yep," I said.

"Timing really sucks."

"Yep," I said, my anger flaring up. "I told him to wait." Then I pressed END.

72

The funeral-home director was the same guy who'd handled Mom's arrangements. He was a warm, amiable guy with hair a few shades too black and a large bristling mustache. His name was Frank—"just like your dad," he pointed out. He showed me into the funeral parlor, which looked like an underfurnished suburban house with oriental rugs and dark furniture, a couple of rooms off a central hallway. His office was small and dark, with a few old-fashioned steel file cabinets and some framed copies of paintings of boats and landscapes. There was nothing phony about the guy; he really seemed to connect with me. Frank talked a little about when his father died, six years ago, and how hard it was. He offered me a box of Kleenex, but I didn't need it. He took notes for the newspaper announcement—I wondered silently who would read it, who would really care—and we came up with the wording. I struggled to remember the name of Dad's older sister, who was dead, even the names of his parents, who I think I'd seen less than ten times in my life and just called "Grandma" and "Grandpa." Dad had had a strained relationship with his parents, so we barely saw them at all. I was a little fuzzy on Dad's long and complicated employment history, and I may have left out a school where he'd worked, but I got the important ones.

Frank asked about Dad's military record, and I only remembered that he'd done basic training in some army base and never went off anywhere to fight and he hated the army with a passion. He asked whether I wanted to have a flag on his coffin, which Dad was entitled to, as a veteran, but I said no, Dad wouldn't have wanted a flag on top of his coffin. He would have railed against it, would have said something like, "The fuck you think I am, John F. Kennedy lying in fucking state?" He asked whether I wanted to have the army play "Taps," which Dad was also entitled to, and he explained that these days there wasn't actually a bugler, they usually played a tape recording at the graveside. I said no, Dad wouldn't have wanted "Taps" either. I told him I wanted the funeral and everything as soon as he could possibly arrange it. I wanted to get it all over with.

Frank called the Catholic church where we had Mom's funeral and scheduled a funeral mass for two days off. There were no out-of-town relatives, as far as I knew; the only survivors were a couple of cousins and an aunt he never saw. There were a couple of guys who I guess could be considered friends of his, even though they hadn't talked for years; they all lived locally. He asked whether Dad had a suit I wanted him to be buried in. I said I thought he might, I'd check.

Then Frank took me downstairs to a suite of rooms where they had caskets on display. They all looked big and garish, just the sort of thing Dad would have made fun of. I remember him ranting once, around the time of Mom's death, about the funeral industry and how it was all a monumental rip-off, how they charged you ridiculously inflated prices for coffins that just got buried anyway, so what was the point, and how he'd heard they usually replaced the expensive coffins with cheap pine ones when you weren't looking. I knew that wasn't true—I'd seen Mom's coffin lowered into the ground with the dirt shoveled over it, and I didn't think any kind of scam was possible unless they came in the middle of the night and dug it up, which I doubted.

Because of this suspicion—that was his excuse, anyway—Dad had picked out one of the cheapest caskets for Mom, cheap pine stained to look like mahogany. "Believe me," he'd said to me in the funeral home when Mom died, when I was a slobbering mess, "your mother didn't believe in wasting money."

But I wasn't going to do that to him, even though he was dead and wouldn't know any different. I drove a Porsche, I lived in a huge apartment in Harbor Suites, and I could afford to buy a nice coffin for my father. With the money I was making from the job he kept ranting about. I picked out an elegant-looking mahogany one that had something called a "memory safe" in it, a drawer where you were supposed to put stuff that belonged to the deceased.

A couple of hours later I drove home and crawled into my never-made bed and fell asleep. Later in the day I drove over to Dad's apartment and went through his closet, which I could tell hadn't been opened in a long time, and found a cheap-looking blue suit, which I'd never seen him wear. There was a stripe of dust on each shoulder. I found a dress shirt, but couldn't find a tie— I don't think he ever wore a tie—so I decided to use one of my mine. I looked around the apartment for things I thought he'd want to be buried with. A pack of cigarettes, maybe.

I'd been afraid that going to the apartment would be hard, that I'd start crying again. But it just made me deeply sad to see what little the old guy had left behind—the faint cigarette stink, the wheelchair, the breathing tube, the Barcalounger. After an excruciating half hour of looking through his belongings I gave up and decided that I wouldn't put anything in the "memory safe." Leave it symbolically empty, why not.

When I got back home I picked out one of my least favorite ties, a blue-and-white rep tie that looked somber enough and I didn't mind losing. I didn't feel like driving back to the funeral home, so I brought it down to the concierge desk and asked to have it delivered.

The next day was the wake. I arrived at the funeral home about twenty minutes before it was to begin. The place was air-conditioned to almost frigid, and it smelled like air freshener. Frank asked if I wanted to "pay my respects" to Dad in private, and I said sure. He gestured toward one of the rooms off the central hall. When I entered the room and saw the open coffin I felt an electric jolt. Dad was lying there in the cheap blue suit and my striped blue tie, his hands crossed on his chest. I felt a swelling in my throat, but it subsided quickly, and I wasn't moved to cry, which was strange. I just felt hollow.

He didn't look at all real, but they never, ever do. Frank, or whoever had done the work, hadn't done a bad job—hadn't put on too much rouge or whatever—but he still looked like one of Madame Tussaud's wax museum displays, if one of the better ones. The spirit leaves the body and there's nothing a mortician can do to bring it back. His face was a fake-looking "flesh tone." There seemed to be subtle brown lipstick on his lips. He looked a little less enraged than he had at the hospital, but they still hadn't been able to make him look peaceful. I guess there was only so much they could do to smooth the furrow from his brow. His skin was cold now, and a lot waxier than it had felt in the hospital. I hesitated a moment before kissing his cheek; it felt strange, unnatural, unclean.

I stood there looking at this fleshy shell, this discarded husk, this pod that had once contained the mysterious and fearsome soul of my father. And I started talking to him, as I figure almost every son talks to his dead father. "Well, Dad," I said, "you're finally out of here. If there really is an afterlife, I hope you're happier there than you were here."

I felt sorry for him then, which was something I guess I was never quite able to feel when he was alive. I remembered a couple of times when he actually seemed to be happy, when I was a lot younger and he'd carry me around on his shoulders. A time when one of his teams had won a championship. The time he was hired by Bartholomew Browning. A few moments like that. But he rarely smiled, unless he was laughing his bitter laugh. Maybe he'd needed antidepressants, maybe that was his problem, but I doubted it. "I didn't understand you so well, Dad," I said. "But I really did try."

Hardly anyone showed up in the three-hour span of time. There were some buddies of mine from high school, a couple with their wives, and two college friends. Dad's elderly Aunt Irene came for a while and said, "Your father was very lucky to have you." She had a faint Irish brogue and wore overpowering old-lady perfume. Seth came early and stayed late, kept me company. He told Dad stories in an attempt to make me laugh, famous anecdotes about Dad's coaching days, tales that had become legend among my friends and at Bartholomew Browning. There was the time he took a marking pen and drew a line down the middle of a kid's face mask, a big lunk named Pelly, then all the way down his uniform to the kid's shoes, and along the grass in a straight line across the field, even though the pen didn't make a mark on the grass, and he said, "You run *this* way, Pelly, you get it? *This* is the way you run."

There was the time when he called time out and he went up to a football player named Steve and grabbed his face mask and said, "Are you stupid, Steve?" Then, without waiting for Steve to reply, he yanked the mask up and down, making Steve's head nod like a doll's. "Yes, I am, Coach," he said in a squeaky imitation of Steve's voice. The rest of the team thought it was funny, and most of them laughed. "Yes, I am stupid."

There was the day when he called time out during a hockey game and started yelling at a kid named Resnick for playing too rough. He grabbed Resnick's hockey stick and said, "Mr. Resnick, if I ever see you spear"—and he jabbed the stick into Resnick's stomach, which instantly made Resnick throw up—"or butt-end"—and he slammed him again in the stomach with the stick—"I will destroy you." And Resnick vomited blood, and then had the dry heaves. Nobody laughed.

"Yeah," I said. "He was a funny guy, wasn't he?" By now I wanted him to stop the stories, and fortunately he did.

At the funeral the next morning, Seth sat on one side of me in the pew, Antwoine on the other. The priest, a distinguished, silver-haired fellow who looked like a TV minister, was named Father Joseph Iannucci. Before the mass he took me aside and asked me a few questions about Dad—his "faith," what he was like, what he did for a living, did he have any hobbies, that sort of thing. I was pretty much stumped.

There were maybe twenty people in the church, some of them regular parishioners who'd come for the mass and didn't know Dad. The others were friends of mine from high school and college, a couple of friends from the neighborhood, an old lady who lived next door. There was one of Dad's "friends," some guy who'd been in Kiwanis with Dad years ago before Dad quit in a rage over something minor. He didn't even know Dad had been sick. There were a couple of elderly cousins I vaguely recognized.

Seth and I were pallbearers along with some other guys from the church and the funeral home. There were a bunch of flowers at the front of the church—I had no idea how they got there, whether someone sent them or they were provided by the funeral home.

The mass was one of those incredibly long services that involve a lot of getting up and sitting down and kneeling, probably so you don't fall asleep. I felt depleted, fogged in, still sort of shell-shocked. Father Iannucci called Dad "Francis" and several times said his full name, "Francis Xavier," as if that indicated that Dad was a devout Catholic instead of a faithless guy whose only connection to the Lord was in taking His name in vain. He said, "We are sad at Francis's parting, we grieve his passing, but we believe that he has gone to God, that he is in a better place, that he is sharing now in Jesus' resurrection by living a new life." He said, "Francis's death is not the end. We can still be united with him." He asked, "Why did Francis have to suffer so much in his last months?" and answered something about Jesus' suffering and said that "Jesus was not conquered or defeated by his suffering." I didn't quite follow what he was trying to say, but I wasn't really listening. I was zoning out.

When it was over, Seth gave me a hug, and then Antwoine gave me a crushing handshake and hug, and I was surprised to see a single tear rolling down the giant's face. I hadn't cried during the whole service; I hadn't cried at all the whole day. I felt anesthetized. Maybe I was past it.

Aunt Irene tottered up to me and held my hand in both of her soft age-spotted hands. Her bright red lipstick had been applied with a shaky hand. Her perfume was so strong I had to hold my breath. "Your father was a good man," she said. She seemed to read something in my face, some skepticism I hadn't meant to show, and she said, "He wasn't a comfortable man with his feelings, I know. He wasn't at ease expressing them. But I know he loved you."

Okay, if you insist, I thought, and I smiled and thanked her. Dad's Kiwanis friend, a hulking guy who was around Dad's age but looked twenty years younger, took my hand and said, "Sorry for your loss." Even Jonesie, the loading dock guy from Wyatt Telecom, showed up with his wife, Esther. They both said they were sorry for my loss.

I was leaving the church, about to get in the limousine to follow the hearse to the graveyard, when I saw a man sitting in the back row of the church. He'd come in some time after the mass had started, but I couldn't make out his face at such a distance, in the dark light of the church's interior.

The man turned around and caught my eye.

It was Goddard.

I couldn't believe it. Astonished, and moved, I walked up to him slowly. I smiled, thanked him for coming. He shook his head, waved away my thanks.

"I thought you were in Tokyo," I said.

"Oh, hell, it's not as if the Asia Pacific division hasn't kept me waiting time and time again."

"I don't . . ." I fumbled, incredulous. "You rescheduled your trip?"

"One of the very few things I've learned in life is the importance of getting your priorities straight."

For a moment I was speechless. "I'll be back in tomorrow," I said. "It might be on the later side, because I'll probably have some business to take care of—"

"No," he said. "Take your time. Go slow."

"I'll be fine, really."

"Be good to yourself, Adam. Somehow we'll manage without you for a little while."

"It's not like—not at all like your son, Jock. I mean, my dad was pretty sick with emphysema for a long time, and . . . it's really better this way. He wanted to go."

"I know the feeling," he said quietly.

"I mean, we weren't all that close, really." I looked around the dim church interior, the rows of wooden pews, the gold and crimson paint on the walls. A couple of my friends were standing near the door waiting to talk to me. "I probably shouldn't say it, especially in here, you know?" I smiled sadly. "But he was kind of a difficult guy, a tough old bird, which makes it easier, his passing. It's not like I'm totally devastated or anything."

"Oh, no, that makes it even harder, Adam. You'll see. When your feelings are that complicated."

I sighed. "I don't think my feelings for him are—were—all that complicated."

"It hits you later. The wasted opportunities. The things that could have been. But I want you to keep something in mind: Your dad was fortunate to have you."

"I don't think he considered himself—"

"Really. He was a lucky man, your father."

"I don't know about that," I said, and all of a sudden, without warning, the shut-off valve in me gave way, the dam broke, and the tears welled up. I flushed with shame as the tears started streaming down my face, and I blurted out, "I'm sorry, Jock."

He reached both of his hands up and placed them on my shoulders. "If you can't cry, you're not alive," Goddard said. His eyes were moist.

Now I was weeping like a baby, and I was mortified and somehow relieved at the same time. Goddard put his arms around me, clasped me in a big hug as I blubbered like an idiot.

"I want you to know something, son," he said, very quietly. "You're not alone."

73

The day after the funeral I returned to work. What was I going to do, mope around the apartment? I wasn't really depressed, though I felt raw, like a layer of skin had been peeled off. I needed to be around people. And maybe, now that Dad was dead, there'd be some comfort in being around Goddard, who was beginning to look like the closest thing I ever had to a father. Not to put myself on a shrink's couch or anything, but something changed, for me, after he showed up at the funeral. I wasn't conflicted or ambivalent anymore about my so-called real mission at Trion, the 'real reason' I was there—because that was no longer the real reason I was there.

At least by my reckoning, I'd done my service, paid my debt, and I deserved a clean slate. I wasn't working for Nick Wyatt any longer. I'd stopped returning Meacham's phone calls or e-mails. Once I even got a message, on my cell phone voice mail, from Judith Bolton. She didn't leave her name, but her voice was instantly recognizable. "Adam," she said, "I know you're going through such a difficult time. We all feel terrible about the death of your father, and please know you have our deepest condolences."

I could just imagine the strategy session with Judith and Meacham and Wyatt, all desperate and angry about their kite who'd slipped his string. Judith would say something about how they should go easy on the guy, he's just lost a parent, and Wyatt would say something foulmouthed and say he didn't give a shit, the clock was ticking, and Meacham would be trying to out-tough-guy his boss about how they were going to hold my feet to the fire and they were going to fuck me over; and then Judith would say no, we have to take a more sensitive approach, let me try to reach out to him. . . .

Her message went on, "But it's extremely important, even in this time of turmoil, for you to remain in constant contact. I want us all to keep everything positive and cordial, Adam, but I need you to make contact today."

I deleted her message as well as Meacham's. They would get the point. In time I'd send Meacham an e-mail officially severing the relationship, but for the time being I thought I'd just keep them dangling while the reality of the situation sank in. I wasn't Nick Wyatt's kite anymore.

I'd given them what they needed. They'd realize that it wasn't worth their while to hang tough.

They might threaten, but they couldn't force me to go on working for them. As long as I kept in mind that there really was nothing they could do, I could just walk away.

I just had to keep that in mind. I could just walk away.

74

My cell phone was ringing even before I pulled into the Trion garage the next morning. It was Flo.

"Jock wants to see you," she said, sounding urgent. "Right now."

Goddard was in his back room with Camilletti, Colvin, and Stuart Lurie, the senior VP for Corporate Development I'd met at Jock's barbecue.

Camilletti was talking as I entered.

". . . No, from what I hear the S.O.B. just flew into Palo Alto yesterday with a term sheet already drawn up. He had lunch with Hillman, the CEO, and by dinner they'd inked the deal. He matched our offer dollar for dollar—I mean, to the *penny*—but in cash!"

"How the *hell* could this happen!" Goddard exploded. I'd never seen him so angry. "Delphos signed a no-shop provision, for Christ's sake!"

"The no-shop's dated tomorrow—it hasn't been signed yet. That's why he flew out there so fast, so he could do the deal before we locked it in."

"Who are we talking about?" I asked softly, as I sat down.

"Nicholas Wyatt," Stuart Lurie said. "He just bought Delphos right out from under us for five hundred million in cash."

My stomach sank. I recognized the name Delphos but remembered I wasn't supposed to. *Wyatt bought Delphos?* I thought, astonished.

I turned to Goddard with a questioning look.

"That's the company we were in the process of acquiring—I told you about them," he said impatiently. "Our lawyers were just about finished drawing up the definitive purchase agreement. . . ." His voice trailed off, then grew louder. "I didn't even think Wyatt had that kind of cash on their balance sheet!"

"They had just under a billion in cash," said Jim Colvin. "Eight hundred million, actually. So five hundred million pretty much empties out the piggy bank, because they've got three billion dollars of debt, and the service on that debt's gotta be two hundred million a year easy."

Goddard smacked his hand down on the round table. "God*damn* it to hell!" he thundered. "What the hell *use* does Wyatt have for a company like Delphos? He doesn't have AURORA. . . . For Wyatt to put his own company on the line like that makes no goddamned sense at all unless he's just trying to screw us over."

"Which he just succeeded in doing," Camilletti said.

"For heaven's sake, without AURORA, Delphos is worthless!" Goddard said.

"Without Delphos, AURORA is fucked," said Camilletti.

"Maybe he knows about AURORA," said Colvin.

"Impossible!" said Goddard. "And even if he knows about it, he doesn't *have* it!"

"What if he does?" suggested Stuart Lurie.

There was a long silence.

Camilletti spoke slowly, intensely. "We're protecting AURORA with the exact same federal security regulations the Defense Department mandates for government contractors dealing in sensitive compartmented information." He stared fiercely at Goddard. "I'm talking firewalls, security clearances, network protection, multilevel secure access—every goddamned safeguard known to man. It's in the goddamned cone of silence. There's just no fucking way."

"Well," Goddard said, "Wyatt somehow found out the details of our negotiations—"

"Unless," Camilletti interrupted, "he had someone inside." An idea seemed to occur to him, and he looked at me. "You used to work for Wyatt, didn't you?"

I could feel the blood rushing to my head, and to mask it, I faked outrage "I used to work *at* Wyatt," I snapped at him.

"Are you in touch with him?" he asked, his eyes drilling into me.

"What are you trying to suggest?" I stood up.

"I'm asking you a simple yes-or-no question—are you in touch with Wyatt?" Camilletti shot back. "You had dinner with him at the Auberge not so long ago, correct?"

"Paul, that's enough," said Goddard. "Adam, you sit down this god-damned instant. Adam had no access whatsoever to AURORA. Or to the details of the Delphos negotiation. I believe today's the first time he's even heard the name of the company."

I nodded.

"Let's move on," Goddard said. He seemed to have cooled off a little. "Paul, I want you to talk to our lawyers, see what recourse we have. See if we can stop Wyatt. Now, AURORA's scheduled launch is in four days. As soon as the world knows what we've just done, there'll be a mad scramble to buy up materials and manufacturers up and down the whole damned supply chain. Either we delay the launch, or . . . I do *not* want to be part of that scramble. We're going to have to put our heads together and look around for some other comparable acquisition—"

"—*No one* has that technology but Delphos!" Camilletti said.

"We're all smart people," Goddard said. "There are always other possibilities." He put his hands on the arms of his chair and got to his feet. "You know, there's a story Ronald Reagan used to tell about the kid who found a huge pile of manure and said, 'There must be a pony around here some-where.'" He laughed, and the others laughed as well, politely. They seemed to appreciate his feeble attempt to defuse the tension. "Let's all get to work. Find the pony."

7 5

I knew what had happened.

I thought things through as I drove home that night, and the more I did the angrier I got, and the angrier I got the faster and more erratically I drove.

If it weren't for the term sheet I'd gotten from Camilletti's files, Wyatt wouldn't have known about Delphos, the company Trion was about to buy. The more I reminded myself of this, the worse I felt.

Damn it, it was time to let Wyatt know it was over. I wasn't working for them anymore.

I unlocked my apartment door, switched on the lights, and headed right for the computer to send an e-mail.

But no.

Arnold Meacham was sitting at my computer, while a couple of tough-looking crew-cut guys were tearing the place apart. My stuff was everywhere. All my books had been taken off the shelves, my CD and DVD players had been taken apart, even the TV set. It looked like someone had gone on a rampage, throwing everything around, wrecking as much as possible, trying to cause maximum damage.

"What the fuck—?" I said.

Meacham looked up calmly from my computer screen. "Don't you *ever* fucking ignore me," he said.

I had to get the hell out of there. I spun around, bounded toward the door just as another of the crew-cut thugs slammed the door shut and stood in front of it, watching me warily.

There was no other exit, unless you counted the windows, a twenty-seven-story drop that didn't seem like a very good idea.

"What do you want?" I said to Meacham, looking from him to the door.

"You think you can *hide* shit from me?" Meacham said. "I don't think so. You don't have a safe-deposit box or a *cubbyhole* that's safe from us. I see you've been saving all my e-mails. I didn't know you cared."

"Of course I have," I said, indignant. "I keep backups of everything."

"That encryption program you're using for your notes of meetings with Wyatt and Judith and me—you know, that was cracked over a year ago. There's far stronger ones out there."

"Good to know, thanks," I said, heavy on the sarcasm. I tried to sound unfazed. "Now, why don't you and your boys get the hell out of here before I call the police."

Meacham snorted and made a hand signal that looked as if he was summoning me over.

"No." I shook my head. "I said, you and your buddies—"

There was a sudden movement I could see out of the corner of my eye, lightning-fast, and something slammed into the back of my head. I sagged to my knees, tasting blood. Everything was tinged dark red. I flung my hand out to grab my attacker, but while my hand was flailing in back of me, a foot slammed into my right kidney. A jagged bolt of pain shot up and down my torso, knocking me flat on the Persian rug.

"No," I gasped.

Another kick, this one to the back of my head, incredibly painful. Pinpoints of light sparkled before my eyes.

"Get 'em off me," I moaned. "Make your—buddy—stop. If I get too woozy, I might get talkative."

It was all I could think of. Meacham's accomplices probably didn't know much if anything of what Meacham and I were involved in. They were just muscle. Meacham wouldn't have told them, wouldn't have wanted them to know. Maybe they knew a little, just enough to know what to look for. But Meacham would want to keep them as much out of the loop as possible.

I cringed, braced myself for another kick to the back of my head, every-thing all white and sparkly, a metallic taste in my mouth. For a moment there was silence; it seemed that Meacham had signaled them to stop.

"What the hell do you want from me?" I asked.

"We're going for a drive," Meacham said.

Meacham and his goons hustled me out of my apartment, down the elevator to the garage, then out a service entrance to the street. I was scared out of my mind. A black Suburban with tinted windows was parked by the entrance. Meacham led the way, the three guys staying close to me, surrounding me, probably to make sure I didn't run, or try to jump Meacham, or anything. One of the guys was carrying my laptop; another had my desktop computer.

My head throbbed, and my lower back and chest were in agony. I must have looked like a mess, all bruised and beaten up.

"We're going for a drive" usually means, at least in Mafia movies, cement boots and a dunk in the East River. But if they'd wanted to kill me, why didn't they do it back in my apartment?

The thugs were ex-cops, I figured out after a while, employed by Wyatt Corporate Security. They seem to have been hired purely for their brute strength. They were blunt instruments.

One of the guys drove, and Meacham sat in the front seat, separated from me by a bulletproof glass enclosure, talking on a phone the whole way.

He'd done his job, apparently. He'd scared the shit out of me, and he and his guys had found the evidence I was keeping on Wyatt.

Forty-five minutes later, the Suburban pulled into Nick Wyatt's long stone driveway.

Two of the guys searched me for weapons or whatever, as if somehow between my apartment and here I could have picked up a Glock. They took my cell phone and shoved me into the house. I passed through the metal detector, which went off. They took my watch, belt, and keys.

Wyatt was sitting in front of a huge flat-panel TV in a spacious, sparely furnished room, watching CNBC with the sound muted, and talking on a cell phone. I glanced at myself in a mirror as I entered with my crew-cut escorts. I looked pretty bad.

We all stood there.

After a few minutes Wyatt ended his call, put the phone down, looked over at me. "Long time no see," he said.

"Yeah, well," I said.

"Look at you. Walk into a door? Fall down a flight of stairs?"

"Something like that."

"Sorry to hear about your dad. But Christ, breathing through a tube, oxygen tanks, all that shit—I mean, shoot me if I ever get like that."

"Be my pleasure," I murmured, but I don't think he heard me.

"Just as well he's dead, huh? Put him out of his fucking misery?"

I wanted to lunge at him, throttle him. "Thanks for your concern," I said.

"I want to thank *you*," he said, "for the information on Delphos."

"Sounds like you had to empty your piggy bank to buy it."

"Always gotta think three moves ahead. How do you think I got to where I am now? When we announce *we've* got the optical chip, our stock's gonna go into orbit."

"Nice," I said. "You've got it all figured out. You don't need me anymore."

"Oh, you're far from done, friend. Not until you get me the specs on the chip itself. And the prototype."

"No," I said, very quietly. "I'm done now."

"You think you're *done*? Man, are you hallucinating." He laughed.

I took a deep breath. I could feel my pulse throbbing at the base of my throat. My head ached. "The law's clear on this," I said, clearing my throat. I'd looked at a bunch of legal Web sites. "You're actually in a lot deeper than me, because you oversaw this whole scheme. I was just the pawn. You ran it."

"The *law*," Wyatt said with an incredulous smile. "You're talking to me about the fucking *law*? That's why you've been saving up e-mails and memos and shit, trying to build a *legal* case against *me?* Oh, man, I almost feel sorry for you. I think you truly don't get it, do you? You think I'm going to let you walk away before you're finished?"

"You got all sorts of valuable intelligence from me," I said. "Your plan worked. It's over. From now on, you don't contact me anymore. End of transaction. As far as anyone's concerned, this never happened."

Sheer terror gave way to a kind of delirious confidence: I'd finally crossed the line. I'd jumped off the cliff and I was soaring in the air, and I was going to enjoy the ride until I hit ground.

"Think about it," I went on. "You've got a whole lot more to lose than I do. Your company. And your fortune. Me, I'm diddlyshit. I'm a small fish. No, I'm plankton."

His smile broadened. "What are you going to do, go to 'Jock' Goddard and tell him you're nothing but a shitty little snoop whose brilliant 'ideas' were spoon-fed him by his chief competitor? And then what do you think he's going to do? Thank you, take you to lunch at his little *diner* and toast you with a glass of Ovaltine? I don't think so."

I shook my head, my heart racing. "You really don't want Goddard to know how you learned all the details of their negotiations with Delphos."

"Or maybe you think you can go to the FBI, is that it? Tell them you were a spy-for-hire for Wyatt? Oh, they'll love that. You know how *understanding* the FBI can be, right? They will squeeze you like a fucking cockroach, and I will deny fucking *everything* and they'll have no choice but to believe me, and do you know why? Because you are a fucking little con man. You're on *record* as a hustler, my friend. I fired you from my company when you embezzled from me, and *everything's* documented."

"Then you're going to have a hard time explaining why everyone at Wyatt recommended me so enthusiastically."

"But no one did, get it? We'd never give a recommendation to a hustler like you. *You,* compulsive liar that you are, you counterfeited our letterhead to forge your own recommendations when you applied to Trion. Those letters didn't come from us. Paper analysis and forensic document examination will establish that without a doubt. You used a different computer printer, different ink cartridges. You forged signatures, you sick fuck." A pause. "You really think we weren't going to cover our asses?"

I tried to smile back, but I couldn't get the trembling muscles of my mouth to cooperate. "Sorry, that doesn't explain the phone calls from Wyatt executives to Trion," I said. "Anyway, Goddard'll see through it. He knows me."

Wyatt's laugh was more like a bark. "He *knows* you! That's a scream. Man, you really don't know who you're dealing with, do you? You are in so far over your fucking head. You think anyone's going to believe that our HR department called Trion with glowing recommendations, after we bounced you out on your ass? Well, do a little investigative work, dickwad, and you'll see that every single phone call from our HR department was rerouted. Phone records show they all came from your own apartment. You made all the HR calls yourself, asshole, impersonating your supervisors at Wyatt, making up all those enthusiastic recommendations. You're a sick fuck, man. You're pathological. You made up a whole fucking story about being some big honcho on the Lucid project, which is provably false. You see, asshole, my security people and theirs will get together and compare notes."

My head was spinning slowly, and I felt nauseated.

"And maybe you should check out that secret bank account you're so proud of—the one where you're so sure we've been depositing funds from some offshore account? Why don't you track down the real source of those funds?"

I stared at him.

"That money," Wyatt explained, "was routed directly from several discretionary accounts at Trion. With your goddamned digital fingerprints on it. You stole money from them, same way you stole from us." His eyes bulged. "Your fucking head is in a goddamned jaw trap, you pathetic sack of shit. Next time I see you, you'd better have all the technical specs for Jock Goddard's optical chip, or your life is fucking *over*. Now get the *fuck* out of my house."

PART EIGHT

BLACK BAG

Black Bag Job: Slang for surreptitious entry into an office or home to obtain files or materials illegally.

—Spy Book: The Encyclopedia of Espionage

77

"This better be important, buddy," Seth said. "It's like after midnight."

"This is. I promise."

"Yeah, you only call when you want something anymore. Or death of a parent, that kinda thing."

He was joking, and he wasn't. Truth is, he had a right to be pissed off at me. I hadn't exactly been in touch with him since I'd started at Trion. And he'd been there when Dad died, through the funeral. He'd been a much better friend than I'd been.

We met an hour later at an all-night Dunkin' Donuts near Seth's apartment. The place was almost deserted, except for a few bums. He was wearing his same old Diesel jeans and a Dr. Dre World Tour T-shirt.

He stared at me. "What the hell happened to you?"

I didn't keep any of the grisly details from him—what was the point anymore?

At first he thought I was making it up, but gradually he saw that I was telling the truth, and his expression changed from amused skepticism to horrified fascination to outright sympathy.

"Oh, man," he said when I'd wound up my story, "you are so lost."

I smiled sadly, nodded. "I'm screwed," I said.

"That's not what I mean." He sounded testy. "You fucking went along with this."

"I didn't 'go along with this.' "

"No, asshole. You fucking had a *choice.*"

"A choice?" I said. "Like what choice? Prison?"

"You took the deal they offered, man. They got your balls in a vise, and you caved."

"What other option did I have?"

"That's what lawyers are for, asshole. You could have told me, I could have gotten one of the guys I work for to help out."

"Help out *how?* I took the money in the first place."

"You could have brought in one of the lawyers at the firm, scare the shit out of them, threaten to go public."

I was silent for a moment. Somehow I doubted it really would have been that simple. "Yeah, well, it's too late for that now. Anyway, they would have denied everything. Even if one of your firm's lawyers agreed to represent me, Wyatt would have set the whole goddamned American Bar Association after me."

"Maybe. Or maybe he would have wanted the whole thing to stay quiet. You might have been able to make it go away."

"I don't think so."

"*I* see," Seth said, oozing sarcasm. "So instead, you bent over and took it. You went along with their illegal scheme, agreed to become a spy, pretty much guaranteed yourself a prison sentence—"

"What do you mean, 'guaranteed' myself a prison sentence?"

"—And then, just to feed your insane ambition, here you are, fucking over the one guy in corporate America who ever gave you a chance."

"Thanks," I said bitterly, knowing he was right.

"You pretty much deserve what you get."

"I appreciate the help and moral support, friend."

"Put it this way, Adam—I may be a pathetic loser in your eyes, but at least I came by my loserdom honestly. What are you? You're a total fraud. You're fucking *Rosie Ruiz.*"

"Huh?"

"She won the Boston Marathon like twenty years ago, set a women's record, remember? Barely broke a sweat. Turned out she'd jumped in half a mile from the finish line. Took the fucking *subway* to get there. That's you, man. The Rosie Ruiz of corporate America."

I sat there, my face growing redder and hotter, feeling more and more miserable. Finally I said, "Are you done yet?"

"For now, yeah."

"Good," I said. "Because I need your help."

78

I'd never been to the law firm where Seth worked, or pretended to work. It took up four floors in one of those downtown skyscrapers, and it had all the trappings people want in a high-end law firm—mahogany paneling, expensive Aubusson carpets, modern art on giant canvases, lots of glass.

He got us an appointment first thing in the morning with his boss, a senior partner named Howard Shapiro who specialized in criminal defense work and used to be a U.S. Attorney. Shapiro was a short, chubby guy, balding, round black glasses, a high voice and rapid-fire delivery, frenetic energy. He kept interrupting me, prodding me to get my story over with, looking at his watch. He took notes on a yellow pad. Once in a while he gave me wary, puzzled looks, as if he was trying to figure something out, but for the most part he didn't react. Seth, who was on good behavior, mostly sat there watching.

"Who beat you up?" Shapiro said.

"His security guys."

He made a note. "When you told him you were pulling out?"

"Before. I stopped returning their calls and e-mails."

"Teach you a lesson, huh?"

"I guess."

"Let me ask you something. Give me an honest answer. Say you get Wyatt what he wants, the chip or whatever it is. You don't think he'll leave you alone?"

"I doubt it."

"You think they're going to keep pushing you?"

"Probably."

"You're not afraid this whole thing might blow up in your face and you'll be left holding the bag?"

"I've thought about it. I know the folks at Trion are mighty pissed off their acquisition fell through. There'll probably be some sort of an investigation, and who knows what'll happen."

"Well, I got more bad news for you, Adam. I hate to tell you, but you're a tool."

Seth smiled.

"I know that."

"It means you have to strike first, or you're hosed."

"How?"

"Say this thing blows up and you're caught. Not unlikely. You throw yourself on the mercy of the court without cooperating, and you're going to go to jail, simple as that. Guarantee it."

I felt like I'd been punched in the stomach. Seth winced.

"Then I'd cooperate."

"Too late. No one's going to cut you any slack. Also, the only proof against Wyatt is *you*—but there'll be lots of proof against you, I bet."

"So what do you suggest?"

"Either they find you, or you find them. I've got a buddy in the U.S. Attorney's office, guy I trust. Wyatt's a big fish. You can serve him up on a silver platter. They'll be very interested."

"How do I know they won't arrest me, throw me in jail too?"

"I'll make a proffer. Call him up, tell him I've got something I think he might be interested in. I'll say, I'm not going to give you any names. If you're not going to work out a deal with my guy, you're not going to see him. You want to deal, you give him a queen for a day."

"What's a 'queen for a day'?"

"We go in, sit down with the prosecutor and an agent. Anything that's said in that meeting cannot be directly used against you."

I looked at Seth, raised my eyebrows, and turned back to Shapiro. "Are you saying I could get off?"

Shapiro shook his head. "With that little prank you pulled at Wyatt, the loading-dock guy's retirement party, we'll have to fashion a guilty plea to something. You're a dirty witness, the prosecutor's going to have to show you didn't get off scot-free. You won't get a total pass."

"More than a misdemeanor?"

"Could be probation, to probation and a felony, to a felony and six months."

"Prison," I said.

Shapiro nodded.

"If they're willing to deal," I said.

"Correct. Look, you're in a shitstorm of trouble, let's speak frankly. The Economic Espionage Act of 1996 made the theft of trade secrets a federal criminal offense. You could get ten years in prison."

"What about Wyatt?"

"If they catch him? Under the Federal Sentencing Guidelines, a judge has to take into account the defendant's role in the offense. If you're a ring-leader, the offense level is increased by two levels."

"So they'll hit him harder."

"Right. Also, you didn't personally benefit materially from the espionage, right?"

"Right," I said. "I mean, I did get paid."

"You just got your Trion salary, which was for the work you did for Trion."

I hesitated. "Well, Wyatt's people continued to pay me, into a secret bank account."

Shapiro stared at me.

"That's bad, right?" I said.

"That's bad," he said.

"No wonder they agreed to it so easily," I groaned, more to myself than to him.

"Yeah," Shapiro said. "You put the hook in yourself. So, you want me to make the call or no?"

I looked at Seth, who nodded. There didn't seem to be any other choice.

"Why don't you guys wait outside," Shapiro said.

We sat in the waiting area outside his office, silent. My nerves were stretched to the breaking point. I called my office and asked Jocelyn to reschedule a couple of appointments.

Then I sat there for a few minutes, just thinking. "You know," I said, "the worst thing about it is, I gave Wyatt the keys so he could rob us blind. He's already derailed our big acquisition, and now he's going to fuck us over totally—and it's all my fault."

Seth stared at me for a long while. "Who's 'us'?"

"Trion."

He shook his head. "You're not Trion. You keep saying 'we' and 'us' when you talk about Trion."

"Slip of the tongue," I said.

"I don't think so. I want you to take a bar of whatever ten-dollar French-milled soap you use now and write on your bathroom mirror, 'I am not Trion, and Trion is not me.'"

"Enough," I said. "You're sounding like my dad now."

"Ever occur to you maybe your dad wasn't wrong about everything? Like a stopped clock's right twice a day, huh?"

"Fuck you."

Then the door opened and Howard Shapiro was standing there. "Sit down," he said.

I could tell from his face that things hadn't gone well. "What'd your buddy say?" I asked.

"My buddy got transferred to Main Justice. His replacement is a real prick."

"How bad?" I asked.

"He said, 'You know what, you take a plea and we'll see what happens.' "

"What's that supposed to mean?"

"It means you take a guilty plea in chambers, and no one will know about it."

"I don't get it."

"If you give him a great case, he's willing to write you a great Five-K. A Five-K is a letter the prosecutor writes to the judge asking him to depart from the sentencing guidelines."

"Does the judge have to do what the prosecutor wants?"

"Of course not. Also, there's no guarantee this prick will really write you a decent Five-K. Be honest, I don't trust him."

"What's his definition of a 'great case'?" asked Seth.

"He wants Adam to make an introduction of an undercover."

"An undercover *agent*?" I said. "That's *insane!* Wyatt'll never go for it. He won't meet with anyone but me. He's not an idiot."

"What about wearing a wire?" Seth asked. "Would he agree to that?"

"*I* won't agree to that," I said. "I get scanned for electronic devices every time I'm in Wyatt's presence. I'd get caught for sure."

"That's all right," said Shapiro. "Our friend in the U.S. attorney's office won't agree to it anyway. The only way he'll play ball is if you introduce an undercover."

"I won't do it," I said. "He'll never go for it. And what guarantee is there that I won't get jail time even if I do?"

"None," Shapiro admitted. "No federal prosecutor is going to give you a one-hundred-percent promise that a judge'll give you probation. The judge may not go for it. But whatever you decide, he's giving you seventy-two hours to make up your mind."

"Or what?"

"Or the chips fall where they may. He'll never give you queen for a day if you don't play by his rules. Look, they don't trust you. They don't think you can do this on your own. And face it, it's their ball."

"I don't need seventy-two hours," I said. "I've already decided. I'm not playing."

Shapiro looked at me strangely. "You're going to keep working for Wyatt."

"No," I said. "I'm going to handle this my own way."

Now Shapiro smiled. "How so?"

"I want to set my own terms."

"How so?" Shapiro said.

"Let's say I get some really concrete evidence against Wyatt," I said. "Serious, hard-core proof of his criminality. Could we take that directly to the FBI and make a better deal?"

"Theoretically, sure."

"Good," I said. "I think I want to do this myself. The only one who's going to get me out of this is me."

Seth half-smiled, reached out and put a hand on my shoulder. " 'Me' meaning 'me,' or 'me' meaning 'we'?"

80

I got an e-mail from Alana saying that she was back, her trip to Palo Alto had been cut short—she didn't explain, but I knew why—and she'd love to see me. I called her at home, and we talked a while about the funeral, and how I was doing, and all that. I told her I didn't much feel like talking about Dad, and then she said, "Are you aware you're in serious trouble with HR?"

My breath stopped. "Am I?"

"Oh, boy. Trion's Personnel Policy Manual expressly forbids workplace romances. Inappropriate sexual behavior in the workplace harms organizational effectiveness through its negative impact on participants and co-workers."

I let my breath out slowly. "You're not in my management chain. Anyway, I felt that we were organizationally quite effective. And I thought our sexual behavior was quite appropriate. We were practicing horizontal integration." She laughed, and I said, "I know that neither one of us has time, but don't you think we'll be better Trion employees if we take off a night? I mean really get out of town. Be spontaneous."

"That sounds intriguing," she said. "Yes, I think that could definitely boost productivity."

"Good. I booked a room for us tomorrow night."

"Where?"

"You'll see."

"Uh-uh. Tell me where," she said.

"Nope. It'll be a surprise. As our fearless leader likes to say, sometimes you just gotta get in the car."

She picked me up in her blue Mazda Miata convertible, drove us out to the country while I gave directions. In the silences I obsessed about what I was about to do. I was into her, and this was a problem. Here I was, using her to try to save my own skin. I was *so* going to hell.

The drive took forty-five minutes, on a stop-and-go road past a parade of identical shopping malls and gas stations and fast-food places, and then a narrow and very winding road through woods. At one point she peered at me, noticed the bruise around my eye, said, "What happened? You get into a fight?"

"Basketball," I said.

"I thought you weren't going to play with Chad anymore."

I smiled, didn't say anything.

Finally we came to a big, rambling country inn, white clapboard with dark green shutters. The air was cool and fragrant, and you could hear birds chirping, and no traffic.

"Hey," she said, removing her sunglasses. "Nice. This place is supposed to be excellent."

I nodded.

"You take all your girlfriends here?"

"Never been here before," I said. "I read about it, and it seemed like the perfect getaway." I put my arm around her narrow waist and gave her a kiss. "Let me get your bags."

"Just one," she said. "I travel light."

I took our bags up to the front door. Inside it smelled of wood fires and maple syrup. The couple who owned and ran the place greeted us like old friends.

Our room was sweet, very country-inn. There was an enormous four-poster bed with a canopy, braided throw rugs, chintz curtains. The bed faced a huge old brick fireplace that clearly got a lot of use. The furnishings were all antiques, the rickety kind that make me nervous. There was a captain's chest at the foot of the bed. The bathroom was enormous, with an old iron clawfoot tub in the middle of the room—the kind that looks great, but if you want to take a shower you have to stand in the tub with a little handheld shower thing and spray yourself the way you wash a dog, and try not to splash water all over the floor. The bathroom was connected to a little sitting area off the bedroom furnished with an oak desk and an old telephone on a rickety telephone table.

The bed squeaked and groaned, as we found out when we both plopped down on it after the innkeeper had left. "God, imagine what this bed has seen," I said.

"A lot of chintz," Alana said. "Reminds me of my grandmother's house."

"Is your grandmother's house as big as this place?"

She nodded once. "This is cozy. Great idea, Adam." She slipped a cool hand under my shirt, stroked my stomach, and then moved south. "What were you saying about horizontal integration?"

A roaring fire was going in the dining room when we came down for dinner. There were maybe ten or twelve other couples already seated at the tables, mostly older than us.

I ordered an expensive red Bordeaux, and I could hear Jock Goddard's words echoing in my head: *You used to drink Budweiser, now you're sipping some first-growth Pauillac.*

The service was slow—there seemed to be one waiter for the whole dining room, a Middle Eastern guy who barely spoke English—but it didn't bother me. We were both sort of blissed-out, floating on a postcoital high.

"I noticed you brought your computer," I said. "In the trunk of your car."

She grinned sheepishly. "I don't go anywhere without it."

"Are you sort of tethered to the office?" I asked. "Pager, cell phone, e-mail, all that?"

"Aren't you?"

"The good thing about having only one boss," I said, "is that it cuts down on some of that."

"Well, you're lucky. I've got six direct reports and a bunch of really arrogant engineers I have to deal with. Plus a huge deadline."

"What kind of deadline?"

She paused, but for just a moment. "The rollout's next week."

"You're shipping a product?"

She shook her head. "It's a demo—a big public announcement, demonstration of a working prototype of the thing we're developing. I mean, it's a really big deal. Goddard hasn't told you about it?"

"He might have, I don't know. He tells me about all kinds of stuff."

"Not the kind of thing you'd forget. Anyway, it's taking up all my time. A real time suck. Night and day."

"Not totally," I said. "You've had time for two dates with me, and you're taking tonight off."

"And I'll pay for it tomorrow and Sunday."

The overworked waiter finally showed up with a bottle of white wine. I pointed out his error, and he apologized profusely and went off to get the right one.

"Why *didn't* you want to talk to me at Goddard's barbecue?" I asked.

She looked at me incredulously, her sapphire-blue eyes wide. "I was serious about the HR manual, you know. I mean, workplace romances really are discouraged, so we've got to be discreet. People talk. People especially love gossiping about who's screwing who. And then if something happens . . ."

"Like a breakup or something."

"Whatever. Then it becomes awkward for everyone."

The conversation was starting to spin in the wrong direction. I tried to bring it back on course. "So I guess I can't just pop in on you one day at work. Show up on the fifth floor unannounced with a bouquet of lilies."

"I told you, they'd never let you in."

"I thought my badge lets me in anywhere in the building."

"Maybe most places, but not the fifth floor."

"Meaning *you* can get onto the executive floor, but I can't get onto yours?"

She shrugged.

"You have your badge with you?"

"They've trained me not to go to the bathroom without it." She pulled it out of her little black purse and flashed it at me. It was attached to a key ring with a bunch of other keys.

I grabbed it playfully. "Not as bad as a passport picture, but I wouldn't submit this head shot to a modeling agency," I said.

I inspected her badge. Hers had the same stuff on it as mine, the 3-D holograph Trion seal that changed color as light passed over it, the same pale blue background color with TRION SYSTEMS printed over and over on it in tiny white letters. The chief difference seemed to be that hers had a red-and-white stripe across the front.

"I'll show you mine if you show me yours," she said.

I took my badge out of my pocket and handed it to her. The basic difference was in the little transponder chip inside. The chip inside the badge was encoded with information that either opened a door lock or didn't. Her card got her into the fifth floor in addition to all the main entrances, the garage, and so on.

"You look like a scared rabbit here." She giggled.

"I think I felt that way on my first day."

"I didn't know employee numbers went this high."

The red-and-white stripe on her card had to be for quick visual identification. Meaning that there must be at least one additional checkpoint beyond waving the badge at the badge reader. Someone had to check you out as you entered. That made things a lot more difficult.

"When you leave to go down to lunch or up to the gym—must be a huge hassle."

She shrugged, uninterested. "It's not too bad. They get to know you."

Right, I thought. That's the problem. You can't get in the door unless the chip inside your proximity access badge has been coded right, and even once you're on the floor, you have to pass by a guard for facial confirmation. "At least they don't make you go through that biometric crap," I said. "We had to do that at Wyatt. You know—the fingerprint scan. A friend of mine at Intel even had to go through a retinal scan every day, and all of a sudden he started needing glasses." This was a total lie, but it got her attention. She looked at me with a curious grin, unsure whether I was joking.

"I'm kidding about the glasses part, but he was convinced all that scanning was going to ruin his eyesight."

"Well, there's this one inner area with biometrics, but only the engineers go in there. It's where they do work on the prototype. But I just have to deal with Barney or Chet, the poor security guards who have to sit in that little booth."

"It can't be as ridiculous as it was at Wyatt in the early stages of the Lucid," I said. "They made us go through this badge-exchange ritual where you had to hand your ID card to the guard, and then the guy gave you a *second* badge to wear on the floor." I was totally bullshitting, parroting back something Meacham had told me about. "So let's say you realize you left your car headlights on, or you forgot something in the trunk of your car, or you want to run down to the cafeteria to grab a bagel or something . . ."

She shook her head absently, snorted softly. She'd run out of what little interest she had in the intricacies of the badge-access system at work. I wanted to pump her for more information—like, do you have to hand your ID card to the guard, or do you just show it to them? If you had to hand the guard your card, the risk was a lot higher of the guard discovering a fake badge. Does the scrutiny get any more lax at night? Early in the morning?

"Hey," she said, "you haven't touched your wine. Don't you like it?"

I dipped a couple of fingertips into my glass of wine. "Delicious," I said.

This little act of stupid juvenile male goofiness made her laugh, loud and whooping, her eyes crinkling into slits. Some women—okay, most women—might have asked for the check at that point. Not Alana.

I was into her.

81

Both of us were stuffed from dinner, a little unsteady from too much wine. Actually, Alana seemed a little more toasted than me. She fell back on the creaky bed, her arms outstretched as if to embrace the whole room, the inn, the night, whatever. That was the moment for me to follow her onto the bed. But I couldn't, not yet.

"Hey, you want me to get your laptop from the car?"

She groaned. "Oh, I wish you hadn't mentioned it. You've been talking about work way too much."

"Why don't you just admit you're a workaholic, too, and be done with it?" I did my AA meeting riff: "Hi, my name is Alana, and I'm a workaholic. 'Hi, Alana!' "

She shook her head, rolled her eyes.

"The first step is always to admit you're powerless over your workaholism. Anyway, I left something in your car, so I'm going down there anyway." I held out my hand. "Keys?"

She was leaning back on the bed, looking too comfortable to move. "Mmph. Okay, sure," she said reluctantly. "Thanks." She rolled over to the edge of the bed, fished her car keys out of her purse, handed the key ring to me with a swanning, dramatic gesture. "Come back soon, huh?"

The parking area was dark and deserted by now. I looked back at the inn, about a hundred feet away, made sure our room didn't look over the parking lot. She couldn't see me.

I popped the trunk of her Miata and found her computer bag, a gray flannel-mohair-textured nylon satchel. I wasn't kidding: I had left something in here, a small knapsack. There was nothing else of particular interest in her trunk. I swung the satchel and knapsack onto my shoulder and got into her car.

I looked back toward the inn again. Nobody was coming.

Still, I kept the interior dome light off and let my eyes get used to the dark. I'd attract less attention this way.

I felt like a creep, but I had to be realistic about my situation. I really didn't have a choice. She was my best way into AURORA, and now I *had* to get inside. It was the only way I could save myself.

Quickly I unzipped the satchel, pulled out her laptop, and powered it on. The car's interior went blue from the computer screen. While I waited for it to boot up, I opened my knapsack and pulled out a blue plastic first aid kit.

Inside, instead of Band-Aids and such, were a few small plastic cases. Each contained a soft wax.

By the blue light I looked at the keys on her key ring. A few looked promising. Maybe one of them would open file cabinets on the AURORA project floor.

One by one, I pressed each key onto a rectangle of wax. I'd practiced this a few times with one of Meacham's guys, and I was glad I did; it took a while to get the hang of it. Now the password prompt on her screen was blinking at me.

Shit. Not everyone password-protected their laptops. Oh, well: at least this wasn't going to be a wasted errand. From the knapsack I pulled out the miniature pcProx reader that Meacham had given me and connected it to my handheld. I pressed the start button, then waved Alana's badge at it.

The little device had just captured the data on Alana's card and stored it on my handheld.

Maybe it was just as well that her laptop was password-protected. There was a limit to how much time I could spend out in the parking lot without her wondering where the hell I'd gone. Just before I shut down her computer, just for kicks, I decided to type in some of the usual-suspect passwords—her birth date, which I'd memorized; the first six digits of her employee number.

Nothing happened. I typed in ALANA, and the password prompt disappeared, and a plain screen came up.

Oh, man, that was easy. I was in.

Jesus. Now what? How much time could I risk spending on this? But how could I pass the opportunity up? It might never come again.

Alana was an extremely well-organized person. Her computer was set up in a clear, logical hierarchy. One directory was labeled AURORA.

It was all here. Well, maybe not all, but it was a gold mine of technical specs on the optical chip, marketing memos, copies of e-mails she'd sent and received, meeting schedules, staff rosters with access codes, even floor plans. . . .

There was so much that I didn't have time even to read through the file names. Her laptop had a CD drive; I had a little spindle of blank CDs in the knapsack. I grabbed one, popped it into her CD drive.

Even on a super-fast computer like Alana's, it took a good five minutes to copy all the AURORA files to a disk. That's how much there was.

"What took you so long?" she said poutily when I returned.

She was under the covers, her naked breasts visible, and she looked sleepy. A Stevie Wonder ballad—"Love's in Need of Love Today"—was playing softly on a little CD player she must have brought.

"I couldn't figure out which was your trunk key."

"A car guy like you? I thought you drove off and left me here."

"Do I *look* stupid?"

"Appearances can be deceiving," she said. "Come to bed."

"I'd never have figured you for a Stevie Wonder fan," I said. Truly, I would never have guessed, given her collection of angry women folk singers.

"You don't really know me yet," she replied.

"No, but give me a little time," I said. I know everything about you, I thought, yet I don't know anything. I'm not the only one keeping secrets. I put her laptop on the oak desk next to the bathroom. "There," I said, returning to the bedroom, taking off my clothes. "In case you're seized with some brilliant inspiration, some amazing brainstorm in the middle of the night."

Naked, I approached the bed. This beautiful naked woman was in bed, playing the role of seductress, when really I was the seducer. She had no idea what sort of game I was playing, and I felt a flush of shame mixed, oddly, with a tug of arousal. "Get up here," she said in a dramatic whisper, staring at me. "I just had a *brainstorm*."

We both got up after eight, unusually late for us hyper-driven type A workaholics—and fooled around in bed for a while before showering and going down to a country breakfast. I doubt people in the country actually eat this way, or they'd all weigh four hundred pounds: rashers of bacon (only at country bed-and-breakfasts does bacon come in "rashers"), mounds of grits, freshly baked hot blueberry muffins, eggs, French toast, coffee with real cream. . . . Alana really chowed down, which surprised me, for such a pencil-thin girl. I enjoyed watching her eat so ravenously. She was a woman of appetites, which I liked.

We went back up the room and fooled around some more, and hung out and talked. I made a point of not talking about security procedures or proximity badges. She wanted to talk about my dad's death and funeral, and even though the subject depressed me, I talked about it a little. Around eleven we reluctantly left, and the date was over.

I think we both wanted it to keep going, but we also needed to get home to our own nests for a while, get some work done, go back to the salt mines, make up for this delicious night away from work.

As we drove, I found myself grooving on the country road, the trees dappled with sunlight, the fact that I'd just spent the night with the coolest and most gorgeous and funniest and sexiest woman I'd ever met.

Man, what the hell was I doing?

8 2

By noon I was back in my apartment, and I immediately called Seth.

"I'm going to need some more cash, man," he said.

I'd already given him several thousand dollars, from my Wyatt-funded account, or wherever the money really came from. I was surprised he'd run through it already.

"I didn't want to fuck around, get cheap stuff," he said. "I got all professional equipment."

"I guess you had to," I said. "Even though it's one-time use."

"You want me to pick up uniforms?"

"Yeah."

"What about badges?"

"I'm working on that," I said.

"Aren't you nervous?"

I hesitated a moment, thought about lying just to bolster his courage, but I couldn't. "Totally," I said.

I didn't want to think about what might happen if things went wrong, though. Some prime real estate in my brain was now being colonized by worry, obsessively working through the plan I'd come up with after meeting with Seth's boss.

And yet there was another part of my brain that wanted to just escape into a daydream. I wanted to think about Alana. I thought about the irony of the whole situation—how this calculated scheme of seduction had led down this unexpected path, how I felt rewarded, wrongly, for my treachery.

I'd alternate between feeling crummy, guilty about what I was doing to her, and being overwhelmed by my attachment to her, something I really hadn't felt before. Little details kept popping into my mind: the way she brushed her teeth, scooping up water from the tap with a cupped hand instead of using a glass; the graceful hollow of her lower back swelling into the cleft of her butt, the incredibly sexy way she applied her lipstick. . . . I thought about her velvet-smooth voice, her crazy laugh, her sense of humor, her sweetness.

And I thought—this was by far the strangest thing—about our future together, a generally scary thought to a guy in his twenties, but somehow this wasn't at all scary. I didn't want to lose this woman. I felt like I'd stopped into a 7-Eleven to buy a six-pack of beer and a lottery ticket, and I'd won the lottery.

And because of that, I never wanted her to find out what I was really up to. That terrified me. That dark, awful thought kept popping up, interrupting my silly fantasy, like one of those kids' clown toys with the weighted bottom that always go *sproing* upright every time you bat them down.

A smudgy black-and-white image would be spliced into my gauzy color fantasy reel—a frame from a surveillance camera: me sitting in my car in the dark parking lot copying the contents of her laptop onto a CD, pressing her keys into the wax, copying her ID badge.

I'd bat back the evil clown doll and there we are on our wedding day, Alana walking down the aisle, gorgeous and demure, escorted by her father, a silver-haired, square-jawed guy in a morning suit.

The ceremony's performed by Jock Goddard as justice of the peace. Alana's family's all in attendance, her mother looking like Diane Keaton in *Father of the Bride*, her sister not as pretty as Alana but sweet, and they're all thrilled—this is a fantasy, remember—that she's marrying me.

Our first house together, a real house and not an apartment, like in an old leafy Midwestern town; I was imagining the great house Steve Martin's family lives in, in *Father of the Bride*. We're both rich high-powered corporate execs, after all. Somewhere in the background, Nina Simone is singing

"The Folks Who Live on the Hill." I'm hoisting Alana effortlessly over the threshold and she's laughing at how cornball and cliché I'm being, and then we boink in every room of the house to initiate the place, including the bathroom and the linen closet. We rent movies together while sitting in bed eating take-out Chinese food from the carton with wooden chopsticks, and every so often I sneak a look at her, and I can't believe I'm actually *married* to this unbelievable babe.

Meacham's goons had brought back my computers and such, which was fortunate, because I needed them.

I popped the CD into my computer with all the stuff I'd copied from Alana's laptop. A lot of it was e-mails concerning the vast marketing potential of AURORA. How Trion was poised to own the "space," as they say in techspeak. The huge increases in computing power it promised, how the AURORA chip really would change the world.

One of the more interesting documents was a schedule of the public demonstration of AURORA. It was to happen on Wednesday, four days from now, at the Visitors Center at Trion headquarters, a mammoth, modernistic auditorium. E-mail alerts, faxes, and phone calls were to go out only the day before to all the media. Obviously it was going to be an immense public event. I printed the schedule out.

But I was intrigued, most of all, by the floor plan and the security procedures that all AURORA team members were given.

Then I opened one of the pullout garbage drawers in the kitchen island. Wrapped in a trash bag were a few objects I'd stored in Zip-Loc bags. One was the Ani DiFranco CD I'd left around my apartment, expecting her to pick it up, as she did. The other was the wineglass she'd used here.

Meacham had given me a Sirchie fingerprint kit, containing little vials of latent print powder, transparent fingerprint lifting tape, and a fiberglass brush. Putting on a pair of latex gloves, I dusted both the CD and the wineglass with a little of the black graphite powder.

By far the best thumbprint was on the CD. I lifted that carefully on a strip of tape, put it in a sterile plastic case.

Then I composed an e-mail to Nick Wyatt.

It was addressed, of course, to "Arthur":

```
Monday evening/Tuesday morning will complete assignment &
obtain samples. Tuesday early morning will hand over at
time and place you specify. Upon completion of assignment
I will terminate all contact.
```

I wanted to strike the right note of resentfulness. I didn't want them to suspect anything.

But would Wyatt himself show up at the rendezvous?

I guess that was the big unanswered question. It wasn't crucial that Wyatt show up, though I sure wanted it to be him. There was no way to force Wyatt to be there himself. In fact, insisting on it would probably just warn him *not* to show. But by now I knew enough of Wyatt's psychology to be fairly confident that he wouldn't trust anyone else.

You see, I was going to give Nick Wyatt what he wanted.

I was going to give him the actual prototype of the AURORA chip, which I was going to steal, with Seth's help, from the secure fifth floor of D Wing.

I had to give him the real thing, the actual AURORA prototype. For a number of reasons it couldn't be faked. Wyatt, being an engineer, would probably know right away whether it was the genuine item or not.

But the main reason was, as I'd learned from Camilletti's e-mails and Alana's files, that for security reasons, the AURORA prototype had been inscribed with a micromachined identification mark, a serial number and the Trion logo, etched with a laser and visible only under a microscope.

That's why I wanted him to be in possession of the stolen chip. The real thing.

Because the moment Wyatt—or Meacham, if it had to be—took delivery of the pilfered chip, I had him. The FBI would be notified far enough in advance to coordinate a SWAT team, but they wouldn't know names or locations or anything until the very last minute. I was going to be in complete control of this.

Howard Shapiro, Seth's boss, had made the call for me. "Forget about dealing with the bureau chief in the U.S. Attorney's office," he said. "Something dicey like this, he's going to go to Washington, and that's going to take forever. Forget it. We go right to the FBI—they're the only ones who'll play the game at this level."

Without naming names, he struck a deal with the FBI. If everything came off successfully, and I delivered Nick Wyatt to them, I'd get probation, and nothing more.

Well, I was going to deliver Wyatt. But it was going to be my way.

8 3

I got into work early on Monday morning, wondering whether this was going to be my last day at Trion.

Of course, if everything went well, this would just be another day, a blip in a long and successful career.

But the chances that everything in this incredibly complicated scheme would go right were pretty small, and I knew it.

On Sunday, I'd cloned a couple of copies of Alana's proximity badge, using a little machine Meacham had given me called a ProxProgrammer and the data I'd captured from Alana's ID badge.

Also, I'd found among Alana's files a floor plan for the fifth floor of D Wing. Almost half the floor was marked with cross-hatching and labeled "Secure Facility C."

Secure Facility C was where the prototype was being tested.

Unfortunately, I had no idea what was *in* the secure facility, where in that area the prototype was kept. Once I got in, I'd have to wing it.

I drove by my dad's apartment to grab my industrial-strength work gloves, the ones I'd used when I worked as a window cleaner with Seth. I was sort of hoping to see Antwoine, but he must have gone out for a while. I got this funny feeling while I was there, like I was being watched, but I wrote it off as just your basic free-floating anxiety.

The rest of Sunday, I'd done a lot of research on the Trion Web site. It was amazing, really, how much information was available to Trion employees—

from floor plans to security badging procedures to even the inventory of security equipment installed on the fifth floor of D Wing. From Meacham I'd gotten the radio frequency the Trion security guards used for their two-way radios.

I didn't know everything I needed to know about the security procedures—far from it—but I did find out a few key things. They confirmed what Alana had told me over dinner at the country inn.

There were only two ways in or out of the fifth floor, both manned. You waved your badge at a card reader to get through the first set of doors, but then you had to show your face to a guard behind a bulletproof glass window, who compared your name and photograph to what he had on his computer screen, then buzzed you through to the main floor.

And even then, you weren't anywhere near Secure Facility C. You had to walk down corridors equipped with closed-circuit video cameras, then into another area set up with not only security cameras but motion detectors, before you came to the entrance to the secure area. That was unmanned, but in order to unlock the door you had to activate a biometric sensor.

So getting to the AURORA prototype was going to be grotesquely difficult, if not impossible. I wasn't even going to be able to get through the first, manned checkpoint. I couldn't use Alana's card, obviously—nobody would mistake me for her. But her card might be useful in other ways once I got onto the fifth floor.

The biometric sensor was even tougher. Trion was on the cutting edge of most technologies, and biometric recognition—fingerprint scanners, hand readers, automated facial-geometry identification, voice ID, iris scans, retina scans—was the next big thing in the security business. They all have their strengths and weaknesses, but finger scans are generally considered the best—reliable, not too fussy or tricky, not too high a rate of false rejections or false acceptances.

Mounted on the wall outside Secure Facility C was an Identix fingerprint scanner.

In the late afternoon, I placed a call, from my cell phone, to the assistant director of the security command center for D Wing.

"Hey, George," I said. "This is Ken Romero in Network Design and Ops, in the wiring group?" Ken Romero was a real name, a senior manager. Just in case George decided to look me up.

"What can I do for you?" the guy said. He sounded like he'd just found a turd in his Cracker Jack box.

"Just a courtesy call? Bob wanted me to give you guys a heads-up that we're going to be doing a fiber reroute and upgrade on D-Five early tomorrow morning."

"Uh huh." Like: why are you telling me?

"I don't know why they think they need laser-optimized fifty micron fiber or an Ultra Dense Blade Server, but hey, it's not coming out of my pocket, you know? I guess they've got some serious bandwidth-hog applications running up there, and—"

"What can I do for you, Mister—"

"Romero. Anyway, I guess the guys on the fifth floor didn't want any disruptions during the workday, so they put in a request to have it done early in the A.M. No big deal, but we wanted to keep you guys in the loop 'cause the work's going to set off proximity detectors and motion detectors and all that, like between four and six in the morning."

The assistant security chief actually sounded sort of relieved that he didn't have to *do* anything.

"You're talkin' the whole darned fifth floor? I can't shut off the whole darned fifth floor without—"

"No, no, no," I said. "We'll be lucky if my guys can get through two, maybe three wiring closets, the way they take coffee breaks. No, we're aiming for areas, lemme see, areas twenty-two A and B, I think? Just the internal sections. Anyway, your boards are probably going to light up like Christmas trees, probably going to drive you guys frickin' bonkers, but I wanted to give you a heads-up—"

George gave a heavy sigh. "If it's just twenty-two A and B, I suppose I can disable those. . . ."

"Whatever's convenient. I mean, we just don't want to drive you guys bonkers."

"I'll give you three hours if you need it."

"We shouldn't need three hours, but I guess better safe than sorry, you know? Anyways, appreciate your help."

84

Around seven that evening I checked out of the Trion building, as usual, and drove home. I got a fitful night's sleep.

Just before four in the morning, I drove back and parked on the street, not in the Trion garage, so there wouldn't be a record of my re-entering the building. Ten minutes later, a panel truck labeled J.J. RANKENBERG & CO—PROFESSIONAL WINDOW CLEANING TOOLS, EQUIPMENT, AND CHEMICALS SINCE 1963 pulled up. Seth was behind the wheel in a blue uniform with a J.J. Rankenberg patch on the left pocket.

"Howdy, cowboy," he said.

"J.J. himself let you have this?"

"The old man's dead," Seth said. He was smoking, which was how I could tell he was nervous. "I had to deal with Junior." He handed me a folded pair of blue overalls, and I slipped them over my chinos and polo shirt, not easy to do in the cab of the old Isuzu truck. It reeked of spilled gasoline.

"I thought Junior hates you."

Seth held up his left hand and rubbed his thumb and fingers together, meaning moolah. "Short-term lease, for a quickie job I got for my girlfriend's dad's company."

"You don't have a girlfriend."

"All he cared was, he doesn't have to report the income. Ready to rock 'n' roll, dude?"

"Press send, baby," I said. I pointed out the D Wing service entrance to the parking garage, and Seth drove down into it. The night attendant in the booth glanced at a sheet of paper, found the company name on the admit list.

Seth pulled the truck over to the lower-level loading dock and we took out the big nylon tote bags stuffed with gear, the Ettore professional squeegees and the big green buckets, the twelve-foot extension poles, the plastic gallon jugs filled with piss-yellow glass cleaner liquid, the ropes and hooks and Ski Genie and bosun chair and the Jumar ascenders. I'd forgotten how much miscellaneous *junk* the job required.

I hit the big round steel button next to the steel garage door, and a few seconds later the door began rolling open. A paunchy, pasty-faced security guard with a bristly mustache came out with a clipboard. "You guys need any help?" he asked, not meaning it.

"We're all set," I said. "If you can just show us to the freight elevator to the roof . . ."

"No problem," he said. He stood there with his clipboard—he didn't seem to be writing anything down on it, he just held it to let us know who was in charge—and watched us struggle with the equipment. "You guys can really clean windows when it's dark out?" he said as he walked us over to the elevator.

"At time-and-a-half, we clean 'em *better* when it's dark out," said Seth.

"I don't know why people get so uptight about us looking in their office windows when they're working," I said.

"Yeah, that's our main source of entertainment," Seth said. "Scare the shit out of people. Give the office workers a heart attack."

The guard laughed. "Just hit 'R,' " he said. "If the roof access door's locked, there should be a guy up there, I think it's Oscar."

"Cool," I said.

When we got to the roof, I remembered why I hated high-rise window cleaning. The Trion headquarters building was only eight stories high, no more than a hundred feet or so, but up there in the middle of the night it might as well have been the Empire State Building. The wind was whipping around, it was cold and clammy, and there was distant traffic noise, even at that time of night.

The security guard, Oscar Fernandez (according to his badge), was a short guy in a navy-blue security uniform with a two-way radio clipped to his belt squawking static and garbled voices. He met us at the freight elevator, shifting his weight awkwardly from foot to foot as we unloaded our stuff, and showed us to the roof-access stairs.

We followed him up the short flight of stairs. While he was unlocking the roof door, he said, "Yeah, I got the word you guys would be coming, but I was surprised, I didn't know you guys worked so early."

He didn't seem suspicious; he just seemed to be making conversation.

Seth repeated his line about time-and-a-half, and we replayed our bit about giving the office workers heart attacks, and he laughed too. He said he guessed it kind of made sense anyway that people didn't want us disrupting their work during normal working hours. We looked like legit window cleaners, we had all the right equipment and the uniforms, and who the hell else would be crazy enough to climb out on the roof of a tall building lugging all that junk?

"I've only been on nights a couple weeks anyway," he said. "You guys been up here before? You know your way around?"

We said we hadn't done Trion yet, and he showed us the basics—power outlets, water spigots, safety anchors. All newly constructed buildings these days are required to have rooftop safety anchors mounted every ten to fifteen feet apart, about six feet in from the edge of the building, strong enough to support five thousand pounds of weight. The anchors usually stick up like plumbing vent pipes, only with a U-bolt on top.

Oscar was a little too interested in how we rigged up our gear. He hung around, watching us fasten the locking steel carabiners. These were attached to half-inch orange-and-white kernmantle climbing rope and connected to the safety anchors.

"Neat," he said. "You guys probably climb mountains in your spare time, huh?"

Seth looked at me, then said, "You a security guard in your spare time?"

"Nah," he said, then he laughed. "I just mean you got to like climbing off tall places and stuff. That would scare the shit out of me."

"You get used to it," I said.

Each of us had two separate lines, one to climb down on, the other a back-up safety line with a rope grab, in case the first one broke. I wanted to do it right, and not just for appearance's sake. Neither one of us felt like getting killed by dropping off the Trion building. During those unpleasant couple of summers when we worked for the window cleaning company we kept hearing about how there was an industry average of ten fatalities a year, but they never told us if that was ten in the world or ten in the state or what, and we never asked.

I knew that what we were doing was dangerous. I just didn't know where the danger was going to come.

After another five minutes or so, Oscar finally got bored, mostly because we stopped talking to him, and he went back to his station.

The kernmantle rope attaches to a thing called a Sky Genie, a kind of long sheet-metal tube in which you wind the rope around a forged aluminum shank. The Sky Genie—gotta love the name—is a descent-control device that works by friction and pays out the rope slowly. These Sky Genies were scratched and looked like they'd been used. I held it up and said, "You couldn't buy us new ones?"

"Hey, they came with the truck, whaddaya want? What are you worried about? These babies'll support five thousand pounds. Then again, you look like you've put on a couple pounds the last few months."

"Fuck you."

"You have dinner? I hope not."

"This isn't funny. You ever look at the warning label on this?"

"I know, improper use can cause serious injury or even death. Don't pay attention to that. You're probably scared to remove mattress tags too."

"I like the slogan—'Sky Genie—Gets You Down.' "

Seth didn't laugh. "Eight stories is nothing, guy. You remember the time when we were doing the Civic—"

"Don't remind me," I interrupted. I didn't want to be a big pussy, but I wasn't into his black humor, not standing up there on the roof of the Trion building.

The Sky Genie got hooked up to a nylon safety harness attached to a waist belt and padded seat board. Everything in the window-cleaning business had names with the words "safety" or "fall-protection" in them, which just reminds you if anything goes even slightly wrong you're fucked.

The only thing we'd set up that was slightly out of the ordinary was a pair of Jumar Ascenders, which would enable us to climb back up the ropes. Most of the time when you're cleaning the windows on a high-rise you have no reason to go back up—you just work your way down until you're on the ground.

But this would be our means of escape.

Meanwhile, Seth mounted the electric winch to one of the roof anchors with a D-ring, then plugged it in. This was a hundred-and-fifteen-volt model with a pulley capable of lifting a thousand pounds. He connected it to each of our lines, making sure that there was enough play that it wouldn't stop us from climbing down.

I tugged on the rope, hard, to check that everything was locked in place, and we both walked over to the edge of the building and looked down. Then we looked at each other, and Seth smiled a what-the-fuck-are-we-doing smile.

"Are we having fun yet?" he said.

"Oh, yeah."

"You ready, buddy?"

"Yeah," I said. "Ready as Elliot Krause in the Port-O-San."

Neither one of us laughed. We climbed onto the guardrail slowly and then went over the side.

8 5

We only had to rappel down two stories, but it wasn't easy. We were both out of practice, we were lugging some heavy tools, and we had to be extremely careful not to swing too far to either side.

Mounted on the building's façade were closed-circuit TV surveillance cameras. I knew from the schematics exactly where they were mounted. I also knew the specs on the cameras, the size of the lenses, their focal range and all that.

In other words, I knew where the blind spots were.

And we were climbing down through one of them. I wasn't concerned about Building Security seeing us rappelling down the side of the building, since they were expecting window cleaners early in the morning. What I was concerned about was that, if anyone looked, they'd realize we weren't actually cleaning any windows. They'd see us lowering ourselves, slowly and steadily, to the fifth floor. They'd see that we weren't even positioning ourselves in front of a window, either.

We were dangling in front of a steel ventilation grate.

As long as we didn't swing too far to one side or the other, we'd be out of camera range. That was important.

Bracing our feet against a ledge, we got out our power tools and set to work on the hex bolts. They were securely fastened, through the steel and into concrete, and there were a lot of them. Seth and I labored in silence, the sweat pouring down our faces. It was possible that someone walking by, a security guard or whoever, might see us removing the bolts that held the vent grate in place and wonder what we were doing. Window cleaners worked with squeegees and buckets, not Milwaukee cordless impact wrenches.

But this time of the morning, there weren't many people walking by. Anyone who happened to look up would probably figure we were doing routine building maintenance.

Or so I hoped.

It took us a good fifteen minutes to loosen and remove each bolt. A few of them were rusted tight and needed a hit of WD-40.

Then, on a signal from me, Seth loosened the last bolt, and we both carefully lifted the grate away from the steel skin of the building. It was super heavy, a two-man job at least. We had to grip it by its sharp edges—luckily I'd brought gloves, a good pair for both of us—and angle it out so that it rested on the window ledge. Then Seth, grasping the grille for leverage, managed to swing his legs into the room. He dropped to the floor of the mechanical equipment room with a grunt.

"Your turn," he said. "Careful."

I grabbed an edge of the grate and swung my legs into the airshaft and dropped to the floor, looking around quickly.

The mechanical room was crowded with immense, roaring equipment, mostly dark, lit only by the distant spill from the floodlights mounted on the roof. There was all kinds of HVAC stuff in here—heat pumps, centrifugal fans, huge chillers and compressors, and other air filtration and air-conditioning equipment.

We stood there in our harnesses, still hooked up to the double ropes, which dangled through the ventilation shaft. Then we unsnapped the harness belts and let go.

Now the harnesses hung in midair. Obviously we couldn't just leave them out there, but we'd rigged them up to the electric winch up on the roof. Seth pulled out a little black remote-control garage-door opener and pressed the button. You could hear this whirring, grinding noise far off, and the harnesses and ropes began to rise slowly in the air, pulled by the electric winch.

"Hope we can get 'em back when we need 'em," Seth said, but I could barely hear him over the thundering white noise in the room.

I couldn't help thinking that this whole thing was little more than a game to Seth. If he was caught, no big deal. He'd be okay. I was the one who was in deep doodoo.

Now we pulled the grate in tight so that, from the outside, it looked like it was in place. Then I took an extra length of the kernmantle, ran it through the grips, then around a vertical pipe to tie the thing down.

The room had gone dark again, so I took out my Mag-Lite, switched it on. I walked over to the heavy-looking steel door and tried the lever.

It opened. I knew that the doors to mechanical rooms were required to be unlocked from the inside, to make sure no one got trapped, but it was still a relief to know we could get out of here.

In the meantime, Seth took out a pair of Motorola Talkabout walkie-talkies, handed me one, and then pulled out from his holster a compact black shortwave radio, a three-hundred-channel police scanner.

"You remember the security frequency? Something in the four hundreds UHF, wasn't it?"

I took a little spiral-bound notebook from my shirt pocket, read off the frequency number. He began to key it in, and I unfolded the floor map and studied my route.

I was even more nervous now than when I was climbing down the side of the building. We had a pretty solid plan, but too many things could go wrong.

For one, there might be people around, even this early. AURORA was Trion's top-priority program, with a big deadline a mere two days off. Engineers worked weird hours. Five in the morning, there probably wouldn't be anyone around, but you never knew. Better to stay in the window-washer uniform, carrying a bucket and a squeegee — cleaning people were all but invisible. Unlikely anyone would stop to ask what I was doing here.

But there was a gruesome possibility that I might run into someone who recognized me. Trion had tens of thousands of employees, and I'd met, I don't know, fifty of them, so the odds were in my favor I wouldn't see someone who knew me. Not at five in the morning. Still . . . So I'd brought along a yellow hard hat, even though window washers never actually wear them, jammed it down on my head, then put on a pair of safety glasses.

Once I was out of this dark little room, I'd have to walk several hundred feet of hallway with security cameras trained on me all the way. Sure, there were a couple of security guys in the command center in the basement, but they had to look at dozens of monitors, and they were probably also watching TV and drinking coffee and shooting the shit. I didn't think anyone would pay me much attention.

Until I reached Secure Facility C, where the security definitely got harsh.

"Got it," Seth said, staring at the police scanner's digital readout. "I just heard 'Trion Security' and something else Trion."

"Okay," I said. "Keep listening, and alert me if there's anything I should know."

"How long you gonna take, you think?"

I held my breath. "Could be ten minutes. Could be half an hour. Depends on how things go."

"Be careful, Cas."

I nodded.

"Wait, here you go." He'd spotted a big yellow wheeled cleaning bucket in the corner, rolled it over to me. "Take this."

"Good idea." I looked at my old buddy for a moment, wanting to say something like "Wish me luck," but then I decided that sounded too nervous and mushy. Instead, I gave him the thumbs-up, like I was cool about all this. "See you back here," I said.

"Hey, don't forget to turn your thingy on," he said, pointing to my Talkabout.

I shook my head at my own forgetfulness and smiled.

Opening the door slowly, I looked out, saw no one coming, stepped into the hall, and closed the door behind me.

Fifty feet up ahead, a security camera was mounted high on the wall, next to the ceiling, its tiny red light winking.

Wyatt said I was a good actor, and now I'd really need to be. I had to look casual, a little bored, busy, and most of all not nervous. That'd take some acting.

Keep watching the Weather Channel or whatever the hell is on now, I mentally willed whoever was in the command center. *Drink your coffee, eat your donuts. Talk basketball or football. Pay no attention to that man behind the curtain.*

My work boots squeaked softly as I walked down the carpeted hall, wheeling the cleaning bucket.

No one else around. That was a relief.

No, I thought, *it's actually better if there're other people walking by. Takes the focus off of you.*

Yeah, maybe. Take what you get. Just hope no one asks where I'm going.

I turned the corner into a large open cubicle-farm area. Except for a few emergency lights, it was dark.

Pushing the bucket through an aisle down the middle of the room, I could see even more security cameras. The signs in the cubicles, the weird unfunny posters, all indicated that engineers worked here. On a shelf above one of the cubicles was a Love Me Lucille doll, staring malevolently at me.

Just doin' my job, I reminded myself.

On the other side of this open area, I knew from the map, was a short corridor leading directly to the sealed-off half of the floor. A sign on the wall (SECURE FACILITY C—ADMITTANCE ONLY TO CLEARED PERSONNEL, and an arrow) confirmed it for me. I was almost there.

This was all going a lot more smoothly than I'd expected. Of course, there were motion detectors and cameras all around the entrance to the secure facility.

But if the call I'd made to Security the day before had worked, they'd have shut off the motion detectors.

Of course, I couldn't be sure of that. I'd know in a few seconds, when I got closer.

The cameras would almost certainly be on, but I had a plan for that.

Suddenly a loud noise jolted me, a high-pitched trill from my Talkabout.

"Jesus," I muttered, heart racing.

"Adam," came Seth's voice, flat and breathy.

I pressed the button on its side. "Yeah."

"We got a problem."

"What do you mean?"

"Get back here."

"Why?"

"Just get the fuck *back* here."

Oh, shit.

I spun around, left the cleaning bucket, started to run until I remembered I was being watched. I forced myself to slow down to a stroll. What the hell could have happened? Did the ropes give us away? Did the ventilation grate drop? Or did someone open the door to the mechanical room, find Seth?

The walk back took forever. An office door swung open just ahead, and a middle-aged guy came out. He was wearing brown double-knit polyester slacks and a short-sleeved yellow shirt, and he looked like an old-line mechanical engineer. Getting an extra-early start on the day, or maybe he'd been up all night. The guy glanced at me, then looked down at the carpet without saying anything.

I was a cleaning guy. I was invisible.

A couple dozen surveillance cameras had captured my image, but I wasn't going to attract anyone's attention. I was a cleaning guy, a mainte-nance guy. I was supposed to be here. No one would look twice.

Finally I reached the mechanical room. I stopped in front of the door, lis-tening for voices, prepared to run if I had to, if someone was in there with Seth, even though I didn't want to leave him there. I could hear the faint squawk of the police scanner, that was all.

I pulled the door open. Seth was standing just on the other side of the door, the radio near his ear.

He looked panicked.

"We gotta get out of here," he whispered.

"What's—"

"The guy on the roof. On the seventh floor, I mean. The security guy who took us to the roof."

"What about him?"

"Must have come back out to the roof. Curious, whatever. Looked down, didn't see us. Saw the ropes and the harnesses, and no window cleaners, and he freaked. I don't know, maybe he got scared something happened to us, who knows."

"What?"

"*Listen!*"

There was squawking over the police scanner, a babble of voices. I heard a snatch: "Floor by floor, over!"

Then: "Bravo unit, come in."

"Bravo, over."

"Bravo, suspected illegal entry, D David wing. Looks like window clean-ers—abandoned equipment on the roof, no sign of the workers. I want a floor-by-floor search of the whole building. This is a Code Two. Bravo, your men cover the first floor, over."

"Roger that."

I stared at Seth. "I think Code Two means urgent."

"They're searching the building," Seth whispered, his voice barely audi-ble over the roar of the machinery. "We have to get the fuck *out* of here."

"How?" I hissed back. "We can't drop the ropes, even if they're still in place! And we sure as hell can't get out through the mantrap on *this* floor!"

"What the hell are we going to *do*?"

I inhaled deeply, exhaled, tried to think clearly. I wanted a cigarette. "All right. Find a computer, any computer. Log on to the Trion Web site. Look for the company security procedures page, see where the emergency points of egress are. I'm talking freight elevators, fire stairs, whatever. Any way we can get out, even if we have to jump."

"Me? So what are *you* going to do?"

"I'm going back out there."

"What? You're fucking *kidding* me. This building is crawling with security guards, you moron!"

"They don't know where we are. All they know is we're *somewhere* in this wing—and there's seven floors."

"Jesus, Adam!"

"I'll never get this chance again," I said, running toward the door. I waved my Motorola Talkabout at him. "Tell me when you find a way out. I'm going into Secure Facility C. I'm going to get what we came for."

8 7

Don't run.

I had to keep reminding myself. Stay calm. I walked down the hall, trying to look blasé when my head was about to explode. Don't look at the cameras.

I was halfway to the big open cubicle area when my walkie-talkie bleeped at me, two quick tones.

"Yeah?"

"Listen, man. It's asking me for an ID. The sign-on screen."

"Oh, shit, right, of course."

"Want me to sign on as you?"

"Oh *God* no. Use . . ." I whipped out the little spiral notebook. "Use CPierson." I spelled it out for him as I kept walking.

"Password? Got a password?"

"MJ twenty-three," I read off.

"MJ . . . ?"

"I assume it's for Michael Jordan."

"Oh, right. Twenty-three's Jordan's number. This guy some kind of amazing hoops player?"

Why was Seth blathering on? He must have been scared out of his mind.

"No," I said, distracted, as I entered the cubicle area. I took off the yellow hard hat and the safety glasses, since I no longer needed them, stowed them under a desk as I passed by. "Just arrogant, like Jordan. They both think they're the best. One of them's right."

"All right, I'm in," he said. "The Security page, you said?"

"Company security procedures. See what you can find out about the loading dock, whether we can get back down there using the freight elevator. That might be our best escape route. I gotta go."

"Hurry it up," he said.

Straight ahead of me was a gray-painted steel door with a small, diamond-shaped window reinforced with wire mesh. A sign on the door said AUTHOR-IZED PERSONNEL ONLY.

I approached the door slowly, at an angle, and looked through the window. On the other side was a small, industrial-looking waiting room, a concrete floor. I counted two CCTV cameras mounted high on the wall near the ceiling, their red lights blinking. They were on. I could also see the little white pods in each corner of the room: the passive infrared motion detectors.

No LED lights on the motion detectors, though. I couldn't be sure, but they seemed to be off. Maybe Security really had shut them down for a few hours.

In one hand I was holding a clipboard, trying to look official, like I was obeying printed instructions. With my other hand I tried the doorknob. It was locked. Mounted on the wall to the left of the door frame was a little gray proximity sensor, just like you saw all over the building. Would Alana's badge open it? I took out my copy of her badge, waved it at the sensor, willing the red light to turn green.

And I heard a voice.

"Hey! You!"

I turned slowly. A Trion security guard was running toward me, another guard lagging behind him.

"Freeze!" the first man shouted.

Oh, shit. My heart leaped in my chest.

Caught.

Now what, Adam?

I stared at the guards, my expression changing from startled to arrogant. I took a breath. In a quiet voice, I said, "You find him yet?"

"Huh?" said the first guard, slowing to a stop.

"Your goddamned intruder!" I said, my voice louder. "The alarm went off five fucking minutes ago, and you guys are still running around like idiots, scratching your asses!" *You can do this*, I told myself. *This is what you do.*

"Sir?" the second guard said. They both were frozen in place, looking at me, bewildered.

"You morons have any idea where the point of entry was?" I was shouting at them like a drill sergeant, tearing them new assholes. "You think we could have made it any easier for you guys? For Christ's sake, you do an exterior perimeter check, that's the first thing you do. Page twenty-three of the god-damned manual! You do that, and you'd find a ventilation grille dislodged."

"Ventilation grille?" said the first one.

"Are we going to have to spray-paint the trail in fucking Day-Glo colors? Should we have given you guys engraved invitations to a Bendix surprise security audit? We've run this drill in three area buildings in the past week, and you guys are the worst bunch of amateurs I've seen." I took the clipboard and the attached pen and began writing. "Okay, I want names and I want badge numbers. You!" The two guards had begun to retreat, backing up slowly. "Get the fuck back here! You think Corporate Security's all about the Krispy Kremes? Heads are going to roll, I promise you that, when we file our report."

"McNamara," the second guard said reluctantly.

"Valenti," said the first.

I jotted down their names. "Badge numbers? Aw, Christ, look—one of you get this goddamned door open, and then both of you, get the hell out of here."

The first one approached the card reader, waved his badge at it. There was a click and the light turned green.

I shook my head in disgust as I pulled the door open. The two guards turned and began loping back down the hall. I heard the first one say to the other sullenly, "I'm going to check with Dispatch right now. I don't like this."

My heart was hammering so loud it had to be audible. I'd bullshitted my way out of that, but I knew all I'd done was to buy a couple of minutes. The

guards would radio in to their dispatch and find out the truth immediately—
there was no "surprise security audit" going on. Then they'd be back with a
vengeance.

I watched the motion detector, mounted high on the wall in this small
lobby area, waiting to see whether a light would flash on, but it didn't.

When the motion detectors were on, they triggered the cameras, shifted
them in the direction of any moving object.

But the motion detectors were off. That meant the cameras were fixed,
couldn't move.

It's funny, Meacham and his guy had trained me to beat security systems
that were more sophisticated than this. Maybe Meacham was right—forget
about the movies, in reality corporate security always tends to be sort of
primitive.

Now I could enter the little lobby area without being seen by the cameras, which were pointed at the door that opened directly into Secure Facility
C. I took a few tentative steps into the room, flattening my back against the
wall. I sidled slowly over to one of the cameras from behind. I was in the camera's blind spot, I knew. It couldn't see me.

And then the Talkabout bleeped to life.

"*Get the hell out!*" Seth's voice screeched. "Everyone's been ordered to
the fifth floor, I just heard it!"

"I—I can't, I'm almost there!" I shouted back.

"*Move it!* Jesus, get the hell out of there!"

"No—I can't! Not yet!"

"Cassidy—"

"Seth, listen to me. You've got to get the hell out of here—stairs, freight
elevator, whatever. Wait for me in the truck outside."

"Cassidy—"

"Go!" I shouted, and I clicked off.

A blast of sound jolted me—a throaty mechanical *hoo-ah* blaring from
an alarm horn somewhere very close.

Now what? I *couldn't* stop here, just feet from the entrance to the
AURORA Project! Not this close!

I had to keep going.

The alarm went on, *hoo-ah, hoo-ah,* deafeningly loud, like an air-raid siren.

I pulled the spray can out of my overalls—a can of Pam spray, that aerosol cooking oil—then leaped up at the camera and sprayed the lens. I could see an oil slick on the glass eyeball. Done.

The siren blared.

Now the camera was blind, its optics defeated—but not in a way that would necessarily attract attention. Anyone watching the monitor would see the image suddenly go blurry. Maybe they'd blame the network wiring upgrade they'd been warned about. The blurred-out image probably wouldn't draw much attention in a bank of TV monitors. That was the idea, anyway.

But now that careful planning seemed almost pointless, because they were coming, I could hear them. The same guards I'd just bamboozled? Different ones? I had no idea, of course, but they were coming.

There were footsteps, shouts, but they sounded far away, just background chatter against the ear-splitting siren.

Maybe I could still make it.

If I hurried. Once I was inside the AURORA laboratory, they probably couldn't come after me, or at least not easily. Not unless they had some kind of override, which seemed unlikely.

They might not even know I was in there.

That is, if I could get in.

Now I circled the room, keeping out of camera range until I reached the other camera. Standing in its blind spot, I leaped up, sprayed the oil, hit the lens dead on.

Now Security couldn't see me through the monitors, couldn't see what I was about to try.

I was almost in. Another few seconds—I hoped—and I'd be inside AURORA.

Getting out was another matter. I knew there was a freight elevator there, which couldn't be accessed from outside. Would Alana's badge activate it? I sure hoped so. It was my only shot.

Damn, I could barely think straight, with that siren blasting, and the voices getting louder, the footsteps closer. My mind raced crazily. Would the security guards even know of the *existence* of AURORA? How closely held was the secret? If they didn't know about AURORA, they might not be able to figure out where I was headed. Maybe they were just running through the corridors of each floor in some wild, uncoordinated search for the second intruder.

Mounted on the wall to the immediate left of a shiny steel door was a small beige box: an Identix fingerprint scanner.

From the front pocket of my overalls I pulled the clear plastic case. Then, with trembling fingers, I removed the strip of tape with Alana's thumbprint on it, its whorls captured in traces of graphite powder.

I pressed the tape gently on the scanner, right where you'd normally put your thumb, and waited for the LED to change from red to green.

And nothing happened.

No, please, God, I thought desperately, my brain scrambled by terror, and by the unbearably loud *hoo-ah* of the alarm. *Make it work. Please, God.*

The light stayed red, stubbornly red.

Nothing was happening.

Meacham had given me a long session on how to defeat biometric scanners, and I'd practiced countless times until I thought I'd gotten it down. Some fingerprint readers were harder to beat than others, depending on what technology they used. This was one of the most common types, with an optical sensor inside it. And what I'd just done was supposed to work ninety percent of the time. Ninety percent of the time this goddamned trick *worked!*

Of course, there's the other ten percent, I thought, as I heard footsteps thunder nearer. They were close, now, that much I knew. Maybe a few yards away, in the cubicle farm.

Shit, it *wasn't* working!

What were the other tricks they'd taught me?

Something about a plastic bag full of water . . . but I didn't have anything like a plastic bag with me. . . . What *was* it? Old fingerprints remained on the surface of the sensor like handprints on a mirror, the oily residue of people who'd been admitted. The old fingerprints could be re-activated with moisture. . . .

Yes, it sounds wacky, but no crazier than using a piece of tape with a lifted print on it. I leaned over, cupped my hands over the little sensor, *breathed* on it. My breath hit the glass, condensed at once. It disappeared in a second, but it was long enough —

A beep, sounding almost like a chirp. A happy sound.

A green light on the box went on.

I'd passed. The moisture from my breath had activated an old fingerprint. I'd fooled the sensor.

The shiny steel door to Secure Facility C slid slowly open on tracks just as the other door behind me opened and I heard, "Stop right there!"

And: "Stay right there!"

I stared at the huge open space that was Secure Facility C, and I couldn't believe what I was seeing. My eyes couldn't make sense of it.

I must have made a mistake.

This couldn't be the right place.

I was looking at the area marked Secure Facility C. I was expecting laboratory equipment and banks of electron microscopes, clean rooms, supercomputers and coils of fiber-optic cable. . . .

Instead, what I saw was naked steel girders, bare unpainted concrete floors, plaster dust and construction debris.

An immense, gutted space.

There was *nothing* here.

Where was the AURORA Project? I was in the right place, but there was nothing here.

And then a thought came to me which made the floor beneath my feet buckle and sway: *Was there in fact no AURORA Project after all?*

"Don't move a fucking *muscle!*" someone shouted from behind me.

I obeyed.

I didn't turn around to face the guards. I froze.

I couldn't move if I wanted to anyway.

88

Slack-jawed, dizzy, I turned slowly and saw a cluster of guards, five or six of them, among them a couple of familiar faces. Two of them were the guys I'd scared off, and they were back, furious.

The security guard, the black guy who'd caught me in Nora's office—what was his name, again? The guy with the Mustang? He was pointing a pistol at me. "Mister—Mister *Sommers?*" he gasped.

Next to him, in jeans and a T-shirt that looked like they'd been thrown on moments ago, his blond hair a tousled mess, was Chad. He was holding his cell phone. I knew at once why he was here: he must have tried to sign on, found that he was *already* signed on, and so he made a call. . . .

"That's Cassidy. Call Goddard!" Chad bellowed at the guard. "Call the goddamned *CEO!*"

"No, man, that's not the way we do it," the guard said, staring, his gun still aimed at me. "Step *back*," he shouted. A couple of other guards were fanning out to either side. He said to Chad, "You don't call the CEO, man. You call the security director. Then we wait for the cops. That's my orders."

"*Call the fucking CEO!*" Chad screamed, waving his cell phone. "I've got Goddard's home number. I don't *care* what time it is. I want Goddard to know what his goddamned executive assistant, this fucking *hustler*, did!" He pressed a couple of buttons on the phone, put it to his ear.

"You asshole," he said to me. "You are so fucked."

It took a long time before anyone answered. "Mr. Goddard," Chad said in a low, deferential voice. "I'm sorry to call so early in the morning, but this is extremely important. My name is Chad Pierson, and I work at Trion." He spoke a few minutes more, and slowly his malevolent grin began to fade.

"Yes, sir," he said.

He thrust the phone at me, looking deflated. "He says he wants to talk to you."

PART NINE

ACTIVE MEASURES

Active Measures: Russian term for intelligence operations that will affect another nation's policies or actions. These can be either covert or open and can include a wide variety of activities, including assassination.

—*Spy Book: The Encyclopedia of Espionage*

8 9

It was close to six in the morning when the security guards put me in a locked conference room on the fifth floor—no windows, only one door. The table was littered with scrawl-covered notepads, empty Snapple bottles. There was an overhead projector, a whiteboard that hadn't been erased, and, fortunately, a computer.

I wasn't a prisoner, exactly. I was being "detained." It was made clear to me that if I didn't cooperate, I'd be turned right over to the police, and that didn't seem to be a very good idea.

And Goddard—sounding weirdly calm—had told me that he wanted to speak with me when he got in. He didn't want to hear anything else, which was good, because I didn't know what to say.

Later I learned that Seth had just made it out of the building, though without the truck. I tried e-mailing Jock. I still didn't know how I could explain myself, so I just wrote:

```
Jock—
Need to talk. I want to explain.
Adam
```

But there was no reply.

I remembered, suddenly, that I still had my cell phone with me—I'd tucked it into one of my pockets, and they hadn't found it. I switched it on.

There were five messages, but before I could check my voice mail, the phone rang.

"Yeah," I said.

"Adam. Oh, shit, man." It was Antwoine. He sounded desperate, almost hysterical. "Oh, man. Oh, shit. I don't want to go back in. Shit, I don't want to go back inside."

"Antwoine, what are you talking about? Start from the beginning."

"These guys tried to break in your dad's apartment. They must've thought it was empty."

I felt a surge of irritation. Hadn't the neighborhood kids figured out yet that there was nothing in my dad's shithole apartment worth breaking in *for*?

"Jesus, are you okay?" I said.

"Oh, *I'm* okay. Two of 'em got away, but I grabbed the slower guy—oh, *shit!* Oh, man, I don't want to get in trouble now! You gotta help me."

This was a conversation I really didn't feel like having, not now. I could hear some kind of animal noise in the background, some sort of moaning or scuffling or something. "Calm down, man," I said. "Take a deep breath and sit down."

"I'm sittin' on the motherfucker right now. What's freaking me out is this fucker says he knows you."

"*Knows* me?" Suddenly I got a funny feeling. "Describe the guy, could you?"

"I don't know, he's a white guy—"

"His face, I mean."

Antwoine sounded sheepish. "Right now? Kinda red and mushy. My bad. I think I broke his nose."

I sighed. "Oh, Jesus, Antwoine, ask him what his name is."

Antwoine put down the phone. I heard the low rumble of Antwoine's voice, followed immediately by a yelp. Antwoine came back on. "He says his name is Meacham."

I flashed on an image of Arnold Meacham, broken and bleeding, lying on my dad's kitchen floor under three hundred pounds of Antwoine Leonard, and I felt a brief, blessed spasm of pleasure. Maybe I *had* been watched when I'd dropped by my dad's apartment. Maybe Meacham and his goons figured I'd hidden something there.

"Oh, I wouldn't worry about it," I said. "I promise you that asshole's not going to cause you any more trouble." If I were Meacham, I thought, I'd go into the witness protection program.

Antwoine now sounded relieved. "Look, I'm really sorry about this, man."

"Sorry? Hey, don't apologize. Believe me, that's the first piece of good news I've heard in a long time."

And it would probably be the last.

I figured I had a few hours to kill before Goddard would show up, and I couldn't just sit there anguishing over what I'd done, or what would be done to me. So I did what I always do to pass the time: I went on the Internet.

That was how I began to put some things together.

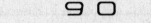

90

The door to the conference room opened. It was one of the security guards from before.

"Mr. Goddard's downstairs at the press conference," the guard said. He was tall, around forty, wore wire-rim glasses. His blue Trion uniform fit badly. "He said you should go down to the Visitors Center."

I nodded.

The main lobby of Building A was hectic with people, loud voices, photographers and reporters swarming all over the place. I stepped out of the elevator into the chaos, feeling disoriented. I couldn't really make out what anyone was saying in the hubbub; it was all background noise to me. One of the doors that led to the huge futuristic auditorium kept opening and closing. I caught glimpses of a giant image of Jock Goddard projected on a screen, heard his amplified voice.

I elbowed my way through the crowd. I thought I heard someone call my name, but I kept going, moving slowly, zombielike.

The auditorium's floor sloped down to a glittering pod of a stage, where Goddard was standing in a spotlight, wearing his black mock turtleneck and brown tweed jacket. He looked like a professor of classics at a small New England college, except for the orange TV makeup on his face. Behind him was a huge screen on which his talking head was projected five or six feet high.

The place was packed with journalists, glaringly bright with TV camera lights.

". . . This acquisition," he was saying, "will double the size of our sales force, and it will double and in some sectors even triple our market penetration." I didn't know what he was talking about. I stood in the back of the theater, listening.

"By bringing together two great companies, we're creating one world-class technology leader. Trion Systems is now without question one of the world's leading consumer electronics companies.

"And I'd like to make one more announcement," Goddard went on. He gave a twinkle-eyed pixie smile. "I've always believed in the importance of giving back. So this morning Trion is pleased to announce the establishment of an exciting new charitable foundation. Beginning with seed money of five million dollars, this new foundation hopes, over the course of the next several years, to put a computer into thousands of public schools in America, in school districts that don't have the resources to provide computers for their students. We think this is the best way to bridge the digital divide. This is a venture that's long been in the works at Trion. We call it the AURORA Project—for Aurora, the Greek goddess of the dawn. We believe the AURORA Project will welcome the dawn of a bright new future for all of us in this great country."

There was a smattering of polite applause.

"Finally, let me extend a warm welcome to the nearly thirty thousand talented and hardworking employees of Wyatt Telecommunications to the Trion family. Thank you very much." Goddard bowed his head slightly and stepped off the stage. More applause, which gradually swelled into an enthusiastic ovation.

The giant projection of Jock Goddard's face dissolved into a TV news broadcast—CNBC's morning financial program, *Squawk Box*.

On half the screen, Maria Bartiromo was broadcasting from the floor of the New York Stock Exchange. On the other half of the screen was the Trion logo and a graph of its share price over the last few minutes—a line that went straight up.

"—as trading in Trion Systems hit record volume," she was saying. "Trion shares have already almost doubled and show no sign of slowing down, after the announcement before the bell this morning by Trion founder and chief executive officer Augustine Goddard that it's acquiring one of its main competitors, the troubled Wyatt Telecommunications."

I felt a tap on my shoulder. It was Flo, elegant, a grave expression on her face. She was wearing a wireless headset. "Adam, can you please come to the Penthouse Executive Reception Suite? Jock wants to see you."

I nodded but kept watching. I wasn't really able to think clearly.

Now the picture on the big screen showed Nick Wyatt being hustled out of Wyatt headquarters by a couple of guards. The wide-angle shot took in the building's reflecting glass, the emerald turf outside, grazing flocks of journalists. You could tell that he was both furious and humiliated as he did the perp walk.

"Wyatt Telecommunications was a debt-plagued company, nearly three billion dollars in debt, when the stunning news leaked out late yesterday that the company's flamboyant founder, Nicholas Wyatt, had signed a secret and unauthorized agreement, without the vote or even the knowledge of his board of directors, to acquire a small California-based startup called Delphos, a tiny company without any revenue, for five hundred million dollars in cash," Maria Bartiromo was saying.

The camera zoomed in closer on the man. Tall and burly, hair gleaming like black enamel, coppery tan. Nick Wyatt in the flesh. The camera moved in even closer. His formfitting dove-gray silk shirt was dappled with flop sweat. He was being trundled into a town car. He had this "What the fuck did they do to me?" expression on his face. I knew the feeling.

"That left Wyatt without enough to cover its debt payments. The company's board met yesterday afternoon and announced the firing of Mr. Wyatt for gross violations of corporate governance, just moments before bondholders forced the sale of the company to Trion Systems at a fire-sale price of ten cents on the dollar. Mr. Wyatt was unavailable for comment, but a spokesman said he was resigning to spend more time with his family. Nick Wyatt is unmarried and has no children. David?"

Another tap on my shoulder. "I'm sorry, Adam, but he wants to see you right now," Flo said.

91

On the way up to the penthouse the elevator stopped at the cafeteria, and a man in an Aloha shirt with a ponytail got in.

"Cassidy," Mordden said. He was clutching a cinnamon-swirl bun and a cup of coffee, and he didn't seem surprised to see me. "The Sammy Glick of the microchip. Word has it that Icarus's wings have melted."

I nodded.

He bowed his head. "It's true what they say. Experience is something you don't get until just after you need it."

"Yep."

He pressed a button and was silent while the doors closed and the cabin ascended. It was just me and him. "I see you're going up to the penthouse. The Executive Reception Suite. I take it you're not receiving dignitaries or Japanese businessmen."

I just looked at him.

"Now perhaps you finally understand the truth about our fearless leader," he said.

"No, I don't think I do. As a matter of fact, I don't even understand *you*. For some reason, you're the one person here who has utter contempt for Goddard, everyone knows it. You're rich. You don't need to work. Yet you're still here."

He shrugged. "By my choice. I told you, I'm fireproof."

"What the hell does that mean, already? Look, you're never going to see my ass again. You can tell me now. I'm outta here. I'm fucking dead."

"Yes, roadkill is, I believe, the term of art around here." He blinked once. "I'll actually miss you. Millions wouldn't." He was making a joke out of it, but I knew he was trying to say something heartfelt. For whatever reason, he'd actually taken a liking to me. Or maybe it was just pity. With a guy like Mordden, it was hard to tell.

"Enough with the riddles," I said. "Will you please explain what the hell you're talking about?"   .

Mordden smirked, did a fairly passable imitation of Ernst Stavro Blofeld. "Since you're about to die, Mr. Bond—" He broke off. "Oh, I wish I could lay it all out for you. But I'd never violate the nondisclosure agreement I signed eighteen years ago."

"Mind putting it in terms my puny earthling mind can comprehend?"

The elevator stopped, the doors opened, and Mordden got out. He put his hand on one of the doors to hold it open. "That nondisclosure agreement is now worth about ten million dollars to me in Trion stock. Perhaps twice that, at today's share price. It certainly wouldn't be in my interest to jeopardize that arrangement by breaking my contractually obligated silence."

"What sort of NDA?"

"As I said, I surely don't wish to jeopardize my lucrative arrangement with Augustine Goddard by telling you that the famous Goddard modem was invented not by Jock Goddard, a rather mediocre engineer if brilliant corporate gamesman, but by yours truly. Why would I want to jeopardize ten million dollars by revealing that the technological breakthrough that transformed this company into a powerhouse of the communications revolution was the brainchild not of the corporate gamesman but of one of his earliest hires, a lowly engineer? Goddard could have had it for free, as my corporate contract stipulated, but he wanted sole credit. That was worth a good deal of money to him. Why should I want to reveal such a thing and thereby tarnish the legend, the sterling reputation of, what was it *Newsweek* once called him, 'Corporate America's Senior Statesman'? Certainly it would not be politic of me to point out the hollowness of Jock Goddard's whole Will Rogers shtick, that down-to-earth cornpone cracker-barrel image that cloaks such ruthlessness. For heaven's sake, that would be like telling you there's no

Santa Claus. Why would I want to disillusion you—and risk my financial bounty?"

"You're telling me the truth?" was all I could think to say.

"I'm not telling you anything," Mordden said. "It wouldn't be in my interest. Adieu, Cassidy."

I'd never seen anything like the penthouse of Trion Building A.

It didn't look at all like the rest of Trion—no choked offices or cluttered cubicles, no industrial-gray wall-to-wall carpeting or fluorescent lights.

Instead, it was a huge open space with floor-to-ceiling windows through which the sunlight sparkled. The floors were black granite, oriental rugs here and there, the walls some kind of gleaming tropical wood. The space was broken up by banks of ivy, clusters of designer-looking chairs and sofas, and right in the center of the room, a giant freestanding waterfall—the water rushed from some unseen fountain over rugged pinkish stones.

The Executive Reception Suite. For receiving important visitors: cabinet secretaries, senators and congressmen, CEOs, heads of state. I'd never seen it before, and I didn't know anyone who had, and no wonder. It didn't look very Trion. Not very democratic. It was dramatic, intimidating, grandiose.

A small round dining table was being set in the area between the indoor waterfall and a fireplace with roaring gas flames on ceramic logs. Two young Latinos, a man and a woman in maroon uniforms, were speaking quietly in Spanish as they put out silver coffee- and teapots, baskets of pastries, pitchers of orange juice. Three place settings.

Baffled, I looked around, but there was no one else. No one waiting for me. All of a sudden there was a *bing*, and a small set of brushed-steel elevator doors on the other side of the room slid open.

Jock Goddard and Paul Camilletti.

They were laughing loudly, both of them giddy, high as kites. Goddard caught a glimpse of me, stopped midlaugh, and said, "Well, there he is. You'll excuse us, Paul—*you* understand."

Camilletti smiled, patted Goddard's shoulder and remained in the elevator as the old man emerged, the doors closing behind him. Goddard strode across the big open space almost at a trot.

"Walk with me to the john, will you?" he said to me. "Gotta wash off this damned makeup."

Silently, I followed him over to a glossy black door that was marked with little silver male-and-female silhouettes. The lights went on as we entered. It was a spacious, sleek rest room, all glass and black marble.

Goddard looked at himself in the mirror. Somehow he seemed a little taller. Maybe it was his posture: he wasn't quite as hunched as usual.

"Christ, I look like fucking Liberace," he said as he worked up soapsuds in his hands and began splashing his face. "You've never been up here, have you?"

I shook my head, watching him in the mirror as he ducked his head down toward the basin and then up again. I felt a strange tangle of emotions—fear, anger, shock—that was so complex that I didn't know what to feel.

"Well, you know the business world," he went on. He seemed almost apologetic. "The importance of theatrics—pageantry, pomp and circumstance, all that crap. I could hardly meet the president of Russia or the crown prince of Saudi Arabia in my shabby little cubbyhole downstairs."

"Congratulations," I said softly. "It's been a big morning."

He toweled off his face. "More theatrics," he said dismissively.

"You knew Wyatt would buy Delphos, no matter what it cost," I said. "Even if it meant going broke."

"He couldn't resist," Goddard said. He tossed the towel, now stained orange-brown, onto the marble counter.

"No," I said. I became aware of my heartbeat starting to accelerate. "Not so long as he believed you were about to announce this big exciting breakthrough on the optical chip. But there never was an optical chip, was there?"

Goddard grinned his little pixie smile. He turned, and I followed him out of the rest room. I kept going: "That's why there were no patents filed, no HR files. . . ."

"The optical chip," he said, almost lunging across the oriental rugs toward the dining table, "exists only in the fevered minds and blotched notebooks of a handful of third-raters at a tiny, doomed company in Palo Alto. Chasing a fantasy, which may or may not happen in your lifetime. Certainly not in mine." He sat at the table, gestured to the place next to his.

I sat, and the two uniformed attendants, who'd been standing against the bank of ivy at a discreet distance, came forward, poured us each coffee. I was more than frightened and angry and confused; I was deeply exhausted.

"They may be third-raters," I said, "but you bought their company more than three years ago."

It was, I admit, an educated guess—the lead investor in Delphos was, according to the filings I'd come across on the Internet, a venture capital fund based in London whose money was channeled through a Cayman Islands investment vehicle. Which indicated that Delphos was actually owned, at a remove of about five shell companies and fronts, by a major player.

"You're a smart fellow," Goddard said, grabbing a sweet roll and tucking into it greedily. "The true ownership chain is pretty damned hard to unwind. Help yourself to a pastry, Adam. These raspberry-and-cream-cheese things are *killer*."

Now I understood why Paul Camilletti, a man who crossed every T and dotted every I, had conveniently "forgotten" to sign the no-shop clause on the term sheet. Once Wyatt saw that, he knew he had less than twenty-four hours to "steal" the company away from Trion—no time to get board approval, even if his board would have approved it. Which they probably wouldn't have anyway.

I noticed the unoccupied third place setting, and I wondered who the other guest would be. I had no appetite, didn't feel like drinking coffee. "But the only way to make Wyatt swallow the hook," I said, "was to have it come from a spy he thought he'd planted." My voice was trembling, and now I was feeling anger most of all.

"Nick Wyatt's a very suspicious man," Goddard said. "I understand him—I'm the same way. He's sorta like the CIA—they never believe a single damned scrap of intel unless they've gotten it by subterfuge."

I took a sip of ice water, which was so cold it made my throat ache. The only sound in this vast space was the splashing and burbling of the waterfall. The bright light hurt my eyes. It felt cheery in here, weirdly so. The waitress approached with a crystal pitcher of water to refill my glass, but Goddard waved a hand. "*Muchos gracias.* You two can be excused, I think we're all set here. Could you ask our other guest to join us, please?"

"It's not the first time you've done this, is it?" I said. Who was it who'd told me that whenever Trion was on the brink of failure, a competitor of theirs always made some disastrous miscalculation, and Trion came back stronger than ever?

Goddard gave me a sidelong glance. "Practice makes perfect."

My head swam. It was Paul Camilletti's resume and bio that gave it away. Goddard had hired him away from a company called Celadon Data, which was at the time the biggest threat to Trion's existence. Soon after, Celadon made a legendary technological gaffe—a Betamax-over-VHS kind of mis-step—and went Chapter Eleven just before Trion scooped them up.

"Before me, there was Camilletti," I said.

"And others before him." Goddard took a swig of coffee. "No, you weren't the first. But I'd say you were the best."

The compliment stung. "I don't understand how you convinced Wyatt the mole idea could work," I said.

Goddard glanced up as the elevator opened, the same one he'd come up on.

Judith Bolton. My breath stopped.

She was wearing a navy suit and white blouse and looked very crisp and corporate. Her lips and fingernails were coral. She came up to Goddard, gave him a quick kiss on the lips. Then she reached over to me, clasped my hand in both of hers. They gave off a faint herbal scent and felt cold.

She sat down on Goddard's other side, unfolded a linen napkin on her lap.

"Adam's curious how you convinced Wyatt," Goddard said.

"Oh, I didn't have to twist Nick's arm, exactly," she said with a throaty laugh.

"You're far more subtle than that," Goddard said.

I stared at Judith. "Why me?" I said finally.

"I'm surprised you ask," she said. "Look at what you've done. You're a natural."

"That and the fact that you had me by the balls because of the money."

"Plenty of people in corporations color outside the lines, Adam," she said, leaning in toward me. "We had lots of choices. But you stood out from the crowd. You were far and away the most qualified. A pitch-perfect gift of blarney, plus father issues."

Anger welled up inside me until I couldn't sit there anymore listening. I rose, stood over Goddard, said: "Let me ask you something. What do you think Elijah would think of you now?"

Goddard looked at me blankly.

"Elijah," I repeated. "Your son."

"Oh, gosh, right, Elijah," Goddard said, his puzzlement slowly turning to wry amusement. "That. Right. Well, that was Judith's inspiration." He chuckled.

The room seemed to be spinning slowly and getting brighter, more washed out. Goddard peered at me with twinkling eyes.

"Adam," Judith said, all concern and empathy. "Sit down, please."

I just stood staring.

"We were concerned," she said, "that you might start to get suspicious if it all seemed to come too easily. You're an extremely bright, intuitive young man. Everything had to make sense, or it would start to unravel. We couldn't risk that."

I flashed on Goddard's lake-house study, the trophies that I now knew were fakes. Goddard's sleight-of-hand talent, the way the trophy somehow got knocked to the floor. . . .

"Oh, *you* know," Goddard said, "the old man's got a soft spot for me, I remind him of his dead son, all that bullshit? Makes sense, right?"

"Can't leave these things to chance," I said hollowly.

"Precisely," said Goddard.

"Very, very few people could have done what you did," Judith said. She smiled. "Most wouldn't have been able to endure the doubleness, straddle the line the way you did. You're a remarkable person, I hope you know that. That's why we singled you out in the first place. And you more than proved us right."

"I don't believe this," I whispered. My legs felt wobbly, my feet unsteady. I had to get the hell out of there. "I don't fucking believe this."

"Adam, I know how difficult this must be for you," Judith said gently.

My head was throbbing like an open wound. "I'll go clear out my office."

"You'll do no such thing," Goddard cried out. "You're not resigning. I won't allow it. Clever young fellows like you are all too rare. I *need* you on the seventh floor."

A shaft of sunlight blinded me; I couldn't see their faces.

"And you'd trust me?" I said bitterly, shifting to one side to get the sun out of my face.

Goddard exhaled. "Corporate espionage, my boy, is as American as apple pie and Chevrolet. For fuck's sake, how do you think America became an economic superpower? Back in 1811, a Yankee named Francis Lowell Cabot sailed to Great Britain and stole England's most precious secret—the Cartright loom, cornerstone of the whole damned textile industry. Brought the goddamn Industrial Revolution to America, turned us into a colossus. All thanks to one single act of industrial espionage."

I turned away, stepped across the granite floor. The rubber soles of my work boots squeaked. "I'm done being jerked around," I said.

"Adam," Goddard said. "You're sounding like an embittered loser. Like your father was. And I know you're not—you're a *winner*, Adam. You're brilliant. You have what it takes."

I smiled, then laughed quietly. "Meaning I'm a lying scumbag, basically. A bullshitter. A world-class liar."

"Believe me, you didn't do anything that isn't done every day in corporations the world over. Look, you've got a copy of Sun Tzu in your office—have you read it? All warfare is based on deception, he says. And business is war, everyone knows that. *Business, at the highest levels, is deception.* No one's going to admit that publicly, but it's the truth." His voice softened. "The game is the same everywhere. You just play it better than anyone else. No, you're not a liar, Adam. You're a goddamned master strategist."

I rolled my eyes, shook my head in disgust, turned back toward the elevator.

Very quietly, Goddard said: "Do you know how much money Paul Camilletti made last year?"

Without looking back, I said: "Twenty-eight million."

"You could be making that in a few years. You're worth it to me, Adam. You're tough-minded and resourceful, you're fucking brilliant."

I snorted softly, but I don't think he heard it.

"Did I ever tell you how grateful I am that you saved our bacon on the Guru project? That and a dozen other things. Let me be specific about my gratitude. I'm giving you a raise—to a million a year. With stock options thrown in, given the way our stock's started to move, you could pull in a neat five or six million next year. Double that the year after. You'll be a fucking multimillionaire."

I froze in my tracks. I didn't know what to do, how to react. If I turned around, they'd think I was accepting. If I kept on walking, they'd think I was saying no.

"This is the solid-gold inner circle," Judith said. "You're being offered something anyone would kill for. But remember: it's not being given to you—you've *earned* it. You were *meant* for this line of work. You're as good at this as anybody I've ever met. These last couple of months, you know what you've been selling? Not handheld communicators or cell phones or MP3 players, but *yourself*. You've been selling Adam Cassidy. And *we're buyers*."

"I'm not for sale," I heard myself say, and I was instantly embarrassed.

"Adam, turn around," Goddard said angrily. "Turn around, *now*."

I obeyed, my expression sullen.

"Are you clear on what happens if you walk away?"

I smiled. "Sure. You'll turn me in. To the cops, the FBI, or whatever."

"I'll do no such thing," Goddard said. "I don't want a goddamned word of this ever made public. But without your car, without your apartment, your salary—you'll have no assets. You'll have nothing. What kind of life is that for a talented fellow like you?"

They own you . . . You drive a company car, you live in company housing. . . . Your whole life ain't yours. . . . My dad, my stopped-clock father, was right.

Judith got up from the table, came over very close to me. "Adam, I understand what you're feeling," she said in a hush. Her eyes were moist. "You're hurt, you're angry. You feel betrayed, manipulated. You want to retreat into the comforting, secure, protective anger of a small child. It's totally understandable—we all feel that way sometimes. But now it's time to put away childish things. You see, you haven't fallen into something. You've *found* yourself. It's all good, Adam. It's all good."

Goddard was leaning back in his chair, arms folded. I could see shards of his face reflected in the silver coffeepot, the sugar bowl. He smiled benevolently. "Don't throw it all away, son. I know you'll do the right thing."

9 3

My Porsche, fittingly, had been towed away. I'd parked it illegally last night; what did I expect?

So I walked out of the Trion building and looked around for a cab, but none was anywhere to be found. I suppose I could have used a phone in the lobby to call for one, but I felt an overwhelming, almost physical need to get out of there. Carrying the white cardboard box filled with the few things from my office, I walked along the side of the highway.

A few minutes later a bright red car pulled over to the curb, slowed down next to me. It was an Austin Mini Cooper, about the size of a toaster oven. The passenger's side window rolled down, and I could smell Alana's lush floral scent wafting through the city air.

She called out to me. "Hey, do you like it? I just got it. Isn't it *fabulous?*"

I nodded and attempted a cryptic smile. "Red's cop bait," I said.

"I never go over the speed limit."

I just nodded.

She said, "Suppose you get down off your motorcycle and give me a ticket?"

I nodded, kept walking, unwilling to play.

She inched her car alongside me. "Hey, what happened to your Porsche?"

"Got towed."

"Yuck. Where're you going?"

"Home. Harbor Suites." Not home for long, I realized with a jolt. I didn't own it.

"Well, you're not *walking* all the way. Not with that *box*. Come on, get in, I'll give you a ride."

"No thanks."

She followed alongside, driving slowly on the shoulder of the road. "Oh, come on, Adam, don't be *mad*."

I stopped, went over to the car, set down my box, put my hands on the car's low roof. Don't be mad? All along I'd been torturing myself because I thought I was manipulating *her*, and she was just doing a goddamned job. "You—they told you to sleep with me, didn't they?"

"Adam," she said sensibly. "Get real. That wasn't part of the job description. That's just what HR calls a fringe benefit, right?" She laughed her swooping laugh, and it chilled me. "They just wanted me to guide you along, pass along leads, that sort of thing. But then you came after *me*. . . ."

"They just wanted you to guide me along," I echoed. "Oh, man. Oh, man. Makes me ill." I picked up the box and resumed walking.

"Adam, I was just doing what they *told* me to do. You of all people should understand that."

"Like we'll ever be able to trust each other? Even now—you're just doing what they want you to, aren't you?"

"Oh, please," said Alana. "Adam, darling. Don't be so goddamned paranoid."

"And I actually thought we had a nice relationship going," I said.

"It was fun. I had a *great* time."

"Did you."

"God, don't take it so seriously, Adam! It's just sex. *And* business. What's wrong with that? Trust me, I wasn't *faking* it!"

I kept walking, looking around for a cab, but there was nothing in sight. I didn't even know this part of town. I was lost.

"Come *on*, Adam," she said, inching the Mini along. "Get in the car."

I kept going.

"Oh, come on," she said, her voice like velvet, suggesting everything, promising nothing. "Will you just get in the *car?*"

ACKNOWLEDGMENTS

Roll the credits. They're woefully long, but this one's been in development and production a long time.

Researching my other novels has taken me around the world and into places like KGB headquarters in Moscow, but nothing prepared me for how strange and fascinating I'd find the world of the American high-tech corporation. No one opened more doors to me, or gave of his time more generously, than my old friend David Hsiao of Cisco Systems, where I was also helped immensely by Tom Fallon, Dixie Garr, Pete Long, Richard Henkus, Gene Choy, Katie Foster, Bill LePage, Armen Hovanessian, Sue Zanner, and Molly Tschang. At Apple Computer, Kate Lepow was enormously helpful. At Nortel, my friend Carter Kersh was a thoughtful (and witty) guide, arranging for me to meet his colleagues, including Martin McNarney, Alyene Mclennan, Matt Portoni, Raj Raman, Guyves Achtari, and Alison Steel. I also had some interesting conversations with Matt Zanner of Hewlett Packard, Ted Sprague of Ciena, Rich Wyckoff of Marimba, Rich Rothschild of Ariba, Bob Scordino of EMC, Adam Stein of Juniper Networks, and Colin Angle of iRobot.

Some very smart friends helped me dream up the financial shenanigans and stealth tactics in the background of the story. They included Roger McNamee, Jeff Bone, Glover Lawrence, and especially my friend Giles McNamee, who brainstormed with me in the spirit of a true unindicted co-conspirator. Nell Minow of The Corporate Library in Washington helped me understand boardroom politics and corporate governance.

In the area of corporate security and intelligence, I got some invaluable assistance from some of the greats in the field, including Leonard Fuld, Arthur Hulnick, George K. Campbell, Mark H. Beaudry, Dan Geer, and the corporate espionage expert Ira Winkler. The legal background of *Paranoia* benefited from the advice of my great friend Joe Teig; Jackie Nakamura of Day Casebeer Madrid & Batchelder (and thanks to Alex Beam for introducing us); and Robert Stein of Pryor Cashman Sherman & Flynn; as well as two of his colleagues, Jeffrey Johnson and particularly Jay Shapiro. Adam's expertise in cool new tech products came from Jim Mann of Compaq, the lead designer of the iPaq; Bert Keely of Microsoft; Henry Holtzman of MIT's Media Lab; Simson Garfinkel; Joel Evans of Geek.com; Wes Salmon of PDABuzz.com; and especially Greg Joswiak, Vice President of Hardware Product Marketing at Apple Computer.

Some of Adam's youthful exploits were inspired by the tales of Keith McGrath, Jim Galvin of the Boston Police, and Emily Bindinger. On Francis X. Cassidy's medical condition, I was helped by my brother, Dr. Jonathan Finder, and Karen Heraty, that angel of a nurse. Jack McGeorge of the Public Safety Group helped me, as always, with numerous technical details. My close friend Rick Weissbourd contributed in all sorts of ways. I've been fortunate to have the help of some excellent research assistants, including John H. Romero, Michael Lane, and the great Kevin Biehl. And my assistant, Rachel Pomerantz, is truly the best.

I'm awed by the enormous enthusiasm and support of the entire talented publishing team at St. Martin's Press, including John Sargent, Sally Richardson, Matthew Shear, and John Cunningham; in marketing, Matthew Baldacci, Jim DiMiero, and Nancy Trypuc; in publicity, John Murphy and Gregg Sullivan; Mike Storrings, Christina Harcar, Mary Beth Roche, Joe McNeely, Laura Wilson, Tom Siino, Tom Leigh, and Andy LeCount. To have a whole publishing house rooting for you is a rare thing in any writer's life, and I extend my deepest thanks to all of them.

Howie Sanders of the United Talent Agency has been an enthusiastic supporter of this book from the beginning. My literary agent, Molly Friedrich, is just all-round terrific: unswervingly loyal, smart, sage, and just really good people.

My brother, Henry Finder, the editorial director of The New Yorker, is a remarkable editor. Fortunately, he's my first reader and editor and collaborator as well; his contribution to this novel was truly immeasurable. And Keith Kahla, my editor at St. Martin's Press, is not only a marvelous editor but also a diplomat, a lobbyist, a tireless advocate, and a behind-the-scenes generalissimo with the patience of a saint. I'm grateful to him more than I can say, and certainly more than he'd allow me to say here.

COMPANY MAN

For my parents, Morris and Natalie Finder

And in loving memory of my in-laws,
Michel and Josephine Souda

That is the thankless position of the father in the family—
the provider for all, and the enemy of all.

—*August Strindberg, 1886*

PART ONE
SECURITY

1

The office of the chief executive officer of the Stratton Corporation wasn't really an office at all. At a quick glance you'd call it a cubicle, but at the Stratton Corporation—which *made* the elegant silver-mesh fabric panels that served as the walls around the CEO's brushed-steel Stratton Ergon desk— "cubicle" was a dirty word. You didn't work in a cubicle in the middle of a cube farm; you multitasked at your "home base" in an "open-plan system."

Nicholas Conover, Stratton's CEO, leaned back in his top-of-the-line leather Stratton Symbiosis chair, trying to concentrate on the stream of figures spewing from the mouth of his chief financial officer, Scott McNally, a small, nerdy, self-deprecating guy who had a spooky affinity for numbers. Scott was sardonic and quick-witted, in a dark, sharp-edged way. He was also one of the smartest men Nick had ever met. But there was nothing Nick hated more than budget meetings.

"Am I boring you, Nick?"

"You gotta ask?"

Scott was standing by the giant plasma screen, touching it with the stylus to advance the PowerPoint slides. He was not much more than five feet tall, over a foot shorter than Nick. He was prone to nervous twitches, anxious shrugs, and his fingernails were all bitten to the quick. He was also rapidly going bald, though he wasn't even out of his thirties; his dome was fringed with wild curly hair. He had plenty of money, but he always seemed to wear the same blue button-down Oxford shirt, fraying at the collar, that he'd worn

since Wharton. His brown eyes darted around as he spoke, sunken in deep
lilac hollows.

As he rattled on about the layoffs and how much they were going to cost
this year versus how much they'd save the next, he fidgeted, with his free
hand, with what remained of his straggly hair.

Nick's desk was kept fastidiously clear by his terrific assistant, Marjorie
Dykstra. The only things on it were his computer (wireless keyboard and
mouse, no pesky rat's nest of wires, a flat-panel screen), a red model truck
with the Stratton logo painted on the side, and framed pictures of his kids.
He kept sneaking glances at the photos, hoping Scott would think he was just
staring into space and concentrating on the interminable presentation.

What's the bottom line, dude? he wanted to say. *Are the guys in Boston going to be happy or not?*

But Scott kept droning on and on about cost savings, about outplacement costs, about metrics, about employees as "units," as bar graphs on a
PowerPoint slide. "Current average employee age is 47.789 years, with a standard deviation of 6.92," Scott said. He noticed Nick's glazed expression as he
touched the screen with the aluminum stylus, and a half smile tugged at the
corner of his mouth. "But hey, age is just a number, right?"

"Is there any good news here?"

"Ahh, it's only money." Scott paused. "That was a joke."

Nick stared at the little display of silver frames. Since Laura's death last
year he cared about two things only: his job and his kids. Julia was ten, and
she beamed with her thousand-watt smile in her school picture, her curly
chestnut hair unruly, her enormous, liquid brown eyes sparkling, her big new
teeth a little crooked, a smile so unself-conscious and dazzling she seemed to
be bursting out of the photo. Lucas was sixteen, dark-haired like his little sister, and unnervingly handsome; he had his mother's cornflower-blue eyes, an
angular jawline. A high school heartthrob. Lucas smiled for the camera, a
smile that Nick hadn't actually seen in person since the accident.

There was just one photo of all four of them, sitting on the porch of the
old house, Laura seated in the middle, everyone touching her, hands on her
shoulder or her waist, the center of the family. The gaping hole, now. Her
amused, twinkling blue eyes looked right at the camera, her expression frank
and poised, seemingly tickled by some private joke. And of course Barney,

their overweight, lumbering Golden/Lab mix, sat on his haunches in front of everyone, smiling his dog smile. Barney was in all the family pictures, even in last Christmas's family photo, the one with Lucas glowering like Charles Manson.

"Todd Muldaur's going to have a shit fit," Nick said, lifting his eyes to meet Scott's. Muldaur was a general partner in Fairfield Equity Partners in Boston, the private-equity firm that now owned the Stratton Corporation. Todd, not to put too fine a point on it, was Nick's boss.

"That's about the size of it," Scott agreed. He turned his head suddenly, and a second later Nick heard the shouts too.

"What the hell—?" Scott said. A deep male voice, somewhere nearby, yelling. A woman's voice, sounded like Marge's.

"You don't have an *appointment*, sir!" Marge was shouting, her voice high and frightened. An answering rumble, the words indistinct. "He isn't here, anyway, and if you don't leave right this *instant*, sir, I'm going to have to call Security."

A hulking figure crashed into one of the silver panels that outlined Nick's workstation, almost tipping it over. A bearded giant in his late thirties wearing a checked flannel shirt, unbuttoned, over a black Harley-Davidson T-shirt: barrel-chested, powerful-looking. The guy looked vaguely familiar. A factory worker? Someone who'd recently been laid off?

Immediately behind him followed Marge, her arms flailing. "You *cannot* come in here!" she shrilled. "Get out of here immediately, or I'll call Security."

The giant's foghorn voice boomed: "Well, whaddaya know, there he is. Boss man himself. The slasher is in."

Nick felt a cold fear wash over him as he realized that the budget meeting might turn out to be the high point of his day.

The guy, probably a worker just laid off in the most recent round of cuts, was staring, wild-eyed.

Nick flashed on news stories he'd read about crazed employees—"disgruntled workers," they were always called—who'd been let go, and then showed up at work and started picking people off.

"I just remembered a phone conference I'm late for," Scott McNally muttered as he squeezed past the intruder. "If you'll excuse me."

Nick got up slowly, raised himself to his full six-two. The crazy bearded guy was considerably bigger.

"What can I do for you?" Nick asked politely, calmly, the way you might try to lull a rabid Doberman pinscher.

"What can you do for me? That's fucking hilarious. There's nothing more you can do for me, or *to* me, asshole."

Marge, hovering directly behind him, her hands flailing, said: "Nick, I'll call Security."

Nick put up his hand to tell her to hold off. "I'm sure there's no need," he said.

Marge squinted at him to indicate her strong disagreement, but she nodded, backed away warily.

The bearded man took a step forward, puffing up his massive chest, but Nick didn't budge. There was something primal going on here: the interloper was a baboon baring his canines, screaming and strutting to scare off a predator. He smelled of rancid sweat and cigar smoke.

Nick fought the strong temptation to deck the guy but reminded himself that, as CEO of Stratton, he couldn't exactly do stuff like that. Plus, if this was one of the five thousand Stratton workers who'd been laid off within the last two years, he had a right to be angry. The thing to do was to talk the guy down, let him vent, let the air out of the balloon slowly.

Nick pointed to an empty chair, but the bearded man refused to sit. "What's your name?" Nick said, softening his voice a bit.

"Old Man Devries woulda never had to ask," the man retorted. "He knew everyone's name."

Nick shrugged. That was the myth, anyway. Folksy, paternal Milton Devries—Nick's predecessor—had been CEO of Stratton for almost four decades. The old man had been beloved, but there was no way he knew ten thousand names.

"I'm not as good with names as the old man was," Nick said. "So help me out here."

"Louis Goss."

Nick extended his hand to shake, but Goss didn't take it. Instead, Goss pointed a stubby forefinger at him. "When you sat down at your fancy computer at your fancy desk and made the decision to fire half the guys in the chair factory, did you even fucking *think* about who these people are?"

"More than you know," Nick said. "Listen, I'm sorry you lost your job—"

"I'm not here because I lost my job—see, I got seniority. I'm here to tell you that you deserve to lose yours. You think just because you waltz through this plant once a month that you know anything about these guys? These are human beings, buddy. Four hundred and fifty men and women who get up at four in the morning to do the early shift so they can feed their families and pay their rent or their mortgages and take care of their sick kids or their dying parents, okay? Do you realize that because of you some of these guys are going to lose their *houses?*"

Nick closed his eyes briefly. "Louis, are you just going to talk at me, or do you want to hear me out?"

"I'm here to give you a little free advice, Nick."

"I find you get what you pay for."

The man ignored him. "You better think seriously about whether you really want to go through with these layoffs. Because if you don't call them off by tomorrow morning, this place is going to grind to a halt."

"What are you trying to say?"

"I got half, maybe three-quarters of the factory floor with me on this. More, once we start. We're all sicking out tomorrow, Nick. And we're staying sick until my buddies get their jobs back." Goss was smiling with tobacco-darkened teeth, enjoying his moment. "You do the right thing, we do the right thing. Everyone's happy."

Nick stared at Goss. How much of this was bluster, how much on the level? A wildcat strike could paralyze the company, especially if it spread to the other plants.

"Why don't you think this over when you're driving home tonight in your Mercedes to your gated community?" Goss went on. "Ask yourself if you feel like taking your company down with you."

It's a Chevy Suburban, not a Mercedes, Nick wanted to say, but then he was struck by that phrase, "gated community." How did Goss know where he lived? There'd been nothing in the newspaper about that, though of course people talked . . . Was this a veiled threat?

Goss smiled, a mirthless, leering grin, saw the reaction on Nick's face. "Yeah, that's right. I know where you live."

Nick felt his rage flare up like a lit match tossed into a pool of gasoline. He sprang out of his seat, lunged forward, his face a few inches from Louis Goss's face. "What the hell are you trying to say?" It took all his self-restraint to keep from grabbing the collar of the guy's flannel shirt and twisting it tight around his fat neck. Up close he realized that Goss's bulk was all flab, not muscle.

Goss flinched, seemed to shrink back a bit, intimidated.

"You think everyone doesn't know you live in a fucking huge mansion in a gated community?" Goss said. "You think anyone else in this company can afford to live like that?"

Nick's anger subsided as quickly as it had surged. He felt a damp sort of relief; he'd misunderstood. The threat that Louis had actually made seemed suddenly tame by comparison. He leaned even closer, poked a finger against Goss's chest, jabbing the little white hyphen between "Harley" and "Davidson."

"Let me ask *you* something, Louis. Do you remember the 'town meeting' at the chair plant two years ago? When I told you guys the company was in a shitload of trouble and layoffs seemed likely but I wanted to avoid them if possible? You weren't sick that day, were you?"

"I was there," Goss muttered.

"Remember I asked if you'd all be willing to cut your hours back so everyone could stay on the job? Remember what everyone said?"

Goss was silent, looking off to one side, avoiding Nick's direct stare.

"You all said no, you couldn't do that. A pay cut was out of the question."

"Easy for you to—"

"And I asked whether you'd all be willing to cut back on your health plan, with your daycare and your health-club memberships. Now, how many people raised their hands to say yeah, okay, we'll cut back? Any recollection?"

Goss shook his head slowly, resentfully.

"Zero. Not a single goddamned hand went up. Nobody wanted to lose a goddamned hour of work; nobody wanted to lose a single perk." He could hear the blood rushing through his ears, felt a flush of indignation. "You think I slashed five thousand jobs, buddy? Well, the reality is, I *saved* five thousand jobs. Because the boys in Boston who own this company now don't fuck around. They're looking at our biggest competitor and seeing that the other guys aren't bending metal, they're not making their furniture in Michigan anymore. Everything's made in China now, Louis. *That's* why they can undercut us on price. You think the boys in Boston don't remind me of that every single goddamned chance they get?"

"I got no idea," Louis Goss muttered, shuffling his feet. It was all he could muster.

"So go right ahead, Louis. Have your strike. And they'll bring in a new CEO who'll make me look like Mister Rogers. Someone who'll shut down all of our plants the second he walks in this building. Then you wanna keep your job, Louis? I suggest you learn fucking *Mandarin*."

Louis was silent for a few seconds, and when he spoke, it was in a small, sullen voice. "You're going to fire me, aren't you?"

"You?" Nick snorted. "You're not worth the severance package. Now, get the fuck back on the line and get the hell out of my . . . work space."

A few seconds after Louis Goss had lumbered away, Marge appeared again. "You need to go home, Nick," she said. "Now."

"Home?"

"It's the police. There's a problem."

2

Nick backed his Chevy Suburban out of his space too fast, not bothering to check whether anyone was behind him, and careened through the parking lot that encircled the headquarters building. Even at the height of the work-day, it stood half-empty as it had for the last two years, since the layoffs began. Gallows humor abounded among the employees these days, Nick knew. The upside of losing half the workforce was, you could always find a parking space.

His nerves felt stretched taught. Acres of empty black asphalt, sur-rounded by a great black field of charred buffalo grass, the remains of a pre-scribed fire. Buffalo grass never needed mowing, but every few years it had to be burned to the ground. The air smelled like a Weber grill.

Black against black against the black of the road, a desolate landscape. He wondered whether driving by the vast swath of scorched earth every day, staring at the charred field through the office windows, left a dark carbon smudge on your psyche.

You need to go home. Now.

When you have kids, they're the first thing you think of. Even a guy like Nick, hardly a worrywart, you get a call from the cops and your imagination takes flight in a bad direction.

But both kids were all right, the cops had assured Marjorie. Julia was on her way back from school, and Lucas—well, Lucas had been in classes today and was doing whatever the hell he did after school these days, which was another issue entirely.

That wasn't it.

Yes, it was another break-in, they'd said, but this time he really needed to come by. What the hell could that mean?

Over the past year or so, Nick had gotten used to the periodic calls from the alarm company or the police. The burglar alarm would go off in the middle of the day. There'd been a break-in. The alarm company would verify that the alarm was genuine by calling home or Nick's office and requesting a code. If no authorized user said it was a false alarm, the company would immediately dispatch the Fenwick police. A couple of cops would then drive by the house, check it out.

Inevitably it happened when no one was there—the crew working on the kitchen were taking one of their frequent days off; the kids were at school; the housekeeper, Marta, was out shopping or maybe picking up Julia.

Nothing was ever stolen. The intruder would force a window or one of the French doors, get inside, and leave a little message.

Literally, a message: words spray-painted in Day-Glo orange, all capital letters formed with the precision of an architect or mechanical engineer: NO HIDING PLACE.

Three words, one on top of another.

Was there any doubt it was a deranged laid-off employee? The graffiti defaced the walls of the living room, the dining room they never used, the freshly plastered walls of the kitchen. In the beginning it had scared the shit out of him.

The real message, of course, was that they weren't safe. They could be gotten to.

The first graffiti had appeared on the heavy, ornate ash-wood front door, which Laura had deliberated over for weeks with the architect, a door that had cost a ridiculous three thousand dollars, a fucking *door*, for God's sake. Nick had made his feelings known but hadn't objected, because it was obviously important to her, for some reason. He'd been perfectly content with the flimsy paneled front door that came with the house they'd just bought. He didn't want to change anything about the house except maybe to shrink it to half its size. There was a saying that was popular at Stratton, which Old Man Devries was fond of repeating: the whale that spouts gets the harpoon. Sometimes he thought about having one of those bronze-looking estate wall plaques made for him by Frontgate, the kind you see on stone entrance pillars in front of McMansions, saying in raised copper letters, SPOUTING WHALE HOUSE.

But to Laura, the front door was symbolic: it was where you welcomed friends and family, and it was where you kept out those who weren't welcome. So it had to be both beautiful and substantial. "It's the *front door*, Nick," she'd insisted. "The first thing people see. That's the *one* place you don't cheap out."

Maybe, on some level, she thought a three-inch-thick front door would make them safer. Buying this insanely big house in the Fenwicke Estates: that was her idea too. She wanted the safety of the gated community. It took only a couple of anonymous threatening phone calls, as soon as the layoffs were announced.

"If you're a target, we're all targets," she said. There was a lot of anger out there, directed at him. He wasn't going to argue with her. He had a family to protect.

Now, with her gone, it felt as if he'd absorbed her neurosis, as if it had penetrated his bones. He felt, sometimes, that his family, what remained of it, was as fragile as an egg.

He also knew that the security of their gated community was little more than an illusion. It was a show, an elaborate charade, the fancy gatehouse and the guards, the private security, the high black iron fence with the spearhead finials.

The Suburban screeched to a stop before the ornately scrolled cast-iron gate beside the brick gatehouse built to resemble a miniature castle. A brass plaque on one of the piers said FENWICKE ESTATES.

That little "e" at the end of Fenwick—he'd always found it pretentious to the point of being irritating. Plus, he was so over the irony here, this posh enclosed neighborhood equipped with the priciest security you could get—the tall wrought-iron perimeter fence with the fiber-optic sensing cable concealed inside the top rail, the pan-tilt-zoom CCTV surveillance cameras, the motion-sensor intruder alarms—where you couldn't stop the loonies from scrambling in through the dense surrounding woods and climbing over the fence.

"Another break-in, Mr. Conover," said Jorge, the day guard. Nice guy, couldn't be nicer. The security guards were all professional in demeanor, all wore sharp uniforms.

Nick nodded grimly, waited for the motor-driven gate to open, ridiculously slow. The high-pitched electronic warning beep was annoying. Everything beeped these days: trucks backing up, dishwashers and clothes dryers, microwaves. It really could drive you crazy.

"Police are there now, you know," said Jorge. "Three cruisers, sir."

"Any idea what it is?"

"No, sir, I don't, I'm sorry."

The damned gate took forever to open. It was ridiculous. In the evening sometimes there was a line of cars waiting to get in. Something had to be done about it. For Christ's sake, what if his house caught fire — would the fire department trucks have to sit here while his house turned to toast?

He raced the engine in annoyance. Jorge shrugged a sheepish apology.

The second the gate was open far enough for the car to get through, he gunned it — the Suburban's pickup never ceased to amaze him — and barreled over the tiger-teeth tire-shredders that enforced one-way traffic, across the wide circular court paved in antique brick in a geometric pattern by old-world Italian stonemasons shipped over from Sicily, past the SPEED LIMIT 20 sign at twice that at least.

The brick pavement turned into glass-smooth macadam road, no street sign. He raced past the old-growth elms and firs, the mailboxes the size of doghouses, none of the houses visible. You had to be invited over to see what your neighbor's house looked like. And there sure as hell weren't any block parties here in Fenwicke Estates.

When he saw police squad cars parked on the street and at the entrance to his driveway, he felt something small and cold and hard forming at the base of his stomach, a little icicle of fear.

A uniformed policeman halted him a few hundred feet from the house, halfway up the drive. Nick jumped out and slammed the car door in one smooth, swift motion.

The cop was short and squat, powerful-looking, seemed to be perspiring heavily despite the cool weather. His badge said MANZI. A walkie-talkie hitched to his belt squawked unceasingly.

"You Mr. Conover?" He stood directly in front of Nick's path, blocking his way. Nick felt a flash of annoyance. My house, my driveway, my burglar alarm: get the fuck out of my way.

"Yeah, that's me, what's going on?" Nick tried to keep the irritation, and the anxiety, out of his voice.

"Ask you some questions?" Dappled sunlight filtered through the tall birches that lined the asphalt lane, played on the cop's inscrutable face.

Nick shrugged. "Sure—what is it, the graffiti again?"

"What time did you leave the house this morning, sir?"

"Around seven-thirty, but the kids are normally out of there by eight, eight-fifteen at the latest."

"What about your wife?"

Nick gazed at the cop steadily. Most of the cops had to know who he was at least. He wondered if this guy was just trying to yank his chain. "I'm a single parent."

A pause. "Nice house."

"Thank you." Nick could sense the resentment, the envy rising off the man like swamp gas. "What happened?"

"House is okay, sir. It's brand-new, looks like. Not even finished yet, huh?"

"We're just having some work done," Nick said impatiently.

"I see. The workers, they're here every day?"

"I wish. Not yesterday or today."

"Your alarm company lists a work number for you at the Stratton Corporation," Officer Manzi said. He was looking down at an aluminum clipboard, his black eyes small and deeply inset like raisins in a butterscotch pudding. "You work there."

"Right."

"What do you do at Stratton?" There was a beat before the policeman looked up and let his eyes meet Nick's: the guy knew damned well what he did there.

"I'm the CEO."

Manzi nodded as if everything now made sense. "I see. You've had a number of break-ins over the last several months, is that correct, Mr. Conover?"

"Five or six times now."

"What kind of security system you have here, sir?"

"Burglar alarm on the doors and some of the windows and French doors. Basic system. Nothing too elaborate."

"Home like this, that's not much of a system. No cameras, right?"

"Well, we live in this, you know, gated community."

"Yes, sir, I can see that. Lot of good it does, keeping out the wing nuts."

"Point taken." Nick almost smiled.

"Sounds like the burglar alarm isn't on very often, sir, that right?"

"Officer, why so many cars here today for a routine—"

"Mind if I ask the questions?" Officer Manzi said. The guy seemed to be enjoying his authority, pushing around the boss man from Stratton. Let him, Nick thought. Let him have his fun. But—

Nick heard a car approaching, turned and saw the blue Chrysler Town and Country, Marta behind the wheel. He felt that little chemical surge of pleasure he always got when he saw his daughter, the way he used to feel with Lucas too, until that got complicated. The minivan pulled up alongside Nick and the engine was switched off. A car door opened and slammed, and Julia shouted, "What are *you* doing home, Daddy?"

She ran toward him, wearing a light-blue hooded Stratton sweatshirt and jeans, black sneakers. She wore some slight variant of the outfit every day, a sweatshirt or an athletic jersey. When Nick went to the same elementary school, more than thirty years before, you weren't allowed to wear jeans, and sweatshirts weren't considered appropriate school attire. But he didn't have time in the mornings to argue with her, and he was inclined to go easy on his little girl, given what she had to be going through since the death of her mother.

She hugged him tight around his abdomen. He no longer hoisted her up, since at almost five feet and ninety-something pounds, it wasn't so easy. In the last year she'd gotten tall and leggy, almost gangly, though there was still a pocket of baby fat at her tummy. She was starting to develop physically, little breast buds emerging, which Nick couldn't deal with. It was a constant reminder of his inadequacy as a parent: who the hell was going to talk to her, get her through adolescence?

The hug went on for several seconds until Nick released her, another thing that had changed since Laura was gone. His daughter's hugs: she didn't want to let him go.

Now she looked up at him, her meltingly beautiful brown eyes lively. "How come there's all these police?"

"They want to talk to me, baby doll. No big deal. Where's your backpack?"

"In the car. Did that crazy guy get in the house again and write bad stuff?"

Nick nodded, stroked her glossy brown hair. "What are you doing home now? Don't you have piano?"

She gave him a look of amused contempt. "That's not till four."

"I thought it was three."

"Mrs. Guarini changed it, like, *months* ago, don't you remember?"

He shook his head. "Oh, right. I forgot. Well, listen, I have to talk to this policeman here. Marta, you guys stay here until the police say it's okay to go in the house, okay?"

Marta Burrell was from Barbados, a mocha-skinned woman of thirty-eight, tall and slender as a fashion model with an air of sultry indifference, or maybe arrogance, her default mode. Her jeans were a little too tight, and she customarily wore high heels, and she was vocal about her disapproval of Julia's daily uniform. She expressed disapproval of just about everything in the household. She was ferociously devoted to the kids, though, and was able to make both of them do things Nick couldn't. Marta had been a superb nanny when the kids were little, was an excellent cook, and an indifferent housekeeper.

"Sure, Nick," she said. She reached for Julia, but the girl scampered off.

"You were saying," Nick said to the cop.

Manzi looked up, fixed Nick with a blank look, bordering on impertinence, but there was a gleam in his eyes; he seemed to be restraining a smile. "Do you have any enemies, Mr. Conover?"

"Only about five thousand people in town."

The policeman's eyebrows shot up. "Excuse me."

"We laid off half our workforce recently, as I'm sure you know. More than five thousand employees."

"Ah, yes," the cop said. "You're not a popular man around here, are you?"

"You could say that."

It wasn't that long ago, Nick reflected, that everyone loved him. People he didn't know in high school started sucking up to him. *Forbes* magazine even did a profile. After all, Nick was the youthful blue-collar guy, the son of a guy who'd spent a life bending metal in the chair factory—business reporters ate that stuff up. Maybe Nick was never going to be beloved at the company like Old Man Devries, but for a while at least he'd been popular, admired, *liked*. A local hero in the small town of Fenwick, Michigan, sort of, a guy you'd point out at the Shop 'n Save and maybe, if you felt bold, walk up to and introduce yourself in the frozen-foods section.

But that was before—before the first layoffs were announced, two years ago, after Stratton's new owners had laid down the law at the quarterly board meeting in Fenwick. There was no choice. The Stratton Corporation was going down the crapper if they didn't cut costs, and fast. That meant losing half its workforce, five thousand people in a town of maybe forty thousand. It was the most painful thing he'd ever done, something he'd never imagined having to do. There'd been a series of smaller layoffs since the first ones were announced, two years ago. It was like Chinese water torture. The *Fenwick Free Press*, which used to publish puff pieces about Stratton, now ran banner headlines: THREE HUNDRED MORE STRATTON WORKERS FACE THE AXE. CANCER VICTIM SUFFERS LOSS OF STRATTON BENEFITS. The local columnists routinely referred to him as "the Slasher."

Nick Conover, local boy made good, had become the most hated man in town.

"Guy like you ought to have better security than that. You get the security you pay for, you know."

Nick was about to reply when he heard his daughter scream.

3

He ran toward the source of the screaming and found Julia beside the pool. Her cries came in great ragged gulps. She knelt on the bluestone coping, her hands thrashing in the water, her small back torquing back and forth. Marta stood nearby, helpless and aghast, a hand to her mouth.

Then Nick saw what had made Julia scream, and he felt sick.

A dark shape floated in cranberry red water, splayed and distended, surrounded by slick white entrails. The blood was concentrated in a dark cloud around the carcass; the water got lighter, pinkish as it got farther away from the furry brown mass.

The corpse wasn't immediately recognizable as Barney, their old Lab/Golden Retriever. It took a second glance, a struggle with disbelief. On the bluestone not far from where Julia knelt, keening, was a blood-slick, carbon-steel Henckels knife from their kitchen set.

Many things immediately made sense, now: the unusual police presence, the questioning, even the absence of Barney's usual barked greeting when Nick arrived.

A couple of policemen were busy taking pictures, talking to one another, their low conversations punctuated by static blasts from their radios. They seemed to be chatting casually, as if nothing unusual had happened. Business as usual to them. No one was expressing sympathy or concern. Nick felt a flash of rage, but the main thing now was to comfort his daughter.

He rushed to her, sank to his knees, put a hand on her back. "Baby," he said. "Baby."

She turned, flung her arms around his neck, let out a wail. Her gasping breath was hot and moist. He held her tight as if he could squeeze the trauma out of her little body, make everything normal again, make her feel safe.

"Oh, baby, I'm so sorry." Her gasps were like spasms, hiccups. He held her even tighter. The copious flow of her tears pooled in the hollow of his neck. He could feel it soak his shirt.

Ten minutes later, when Marta had taken Julia inside, Nick spoke to Officer Manzi. He made no effort this time to contain his fury. "What the *fuck* are you guys going to do about this?" Nick thundered. "What the hell are you waiting for? These break-ins have been going on for months already, and you haven't done a damned thing about it."

"Excuse me, sir," Manzi said blandly.

"You haven't assigned a detective to the case, you haven't done any investigation, you haven't gone through the lists of laid-off Stratton employees. You've had months to stop this fucking madman. What are you waiting for? Does this lunatic have to murder one of my *kids* before you take it seriously?"

Manzi's detachment—did Nick detect a smug sort of amusement, was that possible?—was infuriating. "Well, sir, as I said, you might want to think about upgrading your security—"

"*My* security? What about you guys? Isn't this your goddamned *job?*"

"You said it yourself, sir—you laid off five thousand Stratton employees. That's going to create more enemies than we can possibly protect you against. You should really upgrade your security system."

"Yeah, and what are *you* going to do? How are *you* going to protect my family?"

"I'll be honest with you, sir. Stalking cases are some of our hardest."

"Meaning you pretty much can't do shit, is that right?"

Manzi shrugged. "You said it. I didn't."

4

After the police left, Nick tried for a long while to console his daughter. He called to cancel her piano lesson, then sat with her, talking a bit, mostly hugging. When she seemed stable, Nick left her in Marta's care and returned to the office for a largely unproductive afternoon.

By the time he returned home, Julia was asleep and Marta was in the family room, watching a movie about a baby who talks with Bruce Willis's voice.

"Where's Julia?" Nick asked.

"She's asleep," Marta said sadly. "She was okay by the time she went to bed. But she cried a lot, Nick."

Nick shook his head. "That poor baby. This is going to be hardest on her, I think. Barney was Laura's dog, really. To Julia, Barney . . ." He fell silent. "Is Lucas upstairs?"

"He called from a friend's house, said they're working on their history projects."

"Yeah, right. Working on a nickel bag, more like it. Which friend?"

"I think Ziegler? Um, listen—Nick? I'm kind of nervous being alone in the house—after today, I mean."

"I can't blame you. You lock the doors and windows, right?"

"I did, but this crazy person . . ."

"I know. I'm going to have a new system put in right away so you can put on the alarm while you're inside." Stratton's corporate security director had told Nick he'd drop by later, see what he could do. Anything for the boss. They'd gone too long with a rudimentary security system; it was time to put in something state-of-the-art, with cameras and motion detectors and all that. "You can go to sleep if you want."

"I want to see the rest of this movie."

"Sure."

Nick went upstairs and down the hall to Julia's bedroom, quietly opening the door and making his way through the darkness by memory. Enough moonlight filtered through the gaps in the curtains that, once his eyes adjusted, he could make out his daughter's sleeping body. Julia slept under, and with, an assortment of favorite blankets, each of which she'd given names to, as well as a rotating selection of stuffed animals and Beanie Babies from her vast menagerie. Tonight she was clutching Winnie the Pooh, who'd been given to her when she was a few days old, now frayed and matted and stained.

Her choice of sleeping partner was a pretty reliable indicator of her mental state: Elmo when she was feeling sprightly; Curious George when she was feeling mischievous; her little Beanie Baby koala, Eucalyptus, when she wanted to nurture someone needier than herself. But Pooh always meant she was feeling especially fragile and in need of the ultimate comfort of her longest-serving pal. For several months after her mommy's death, she slept with Pooh every night. Recently, she'd traded in Pooh for some of the other guys, which was a sign that she was starting to feel a little stronger.

Tonight, though, Pooh was back in her bed.

He touched her sweaty curls, breathed in the sweet baby-shampoo aroma mixed with the slightly sour smell of perspiration, and kissed her damp forehead. She murmured but did not stir.

A door opened and closed somewhere in the house, followed immediately by the thud of something being dropped to the floor. Nick was instantly alert. Heavy, bounding footsteps on the carpeted stairs told him it was Lucas.

Nick navigated a path through the minefield of books and toys and closed the door quietly behind him. The long hall was dark, but a stripe of yellow light glared through the crack under Lucas's bedroom door.

Nick knocked, waited, then knocked again.

"Yeah?"

The depth and timbre of his son's voice always startled him. That and the surly edge to it, in the last year. Nick opened the door and found Lucas lying back on his bed, boots still on, iPod earbuds in his ears.

"Where've you been?" Nick asked.

Lucas glanced at him, then found something in the middle distance that was more interesting. "Where's Barney?"

Nick paused. "I asked you where you've been, Luke. It's a school night."

"Ziggy's."

"You didn't ask me if you could go over there."

"You weren't around to ask."

"If you want to go over to a friend's house, you've got to clear it in advance with me or Marta."

Lucas shrugged in tacit acknowledgment. His eyes were red and glassy, and now Nick was fairly certain he'd been getting high. This was an alarming new development, but he hadn't yet confronted his son about it. He'd been putting it off simply because it was one more mountain to climb, a showdown that would require unwavering strength he didn't have. There was so much going on at work, and there was Julia, who was frankly a hell of a lot easier to console, and then there was his own sadness, which sapped his ability to be a good and understanding dad.

He looked at Lucas, could hear the tinny, percussive hiss coming from the earphones. He wondered what kind of crappy music Lucas was listening to now. He caught a whiff of stale smoke in the room, which smelled like regular cigarettes, though he wasn't sure.

There was a baffling disconnect between Lucas on the inside and Lucas on the outside. Externally, Lucas was a mature sixteen, a tall and handsome man. His almost feminine prettiness had taken on a sharp-featured masculinity. His eyebrows, above blue eyes with long lashes, were dark and thick. The Lucas inside, though, was five or six: petulant, easily wounded, expert at finding insult in the most unexpected places, capable of holding grudges to the end of time.

"You're not smoking, are you?"

Lucas cast his father a look of withering contempt. "Ever hear of second-hand smoke? I was around people who were smoking."

"Ziggy doesn't smoke." Kenny Ziegler was a big, strapping blond kid, a swimmer who was Lucas's best friend from when he was still on the swim team. But ever since Lucas had quit swimming, six months or so ago, he hadn't been hanging out with Ziggy nearly as much. Nick doubted that Lucas had actually spent the afternoon and evening at Ziggy's house. Somewhere else: some other friend, probably.

Lucas's stare was unwavering. His music squealed and hissed.

"You got homework?" Nick persisted.

"I don't need you to monitor me, Nick." Nick. That was something else new, calling his father by his first name. Some of Lucas's friends had always called their own parents by their first names, but Nick and Laura had always insisted on the traditional "Mom" and "Dad." Lucas was just trying to push his buttons. He'd been calling him Nick for the last month or so.

"Can you please take those earphones out when I'm talking to you?"

"I can hear you just fine," Lucas said. "Where's Barney?"

"Take off the earphones, Luke."

Lucas yanked them out of his ears by the dangling wire, let them drop on his chest, the tinny sound now louder and more distinct.

"Something happened to Barney. Something pretty bad."

"What are you talking about?"

"We found him . . . Someone killed him, Luke."

Lucas whipped his legs around until he was perched on the edge of the bed, looking as if he were about to launch himself toward Nick.

"*Killed* him?"

"We found him in the pool today—some nut . . ." Nick couldn't continue, couldn't relive the gruesome scene.

"This is the same guy who keeps breaking in, isn't it? The spray-paint graffiti guy."

"Looks that way."

"It's because of *you*!" Lucas's eyes widened, gleaming with tears. "All those people you fired, the way everyone in town hates you."

Nick didn't know how to answer.

"Like half the kids in school, their parents got laid off by you. It's fucking embarrassing."

"Lucas, listen to me—"

Lucas gave him a ferocious look, eyes bulging, teeth bared, as if Nick was the one who'd killed Barney. "Why don't you get the fuck out of my room," he said, his voice cracking.

Nick's reaction surprised himself. If he'd talked that way to his father, he'd have had the shit beaten out of him. But instead of flying into a fury, he was instead overcome by calm, patient sorrow—his heart ached for the kid, for what he'd had to go through. "Lucas," Nick said, so softly it was almost a whisper, "don't you ever talk to me like that again." He turned around and quietly closed the door behind him. His heart wasn't in it.

Standing in the hallway just outside her adored older brother's room was Julia, tears streaming down her face.

5

It wasn't long after Nick had finally gotten Julia back to sleep—picking her up, hugging her, snuggling with her in her bed—that there was a quick rap on the front door.

Eddie Rinaldi, Stratton's corporate security director, was wearing a tan fleece jacket and a pair of jeans and smelled like beer and cigarettes. Nick wondered whether Eddie had just come over from his usual hangout, Victor's, on Division.

"Shit, man," Eddie said. "That sucks, about the dog."

Eddie was a tall, lanky guy, edgy and intense. His frizzy brown hair was run through with gray. He had pitted cheeks and forehead, the legacy of a nasty case of acne in high school. He had gray eyes, flared nostrils, a weak mouth.

They'd been high school teammates—Eddie was the right wing on the same hockey team on which Nick, the captain, played center—though they'd never been especially close. Nick was the star, of the team and of the high school, the big man on campus, the good-looking guy all the girls wanted to go out with. Eddie, not a bad hockey player, was a natural cut-up, half-crazy, and with a face full of zits he wasn't exactly dating the prom queen. The joke about Eddie among some on the team was that he'd been left on the Tilt-A-Whirl a bit too long as a baby. That wasn't quite fair; he was a goofball who just scraped by in school, but he had a native cunning. He also looked up to Nick, almost hero-worshiped him, though his idolatry always seemed tinged with a little jealousy. After high school, when Nick went to Michigan State, in East Lansing, Eddie went to the police academy in Fraser and lucked out, got a job with the Grand Rapids PD, where after almost two decades he hit a bad patch. As he'd explained to Nick, he'd been accused of brutalizing a suspect—a bullshit charge, but there it was—banished to a desk job, busted down the ranks until the publicity blew over, or so he was assured by the police chief. But he knew his career was as good as done for.

Nick, by then CEO of Stratton, stepped in and saved his ass, offering Eddie a job he was maybe underqualified for, assistant director of corporate security, in charge of background checks, pilferage investigations, that sort of thing. Just as Nick had assured the longtime security director, a white-haired sergeant who'd retired from the Fenwick force, Eddie had poured himself into the job, deeply grateful to Nick and eager to redeem himself.

Two years later, when the security director took early retirement, Eddie moved into the top job. Sometimes Nick thought it was like the old hockey days: Nick, the star, the power forward as they called him, with his hundred-mile-an-hour slap shot, taking the face-offs, making a pass through nine sticks as if he were threading a needle; and Eddie, grinning wildly as he did wild stunts like kicking an opponent's skates out from under him, spearing guys in the gut, carving some other guy's face with his stick, skating up and down the wing with a jittery juking craziness.

"Thanks for coming over," Nick said.

"First I want to see the kitchen."

Nick shrugged, led him down the hall. He switched on the light and peeled back one of the heavy plastic sheets, taped to the doorjamb, which served as a dust barrier between the kitchen and the rest of the house.

Nick stepped through, followed by Eddie, who gave a low whistle, taking in the glass-fronted cabinets, the Wolf commercial range. He set down the little nylon gym bag he'd been carrying. "Jeez Louise, this gotta cost a fortune."

"It's ridiculous."

He switched one of the burners on. It *tick-ticked* and then ignited, a powerful roar of blue flame coming out. "Man, serious gas pressure. And you don't even cook."

"Had to bring in a new line for that. Tore up the lawn, had to reseed and everything."

"Shit, how many sinks you got?"

"I think they call that one a prep sink, and that one's for dishes."

"The dishwasher's gonna go in there?"

"Yeah." Fisher & Paykel, was that it? Another result of Laura's star-searches for the best appliances ever. *It's two drawers*, she'd told him, *so you can run smaller loads*. Okay, whatever.

Eddie tugged at a handle, releasing a slab of rock maple. "This a knife drawer?"

"Built-in cutting board."

"Sweet. Don't tell me you picked all this shit out."

"Laura designed the whole thing, picked out every appliance, the color scheme, the cabinets, everything."

"Tough to cook without a kitchen counter, you know."

"That's coming."

"Where do you keep the booze?"

Nick touched the front of a cabinet. It popped open, revealing an array of liquor bottles.

"Neat trick."

"Magnetic touch-latch. Also Laura's idea. Scotch?"

"Sure."

"Rocks, right?" Nick held a tumbler against the automatic icemaker on the door of the Sub-Zero and watched as the cubes *chink-chink-chinked* against the glass. Then he poured a healthy slug of Johnny Walker, handed it to Eddie, and led the way out of the kitchen.

Eddie took a long sip, then gave a contented sigh. "Hey, Johnny, Daddy's home. What are you drinking, buddy?"

"Better not. I've been taking a pill to sleep, not supposed to mix it with alcohol."

They left the kitchen, entered the dark back corridor, illuminated only by the orange glow from the switch plates. Nick switched on the lamp on the hall table, another of the millions of little details about this house that reminded him of Laura every single day. She'd spent months looking for the perfect alabaster lamp until she found it one day in an antiques store on the Upper East Side of Manhattan when she'd accompanied him on a business trip. The shop dealt only with the trade, decorators and interior designers, but she'd sweet-talked her way in, then spotted the lamp. The base was carved of alabaster quarried in Volterra, Italy, she'd explained, when Nick asked why it had cost so freaking much. To Nick it just looked like white rock.

"Aw, don't take pills, man. You know what you need to help you sleep?"

"Let me guess." The lights in his study came on automatically as they entered, pinpoints in the ceiling and little floods that washed the hand-plastered walls, the huge Sony flat-panel TV mounted on the facing wall, the French doors that opened onto the freshly seeded lawn.

"That's right, Nicky. Pussy. Look at this place. Incredible."

"Laura."

Eddie sank into one of the butter-soft leather Symbiosis chairs, took a swig of his Scotch, and placed it noisily down on the slate-topped side table. Nick sat in the one next to him.

"So I picked up this chick Saturday night at Victor's, right? I mean, I must've had my beer goggles on, because when I woke the next morning she—well, she had a great personality, know what I'm saying? I mean, the bitch must have fell off the ugly tree and hit every branch on the way down." He gave a dry, wheezing cackle.

"But you got a good night's sleep."

"Actually no, I was shit-faced, man. Point is, Nick, you gotta get out there and start dating. Get back on the trail of tail. But man, watch out, there's a lot of skanks out there."

"I don't feel like it yet."

Eddie tried to soften his voice, though it came out more as an insinuating rasp. "She died a year ago, Nicky. That's a long time."

"Not if you're married seventeen years."

"Hey, I'm not talking about getting *married* again. I'm the *last* one to tell you to get married. Look at me—I don't buy, I lease. Trade 'em in regularly for the latest model."

"Can we talk about my security system? It's late, and I've had a long day."

"All right, all right. My systems guy's a total fucking wizard. He put in my home system."

Nick's brows shot up.

"I mean, I paid for it out of my own pocket, come on. If he can get the equipment, I'll have him put one in tomorrow."

"Cameras and everything?"

"Shit. We're talking IP-based cameras at the perimeter and at all points of entry and egress, cameras inside, overt and covert."

"What's IP?"

"Internet-something. Means you can get the signal over the Internet. You can monitor your house from your computer at work—it's amazing shit."

"Back up to tape?"

"No tape. All the cameras record to a hard drive. Maybe put in motion sensors to save on disk space. We can do remote pan-and-tilt, real-time full-color streaming video at seven and a half frames per second or something. The technology's totally different these days."

"This going to keep my stalker out?"

"Put it this way, once he sees these robot cameras swiveling at him as he approaches the house, he'll turn and run, unless he's a total whack job. And at the very least, we get a bunch of high-quality images of him next time he tries to break in. Speaking of which, I saw some serious cameras around the guard booth down the road. Looks like you got cameras all around the perimeter fence, not just at the entrance. We mighta got lucky, got a picture of him. I'll talk to the security guys down there first thing in the morning."

"You don't think the cops already did that?"

Eddie made a *pfft* sound. "Those guys aren't going to do shit for you. They'll do the bare minimum, or less."

Nick nodded. "I think you're right."

"I know I'm right. They all hate your fucking guts. You're Nick the Slasher. You laid off their dads and their brothers and sisters and wives. I bet they love seeing you get some serious payback."

Nick exhaled noisily. "What do you mean, 'unless he's a total whack job'?"

"That's the thing about stalkers, man. They don't necessarily obey the rules of sanity. Only one thing can give you total peace of mind if he comes around again." He unzipped the black nylon gym bag and took out a small oil-cloth bundle. He unwrapped it, revealing a blunt matte-black semi-automatic pistol, squarish and compact, ugly. Its plastic frame was scratched, the slide nicked. "Smith and Wesson Sigma .380," he announced.

"I don't want that," Nick said.

"I wouldn't rule anything out, I were you. Anyone who'd do that to your dog might well go after your kids, and you gonna tell me you're not going to protect your family? That's not the Nick *I* know."

6

Nick slipped into the dark theater—the FutureLab, they called it—and took a seat at the back. The Film was still playing on the giant curved movie screen, a high-gain, rear-projection video screen that took up an entire curved front wall. The darkness of the theater was soothing to his bleary morning eyes.

Jangly techno music emanated in surround sound from dozens of speakers built into the walls, ceiling, and floor. Watching this beauty reel, you were careening through the Kalahari Desert, down a narrow street in Prague, flying over the Grand Canyon, close enough to the walls to be scraped by the jagged rocks. You were whizzing through molecules of DNA and emerging in a City of the Future, the images kaleidoscopic, futuristic. "In an interlinked world," a mellifluous baritone confided, "knowledge reigns supreme." The Film was about the future of work and life and technology; it was totally abstract and cerebral and very trippy. Not a stick of furniture was anywhere to be seen.

Only some customers were shown The Film. Some visitors, particularly Silicon Valley types, were blown away by it and, when the lights came up, wanted to chatter on and on about the "seamless integration" between office furniture and technology, about the Workplace of the Future, ready to sign on the dotted line right then and there.

Others found it pretentious and annoying, didn't get it at all. Like this morning's audience, a delegation of nine high-level executives from the Atlas McKenzie Group. It was one of the world's largest financial services companies, had its spindly tendrils in everything from banking to credit cards to insurance, in more than a hundred countries and territories. Nick watched them squirm in their seats, whispering to each other. They included the Senior VP of Real Estate and the VP for Facilities Management and assorted minions. They'd been flown up from Chicago the day before on the Stratton corporate jet, been given the full-out tour by Stratton's Guest Experience Team. Nick had had lunch with them, shown them around the executive offices himself, given them his standard pitch about the flattening of the corporate pyramidal hierarchy and how the work environment was moving from individual to the collaborative community, all that stuff.

Atlas McKenzie was building an immense office tower in Toronto. A million square feet, a third of which would be their new corporate headquarters, which they wanted outfitted from scratch. That meant at least ten thousand workstations, at least fifty million bucks up front, and then there was the ten-year maintenance contract. If Stratton got the deal, it would be a huge win. Beyond huge. Unbelievable. Then there were all the Atlas McKenzie offices around the world, which could well be standardized on Stratton — Nick couldn't even calculate how much that could mean.

All right, so The Film was flopping. They might as well have been watching some subtitled art house film set in a small Bulgarian village.

At least yesterday afternoon they'd been totally jazzed by the Workplace of the Future exhibit. Visitors always were, without exception. You couldn't help but be. It was a fully functional mock-up of a workstation, eight by ten, that looked a lot more like a network news anchor set than some cubicle out of Dilbertland. The visitors were given ID tags to wear that contained an embedded chip, which communicated with an electronic sensor so that when you entered the space, the overhead lights changed from blue to green. That way, co-workers could tell from way across the floor that you were at your desk. As soon as you sat down, an electronic message was flashed to your team members — in this case, the laptops provided to the visitors — telling them you were in. Amazing what Stratton's engineers came up with, he'd often marveled. In front of the worker's desk in the Workplace of the Future was a six-foot-long wraparound computer monitor, superhigh resolution, on which appeared a page of text, a videoconference window, and a PowerPoint slide. Clients saw this and coveted it, the way some guys drool over Lamborghinis.

They were running about ten minutes behind, so Nick had to sit through The Talk. The screen faded to black, and slowly, slowly, the lights in the Lab came up. Standing at the brushed-aluminum podium was Stratton's Senior Vice President for Workplace Research, a very tall, slender woman in her late thirties with long, straight blond hair cut into severe bangs and giant horn-rim glasses. She was Victoria Zander—never Vicky or Tori, only Victoria. She was dressed dramatically, in all black. She could have been a beatnik from the fifties, a pal of Jack Kerouac's on the road.

Victoria spoke in a mellifluous soprano. She said, "Your corporate headquarters is one of the most powerful branding tools you have. It's your opportunity to tell your employees and your visitors a story about *you*—who you are, what you stand for. It's your *brandscape*. We call this the *narrative office*." As she talked, she jotted down key phrases—"smart workplace" and "heartbeat space" and "Knowledge Age"—on a digital whiteboard set into the wall in front of her, and her notes, zapped instantly into computer text, appeared on the laptops in front of the folks from Atlas McKenzie. She said, "Our model is *wagons around the campfire*. We live our private lives in our own wagon but come together at suppertime."

Even after hearing it a dozen times, Nick didn't understand all of her patter, but that was okay; he figured that no one else did either. Certainly not these guys from Chicago, who were probably rolling their eyes inwardly but didn't want to admit their lack of sophistication. Victoria's loopy little graduate seminar was intimidating and probably soared over their heads too.

What these guys understood was modular wiring infrastructure and preassembled components and data cables built into access floors. That was where they lived. They didn't want to hear about brandscapes.

He waited patiently for her to finish, increasingly aware of the visitors' restlessness. All he had to do was a quick meet-and-greet, make sure everyone was happy, chat them up a bit.

Nick didn't actually get involved in selling since he became CEO, not in any real hands-on way. That was handled on the national accounts level. He

just helped close the deal, nudged things along, assured the really big customers that the guy at the top cared. It was remarkable how far a little face
time with the CEO went with customers.

He was normally good at this, the firm handshake and the clap on the
back, the no-bullshit straight answer that everyone always found so refreshing. This morning, though, he felt a steady pulse of anxiety, a dull stom-
achache. Maybe it was a rebound reaction to the Ambien he'd taken last
night, that tiny sliver of a pill that lulled him to sleep. Maybe it was the three
cups of coffee instead of his usual two. Or maybe it was the fact that Stratton
really, *really* needed this deal.

After Victoria finished her presentation, the lights came up, and the two lead
guys from Atlas McKenzie went right up to him. One, the Senior VP of Real
Estate, was a slight, whey-faced man of around fifty with full, almost female
lips, long lashes, a permanently bland expression. He didn't speak much. His
colleague, the VP for Facilities Management, was a stubby man, all torso,
with a heavy five-o'clock shadow, a beetle brow, obviously dyed jet-black hair.
He reminded Nick of Richard Nixon.

"And I thought you guys just did chairs and filing cabinets," said Nixon,
flashing bright white teeth with a prominent center gap.

"Far from it," Nick chuckled. They knew better; Stratton had been court-
ing them for months, making their business case, running a long series of offsite meetings that Nick had thankfully been spared. "Listen, if you need to
check your e-mail or your voice mail or whatever, we've got a wireless camp-
site down the hall."

The whey-faced man, whose name was Hardwick, sidled up to Nick and
said silkily, "I hope you don't mind a rather direct question."

"Of course not." The delicate-featured, blank-faced Hardwick was a
killer, a genuine corporate assassin; he could have been an apparatchik out of
the old Soviet Politburo.

Hardwick unzipped a Gucci leather portfolio and pulled out a clipping.
Nick recognized it; it was an article from *Business Week* headlined, "Has Midas Lost His Touch?" There was a picture of the legendary Willard Osgood,

the crusty old founder of Fairfield Equity Partners—the man who'd bought Stratton—with his Coke-bottle glasses and leathery face. The article focused mostly on "the millions in pretax losses incurred by Stratton, once the fastest growing office-furniture company in the U.S." It talked about Osgood's "vaunted Midas touch for picking quality companies and growing them steadily over the long term" and asked, "What happened? Will Osgood stand idly by while one of his investments falls off a cliff? Not likely, say insiders."

Hardwick held the clipping up for a few seconds. "Is Stratton in trouble?" he asked, fixing Nick with a watery stare.

"Absolutely not," Nick replied. "Have we had a couple of lousy quarters? Hell, yeah—but so have Steelcase and Herman Miller and all the other players. We've been through two years of layoffs, as you know, and the severance costs are a bear. But we're doing what we've got to do to stay healthy in the long term."

Hardwick's voice was almost inaudible. "I understand that. But you're not a family-run company like you used to be. You're not running the whole show. I'm sure Willard Osgood's breathing down your neck."

"Osgood and his people pretty much leave us alone," Nick said. "They figure we know what we're doing—that's why they acquired us." His mouth was dry. "You know, they always like to give their companies enough rope."

Hardwick blinked, lizardlike. "We're not just buying a hell of a lot of workstations from you folks, Nick. We're buying a ten-year service contract. Are you going to be around a year or two from now?"

Nick placed a hand on Hardwick's bony shoulder. "Stratton's been around for almost seventy-five years," he said, "and I can assure you, it's going to be here long after you and I are gone."

Hardwick gave a wan smile. "I wasn't asking about Stratton. I'm asking if *you're* going to be around."

"Count on it," Nick said. He gave Hardwick's shoulder a squeeze as, out of the corner of his eye, he saw Eddie Rinaldi leaning against the wall by the entrance to the Lab, arms folded.

"Excuse me for a second," Nick said. Eddie rarely dropped by, and when he did it was always something important. Plus, Nick didn't mind taking a break in this awkward exchange.

He went up to Eddie. "What's up?"

"I got something for you. Something you better take a look at."

"Can it wait?"

"It's about your stalker. You tell me if you want to wait."

7

Eddie sat down in front of Nick's computer as if it were his own and pecked at the keyboard with two fingers. He was surprisingly adept for someone who'd never learned how to type. As he navigated through the corporate intranet to the Corporate Security area, he said, "The boys in the guard booth at your little concentration camp were more than happy to help out, of course."

"You're talking about Fenwicke Estates." Eddie smelled of cigarettes and Brut, the cologne he'd worn back in high school. Nick didn't even know they still made Brut.

"Now, *they've* got a nice setup there—high-definition, high-res Sony digital video cams positioned at the entrance and exit. Backlight compensation. Thirty frames a second. The cops didn't even ask to look at their hard-disk recorder, know that?"

"Like you said."

"Shit, they didn't even do the bare minimum, for appearances' sake. Okay." A color photo appeared on the monitor of a lanky, bespectacled figure. Eddie clicked the mouse a few times, zooming in on the figure. He was a man of around sixty with a deeply creased face, a small, tight mouth, close-cropped gray hair, eyes grotesquely magnified by the lenses of heavy-framed black glasses. Nick's heart began to thud. A few more mouse clicks, and the man's grim face took up most of the screen. The resolution wasn't bad. The man's face was clearly visible.

"Recognize him?" Eddie said.

"No."

"Well, he knows who you are."

"No doubt. What, did he just walk through? Some security."

"Climbed the fence in the wooded section, actually. Cameras there get triggered by motion sensors. No alarms there—they'd get way too many false alarms with all the animals and shit—but cameras up the wazoo."

"Great. Who is he?"

"His name is Andrew Stadler."

Nick shrugged. He'd never heard the name.

"I narrowed it down by laid-off male employees in their fifties or older, especially with outplacement irregularities. Man, I spent most of the morning looking at mug shots. My eyes are crossing. But hey, that's why I get the big bucks, right?"

Eddie double-clicked the mouse, and another photo appeared on a split screen beside the surveillance image. It was the same man, a little younger: the same heavy black glasses with the ogling eyes, the same slit of a mouth. Under this photograph was the name ANDREW M. STADLER and a social-security number, a date of birth, a Stratton employee number, a date of hire.

Nick asked, "Laid off?"

"Yes and no. They sat him down for the layoff meeting and he quit. You know, said, 'After all I've done for this company?' and 'Fuck you,' and like that."

Nick shook his head. "Never even seen the guy before."

"Spend a lot of time at the model shop?"

The model shop was where a small crew of workers—metal-benders, solderers, woodworkers—built prototypes of new Stratton products, in editions of one or two or three, from specs drawn up by the designers. The model-shop employees tended to be odd sorts, Nick had always thought. They'd all done time on the factory floor, bending metal, and they were good with their hands. They also tended to be loners and perfectionists.

"Andrew Stadler," Nick said, listening to the sound of the name, scanning the data on the man's file. "He was with the company thirty-five, thirty-six years."

SECURITY 39

"Yep. Started as an assembler on the old vertical-file-cabinet line, became a welder. Then he became a specialist level two—worked by himself in the chair plant repairing the returns. Refused to work on any of the progressive build lines because, he said, he hated listening to other people's music. Kept getting into fights with his floor supervisor. They learned to leave him alone and let him do his work. When there was an opening in the model shop five years ago, he put in for it, and they were glad to get rid of him." With another couple of clicks, Eddie brought up Stadler's employee reviews. Nick leaned closer to read the small type. "What's this about hospitalization?"

Eddie swiveled around in Nick's chair and looked up, his half-wild eyes staring. "He's a fucking nutcase, buddy. A brainiac and a maniac. The guy's been in and out of the locked ward at County Medical."

"Jesus. For what?"

"Schizophrenia. Every couple of years he stops taking his meds."

Nick let his breath out slowly.

"Okay, Nick, now here's the scary part. I put in a call to the Fenwick PD. Something like fifteen years ago, Stadler was questioned in the possible murder of an entire family that lived across the street."

Nick felt a sudden chill. "What does that mean?"

"Family called Stroup, neighbors, used to hire this guy to do repairs, odd jobs. Mister Fix-It—guy's a mechanical genius, could fix anything. Maybe they got into some kinda fight, maybe they looked at him wrong, who knows, but one night there's a gas leak in their basement, something sets it off, whole house blows."

"Jesus."

"Never proven if the whole thing was an accident or this wacko did it, but the cops suspected he did. Never could prove it, though. Had to let him go—no evidence. Just strong suspicion. Nick, this guy Stadler is one dangerous motherfucker. And I'll tell you something else you're not going to want to hear. This fruitcake's got a gun."

"What?"

"There's an old safety inspection certificate in his name—found it in the county records. Like twenty years old. And no record of sale, which means he's still got it."

"Jesus. Get a restraining order."

Eddie made a soft, dismissive *pfft* sound. "Come on, man, TROs are bullshit. Piece of paper."

"But if he tries to go on my property again—"

"You can get him arrested for *trespassing*, man. Not for stalking. Big fucking deal. You think that's going to stop a goddamned psychopath? Guy who eviscerated your goddamned dog? Guy who hears voices, wears a tinfoil hat?"

"Jesus Christ, Eddie. We got a time-stamped image of this nut climbing the fence right around the time my dog got killed. The cops got a knife that might have prints on it. They got enough to charge the guy with my dog's death."

"Yeah, and what have they done, right? They haven't done shit."

"So how do we make them take action?"

"I don't know, man. Got to apply some serious pressure. But they're going to be busy covering their big fat asses, so they're not exactly going to snap to. I say we scare the shit out of this loon first. Once the police get involved in any real way, we gotta keep hands off Stadler. But in the meantime, we got to make sure you and your family are safe."

Nick considered for a moment. "All right. But don't do anything that'll compromise me in any way. So no getting rough with him. I just want the fucker locked up somewhere."

"Fine with me. I'll track the guy down. Meantime, my man Freddie's going over to your house this afternoon to get started on the new system. I'm having him put a rush on it."

Nick glanced at his watch. He had to head over to the monthly meeting of the Compensation Committee. "Great."

"And hey, if all else fails, remember my little loaner."

Nick lowered his voice, aware that Marjorie was at her desk on the other side of the partition and might be able to hear their voices. "I don't have a permit, Eddie."

Eddie gave a slow shake of his head. "Permit? Come on, man. You know how long it takes to go through the hoops, do all the paperwork? You can't wait that long. Look, carrying an unlicensed weapon is a misdemeanor, okay? A hundred-buck fine. And that's if you get caught. Which you won't, because you won't have to use it. Isn't that worth it to protect your family from that sick fuck? A hundred bucks?"

"All right. Get out of here—I need to check my e-mail, and then I've got three meetings stacked up."

Eddie rose. "Man, you got some fancy computer equipment up here. I could use some monitors like this for my department."

"Not up to me," Nick said. "I'm just a figurehead."

8

Scott McNally lived in a decent-sized, but perfectly ordinary, house in the Forest Hills section of Fenwick where many of the Stratton execs lived. A successful accountant could have lived here. It was a generic white colonial with green shutters, a two-car garage, a rec room, a finished basement. It was decorated generically too. Everything—the dining room set, the couches and chairs and rugs—seemed to have been bought all at once, at the same mid-priced home-furnishings store. Obviously Eden, Scott's trophy wife, didn't share Laura's interest in design.

Nick and Laura had talked about Scott's house once. He admired the fact that Scott, who was loaded from his McKinsey days, didn't try to show it off like so many financial types. Money to Scott wasn't something you spent. It was like frequent-flyer miles you never use. Still, Nick couldn't put his finger on what felt funny about Scott's house until Laura pointed out that it looked somehow *temporary*, like those short-term furnished corporate apartments.

As soon as they arrived, the kids dispersed, Julia to the bedroom of one of Scott's twin twelve-year-old daughters, and Lucas to the rec room to sit by himself and watch TV. Scott was manning the immense, stainless-steel charcoal grill, the only remotely expensive thing he seemed to own. He was wearing a black barbecue apron with a yellow hazard sign on the front of it that said DANGER MEN COOKING, and a matching DANGER MEN COOKING baseball cap.

"How's it going?" Nick said as they stood in the smoke.

"Can't complain," Scott said. "Who'd listen?"

"Think that grill's big enough?"

"A cooking surface of eight hundred and eighty square inches, big enough to burn sixty-four burgers at once. Because you just never know." He shook his head. "That's the last time I let Eden go shopping at Home Depot."

"How *is* Eden these days?"

"The same, only more so. She's become a real fitness nut. If it were up to her, we'd be feasting on texturized tofu, spirulina, and barley green juice. Her latest obsession is this Advanced Pilates course she's taking. I don't quite get how that works. Does it keep getting more advanced? Can you do graduate work in Pilates, end up with a doctorate?"

"Well, she looks great."

"Just don't call her arm candy. She'd rather be thought of as arm tempeh." Scott checked that all the knobs were set to high. "You know, I'm always kind of embarrassed when you come over. It's like the feudal lord leaving his castle to go visit the peasants in their hovels. We should be roasting a boar, really. Maybe a stag." He looked at Nick. "What would you like to drink? A flagon of mead, my liege?"

"A beer would do it."

Scott turned and began shouting to his portly nine-year-old son, who was sitting by himself on the back porch making immense bubbles using a strange gadget, a long pole with a cloth strap dangling off it. "Spencer! Spencer, will you get over here, please?"

"Aww!" Spencer whined.

"Right now!" Scott shouted. Lowering his voice a bit, he said, "Eden can't wait until he's old enough to send to Andover."

"Not you, though."

"I barely notice the kid," he said with a shrug. If Nick didn't know Scott better, he wouldn't realize Scott was kidding, doing his usual shtick. When his son was within speaking range, he said, "Spencer, could you please get Mr. Conover one of those brown bottles of beer?" To Nick he said, "You'll love this beer. It's a Belgian Abbey ale that's brewed in upstate New York."

"Got any Miller?"

"Ah, the Champagne of Beers. What I'd like to find is the beer of champagnes. I think Eden bought some Grolsch, if that'll work."

"Sure."

"Spencer, look for the green bottles that have the funny metal tops with the rubber stoppers on them, got it?"

"Dad, it's not supposed to be good for you to eat barbecued meats." Spencer folded his arms across his chest. "Do you know that barbecuing at high heat can create polycyclic aromatic hydrocarbons, which are known to be mutagens?"

Nick stared at the kid. How the hell do you learn to *pronounce* that stuff?

"Now, that's where you're wrong, son," said Scott. "They *used* to think that aromatic hydrocarbons were bad. Now they know that they're the best thing for you. What do they teach you in school, anyway?"

Spencer looked stymied, but only momentarily. "Don't say I didn't warn you if you get cancer later in life."

"I'll be dead by then, son."

"But Dad—"

"Okay, kid, so here's your burger," Scott said blithely, holding up one of the raw patties. "Go fetch yourself a bun and some ketchup, okay? So instead of cancer, you'll get salmonella and *E. coli* bacteria. Mad cow too, if you're really lucky."

Spencer seemed to get his father's sense of humor but wouldn't let on. "But I thought *E. coli* naturally colonizes the human intestine," he said.

"You don't stop, do you? Go play in traffic. But first get Mr. Conover his beer."

The boy trudged reluctantly away.

Scott chuckled. "Kids these days."

"Impressive," was all Nick could think to say.

"I'm sorry you don't want to try this Belgian ale," Scott said. "I discovered it at that dude ranch in Arizona I went to last month with my old college buddies, remember?"

"You didn't exactly rave about the place."

"Ever smell a horse up close? Anyway, I liked the beer."

"So, Spencer's a little scary, huh?"

"I guess. We first had an inkling of that when he was three and he started composing haiku using the letters from his alphabet soup."

"I don't think you appreciate how cooperative he is. If I'd asked Luke to go fetch me a beer he would have ripped my face off."

"Tough age. By the time Spencer turns sixteen we'll probably see him just once a year, at Christmas. But yeah, he's usually well behaved, and he's into math just like his dad. Of course, later, when he turns into Jeff Dahmer, we'll discover the dissected remains of dogs and cats in the backyard." He started to chuckle, and then his face fell. "Oh, shit, Nick, I forgot about your dog. I'm sorry."

"Don't worry about it."

"I can't believe I said that."

"You might want to turn the burgers. They're burning."

"Oh, right." He wrestled with a big metal spatula. "Nick, the cops have any idea who did it?"

Nick hesitated, then shook his head. "They're guessing it's a downsized employee. But I could've told 'em that."

"That narrows it down to five thousand and sixty-seven. You don't have a security system?"

"Not good enough, obviously. I mean, we're in a gated community."

"Jesus, that could happen to us too."

"Thanks for being so sensitive."

"No, I mean—sorry, but as the CFO I'm just as responsible as you are for the layoffs, and—God, you must be spooked as shit."

"Of course I am. But most of all I'm fucking pissed off."

"The cops aren't going to do anything, are they?"

"They all know someone we laid off. Alarm goes off at my house, they're not going to get off their stools at Dunkin' Donuts."

Spencer ran across the lawn with a bottle of beer in one hand and a glass in the other. "Here you go, Mr. Conover," he said, handing the beer and glass to Nick.

"Thanks, Spencer." Nick set down the glass and struggled with the complicated top of the Grolsch. He'd actually never had a bottle of the stuff outside of a bar, where they poured it for you.

Spencer circled his pudgy little arms around his dad's waist. Scott reached out his free hand and grabbed his son back, made a grunting sound.

"Hey, sweetie," he said. His face was red from the heat, and he blinked the smoke out of his eyes.

"Hey, Dad."

Nick smiled. So Spencer was a little kid, too, not just a *Jeopardy* champ.

"Shit," Scott said, as one of his burgers slipped through the grate and into the fire.

"Do this often?"

"It's my only hobby. Understand, my idea of a good time is filling out my tax return using Roman numerals." He fiddled some more with the metal spatula. "Shit," he said again, as another burger dropped into the flames. "You like well done?"

9

The architect who was doing the renovations to the Conovers' kitchen was a stodgy but affable man named Jeremiah Claflin. He wore round black glasses of the sort that some of the famous architects affected—that Japanese guy, that Swiss guy, Nick forgot their names if he ever knew them—and his white hair contrasted pleasantly with his ruddy face and curled over his shirt collar. Laura had interviewed him and several other architects from Fenwick and the surrounding towns as intensively as she'd interviewed nanny candidates years ago. It was important to her that the architect she hired not only had a portfolio of projects she admired, but also wasn't too stubborn, too much of an *artiste* that he wouldn't do exactly what she wanted.

Nick got along with Claflin, as he got along with just about everyone, but he realized early on that the architect found Nick frustrating. Sure, he was pleased to be working on the house that belonged to Stratton's CEO— that gave him certain bragging rights—and since Laura had chosen nothing but the most high-end, most ridiculously expensive appliances and cabinets and all that, Claflin was making a boatload of money for not that much design work. But Nick wasn't all that interested in the fussy little details that Laura had had such patience for, and there sure as hell were a million fussy little details. The decisions never seemed to end. Did he want the kitchen counters to have a full bullnose or half bullnose or an ogee edge? How much of an overhang? How tall did he want the backsplash to be? A self-rimming sink or an undermount? What about the height of the countertop? Jesus, Nick had a company to run.

Claflin was forever faxing him drawings and lists of questions. Nick would inevitably tell the architect to just do whatever Laura had told him to do. He really didn't give a damn about what the kitchen looked like. What he cared about—was obsessed about, really—was that it be done precisely the way Laura wanted. The renovations had been Laura's last big project, pretty much all she thought about, talked about, in the months before the accident. Nick suspected that part of the reason she'd poured so much of herself into it was that the kids were getting older, and being a mom was no longer a full-time job. After Lucas was born, she'd quit her job teaching art history at St. Thomas More College. She tried to get her teaching position back when the kids were older, but she couldn't. She'd been mommy-tracked. She missed teaching, missed the intellectual engagement.

Laura was by far the smarter one in the marriage. Nick had gone to Michigan State on a full-boat hockey scholarship, busted his hump to get C's and B's, while Laura had breezed through Swarthmore *summa cum laude*. It was like she had a deep well of creative energy inside her that needed to be tapped or she'd go crazy, and the renovations filled a need for her.

But there was more to it: Laura had wanted to knock down the sterile old kitchen, which looked like no one ever used it, and turn it into a hearth, a great room where the whole family could gather. Laura, who was an excellent cook, could make dinner while the kids did their homework or hung out around the kitchen island. The whole family could be together comfortably.

The least Nick could do to honor her was to make sure the damned kitchen was done the way she wanted.

Their marriage had been far from perfect—hell, they'd been arguing the night she was killed, as he'd never forget—but Nick had learned you choose your battles. You made unspoken deals sometimes, ceded turf. Laura, who'd grown up in a shambling Victorian on the Hill, a pediatrician's kid, wanted to live a certain way, namely better than the way in which she'd been brought up. She wanted the elegance and style she never had growing up in a house that was always in some state of chaos and disrepair. She subscribed to *Architectural Digest* and *Elle Décor* and half a dozen other magazines that all looked the same, and she was always tearing out photos and two-page spreads and adding them to a steadily thickening file folder that she might as well have labeled DREAM HOUSE. To Nick, having a house with more than two bedrooms and a backyard and a kitchen you didn't eat in already bordered on unimaginable luxury.

Claflin was waiting for him in the kitchen when he arrived, twenty minutes late. From the family room Nick could hear Julia and her best friend, Emily, playing a computer game called *The Sims* in which they created their own creepily real-looking human beings and bent them to their will. Julia and Emily were shrieking with laughter over something.

"Busy day?" Claflin asked. His tone was jovial, but his eyes betrayed annoyance at being kept waiting.

Nick apologized as he shook the architect's hand, and then his eye was immediately caught by something. The countertops were in. He went up to the island and realized that, even to his untrained eye, something looked wrong.

"I see they've put a new alarm system in," Claflin said. "Fast work."

Nick nodded. He'd noticed the white touch pads on the wall as he entered. "The island," he said. "That's not what Laura wanted."

She'd designed a big island in the center of the kitchen around which the whole family could gather, sitting on stools, while she made dinner. But you sure as hell couldn't sit at this thing. It had walls of black granite that came up about two feet, no overhang, no place for stools.

Claflin beamed. "None of your guests will have to see the cooking mess from the dining table," he said. "Yet it works perfectly as a food-prep station. Clever, don't you think?"

Nick hesitated. "You can't sit at it," he said.

"True," Claflin conceded, his smile fading, "but there's no unsightly mess. That open-kitchen thing, that's the big problem with this great-room design that no one talks about. You have this stunning kitchen with all the best appliances, and this big farmhouse table where your guests eat their dinner, and what do they end up looking at? A mess of dirty pots and pans on the counters and island. This solves that problem."

"But the kids can't sit around it."

"Believe me, that's trivial compared to—"

"Laura wanted everyone to be able to sit around the kitchen island. She wanted to be able to see the kids hanging out here, doing their homework or reading or talking or whatever while she was making dinner."

"Nick," Claflin said slowly, "you don't cook, right? And Laura's—well, she's . . ."

"Laura wanted this big, open, hang-out kitchen," Nick said. "That's what she wanted, and that's what we're going to have."

Claflin looked at him for a few seconds. "Nick, I faxed you the specs, and you signed off on them."

"I probably didn't even look at them. I told you we're doing everything exactly according to Laura's wishes."

"This has already been cut. We can't . . . send it *back*. You own it."

"I really don't give a shit," Nick said. "You get the stone guy back here and have him recut it the way Laura wanted."

"Nick, there's a logic to this design that—"

"Just do it." Nick's voice was arctic. "Are we clear?"

10

As soon as Claflin left, Julia entered the kitchen. She was wearing a gray sweatshirt emblazoned with the arch-shaped logo of the Michigan Wolverines. Her friend was still sitting at the computer in the family room, busily tyrannizing the lives of her Sims family like some high-tech Hitler.

"Daddy, are you the president of Stratton?"

"President and CEO, baby, don't you know that? Give me a hug."

She ran to him as if she'd been waiting for permission, threw her arms around him. Nick leaned over and gave her a kiss on her forehead, thought: *She's just figuring this out?*

"Emily says you fired half the people in Fenwick."

Emily looked up from the computer screen, stole a furtive glance at Nick.

"We had to lay a lot of really good people off," Nick said. "To save the company."

"She says you fired her uncle."

Ah, so that was it. Nick shook his head. "I didn't know that. I'm sorry to hear it, Emily."

Emily gave him an imperious, condescending look, almost withering, quite remarkable for a ten-year-old girl. "Uncle John's been unemployed for almost two years. He says he gave everything to Stratton and you ruined his life."

Nick wanted to respond—*it wasn't me, and anyway we provided extensive outplacement counseling, you know*—but once you start debating with ten-year-olds you might as well hang it up. He was saved by the honk of a car horn. "Okay, Em, you'd better get going. You don't want to keep your mom waiting."

Emily's mom drove a brand-new gold Lexus LX 470 roughly half as long as a city block. She wore a white Fred Perry tennis shirt, white shorts, a Fenwick Country Club windbreaker, expensive-looking white tennis shoes. She had great, tanned legs, short auburn hair coiffed in a high-fashion cut, a giant glittering diamond engagement ring. Her husband was a plastic surgeon who was rumored to be having an affair with his receptionist, and if even Nick, who was completely out of the gossip stream, had heard it, it was probably true.

"Hello, Nick." Her cigarette-husky voice was chilly and bone-dry.

"Hi, Jacqueline. Emily should be out in a second. I had to tear her away from the computer."

Jacqueline smiled in an artful semblance of sociability. Nick knew her only enough to say hi: maintaining friendships among the school parents had been Laura's job. Not that long ago, Jacqueline Renfro would light up when she saw him at school plays and parents' nights, as if he were a long-lost friend. But people didn't suck up to him so much anymore.

"How's Jim?" he said.

"Oh, you know," she said airily. "When people lose their jobs they don't get Botox quite as often."

"Emily mentioned that her uncle got laid off from Stratton. Is he your brother or Jim's?"

She paused, then said sternly, "Mine, but Emily shouldn't have said that. Honestly, she has no manners. I'll talk to her."

"No, no—she was saying what was on her mind. Where'd your brother work?"

"I don't—" she faltered, then she called out, "Emily, what is *taking* you so long?"

They stood in awkward silence for a moment until her daughter emerged from the house, struggling under the weight of a backpack the size of a Sherpa's.

Julia didn't look up from the computer monitor as Nick approached and asked, "Where's your brother?"

"I don't know."

"You finish your homework?"

Julia didn't answer.

"You heard me, right?"

"What?" What was it with the selective hearing? He could whisper "Krispy Kreme" in the kitchen and she'd come bounding.

"Your homework. We're eating dinner in half an hour — it's Marta's night off. Turn off the computer."

"But I'm in the middle —"

"Save it and shut down. Come on, sweetie."

He went to the foot of the stairs and shouted up for Lucas. No reply. The house was so unnecessarily big, though, that sound didn't carry far. Nick went upstairs, past Laura's study, its door unopened since her death, to Lucas's room.

He knocked. The door, slightly ajar, opened inward a few inches. He pushed it open the rest of the way, called, "Luke?" No answer; no Lucas here. His desk lamp was on, a textbook open. He walked over to see which textbook it was, inadvertently bumping against the desk. The iMac's flat panel screen came out of sleep mode, displaying a profusion of colorful flesh-tone photographs. Nick looked again and saw naked bodies in various sexual contortions. He came closer to get a closer look.

The entire screen was taken up with pop-up windows of slutty-looking women with huge boobs in garish shades of pink and orange. "Real Amateur Pussy," one window read, the word "real" flashing red like a neon sign.

Nick's first reaction was a very male one: he looked even closer, intrigued, felt a stirring he hadn't felt in months. Immediately after, though, he felt disgusted at the tawdriness of the images — who were these girls who were willing to do this stuff for all the heavy-breathing Internet world to see? And then the realization washed over him that this was Lucas's computer, that his son was looking at all this stuff. If Laura had discovered this, she would have freaked out, called him at work, demanded that he come home at once and have a Talk with his son.

Whereas Nick didn't know what to think, how to react. He was at a loss. The kid was sixteen, and developmentally a fairly advanced sixteen at that. Of course he was interested in sex. Nick remembered when he and a buddy, around the same age, had found a matted, waterlogged *Playboy* in the woods. They'd dried it out carefully, pored over it as if it were the Dead Sea Scrolls, hid it in Nick's garage. Looking back on it now, it was amazing how different smut was in those days, how innocent, though it sure didn't seem it at the time. The photos in *Playboy* were so heavily airbrushed that it was something of a shock when Nick first got an up-close glimpse of his first real-life tits not long afterward, in the finished basement of his first real girlfriend, Jody Catalfano. Jody, the cutest girl in the class, had been after him for months, was ready long before he was. Her breasts were far smaller than the voluptuous babes in *Playboy*, her nipples larger and darker with a few stray hairs around the edges of the aureoles.

But this stuff, garish and flashing, was way too *real*, somehow. It was more blatant, more perverted than anything from Nick's fevered adolescence. And here it was, a couple of mouse clicks away. It wasn't half-buried under dead leaves in the woods, didn't require conservation efforts or concealment in an empty Pennzoil box in a garage. On some level it was almost sickening. And what if Julia had wandered in here and seen it?

He picked up Lucas's desk phone and called his son's cell.

Lucas answered after five rings, fumbling with the phone a long time. "Yeah?" In the background was loud music, raucous voices.

"Luke, where the hell are you?"

A pause. "What's up?"

"What's *up*? It's suppertime."

"I ate already."

"We have dinner together, remember?" This "dinner together" thing had become one of Nick's recent obsessions, particularly since Laura was gone. He sometimes felt that if he didn't insist on it, the remains of his family could all fly away by centrifugal force.

Another pause. "Where are you, Luke?"

"All right," Lucas said and hung up.

An hour later, Lucas still wasn't home. Julia was hungry, so the two of them sat down to dinner at the small round table that had been temporarily placed in one corner of the kitchen, away from most of the construction. Marta had set the table for the three of them before going out for the evening. In the warm oven was a roast chicken, tented with foil. Nick brought the chicken and rice and broccoli to the table, remembering to put trivets under the chicken pan so he didn't scorch the table. He expected a fight over the broccoli, and he got it. Julia would accept only rice and a chicken drumstick, and Nick was too wiped out to argue.

"I like Mommy's better," Julia said. "This is too dry."

"It's been in the oven for a couple of hours."

"Mommy made the best fried chicken."

"She sure did, baby," Nick said. "Eat."

"Where's Luke?"

"He's on his way back." *Taking his damned time of it too,* Nick thought.

Julia stared at the chicken leg on her plate as if it were a giant cockroach. Finally, she said, "I don't like it here."

Nick thought for a moment, unsure how to respond. "Like it where?"

"Here," she said unhelpfully.

"This house?"

"We don't have any neighbors."

"We do, but . . ."

"We don't know any of them. It's not a neighborhood. It's just . . . houses and trees."

"People do keep to themselves here," he conceded. "But your mommy wanted us to move here because she thought it would be safer than our last house."

"Well, it's not. Barney . . ." She stopped, her eyes welling up with tears, resting her chin in her hands.

"But we will be now, with this new security system in."

"Nothing like that ever happened in our old house," she pointed out.

The front door opened, setting off a high alert tone, and a few seconds later Lucas trundled noisily into the kitchen, threw his backpack down on the floor. He seemed to get taller and broader by the day. He wore a dark blue Old Navy sweatshirt, baggy cargo pants with the waistband of his boxer shorts showing, and some white scarflike thing under his backwards baseball cap.

"What's that on your head?" Nick asked anyway.

"Do-rag, why?"

"That like a hip-hop thing?"

Lucas shook his head, rolled his eyes. "I'm not hungry," he said. "I'm going upstairs."

"Sit with us anyway, Luke," Julia pleaded. "Come on."

"I've got a lot of homework," Lucas said as he left the kitchen without turning back.

11

Nick followed his son upstairs. "We have to have a talk," he said.

Lucas groaned. "What now?" When he reached the open door to his room, he said, "You been in here?"

"Sit down, Luke."

Lucas noticed the computer monitor facing the door, and he leaped toward it, spun it away. "I don't want you going in my room."

"Sit down."

Lucas sat on the edge of his bed, hunched over with his elbows propped on his knees, his chin resting on his hands, a gesture that Julia had recently started imitating. He stared malevolently.

"You're not allowed to go to porn sites," Nick said.

Lucas blinked. His angry blue eyes were crystal clear, innocent and pure. He was trying to grow something under his chin, Nick noticed. For a moment Lucas seemed to be debating whether to own up to the evidence so prominently on display. Then he said: "There's nothing there I don't know about, Nick. I'm sixteen."

"Cut out the 'Nick' stuff."

"Okay, *Dad*," he said with a surly twist. "Hey, at least I'm not going to snuff or torture sites. You should see the shit that's out there."

"You do that again and your Internet access gets cut off, understand?"

"You can't do that. I need e-mail for school. It's required."

"Then I'll leave you with just AOL with whatever those controls are."

"You can't *do* that! I got to do research on the Internet."

"I'll bet. Where were you this afternoon?"

"Friend's."

"Sounded like a bar or something."

Lucas stared as if he weren't going to dignify this with a response.

"What happened to Ziggy?"

"Ziggy's an asshole."

"He's your best friend."

"Look, you don't know him, all right?"

"Then who are these new kids you're hanging out with?"

"Just friends."

"What are their names?"

"Why do you care?"

Nick bit his lip, thought for a moment. "I want you to go back to Underberg." Lucas had seen a counselor for four months after Laura's death until he quit, complaining that Underberg was "full of shit."

"I'm not going back there. No way."

"You've got to talk to someone. You won't talk to me."

"About what?"

"For God's sake, Lucas, you've just been through one of the most traumatic things a kid can go through. Of course you're having a hard time. You think it's any easier on your sister, or on me?"

"Forget it," Lucas said, raising his voice sharply. "Don't even go there."

"What's that supposed to mean?"

Lucas shot him a pitying look. "I got homework," he said, getting up from the bed and walking over to his desk.

Nick poured himself a Scotch on the rocks, sat in the family room and watched TV for a while, but nothing held his interest. He started feeling a mild, pleasant buzz. Around midnight he went up to his room. Both Julia's and Lucas's lights were off. The newly installed alarm touch pad in his bedroom glowed green, announced READY in black letters. *Ready for what?* he thought. The installer had called him and given him the ten-minute low-down that afternoon. If a door was open somewhere, it would say something like FAULT—LIVING ROOM DOOR. If someone moved downstairs it would say, FAULT—MOTION SENSOR, FAMILY ROOM or whatever.

He brushed his teeth, stripped down to his shorts, and climbed into the king-size bed. Next to Laura's side of the bed was the same stack of books that had been there since the night of the accident. Marta dusted them off but knew enough not to put them away. The effect was as if she were away on a business trip and might come back in, keys jingling, at any moment. One of the books, Nick always noticed with a pang, was an old course catalog from St. Thomas More College that had a listing for her art history class. She used to look at it sometimes at night, regretful.

The sheets were cool and smooth. He rolled over something lumpy: one of Julia's Beanie Babies. He smiled, tossed it out of the way. Lately she'd taken to leaving a different Beanie Baby in his bed each night, a little game of hers. He guessed it was her way of sleeping with Daddy, by proxy, since she hadn't been allowed to sleep in the parental bed for some time.

He closed his eyes, but his mind raced. The Scotch hadn't helped at all. A jerky, low-quality movie kept playing in his mind: The cop saying, *Do you have any enemies, Mr. Conover?* Julia's hot, wet tears soaking his shirt by the side of the pool.

Fifteen, twenty minutes later he gave up, switched on the bathroom light, and fished out an Ambien from the brown plastic pharmacy bottle and dry-swallowed it.

He turned on the bedside lamp and read for a while. Nick wasn't a reader, never read fiction, only enjoyed biographies but didn't have time to read anything anymore. He hated reading those books on business manage-ment that so many of his Leadership Team kept on their shelves.

After a while he began feeling drowsy, finally, and turned off the light.

He had no idea how much later it was when he was awakened by a rapid beeping tone. Eddie's installers had set the system to go off only in his bed-room or his study, and not too loud, when he was in the house.

He sat up, his heart pounding, his head filled with sludge. For a moment he didn't know where he was or what that strange insistent beeping was.

When he realized where it was coming from, he leaped out of bed and squinted at the green touch pad's LED.

It was flashing: ALARM***PERIMETER***ALARM.

Keeping his footsteps light, in order not to wake the kids, he went downstairs to investigate.

12

Nick padded barefoot downstairs, the house dark and silent. He glanced at one of the new touch pads at the foot of the stairs. It too was flashing: ***ALARM***PERIMETER***.

His brain felt viscous and slow. It was an effort to think clearly. Only the rapid beating of his heart, the adrenaline-fueled anxiety, kept him moving forward.

He paused for a moment, considering which way to go.

Then a light came on *inside* the house, flooding him with panic. He walked quickly toward the light—his study?—until he remembered that the software that ran the cameras had been programmed to detect pixel changes, shifts in light or movement. Not only did the cameras start recording when there was a change in light, but the software was connected to a relay that automatically switched on a couple of inside lights, to scare off potential intruders by making them think someone in the house had been awakened, even if no one was home.

He slowed his pace but kept going, trying to think. The motion-sensor software worked by zones. That meant that whoever or whatever was there was on the side of the lawn nearest his study. Eddie's guy had set up the system so that the alarm company wasn't alerted unless the house itself was broken into, since a large animal moving across the lawn was enough to set off the perimeter alarm. Otherwise there'd be too many false alarms. But if something did cross the lawn, the cameras started and the lights went on.

A deer. Probably that was all it was.

Still, he had to be sure.

He kept going through the family room, down the hall to his study. The lights were on.

He slowed as he entered the study, the sludge in his head starting to clear. No one was here, of course. The only sound was the faint hum from his computer. He looked at the French doors and the darkness beyond. Nothing there; nothing outside. A false alarm.

The room went dark, startling him momentarily, until he remembered that the lights were also programmed to go off after two minutes. He walked through the study, approaching the glass panes of the French doors, staring out.

He could see nothing.

Nothing out there but watery moonlight glinting on the trees and shrubbery.

He glanced back at the illuminated face of his desk clock. Ten minutes after two. The kids were asleep upstairs, Marta presumably back from her night out and asleep in her bedroom in the wing off the kitchen. He glanced back out through the windowpanes, checking again.

After a few seconds he turned to leave the study.

The lawn outside lit up. The floodlights came on, jolting Nick. He spun back around, looked outside, saw a figure approaching from a stand of trees.

He moved closer to the glass, squinted. A man in some kind of trench coat that flapped as he walked. He was crossing the lawn slowly, headed directly toward Nick.

Nick went to the touch pad and deactivated the alarm system. Then he reached for the French doors' lever handle, thought for a moment, and went to his desk. He took the key from the middle drawer and unlocked the bottom one, slid it open, took out the pistol.

He removed it from its oilcloth.

Blood rushed through his head; he could hear it in his ears.

Despite assuring him he'd never have to use the thing, Eddie had left it loaded. Now Nick gripped the weapon, pulled back the slide to chamber the first round, as Eddie had instructed, let the slide go.

He turned slowly, the weapon at his side, careful to keep his finger away from the trigger. With his left hand he turned the handle and opened the French doors. He stepped outside, the soil of the newly seeded lawn cold against his bare feet.

"Stop right there," he called.

The man kept advancing. Now Nick could make out his heavy black eyeglasses, his ogling eyes, his brush-cut gray hair, his bent figure. The man, his name was Andrew Stadler, walked straight ahead, heedlessly.

Nick raised the gun, barked: *"Freeze!"*

Under the flapping trench coat, Stadler wore white pants, a white shirt. He was muttering to himself, all the while staring at Nick as he came closer and closer.

He's a fucking nutcase, buddy . . .

The guy kept coming, goggling eyes staring as if he didn't even see the gun, or if he did, he didn't give a shit.

Eddie's words. *A maniac. The guy's been in and out of the locked ward at County Medical.*

"Don't you fucking take another step!" Nick shouted.

Now the man's mutterings were starting to become distinct. The man raised his hand, pointed a finger at Nick, his expression malevolent, enraged. "Never safe," the man croaked. He smiled, his hands fluttering to his sides, to his coat pockets. The smile was like a twitch: it came and disappeared several times in succession, no logic to it.

Stadler was questioned in the possible murder of an entire family that lived across the street.

"One more step, and I shoot!" Nick shouted, raising the weapon with both hands, aiming at the center of the lunatic's body.

"You're never going to be safe," the man in white said, one hand fumbling in his pocket, now *rushing* toward Nick, toward the open door.

Nick squeezed the trigger, and everything seemed to happen all at once. There was a popping sound, loud but not nearly as loud as he'd expected. The pistol bucked in his hands, flew backward at him. An empty shell casing flew off to one side. Nick could smell gunpowder, sulfuric and acrid.

The maniac stumbled, sank to his knees. A dark blotch appeared on his white shirt, a corona of blood. The bullet had entered his upper chest. Nick watched, his pulse racing, still gripping the pistol in both hands, leveling it at the man until he could be sure the man was down.

Suddenly, with surprisingly agility, the madman sprang to his feet with a throaty growl, shouting, "No!" in an aggrieved, almost offended voice. He propelled himself toward Nick, said, *"Never—safe!"*

The man was less than six feet away now, and Nick fired, aiming higher this time, wild with fear and resolve. He was able to stabilize the weapon better now, felt a spray of powder sting his face, and he saw the man tumble backward and to one side, mouth open, but this time he did not break his fall. He landed on his side, legs splayed at a funny angle, expelling a guttural, animallike sound.

Nick froze, watched in silence for a few seconds.

His ears rang. Gripping the weapon in both hands, he stepped to one side to see the man's face. The lunatic's mouth was gaping, blood seeping over his lips, his chin. The black glasses had fallen off somewhere; now the eyes, much smaller without the magnification of the lenses, stared straight ahead.

The man exhaled with a rattling noise and was silent.

Nick stood, dazed, flooded with adrenaline, even more terrified at this moment than he had been a minute earlier. He pointed the pistol, almost accusingly, at the man and walked slowly up to him. Nick thrust out his right foot, nudged the man's chest, testing.

The man rolled backward, his mouth open, a mouthful of silver fillings glinting, the eyes now staring into the night sky, blood seeping. The high metallic ringing in Nick's ears had begun to subside, and everything was strangely, eerily silent. From very far away, Nick thought he could hear a faint rustling of leaves. A dog now barked, far in the distance, then stopped.

The man's chest was not moving; he was not breathing. Nick leaned over him, the pistol now dangling in his left hand by his side. He placed his right forefinger on the man's throat and felt no pulse. This was no surprise; the staring eyes had already announced that the maniac lay dead.

He's dead, Nick thought. I've killed him.

I've killed a man.

He was suffused with terror. I killed this guy. Another voice in his head began to plead, defensive and frightened as a little boy.

I had to. I had no choice. I had no fucking choice.

I had to stop him.

Maybe he's just unconscious, Nick thought desperately. He felt the man's throat again, couldn't find the pulse. He grabbed one of the man's rough, dry hands, pressed against the inside of his wrist, felt nothing.

He let go of the hand. It dropped to the ground.

He poked again at the man's chest with his toes, but he knew the truth.

The man was dead.

The crazy man, this stalker, this man who would have dismembered my children the way he butchered my dog, lay dead on the freshly seeded lawn, surrounded by tiny sprouts of grass that poked out sparsely from the moist black earth.

Oh, Jesus God, Nick thought. I've just killed a man.

He stood up but felt his knees give way. He sank to the ground, felt tears running down his cheeks. Tears of relief? Of terror? Not, certainly not, of despair or of sadness.

Oh, please, Jesus, he thought. What do I do now?

What do I do now?

For a minute, maybe two, he remained on his knees, sunken in the soft ground. It was as if he were in a church, a place he hadn't been in decades, praying. That was what it felt like. He was praying on the soft, hydroseeded lawn, his back turned to the crumpled body. For a few seconds he wondered if he was going to lose consciousness, pass out on the soil. He waited for a sound, the sound of someone in the house, awakened by the gunshots, running out to see what had happened. The kids couldn't see this, mustn't be allowed to see it.

But not a sound. No one had awakened, not even Marta. Gathering his strength, he rose, dropping the weapon to the ground, moving back toward the study as if in a trance. The lights came on: the motion sensor software again.

He could barely stand. He sank into his desk chair, folding his arms on the desk, resting his head on his arms. His mind was racing, but to no purpose; he was not thinking clear thoughts. His brains felt scrambled.

He was terrified.

What do I do now?

Who can help me? Who do I call?

He lifted the handset on his desk phone, pressed the number nine.

Nine-one-one. The police.

No, I can't. Not yet. He hung up.

Must think. What do I tell them? Everything depends on this. Was it self-defense pure and simple?

The police, who despised him so much, would be looking to hang him. Once they showed up, they'd be asking all sorts of questions, and one wrong answer might put him in prison for years. Nick knew that, given how groggy and out of it he was, he might well be railroaded by the cops.

He needed help.

He picked up the handset again, punched the cell number of the one person who would know what to do now.

Dear God, he thought as the phone rang.

Help me.

Eddie's voice was sleep-thickened, clipped. "Yeah?"

"Eddie, it's Nick."

"Nick—Jesus, it's fucking—"

"Eddie, I need you to come over to my house. Right now." He swallowed. A cool breeze swept through the room from the open doors, making him shiver.

"Now? Nick, are you out of your—"

"Now, Eddie. Oh, God. Right now."

"What the hell is it?"

"The stalker," Nick said. His mouth was dry, and the words stuck in his throat.

"He's *there*?" For a few seconds, Nick couldn't answer. Eddie went on, "Christ, Nick, what *is* it? My God, don't tell me he got to your *kids*!"

"I—I gotta call nine-one-one, but—I need to know what to *tell* them, and—"

"What the fuck *happened*, Nick?" Eddie barked.

"I killed him," Nick heard himself say softly. He paused to think of how to explain it, blinked a few times, then fell silent. What was there to say, really? Eddie had to have figured it out.

"*Shit*, Nick—"

"When I call the cops, they're going to—"

"Nick, you listen to me," Eddie interrupted. "Do *not* pick up the phone again. I'll be there in ten minutes."

The phone slipped from Nick's hand as if his fingers were greased. He felt a sob welling up.

Please, dear God, Nick thought. Make this go away.

13

Standing in the shadowed recesses of the front porch, Nick sipped from a mug of instant coffee and waited. Apart from physical sensations—the chill of the night air, the warmth of the mug against his palms, the gusts of wind—he felt nothing. He was beyond numb. He was a husk, an empty body standing on a porch at night while above him hovered Nick Conover, watching in disbelief. This hadn't happened. This was a nightmare that, even as he experienced it in real time, he told himself was merely a bad dream that he'd awaken from, soon enough, but not before he moved through the twisting, steadily more awful script. At the same time he understood that it wasn't a dream. Any minute now, Eddie's car would pull into the driveway and Nick, by telling another person, seeking his advice, would make it real.

As if on cue, Eddie's Pontiac GTO coasted quietly up the driveway, headlights extinguished. Eddie got out, shut the door quietly, jogged up to Nick. He was wearing sweatpants and a tan Carhartt jacket.

"Nicky, tell me exactly what happened?" Eddie's face was creased, unfamiliarly, with concern. His shoulders were hunched. His breath stank of stale booze; he looked like he'd been asleep.

Nick chewed the inside of his cheek, looking away.

Eddie twisted his head to one side. "All right. Where is he?"

———

"Okay," Eddie said. "Okay."

His hands made strange, resolute chopping motions in the air. "Okay." He stood over the crumpled body. The floodlights at his back cast a long, spindly shadow.

"Do you think anyone heard?" His first question. A strange one, it seemed to Nick. Not "what happened?"

Nick shook his head. He spoke in a low voice, hoping Eddie would do the same. "Marta or the kids would have gotten up if they did."

"Neighbors?"

"Hard to say. The security guys down at the booth normally drive up if they think there's a problem."

"No lights went on at any of the neighbors' houses?"

"Look for yourself. Our nearest neighbor is hundreds of feet away. Trees and everything between us. I can't see them, they can't see me."

Eddie nodded. "The Smith and Wesson's a .380. Makes kind of a loud popping noise." He leaned over to peer more closely at Stadler. "Did he enter the house?"

"No."

Eddie nodded again. Nick couldn't tell from his expression whether that was good or not.

"He see you?"

"Sure. I was standing right here."

"You told him to stop."

"Of course. Eddie, what the hell am I—"

"You did the right thing." His voice was low, soothing. "You had no fucking choice."

"He kept on going. He wouldn't stop."

"He would have attacked your kids if you didn't stop him."

"I know."

Eddie let out a long, slow breath, a little quaver in it. "Shit, man."

"What?"

"Shit."

"It was self-defense," Nick said.

Eddie drew closer to Stadler's corpse. "How many shots?"

"I think two."

"Chest and the head. The mouth."

Nick noticed that the bleeding had stopped. It looked black in the artificial light. The man's skin was white and waxen, his eyes staring.

"You must have a tarp here, all the construction."

"A tarp?"

"Canvas. Or plastic, better."

"A tarp?"

"A tarpaulin, Nick. You know. A big heavy plastic sheet. Or contractor bags if you have them. You must have those around."

"What for?"

"The hell do you think? Any idea how hard it is to carry a dead body?"

Nick felt a spasm of fear in his abdomen. "We got to call the cops, Eddie."

Eddie looked at Nick incredulously. "You are fucking kidding me. You think you even have a choice here?"

"What the hell else are we going to do?"

"Then what'd you call me for, Nick?"

"I—" He had a point, of course. "This is bad, Eddie. Really bad."

"You just used my fucking gun. To kill a guy, okay? Are you hearing me? My gun. We really don't have a choice."

14

Nick stared, didn't know what to say, went back into the study, Eddie right behind him. Nick sat in one of the side chairs, rubbed the heels of his hands into his eyes.

"It was self-defense," he repeated.

"Maybe."

"Maybe? What are you talking about, maybe? This guy was dangerous."

"Did he have a gun?"

"No. But how the hell could I have known that?"

"You couldn't," Eddie conceded. "Maybe you saw something glint, a knife or a gun or something, you couldn't be sure."

"I saw him reach in his pocket. You told me the guy has a gun—I figured he was reaching for a weapon."

Eddie nodded, turned grimly toward the doors, and stepped back into the inky blackness. He returned a minute or so later, some objects in his cupped hands. He dumped them onto the coffee table. "Wallet, key ring. No knife, no gun, no nothing on the guy."

"I didn't fucking *know* that," Nick said. "He kept saying, 'You're not safe.'"

"Nick, of *course* you didn't know. Jesus, I mean, you were dealing with a fucking psycho, a guy's gotta do what a guy's gotta do. That's not it."

"The truth is, you lent me your gun as protection," Nick said. "Temporarily. You said it's a misdemeanor."

Eddie slammed his fist into his palm. "You still don't fucking get it, do you? You killed the dude outside the house, not inside."

"He was trying to get in, believe me."

"*I* know that. You're allowed to use physical force to terminate attempted commission of criminal trespass." The words sounded unnatural, halting, coming out of his mouth, as if he'd memorized them during his cop days. "But not deadly physical force. That's the premises law. See, Nick, the law says deadly physical force can only be used in the face of deadly physical force."

"But given the guy's record—"

"I'm not saying you wouldn't have a chance of beating this. But what the hell you think's going to happen to you, huh?"

Nick finished his mug of coffee. The caffeine only went so far in counteracting the sleeping pill; it was adrenaline and fear that were keeping him functioning. "I'm the CEO of a major corporation, Eddie. I'm a respected member of the community."

"You're fucking Nick the Slasher!" Eddie hissed. "What the fuck do you think's going to happen to you? And to your family? Think about it. You think the cops are going to cut you any slack?"

"The law's the law."

"Shit! Don't talk to me about the law, Nick. I know the law. I know how it gets twisted and bent if the cops want it to. I've done it, okay?"

"Not all cops," Nick said.

Eddie flashed him a look of barely concealed hostility. "Put it to you this way. The locals'll have no choice but to charge you, right?"

"Maybe."

"For absolute fucking sure. And when it comes to trial—and it will, you can be sure of that—yeah, you might beat it. Maybe. After ten months of a *nightmare*. Yeah, you could get lucky, get a reasonable prosecutor, but even they're going to face all sorts of pressure to string up Nick the Slasher. You're going to be facing a jury of twelve people who all hate your guts—man, the thought of locking you up . . . I mean, in a town this size, there isn't going to be a juror in the pool who doesn't know someone, a friend or a relative, that you fired, right? You saw what that jury did to Martha Stewart for a little insider trading. You fucking murdered an old man, are you with me yet? A sick old man."

"The bottom line is, I'm innocent." Nick was feeling ill again, thought he might throw up, looked around for his metal wastebasket in case he did.

"You don't get to say what the bottom line is, okay?"

"But it was fucking *self-defense!*"

"Hey, don't argue with *me!* I'm on *your* side. But it's homicide, Nick. Manslaughter at a minimum. You say it's self-defense, but you got no witnesses, you got no injuries, and you got a dead guy who was unarmed. I don't care how much money you spend on a lawyer—you get tried here, in Fenwick. And what the hell you think's going to happen to your kids during this goddamned media circus, huh? You have any fucking *idea* what this is going to do to them? You think it's hard for them, dealing with Laura and the lay-offs and everything? Imagine you on trial for murder. A fucking lynch mob, Nick. You want to put your kids through that?"

Nick didn't reply. He felt frozen in the chair, completely at a loss.

"They're probably going to send you away, Nick. Five, ten years if you're lucky. Sentence like that, you're going to miss your kids' childhood. And they grow up with a jailbird father. They don't have a mom, Nick. All they got is you. You gonna play Russian roulette with your kids, Nick?"

Eddie's stare was unrelenting, furious.

Finally, Nick spoke. "What are you suggesting?"

PART TWO
TRACE EVIDENCE

15

Audrey Rhimes's pager shrilled in the semidarkness.

She jolted awake, out of a blissful dream of her childhood, a warm summer day, going down a Slip 'N Slide that went on and on and on, in her family's steeply canted backyard. Ordinarily 6:30 A.M. wasn't early at all, but her shift had ended at midnight, and after that came the usual unpleasantness with Leon, so she'd gotten maybe four hours of sleep.

She felt raw, vulnerable like a freshly hatched chick.

Audrey was a woman who liked routine, schedule, regularity. This was a personality trait that didn't go well with her job as a detective with the Fenwick Police Major Case Team. Calls could come at any time of day or night. Though she could no longer remember why, this was a job she'd wanted, a job she fought for. She was not just the only African-American member of the Major Case unit but the only woman—the real difficulty, it turned out.

Leon groaned, rolled over, buried his head beneath a pillow.

She slipped out of bed and moved silently through the dim bedroom, narrowly avoiding a cluster of empty beer cans that Leon had left there. From the kitchen phone she called Dispatch.

A body discovered in a Dumpster on the five hundred block of Hastings. A section of town where all of the town's vice seemed to be concentrated, all the prostitution and drugs and violence and shootings. A dead body there could mean any of a number of things, including drugs or gangs, but the odds were that it meant very little. Was this hard-hearted of her? She preferred not to think so. At first she'd been shocked at the reactions of the survivors, even the mothers, who seemed to be almost resigned to losing a son. They'd already lost their sons. Few of them pleaded their sons' innocence. They knew better.

When Audrey learned who'd be picking her up this morning, whom she'd been partnered with on this case—the loathsome Roy Bugbee—she felt her body go rigid with annoyance. More than annoyance, she had to admit to herself. Something stronger. This was not a worthy feeling, not a generous impulse.

Silently, as she dressed—she kept a clean outfit in the parlor closet—she recited one of her favorite verses of scripture, from Romans 15: "Now the God of patience and consolation grant you to be likeminded one toward another, according to Christ Jesus." She loved this line, even as she realized she didn't yet fully understand it. But she knew it meant that the Lord first teaches us what is true consolation and true patience, and then He instills this in our hearts. Reciting this to herself got her through Leon's recent sulking fits, his drinking problem, lent her a much-needed serenity. Her goal had been to reread the entire Bible by year's end, but the irregularity of her schedule made that impossible.

Roy Bugbee was a fellow detective in Major Cases who had an unaccountable loathing toward her. He didn't know her. He knew only her outward appearance, her sex, and the color of her skin. His words cut her, though never as deeply as Leon's.

She gathered her equipment, her Sig-Sauer and her handcuffs, rights cards and IBO request forms and her PT, her handheld radio. While she waited, she sat in Leon's favorite chair, the worn rust BarcaLounger, and opened her old leather-bound King James Bible, her mother's, but there was barely time to find her place before Detective Bugbee pulled up in his city car.

He was slovenly. The car, which he was lucky enough to have at his disposal—she hadn't been given one—was littered with pop cans and Styrofoam Quarter Pounder boxes. It smelled of old French fries and cigarette smoke.

He didn't say hello or good morning. Audrey said good morning to him, however, determined to rise above his pettiness. She sat in uncomfortable silence, amid the squalor, observing the scattering of ketchup packets on the floor around her feet and hoping that none of them was on the seat beneath her plum business suit. It would never come out.

After a few minutes he spoke as he flicked the turn signal at a red light. "You got lucky, huh?" Bugbee's blond hair was slicked back in a pompadour. His eyebrows were so pale they were almost invisible.

"Pardon me?"

His laugh was raucous. "I don't mean with your husband. If Owens wasn't drunk on his ass when Dispatch called, you'da been assigned to him. But lucky you, you get me."

"Mm hm," she said, her tone pleasant. When she first arrived at Major Cases, only two of the men would talk to her, Owens being one of them. The others acted as if she wasn't even there. She'd say, "Good morning," and they wouldn't answer. There was no women's bathroom, of course—not for one woman—so she had to share the men's. One of the guys kept urinating right on the toilet seat just to make it unpleasant for her. Her fellow detectives thought it was hilarious. She'd heard it was Bugbee, and she believed it. He'd done "practical jokes" on her she didn't like to think about. Finally she'd had to resort to using the bathroom downstairs in the warrant unit.

"Body found in a Dumpster on Hastings," Bugbee continued. "Wrapped up like a burrito in Hefty bags."

"How long has it been there?"

"No idea. You better not go blow your cookies on me."

"I'll do my best. Who found it, one of the homeless looking for food?"

"Trash guy. You lose it like you did with that little black girl, you'll get yanked off the case, I'll see to it."

Little Tiffany Akins, seven years old, had died in her arms a few months earlier. They'd got her father cuffed, but her mother and her mother's boyfriend had already died of their gunshot wounds by the time Major Cases showed up. Audrey could not keep herself from weeping. The beautiful little girl, wearing SpongeBob pajamas, could have been her own child if she'd been able to have kids. She didn't understand what kind of father would be so blinded by rage and jealousy that he'd kill not only his estranged wife and her lover but his own daughter too.

She recited to herself: *Now the God of patience and consolation grant you to be likeminded one toward another* . . .

"I'll do my best, Roy," Audrey said.

16

The crime scene was a small blacktopped parking lot behind a ratty little diner called Lucky's. A yellow streamer of evidence tape secured the area, barricaded off a small gathering of the usuals. It was remarkable, Audrey thought, and not a little sad, that this unknown vagrant was getting in death the kind of attention that he surely never got when it could have made a difference. A man wanders through the streets alone and unnoticed and despairing. Now, with the life gone out of his body, a crowd gathers to pay him the respect he'd never received in life.

No TV cameras here, though. No Newschannel Six truck. Maybe not even a reporter from the *Fenwick Free Press*. No one wanted to come down to the five hundred block of Hastings at six in the morning to report on the discovery of some vagrant's body.

Roy Bugbee parked the city car on the street between two patrol cars. They got out without exchanging another word. She noticed the white van belonging to the Identification Bureau Office, meaning that the crime-scene techs were already there. Not the Medical Examiner yet. The uniformed first officer, who'd notified Dispatch, was swanning around self-importantly, warding off neighborhood gawkers, clearly enjoying the biggest thing that had happened to him all week. Maybe all month. He approached Audrey and Bugbee with a clipboard and demanded that they sign in.

Her eye was caught by a flash of light, then another. The IBO evidence tech on the scene was Bert Koopmans. She liked Koopmans. He was smart and thorough, obsessive-compulsive like the best crime-scene techs, but without being arrogant or difficult. Her kind of cop. Something of a gun nut, maintained his own personal Web site on firearms and forensics. He was a lean man in his fifties with a receding hairline and thick Polar Gray spectacles. He was snapping pictures, switching between Polaroid and digital and 35mm and video like some crazed paparazzi.

Her boss, Sergeant Jack Noyce, the head of the Major Case Team, was talking on his Nextel phone. He saw Audrey and Bugbee duck under the yellow tape, held up a finger to ask them to wait. Noyce was a round-faced, stout man with melancholy eyes, gentle and sweet natured. He'd been the one who'd talked her into putting in for Major Cases. He said he wanted a woman on the squad. Never had he admitted it might have been a mistake. He was her steadfast defender, and she did him the favor of never going to him with the petty insults of her colleagues. From time to time he'd hear about something and would take her aside, promise to talk to them. He never did, though. Noyce preferred to avoid confrontation, and who could blame him, really?

He ended the call and said, "Unknown older white male, sixties maybe, gunshot wounds to the head and chest. Waste Management guy spotted it after he loaded the Dumpster on his frontloader. First pickup too. What a way to start your day."

"Before or after he tipped the trash into the hopper, boss?" asked Audrey.

"He noticed it before. Left the contents intact, stopped a patrol car."

"Coulda been a lot worse," Bugbee said. "Coulda put it through the compactor, huh?" He chortled, winked at his boss. "'Stead of a burrito we'd have a quesadilla. Ever see a body like that, Audrey? You'd really blow lunch."

"You make a very good point there, Roy," Noyce said, smiling thinly. Audrey had always suspected that her boss shared her dislike of Roy Bugbee but was too polite to let on.

Bugbee put a comradely hand on Noyce's shoulder as he strutted past.

"I'm sorry about that," Noyce said under his breath.

Audrey didn't entirely understand what he was sorry about. "He's got a unique sense of humor," she said, taking a stab.

"Owens was intoxicated, according to Dispatch. Bugbee was next on the call list. I wouldn't have partnered you two, but . . ." He shrugged, his voice trailing off.

Noyce waved at someone. Audrey turned to look. Curtis Decker, the body mover, was getting out of his old black Ford Econoline van. Decker, a small man of ghostly pallor, had a funeral home in Fenwick and was also the town's conveyance specialist. He'd been transferring bodies from crime scenes to the morgue at Boswell Medical Center for twenty-seven years. Decker lighted a cigarette, leaned back against his van, chatting idly to his assistant, waiting his turn.

Noyce's phone chirped. He picked it up, said, "Noyce," and Audrey silently excused herself.

Bert Koopmans was painstakingly brushing powder on the rim of the battered dark-blue Dumpster. Without turning his head from his work, he said, "Morning, Aud."

"Good morning, Bert." As she drew closer to the Dumpster, she caught a whiff of a ripe stench, which mingled with the odor of bacon that wafted from the open service entrance door.

The asphalt was littered with cigarette butts. This was where the busboys and short-order cooks smoked. There were a few jagged shards from a brown beer bottle. She knew there wasn't likely to be any evidence here, no shell casings or anything, since the body had been dumped.

"Partnered with Bugbee on this, I see."

"Mm-hmm."

"The Lord trieth the righteous."

She smiled, her eyes straying to the body in the Dumpster, wrapped tightly in black trash bags. It did look a little like a take-out burrito. The bundle lay atop a foul mound of slimy lettuce heads and banana peels, a discarded submarine sandwich, next to a giant empty tin of Kaola Golden Solid Vegetable Griddle Shortening.

"Was it right on top like that?" she asked.

"No. Buried under a bunch of trash."

"I assume you haven't found anything, shell casings or whatever."

"I didn't really look that hard. There's eight cubic yards of garbage in there. I figure that's a job for the uniformed guys."

"You already print the bags?"

"Huh," Koopmans said. "Hadn't thought of it." Meaning: Of course, what do you think?

"So what's your take, smart guy?"

"On what?"

"You unwrap that package up there, Bert?"

"First thing I did."

"And? A mugging? Did you find a wallet or anything?"

Koopmans finished dusting a patch, carefully replaced his brush in the kit. "Just this." He held up a plastic sandwich bag.

"Crack cocaine," she said.

"Off-white chunky material in a baggie, to be precise."

"Which looks like crack. Like eighty dollars' worth."

He shrugged.

"A white guy in this part of town," she said, "has to be a drug deal."

"If the deal went bad, how come he got to keep the crack?"

"Good question."

"Where's your partner?"

She turned, saw Bugbee smoking, laughing raucously with one of the uniforms. "Hard at work interviewing witnesses, looks like. Bert, you'll get this stuff tested, right?"

"Standard procedure."

"How long does it take to get back results?"

"Few weeks, given the MSP's work load." The Michigan State Police lab did all the drug testing.

"You happen to have one of those field test kits with you?"

"Somewhere, sure."

"Can I have a pair of gloves? I left mine in the car."

Koopmans reached into a nylon rucksack beside him and pulled out a blue cardboard box, from which he yanked a pair of latex gloves. She snapped them on. "Could you hand me that baggie?"

Koopmans gave her a questioning look but handed over the bag of crack. It was one of those Ziploc kinds. She pulled it open, removed one of the individually wrapped chunks—five or six in there, she noticed—and peeled off the plastic wrap.

"Don't start doing my work," Koopmans said. "Leads to worse things.

Pretty soon you'll be squinting into a microscope and bitching about detectives."

With one gloved index finger she scraped at an edge of the off-white rock. Strange, she thought. A little too round-looking, too perfect a formation. Only one side was jagged. Then she touched her forefinger to her tongue.

"What the hell are you doing?" Koopmans said, alarmed.

"Thought so," she said. "Didn't numb my tongue like it's supposed to. This isn't crack. These are lemon drops."

Koopmans gave a slow smile. "Still need me to get the test kit?"

"That's okay. Could you help me up the side of this Dumpster, Bert? Of all the days I picked to wear my good shoes."

17

Another ordinary morning at the office. Arrive at the Stratton parking lot at seven-thirty. Check e-mail, voice mail. Return a few calls, leave voice mails for people who won't be in their offices for at least another hour.

You have killed a man.

Just another ordinary day. Business as usual.

The day before, Sunday, he'd even fantasized about going to church, to confession, which he hadn't done since he was a kid. He'd never do it, he knew, but in his mind he rehearsed his confession, imagined the dark confessional booth, that musty cedar-vanilla smell, the scuffling footsteps outside. "Forgive me, Father, for I have sinned," he says. "It has been thirty-three years since my last confession. I have committed these sins. I have taken the Lord's name in vain. I have gazed lustfully upon other women. I have lost patience with my kids. And, oh yeah, I killed a man." What would Father Garrison say about that? What would his own father have made of it?

He heard Marge's voice, intercepting the early morning calls like the pro she was. "He *is* in the office, yes, but I'm afraid he's in conference just now . . ."

How much had he slept in the past two days? He was in one of those weird, wobbly all-nighter states poised between calm and despair, and despite the coffee he'd had, he felt a sudden surge of weariness. He would have been tempted to close his office door and lay his head on his desk, except there was no door.

And it wasn't an office, really, at all. Certainly not what he used to imagine a CEO's office would look like. Which wasn't to say he'd ever spent much time thinking about being CEO of Stratton, or CEO of anything for that matter. As a kid, sitting at supper at his parents' Formica kitchen table, inhaling the acrid must of machine oil that emanated from his dad's hair and skin even after his father had taken his post-shift shower, Nick used to imagine one day working alongside Dad on the Stratton shop floor, bending metal at the brake machine. His father's gnarled stubby fingers, with the crescents of black grime still lodged under his fingernails, fascinated him. These were the fingers of a man who knew how to fix anything, could open a Mason jar that had been rusted shut, could build a fort out of spare lumber, nestled securely in the oak in their tiny backyard, that was the envy of all the neighbor kids. They were the hands of a worker, a guy who came home from the factory exhausted but then went right to work again, after his shower, around the house, tumbler of whiskey in one hand: fixing the dripping sink, a wobbly table leg, a lamp whose socket had a short. Dad liked fixing things that were broken, liked restoring order, getting things to work right. But more than anything, he liked being left alone. Working around the house was his way to get what he really wanted: a cone of silence around him, his thoughts kept to himself, not having to talk to his wife or son. Nick Conover only realized this about his dad much later when he saw it in himself.

He never thought one day he'd be running the company his father spoke of, the rare times he did speak, with such awe and disgruntlement. They barely knew anyone who *didn't* work for Stratton. All the neighbor kids, all the grown-ups his parents ever saw or talked about, they all worked at Stratton. Dad always groused about fat old Arch Campbell, the nasty round-shouldered factory manager who tyrannized the day shift. Complaining about Stratton was like complaining about the weather: you were stuck with whatever you got. It was the big annoying extended family you could never escape from.

When he was around fourteen or fifteen, Nick's junior-high class took the obligatory tour of Stratton — as if any of the kids needed a close look at the company that dominated their parents' supper conversations, the company whose logo was sewn in red on their white baseball caps, on team uniforms, emblazoned in neon over the arched entrance to the high school stadium. Walking through the chair factory, cavernous and thundering, deafeningly loud, might have been fun if most of the kids hadn't already been taken there at one time or another by their dads. Instead, it was the headquarters building that fascinated the rambunctious eighth-graders, finally intimidated them into a respectful awed silence.

At the climax of the tour they were crowded into the anteroom of the immense office suite of the president and chief executive officer, Milton Devries. This was the inner sanctum, the beating heart of the company that they realized, even as kids, ruled their lives. It was like being taken into King Tut's tomb; it was that alien, that fascinating, that intimidating. There, Devries's frightening mastiff-faced secretary, Mildred Birkerts, gave them a grudging little memorized talk, punctuated by the occasional dyspeptic scowl, about the vital function of the chief executive officer at Stratton. Craning his neck, Nick caught an illicit glimpse of Devries's desk, an acre of burnished mahogany, bare except for a gold desk set and a perfectly neat pile of papers. Devries wasn't there: that would have been too much. He saw huge windows, a leafy private balcony.

When, years later, Milton Devries died, Nick—who'd become the old man's favorite vice president—was summoned by Milton's widow, Dorothy, to her dark mansion on Michigan Avenue, where she told him he was the next CEO. Her family owned Stratton, so she could do that.

With great discomfort, Nick had moved into the old man's Mussolini-size office, with the floor-to-ceiling windows, the Oriental rugs, the immense mahogany desk, the outer office where *his* executive assistant, Marjorie Dykstra, would guard his privacy. It was like living in a mausoleum. Of course, by then, Stratton had changed. Now everyone wanted to stuff as many employees as possible into a building, and Stratton had gone to the open-plan system, that fancy term for cubicles and all the furnishings that went with them. No one really liked the cube farm, but at least Stratton's designs were elegant, cool, and friendly, 120-degree angles, the panels not too tall, all the computer cables and electrical wires and stuff hidden in the floors and panels.

One day a visitor looked around Nick's office and made a crack. He was head of worldwide purchasing for IBM, a harried-looking guy with a sharp tongue, who'd surveyed Nick's mahogany chamber and muttered dryly, "Oh, I see—you get the fancy digs while everyone *else* gets the 'open plan.'"

The next day Nick had ordered the executive floor completely remod-

eled, switched to the open plan too, over the howls of protest from his entire
executive management team. They'd busted their humps for years to finally
land the big office with the private balcony and now they were all getting *cubicles*? This was a joke, right? You couldn't do this.

But he did. Of course, everyone on the fifth floor got the best of the best,
the elegant, high-end Ambience Office System with its silver mesh fabric
panels on brushed aluminum frames, sound-absorbing panel walls, and the
top-of-the-line leather Stratton Symbiosis chairs, the harp-back beauties that
had pretty much taken the place of the Aeron chair in fancy offices around
the world, much coveted, just added to the permanent collection of the Museum of Modern Art.

Eventually people got used to the new arrangement. The complaints
stopped. It got a little easier when *Fortune* did a big spread on the Stratton executive offices, on how they were walking the walk as well as talking the talk.
It got easier still when delegations of design-school students started coming
to gape at the executive offices, marvel at how *edgy* they were.

The new offices were pretty damned cool, it was true. If you had to work
in cubicles, this was the best damned cube farm money could buy. So now,
Nick had often reflected, you had guys sitting in cubicles thinking about . . .
cubicles.

Of course, there really wasn't any privacy anymore. Everyone knew
where you were, when you went out to lunch or to work out, who you were
meeting with. If you yelled at someone on the phone, everyone heard it.

The bottom line was, when Steve Jobs from Apple Computer came in
for a meeting, or Warren Buffett flew in from Omaha, they could see that the
top executives of Stratton weren't hypocrites. They ate the same dog food
they were selling. That was the best sales pitch of all.

So now Nick Conover's office was a "workstation" or a "home base." The
new arrangement was less grandiose, suited him more. It wasn't a big sacrifice. Most days he liked it a lot more anyway.

Only this wasn't one of them.

"Nick, are you all right?"

Marjorie had come over to make sure he had the stapled agenda for

Nick's 8:30 meeting of his Executive Management Team. She was dressed elegantly, as always; she was wearing a lavender suit, the short string of pearls he'd bought as a gift for her a few years before. She wafted a faint cloud of Shalimar.

"Me? Oh, I'm fine, Marge, thanks."

She wasn't moving. She stood there, cocked her head. "You don't look it. Have you been sleeping?"

Rough couple of nights, he almost said. Immediately he could hear her repeating back the words in a courtroom. *He said he'd had a couple of rough nights, but he didn't elaborate*. "Ah, Lucas is driving me crazy," he said.

A knowing smile. She'd raised two boys and a girl pretty much by herself and rightly considered herself an expert. "Poor kid's in a tough place."

"Yeah, called adolescence."

"Anything you want to talk about?"

"I'd love to, later on," Nick said, knowing that would never happen; he'd make sure of it.

"Right, the EMT meeting. You all set for that, Nick?"

"I'm all set."

Was it possible to look like a murderer? Was it visible on his face? It was stupid, it made no sense, but in his dazed, scrambled egg–brain state, he worried about it. In the EMT meeting, he barely spoke, because he could barely concentrate. He remembered the time when the family was camping in Taos, and a snake got into their cabin. Laura and the kids screamed, and she begged Nick to get a shovel and kill the vile thing. But he couldn't. He couldn't bring himself to do it. It wasn't a venomous snake—it was a Western coachwhip—but Laura and the kids kept demanding that he get the shovel. Finally he reached down, picked it up, and threw it, twisting and wriggling, out into the desert.

Couldn't kill a snake, he thought.

Some irony in that.

He strode out of the room as soon as the meeting was over, avoiding the usual post-meeting entanglements.

Back at his desk, he went on the Stratton intranet and checked Eddie Rinaldi's online Meeting Maker to see what his schedule was. They hadn't talked since Eddie had driven away with the body in the trunk of his car.

Every time the phone rang, all Saturday and Sunday, he flinched a little, dreading that it might be Eddie. But Eddie never called, and he never called Eddie. He assumed everything had gone okay, but now he wanted the assurance of knowing. He thought about e-mailing Eddie to tell him he wanted to talk, but then decided against it. E-mails, instant messages, voice mails— they were all recorded somewhere. They were all evidence.

18

The only reason Audrey attended autopsies was that she had no choice. It was department policy. The Medical Examiner's office required that at least one detective on a case be present. She told herself she didn't see the need, since she knew she could ask the pathologist anything she wanted, anything that wasn't in the path report.

In truth, of course, it made perfect sense to have a detective there. There were all sorts of things you found out at an autopsy that didn't appear in the sterile lines of a report. Even so, they were the part of her job she most disliked. The dissection of bodies made her queasy. She was always afraid she might have to vomit, though she hadn't done so since her first one, and that was a terribly burned female.

But that wasn't what she hated most about autopsies. She found them deeply depressing. This was where you saw the human body devoid of its spirit, its soul, a carapace of flesh meted out in grams and liters. To her, on the other hand, homicide cases were about setting things right. Solving the crime didn't always heal the wounds of the victim's family—often it didn't— but it was her way of restoring some kind of moral order to a deeply messed-up world. She'd taped a sign to her computer at work, a quote from one Vernon Geberth, whose name was well known to all homicide investigators, the author of a classic text, *Practical Homicide Investigation*. It said, "Remember: We work for God." She believed this. She felt deeply that, as much as she was troubled by her work—and she was, most of the time—she really was doing God's work here on earth. She was looking for the one lost sheep. But autopsies required a detachment she preferred not to have.

So she uneasily entered this white-tiled room that stank of bleach and formaldehyde and disinfectant, while her partner got to make phone calls and do interviews, though she wondered just how hard Roy Bugbee was working to solve this case of what he called "a shitbird crackhead." Not too hard, she figured.

The morgue and autopsy room were located in the basement of Boswell Medical Center, concealed behind a door marked PATHOLOGY CONFERENCE ROOM. Everything about this place gave her the heebie-jeebies, from the stainless-steel gurney on which the victim's nude body had been placed, head a few inches higher than the feet to facilitate drainage of bodily fluids, to the handheld Stryker bone saw on the steel shelf, the garbage disposals in the stainless-steel sink, the organ tray whose plastic drainage tube, once clear, was now discolored brown.

The assistant medical examiner, one of three attached to the department, was a young doctor named Jordan Metzler, strikingly handsome and he knew it well. He had a head of dark curly hair, great brown eyes, a strong nose, full lips, a dazzling smile. Everyone knew he wasn't long for this job, or this town: he'd recently been offered a job in pathology at Mass General, in Boston. In a matter of months he'd be sitting at some fancy restaurant on Beacon Hill, regaling a beautiful nurse with tales of this backwater town in Michigan where he'd been stuck the last couple of years.

"Audrey's in the *house!*" he crowed as she entered. "'S'up, Detective?"

What was it with white guys who felt compelled to use black slang when African-Americans were around? Did they think it made them seem cool, instead of ridiculous? Did they think that made black folks connect with them better? Did Metzler even notice that she didn't talk that way?

She smiled sweetly. "Dr. Metzler," she said.

He found her attractive; Audrey could tell by the way he grinned at her. Her antennae still worked, even after eight years of marriage to Leon. Like most women, she was adept at reading males; sometimes she was convinced she knew them better than they knew themselves. Eight years of marriage to Leon hadn't knocked the self-esteem out of her, not even the terrible last couple of years. She knew that men had always been drawn to her, because of her looks. She didn't consider herself beautiful, far from it, but she knew she was pretty. She took care of herself, she exercised, she never went without makeup and she was adept at choosing the right lipstick for her skin tone. She liked to think that it was her deep abiding faith that kept her looking good, but she had seen enough women of equally deep abiding faith at church, women whose looks only God could love, to know better.

"Have you found any bullets?" she asked.

"Well, we've got two in there, X-ray shows. No exit wounds. I'll get 'em. You don't have an ID on this one yet, do you?"

She found herself avoiding looking at the body, the wrinkled flesh and the yellow-brown toenails, which meant she had to keep looking at Metzler, and she didn't want to send him the wrong signals. Not a horn-dog like him.

"Maybe we'll get lucky and score a hit on AFIS," she said. The crime scene techs had just finished fingerprinting the victim, having collected whatever trace evidence they could find on the body, scraping and clipping the fingernails and all that. Since the body was unidentified, they'd run the prints right away through the Michigan Automated Fingerprint Identification System in Lansing.

She asked, "Evidence of habitual drug use?"

"You mean needle marks or something? No, nothing like that. We'll see what tox finds on the blood."

"Look like a homeless guy to you?"

He jutted his jaw, frowned. "Not based on his clothes, which didn't smell unusually bad. Or grooming or dental care or hygiene. I'd guess no. In fact, the guy's pretty clean. I mean, he could take better care of his cuticles, but he looks more like a house case than a police case." That was what the pathologists called the autopsies they did on hospital patients, whose bodies were always clean and well scrubbed when they got here.

"Any signs of struggle?"

"None apparent."

"The mouth looks sort of bashed in," she said, forcing herself to look. "Broken teeth and all. Is it possible he got hit with, say, the butt of the gun?"

Metzler looked amused by her hypothesis. "Possible? Anything's *possible*." He probably sensed that he'd come off as too arrogant, so he softened his tone. "The teeth are chipped and cracked, not pushed in. That's consistent with a bullet. And there's no trauma to the lips—no swelling or bruising you'd find if there was a blunt-force injury. Also, there's the little matter of the bullet hole in his palate."

"I see." She let him enjoy his moment of superiority. The fragile male ego needed to be flattered. She had no problem with that; she'd been doing that all of her adult life. "Doctor, what do you estimate as the time of death? We found the body at six—"

"Call me Jordan." Another dazzling smile. He was working it. "We can't tell. It's in full rigor at this point."

"At the crime scene you said there was no rigor mortis, and since rigor doesn't really start setting in until three, four hours after death, I figured—"

"Nah, Audrey, there's too many other factors—physique, environment, cause of death, whether the guy was running or not. Doesn't really tell you anything."

"What about the body temperature?" she pointed out, careful to sound tentative. She wanted answers from the pathologist; she had no interest in showing him up.

"What about it?"

"Well, at the scene, didn't you take a body temperature reading of ninety-two? That means it dropped around six degrees, right? If the body temperature drops one point five to two degrees per hour after death, I estimate the victim had been killed three or four hours before the body was found. Does that sound about right to you?"

"In a perfect world, sure." Dr. Metzler smiled, but this time it was the look a parent might give a five-year-old asking if the moon was made of green cheese. "It's just not an accurate science. There are too many variables."

"I see."

"You seem more versed in forensics than a lot of the cops who come in here."

"It's an important part of my job, that's all."

"If you're interested, I'd be willing to teach you a little, help you out. No sense me having all this information in my head if I can't share it with someone who so clearly wants to learn."

She nodded, smiled politely. The burdens of being so smart, she wanted to say.

"I wonder whether they really appreciate you on the Major Case Team." He pretended to adjust the perforated stainless-steel tubing around the perimeter of the examination table, which washed the fluids off the body during the autopsy.

"I've never felt unappreciated," she lied. For the first time she noticed the toe tag on the body's left foot. It said "Unknown John Doe #6." Wasn't that, what was the word? A "John Doe" *was* unknown, wasn't it?

"Somehow I doubt your beauty helps you in your line of work."

"That's very kind of you, Doctor," she said, casting around desperately for a question in order to change the subject, but her mind had gone blank.

"Not kind at all. Accurate. You're a fine-looking woman, Audrey. Beauty *and* brains—not a bad combination at all."

"Why, you sound just like my husband," she said lightly. He'd never actually said anything remotely like that, but she wanted the pathologist to get the message without hammering him over the head about it, and that was the first thing she thought of.

"I saw your ring, Audrey," he said, giving her a smile that seemed more than playful.

The man was cutting up a dead body, for heaven's sake. This wasn't exactly a singles bar.

"You're too kind," she said. "Doctor, do the gunshot wounds give you any sense of the distance from the shooter?"

Metzler smiled to himself awkwardly as he studied the body on the table before him. He took a steel scalpel from the metal shelf attached to the table and, with maybe a little too much force, carved a large Y-shaped incision from the shoulders all the way down to the pubic bone. He was clearly trying his best to accept defeat gracefully. "There's no stippling, no powder burns, no tattooing, no soot," he said. His voice had changed; now he was all business.

"So they're not contact wounds?"

"Neither contact nor intermediate range." He began trimming back the skin and the muscle and tissue below.

"So what does that tell us distancewise?"

He was silent for a good thirty seconds as he worked. Then he said, "Actually, Detective, that tells us nothing except that the muzzle was more than three feet from the wound. Certainly not without determining the caliber of the bullet, the type of ammo, and then test-firing the gun. It could have been fired from three feet away, or a hundred feet. You can't tell." ›

The glistening rib cage exposed, he positioned the round jagged-toothed blade above the bone and flicked the switch to start it. Above the high-pitched mechanical whine, he said, "You might want to stand back, Detective. This can get a little messy."

19

As badly as he wanted to, Nick couldn't easily cancel the weekly number-crunching lunch with Scott McNally, not with the big quarterly board meeting coming up. He felt feverish, clammy, nauseated. He felt, unusually for him, antisocial. His normal ebullience had been tamped down. He felt the beginnings of a raging headache, and he hadn't had a headache in years. He felt hung over, his stomach roiling. Coffee upset his stomach now, even though he needed it to stay awake and alert.

A chef from the corporate cafeteria had set out lunch for the two of them at the small round table adjacent to his home base. It was the usual—an eggplant Parmesan sub and a salad for Scott, a tuna sandwich and a cup of tomato soup for Nick. Folded linen napkins, glasses of ice water and a glass pitcher, Diet Cokes for both of them. Nick normally just ate a sandwich at his desk unless he had to do a working lunch. And until Laura's death, she always packed his lunch—a tuna fish sandwich, a bag of Fritos, carrot sticks—and put it in his briefcase. It was a little tradition that went back to their earliest days, when they had no money, and he'd gotten used to it. It was one of those little things Laura liked to do for him, even when she was teaching college and barely had time in the morning before class to make his lunch. She always put a little mash note in the paper lunch bag, which always made him smile when he came upon it, like the prize in a Crackerjacks box. There'd been times when he'd been having an informal lunch with Scott or another of his executives and one of Laura's notes had fluttered out, to Nick's embarrassment and secret pride. He'd saved every single one of her notes, without telling her. After her death, he'd come very close to throwing them away or burning them or something, because it was just too excruciating to have them around. But he couldn't bring himself to do that. So a neat pile of yellow Post-it notes in Laura's beautiful handwriting lay in the bottom drawer of his desk at work, secured with a rubber band. Sometimes he'd been tempted to take them out and look through them, but in the end, he couldn't. It was too painful.

"You look wiped out," Scott said, tucking right in to his sub. "You getting sick?"

Nick shook his head, took a careful sip of ice water, its coldness making him shiver. "I'm fine."

"Well, this ought to help," Scott said. "I know how you feel about the numbers. You might want to grab a pillow." He produced a couple of Velo-bound documents, slid one in front of Nick, next to his lunch plate.

Nick glanced at it. Income statement, cash-flow statement, and balance sheet.

"Check it out," Scott said. "Man, I love the way they toast the bun. Grill it, maybe, I don't know." He took a slug of Diet Coke. "You're not eating?"

"Not hungry."

Nick skimmed through the statements without interest while Scott examined the Diet Coke can. "I hear the artificial sweetener in this stuff can cause mood disorders in rats," he said.

Nick grunted, not listening.

"Ever seen a depressed rat?" Scott went on. "Curled up in a ball and everything? Some days they just don't feel the maze is worth it, you know?" He took a large bite of his sub.

"What's Stratton Asia Ventures?" Nick asked.

"You read footnotes. Very good. It's a subsidiary corporation I've formed to invest in Stratton's Asia Pacific ops. We needed a local subsidiary for permitting and to take advantage of certain tax treaties with the U.S."

"Nice. Legal?"

"Picky, picky," Scott said. "Of course legal. Clever doesn't mean illegal, Nick."

Nick looked up. "I don't get it," he said. "Our earnings are *up*?"

Scott nodded, chewing his huge mouthful, made some grunting noises indicating he wanted to speak but couldn't. Then he said, mouth still half full of food, "So it appears."

"I thought—Jesus, Scott, you told me we were in the toilet."

Scott shrugged, gave an impish smile. "That's why you've got me around. You know I always come to play. I'm bringing my A game, huh?"

"Your 'A game'? Scott, did you ever play a competitive sport in your life?"

Scott tilted his head to one side. "What are you talking about? I was point guard on the Stuyvesant math team."

"Wait a second." Nick went back to the beginning of the booklet, began reading over the numbers more closely. "All right, hold on. You're telling me our *international* business is up twelve percent? What gives?"

"Read the numbers. The numbers don't lie. It's all there in black and white."

"I just talked with George Colesandro in London last week, and he was pissing and moaning all over the place. You telling me he was reading the numbers wrong? Guy's got a fucking microprocessor for a brain."

Scott shook his head. "Stratton UK reports in pounds, and the pound's way up against the dollar," he said with his Cheshire-cat smile. "Gotta use the latest exchange rate, right?"

"So this is all hocus-pocus. Foreign exchange crap." Nick's nerve endings were raw, and it felt good somehow to think about something besides Friday night. At the same time, though, what Scott seemed to be doing was unbelievable. It was smarmy. "We're not up at all—we're down. You're—you're juggling the numbers."

"According to GAAP, we're supposed to use the correct exchange rates." GAAP stood for Generally Accepted Accounting Principles, but bland and jargony as it sounded, it had the force of law.

"Look, Scott, it's not apples to apples. I mean, you're using a different exchange rate than the one you used last quarter. You're just making it *look* like we did better." Nick rubbed his eyes. "You did the same thing in Asia Pacific?"

"Everywhere, sure." Scott's eyes were narrowed, apprehensive.

"Scott, this is fucking *illegal*." Nick slammed the booklet down on the table. "What are you trying to do to me?"

"To *you*? This isn't *about* you." Red-faced, Scott was looking down at the table as he spoke. "First of all, there's nothing illegal about it. Call it pushing the envelope a little, maybe. But let me tell you something. If I don't pretty these numbers up a little, our friends from Boston are going to come down on you like Nazi storm troopers. They are going to parachute in and tear this place up. I'm telling you this is a perfectly legitimate way to spin the numbers."

"You're—you're putting lipstick on a pig, Scott."

"Well, a little lip *gloss*, maybe. Look, when company comes over for dinner, you clean house, right? Before you sell your car, you take it to the car wash. None of the board members are going to look this close."

"So you're saying we can get *away* with it," Nick said.

Scott shrugged again. "What I'm saying, Nick, is that everyone's job is at risk here, okay? Including yours and mine. This way, at least, we buy ourselves a little time."

"No. Uh-uh," Nick said, drumming his fingertips on the clear plastic cover. "We give it to 'em straight. You got me?"

Scott's face flushed, as if he were embarrassed or angry, or both. He was clearly straining hard to sound calm, like it was taking enormous effort to keep from raising his voice to his boss. "Gosh, and I was hoping to have a corporate tax loophole named after me," he said after a pause.

Nick nodded, dispensed a grudging smile. He thought of Hutch, the old CFO. Henry Hutchens was a brilliant accountant, in his green-eyeshade, bean-counting way—no one knew the intricacies of the good old-fashioned balance sheet the way he did—but he knew little about structured finance and derivatives and all the shiny new financial instruments you had to use these days to stay afloat.

Hutch would never have done anything like this. Then again, he probably wouldn't have known how.

"You told me we're having dinner tonight with Todd Muldaur, remember?"

"Eight o'clock," Nick said. He was dreading it. Todd had called just a few days ago to mention he was passing through Fenwick, as if anyone ever "passed through" Fenwick, and wanted to have dinner. It couldn't be a good thing.

"Well, I told him I'd get him the updated financials before dinner."

"Fine, but let's make sure we're on rock-solid foundations here, okay?"

"In accounting?" Scott shook his head. "No such thing. It's like that story about the famous scientist who's giving a lecture on astronomy, and afterward an old lady comes up to him and tells him he's got it all wrong—the world is really a big flat plate resting on the back of a giant turtle. And the scientist says, 'But what's *that* turtle standing on?' And the old lady says, 'You're very clever, young man, very clever, but it's no use—it's turtles all the way down.'"

"Is that meant to be reassuring?"

Scott shrugged.

"I want you to give Todd the real, unvarnished numbers, no matter how shitty they look."

"Okay," Scott said, looking down at the table. "You're the boss."

20

Audrey's desk phone was ringing as she approached her cubicle. She glanced at the caller ID and was glad she did, because it was a call she didn't want to take.

She recognized the phone number. The woman called her every week, regular as clockwork, had done so for so many weeks Audrey had lost count. Once a week since the woman's son was found murdered.

The woman, whose name was Ethel Dorsey, was a sweet Christian woman, an African-American lady who'd raised four sons on her own and was justifiably proud of that, convinced herself she'd done a good job, had no idea that three of her boys were deep into the life of gangs and drugs and cheap guns. When her son Tyrone was found shot to death on Hastings, Audrey recognized right away that it was drug-related. And like a lot of drug-related murders, it went unsolved. Sometimes people talked. Sometimes they didn't. Audrey had an open file, one less clearance. Ethel Dorsey had one less son. But here was the thing: Audrey simply couldn't bring herself to tell poor devout Ethel Dorsey the truth, that her Tyrone had been killed in some bad drug deal. Audrey remembered Ethel's moist eyes, her warm direct gaze, during the interviews. The woman reminded Audrey of her grandmother. "He's a good boy," she kept saying. Audrey couldn't break it to her that her son had not only been murdered, but he'd been a small-time dealer. For what? Why did the woman need to have her illusions shattered?

So Ethel Dorsey called once a week and asked, politely and apologetically, was there any progress on Tyrone? And Audrey had to tell her the truth: No, I'm sorry, nothing yet. But we haven't given up. We're still working, ma'am.

Audrey couldn't bear it. Because she realized that they'd probably never find Tyrone Dorsey's killer, and even if they did, it would bring no peace to Ethel Dorsey. Yet even a lowlife drug dealer was someone's son. Everyone matters, or else no one matters. Jesus told of the shepherd who kept searching for the one lost lamb, leaving his flock behind. For this purpose, Christ said, I was born.

Today she couldn't even bring herself to pick up the phone and talk to the woman. She looked at the photo of Tyrone she'd taped to the side wall of the cubicle, alongside the pictures of all the other victims whose cases she was working or had worked. As she waited for the phone to stop ringing, she noticed a folded square of paper that had been placed on top of the brown accordion file at the center of her desk. "UNKNOWN WHITE MALE #03486," the file had been labeled in her neat capital letters.

The white square of paper, folded a little unevenly into a makeshift card. On the front a black-and-white image of some generic church, a cheesy graphic that looked like clip art downloaded off the Internet. Below it, in Gothic lettering done on someone's computer, the words "Jesus Loves You."

She opened it, knowing more or less what she'd find. Inside it said, "But Everyone Else Thinks Your an Asshole."

She crumpled up Roy Bugbee's inane little prank, misspelling and all, and tossed it into the metal wastebasket. She glanced, for the five-hundred-thousandth time, at the index card taped to her computer monitor, the card starting to go sepia at the edges, her lettering neat and fervent: "Remember: We work for God." She wondered who Roy Bugbee thought he worked for.

Bugbee sauntered in an hour or so later, and they sat in an empty interview room.

"Strikeout on AFIS," he announced, almost proudly. "Nada."

So the old man's prints didn't match any of the fingerprint records in Lansing, neither the Tenprint Database nor the unsolved ones in the Latent

Database. No real surprise there. The victim's prints would only be in AFIS if he'd been arrested for something.

She said, "The rounds that were fired were .380s, according to Bert Koopmans. Brass-jacketed."

"Oh, that's helpful," said Bugbee, deadpan. "Narrows it down to about a thousand possible weapons."

"Well, not really." Audrey ignored his sarcasm, proceeded on the assumption that Roy just didn't know what he was talking about. "Once the MSP in Grand Rapids takes a look at it, they'll winnow it down a whole lot more for us." The Forensic Science Lab of the Michigan State Police, in Grand Rapids, handled the firearms investigations for the police in this part of the state. Their examiners were good, trained in identifying weapons and ammunition using all sorts of tools, including IBIS, the Integrated Ballistics Identification System database, which was managed by the Bureau of Alcohol, Tobacco, and Firearms.

"That shouldn't take more than six months," said Bugbee.

"Actually, I was hoping that when you drive it over there, you could press them to speed it up."

"Me?" Bugbee laughed. "I think *you* ought to drive to Grand Rapids, Audrey. Pretty woman like you, bat your little eyes at them, ask 'em to put it on the top of the heap."

She breathed in. "I'll drive it over there," she said. "Now, what about informants?"

"None of the snitches know a damned thing about some old guy trying to buy crack down the dog pound," he said grudgingly, as if it annoyed him to part with the information. Why that section of town was called the "dog pound" Audrey didn't remember if she ever knew. It just was.

"But the crack in the guy's pocket was fake."

"Yeah, yeah," Bugbee said with a wave of his hand. "Oldest trick in the book. White guy, easy mark, goes down to the dog pound to buy rock, and some zoomer sells him flex made outta candle wax and baking soda."

"Horehound lemon drops broken up, actually." So Bert Koopmans had told her.

"Whatever, don't make no difference. White guy argues with the zoomer who says, who needs this shit? and wastes the guy. Takes his wallet while he's at it and takes off. Open and shut."

"And leaves the lemon drops."

Bugbee gave a "lay off" shrug. He leaned back in the steel chair until his head was resting against the wall.

"And then instead of leaving the body in an alley somewhere, he goes to the trouble of wrapping it in garbage bags and then lifting it into a Dumpster, which isn't easy."

"Coulda been two guys."

"Wearing surgical gloves."

"Hmm?" He looked annoyed.

"The lab found traces of surgical-grade cornstarch on the trash bags consistent with the use of latex gloves."

Bugbee probed a seam in the sheetrock wall with a lazy forefinger. "Probably the lab's."

"I think they're more careful than that," she said, thinking: *Come on, Roy, did you even think this one through? Are you working this case?* She felt a pulse of annoyance, then willed herself back to serenity. "I kind of doubt many crackheads have surgical gloves lying around."

Bugbee exhaled showily. "Is Noyce in this room?"

"Excuse me?"

"I said, I don't see Sergeant Noyce standing here, so if you're trying to show off, no one's watching, okay?"

Audrey swallowed, heard her inner voice begin, *Now the God of patience and consolation grant you . . .* and then she interrupted that inward sensible voice and spoke in a voice even softer than usual: "Roy, I'm not here to impress you. I'm here to do my job."

Bugbee brought his chair forward, sat up straight, gave her a sleepy-eyed look.

She could hear her heart thudding. "Now, I know you don't like me, for whatever reason, but I'm not going to apologize to you for being who I am and what I am. I'm afraid you're just going to have to deal with it. I don't judge you, and you shouldn't judge me. You don't sign my paycheck on Fridays. If you want off of this case, talk to Noyce. Otherwise, let's both try to be professionals, okay?"

Bugbee looked as if he was debating shoving the table at her or getting up and slamming the door. A couple of seconds of silence passed. Then he said, "You don't judge me, huh? Christers like you, that's all you do. You're always ticking off everyone's little infractions like some hall monitor at school. It's all about feeling superior, isn't it, Audrey? Like you got the Big Guy on your side. All that praying you do, it's about sucking up to the Big Boss in the Sky. Ass-kissing your way to heaven, right?"

"That's enough, Roy," she said.

A pounding on the door, and it swung open. Sergeant Noyce stood there, squaring his shoulders, looking from one to the other. "May I ask you two something?" he said. "Did either one of you check the missing persons database?"

"I called Family Services this morning," Audrey said, "but they had nothing."

"You've got to keep checking, you know," Noyce said. "These things sometimes take a day or more to get posted."

"You got a possibility?" Bugbee asked.

"It's a lead, a pretty decent one," Noyce replied. "I'd say it's worth a look."

21

Nick called Eddie, didn't IM him, still feeling paranoid about what kind of records were stored on the corporate server.

They met at the southwest building entrance, outside of the Security offices, Eddie's idea. Eddie didn't want to talk inside the building. What did that mean, Nick wondered, if his own security chief didn't feel safe talking in there?

They walked along the paved path that encircled one of the parking lots. The air had a faint manure smell, from all the surrounding farms, mixed with the charred scent of the burnt buffalo grass.

"What's up?" Eddie said, lighting up a Marlboro. "Dude, you look worried."

"Who, me?" Nick said, grimacing. "What's to worry about?"

"Come on. Everything's under control."

Nick looked around, made sure no one was walking remotely near. "What'd you do with . . . him?"

"You don't want to know."

Nick was silent, listened to the scuff of Eddie's shoes on the pavement. "No, I do. I want to know."

"Nick, believe me, it's better this way."

"Did you get rid of the gun, or do you still have it, or what?"

Eddie shook his head. "The less you know, the better."

"All right, listen. I've been thinking a lot about it, and I think—I've got to go to the cops. There's just no other way. What happened was legally defensible. It'll be a goddamned mess, but with a smart enough attorney, I think I can tough it out."

Eddie gave a low, dry chuckle. "Oh, no, you don't," he said. "You can't put that toothpaste back in the tube."

"Meaning what?"

"Friday night you wanted it to go away. I made it go away." He seemed to be straining to keep his tone civil. "At this point, we've got a serious cover-up, involving both of us."

"A cover-up devised in a panic—"

"Look, Nick," Eddie said. "I don't swim in your toilet, you don't pee in my pool, understand?"

"Huh?"

"I don't tell you how to run Stratton. You don't tell me about crime and cops and all that shit. This is my area of expertise."

"I'm not telling you what to do," Nick said. "I'm telling you what *I'm* going to do."

"Any decision you make involves me too," Eddie said. "And I vote no. Which means you don't do a damned thing. What's done can't be undone. It's just too fucking late."

22

They pulled up in front of a modest house on West Sixteenth in Steepletown, Audrey feeling that jellyfish wriggling in her belly, the thing she always felt when she first met a survivor of a homicide. The spill of raw grief, disbelief, fathomless pain—she could hardly stand it. You had to distance yourself from all that, or you'd go crazy, Noyce had warned her early on. We all do. What looks to the outside world like cynicism, hardness, that's what it is. Protective insulation. You'll learn it.

She never did.

The investigative work, even the routine stuff that phone-it-in types like Roy Bugbee had no patience for, she enjoyed. Not this. Not feeling the hot spray of another human being's agony up close and being unable, fundamentally, to do anything about it. I'll find your dad's murderer, I'll track down the kids who killed your daughter, I'll uncover the guy who popped your father in the 7-Eleven—that was the most she could promise, and it helped, but it didn't heal.

So a missing persons report had been called in to the police by a woman whose father had never come home Friday night. The physical description— age, height, weight, clothing—matched the murder victim found in the Dumpster on Hastings. Audrey knew this was it. The Family Services Division had called the daughter, which was the protocol, to say in their most diplomatic, tender way—they were good at this—that a body had been found, and there was a chance, just a chance, that it was her father, would she be so kind as to come down to the police morgue at Boswell Medical Center and help them identify a body, rule it out?

The aluminum screen door slammed, the woman coming toward them, even before Audrey was out of the Crown Vic. She was a small woman, even tiny, and from twenty feet she looked like a little girl. She wore a white T-shirt, faded and paint-splotched jeans, a ragged jeans jacket. Her brown hair was cut in a spiky sort of hairdo that Audrey associated with punk rockers and artists. Her hands flopped from side to side as she walked, making her look a little like some neglected rag doll.

"You must be from the police," she said. Her brown eyes were large and moist. Up close she was actually quite beautiful and even more fragile. She looked to be in her mid- to late twenties. She had that glazed look of disbelief that Audrey had seen dozens of times in the faces of victim's families. Her voice was deeper than Audrey had expected, its timbre oddly soothing.

"I'm Audrey Rhimes." She extended a hand, beamed a look of compassion. "That's my partner, Roy Bugbee."

Roy, standing beside the open driver's side door, did not come around to shake the daughter's hand, probably figuring that it would be overkill. He gave a quick wave, a tight smile. Move your butt over here, Audrey thought. The man had no manners, no compassion. He didn't even have the ability to fake it.

"Cassie Stadler." Her palm was warm and damp, and her eye makeup was smudged. She got into the backseat of the cruiser. Bugbee drove.

The object here was to low-key it, to reduce the woman's anxiety if at all possible. She's being driven over to the city morgue to identify a body that might be her father's, for God's sake; probably nothing could diminish her anxiety. Cassie Stadler probably knew just as surely as Audrey knew. But Audrey kept speaking, turning around to face the passenger, who sat in the middle of the back seat, staring glassily ahead.

"Tell me about your father," she said. "Does he tend to go out at night?" She hoped the present tense would just slip in there unobserved, silently reassuring.

"No, not really," Cassie Stadler said, and fell silent.

"Does he get disoriented from time to time?"

She blinked. "What? I'm sorry. Disoriented? Yes, I guess he does, sometimes. His . . . his condition."

Audrey waited for more. But Bugbee, heedless, broke in, his voice booming. "Did your father go down to the Hastings Street area often, to your knowledge?"

A series of expressions flashed in this lovely woman's dark eyes, a slide show: puzzlement, hurt, annoyance, sorrow. Audrey, embarrassed, averted her gaze and turned back around in her seat, facing forward.

"It's him, isn't it?" was all the daughter finally said. "My daddy."

They pulled into the hospital parking garage in silence. Audrey had never done one of these before. Identifying a body in the morgue — it was not at all common, thank God, no matter what you saw on TV. There were no sliding drawers at the morgue either, none of those hokey gothic touches. But death was gruesome, unavoidably so.

The body lay on a steel gurney covered with a green surgical sheet, the room sterile and air-conditioned to a chill and smelling of formalin. Jordan Metzler, polite if distant, pulled back the green cloth as matter-of-factly as if he were turning down a bed, exposing the head and neck.

Beneath that spiky mane, Cassie Stadler's perfect little doll face crumpled, and no one had to say anything.

23

Audrey found an empty room in the hospital basement where the three of them could talk. It was an employees' lounge: a collection of chairs uphol-stered in different institutional fabrics, a short couch, a coffee machine that looked as if no one ever used it, a TV. She and Bugbee moved chairs into a cluster. A couple of open soda cans were clustered on an end table. She found an almost-empty box of Kleenex. Cassie Stadler's narrow shoulders bobbed; she sobbed silently, with all her body. Bugbee, who'd obviously learned how to distance, sat impatiently with a clipboard on his lap. Audrey couldn't take it anymore, put her arms around the woman, murmuring, "Oh, it's so hard, I know it."

Cassie took in great gulps of air, her head bent. Eventually she looked up, saw the Kleenex box and pulled out a few tissues, blew her nose.

"I'm sorry," she said. "I didn't think . . ."

"Don't apologize, sweetheart," Audrey said. "What a terrible time for you."

Cassie took out a pack of cigarettes and shook one out. "Okay if I smoke?"

Audrey nodded, gave Bugbee a sidelong glance. Smoking wasn't allowed in here, but she wasn't going to make a point of it, not with this poor woman at this time, and fortunately neither was Bugbee, who nodded as well.

Cassie took out a cheap plastic lighter and lit up, then exhaled a cloud of smoke. "He was shot in—in the mouth?"

A funeral home would have done some reconstruction, skillfully applied makeup. The face would have looked artificial in that way that all dead bodies look at funeral homes, but at least she'd have been spared the brutal sight.

"That's right," Bugbee said. He didn't elaborate, didn't say twice, didn't say Stadler had also been shot in the chest. He was following standard procedure, which was to give out as little information as possible, in case a withheld detail could help them, down the line, confirm the killer.

"God!" she erupted. "Why? Who'd *do* that to my daddy?" She took another puff, took an empty Coke can off the end table and tapped out the ash into its small opening.

"That's what we want to find out," Audrey said. *Daddy*: it stabbed her, hearing that from a grown woman. She thought of her own daddy, remembered his smell of tobacco and sweat and Vitalis. "We need your help. I know this is a painful time, and you probably don't want to talk at all, but anything you can think of will help."

"Miss Stadler," asked Bugbee, "was your father a drug user?"

"Drugs?" She looked puzzled. "What kind of drugs?"

"Such as crack?"

"Crack? My *dad*? Never."

"You'd be surprised at who uses drugs like crack cocaine," Audrey put in hastily. "People you'd never ever think of as users, people from all walks of life. Prominent citizens even."

"My dad didn't even know about that world. He was a simple guy."

"But it's possible he kept things from you," Audrey persisted.

"Sure, possible, but I mean—crack? I'd have noticed," Cassie said, expelling smoke through her nostrils like the twin plumes of a fire-breathing dragon. "I've been living with him for almost a year, I'd have seen something."

"Maybe not," Bugbee said.

"Look, I don't do drugs myself, but I sure know people who do. I mean, I'm an artist, I live in Chicago, it's not unheard of, you know? Dad had none of the signs. He—it's absurd, really."

"You're originally from here?" Audrey asked.

"I was born here, but my parents divorced when I was a kid, and I went to live with my mom in Chicago. I come . . . came back here to visit Dad pretty often."

"What made you come back to stay?"

"He called me and told me he'd just quit his job at Stratton, and I was worried about him. He's not well, and my mom passed away four or five years ago, and I knew he needed someone to take care of him. I was afraid he couldn't cope."

"When Detective Bugbee asked you about drugs just now, you hesitated," Audrey said. "Was he on any kind of medication?"

She nodded, passed a hand over her eyes. "A number of meds including Risperdal, an antipsychotic."

"Psychotic?" Bugbee blurted out. "Was he psychotic?"

Audrey briefly closed her eyes. The guy never failed to do or say the wrong thing.

Cassie turned slowly to look at Bugbee as she snubbed out the cigarette on the top of the Coke can, then dropped it through the opening. "He suffered from schizophrenia," she said absently. "He suffered from it for most of my life." She turned to Audrey. "But it was more or less under control."

"Did he ever disappear for stretches of time?" asked Audrey.

"No, not really. He'd go out for walks once in a while. I was glad when he got out of the house. This last year has been hard for him."

"What did he do at Stratton?" Bugbee asked.

"He was a model builder."

"What's that mean?"

"He worked in their model shop making prototypes of products they were working on, the latest chairs or desks or whatever."

"He quit, didn't get laid off?" Bugbee said.

"They were about to lay him off, but he just sort of blew up and quit before they could do it."

"When did you last see him?" Audrey asked.

"At supper Friday night. I—I'd just made supper for us, and he usually watches TV after supper. I went to the room I've been using as a studio and painted."

"You're an artist?"

"Sort of. Not as serious as I used to be, but I still paint. I never got a gallery or anything. I support myself by teaching Kripalu yoga."

"Here?"

"In Chicago I did. I haven't worked since I got to Fenwick."

"Did you see him before you went to sleep?" Audrey asked.

"No," she said sadly. "I fell asleep on the couch in there—I do that fairly often, when a painting's not working and I want to think about it, sometimes I just fall asleep and wake up in the morning. That's what happened Saturday morning—I got up and had breakfast, and when he wasn't down by ten I started to worry about him, so I went to his room, but he was gone. I—will you excuse me? I'm thirsty—I need—"

"What can we get you, honey?" said Audrey.

"Anything, just—I'm so thirsty."

"Water? Pop?"

"Something with sugar in it." She smiled apologetically. "I need a hit of sugar. Sprite, Seven-Up, anything. Just no caffeine. It makes me crazy."

"Roy," Audrey said, "there's a vending machine down the hall—could you . . . ?"

Bugbee's eyebrows went up, a nasty smile curling the corners of his mouth. He looked like he was about to say something unpleasant. But she wanted a little time alone with this woman. She had a feeling Cassie would open up more easily with her alone.

"Sure," Roy said after a long pause. "Happy to."

When the door closed, Audrey cleared her throat to speak, but Cassie spoke first.

"He has it in for you, doesn't he?"

Good God, was it that obvious? "Detective Bugbee?" Audrey said, feigning surprise.

Cassie nodded. "It's like he can barely contain his contempt for you."

"Detective Bugbee and I have a very good working relationship."

"I'm surprised you put up with him."

Audrey smiled. "I'd prefer to talk about your father."

"Of course. I'm sorry. I just—noticed." She was weeping again, wiping a hand across her eyes. "Detective, I—I have no idea in the world who might have killed my daddy. Or why. But I have a feeling that if anyone can find out, you can."

Audrey felt tears come into her eyes. "I'll do my best," she said. "That's all I can promise."

24

Terra was the finest restaurant in Fenwick, the place you went to celebrate special occasions like birthdays, promotions, a visit of a special old friend. It had the slightly forbidding air of an expensive place where it was assumed you didn't go often. Men were expected to wear ties. There was a maitre d' and a sommelier who wore a big silver taste-vin on a ribbon around his neck like an Olympic medal. The waiters ground pepper for you in a mill the size of a Louisville Slugger. The tablecloths were heavily starched white linen. The menu was immense, leather-bound, and required two hands. The wine list itself, a separate leather-bound folio, was twenty pages long. Nick had taken Laura here for her birthday, a few weeks before the accident; it was her favorite place. She loved their signature dessert, a molten chocolate cake that oozed chocolate like lava when you spooned into it. Nick found Terra stuffy and nervous-making, but the food was always great. From time to time he'd take important clients here.

Dinner tonight was with his most important client: his boss, the managing partner from Fairfield Equity Partners in Boston. Nick hadn't particularly liked Todd Muldaur when he first met him, in the company of Fairfield's founder, Willard Osgood. But Osgood always placed one of his deputies in charge of the companies his firm owned, and Todd was the man he picked.

Not long after Dorothy Devries had tapped Nick as her husband's successor as CEO, she'd summoned Nick back to her old dark mansion to announce that the family was facing a huge tax bill and had to sell. It was up to

Nick to find the ideal buyer. There was no shortage of interested bidders. The Stratton Corporation had no debt, steady profits, a major market share, and a famous name. But plenty of the buyout firms wanted to buy Stratton, gussy it up, then turn it around for a quick sale to someone else. Spin it off, maybe take it public—who the hell knew what those rape-and-pillage folks might do. Then the call came from the famous Willard Osgood, who had a reputation for buying companies and holding on to them forever, letting them run themselves. Willard Osgood: "the man with the Midas Touch," as *Fortune* magazine called him. The perfect solution. Osgood even flew in to Fenwick—well, he flew in to Grand Rapids in his private jet and then was driven out to Fenwick in a plain old Chrysler sedan—and came a-courtin' on the widow Devries and Nick. He charmed the pants off Dorothy Devries (she was partial to pantsuits, actually), and won over Nick as well. Willard Osgood was as plainspoken and unpretentious in person as he was in all his interviews. He was a lifelong Republican, an archconservative, just like Dorothy. He told her his favorite holding period was forever. Rule number one, he said, is never lose money; rule number two is never forget rule number one. He really won her over when he said it's better to buy a great company at a fair price than a fair company at a great price.

The deputy he brought with him, Todd Muldaur, a straw-haired Yale football jock who'd done time at the big management-consulting firm McKinsey, didn't say too much, but there was something about him Nick didn't like. He didn't like Todd's swagger. But hey, it was Osgood who ran the show, Nick figured. Not Muldaur.

Of course, now it was Todd who presided over the quarterly board meetings, Todd who read the monthly financial reports and asked all the questions, Todd who had to sign off on the major decisions. After that first meeting with Willard Osgood, Nick never saw the old guy again.

Nick arrived a few minutes early. Scott McNally was already at the table, nursing a Diet Coke. He'd changed out of his frayed blue button-down shirt into a crisp blue-and-white broad-striped one, a red tie, a good dark suit. Nick was wearing his best suit too, which Laura had picked out for him at Brooks Brothers in Grand Rapids.

"Muldaur give you any sense of what he's here for?" Nick asked as he sat down. This was just about the last place he wanted to be, eating at a fancy restaurant when he had no appetite, being social with some strutting asshole when he just wanted to be home in bed.

"No idea. He didn't say."

"He told me he wanted to 'touch base' in advance of the board meeting."

"Gotta be the updated financials I just sent him. They can't be happy about our numbers either."

"Still, no need for a personal visit."

Scott lowered his head, muttered, "He just walked in." Nick looked up, saw the big blond man coming their way. Both he and Scott stood.

Scott stepped around the table, went up to Muldaur, gave him a hearty two-handed shake. "Hey, bud!"

"Scotty! My man!"

Muldaur extended his beefy hand to Nick and gave him one of those unnecessarily crushing handshakes, grabbing his fingers just below the knuckles in such a way that Nick couldn't shake back. Nick hated that. "Nice to see you," Todd said.

Todd Muldaur had a big square jaw, a button nose, and turquoise eyes that were bluer than they'd been last time Nick had seen him, in a glass-walled conference room at Fairfield's offices on Federal Street in Boston. Had to be colored contacts. He had the lean, drawn face of a guy who ate a lot of protein, worked out regularly. He wore a dove-gray suit that looked expensive. "So, this must be the one good restaurant in town, huh?"

"Nothing but the best for our friends from Boston," Nick said affably as they sat down.

Todd took the big white linen napkin, unfolded it, and put it in his lap. "Gotta be good," he said sardonically. "The American Automobile Association gives this place its 'prestigious Four Diamond Award,' it says out front."

Nick smiled and imagined punching Todd's face out. He noticed a couple being seated a few tables over and recognized them. The man had been a senior manager at Stratton until last year, when his division had been shut down in the layoffs. The guy was in his fifties, with two kids in college, and despite the best efforts of the outplacement service Stratton had hired, hadn't been able to find another job.

That familiar sinking feeling came over him. Nick excused himself, and went over to say hello.

It was the man's wife who saw him first. Her eyes widened briefly. She turned away, said something quickly to her husband, then stood up, but not to greet him.

"Bill," Nick said.

Now the man rose without saying anything, and he and his wife turned and walked out of the dining room. For a few seconds, Nick stood there, his face burning. He wondered why he subjected himself to this kind of snub. It happened often enough for him to know better. Maybe, on some level, he felt he deserved it.

By the time he returned to his table, Todd and Scott were deep in conversation about the good old days at McKinsey. Nick hoped that neither man had seen what had just happened.

It had been Todd who'd insisted that Stratton replace their old CFO, Henry "Hutch" Hutchens, with Scott McNally. Nick had gone along quite happily, but it annoyed him sometimes that Scott was so friendly with Muldaur.

"Whatever happened to that guy Nolan Bennis?" Scott was saying. "Remember him?" He smiled at Nick. "Another McKinseyite. You wouldn't believe this dweeb." He turned back to Todd. "Remember that Shedd Island retreat?" He explained to Nick: "McKinsey always used to rent out this really posh hotel on this superexclusive island off the coast of South Carolina, for a retreat with top clients. So this guy Nolan Bennis is out there on the tennis court with some Carbide guys, and I swear to God, he's wearing black socks and penny loafers. Couldn't play for shit. Really stank up the place. We heard about that for months—what an embarrassment. I mean, the guy was a total loser. You couldn't take him out in public. He still at McKinsey?"

"You obviously didn't see the latest *Forbes* Four Hundred," Todd said.

"What are you talking about?" Scott said, a quizzical look on his face.

"Nolan Bennis is the CEO of ValueMetrics. Worth four billion dollars now. He bought the Shedd Island hotel a couple of years ago, along with about five hundred acres on the island."

"I always thought that guy would go places," Scott said.

"Gotta love this menu," Todd said. "Duck breast with raspberry coulis. I mean, how 1995 can you get? I'm getting nostalgic here."

The waitress approached their table. "May I tell you about our specials tonight?" she said. The woman looked familiar to Nick, though he couldn't quite place her. She glanced at Nick, looked away quickly. She knew him too. Not another one.

"We have a Chilean sea bass with roasted cauliflower, pancetta, and tangerine juice for twenty-nine dollars. There's a pistachio-crusted rack of lamb with celery root puree and wild mushrooms. And the catch of the day is a seared tuna—"

"Let me guess," Todd broke in. "It's 'sushi quality,' and it's served rare in the center."

"That's *right*!" she said.

"Where have I heard that before?"

"You look familiar," Nick said, feeling bad for the woman.

Her eyes flitted to him and then away. "Yes, Mr. Conover. I used to work for Stratton, in Travel."

"I'm sorry to hear that. You doing okay?"

She hesitated. "Waitressing pays less than half what I was making at Stratton, sir," she answered tightly.

"It's been tough all around," Nick said.

"I'll give you gentlemen a few more minutes to decide," she said, and moved quickly away.

"Is she going to spit in our salads?" Todd said.

"You guys don't need me to tell you we got a real problem here," Todd said.

"No question," Scott agreed quickly.

Nick nodded, waited.

"A bad quarter or two, blame it on a lousy economy," Todd said. "But it keeps happening, it begins to look like a death spiral. And we can't afford that."

"I understand your concern," Nick said, "and believe me, I share it. I want to assure you that we've got things under control. We've got a major customer coming in tomorrow—I mean *major*—and it looks good for signing them up. That contract alone will turn things around."

"Hey, we can always hope lightning strikes," Todd said. "Maybe you'll get lucky. But let me tell you something. Corporations may be based on continuity, but capital markets are all about *creative destruction*. If you're unwilling to change, you'll be drawn into that big slide toward mediocrity. As CEO, you've got to overcome the organizational inertia. Unclog those corporate arteries. Free the flow of fresh ideas. Even the best boats need rocking, man. That's the magic of capitalism. That's what Joseph Schumpeter said years ago."

"Didn't he used to play for the Bruins?" Nick said, deadpan.

"There's the quick, and there's the dead, Nick," Todd said.

"Well, I don't know about 'creative destruction,'" Nick said, "but I know we're all basically in sync. That's why we sold the company to Fairfield. You guys are value investors with the long view—that's the only reason I was able to convince Dorothy Devries to sell to you. I always remember what Willard said to Dorothy and me, in the parlor of her house on Michigan Avenue—'We want to be your partner, your sounding board. We don't want to run the business—we want you to run the business. We may have to go through some pain together, but we're all in this for the long haul.'"

Todd smiled slyly. He got what Nick was doing, invoking the words of the ultimate boss like Holy Scripture. "That sounds just like Willard. But you gotta understand something—the old man's been spending an awful lot of time fly-fishing in the Florida Keys these days. Guy loves fly-fishing—last year or so, he seems to think a lot more about tarpon and bonefish than P and Ls."

"He's retiring?"

"Not yet, but soon. All but. Which means he leaves the heavy lifting to us, the poor suckers who have to go to work every day and do the dirty work while he's standing in the bow of his Hell's Bay, casting his line. The world has changed, Nick. Used to be all the big institutional investors would write us a twenty-million-dollar check, maybe a hundred-million-dollar check, and let us do our job. At the end of six years, ten years, they cash out, everyone's happy. Not anymore. Now they're all looking over our shoulders, calling all the time. They don't want to see one of our major investments turn sour. They want to see results yesterday."

"They ought to go to your Web site," Nick said. Fairfield Equity Partners actually had an animated Flash movie on its Web site, the Aesop's fable of the tortoise and the hare, made to look like a storybook. It was beyond corn-ball. "Tell 'em to check out the tortoise-and-the-hare story. Remind 'em about the long view."

"These days, the tortoise gets made into turtle soup, buddy," Todd said.

Scott laughed a bit too loud.

"Don't worry," Nick said, "that's not on the menu."

Todd didn't smile. "The kind of companies we like are healthy compa-nies that are growing. We don't believe in catching a falling knife."

"We're not a falling knife, Todd," Nick said calmly. "We're going through some adjustments, but we're on the right path."

"Nick, the quarterly board meeting is in a couple of days, and I want to make sure the board sees a comprehensive plan to turn things around. I'm talking plant consolidation, selling off real estate, whatever. Creative de-struction. I don't want the board losing confidence in you."

"Are you implying what I think you're implying?"

Todd cracked a victorious smile. "Hell no, Nick! Don't take me the wrong way! When we bought Stratton, we weren't just buying some outdated factories in East Bumfuck, Michigan, with equipment out of 1954. We were buying a *team*. That means you. We want you to hang in there. We just need you to start thinking different. A balls-out, warp-speed effort to come up with a way to change the trend line."

Scott nodded sagely, chewing his lower lip, twirling a few strands of his hair behind his right ear. "I get what you're saying, and I think I've got some interesting ideas."

"What I like to hear. I mean, hell, there's no reason for you to have all your components made in the U.S. when you can get 'em at half the price from China, you know?"

"Actually," Nick said, "we've considered and rejected that, Todd, because—"

Scott broke in, "I think it's worth taking up again."

Nick gave him a black look.

"I knew I could count on you guys. Well, who's up for dessert? Let me guess—the dessert trend that swept Manhattan in 1998 has finally made it to Fenwick: molten chocolate cake?"

After they said goodbye to Todd and watched him drive away in his rented Lincoln Town Car, Nick turned to Scott. "Whose side are you on, anyway?"

"What are you talking about? You've got to keep the boss happy."

"I'm your boss, Scott. Not Todd Muldaur. Remember that."

Scott hesitated, seemingly debating whether to argue. "Anyway, who says there's sides? We're all in this together, Nick."

"There's always sides," Nick said quietly. "Inside or outside. Are you with me?"

"Of course, Nick. Jesus. Of course I'm on your side, what do you think?"

25

Leon was watching TV and drinking a beer. That was pretty much all he did these days, when he wasn't sleeping. Audrey looked at her husband, slouched in the middle of the couch, wearing pajama bottoms and a white T-shirt that was too tight over his ever-expanding beer gut. The thirty or forty pounds he'd put on in the past year or so made him look ten years older. Once she would have said he was the hardest-working man she'd ever met, never missed a day of work on the line, never complaining. Now, with his work life taken away from him, he was lost. Without work, he retreated into a life of sloth; there was no in-between for him.

She went over to the couch and kissed him. He hadn't shaved, hadn't bathed either. He didn't turn his head to kiss her; he received her kiss, his eyes not even moving from the screen. After a while, Audrey standing there, hands on her hips, smiling, he said, "Hey, Shorty," in his whiskey-and-cigarettes voice. "Home late."

Shorty: his term of endearment almost since they'd started going out. He was well over six feet, she was barely five, and they did look funny walking together.

"I called and left you a message," she said. "You must have been in conference." He knew she meant asleep. That was how she dealt with Leon's newfound lifestyle. The idea of his sitting around watching TV and sleeping during the day, when they had a mortgage to pay—it was infuriating to her. She knew she wasn't being entirely reasonable about it. The poor guy had been laid off from his job, and there wasn't a company for hundreds of miles around that was looking to hire an electrostatic powder-coating technician. Still, half the town had been laid off, and plenty of people had managed to get jobs working for Home Depot or bagging groceries at the Food Town. The pay was lousy, but it was better than nothing, and certainly better than sleeping on the couch all day.

He didn't answer. Leon had deep-set eyes, a large head, a powerful build, and once, not that long ago, he would have been considered a fine-looking man. Now he looked beaten down, defeated.

"You . . . get my message about dinner?" Meaning, of course, that she wanted him to make dinner. Nothing complicated. There was frozen hamburger he could defrost in the microwave. A package of romaine hearts he could wash for salad. Whatever. But she smelled nothing, no food cooking, and she knew the answer before he spoke.

"I ate already."

"Oh. Okay." She'd left him a message around four, as soon as she knew she'd be staying late, way before he ever ate supper. She suppressed her annoyance, went into the kitchen. The small counter was stacked so high — dirty plates, glasses, coffee mugs, beer bottles — that you couldn't even see the swirly rose Formica surface. How, she marveled, could one person create such a mess in a day? Why did he refuse to clean up after himself? Did he expect her to be breadwinner and wife and housekeeper all at the same time? In the plastic trash bucket was a discarded Hungry Man box and plastic compartmented tray, crusted with tomato sauce goo. She reached down, felt it. It was still warm. He'd just eaten. Not hours ago. He'd been hungry and just made himself dinner, didn't make anything for her even though she'd asked him to. Well, exactly *because* she'd asked him to, probably.

Returning to the living room, she stood there, waiting to get his attention, but he kept watching the baseball game. She cleared her throat. Nothing.

She said, "Leon, honey, can I talk to you for a second?"

"Sure."

"Could you look at me?"

He muted the TV, finally, and turned.

"Baby, I thought you were going to make us both supper."

"I didn't know when you were getting back."

"But I said . . ." She bit her lip. She was not going to yell at him. She was not going to be the one to start the quarreling, not this time. She softened her voice a bit. "I asked you to make dinner for us, right?"

"I figured you'd eat whenever you got home, Shorty. Don't want to make something's gonna get cold."

She nodded. Paused. By now she knew the script by heart. But our deal, our agreement, was that you make dinner, clean up, you know I can't do everything. And he says, How come you can't do what you did before? You had time to do that stuff before. And she says, I need help, Leon, that's the point. I get home exhausted. And he says, How do you think I feel, sitting here like a good-for-nothing piece of shit? At least you got a job.

That worked for a long time, that guilt thing. But then he began to take it to another level, talking about how cooking and cleaning, that was woman's work, and how come all of a sudden he's expected to do woman's work, was this all because he wasn't bringing home a paycheck? And by now she wants to scream, woman's work? Woman's work? What makes this woman's work? And can't you at least pick up after yourself? And so it would go, tedious and mind-numbing and pointless.

"Okay," she said.

She was working six cases, three of them active, one a homicide. You couldn't really focus on more than one at a time; tonight was Andrew Stadler. She placed the accordion file on the couch next to her, and while Leon watched the Tigers and drank himself into a stupor, she read over the files. She liked to read case files just before she went to sleep. She believed that her unconscious kept working on things, poking and prodding, turning things over with its gimlet eye, saw things more clearly than she did awake.

How Andrew Stadler's body ended up in a Dumpster on the five hundred block of Hastings baffled her. So did the fake crack. His diagnosed schizophrenia—did that fit in anywhere? Obviously she'd have to talk to his boss at Stratton, and the Employee Relations director too. See if there'd been any indication of drug use.

She was tempted to ask Leon about Stratton, about the model shop, if he knew anything about it. Maybe he'd even run across Stadler in the factory some time, or knew someone who knew him. She was, in fact, just about to say something when she turned to look at him, saw his glazed eyes, his defeated face, and decided not to. Any little thing she mentioned about the job these days was like probing a bad tooth for him. It reminded him of how she had a job she was involved in, and how he didn't.

Not worth the pain, she decided.

When the game was over, he went to bed, and she followed. As she brushed her teeth and washed her face, she debated whether to put on her usual long T-shirt or a teddy. They hadn't had sex in more than six months, and not because she didn't want it. He'd lost all interest. But she needed it, needed to regain that physical closeness. Otherwise . . .

By the time she got into bed, Leon was snoring.

She slipped in beside him, clicked off her bedside lamp, and was soon asleep.

She dreamed of Tiffany Akins, dying in her arms. The little girl in the SpongeBob pajamas. The girl who could have been her own. Who could have been herself. She dreamed of her father, of that moment when Cassie Stadler called her father Daddy.

And then her gimlet-eyed subconscious kicked something upstairs, and her eyes came open. She sat up slowly.

It was all too clean. An *absence* of evidence.

Not just the daubs of pharmaceutical-grade starch on the plastic bags wrapped around the body. This indicated that the body had been moved by someone wearing surgical gloves, someone who was careful about not leaving fingerprints. That in itself revealed a degree of caution not often found in drug murder cases. But neither was there any particulate matter on the body, no fibers, none of the normal trace evidence you always found on the body of a victim. Even the treads on the victim's shoes, where you always found dirt, had been brushed clean.

She remembered, too, how clean the body was at the autopsy. She remembered the pathologist saying, "He looks more like a house case than a police case."

That was it; that was the anomaly. The body had been fastidiously cleaned, gone over by an expert. By someone who *knew* what the police looked for.

Andrew Stadler's body hadn't been disposed of by some crack dealer in a panic. It had been carefully, methodically placed in a Dumpster by someone who knew what he was doing.

It took her a long time to fall back asleep.

26

"This stuff tastes like twigs," Julia said.

Nick couldn't stop himself from laughing out loud. The front of the box had a photograph of two smiling people, a little Asian girl and a blond Nordic-looking boy. They weren't smiling about the cereal, that was for sure.

"It's good for you," he said.

"How come I always have to have healthy cereal? Everyone else in my class gets to have whatever they want for breakfast."

"I doubt that."

"Paige gets to have Froot Loops or Cap'n Crunch or Apple Jacks every morning."

"Paige . . ." Normally the parental responses came quickly to him, auto-pilot, but this morning he wasn't thinking very clearly. He worried about taking the sleeping pill so many days in a row. It was probably addictive. He wondered whether Julia or Lucas or Marta had heard anything two nights before. "Paige doesn't do well in school because she doesn't start off her day with a healthy breakfast." Sometimes he couldn't believe the crap he said aloud, the shameless propaganda. When he was a kid, he ate whatever the hell he wanted for break-fast, sugary shit like Quisp and Quake and Cocoa Puffs, and he did just fine in school. He didn't know, actually, if all kids were forced to eat healthy breakfasts by their parents these days, or it was just Laura who'd insisted on it. Whatever, he observed the Law of Healthy Breakfast as if it were the Constitution.

"Paige is in my math group," Julia countered.

"Good for her. I don't care if she eats chocolate cake for breakfast." The TV had been set up on a table in this temporary corner of the kitchen. The *Today* show was on, but right now there was a local commercial for Pajot Ford, always an annoying ad. John Pajot, the owner, was also the pitchman— hell, he paid for the ads, he could star in them if he wanted to—and he always did them wearing a hunting outfit. He made puns about saving "bucks" and "racking up" savings.

"Where's your brother?" he asked.

She shrugged, staring balefully at the cereal. It actually did look like stuff gathered from the ground in a forest. "Asleep, probably."

"All right, just have some yogurt, then."

"But I don't like the kind we have. It doesn't taste good."

"It's what we have. That's your choice. Yogurt or . . . twigs."

"But I like strawberry."

"I'll ask Marta to get more strawberry. In the meantime we have vanilla. It's good." Marta was doing laundry. He'd have to remember to ask her to add strawberry yogurt to her shopping list. Also some healthy cereal that didn't taste like twigs.

"No, it's not. It's the organic kind. Their vanilla tastes funny."

"It's that or string cheese, take your choice."

Julia sighed with bottomless frustration. "String cheese," she said sullenly.

The local news segment came on, and the anchorman, a lean-faced, slick-looking guy with shoe-polish black hair, said something about "found brutally murdered."

"Where's the remote?" asked Nick. When Julia was in hearing range, he normally muted any TV stories about murders or gruesome crimes or child molestation. She reached for it between the carton of organic one-percent milk and the sugar bowl, handed it to her father. He grabbed it, searched for the tiny mute button—why didn't they make the damned mute button bigger, and a different color?—but as he was about to press it, he saw the graphic on the screen. A photograph of a horribly familiar face, the words "Andrew Stadler." He froze, stared, his heart pounding.

He heard: "Dumpster behind Lucky's Restaurant on Hastings Street."

He heard: "Thirty-six years at the Stratton Company until he was laid off last March."

"What's the matter, Daddy?" Julia asked.

He heard something about funeral arrangements. "Hmm? Oh, nothing. One of our Stratton employees died, baby. Come on, get yourself some string cheese."

"Was he old?" she asked, getting up.

"Yeah," Nick said. "He was old."

Marge was already at her desk when he arrived, sipping coffee from a Stratton mug and reading a novel by Jane Austen. She flipped the paperback closed apologetically. "Oh, good morning," she said. "Sorry, I was hoping to finish this before my book group meets tonight."

"Don't let me stop you."

A copy of the *Fenwick Free Press* had been placed on his desk next to his keyboard. A front-page headline read: "Longtime Stratton Employee a Probable Homicide." Marjorie must have placed it there, folded so that the Stadler article faced up.

He hadn't bothered to look at the paper this morning before leaving the house; it had been too hectic. Luke hadn't gotten up, so Nick had gone to his room to awaken him. From under his mound of blankets and sheet, Luke had said he had study hour first period and was going to sleep in. Instead of arguing, Nick simply closed Luke's bedroom door.

Now he picked up the article and read it closely. Once again his heart was drumming. Not much here in the way of details. ". . . body discovered in a Dumpster behind a restaurant on Hastings Street." Nothing about it being wrapped in plastic; Nick wondered whether Eddie had, for some reason, removed the trash bags. "Apparently shot several times," though it didn't say where the man had been shot. Surely the police hadn't released to the paper everything they knew about the case. As nerve-wracking as it was to read, Nick found it oddly reassuring. The details formed a convincing picture of an unemployed man who'd been murdered in a rough part of town, probably having been involved in some street crime. There was a photo of Stadler taken at least twenty years ago: the same glasses, the same tight mouth. You'd read the article, shake your head sadly over how the loss of a job had caused an already troubled man to spiral into drugs or crime or something, and you'd move on to the sports.

Nick's eyes filled with tears. This is the man I killed. A man who left behind one child—"a daughter, Cassie, twenty-nine, of Chicago"—and an ex-wife who'd died four years earlier. A modest, quiet-living man, worked in a Stratton factory for his entire adult life.

He was suddenly aware of Marge standing there, looking worriedly at him. She'd said something.

"Excuse me?"

"I said, it's sad, isn't it?"

"Terribly sad," Nick said.

"The funeral's this afternoon. You have a telcon with Sales, but that can be rescheduled."

He nodded, realizing what she was saying. Nick usually attended the funerals of all Stratton employees, just as old man Devries had done. It was a tradition, a ceremonial obligation of the CEO in this company town.

He'd have to go to Andrew Stadler's funeral. He didn't really have a choice.

27

"You're not helping me any," Audrey said.

Bert Koopmans, the evidence tech, turned at the sink where he was washing his hands. There was something birdlike about the way he inclined his head, gawked at her. He was tall, almost spindly, with small close-set eyes that always looked startled.

"Not my job," he said, dry but not unfriendly. "What's the problem?"

She hesitated. "Well, you really didn't find anything on the body, when it comes right down to it."

"What body are we talking about?"

"Stadler."

"Who?"

"The guy in the Dumpster. Down on Hastings."

"The tortilla."

"Burrito, really."

He allowed a hint of a smile. "You got everything I got."

"Did the body strike you as too . . . clean?"

"Clean? You talking hygiene? I mean, the guy's fingernails were filthy."

"That's not what I mean, Bert." She thought a minute. "The dirt under his fingernails—that got tagged, right?"

"No, I lost it," Bert said, flashing her a look. "You forget who you're talking to? Like this was one of Wayne's cases?" Not all the techs were as meticulous, as obsessive-compulsive as Koopmans. He walked over to a black file cabinet, pulled it open, selected a folder. He scanned a sheet of paper. "Pubic hairs, head hairs, fingernails left hand, fingernails right hand. Fibers from shoe left, fibers from shoe right. Unidentified substance under fingernails right hand, unidentified substance under fingernails left hand. Want me to keep going?"

"No, thanks. What's the unidentified substance?"

Another look. "If I knew what it was, think I'd call it unidentified?"

"Are we talking skin or blood or dirt?"

"You try my patience, Detective. Skin and blood, these are substances I've seen before, believe it or not."

"Dirt you've seen before too."

He shrugged one shoulder. "But dirt isn't dirt. It's . . . stuff. It's anything. I made a note that it had a kind of greenish hue to it."

"Green paint? If Stadler scraped his fingernails against the side of a house, say . . . ?"

"Paint I would have recognized." He handed her the chain-of-custody sheet. "Here. Why don't you take a walk down to Property and get the shit. We can both take a look."

The guy who ran the Property room was a clock-puncher named Arthur something, a flabby white man with a toothbrush mustache who wore coveralls. She pushed the buzzer, and he took his time coming around to the window. She handed him the pink copy of the Property Receipt, explaining that she only wanted item number fifteen. All the evidence—the pulled head hair, pulled pubic hair, the two vials of blood—was kept in a big refrigerator. Arthur returned a few minutes later and could not have looked more bored. As he went through the ritual of scanning the bar code label on the five-by-seven evidence envelope marked "Nail Clippings From Autopsy," then the bar code on the wall chart to capture her name and number, Audrey heard Roy Bugbee's voice.

"That looks like the Stadler case," Bugbee said.

She nodded. "You working Jamal Wilson?"

Bugbee ignored her question. As the property guy slid the envelope under the window, Bugbee snatched it before Audrey could get to it. "Nail clippings, eh?"

"Just some more trace evidence I'm running past IBO again."

"Why do I get the crazy feeling we're not partnering on this, Audrey?"

"There's no end of things I'd appreciate your help on," she said uneasily.

"Right," Bugbee said. "You going over to IBO right now?"

Koopmans, who seemed surprised to see Roy Bugbee, placed two sheets of copy paper on the counter in the long narrow lab room where they fumed for fingerprints. He slit the bottom of each little envelope with a disposable scalpel and tapped out the contents onto the paper.

"Like I said, green dirt," Koopmans said. He and Audrey both wore surgical masks so that their breath wouldn't blow away the dirt. Bugbee did not.

Audrey peered closely. "Would it help to put it under a binocular microscope?"

"Happy to. But I've already done it, and there's nothing more to see." He sifted the tiny pile with a wooden applicator. "Sand, some kind of fine green powder, some fragments of what looks like pellets, maybe. Take it over to the state lab, if you want, but they're just going to tell you what I've just said. And it'll take 'em six weeks to tell you."

"Christ," said Bugbee, "you don't need a microscope for this shit."

"Oh, is that right," said Koopmans, giving Audrey a quick look.

"You don't have a lawn, obviously," Bugbee said. "That's hydroseed."

"Hydroseed," said Koopmans.

"Which is what, exactly?" Audrey asked.

"It's grass seed and, I don't know, ground-up newspaper and shit they spray. To start a new lawn. Hate the shit, myself—full of weed seed. I call it 'hydroweed.'"

"But it's green," Audrey said.

"That's the dye powder," Koopmans said. "And the pellets—that's the mulch." He pulled at his chin with his thumb and forefinger.

"Well, you saw the Stadler home," Audrey said. "I didn't see any hydroseed, did you?"

"Naw," said Bugbee, cocky. "A shitty lawn. All crabgrass and broadleaf weeds. Guys notice stuff like that."

"If you're lawn-obsessed," Koopmans said. "Is it possible your guy had some part-time job doing landscaping work or something?"

"No," Audrey said. "He could barely hold on to his job at Stratton. No, I suspect he got that stuff under his fingernails from wherever he went. Maybe—probably—the night he was killed."

28

The Mount Pleasant Cemetery was not the biggest burial ground in Fenwick Township, nor especially well tended. It sat on a high bluff above a busy highway and seemed forlorn, even for a cemetery. Nick had never been here before. Then again, he hated cemeteries and avoided them whenever possible. When he had to attend a funeral, he went to the church or funeral home and missed this part. Laura's death had made burials harder, not easier.

But he was late. He'd missed the service at the funeral home, having been unable to reschedule a major teleconference with the CEOs of Steelcase and Herman Miller to discuss a lobbying effort against an idiotic bill before Congress.

He parked his Suburban along a curb near where a ceremony was going on. There was a small clutch of people in dark clothing, maybe ten or twelve people in all. There was a pastor, a black woman, an elderly couple, five or six guys who might have worked with Stadler, a pretty young woman who had to be the man's daughter. She was petite, with big eyes and short, sort of chopped-looking punk hair. The paper had said she was twenty-nine and lived in Chicago.

Nick approached tentatively, heard the pastor, standing beside the casket, say: "Bless this grave that the body of our brother Andrew may sleep here in peace until You awaken him to glory, when he will see You face to face and know the splendor of the eternal God, who lives and reigns, now and forever." The roaring traffic obliterated some of his words.

A couple of the mourners turned to look at him. The Stratton guys rec-ognized him, their eyes lingering a moment longer. Nick thought he saw sur-prise, maybe a flash or two of indignation, though he wasn't sure. The beautiful daughter looked dazed, like a deer caught in the headlights. Near her stood the black woman, who was quite attractive as well. She looked at Nick, her glance piercing, tears running down her cheeks. Nick wondered who she was. There weren't that many blacks in town.

He wasn't prepared for the sight of the burnished mahogany casket, sit-ting atop the lowering device, Nick remembered from Laura's burial, which was hidden behind drapes of green crushed velvet. It jolted him. Somehow it was even more brutal, that tall, rounded mahogany coffin, than seeing An-drew Stadler's dead body crumpled on his lawn. It was more final, more *real*. This was a man with a family—a daughter, at least—and friends. He might have been a dangerous, unmedicated schizophrenic—but he was some-body's daddy too. This lovely young woman with the spiky hair and porcelain skin. Tears sprang to Nick's eyes. He was embarrassed.

The black woman glanced at him again. Who was she?

The Stratton guys looked at him again, no doubt noticing his tears and inwardly rolling their eyes at the hypocrisy. Slasher Nick weeping at the grave of a guy he laid off, they had to be thinking.

When it was over, and the coffin was lowered smoothly and silently into the grave, the mourners began tossing clods of earth and flowers onto the cof-fin. Some of them embraced the daughter, clutching her hand, murmuring condolences. When the moment seemed right, he approached her.

"Ms. Stadler, I'm Nick Conover. I'm the—"

"I know who you are," she replied coolly. She had the tiniest stud on the right side of her nose, a glint of light.

"I didn't know your father personally, but I wanted to tell you how sorry I am. He was a valued employee."

"So valued that you fired him." She spoke in a quiet tone, but her bitter-ness was obvious.

"The layoffs have been difficult for all of us. So many deserving people lost their jobs."

She sighed as if the subject wasn't worth discussing any further. "Yeah, well, everything started to fall apart for my dad when he got forced out."

He'd steeled himself against anger, given how often he met former Stratton employees, but this he wasn't quite prepared for, not here in a cemetery, from a woman who was burying her father. "It's a terrible thing he had to go through." He noticed the black woman watching the exchange with interest, though she was far enough away that she might not have been able to hear what they were saying.

Stadler's daughter smiled ruefully. "Let's get one thing straight, Mr. Conover. As far as I'm concerned, you killed my dad."

29

Leon's oldest sister, LaTonya, was a very large woman with an imperious way about her, adamant in all her opinions, though maybe you had to be to raise six kids. Audrey liked being around her—she was everything Audrey wasn't, bawdy where Audrey was respectful, profane where Audrey was polite, stubborn where Audrey was compliant. Things might not have been so good with Leon, but that didn't affect their friendship. Sisterhood was stronger. LaTonya didn't have much respect for her younger brother anyway, it seemed.

Fairly often Audrey baby-sat the three younger Saunders kids. Most of the time she enjoyed it. They were good kids, a twelve-year-old girl and two boys, nine and eleven. No doubt they ran roughshod over her, took advantage of her good nature, got away with stuff their drill-sergeant mother would never let them. But that, she figured, was what aunts were for. It didn't escape her, either, that LaTonya herself took advantage of Audrey, asking her to sit way more than she should, because LaTonya understood what was never said aloud, that her kids were the only kids Audrey would ever have.

LaTonya arrived home an hour later this evening than she'd said she would. She was taking a motivational training seminar at the Days Inn on Winsted Avenue, learning to start a home business. Her husband, Paul, managed the service department of a GMC dealership and usually worked late, didn't get home until eight. Audrey didn't mind, really. She'd just come off a long shift, which included attending the Andrew Stadler funeral, and would rather spend a few hours with her niece and nephews than at home with Leon, to be honest. Or thinking about poor Cassie Stadler. You had to take a break sometimes.

LaTonya was lugging a huge cardboard box heaped with white plastic bottles. Her moon-shaped face was beaded with sweat. "This here," she announced as the screen door slammed behind her, "is going to liberate us from debt."

"What is it?" Audrey asked. Camille was practicing her piano in the den by now and the two boys were watching TV.

"Hey, what's this? What the *hell* is *this*?" LaTonya hollered at her sons as she dropped the box on the kitchen table. "I don't care how much of a pushover your Auntie Audrey is, we have a rule about the TV. Turn that goddamned set off, and get to your homework, right now!"

"But Audrey said we could!" protested Thomas, the younger son. Matthew, experienced enough to know never to argue with their mother, scampered upstairs.

"I don't give a shit what Audrey said, you know the rules!" she thundered. She turned to Audrey, her voice softening. "It's weight-loss supplements. In a year or two, I'm not going to *need* Paul's salary. Not that there's much of that."

"Weight-loss supplements?"

"Thermogenic," LaTonya said. It was clear she had just learned the word. "Burns the fat off. Stokes up your metabolism. Blocks carbs too. And it's all natural."

"Sistah, you got to be careful with those make-money-at-home schemes," Audrey said. It was funny, when she was around LaTonya she found herself talking black, the rhythms of her speech changing. She was acutely aware that LaTonya considered Audrey saditty, or conceited.

"Careful?" LaTonya gasped. "This is the wellness industry we're talking about. In five years it's going to be a *trillion*-dollar industry, and I'm getting on the elevator at the ground floor." She opened a new box of Ritz crackers, offered it to Audrey, who shook her head. LaTonya tore open the wax paper on one of the cracker rolls and grabbed a handful.

"LaTonya, can I talk to you for a second?"

"Mmmph?" LaTonya replied through a mouthful of cracker.

"It's the way you talk to your kids. The language. I don't think children should hear that kind of language, particularly from a parent."

LaTonya's eyes widened in indignation. She put her hands on her hips. She chewed, swallowed, then said, "Audrey, baby, I love you, but they're my kids, you understand? Not yours. Mine."

"But still," Audrey said, regretting she'd said anything, wanting to take it back.

"Honey, these little buggers respect strong words. If you had kids, you'd understand." LaTonya saw the wounded look in Audrey's face. "I'm—I'm sorry, I didn't mean it the way it came out."

"That's okay," Audrey said with a dismissive shake of the head. "I shouldn't have said anything."

LaTonya was holding up one of the big white plastic bottles. "*This* you need," she said.

"*I* need?"

"For your no-good, lazy-ass husband. My brother. Least he can do while he's sitting on his butt is take some of these thermogenic supplements. Twenty-four ninety-five. You can afford it. Tell you what: I'll give you my discount. Sixteen fifty. Can't do better than that."

30

Audrey didn't much like the security director of the Stratton Corporation, an ex-cop named Edward Rinaldi. For one thing, there was his initial unwillingness to meet her, which she found peculiar. She was investigating the death of a Stratton employee, after all. How packed could his schedule really be? On the phone, after she'd told him what she wanted, he'd said he was "raked."

Then there was his reputation, which was a little hinky. She always did her homework, of course, and before coming to Stratton headquarters, she called around, figuring that the security director of the biggest company in town had to be known to at least the uniform division of the police. She learned that he was a local boy, went to high school with Nicholas Conover, Stratton's CEO. That he'd joined the force in Grand Rapids. His dealings with the Fenwick police were limited to pilferage cases and vandalism at Stratton. "That guy?" a veteran patrol cop named Vogel told her. "He never woulda made it here. We'd have kicked him out on his ass."

"How come?"

"Smartass. Got his own rule book, know what I'm saying."

"I don't think I do, no."

"I don't want to spread rumors. Ask around in GR."

"I will, but you've dealt with him yourself, haven't you?"

"Ah, he was all over us on some vandalism deal at the CEO's house like it was our fault, instead of some whacked laid-off employee."

"All over you how?"

"He wanted the priors on this employee."

"Who?"

Vogel seemed surprised. "What're you talking, your guy, of course, right? That Stadler guy, isn't that why you called me?"

Suddenly Edward Rinaldi was becoming more interesting.

When she called Grand Rapids, she had a harder time finding someone who'd talk to her about Edward Rinaldi, until a lieutenant there named Pettigrew confided that Rinaldi was not missed. "Put it this way," the lieutenant said cagily, "he lived pretty good."

"Meaning what?"

"Meaning his income wasn't necessarily limited to his salary."

"We talking bribes, Lieutenant?"

"Could be, but that's not what I mean. I'm just saying that not all the evidence from drug busts made it to the property room."

"He was a user?"

The lieutenant chuckled. "Not so far as I know. He seemed a lot more interested in the shoeboxes full of cash. But he was booted out without a formal IA investigation, so that's just rumor."

It was enough to make her wary of the man.

But most of all she didn't like Rinaldi's manner—the evasiveness, the shiftiness in his eyes, the quick and inappropriate grins, the intensity of his stare. There was something vulgar, something scammy about the man.

"Where's your partner?" he asked after they'd chatted a few minutes. "Don't you guys always work in teams?"

"Often." He and Bugbee would have hit it off just fine, she thought. Cut from the same bolt of polyester fabric.

"You're Detective Rhimes? As in LeAnn Rimes?"

"Spelled differently," she said. "Did Andrew Stadler vandalize your CEO's house, Mr. Rinaldi?" she asked, coming straight to the point.

Rinaldi looked away too quickly, searched the ceiling as if wracking his brain, furrowed his brow. "I have no idea, Detective."

"You wanted to know his priors, Mr. Rinaldi. You must have had some suspicion."

Now he looked straight at her. "I like to do a thorough job. I investigate all possibilities. Same as I'm sure you do."

"I'm sorry, I don't quite understand. You did suspect Mr. Stadler, or you didn't?"

"Look, Detective. My boss's house gets vandalized in a particularly sick and twisted way, first thing I'm gonna do is go through the rolls of people who got the ax here, right? Anyone who made any threats during their out-placement interviews, all that. I find out that one guy who got laid off has a mental history, I'm gonna look a little more closely. Make sense?"

"Absolutely. So what did you find when you looked closely?"

"What'd I find?"

"Right. Did he make any threats during his outplacement?"

"Wouldn't surprise me. People do, you know. People lose it, time like that."

"Not according to his boss at the model shop, the fellow who conducted the outplacement interview along with someone from HR. He said Stadler quit, but he wasn't violent."

Rinaldi guffawed. "You trying to trap me or something, Detective? Forget it. I'm telling you this guy was in and out of the loony bin."

"He was diagnosed with schizophrenia, is that right?"

"What do you want from me? You want to know if this guy Stadler was the sick fuck who went to my boss's home and killed his dog, I have no idea."

"Did you talk to him?"

Rinaldi waved his hand. "Nah."

"Did you ask the police to investigate him?"

"For what? Get the poor guy in trouble, for what?"

"You just said it wouldn't surprise you if he made threats during his out-placement interview."

Rinaldi spun his fancy chair around and looked at his computer screen, squinted his eyes. "Who's the head of Major Cases now? Is it Noyce?"

"Sergeant Noyce, that's right."

"Say hi for me. Nice guy. Good cop."

"I will." Was he threatening to pull strings? Wouldn't work if he did, she thought. Sergeant Noyce barely knew him. She'd asked her boss about Ri-naldi. "But as to my question, Mr. Rinaldi—you never talked to Stadler, never pointed him out as a potential suspect in the incident at Mr. Conover's home?"

Rinaldi shook his head again, gave a thoughtful frown. "I had no reason to think he was the one," he said reasonably.

"So that situation is unresolved, what happened at Mr. Conover's home?"

"You tell me. Fenwick PD doesn't seem optimistic about solving it."

"Did you ever meet Andrew Stadler or talk with him?"

"Nope."

"Or Mr. Conover? Did he ever meet with Stadler or talk with him?"

"I doubt it. The CEO of a company this size doesn't usually meet most of his employees, except maybe in group settings."

"Then it was very kind of him to attend Mr. Stadler's funeral."

"Did he? Well, that sounds like Nick."

"How so?"

"He's very considerate about his employees. Probably goes to all funerals of Stratton workers. Town like this, he's a public figure, you know. Part of his job."

"I see." She thought for a moment. "But you must have run names by Mr. Conover, names of laid-off employees, to see if any of them rang a bell."

"I usually don't bother him at that level, Detective. Not unless I have a firm lead. I let him do his job, and I do mine. No, I wish I could help you. The guy worked for Stratton for, what, like thirty-five years. I just hate to see a loyal employee come to an end like that."

31

"Yo," Scott said, appearing from behind Marge's side of the divider panel next to Nick's desk. "Looking for some exciting reading? The board books are ready."

Nick looked up from his screen, a testy e-mail exchange with his general counsel, Stephanie Alstrom, about some tedious and endless battle with the Environmental Protection Agency over the emissions of certain volatile organic compounds in an adhesive used in the manufacture of one of the Stratton chairs that they'd discontinued anyway.

"Fiction or nonfiction?" he said.

"Nonfiction, unfortunately. Sorry it's so last minute, but I had to redo all the numbers the way you wanted."

"Sorry to be so unreasonable," Nick said sardonically. "But I'm the guy on the hot seat."

"Muldaur and Eilers are arriving at the Grand Fenwick this afternoon," Scott said, "and I told them I'd get the board books over there before dinner tonight so they could look 'em over. You know those guys—there's going to be questions, the second they see you. Just so long as you're ready to face them."

The board of directors always had dinner in town the night before the quarterly board meeting. Dorothy Devries, the founder's daughter and the only member of the Devries family on the board, usually hosted them at the Fenwick Country Club, which she more or less owned. It was always a stiff and awkward occasion, with no overt business transacted.

"Ah, Scott, I'm going to have to miss it tonight." He stood up, feeling rubbed raw, his headache full blown now.

"You're—you're kidding me."

"It's the fourth-grade school play tonight—they're doing *The Wizard of Oz*, and Julia's got a big part. I really can't miss it."

"Please tell me you're joking, Nick. The *fourth-grade play?*"

"I missed her school play last year, and I've missed the art exhibit and just about every school assembly. I can't miss this too."

"You can't get someone to videotape it?"

"Videotape it? What kind of dad are you?"

"Absentee and proud of it. My kids respect me more for being distant and unavailable."

"Now. Wait 'til they get into therapy. Anyway, you know as well as I do that nothing ever gets done at those dinners."

"It's called schmoozing. A Yiddish word that means saving your job."

"They're going to fire me because I didn't have dinner with them? If they do, Scott, they're just looking for an excuse anyway."

Scott shook his head. "Okay," he said, looking down at the floor. "You're the boss. But if you ask me—"

"Thanks, Scott. But I didn't ask you."

32

Audrey sat at her desk, staring at her little gallery of photographs, and then phoned the Michigan State Police crime lab in Grand Rapids.

Yesterday she'd driven almost two hours to Grand Rapids and handed the bullets, in their little brown paper evidence envelopes, to a crime lab tech who looked barely old enough to be shaving. Trooper Halverson had been polite but all business. He asked her if there were any shell casings, as if she'd maybe forgotten. She told him they hadn't recovered any, found herself actually apologizing to the boy. She asked how long it would take, and he said their caseload was huge, they were badly understaffed, their backlog was running a good three or four months. Luckily, Sergeant Noyce knew one of the Ramp Rangers, as they called the Michigan highway patrolmen, and when she reminded him of that—subtly, delicately—Trooper Halverson had said he'd try to get right to it.

On the phone, Trooper Halverson sounded even younger. He didn't remember her name, but when she read off the lab file number, he pulled it up on the computer.

"Yes, Detective," he said, tentative. "Um, well, let's see here. Okay. They're .380, brass-jacketed, like you said. The rifling looks to be six left. Gosh, you guys didn't turn up any casings?"

"The body was dumped. So, as I said, unfortunately, no."

"It's just that if you had a casing we could really learn a whole lot more," he said. He spoke as if she were holding the cartridge casings back and maybe just needed a little persuasion to hand them over. "The casings tend to take imprints so much better than the bullets."

"No such luck," she said. She waited patiently while he went through the measurements and specs from his microscope exam. "So, um, based on the land and groove widths, the GRC database spits out like twenty different possible models that might've been the weapon in question." The GRC, she recalled, was the General Rifling Characteristics database, put out by the FBI every year or so on a CD.

"Twenty," she said, disappointed. "That doesn't narrow it down too much."

"Mostly Colts and Davis Industries. A lot of street guns look like this. So I'd say you're looking for a Colt .380, a Davis .380, or a Smith and Wesson."

"There's no way to narrow it down any more? What about the ammunition?"

"Yes, ma'am, these are hollow-point brass-jacketed bullets. There are some indications that they're Remington Golden Sabers, but don't hold me to it. That's problematic."

"Okay."

"And also—well, I probably shouldn't say this."

"Yes?"

"No, I'm just saying. Personal observation here. The land width is between .0252 and .054. The groove measurement is between .124 and .128. So it's pretty tight. That tells me the weapon that fired it is a pretty decent one, not just some Saturday night special. So I'm thinking maybe it's the Smith and Wesson, because they're a good manufacturer."

"How many possible Smith and Wesson models are we talking about?"

"Well, Smith and Wesson doesn't make any .380s any more. The only one they ever made was the baby Sigma."

"Baby Sigma? That's the name of the gun?"

"No, ma'am. I mean, you know, they have a product line called the Sigma, and for a couple of years—like the mid-to-late nineties—the bottom end of the Sigma line was a .380 pocket pistol that people sometimes called the 'baby' Sigma."

She wrote down "S&W Sigma .380."

"Okay, good," she said, "so we're looking for a Smith and Wesson Sigma .380."

"No, ma'am. I didn't say that. No suspect weapons should be overlooked."

"Of course, Trooper Halverson." The troops were supercareful about what they told you, because they knew that everything had to stand up in a court of law, everything had to be carefully documented, and there couldn't be any guesswork. "When do you think you might know more?"

"Well, after our IBIS technician enters it."

She didn't want to ask how long that would take. "Well, anything you can do to put wings on this, Trooper, would be much appreciated."

33

The brand-new Fenwick Elementary School auditorium was fancier than a lot of college theaters: plush stadium seating, great acoustics, professional sound system and lighting. It was called the Devries Theater, a gift from Dorothy Stratton Devries, in honor of her late husband.

When Nick had gone to Fenwick Elementary, there hadn't even been an auditorium. School assemblies had been held in the gym, all the kids sitting on the splintery wooden bleachers. Now it seemed like the fourth-grade class was doing its annual play in a Broadway theater.

Looking around, Nick was glad he'd come. All the parents were here, grandparents too. Even parents who rarely came to any of their kids' school events, like Emily Renfro's plastic-surgeon dad, Jim. Jacqueline Renfro was a class mom or something, but her husband was usually too busy doing face-lifts or screwing his receptionist to show up. A number of the parents had mini videocams, ready to film the production on compact digital tape that no one would ever bother to watch.

He was late as usual. Everywhere he went, he seemed to arrive late these days. Marta had dropped Julia off an hour ago so she and the rest of the fourth-graders could get into their handmade costumes, which they'd been working on in art class for months. Julia was excited about tonight because she got to play the Wicked Witch of the West—her choice, a role she'd auditioned for and then pleaded for. Not for her Dorothy, which all the other girls wanted. Nick's little tomboy had no interest in playing a wimpy character wearing a braided wig and a gingham dress. She knew that the witch part was the scene-stealer. He liked that about her.

She didn't expect him to be here. He'd already told her a couple of times that he had a work dinner he had to go to and couldn't get out of. She was disappointed, but resigned. So she'd be all the more excited when she saw her daddy here. In truth, of course, Nick considered sitting through the school play, one of those unpleasant parental obligations like changing a poopy diaper, or going to "The Lion King On Ice" (or *anything* on ice, for that matter), or watching the *Teletubbies* or *The Wiggles* and not letting on how creepy they were.

The back sections of the theater had been cordoned off, and there didn't seem to be any available seats in the front. He peered around, saw a few spaces here and there, a sea of averted glances, a few unfriendly faces. Maybe he was being a little paranoid. Guilt burned on his face as visibly as a scarlet letter. He was convinced people knew what he'd done just by looking at him.

But that wasn't it, of course. They hated him for other reasons, for being Slasher Nick, for being the local hero who'd turned on them. He saw the Renfros, caught their icy glares before they looked away. Finally he saw one friendly face, a buddy of his from high school days whose son was in Julia's class.

"Hey, Bobby," he said, sitting down in the seat Bob Casey had freed up by moving his jacket. Casey, a bald, red-faced guy with an enormous beer gut, was a stockbroker who'd tried to hit Nick up for business several times. He was a wisenheimer whose chief claim to fame since high school was his ability to memorize long stretches of dialogue from Monty Python or any of the National Lampoon or Airplane movies.

"There he is," Casey said heartily. "Big night, huh?"

"Oh, yeah. How's Gracie?"

"Doin' good. Doin' good."

A long, uncomfortable silence followed. Then Bob Casey said, "Ever see anything like this theater? We never had anything like this."

"We were lucky to use the gym."

"Luxury!" Casey said in his Monty Python voice. "Luxury! We had to walk thirty miles to school every morning in a blizzard—uphill, both ways. And we loved it!"

Nick smiled, amused but unable to laugh.

Casey noticed Nick's subdued response and said, "So, you've had a hard year, huh?"

"Not as hard as a lot of people here."

"Hey, come on, Nick. You lost your wife."

"Yeah, well."

"How's the house?"

"Almost done."

"It's been almost done for a year, right?" he gibed. "Kids okay? Julia seems to be doing good."

"She's great."

"I hear Luke's having a hard time of it."

Nick wondered how much Bob Casey knew about Luke's troubles— probably more than Nick did himself. "Well, you know. Sixteen, right?"

"Tough age. Plus, only one parent and all that."

The production was about what you'd expect for a fourth-grade play—an Emerald City set they'd all painted themselves, the talking apple tree made out of painted corrugated cardboard. The music teacher playing sloppily on the Yamaha digital piano. Julia, as the Witch, froze up, kept forgetting her lines. You could almost hear the parents in the audience *thinking* them out loud for her—"Poppies!" and "I'll get you, my pretty!"

When it was over, Jacqueline Renfro seemed to go out of her way to find Nick and say, "Poor Julia." She shook her head. "It can't be easy for her."

Nick furrowed his brow.

"Well, only one parent, and you hardly ever there."

"I'm there as much as I can," he replied.

Jacqueline shrugged, having made her point, and moved on. But her husband, Jim, lagged behind. He wore a brown tweed jacket and a blue button-down shirt, looking like he was still a Princeton undergrad. He pointed a finger at Nick and winked. "Can't imagine how I'd get by without Jackie," he said in a confiding tone. "I don't know how you get by. Still, Julia's a great kid—you're very lucky."

"Thanks."

Jim Renfro was smiling too hard. "Of course, the thing about family is, when they get to be too much, you can't exactly downsize them." A cheery, self-satisfied wink. "Am I right?"

Any number of responses occurred to Nick—too many. None of them nonviolent. He had this strange feeling of a lid coming off, the bleed valves blowing.

At that point, Julia came running up, still wearing her pointed black construction-paper hat and her green face makeup. "You came!" she said.

He threw his arms around her. "I couldn't miss this."

"How was I?" she asked. There wasn't a drop of concern in her voice, no awareness that she'd messed up. She was bursting with pride. He loved this little girl.

"You were great," he said.

34

In the car on the way home, Nick's cell phone went off, a weird synthesized, symphonic fanfare that he'd never bothered to reprogram.

He glanced at the caller ID, saw that it was Eddie Rinaldi. He picked it up from the cradle, not wanting Julia to hear whatever Eddie had to say over the speakers. She was sitting in the backseat of the Suburban, poring over the *Wizard of Oz* program in the darkness. She still had the green zinc-oxide face makeup on, and Nick could see a bedtime struggle ahead when he made her clean it off.

"Hey, Eddie," he said.

"There you are. You had the phone off?"

"I was watching Julia's school play."

"Okay," he said. Eddie, who had no kids, no plans to have any, and no interest in them, never asked about his kids beyond the bare minimum required. "I was thinking of dropping by."

"Can't it wait?"

A pause. "I think not. We should talk. Only take five minutes, maybe."

"There a problem?" Nick was suddenly on edge.

"No, no. No problem. Just, we should talk."

Eddie sprawled in the easy chair in Nick's study, legs splayed wide as if he owned the place.

"A homicide detective came to talk to me," he said casually.

Nick felt his insides go cold. He leaned forward in his desk chair. Here they sat, just a few feet from where it had happened. "What the fuck?" he said.

Eddie shrugged, no big deal. "Standard operating procedure. Routine shit."

"*Routine?*"

"She's just covering all the bases. Got to, sloppy if she didn't."

"It's a woman." Nick focused on the anomaly, avoiding the main issue: *a homicide detective was on the case, already?*

"Negro lady." Eddie could have put it much more crudely. His racism was no secret to anyone, but maybe he'd learned over the years that it wasn't socially acceptable, not even around his old buddies. Or maybe he didn't want to antagonize Nick at the moment.

"I didn't know the Fenwick police had any."

"I didn't either."

A long silence in which Nick could hear the ticking of the clock. A silver clock, engraved FENWICK CITIZEN OF THE YEAR, awarded to him three years ago. When everything was going great. "What'd she want?"

"What do you think? She wanted to ask about Stadler."

"What *about* Stadler?"

"You know, what you'd expect. Did he make any threats, whatever."

Eddie was being evasive, and Nick didn't like it. Something didn't sit right. "Why was she talking to you?"

"Hey, man, I'm the security director, remember?"

"No. There has to be some more specific reason she went to talk to you. What are you leaving out, Eddie?"

"Leaving out? I'm leaving nothing out, buddy. I mean, look, she knew I asked some guys on the job about Stadler."

So that was it. By doing his background check on Stadler, he'd in effect tipped his hand to the police. "Shit."

"Come on. I never talked to the guy."

"No," Nick said, one hand cupping his chin. "You call the cops, asking about some downsized employee who slaughtered your boss's dog, then the guy turns up dead a couple days later. This doesn't look good."

Eddie shook his head, rolling his eyes in contempt. "Like this is, what, the Mafia or something? Get real. The guy goes off the deep end, doing sick shit, matter of time before he pisses off the wrong guy."

"Yeah."

"In the dog pound, I mean, come on. Look, they got nothing tying Stadler to me—or to you."

"Then what was she asking about?"

"Ah, she wanted to know if you'd ever talked to Stadler, had any contact with the guy. Told her you probably didn't even know who the guy was. Pretty much true."

Nick inhaled slowly, tried to calm himself, held his breath. "And if I did? What's the assumption here, that I went after the guy, *killed* him?" Nick heard the aggrieved tone in his own voice, as if he were actually starting to believe himself innocent.

"Nah, she's just looking for scraps. Anyway, don't worry, I handled her fine. Believe me, she left knowing she's barking up the wrong tree."

"How do you know?"

"I can tell, come on. Get serious here, Nick. The CEO of Stratton murdered one of his employees? I don't *think* so. No one's going to believe that for a second."

Nick was silent for a long while. "I hope so."

"I just wanted to keep you in the loop. In case she comes to talk to you."

Nick, his chest tightening, said, "She said she was going to?"

"No, but she might. Wouldn't surprise me."

"I'd never even heard the name," Nick said. "Right? You tell her otherwise?"

"Exactly. Told her you're a busy guy, I do my job, you don't get involved."

"Right."

"So you figured maybe some downsized employee went wacko, killed your dog, but you called the cops, figured they'd handle it, you had no idea who it mighta been."

"Right."

"Guy turns up dead, mighta been the same guy, mighta been different, you have no idea. Like that."

Nick nodded, rehearsing the answer in his mind, turning it over and over, poking at the soft spots. "There's nothing tying me to this thing?" he said after a few moments.

A long silence. Eddie replied with a kind of smoldering indignation. "I did my job, Nick, you clear?"

"I don't doubt it. I'm asking you to think like a cop. Like a homicide cop."

"That's how I think, man. Like a cop."

"No prints, nothing like that, on the . . . body? Fibers, DNA, whatever?"

"Nick, I told you, we're not going to talk about this."

"We are now. I want to know."

"The body was clean, Nick," Eddie said. "Okay? Clean as a whistle. Clean as I could get it in the time we had."

"What about the gun?"

"What about it?"

"What'd you do with it? You don't still have it, do you?"

"Like I'm a stupid fuck? Come on, man."

"Then where is it?"

Eddie let out a puff of air, made a sound like *pah*. "Bottom of the river, you really want to know." Fenwick, like so many towns in Michigan, was built on the shores of one of the many waterways leading into Lake Michigan.

"Shell casings too?"

"Yup."

"And if it turns up?"

"You realize how unlikely that is?"

"I'm saying."

"Even if they do find it, they got no way to connect it to me."

"Why not? It's your gun."

"It's a goddamned drop gun, Nick."

"A what?"

"A throw-down. A piece I picked up at a scene in GR. Some crack dealer, who the hell knows where he got it. Point is, there's no record anywhere. No paperwork, no purchase permit, nothing. Clean."

Nick had heard of cops picking up guns they found at crime scenes, keeping them, but he knew you weren't supposed to do that, and it made him nervous to hear Eddie admit to it. If he did that, what else did he do?

"You sure," Nick said.

"Sure as shit."

"What about the security cameras?"

Eddie nodded. "Hey, I'm a pro, right? Took care of that too."

"How?"

"Why do you need to know?"

"I need to know. My own fucking security cameras recorded me killing the guy."

Eddie closed his eyes, shook his head in irritation. "I reformatted the hard drive on the digital video recorder. That night's gone. Never happened. System started recording next day—makes sense, right? Since we just put it in the day before."

"Not a trace?"

"Nada. Hey, don't worry about it. The lady comes to talk to you, you co-operate, tell her everything you know, which is a big fat zero, right?" Eddie gave his dry cackle.

"Right. I know she talked to you?"

Eddie shrugged. "Play it either way. Let's say, no, I didn't get around to it. Got nothing to do with you, right?"

"Right."

Eddie got up. "Nothing to worry about, man. Get some sleep. You look like shit."

"Thanks." Nick got up, to walk Eddie out, then thought of something. "Eddie," he said. "That night. You said it was your gun, tied everything to you, right? That's why I didn't have a choice."

Eddie's eyes were dead. "Yeah?"

"Now you tell me the gun was clean. No connection to you at all. I don't get it."

A long silence.

"Can't take chances, Nicky," Eddie finally said. "Never take chances."

Nick walked Eddie out of his study, heard footfalls on the carpeting. Saw a jeans-clad leg, a sneaker, disappear up the stairs.

Lucas.

Just getting home? Was it possible that he'd overheard their conversation? Nah, he'd have had to have stood outside the study door, listening. Lucas didn't do that, the main reason being that he had no interest in what his dad was up to.

Still.

Nick wondered, a tiny wriggle of worry.

35

•

Driving to work the next morning, Nick was in a foul mood. The news that a homicide detective was poking around the corporation had sent him spiraling into a tense, sleepless night. He thrashed around in the big bed, got up repeatedly, obsessed about that night.

What Happened That Night—that was how he thought of it now. The memory had receded to attenuated, kaleidoscopic images: Stadler's leering face, the gunfire, the body sprawled on the ground, Eddie's face, carrying the body wrapped in black trash bags.

He was out of pills, which was just as well; any more of them, he figured, and he was headed for the Betty Ford clinic. He tried to think about work stuff, anything but that night. But that just meant the board meeting in the morning. Board meetings always made him tense, but this time he knew that the shit was about to rain down.

On the way into work he stopped at a light next to a gleaming silver S-Class Mercedes. He turned to admire it and saw that the driver was Stratton's VP of sales, Ken Coleman. Nick rolled down his passenger's side window, tapped on his horn until he got Coleman's attention. When Coleman—forty-one, a good seventy pounds overweight, a bad hairpiece—rolled down his window, his face lit up.

"Hey, Nick! Looking pretty slick."

"Board meeting. New car, Kenny?"

Coleman's grin got even wider. "Got it yesterday. You like?"

"Must list for a hundred grand, right?"

Coleman, always hyper, nodded fast, up and down and up and down like some bobble-head doll. "Over. Fully loaded. Like, AMG sports package and, I mean, heated *steering wheel*, you know?" The top sales guys at Stratton made more than Nick did. He didn't resent it; someone had to do the soul-destroying shit they did.

The light turned green, but Nick didn't move. "Buy or lease?" he asked.

"Well, lease. I always lease, you know?"

"Good. Because it's going back to the dealer."

Coleman cocked his bobble head, a movement like a terrier, almost comic. "What?"

Behind him, someone honked a horn. Nick ignored it. "We laid off five thousand workers, Ken. Half the company. To cut costs, save Stratton. Pretty much wiped out the town. So I don't want a member of my executive man-agement team driving around town in a fucking hundred-thousand-dollar Mercedes, understand?"

Coleman stared in disbelief.

Nick went on, "You take that back to the dealership by close of business today and tell 'em you want a fucking Subaru or something. But I don't want to see you behind that heated steering wheel again, you understand?"

Nick gunned the engine and took off.

The five members of the board of directors of the Stratton Corporation, and their guests, were gathered in the anteroom to the boardroom. Coffee was be-ing served from vacuum carafes, and not the institutional food-service blend that was served in the Stratton employee cafeteria, either. It was brewed from Sulawesi Peaberry beans fresh-roasted by Town Grounds, Fenwick's best cof-fee place. Todd Muldaur had complained about the coffee at the first board meeting after the buyout, poked fun at the Bunn-O-Matic. Nick thought Todd was being ridiculous, but he ordered the change. That, and little cold bottles of Evian water, melon slices, raspberries and strawberries, fancy pas-tries trucked in from a famous bakery in Ann Arbor.

Todd Muldaur, in another of his expensive suits, was at the tail end of a joke when Nick arrived, holding forth to Scott, the other guy from Fairfield

Partners, Davis Eilers, and someone Nick had never seen before. "I told him the best way to see Fenwick is in your rearview mirror," Todd was saying. Eilers and the other guy laughed raucously. Scott, who'd noticed Nick's approach, just smiled politely.

Davis Eilers was the other deal partner, a guy who had a lot of operational experience. He'd done his time at McKinsey like Todd and Scott, only he'd played football at Dartmouth, not Yale. He later ran a number of companies, sort of a CEO-for-hire.

Todd turned, saw Nick. "There he is." He tipped his cup at Nick. "Great coffee!" he said expansively and gave a wink. "Sorry to miss you last night. Busy being a dad, huh?"

Nick shook Todd's hand, then Scott's, then Eilers's. "Yeah, couldn't get out of it. My daughter's school play, you know, and given—"

"Hey, you got your priorities straight," Todd said with an excess of sincerity. "I respect that."

Nick wanted to toss the cup of hot Sulawesi Peaberry in the guy's face, but he just looked straight in Todd's too-blue eyes and smiled appreciatively.

"Nick, I want you to meet our new board member, Dan Finegold." A tall, handsome guy, athletic-looking. A thatch of dark brown hair starting to silver over. What was it with Fairfield Equity Partners? It was a fucking frat.

Dan Finegold's handshake was a crusher.

"Don't tell me Yale football too," Nick said cordially. Thinking: *our new board member? Like, were they going to tell me? Just spring it on me?*

"Yale baseball, actually," said Todd, clapping both men on their shoulders, bringing them together. "Dan was a legendary pitcher."

"Legendary, my ass," said Finegold.

"Hey, man, you *were*," Todd said. He looked at Nick. "Dan's got twenty years' experience in the office-supply space, with all the scar tissue. I'm sure you know OfficeSource—that was his baby. When Willard bought it, he grabbed Dan for Fairfield."

"You like Boston?" Nick asked. He couldn't think of anything else to say. He couldn't say what he was really thinking, which was: Why are you here, and who invited you onto the board, and what's really going on here? Fairfield had the right to put whomever they wanted on the board, but it wasn't exactly cool for them to just show up with a new board member in tow. They hadn't done it before. It wasn't a good precedent, or maybe that was the point.

"It's great. Especially for a foodie like me. Lot of happening restaurants in Boston these days."

"Dan's part owner of an artisanal brewery in upstate New York," said Todd. "They make the best Belgian beer outside of Belgium. Abbey ale, right?"

"That's right."

"Welcome to the board," Nick said. "I'm sure your expertise in Belgian beer's going to come in handy." Something about Belgian beer and Abbey ale sounded familiar, but he couldn't place it.

Todd took Nick by the elbow as they walked to the boardroom. He spoke in a low voice. "Bummer about Atlas McKenzie."

"Huh?"

"Scott told me last night."

"What are you talking about?"

Todd gave him a quick, curious glance. "The deal," he said under his breath. "How it fell through."

"*What?*" What the hell was he talking about? The Atlas McKenzie deal was all but inked. This made no sense!

"Don't worry, it's not going to come up this morning. But still, a *major* bummer, huh?" In a louder voice, he called out, "Mrs. Devries!"

Todd turned away and strode up to Dorothy Devries, who had just entered the boardroom. Todd clasped her small hand in both of his large ones and waited until she turned her cheek toward him before he kissed it.

Dorothy was wearing a Nancy Reagan burgundy pants suit with white piping around the lapels. Her white hair was a perfect cumulus cloud with just a hint of blue rinse in it, which brought out the steely blue of her eyes. Fairfield Partners had left Dorothy Stratton Devries a small piece of the company and a seat on the board, which was a condition of hers that Willard Osgood had no quibble with. It looked good to have the founder's family still connected to Stratton. It told the world that Fairfield still respected the old ways. Of course, Dorothy had no power. She was there for window dressing, mostly. Fairfield owned ninety percent of Stratton, controlled the board, ran the show. Dorothy, a sharp cookie, understood that, but she also understood that, outside the boardroom at least, she still possessed some moral authority.

Her dad, Harold Stratton, had been a machinist for the Wabash Railroad, a tinsmith's apprentice, a steeplejack. He worked as a machinist at Steelcase, in Grand Rapids, before he started his own company with money provided by his rich father-in-law. His big innovation had been to develop a better roller suspension for metal file cabinets—progressive roller bearings in a suspension-file drawer. His only son had died in childhood, leaving Dorothy, but women didn't run companies in those days, so eventually he turned it over to Dorothy's husband, Milton Devries. She'd spent her later years in her big, dark mansion in East Fenwick as the town matriarch, a social arbiter as fearsome as only a small-town society queen can be. She was on every board in town, chair-woman of most of them. Even though she liked Nick, and made him the CEO, she still looked down on him as being from a lower social class. Nick's dad, after all, had worked on the shop floor. Never mind that Dorothy was but one generation away from having machinist's grease on her own fingers.

Nick, reeling from Todd's casual revelation, saw Scott sitting down at his customary place at the oval mahogany board table. As Nick approached him, put a hand on his shoulder, he heard Todd saying, "Dorothy, I'd like you to meet Dan Finegold."

"Hey," Nick whispered, standing immediately behind Scott, "what's this about Atlas McKenzie?"

Scott craned his neck around, eyes wide. "Yeah, I just got the call on my cell at dinner last night—Todd happened to be there, you know . . ." His voice trailed off. Nick remained silent. Scott went on: "They went with Steelcase— you know, that joint venture Steelcase has with Gale and Wentworth—"

"They called *you*?"

"I guess I was on Hardwick's speed-dial, all those negotiations at the end—"

"You get bad news, you tell me first, understand?"

Nick could see Scott's pale face flush instantly. "I—of course, Nick, it was just that Todd was right there, you know, and—"

"We'll talk later," Nick said, giving Scott a shoulder squeeze too hard to be merely companionable.

He heard Dorothy Devries's brittle laugh from across the room, and he took his place at the head of the table.

The Stratton boardroom was the most conservative place in the head-quarters—the immense mahogany table with places for fifteen, even though there hadn't been fifteen board members since the takeover; the top-of-the-line black leather Stratton Symbiosis chairs, the slim monitors at each place that could be raised and lowered with the touch of a button. It looked like a boardroom in any big corporation in the world.

Nick cleared his throat, looked around at the board, and knew he was not among friends anymore. "Well, why don't we get started with the CFO's report?" he said.

36

Something about the way Scott went through his depressing presentation—his dry, monotone, doom-and-gloom voice-over to the PowerPoint slides projected on the little plasma screens in front of everyone—was almost defiant, Nick thought. As if he knew full well he was hurling carrion to the hyenas.

Of course, they didn't need his little dog-and-pony show, since they'd all gotten the charts in their black loose-leaf board books, FedExed to everyone yesterday, or couriered over to their hotel. But it was a board ritual, it had to go into the minutes, and besides, you couldn't assume that any of them had actually read through the materials.

Nick knew, however, that Todd Muldaur had read the financials closely, the instant he got them in Boston, the way some guys grab the sports section and devour the baseball box scores. Todd probably didn't wait even for the printouts; he'd surely gone through the Adobe PDF files and Excel spreadsheets as soon as Scott had e-mailed them.

Because his questions sounded awfully rehearsed. They weren't even questions, really. They were frontal assaults.

"I don't believe what I'm seeing here," he said. He looked around at the other board members—Dorothy, Davis Eilers, Dan Finegold—and the two "invited guests" who always attended the first half of the board meeting: Scott, and the Stratton general counsel who was here in her capacity as board secretary. Stephanie Alstrom was a small, serious woman with prematurely gray hair and a small, pruned mouth that seldom smiled. There was something juiceless, almost desiccated about Stephanie. Scott had once described her as a "raisin of anxiety," and the description had stuck in Nick's mind.

"This is a train wreck," Todd went on.

"Todd, there's no question these numbers look bad," Nick tried to put in.

"*Look* bad?" Todd shot back. "They *are* bad."

"My point is, this has been a challenging quarter—hell, a challenging year—for the entire sector," Nick said. "Office furniture is economically sensitive, we all know that. Companies stop buying stuff practically overnight when the economy slows."

Todd was staring at him, rattling Nick momentarily. "I mean, look, new office installations have plummeted, business startups and expansions have slowed to almost nothing," Nick went on. "Last couple of years, there's been serious overcapacity in the office furniture sector, and that, combined with weaker demand across the board, has put serious downward pressure on prices and profit margins."

"Nick," Todd said. "When I hear the word 'sector,' I reach for my barf bag."

Nick smiled involuntarily. "It's the reality," he said. He folded his arms, felt something crinkle in one of the breast pockets of his suit.

"If I may quote Willard Osgood," Todd went on, "'Explanations aren't excuses.' There's an *explanation* for everything."

"Uh, in all fairness to Nick," Scott put in, "he's just seeing these numbers for the first time."

"*What?*" said Todd. "Today? You mean, *I* saw these numbers before the CEO?" He turned to Nick. "You got something more important on your mind? Like, your daughter's *ballet recital* or something?"

Nick gave Scott a furious look. Yeah, it's the first time seeing the *real* numbers, he thought. Not the fudged ones you wanted to fob off on them. Nick was sorely tempted to let loose, but who knew where that might lead? Nervously, he fished inside the breast pocket of his suit and found a scrap of paper, pulled it out. It was a yellow Post-it note. Laura's handwriting: "Love you, babe. You're the best." A little heart and three X's. Tears immediately sprang to his eyes. He so rarely wore this suit that he must not have had it dry-cleaned last time he wore it, before Laura's death. He slipped the note carefully back where he'd found it.

"Come on, now, Todd," said Davis Eilers. "We're all dads here." Noticing Dorothy, he said, "Or moms." He ignored Stèphanie Alstrom, who had no kids and wasn't married and seemed to shrink into herself as she tapped away at her laptop.

Calm, Nick told himself, blinking away the tears. *Stay calm.* The room revolved slowly around him. "Scott means the final figures, Todd, but believe me, there's no surprise here. I take heart from the fact that our profit margins are still positive."

"No surprise?" Todd said. "No *surprise?* Let me tell you something, I don't really care how the rest of the sector's doing. We didn't buy Stratton because you're like everyone else, because you're *average.* We bought you because you were marquee. Same reason we use Stratton chairs and work panels and all that in our own offices in Boston, when we could have bought anything. Because you were the best in your space. Not just good enough. As Willard's so fond of saying, ' "Good enough" is *not* good enough.' "

"We're still the best," Nick said. "Bear in mind that we did our layoffs early—at your insistence, let me remind you. Everyone else waited. We got ahead of the curve."

"Fine, but you're still not delivering on your plan."

"To be fair," Scott pointed out, "Nick's plan didn't assume the economy was going to get worse."

"Scott," Todd said in a deadly quiet voice, "Nick's the CEO. He should have anticipated turns in the economy. Look, Nick, we always like to give our CEOs a lot of rope." He gave Nick a steady blue stare. What did that mean, anyway? Give a man enough rope and he'll hang himself—was that it? "We don't want to run your business—we want *you* to run your business," Todd went on. "But not if you're going to run it into the ground. At the end of the day, you work for us. That means that your job is to protect our investors' capital."

"And the way to protect your capital," Nick said, straining to remain civil, "is to invest in the business now, during the downturn. Now's the time to invest in new technology. That way, when the economy comes back, we kick butt." He looked at Dorothy. "Sorry." She didn't respond, her icy blue eyes focused on the middle distance.

Todd, leafing through his board book, looked up. "Like spending thirty million dollars in the last three years in development costs for a new *chair?*"

"A bargain," Nick said. "Design and retooling costs, twenty-six patents, two separate design teams. And that's actually less than Steelcase spent on their Leap chair, which turned out to be a great investment. Or Herman Miller spent on developing the Aeron chair. I mean, don't forget, product design and development is a core value at Stratton." Todd was silent for a moment. *Score one for the defense.* Before he could reply, Nick went on: "Now, if you want to continue this discussion, I'd like to move that we go into executive session." The motion was seconded and approved by voice vote. This was the point when Scott, as an invited guest but not a board member, normally got up to leave. Nick caught his eye, but Scott's expression was opaque, unreadable. He wasn't gathering his things, wasn't getting up.

"Listen, Nick, we're going to ask Scott to stay," Todd said.

"Really?" was all Nick could think to say. "That's—that's not the protocol."

Now Davis Eilers, who'd barely said a word, spoke up. "Nick, we've decided that it's time that Scott join the board formally. We really feel that Scott's become an important enough part of the management team that we'd like his official participation on the board. We think he can add a lot of value."

Nick, stunned, swallowed hard as he racked his brain for something to say. He tried to catch Scott's eye again, but Scott was avoiding his glance. He nodded, thought. The Dan Finegold thing was outrageous. But now, adding Scott as a board member without even telling him in advance, let alone pretending to seek his opinion? He wanted to call them on it, bring it all out into the open, but all he said was, "Well, he can certainly add value."

"Thanks for understanding," Eilers said.

"Uh, Nick, we're going to be making a few changes going forward," Todd said.

As opposed to what? Nick thought. *Going backward?* He said, "Oh?"

"We think this board should be meeting every month instead of quarterly."

Nick nodded. "That's a lot of travel to Fenwick," he said.

"Well, we can alternate between Boston and Fenwick," Todd said. "And we'll be looking to see the financials weekly instead of monthly."

"I'm sure that can be arranged," Nick said slowly. "As long as Scott doesn't mind." Scott was examining his board book closely and didn't look up.

"Nick," said Davis Eilers, "we've also been thinking that, if and when you decide to fire any of your direct reports—any of the executive managers—that's going to require board approval."

"Well, that's not what my contract says." He could feel his face start to prickle.

"No, but it's an amendment we'd be in favor of. Sort of making sure we're all on the same page, personnelwise. Like they say, the only constant is change."

"You guys are hiring me to do the best job I can," Nick said. "Enough rope, like you always say. And you just said you want me to run the company—you don't want to run it yourself."

"Of course," Eilers said.

Todd said, "We just don't want any surprises. You know, keep things running smoothly." He'd adopted a reasonable tone, no longer combative. He knew he'd won. "We've got an almost-two-billion-dollar company to run. That's a big job for anyone, even someone who's paying full attention. Hey, it's like football, you know? You may be the quarterback, but you're not going to have a winning team without linesmen and receivers and running backs—and coaches. Think of us as your coaches, right?"

Nick gave a slow, faint smile. "Coaches," he said. "Right."

When the board meeting came to an end an hour and a half later, Nick was the first to leave the room. He needed to get the hell out of there before he lost it. That wouldn't be good. I'm not going to quit, he told himself. Make them fire me. Quit and you get nothing. Get fired without cause, and the payoff was considerable. Five million bucks. That was in the contract he'd negotiated when he sold to Fairfield, when the idea of getting fired seemed like science fiction. He was a rock star then; they'd never dump him.

As he left, he noticed two people seated just outside the boardroom, a thuggy-looking blond man in a bad suit and a well-dressed, attractive black woman.

The woman Rinaldi had told him about.

The homicide detective.

The woman he'd seen at Stadler's funeral.

"Mr. Conover," she called out. "Could we talk to you for a few minutes?"

PART THREE
GUILT

37

Nick took them into one of the conference rooms. Talking at his home base was out of the question, given the way anyone, including Marjorie, could listen in.

He took the lead. He sat at the head of the table. The moment the two homicide detectives sat, he began speaking. He adopted a calm, authoritative tone, brisk but cordial. He was the head of a major corporation with a million things going on, and these two cops were here without an appointment, without even giving him the courtesy of a heads-up call. Yet he didn't want to diminish the importance of what they were doing. They were investigating the murder of a Stratton employee. He wanted them to feel that he took this seriously. It was a delicate balancing act.

He was scared shitless. He didn't like the fact that they'd just shown up at his workplace. There was something aggressive, almost accusatory about that. He wanted to let them know, through his tone and his attitude, that he didn't appreciate this, while at the same time communicating his respect for their mission.

"Detectives," he said, "I can spare maybe five minutes. You've caught me on my busiest day."

"Thanks for seeing us," said the black woman. The blond man blinked a few times, like a Komodo dragon admiring a delicious-looking goat, but said nothing. Nick could tell that he was going to be trouble. The black woman was sweetly apologetic, an obvious pushover. The blond man—Busbee? Bugbee?—was the one to watch.

"I wish you'd called my office and made an appointment. I'd be happy to talk to you at greater length another time."

"This shouldn't take that long," said the blond man.

"Tell me what I can do for you," Nick said.

"Mr. Conover, as you know, an employee of the Stratton Company was found dead last week," said the black woman. She was quite pretty, and there was something serene about her.

"Yes," Nick said. "Andrew Stadler. A terrible tragedy."

"Did you know Mr. Stadler?" she went on.

Nick shook his head. "No, unfortunately. We have five thousand employees—as many as ten thousand two years ago, before we had to let so many people go—and I can't possibly get to know everyone. Though I wish I could." He smiled wistfully.

"Yet you went to his funeral," she pointed out.

"Of course."

"You always go to the funerals of Stratton employees?" said the blond detective.

"Not always. When I can, though. I don't always feel welcome, not anymore. But I feel it's the least I can do."

"You never met Mr. Stadler, is that right?" the black woman said.

"Right."

"You were aware of his . . . situation, though, isn't that right?" she continued.

"His situation?"

"His personal troubles."

"I heard later that he'd been hospitalized, but plenty of people have mental illness and aren't violent."

"Oh?" the black detective said quickly. "How did you know he'd been hospitalized? Did you see his personnel file?"

"Didn't I read it in the newspaper?"

"There wasn't anything in the paper about that," said the blond man.

"Must've been," Nick said. There *had* been something in the paper, hadn't there? "Said something about a 'troubled emotional history' or something, right?"

"Nothing about hospitalization," the blond man said firmly.

"Someone must have mentioned it to me, then."

"Your corporate security director, Edward Rinaldi?"

"Possibly. But I don't recall."

"I see," the black woman said, jotting something down.

"Mr. Conover, did Edward Rinaldi tell you he thought Andrew Stadler was the guy who killed your dog?" the blond cop asked.

Nick squinted, as if trying to recall. He remembered asking Eddie about this.

Told her you didn't even know who the guy was. Pretty much true.

"I never even heard the name," Nick had said. *"Right? You tell her otherwise?"*

"Exactly. Told her you're a busy guy, I do my job, you don't get involved."

"Eddie didn't mention any names to me," Nick said.

"Is that right?" the woman said, sounding surprised.

Nick nodded. "To be honest, it's been a rough year. I'm the head of a company that's had to let half its employees go. There's a lot of anger out there, understandably."

"You're not the most popular man in town," she suggested.

"That's putting it mildly. I've gotten angry letters from downsized employees, really heartbreaking letters."

"Threats?" she asked.

"Could be, but I wouldn't know about them."

"How could you not know about threats?" the male cop said.

"I'm not the first to open my mail here. If I get a threatening letter, it goes right to Security—I never see it."

"You don't want to know?" he said. "Me, I'd want to know."

"Not me. Not unless I need to know for some reason. The less I know, the better."

"Really?" said the blond man.

"Really. I don't like to go around feeling paranoid. There's no point in it."

"Did Mr. Rinaldi tell you why he was looking into Mr. Stadler's background?" the black woman persisted.

"No. I didn't even know he was."

"He didn't tell you later he'd been looking into Stadler?" she persisted.

"Nope. He never told me anything about Stadler. I mean, I had no idea—*have* no idea—what Eddie was looking into. He does his job and I do mine."

"Mr. Rinaldi never even mentioned Stadler's name to you?" the woman said.

"Not that I recall, no."

"I'm confused," she said. "I thought you just said Mr. Rinaldi might have told you about Andrew Stadler's hospitalization. Which would sort of require him to mention Stadler's name, right?"

Nick felt the tiniest trickle of sweat run slowly down his earlobe. "After the news of Stadler's death came out, Eddie may have mentioned his name to me in passing. But I really don't recall."

"Hmm," the woman said. A few seconds of silence went by.

Nick ignored the sweat trickle, not wanting to call attention to it by brushing it away.

"Mr. Conover," said the blond man, "your house has been broken into a bunch of times in the last year, right? Since the layoffs began?"

"Several times, yes."

"By the same person?"

"It's hard to say. But I'd guess yeah, the same person."

"There was graffiti and such?"

"Graffiti spray-painted inside my house, on the walls."

"What kind of graffiti?" the black detective asked.

" 'No hiding place.' "

"That's what they wrote?"

"Right."

"Did you receive any death threats?"

"No. Ever since the layoffs started, two years ago, I've gotten occasional threatening phone calls, but nothing quite that specific."

"Well, your family dog was killed," said the blond detective. "That's sort of a death threat, wouldn't you say?"

Nick considered for a moment. "Possibly. Whatever it was, it was a sick, depraved thing to do." He worried that he'd just gone too far: had be just betrayed his anger? Yet how else would he be expected to react? He noticed that the black woman wrote something down in her notebook.

"The Fenwick police have any idea who did this?" the guy said.

"No idea."

"Does Mr. Rinaldi get involved in your personal security, outside the corporation?" the black detective asked.

"Informally, yeah," Nick said. "Sometimes. After this last incident, I asked him to put in a new security system."

"So you must have discussed the incident with him," she said.

Nick hesitated, a beat too long. What did Eddie tell them, exactly? Did Eddie tell them he came over to the house after Barney was slaughtered? He wished he'd talked to Eddie longer, found out everything he'd said. Shit. "A bit. I asked his advice, sure." He waited for the inevitable next question—inevitable to him, at least: did Eddie Rinaldi come to his house after Barney had been discovered in the pool? And what was the right answer?

Instead, the black detective said, "Mr. Conover, how long ago did you move into Fenwicke Estates?"

"About a year ago."

"After all the layoffs were announced?" she went on.

"About a year after."

"Why?"

Nick paused. "My wife insisted."

"Why was that?"

"She was concerned."

"About what?"

"That our family might be threatened."

"What made her so concerned?"

"Instinct, mostly. She knew there were a few people who might want to do us harm."

"So you did hear about threats," the black woman said. "But you just said you didn't know about any—you didn't *want* to know about them."

Nick folded his hands on the table. He was feeling increasingly frantic, trapped like some cornered animal, and he knew the only way to respond was to sound both reasonable and blunt. "Did I hear about specific threats? No. Did I hear that there *were* threats—that a few isolated fringe cases might have it in for me and my family? Sure. People talk. Rumors spread. I wasn't going to wait to see if there was any basis in these rumors. And I can tell you my wife sure as hell wasn't going to wait."

The two detectives seemed to accept his answer. "Before you moved to your new house, Mr. Conover, did you have any break-ins?"

"Not till we moved to Fenwicke Estates."

The blond detective smiled. "Guess the . . . *gated community* . . . didn't give you much protection, huh?" He put a surly spin on the words "gated community," made no attempt to conceal a note of smugness.

"Just takes longer to get in and out of," Nick admitted.

The blond guy chuckled, shook his head. "Costs a lot more, though, I bet."

"There you go."

"But you can afford it."

Nick shrugged. "Wasn't my idea to move there. It was my wife's."

"Your wife," said the black woman. "She—she passed away last year, isn't that right?"

"That's right."

"Nothing suspicious about her death, was there?"

A pause. "No, nothing suspicious," Nick said slowly. "She was killed in a car accident."

"You were driving?" she asked.

"She was driving."

"Nothing—was alcohol involved?"

"The other driver, yeah," Nick said. "A semi. He'd been drinking."

"But not you."

"No," he said. "Not me." He compressed his lips, then looked at his watch. "I'm afraid—"

The blond guy stood up. "Thanks for taking the time."

But the black woman remained seated. "Just a couple more things, sir?"

"Can we continue this some other time?" Nick said.

"Just—just another minute, if you don't mind. We don't want to leave any stone unturned. Do you own any guns, Mr. Conover?"

"Guns?" Nick shook his head. He hoped his face hadn't reddened.

"No handguns at all?"

"Nope. Sorry."

"Thank you. And last Tuesday night, where were you?"

"At home. I haven't traveled anywhere in ten days or so."

"What time did you go to sleep, do you remember?"

"Last Tuesday?"

"A week ago."

Nick thought a moment. "I went out for dinner Wednesday night. Tuesday I was at home."

"Do you remember what time you went to sleep?"

"I can't—well, I'm normally asleep by eleven, eleven-thirty."

"So you'd say by eleven-thirty you were in bed?"

"That sounds about right." She was smart, Nick realized. Smarter, he saw now, than the blond guy, who was all posture and attitude.

"Sleep through the night?"

"Sure." *Jesus*, he thought. What was she implying?

"Okay, great," she said. She got up. "That's all we need. We appreciate your taking the time to talk to us."

Nick rose, shook their hands. "Anytime," he said. "Just next time, give me some notice."

"We will," the black woman said. She stopped, appeared to hesitate. "I'm sorry to take up your time, Mr. Conover. But you know, our victims aren't just victims—they're human beings. Whatever their problems, whatever their difficulties, a man is dead. Someone who mattered to someone. We're all beloved by someone, you know."

"I'd like to think so," Nick said.

38

As soon as Nick showed the two homicide cops to the elevator, he returned to the boardroom, hoping to catch Todd Muldaur, but the room was empty. Todd and the others had left. He returned to his office area—hell, his *cubicle*—taking an indirect route, past Scott's area.

"Afternoon, Gloria," he said to Scott's admin, a small, hypercompetent woman with a broad face and blond hair cut in bangs. "Scott in?"

"Good afternoon, Mr. Conover. Scott's right—"

"Hey, Nick," Scott said, emerging from behind his panel. "Man, that was a rough ride today, huh?"

"Tell me about it," Nick said blandly. He kept on going, toward Scott's desk, to the round table where Scott held his conferences.

"That put root canals in a whole new perspective," Scott said. He began lifting piles of papers off the round table, moving them to a credenza next to his desk. "So what'd you think of that new guy, Finegold?"

"Seems nice enough," Nick said guardedly, standing at the table, waiting for Scott to finish clearing away the papers.

"That guy's rolling in it, you know. I mean, totally loaded. You know he hired that boy band 'N Sync to play at his daughter's bat mitzvah a couple of years back, when they were still hot?"

"He's a hot spare," Nick said.

"A what?"

"A hot spare. Disk drive fails, you swap it with a spare, all ready to go. Plug-'n'-play. Ready to go."

"Dan? Oh—no, I'm sure they're just trying to strengthen the bench. Is that the right sports term? He's a great guy, actually—tell you a funny story, when he was at—"

"I had to learn about Atlas McKenzie from *Todd*?" Nick broke in. "What the hell's up with that?"

Scott's face colored; he examined the tabletop. "I told you, I got the call from Hardwick on my way over to dinner," he said. "I tried you on your cell, but I guess it was off."

"You didn't leave a message."

"Well, it's—it wasn't the sort of thing you want to leave in a voice mail, you know—"

"And you didn't e-mail me? You didn't call me this morning before the board meeting? You let me find out from *Todd* fucking *Muldaur*?"

Scott's hands flew up, palms out. "I didn't have a chance—"

"And you didn't have a *chance* to tell me they wanted to put you on the board?" Nick said.

Scott stared at the white Formica tabletop as if he'd just seen something alarming there. "I didn't," he began, falteringly.

"*Don't* tell me you didn't know that was going to happen. Why the hell didn't you mention it to me? You couldn't reach me on my cell, that it?"

"It—it wasn't my place, Nick," Scott said. He looked up at last, face gone burgundy, eyes watering. His voice was meek but his expression was fierce.

"Not your place? The fuck are you telling me? You knew they were going to put you on the board and it wasn't your place to tell me that? You kept their little secret, embarrassed me in front of the board?"

"Hey, come on, Nick, calm down," Scott said. "All right? It was complicated—I mean, maybe I should have said something, in retrospect, but Todd wanted me to keep it—Nick, you should take it up with Todd."

Nick got up. "Yeah," he said. "I just might do that."

Don't fuck with me, he thought. Almost said it, but at the last second something stopped him.

———

As he returned to his desk, Marge stopped him, holding up an envelope.

"This just came in from HR," she said. "That check you requested."

"Thanks," he said, taking the envelope as he resumed walking.

"Nick," she said.

He stopped, turned around.

"That check—for Cassie Stadler?"

"Yeah?"

"That's a lot of money. It's for her dad's severance pay, isn't it? Which he lost when he quit?"

Nick nodded.

"The company isn't obligated to pay that, right?"

"No, it's not."

"But it's the right thing to do. It's—that's nice, Nick." There were tears in her eyes.

Nick nodded again, returned to his desk. He immediately picked up his handset and called Todd Muldaur's cell phone. It rang three times, four, and just as Nick was about to hang up, Todd's voice came on. "This is Todd."

It sounded like a prerecorded voice-mail message, so Nick waited a second before saying, "Todd, it's Nick Conover."

"Oh, hey, Nick, there you are. You bolted before I had a chance to say goodbye, dude."

"Todd, are you trying to squeeze me out?"

A beat. "What makes you say that?"

"Come on, man. What happened in there, in the board meeting. Bring in Finegold, your hot spare, putting Scott on the board without giving me a heads-up. The monthly board meetings, the weekly financials. Changing the rules of the game like that. Taking away my ability to change my team the way I see fit. What, you think I'm an idiot?"

"Nick, we don't need to squeeze you out," Todd said, his voice gone steely. "If we wanted you gone, you'd be gone."

"Not without a pretty damned huge payday."

"A rounding error at Fairfield Partners, buddy."

"Five million bucks is a rounding error to you guys?"

"Nick, I meant what I said. We want to bring more to the table. Strengthen the team."

"You don't trust me to run the company, you should just come out with it."

Todd said something, but the signal started to break up ". . . the way," he was saying.

"Say again?" Nick said. "I lost you there."

"I said, we trust you, Nick. We just don't want you getting in the way."

"In the *way*?"

"We need to make sure you're responsive, Nick. That's all. We want to make sure you're on board."

"Oh, *I'm* on board," Nick said, deliberately ambiguous, insinuating. He didn't know what that was supposed to mean, exactly, except that he hoped it sounded vaguely threatening.

"Excellent," Todd said. His voice got all crackly again as the signal weakened. A fragment: ". . . to hear."

"Say again?" Nick said.

"Man, do you guys have, like, one cell tower out here in cow town? I swear, the reception *sucks*. All right, I better go. I'm losing you." Then the line went dead.

For a long time, Nick stared at the long blue Stratton check he'd had the treasurer's office cut for Cassie Stadler: a payoff, pure and simple. Andrew Stadler had quit before being laid off; legally, he wasn't entitled to any severance. But what was legal, and what the courts might decide—if Cassie Stadler decided to press the issue—were two separate things. Better to pre-empt, he'd decided. Be generous. Show her that her father's employer meant well, that Stratton was willing to go above and beyond what it was required to do.

That was all there was to it, he told himself.

Keep the woman happy. No one wanted a lawsuit.

And he remembered what that black woman detective had said as she left. "We're all beloved by someone," she'd said. She had a point. As crazy, as deranged as Andrew Stadler was, he'd been loved by his daughter.

He hit the intercom button. "Marge," he said. "I need you to call Cassie Stadler for me."

"I believe she's living in her father's house," came Marge's voice over the speakerphone.

"Right. Tell her I want to stop by. I have something for her."

39

Sergeant Jack Noyce pulled Audrey into his glass-walled office, which was not much bigger than Audrey's cubicle. He had it outfitted with an expensive-looking sound system, though, a top-of-the-line DVD player and speakers. Noyce loved his audio equipment, and he loved music. Sometimes Audrey would see him with his headphones on, enjoying music, or listening to the speakers with the office door closed.

As head of the Major Case Team, he had all sorts of administrative responsibilities and more than a dozen cops to supervise, and he spent much of his day in meetings. Music—Keith Jarrett, Bill Evans, Art Tatum, Charlie Mingus, Thelonious Monk, all the jazz piano greats—seemed to be his only escape.

A piece was playing quietly on Noyce's stereo, a beautiful and soulful rendition of the ballad "You Go to My Head," a pianist doing the melody.

"Tommy Flanagan?" Audrey said.

Noyce nodded. "You close your eyes, and you're back in the Village Vanguard."

"It's lovely."

"Audrey, you haven't said anything about Bugbee." His sad eyes, behind thick aviator-framed glasses, shone with concern.

"It's okay," she said.

"You'd tell me if it wasn't, right?"

She laughed. "Only if I couldn't take it anymore."

"'The practical jokes seem to have stopped."

"Maybe he got tired of them."

"Or maybe he's learned to respect you."

"You give him way too much credit," she said with a laugh.

"And you're the one who's supposed to believe in the possibility of redemption. Listen, Audrey—you guys went over to Stratton?"

"Now don't tell me he's filling you in on every step we take."

"No. I got a call from the security director at Stratton."

"Rinaldi."

"Right. You talked to him, and then you both went over to talk to Nicholas Conover."

"What'd he call you for?"

"He says you just showed up and waited for Conover outside a board meeting? That true?"

She felt a prickle of defensiveness. "That was my decision. I wanted to avoid any prepared answers, any coordination."

"I'm not following." Noyce took off his glasses and began rubbing at them with a little cleaning cloth.

"I'd already talked to Rinaldi, and something didn't sit right with me. I can't explain it."

"You don't need to. Gut instinct."

"Right."

"Which ninety percent of the time doesn't pan out. But hey." He smiled. "You take what you get."

"I didn't want Rinaldi talking to his boss and getting his story straight."

"So you just ambushed the CEO outside the boardroom?" Noyce laughed quietly.

"I just thought if we set up a meeting with him in advance, he'd call his security director and say, what's this about?"

"Still not following. You telling me you think the CEO of Stratton's got something to do with this case?"

She shook her head. "No, of course not. But there may be some connection. A couple of days before Stadler's death, there was an incident at Nicholas Conover's house. Someone slaughtered the family dog and dumped it in the swimming pool."

Noyce winced. "My God. Was it Stadler?"

"We don't know. But this was just the latest of a long series of incidents at the Conover house since they moved in, about a year ago. Up till now it's been graffiti, nothing stolen, no violence. But each time, our uniformed division was notified—and we haven't done a thing. They didn't even print the knife that was used to kill the dog. From what I hear, there wasn't a lot of motivation to do anything about it, given the way people feel about Conover."

"Well, yeah, but that's not right."

"So just before Stadler's death, Rinaldi got in touch with our uniformed division to ask about this guy Andrew Stadler and find out if he had any priors."

"And were there any?"

"A long time ago Stadler was questioned in connection to the death of a neighbor family, but nothing ever came of it."

"What got Rinaldi interested in Andrew Stadler?"

"Rinaldi said he went through the list of people they laid off—and it's a long list, like five thousand people—to see who might have exhibited signs of violence."

"Stadler did?"

"Rinaldi was evasive on that point. When I interviewed Stadler's supervisor, at the model shop where he worked, the guy said Stadler wasn't violent at all. Though he did quit in anger, which meant he lost the severance package. But Rinaldi said he found that Stadler had a history of mental illness."

"So he suspected Stadler of being Conover's stalker."

"He denies it, but that's the feeling I got."

"So you think Conover or Rinaldi had something to do with Stadler's murder?"

"I don't know. But I do wonder about this Rinaldi fellow."

"Oh, I know about Rinaldi."

"He said you're friends, you two."

Noyce chuckled. "Did he, now."

"He didn't exactly play by the rules on the GRPD. He was squeezed out on suspicions of holding onto cash in a drug bust."

"How do you know that?" Noyce was suddenly intrigued.

"I called Grand Rapids, asked around until I found someone who knew him."

Noyce frowned, shook his head. "I'd rather you didn't call GR."

"Why not?"

"People talk. Rumors spread like wildfire. Things could get back to Rinaldi, and I don't want him knowing that we've been asking around about him. That way we're more likely to catch him in a lie."

"Okay, makes sense."

"You saying you like Rinaldi for the Stadler homicide?"

"That's not what I'm saying. Edward Rinaldi's an ex-cop, and a guy like that may know people, you know?"

"Who might have done a hit on some loony ex-employee?" Noyce replaced his glasses, raised one brow.

"Far-fetched, right?"

"Just a little."

"But no more unlikely than a crack-related murder involving a guy who doesn't fit the profile of a crackhead, had no crack in his bloodstream, and had fake crack in his pocket. A setup, in other words."

"You make a good point."

"Also, no fingerprints anywhere on the plastic wrapped over the body. Traces of talc indicating that surgical gloves were used to move the body. It's all very strange. I'd like to get Rinaldi's phone records."

Noyce gave a long sigh. "Man, you're opening a can of worms with Stratton."

"What about Rinaldi's personal phone records—home, cell, whatever?"

"Easier."

"Could you sign off on that?"

Noyce bit his lip. "Sure. I'll do it. You got an instinct, I like to go with it. But Audrey, listen. The Stratton Corporation has a lot of enemies in this town."

"Tell me about it."

"That's why I want to be fair. I don't want it to look like we're going after them arbitrarily, trying to embarrass them. Bowing to public pressure, pandering. Nothing like that. I want us to play fair, but just as important, I want the *appearance* of fairness, okay?"

"Of course."

"Just so long as we're on the same page here."

40

Cassie Stadler's house was on West Sixteenth Street, in the part of Fenwick still known as Steepletown because of all the churches that used to be there. It was an area Nick knew well; he'd grown up here, in a tiny brown split-level with a little scrubby lawn, a chain-link fence keeping out the neighbors. When Nick was a kid, Steepletown was blue-collar, most of the men factory workers employed at Stratton. Mostly Polish Catholic, too, though the Conovers were neither Polish nor members of Sacred Heart. This was a place where people kept their money in mattresses.

He was overcome by a strange, wistful nostalgia driving through these streets. It all looked and smelled so familiar, the American Legion hall, the bowling alley, the pool hall. The triple-deckers, the aluminum siding, Corky's Bottled Liquors. Even the cars were still big and American. Unlike the rest of Fenwick, which had gone upscale and fancy, vegan and latte, with all the galleries and the SUVs and the BMWs, something uncomfortable and ill fitting about it, like a little girl playing dress up in her mother's high heels. Just before he parked the car at the curb in front of the house, a song came on the radio: Billy Joel's "She's Always a Woman." One of Laura's favorites. She'd taught herself to play it on the piano, not badly at all. She'd sing it in the shower—"*Oh, she takes care of herself . . .*"—badly, off-key, in a thin, wobbly voice. Hearing it caused a lump to rise in Nick's throat. He switched the radio off, couldn't take it, and had to sit there in the car for a few minutes before he got out.

He rang the doorbell: six melodious tones sounding like a carillon. The door opened, a small figure emerging from the gloom behind the dusty screen door.

What the hell am I doing? he thought. Jesus, this is insane. The daughter of the man I killed.

Everyone is beloved by someone, the cop had said.

This is that someone.

"Mr. Conover," she said. She wore a black T-shirt and worn jeans. She was slim, even tinier than he remembered from the funeral, and her expression was hard, wary.

"May I come in for a second?"

Her eyes were red-rimmed, raccoon smudges beneath. "Why?"

"I have something for you."

She stared some more, then shrugged. "Okay." The bare minimum of politeness, nothing more. She pushed open the screen door.

Nick entered a small, dark foyer that smelled of mildew and damp carpeting. Mail lay in heaps on a trestle table. There were a few homey touches—a painting in an ornate gold frame, a bad seascape, looked like a reproduction. A vase of dried flowers. A lamp with a fringed shade. A sampler in a severe black frame, done in needlepoint or whatever, that said LET ME LIVE IN THE HOUSE BY THE SIDE OF THE ROAD AND BE A FRIEND TO MAN, over a stitched image of a house that looked a good deal nicer than the one it hung in. It seemed as if nothing had been moved, or dusted, in a decade. He caught a glimpse of a small kitchen, a big old white round-shouldered refrigerator.

She backed up a few steps, standing in a cone of light from a torchiere. "What's this all about?"

Nick produced the envelope from his jacket pocket and handed it to her. She took it, gave a puzzled look, examined the envelope as if she'd never seen one before. Then she slid out the pale blue check. When she saw the amount, she betrayed no surprise, no reaction at all. "I don't get it."

"The least we can do," Nick said.

"What's it for?"

"The severance pay your father should have gotten."

Realization dawned in her eyes. "My dad quit."

"He was a troubled man."

She flashed a smile, bright white teeth, that in another context would have been sexy. Now it seemed just unsettling. "This is so interesting," she said. Her voice was velvety smooth, pleasingly deep. There was something about her mouth, the way it curled up at the ends even when she wasn't smiling, giving her a kind of knowing look.

"Hmm?"

"This," she said.

"The check? I don't understand."

"No. You. What you're doing here."

"Oh?"

"It's like you're making a payoff."

"A payoff? No. Your father should have been counseled better at his outplacement interview. We shouldn't have let him walk out without the same severance package everyone else got, whether he quit or not. He was angry, and rightly so. But he was a longtime employee who deserved better than that."

"It's a hell of a lot of money."

"He worked for Stratton for thirty-six years. It's what he was entitled to. Maybe not legally, but morally."

"It's guilt money. *Schuldgeld,* in German, right?" Those corners of her mouth turned all the way up in a canny smile. Closer to a smirk, maybe. "The word guilt has the same root as the German word for money, *Geld.*"

"I wouldn't know." He felt his insides clutch tight. "I just didn't think you should be left high and dry."

"God, I don't know how you can stand doing what you do."

She has the right to go after me, Nick thought. *Let her. Let her rant, do her whole anti-corporate thing. Trash Stratton, and me. Make her feel better. Maybe that's why you're here: masochism.*

"Ah, right," he said. " 'Slasher Nick' and all that."

"I mean, it can't be easy. Being hated by just about everyone in town."

"Part of my job," he said.

"Must be nice to have one."

"Sometimes yes, sometimes no."

"Life must have been a lot easier a couple of years ago when everyone loved you, I bet. You must have felt you were really in the groove, hitting on all cylinders. Then all of a sudden you're the bad guy."

"It's not a popularity contest." *The hell was this?*

A mysterious smile. "A man like you wants to be liked. *Needs* to be liked."

"I should be going."

"I'm making you uncomfortable," she said. "You're not the introspective type." A beat. "Why are you really here? Don't trust the messenger service?"

Nick shook his head vaguely. "I'm not sure. Maybe I feel really bad for you. I lost my wife last year. I know how hard this can be."

When she looked up at him, there seemed to be a kind of pain in the depths of her hazel eyes. "Kids?"

"Two. Girl and a boy."

"How old?"

"Julia's ten. Lucas is sixteen."

"God, to lose your mother at that age. I guess there's always enough pain to go around at the banquet of life. Plenty of seconds, right?" She sounded as if the wind had suddenly gone out of her.

"I've got to get back. I'm sorry if it bothered you, me coming by like this."

Suddenly she sank to the floor, collapsing into a seated position on the wall-to-wall carpet, canting to one side. Her legs folded up under her. She supported herself with one arm. "Jesus," she said.

"You okay?" Nick came up to her, leaned over.

Her other hand was against her forehead. Her eyes were closed. Her translucent skin was ashen.

"Jesus, I'm sorry. All the blood just left my head, and I . . ."

"What can I get you?"

She shook her head. "I just need to sit down. Light-headed."

"Glass of water or something?" He kneeled beside her. She looked like she was on the verge of toppling over, passing out. "Food, maybe?"

She shook her head again. "I'm fine."

"I don't think so. Stay there, I'll get you something."

"I'm not going anywhere," she said, her eyes unfocused. "Forget it, don't worry about it. I'm fine."

Nick got up, went into the kitchen. Dirty dishes were piled up in the sink and on the counter next to it, a bunch of Chinese takeout cartons. He looked around, found the electric stove, a kettle sitting on one burner. He picked it up, felt it was empty. He filled it in the sink, shoving aside some of the stacked plates to make room for the kettle. It took him a couple of seconds to figure out which knob on the stove turned on which burner. The burner took a long time to go from black to orange.

"You like Szechuan Garden?" he called out.

Silence.

"You okay?" he said.

"It's pretty gross, actually," she said after another pause, voice weak. "There's like two, maybe three Chinese restaurants in this whole town, one worse than the next." Another pause. "There's more than that on my *block* in Chicago."

"Looks like you get a lot of takeout from there anyway."

"I can walk to it. I haven't felt much like cooking, since . . ."

She was standing at the threshold to the kitchen, entered slowly and un-steadily. She sank down in one of the kitchen chairs, chrome with a red vinyl seat back, the table red Formica with a cracked ice pattern and chrome banding around the edge.

The teakettle was making a hollow roaring sound. Nick opened the re-frigerator—"Frigidaire" on the front in that great old squat script, raised metal lettering, reminding Nick of the refrigerator in his childhood home—and found it pretty much empty. A quart of skim milk, an opened bottle of Australian chardonnay with a cork in it; a carton of eggs, half gone.

He found a rind of Parmesan cheese, a salvageable bunch of scallions.

"You got a grater?"

"You serious?"

41

He set the omelet on the table before her, a fork and a paper napkin, a mug of tea. The mug, he noticed too late, had the old 1970s Stratton logo on one side.

She dug into it, eating ravenously.

"When's the last time you ate today?" Nick asked.

"Right now," she said. "I forgot to eat."

"Forgot?"

"I've had other things on my mind. Hey, this isn't bad."

"Thank you."

"I wouldn't have figured you for a chef."

"That's about the extent of my cooking ability."

"I feel way better already. Thank you. I thought I was going to pass out."

"You're welcome. I saw some salami in there, but I thought you might be a vegan or something."

"Vegans don't eat eggs," she said. "Yum. God, you know, there's some kinds of ribbon worms that actually eat themselves if they don't find any food."

"Glad I got here in time."

"The head of Stratton makes a mean omelet. Wait till the newspapers get hold of that."

"So how did you end up in Chicago?"

"Long story. I grew up here. But my mom grew tired of my dad's craziness, when I was like nine or ten. That was before he was diagnosed as schizophrenic. She moved to the Windy City and left me here with Dad. A couple of years later, I went to live with her and her new husband. Hey, this is my house, and I'm not being much of a hostess."

She got up, went over to one of the lower cabinets, opened the door. It held a collection of dusty bottles, vermouth and Bailey's Irish Cream and such. "Let me guess—you're a Scotch kinda guy."

"I've got to get home to the kids."

"Oh," she said. "Right. Sure." Something waiflike and needy in her face got to him. He'd told Marta an hour or so; another hour wouldn't be a big deal.

"But maybe a little Scotch would be okay."

She seemed to light up, leaned over and pulled out a bottle of Jameson's. "Irish, not Scotch—okay?"

"Fine with me."

She pulled out a cut-glass tumbler from the same cabinet. "Whoo boy," she said, blowing a cloud of dust out of it. She held it under the running tap in the sink. "I'm going to say rocks."

"Hmm?"

"Ice cubes. You drink your whiskey on the rocks." She went to the antique Frigidaire, opened the freezer, took out the kind of ice tray Nick hadn't seen in decades, aluminum with the lever you pull up to break the ice into cubes. She yanked back the handle, making a scrunching sound that sounded like his childhood. Reminded him of his dad, who liked his Scotch on the rocks, every night and too much of it.

She plopped a handful of jagged cubes into the glass, glugged in a few inches of whiskey, came over and handed it to him. She looked directly into his eyes, the first time she'd done that. Her eyes were big and gray-green and lucid, and Nick felt a tug in his groin. He immediately felt a flush of shame. *Jesus*, he thought.

"Thanks," he said. The glass had FAMOUS GROUSE etched into it. It was the kind of thing you get at a liquor store packed with the bottle, a promotional deal.

"How about you?"

"I hate whiskey," she said. The kettle began whistling shrilly. She pulled it off the burner, found a carton of teabags in a drawer, and poured herself a mug of herbal tea.

"How does it feel being home?" The whiskey had a pleasant bite to it, and he felt its effect immediately. He didn't recall when he'd last eaten anything himself, actually.

"Strange," she said, sitting down at the table. "Brings a lot of things back. Some good things, some not good things." She looked at him. "I don't expect you to understand."

"Try me."

"Do you know what it's like to have a parent with severe mental illness? The whole point is, you're a child, so you don't grasp what's going on."

"Right. How could you?"

Cassie closed her eyes, and it was as if she were in some other place. "So you're his beloved daughter, and he hugs you like nobody can hug you and he puts his forehead to yours and you feel so safe, and so loved, and everything's right with the world. And then, one day, he's different—except, as far as he's concerned, *you're* different."

"Because of the disease."

"He looks at you and you're a stranger to him. You're not his beloved daughter now. Maybe you resemble her, but he's not fooled, he knows you've been replaced by someone or something else. He looks at you and he sees a Fembot, you know? And you say, 'Daddy!' You're three or four or five and you throw your arms open, waiting for your super-special hug. And he says, 'Who are you? Who are you *really*?' and he says, 'Get away! Get away! Get away!' " Her mimicry was uncanny; Nick was beginning to glimpse the nightmare she had endured. "You realize that he's *terrified* of you. And it's different from anything you've ever experienced. Because it isn't what happens when, you know, you misbehave, and Mommy or Daddy turns red and you get yelled at. Every kid knows what that's like. They're mad. But you know they still love you, and they're still aware of your *existence*. They don't think you're an alien. They're not frightened of you. It's different when a parent has schizophrenia. It steals over them, and suddenly you don't exist to them any longer. You're not a daughter anymore. Just some impostor. Just some intruder. Some . . . outsider. Someone who doesn't belong." She smiled sadly.

"He was ill."

"He was ill," Cassie repeated. "But a child doesn't understand that. A child *can't* understand it. Even if anybody had explained to me, I probably wouldn't have understood." She sniffed, her eyes flooded with tears. She frowned, turned away, wiped her eyes with her T-shirt, exposing her flat belly, a tiny pouting navel. Nick tried not to look.

"Nobody ever told you what was going on?"

"When I was maybe thirteen, I finally figured it out. My mother didn't want to deal, and her way of not dealing meant you didn't talk about it. Which is pretty crazy, too, when you think about it."

"I can't imagine what you had to go through." And he couldn't—not what she'd had to go through, nor what her father's death was causing her to relive. He ached to do something for her.

"No, you can't imagine. But it messes with your head. I mean, it messed with mine."

She tucked her chin in close to her chest, ran her fingers through her spiky hair, and when she looked up, her cheeks were wet. "You don't need this," she said, her voice thick with tears. "I think you should go."

"Cassie," he said. It came out in a whisper, sounded far more intimate than he'd intended.

For a while, her breaths came in short little puffs. When she spoke again, her voice was strained. "You need to be there for your kids," she said. "There's nothing more important than family, okay?"

"Not much of a family these days."

"Don't say that," Cassie said. She looked up at him, eyes fierce. "You don't *fucking* talk that way, *ever*." Something had flared up inside her, like a whole book of matches, and then subsided almost as quickly. But who could blame the woman, having so recently put her father in the ground? And then he remembered why.

"Sorry," he said. "It hasn't been easy for the kids, and I'm not exactly doing my job."

"How'd she die?" Her voice was soft. "Their mother."

He took another sip. A quick scene played in his head, jittery, badly spliced film. The pebbles of glass strewn throughout Laura's hair. The spiderwebbed windshield. "I don't like to talk about it."

"Oh, I'm sorry."

"Don't apologize. Natural question."

"No, you're—crying."

He realized that he was, and as he turned his face, embarrassed, cursing the booze, she got up from her chair, came up to him. She put a small warm hand on his face, leaned close to him, and put her lips on his.

Startled, he backed away, but she moved in closer, pressed her lips against his, harder, her other hand pressed against his chest.

He turned his head away. "Cassie, I've got to get home."

Cassie smiled uncomfortably. "Go," she said. "Your kids are waiting."

"It's the babysitter, actually. She hates it when I come home later than I promised."

"Your daughter—what's her name, again?"

"Julia."

"Julia. Sweet name. Go home to Julia and Luke. They need you. Go back to your gated community."

"How'd you know?"

"People talk. It's perfect."

"What?"

"You living in a gated community."

"I'm not really the gated-community type."

"Oh, I think you are," she said. "More than you know."

42

LaTonya's twelve-year-old daughter, Camille, was practicing piano in the next room, which made it hard for Audrey to concentrate on what her sister-in-law was saying. LaTonya was speaking in a low voice, uncharacteristically for her, while she removed a sweet-potato casserole from the oven.

"Let me tell you," LaTonya said, "if Paul didn't have a steady income, I don't know how we'd get by with three kids still in the house."

Audrey, who'd noticed the kitchen piled high with cartons of thermogenic fat-burning supplements, said, "But what about the vitamins?"

"Shit!" LaTonya shouted, dropping the casserole to the open oven door. "These damned oven mitts have a hole in them—what the hell good are they?"

Thomas, who was nine, ran in from the dining room where he and Matthew, eleven, were allegedly setting the table, though mostly just clattering the dishes and giggling. "You okay, Mom?"

"I'm fine," LaTonya said, picking up the casserole again and putting it on the stovetop. "You get back out there and finish setting the table, and you tell Matthew to go tell your father and Uncle Leon to get off their lazy butts and come in to dinner." She turned to Audrey, a disgusted look on her face. "Once again, I'm ahead of the curve."

"How so?"

"These thermogenic supplements. Fenwick is a backward, fearful community," she said gravely. "They do *not* want to try new things."

"And now you're stuck with all these bottles."

"If they think I'm paying for them, they've got another think coming. I'm going to ask you to read the small print on my agreement, because I don't think they can get away with it."

"Sure," Audrey said without enthusiasm. The last thing she wanted to do was get involved in extricating LaTonya from another mess she'd created. "You know, the money isn't the worst part," Audrey said. "I mean, it's not easy, but we can get by."

"Not having kids," LaTonya pointed out.

"Right. It's dealing with Leon."

"What the *hell* does he do all day?" LaTonya demanded, one hand on her left hip, waggling the other hand to cool it off.

"He watches a lot of TV and he drinks," Audrey said.

"You see, I knew this would happen. We spoiled him growing up. The baby of the family. Anything he wanted, he got. My momma and me, we waited on him hand and foot, and now you're paying the price. You hear what I hear?"

"I don't hear anything."

"Exactly." She shouted, earsplittingly loud, "Camille, you've got twenty more minutes of practicing, so don't stop now!"

An anguished, garbled protest came from the next room.

"And you don't get any supper until you're done, so *move* it!" She glowered at Audrey. "Honestly, I don't know what's wrong with her ownself. She pays me no mind at all."

Dinner was meat loaf, macaroni and cheese, collards, and sweet-potato casserole, everything heavy and greasy but delicious. Leon sat next to his sister at one end of the table, LaTonya's husband at the other, the two squirming boys on one side facing Audrey and Camille's empty place.

The sound of the piano came from the living room, sporadic, sullen. Brahms, Audrey recognized. A pretty piece. A waltz, maybe? Her niece was struggling with it.

Thomas squawked with laughter over something, and Matthew said, "Fuck you!"

LaTonya exploded: "Don't you *ever* use language like that in this house, you hear me?"

The two boys fell instantly silent. Matthew, looking like a whipped puppy, said, "Yes, ma'am."

"That's right," LaTonya said.

Audrey caught the younger boy's eye and gave him a mildly disapproving look that was still, she hoped, filled with auntly love.

Leon was stuffing his face meanwhile. He said, "I wish I could eat supper here every night, LaTonya."

She beamed, then caught herself. "Is there any reason you can't get yourself a job?"

"Doing what?" Leon said, dropping his fork dramatically. "Operating an electrostatic spray gun at the Seven-Eleven, maybe?"

"Doing something," LaTonya said.

"Doing something?" Leon said. "Like what? Like what do you think a guy with my skills can do here?"

"Your skills," LaTonya scoffed.

"How do you think it feels getting laid off?" Leon said, his voice rising. "Do you have any idea? How do you think I feel about myself?"

"I'll tell you how I feel about you sitting around doing absolutely nothing," LaTonya said. She cocked her head. "Camille," she shouted, "what are you doing?"

Another muffled cry.

"We're all eating in here," LaTonya yelled. "We're likely to finish dinner without you, rate you're practicing."

Camille screamed back, "I can't stand it!"

"You can yell all you want," LaTonya bellowed. "Won't make any difference. You're not getting over on me."

"Let me talk to her," Audrey said. She excused herself from the table, went into the next room.

Camille was weeping at the piano, her head resting on her elbows atop the keys. Audrey sat down at the bench next to her. She stroked her niece's hair, lingering on the kitchen, that kinky hair at the nape of her neck. "What is it, honey?"

"I can't stand it," Camille said. She sat up. Her face was streaked with tears. She looked genuinely upset; it was no act. "I don't understand this. This is torture."

Audrey looked at the sheet music. Brahms's Waltz in A Minor. "What don't you get, baby?"

Camille touched the music with a pudgy, tear-damp finger, making a tiny pucker.

"The trill, is that it?"

"I guess."

Audrey nudged Camille over a bit and played a few measures. "Like that?"

"Yeah, but I can't do that."

"Try this." Audrey played the trill slowly. "Down an octave."

Camille placed her fingers on the keyboard and tried.

"Like this," Audrey said, playing again.

Camille imitated her. Close enough. "That's it, baby. You got it. Try it again."

Camille played it, got it right.

"Now go back a couple of measures. To here. Let me hear it."

Camille played the first two lines of the second page.

"Boy, are you a fast learner," Audrey marveled. "You don't even need me anymore."

Camille smiled faintly.

"When's your recital?"

"Next week."

"What are you doing besides this?"

"Little Prelude."

"Beethoven?"

Camille nodded.

"Can I come?"

Camille smiled again, this time a happy grin. "You think you have time?"

"I'll make time, baby. I'd love to. Now, hurry up and finish. I'm getting lonely at the table without you."

———

Paul looked up as Audrey entered the dining room. He was a pigeon-chested man with sunken cheeks, a recessive gene but a sweet-natured guy. Camille was back at the Brahms, strong and enthusiastic. "I don't know what you threatened her with, but sounds like it worked," he said.

"She probably pulled out her handcuffs," said LaTonya.

"Probably her gun," Leon mumbled. He seemed to have calmed down in the meantime, retreated back into his old, monosyllabic self.

"No," Audrey said, sitting down. "She just needed a little help figuring something out."

"I want an ice cream sundae for dessert," the younger boy said.

"I'll be the judge of that," said LaTonya. "Right now it's looking awful grim for you."

"How come?"

"You got more than half your meat loaf left. Now Audrey, what are you working on these days?"

"It's not dinner-table conversation," Audrey said.

"I don't mean the gory details."

"I'm afraid it's all gory details," Audrey said.

"She's working on that murder of the Stratton worker got murdered down on Hastings," Leon said.

Audrey was amazed he even knew what she was working on. "People aren't supposed to know what I'm doing," she told him.

"We're all family here," said LaTonya.

"Right, but still," said Audrey.

"No one's going to say anything, my seddity sister," LaTonya said. "You think we know anybody? This guy fell off the edge, that right? Get into crack and other poisons like that?" She cast an evil eye at her two sons.

"I met the guy," Leon said.

"Who?" said Audrey. "Andrew Stadler?"

Leon nodded. "Sure. He kept to himself, but I talked to him in the break room once or twice." Leon reached for the macaroni and cheese and shoveled a huge lump onto his plate, a third helping. "Couldn't meet a nicer guy."

"A troubled man," Audrey said.

"Troubled?" said Leon. "I don't know. Gentle as a lamb, I'll tell you that."

"Really?" said Audrey.

"Gentle as a lamb," Leon said again.

"I'm done," Camille announced, entering the room and sitting down next to Audrey. She found Audrey's hand under the table and gave it a little secret squeeze. Audrey's heart fluttered for a moment.

"Took you long enough," said LaTonya. "I hope you learned your lesson."

"You sounded great," Audrey said.

43

Nick got in a little earlier than usual, got a cup of coffee from the executive lounge, and checked his e-mail. As usual, his inbox was cluttered with offers for Viagra and penis enlargement and low-interest mortgages, the subject headings inventively misspelled. The putative wives and sons of various deceased African heads of state urgently sought his assistance in transferring millions of dollars out of their country.

He thought about this woman, Cassie Stadler. She was not only seriously attractive, but she was unlike any woman he'd ever met before. And she—who, of course, had no idea what he'd done—was clearly as attracted to him as he was to her.

No message from the Atlas McKenzie guys—the mammoth deal that had unaccountably fallen through—but that didn't surprise him. He was going to have to confront them on it, find out what the reason was, see if there was a way to sweet-talk them back on board.

Marjorie wasn't in yet, so Nick placed the calls himself. It was 7:10 A.M. The Atlas McKenzie guys were usually in by then. Ten digits away. Not a lot of work to press those ten digits on the telephone keypad. How many calories did this take? Nick imagined a tiny scrap of the twiggy cereal Julia wouldn't eat: *that* many calories. Why wouldn't he place his own calls?

The woman on the other line was really sorry. Mr. Hardwick was still in conference. Nick imagined Hardwick making throat-cut, I'm-not-in gestures.

There it was. *That* was a reason not to place your own calls. To spare yourself the humiliation of dissembling secretaries. The smile in the voice that accompanied the singsongy formula *I'm sorry*. The micro–power trip of putting one over on a CEO. Fun for the whole family. He wondered whether the waitress at Terra really had spit in his arugula salad. She'd brightened a little when she brought it out, hadn't she?

Nick felt a little acid come up his gullet as he stared at the silver-mesh fabric panels in front of him. There were certain things that money and position protected you from. There were certain things that it didn't. When his driver's license needed renewing a couple of years ago, he didn't stand in line at the DMV, the way he once had to. The CEO of a major corporation didn't wait in line at the DMV. Some young staffer from the corporate counsel's office did, and it got taken care of. Nick couldn't remember the last time he'd waited in line for a taxi at an airport. Senior execs had cars; you looked for the guy holding a sign that said CONOVER. And senior execs of major corporations didn't haul their own baggage. That got taken care of, too, even when Nick was flying commercial. But when the weather was bad, it was bad for you too. When your car was stuck in traffic, it didn't matter what your company's valuation was; traffic was traffic. Those things were the Levelers. The things that reminded you that you lived in the same world and were going to end up in the same place as everybody else. You thought you were a master of the universe, but you were just lording it over a little box of dirt, the tyrant of a terrarium. Having a kid who hated you—that had to be a leveler too. And so was sickness.

And so was death.

Next he tried MacFarland—that was the name of the Nixon look-alike. But his assistant apologized: Mr. MacFarland was traveling. "I'll be sure to let him know that you called," MacFarland's assistant told him, with the bright artificiality of someone from a casting director's office. Don't call us; we'll call you.

Twenty minutes later came the faint settling-in noises, the heavy vanilla smell of Shalimar: Marjorie was in.

Nick got up, stretched, stepped around the partition. "How's the novel coming?" He tried to remember the title. "*Manchester Abbey*, was it?"

She smiled. "We did *Northanger Abbey* a few weeks ago. This week is *Mansfield Park*."

"Got it," Nick said.

"I think Jane Austen wrote *Northanger Abbey* first, but it didn't come out until after her death," Marjorie said, turning on her computer. She said distantly, "Amazing what comes out after people die."

Nick felt as if someone had touched his neck with an ice cube. His smile faded.

"*Persuasion* did too," she went on. "And *Billy Budd*, which we read last year. I didn't know you had such an interest, Nick. You ought to come to our book club."

"Let me know when you decide to do the Chevrolet Suburban Owner's Manual—that's what *I* call a book," he said. "Listen, I'm expecting a call from those Atlas McKenzie guys. Hardwick, MacFarland. Let me know when they're on the line. Wherever I am, I'll take the call."

Nick spent the next couple of hours in conference rooms, two back-to-back, bun-numbing meetings. There was the supply-chain-management team, whose seven members had reached an important conclusion: Stratton needed to diversify its suppliers of metallic paint. They were bubbling with excitement as they reviewed the considerations they had taken into account, like they'd discovered penicillin. Then there was the industrial-safety team, which always had more lawyers than engineers, more concerned about lawsuits than limbs. Nobody came to spring him. No message from Marjorie.

He gave Marjorie a questioning look as he made his way back to his desk.

"The Atlas McKenzie people—they were supposed to get back this morning?" she asked.

Nick sighed. "I'm beginning to feel like I'm getting the bum's rush. I phoned first thing today, you know, and they said Hardwick's in conference, MacFarland's on the road, they'll get back to me." Then again, they were supposed to return his call from yesterday too. Apparently they had other priorities.

"You think they're trying to dodge you."

"Could be."

"Want to get them on line?" Marjorie looked sunny but sly. It was a good look.

"Yup."

"Let me have a go."

Nick took a few more steps toward his desk as Marjorie made a couple of phone calls. He couldn't hear everything. "That's right," she was saying. "United Airlines. We've located the lost baggage, and he gave us a cell number to call him at. James MacFarland, yes. He seemed frantic. But the clerk must have written it down wrong . . ."

A minute later, an intercom tone told Nick to pick up his Line 1.

"Jim MacFarland?" Nick said as he answered the phone.

Cautiously: "Yes?"

"Nick Conover here."

"Nick. Hey." Friendly, but with a tremor of unease.

Nick wanted to say, *Do you realize the amount of money and man-hours we've spent designing your goddamn prototypes? And you can't be bothered to return my calls?* Instead he tried to sound breezy. "Just wanted to touch base," he said. "About where things stood."

"Yeah," MacFarland said. "Yeah. I meant to give you a call about that. About the current thinking."

"Lay it on me."

A deep breath. "Thing is, Nick—well, we hadn't realized that Stratton's on the block. Which kind of changes the picture for us."

"On the block? Meaning what?" Nick struggled to keep his voice calm. At the start of his career, Nick figured that being the boss meant not having to kiss ass. A nice thought, anyway. Turned out there was always somebody whose ass you had to kiss. The commander in chief of the free world had to suck up to farmers in Iowa. *It's good to be the boss*—wasn't that what they said? But every boss had a boss. Turtles all the way down. Asses all the way up.

That was how it felt sometimes, anyway. That was how it felt just now.

"It's just that Hardwick's always real concerned about stability when it comes to sourcing and support," MacFarland was saying. "We hadn't realized things were in flux that way. It's not like you had a big 'For Sale' sign over the front door, right?"

Nick was dumbfounded. "Stratton's not for sale," he said simply.

There was a moment of silence on the other end. "Huh." Not the sound of agreement. "Look, Nick, you didn't hear this from me. We use the same law firm in Hong Kong that Fairfield Partners does. And, you know, people talk."

"That's *bullshit*," Nick said.

"What it is, is water under the bridge."

"Come on. I'm the CEO of the company. If Stratton was being sold, you'd think I'd know, right?"

"You said it." The chilling thing was that MacFarland sounded kindly, sympathetic, like an oncologist breaking the news of a bad diagnosis to a favorite patient.

44

Marjorie poked her head around at ten thirty.

"Remember, you've got a lunch at half past with Roderick Douglass, the Chamber of Commerce guy," she said. "He'll be wanting to hit you up again. Then there's the meeting with the business development execs right after."

Nick swiveled around and looked out the window. "Right, thanks," he said, distracted.

It was a beautiful day. The sky was blue, deepened a little by the tint of the glass. There was enough of a breeze to flutter the leaves of the trees. A jet was making its way across the sky, its double contrails quickly turning into smudgy fluff.

It was also the seventh day in a row that Andrew Stadler hadn't been alive to see.

Nick shivered, as if a gust of cool air had somehow made it through the building's glass membrane. Cassie Stadler's fragile, china-doll face now filled his mind. *What did I do to you?* He remembered the look of infinite hurt in her eyes, and he found himself dialing her number before he was even conscious of having decided to.

"Hello." Cassie's voice, deep and sleepy-sounding.

"It's Nick Conover," he said. "Hope I'm not calling you too early."

"Me? No—it's—what time is it?"

"I woke you up. I'm sorry. It's ten thirty. Go back to sleep."

"No," she said hastily. "I'm glad you called. Listen, about yesterday—"

"Cassie, I'm just calling to make sure you're okay. When I left, you didn't look so great."

"Thanks."

"You know what I mean."

"I—it helped, talking to you. Really helped."

"I'm glad."

"Would you like to come over for lunch?"

"You mean today?"

"Oh, God, that's ridiculous, I can't believe I just said that. You're this big CEO, you've probably got lunch meetings scheduled every day until you're sixty-five."

"Not at all," he said. "My lunch meeting just canceled, in fact. Which means a sandwich at my desk. So, yeah, I'd love to get out of the office, sure."

"Really? Hey, great. Oh—just one little thing."

"You don't have any food in your refrigerator."

"Sad but true. What kind of host am I?"

"I'll pick something up. See you at noon."

When he hung up, he stopped by his assistant's desk. "Marge," he said, "could you cancel my lunch meetings?"

"Both of them?"

"Right."

Marjorie smiled. "Going to play hooky? It's a beautiful day."

"Hooky? Does that sound like me?"

"Hope springs eternal."

"Nah," he said. "I just need to run a couple of errands."

45

The house on West Sixteenth, in Steepletown, was even smaller than he remembered it. A dollhouse, a miniature, almost.

Two stories. White sidings that could have been aluminum or vinyl, you'd have to tap to be sure. Black shutters that weren't big enough to pretend to be shutters.

Nick, holding a couple of brown bags from the Family Fare supermarket he'd stopped at on the way over, rang the bell, heard the carillon tones.

It was almost half a minute before Cassie came to the door. She was in a black knitted top and black stretchy pants. Her face was pale, and sad, and perfect. She was wearing glossy orange lipstick, which was a little strange, but it looked right on her. She also looked better, more rested, than she had yesterday.

"Hey, you actually came." Cassie opened the door, and walked him past the vase with the dried flowers and the framed embroidered sampler to the small living room. He could hear "One Is the Loneliest Number" come from the small speakers of a portable CD player. Not the old Three Dog Night version. A modern cover. A woman with a voice like clove cigarettes. Cassie switched it off.

Nick unloaded the stuff he'd bought—bread, eggs, juice, milk, bottled water, fruit, a couple of bottles of iced tea. "Toss whatever you don't like," he said. Then he unwrapped a couple of sandwiches, placing them ceremoniously on paper plates. "Turkey or roast beef?"

She looked doubtfully at the roast beef. "Too bloody," she said. "I like my meat burned to a crisp, basically."

"I'll have it," Nick said. "You have the turkey."

They ate together in silence. He folded up the Boar's Head delicatessen wrappers into neat squares, a form of fidgeting. She finished most of her iced tea and toyed with the cap. It was a little awkward, and Nick wondered why she'd invited him over. He tried to think of something to say, but before he could, she said, "Hey, you never know what you're going to learn from a bottle cap. It says here, 'Real Fact'—the last letter added to the English-language alphabet was the 'J.'"

Nick tried to think of something to say, but before he could, she went on: "Aren't you supposed to be running a Fortune Five Hundred company or something?"

"We're not a public company. Anyway, I had a boring lunch I canceled."

"Now I feel guilty."

"Not at all. I was happy to have an excuse to miss it."

"You know, you really surprised me yesterday."

"Why?"

"It wasn't very 'Nick the Slasher.' I guess people are never what you expect. Like they say, still waters—"

"Get clogged with algae?"

"Something like that. You know how it is—you see someone who seems so desperate, and you just have to reach out and help."

"You don't seem desperate."

"I'm talking about you."

Nick reddened. "Excuse me?"

She got up and put the kettle on. Standing at the stove, she said, "We've both suffered a loss. It's like Rilke says—when we lose something, it circles around us. 'It draws around us its unbroken curve.'"

"Huh. I used to have a Spirograph set when I was a kid."

"I guess I figured you for the typical company man. Until I met you. But you know what I think now?" Her gaze was calm but intent. "I think you're actually a real family man."

He cleared his throat. "Yeah, well, tell that to my son. Tell that to Lucas."

"It's a bad age for a boy to lose his mom," Cassie said quietly. She took a teapot down from a cabinet, then some mugs.

"Like there's a good one?"

"The kid probably needs you badly."

"I don't think that's how he sees it," Nick said, a little bitterly.

Cassie looked away. "You're saying that because he's isolated and he's angry, and he turns on you. Am I right? Because you're safe. But you'll get through it. You love each other. You're a family."

"We were."

"You know how lucky your kids are?"

"Yeah, well."

She turned to face him. "I'll bet being a CEO is sort of like being head of a family too."

"Yeah," Nick said acerbically. "Maybe one of those Eskimo families. The kind that puts Grandma on the ice floe when she's not bringing in the whale blubber anymore."

"I bet the layoffs were hard on you."

"Harder on the people who got laid off."

"My dad had a lot of problems, but I think having a job helped him keep it together. Then when he found out they don't want him anymore, he fell apart."

Nick felt as if there was a metal strap around his chest and it was steadily tightening. He nodded.

"I was mad at Stratton," Cassie said. "Mad at you, is the truth. Maybe because I'm a girl, I take these things too personally. But it might have had a bad effect on him. Someone with a thought disorder, it's hard to know."

"Cassie," Nick started, but whatever he was going to say died in his throat.

"That was before I met you, though. You didn't want to do this. The people in Boston made you. Because, end of the day, Stratton is a business."

"Right."

"But it's never just a business to you, is it? See, I just realized something. Being a Stratton employee in the past couple of years must have been like being the daughter of a schizophrenic. One day you're a beloved family member, the next you're a unit, a cost center, something to be slashed." She leaned against the counter, her arms folded.

"I'm sorry about your dad," Nick said. "More sorry than I can tell you." *With more to be sorry about than I can tell you.*

"My daddy . . ." Cassie's voice was hushed, halting. "He didn't—he didn't want to be the way he was. It would just take over him. He wanted to be a good father like you. He wanted . . ." Cassie's breathing started to become ragged, and Nick realized that she was weeping. Her face was red, bowed, and she put a hand over her eyes. Tears rolled copiously down her cheeks.

Nick got up suddenly, his chair scraping against the linoleum floor, and put his arms around her.

"Oh, Cassie," he said softly. "I'm sorry."

She was tiny, birdlike, and her shoulders were narrow and bony. She made a sound like she was hiccupping. She smelled like something spicy and New-Agey—patchouli, was that it? Nick was ashamed to realize he was getting aroused.

"I'm sorry," he said again.

"Stop saying that." Cassie looked up at him and smiled wanly through her tears. "It's got nothing to do with you."

Nick remembered a time when he was trying to fix a lamp socket he'd thought was switched off. An eerie, hair-erecting, tingling feeling had swept through his arm, and it had taken him a second to identify the sensation as house current that was leaking through the screwdriver. He felt something like that now, guilt washing through his body like an electrical flux. He didn't know how to respond.

But Cassie said, "I think you're a good man, Nicholas Conover."

"You don't know me," he said.

"I know you better than you think," she said, and he felt her arms squeezing against his back, pulling him toward her. Then she seemed to be standing on tiptoes, her face close to his, her lips pressing against his.

The moment for refusing, for backing out, came and went. Nick's response was almost reflexive. This time he kissed her back, her tears sticky against his face, and his hands moved downward from her shoulders.

"Mmm," she said.

The teakettle started whistling.

For a long time afterward, she lay on top of him in the slick of their perspiration, her mouth pressed against his chest. He could feel her heartbeat, fast as a bird's, slowing gradually. He stroked her hair, nuzzled her porcelain neck, smelling her hair, a conditioner or whatever. He felt her breasts against his stomach.

"I don't know what to say," Nick began.

"Then keep silent." She smiled, lifted herself up on her elbows until she was sitting upright on him. She lightly scratched her fingernails across his upper chest, tangling them in his chest hair.

Nick shifted his butt against the coarse-textured couch in the living room. He rocked upward, enfolded her in an embrace, leaned forward until he was sitting up too.

"Strong guy," she said.

Her breasts were small and round, the nipples pink and still erect like little upturned thumbs. Her waist was tiny. She reached across him to the table next to the couch, and as she did, her breasts brushed against his face. He gave them a quick kiss. She retrieved a pack of Marlboros and a Bic lighter, took one out of the pack and waved it at him, offering.

"No, thanks," Nick said.

She shrugged, lighted the cigarette, took in a lungful of air and spewed out a thin stream of smoke.

" 'Let me live in a house by the side of the road and be a friend to man,' " Nick quoted.

"Yep."

"Needlepoint by Grandma?"

"Mom got it in some junk store. She liked what it said."

"So how long has it been since you left this place?"

"I just turned twenty-nine. Left when I was around twelve. So, a long time. But I came back to visit Dad a bunch of times."

"School in Chicago, then."

"You're trying to piece together the Cassie Stadler saga? Good luck."

"Just wondering."

"My mom remarried when I was eleven. An orthodontist. Had a couple of kids of his own, my age, a little older. Let's just say it wasn't the Brady Bunch. Dr. Reese didn't exactly take to me. Neither did the little Reese's pieces, Bret and Justin. Finally shipped me off to Lake Forest Academy, basically to get me out of the way."

"Must have been tough on you."

She inhaled, held a lungful of smoke for several seconds. Then, as she let it out, she said, "Yes and no. In some ways, they did me a favor. I actually flourished at the academy. I was a precocious kid. Got a Headmaster scholarship, graduated top of the class. Should have seen me when I was seventeen. A real promising young citizen. Not the head case you see before you."

"You don't seem like a head case to me."

"Because I don't drool and wear bad glasses?" She crossed her eyes. "Fools them every time."

"You talk about it like it's a big joke."

"Probably it *is* a joke. Some cosmic joke that's just a little over our heads. God's joke. Nothing to do but to smile and nod and try to pretend that we get it."

"You can go pretty far in life doing that," Nick said. He sneaked a glimpse at his wristwatch, saw it was after two already. With a jolt, he realized he had to get back to the office.

She noticed. "Time to go."

"Cassie, I—"

"Just go, Nick. You've got a company to run."

46

Dr. Aaron Landis, the clinical director of mental health services for County Medical, seemed to wear a permanent sneer. Audrey realized, though, that there was something not quite right about the man's face, a crookedness to the mouth, a congenital deformity that made him look that way. His gray hair resembled a Brillo pad, and he had a receding chin that he tried to disguise, not very successfully, with a neatly trimmed gray beard. At first Audrey felt a bit sorry for the psychiatrist because of his homeliness, but her compassion quickly faded.

His office was small and messy, so heaped with books and papers that there was scarcely room for the two of them to sit. The only decoration was a photograph of a plain-looking wife and an even plainer son, and a series of colorful scans of a human brain, purple with yellow-orange highlights, on curling slick paper, thumbtacked along one wall.

"I don't think I understand what you're asking, Detective," he said.

She had been as clear as day. "I'm asking whether Andrew Stadler exhibited violent tendencies."

"You're asking me to breach doctor-patient confidentiality."

"Your patient is dead," she said gently.

"And the confidentiality of his medical records survives his death, Detective. As does physician-patient confidentiality. You know that, or if you don't, you should. The Supreme Court upheld that privilege a decade ago.

More important, it's part of the Hippocratic oath I took when I became a doctor."

"Mr. Stadler was murdered, Doctor. I want to find his killer or killers."

"An effort I certainly applaud. But I don't see how it concerns me."

"You see, there are a number of unanswered questions about his death that might help us determine what really happened. I'm sure you want to help us do our job."

"I'm happy to help in any way I can. Just so long as you don't ask me to violate Mr. Stadler's rights."

"Thank you, Doctor. Then let me restate my question. Speaking generally. Do most schizophrenics tend to be violent?"

The psychiatrist looked upward for a moment, as if consulting the heavens. He exhaled noisily. Then he fixed her with a sorrowful look. "That, Detective, is one of the most pernicious myths about schizophrenia."

"Then maybe you can enlighten me, Doctor."

"Schizophrenia is a chronic recurring psychotic illness that begins in early adulthood, as a rule, and lasts until death. We don't even know if it's a single disease or a syndrome. Myself, I prefer to call it SSD, or schizophrenia spectrum disorder, though I'm in the minority on this. Now, the defining symptoms of schizophrenia are thought disorder, a failure of logic, reality distortion, and hallucinations."

"And paranoia?"

"Often, yes. And a psychosocial disability. So let me ask *you* something, Detective. You see a good deal of violence in your work, I'm sure."

"Yes, I do."

"Is most of it inflicted by schizophrenics?"

"No."

"My point. Most violent crimes are not committed by persons with schizophrenia, and most persons with schizophrenia don't commit violent crimes."

"But there's a—"

"Let me finish, please. The vast majority of patients with schizophrenia have never been violent. They're a hundred times more likely to commit *suicide* than homicide."

"So are you saying that Andrew Stadler was not a violent man?"

"Detective, I admire your persistence, but the backdoor approach won't work either. I will not discuss the particulars of his case. But let me tell you what the real correlation is between schizophrenia and violence: schizophrenia increases the likelihood of being the *victim* of a crime."

"Exactly. Mr. Stadler was the victim of a terrible crime. Which is why I need to know whether he might have provoked his own death by killing an animal, a family pet."

"If I knew that, I wouldn't tell you."

"I'm asking whether he was capable of such an act."

"I won't tell you that either."

"Are you saying that schizophrenics are never violent?"

After a long pause, he said: "Obviously there are the exceptions."

"Was Andrew Stadler one of those exceptions, Doctor?"

"Please, Detective. I won't discuss the particulars of Mr. Stadler's medical records. I don't know how much more clear I can be."

Audrey sighed in exasperation. "Then let me ask you a purely hypothetical question, all right?"

"Purely hypothetical," Dr. Landis repeated.

"Let's take a . . . *hypothetical* case in which an individual repeatedly breaks into a family's house in order to write threatening graffiti. Is able to do so, cleverly and without leaving any evidence, despite the security provided by the gated community in which this family lives. And has even slaughtered the family's pet. What sort of person might do this, would you say?"

"What sort of *hypothetical* individual?" He attempted a smile, which twisted unpleasantly. "Someone, I would say, who's extremely intelligent, high-functioning, capable of higher-order thinking and goal-governed behavior, and yet has pervasive impulse-control problems, marked mood swings, and is highly sensitive to rejection. There may be, say, a great fear of abandonment, derived from difficulties in childhood feeling connected to important persons in one's life. He might have absolutely black-and-white views of others—might tend to idealize people and then suddenly despise them."

"And then?"

"And then he might be subject to sudden and unpredictable rages, brief psychotic episodes, with suicidal impulses."

"What might set him off?"

"A situation of great stress. The loss of someone or something important to him."

"Or the loss of a job?"

"Certainly."

"Can a schizophrenic exhibit this pattern of behavior you're describing?"

Dr. Landis paused for a long moment. "Conceivably. It's not impossible." Then he gave a creepy sort of smile. "But what does all this have to do with Andrew Stadler?"

47

"Grover Herrick," Marjorie said over the intercom the next morning.

Grover Herrick was a senior procurement manager at the U.S. General Services Administration, which did purchasing for federal agencies. He was also the point man for an enormous contract Stratton had negotiated for the Department of Homeland Security. DHS now encompassed the Coast Guard, Customs, Immigration and Naturalization Service, and the Transportation Security Administration—thousands of offices, a hundred and eighty thousand employees, and a major infusion of federal cash. The contract was second in value only to the Atlas McKenzie deal, and had been in the works almost as long.

You didn't keep a GSA procurement manager on hold for long. That was one rule. Another was that anytime Grover Herrick wanted to talk to the CEO, Grover Herrick talked to the CEO. On half a dozen occasions in the past year, Nick fulfilled his duties as Stratton's chief executive by feigning interest as Grover talked about the sailboat he was going to buy as soon as he retired, and pretending to care about the difference between a ketch and a yawl. If Herrick had wanted to talk about hemorrhoids, Nick would have boned up on that topic too.

This time, though, there were no preliminaries.

"Nick," the GSA man said, "Gotta tell you, it looks like we're going with Haworth."

Nick felt gut-punched. It was all he could do not to double over. "You're *kidding*."

"I think you know by now when I'm kidding." There was a pause. "Remember when I told you the story about dropping the Thanksgiving turkey in front of all the guests, and how my wife had the presence of mind to say, 'Never mind, just bring out the other bird'? *That* I was kidding about."

"Fucking *Haworth*?"

"Well, what the hell did you *think* would happen?" Herrick's voice was a squawk of indignation. "You were going to have us ink the deal, move the company to *Shenzhen*, and then what? Have us outfit Homeland Security offices with desks from *China*?"

"What—?" Nick managed to choke out.

"When were you planning on telling us? I can think of some Senators who'd have a ball with that—but politics aside, it's completely against GSA procurement guidelines. Can't happen. Don't pretend you've forgotten about 41 USC 10. You guys oughta have the Buy American Act tattooed on your forehead."

"Wait a minute—who told you Stratton's going offshore?"

"What does it matter? Where there's smoke, there's fire. We liked Stratton. Great American company. I can see the temptation to cash in, put everything on a fast boat to China. Still think it's a mistake, though. My personal opinion."

"What you're saying doesn't make any sense. We're not going anywhere. I don't care what you've heard."

Herrick ignored him. "What was the game plan—inflate revenues with a hefty GSA prepayment, jack up the purchase price, figure the Heathen Chinese wouldn't figure out the game? Strategic vision, huh? I guess that's why you get the big bucks."

"*No*, Grover. This is bullshit."

"I told you before. We really liked you guys. We liked Haworth, too, but the Stratton price points looked better, all in. We just didn't realize your price points came courtesy of cheap Chinese labor."

"Listen to me, Grover." Nick tried to cut him off, to no avail.

"Thing that chafes my ass is, you guys wasted a *hell* of a lot of my time. Got half a mind to bill you for it."

"Grover, *no*."

"Happy sailing, Nick," the GSA man said, and he hung up.

Nick cursed loudly. He wanted to fling the phone across the room—across *a* room—but the Ambience system didn't really lend itself to boss-man theatrics.

Marjorie came over. "Something going on that I should know about?"

"That's pretty much *my* question, Marge," Nick said, struggling to regain his composure.

He walked across the executive floor to Scott's area, taking a back way in order to bypass Gloria, Scott's admin. As he approached, he heard Scott talking on the phone.

"Well, sure," Scott was saying. "We'll give it a try, Todd man, why not?"

Nick advanced until he was in Scott's line of sight.

Scott noticed him now, seemed to flinch just a bit, but instantly recovered: widening his eyes and smiling, raising his chin by way of greeting. "Right," he said, more loudly. "Sounds like a great trip. Gotta go." He hung up and said to Nick, "Hey, my liege, welcome to the low-rent district."

"How's Todd?" Nick said.

"Ah, he's trying to set up a golf trip to Hilton Head."

"I didn't know you golf."

"I don't." He laughed uncomfortably. "Well, badly. But that's why they love having me around. Makes them look like Tiger Woods."

" 'They' being Todd and the other Fairfield boys?"

"Todd and his wife and Eden and another couple. Anyway."

"I had an interesting talk with MacFarland at Atlas McKenzie."

"Oh, yeah?" Scott's expression seemed wary.

"Yeah. Learn something new everyday. You know why they decided not to go with us?"

"Gotta be price, what else. Not quality, that's for sure. But you get what you pay for."

"MacFarland seems to think we're on the block. Now, why would he think that?"

Scott spread out his palms.

"Atlas McKenzie uses the same Hong Kong law firm as Fairfield, which is how they heard."

"That's *crazy.*"

"Funny thing is, I heard something sort of similar from the guy at GSA just now."

"GSA?" Scott said, swallowing.

"The Homeland Security deal? That just fell apart too."

"Shit."

"And you know why? They need Made-in-America, and they heard a rumor we're going to be offshoring our manufacturing to China. Isn't that the craziest thing?"

Scott, picking up on Nick's bitter sarcasm, sat up straight in his chair and said solemnly, "If Todd and those guys were planning a move like that, don't you think they'd at least mention it to me?"

"Yeah, I do, actually. Have they?"

"Obviously not—I would have told you right away."

"Would you?"

"Of course—Jesus, Nick, I can't believe people listen to stupid rumors like that. I mean, it's no different from those idiotic rumors about the deep-fried chicken head in the box of Chicken McNuggets, or the bonsai kittens, or how the moon walk was a fraud—"

"Scott."

"Look, I'll make some calls, look into it for you, okay? But I'm sure there's nothing to it."

"I hope you're right," Nick said. "I really hope you're right."

48

Eddie didn't stand up when Nick came to his office that afternoon. Just gave him a mock salute, as he leaned back in his Symbiosis chair with his feet on his desk. On the silver-mesh fabric wall behind him was a poster with the words "MEDIOCRITY. It Takes a Lot Less Time and Most People Won't Notice the Difference Until It's Too Late." Above the slogan was a photograph of the Leaning Tower of Pisa. It was one of those wiseass spoofs of corporate workplace propaganda, but Nick sometimes wondered how much irony Eddie really meant.

"I get a promotion?" Eddie asked. "I mean, with you coming down here instead of making me come up."

Nick pulled up a small, wheeled stool. "They call it Management by Walking Around. MBWA."

"Lot to be said for MBSOYA. Management by Sitting on Your Ass."

Nick forced a smile, and told him about what MacFarland and Grover Herrick had said, skipping the incidentals.

"Fuck me," Eddie said. "Gotta be bullshit, right? You talk to Scott McNally about this?"

"He says there's nothing to it. But he knows more than he's telling me. I'm sure of it."

Eddie nodded slowly. "If you're out, I'm out, right?"

"Who said anything about my being out? I just want you to see what Scott's up to, that's all."

Eddie grinned slowly. "You want an assist, I'll fire you the puck and cross-check the assholes. I'll even break the fucking stick over their heads."

"A little e-mail surveillance should do it, Eddie."

"I'll get one of the techs to pull his e-mail records off the server, right? Just get me a few keywords."

"That sounds like a start."

"Oh, sure. Phone records, all that stuff. Easy peasy. But boy, you sure do have a knack for stepping in the shit." Eddie's skin formed webbing around his eyes as he smiled. "Good thing you got a friend who doesn't mind cleaning your shoes."

"You'll let me know if you find anything."

"That's what friends are for."

Nick didn't meet his eyes. "And not a word to anyone."

"Back at ya, buddy."

Nick hesitated for a moment, then wheeled the stool close to Eddie's desk. "Eddie, did you tell the cops you went over to my house after we found my dog?"

Eddie peered at him for a while. "They didn't ask me. I don't volunteer information. That's cop interview lesson number one."

Nick nodded. "They didn't ask me either. Not yet. But in case it comes up, I want to make sure we have a consistent story, okay? I asked you to come over, and you did. Only natural that I'd give you a call. You're my security director."

"Only natural," Eddie repeated. "Makes sense. But you got to calm down, buddy. You worry too much."

49

When he returned to the executive floor, Marjorie stopped him and handed him a slip of paper, a concerned look in her face. "I think you need to return this call right away," she said.

Principal J. Sundquist, she had written in her clear, elegant script, and then the telephone number.

Jerome Sundquist. Twenty-five years ago, he'd been Nick's high school math teacher. Nick remembered him as a rangy guy—a former tennis pro— who bounced around the classroom and was pretty good at keeping up the Math Is Fun act. To his students, he was Mr. Sundquist, not "Jerome" or "Jerry," and though he was reasonably laid back he didn't pretend to be pals with the kids in their chair desks. Nick half-smiled as he remembered those chair desks, with the little steel basket for books under the seat, and a "tablet arm" supported by a continuous piece of steel tube that ran from the back supports to the crossover legs. They were manufactured, back then as they were now, right in town, at Stratton's chair plant, a few miles down the road. Nick hadn't seen the numbers recently, but they listed for about a hundred and fifty, on a unit cost of maybe forty. Basically, it was the same design today.

Jerome Sundquist hadn't changed that much, either. Now he was the school principal, not a young teacher, and allowed himself a little more sententiousness than he used to, but if you were a high school principal that was pretty much part of the job description.

"Nick, glad you called," Jerome Sundquist said, in a tone that was both cordial and distant. "It's about your son."

Fenwick Regional High was a big brick-and-glass complex with a long traffic oval and the kind of juniper-and-mulch landscaping you found at shopping centers and office parks—nothing fancy, but somebody had to keep it up. Nick remembered when he came home after his first semester at Michigan State, remembered how *small* everything seemed. That's how it should have felt when he visited his old high school, but it didn't. The place was *bigger*—lots of add-ons, new structures, new brick facings on the old ones—and somehow plusher than it was in the old days. Plenty of it had to do with how Stratton had grown over the past couple of decades, with a valuation that broke two billion dollars three years ago. Then again, the higher you got, the longer the fall to the bottom. If Stratton collapsed, it would bring a lot of things down with it.

He stepped through the glass double doors and inhaled. As much as the place had changed, it somehow *smelled* the same. That grapefruit-scented disinfectant they still used: maybe they'd ordered a vat in 1970 and were still working through it. Some sort of faint burnt-pea-soup odor wafting from the cafeteria, as ineradicable as cat piss. It was the kind of thing you only noticed when you were away from it. Like the first day of homeroom after summer vacation, when you realized that the air was heavy with hair-styling products and eggy breakfasts and cinnamon Dentyne and underarm deodorant and farts—the smell of Fenwick's future.

But the place had changed dramatically. In the old days everyone came to school on the bus; now the kids were either dropped off in vans or SUVs or drove to school themselves. The old Fenwick Regional had no blacks, or maybe one or two a year; now the social leaders of the school seemed to be black kids who looked like rappers and the white kids who tried to. They'd added a sleek new wing that looked like something out of a private school. In the old days there used to be a smoking area, where longhaired kids in Black Sabbath T-shirts hung out and puffed and jeered at the jocks like Nick. Now smoking was outlawed and the Black Sabbath kids had become Goths with nose rings.

Nick hadn't spent much time in the principal's office when he was a student, but the oatmeal curtains and carpeting looked new, and the multicultural photographs of tennis champs on the court—the Williams sisters, Sania Merza, Martina Hingis, Boris Becker—was very Jerome Sundquist.

Sundquist stepped around from his desk and shook Nick's hand somberly. They sat down together on two camel-colored chairs. Sundquist glanced at a manila file he had left on his desk, but he already knew what was in it.

"Love what you've done with the place," Nick said.

"My office, or the school?"

"Both."

Sundquist smiled. "You'd be surprised how many two-generation families the school has now, which is a nice thing. And obviously the district has been very lucky in a lot of ways. When the parents prosper, the schools prosper. We're all hoping the downturn isn't permanent. I appreciate you've got a lot on your shoulders right now."

Nick shrugged.

"You were a pretty good student, as I recall," Sundquist said.

"Not especially."

Sundquist looked amused, tilted his head. "Okay, maybe 'indifferent' would be closer to the mark. I don't think I ever persuaded you about the glories of polar coordinates. Your interest in trig was more practical. All about what angle you could use to slap a puck between the goalie's legs."

"I remember your trying to sell me on that at the time. Nice try, though."

"But you always did okay on the exams. And, Christ, you were a popular kid. The school's blue-eyed boy. Brought Fenwick Regional to the state semifinals, twice, isn't that right?"

"Semifinals one year. Finals the next."

"That's one area where we haven't kept up. Caldicott has kicked our ass for the past four years."

"Maybe you need a new coach."

"Mallon is supposed to be good. Gets paid more than me, anyway. It's always hard to know when to blame the coach and when to blame the players." Sundquist broke off. "I know how busy you are, so let me get right to the point."

"Luke's been having problems," Nick said with a twinge of defensiveness. "I realize that. I want to do whatever I can."

"Of course," Sundquist said, sounding unconvinced. "Well, as I told you, Lucas is being suspended. A three-day suspension. He was caught smoking, and that's what happens."

So Lucas would have even more time to light up. That was really going to make things better. "I remember when there used to be a smoking area."

"Not anymore. Smoking is forbidden on the entire campus. We've got very tough rules on that. All the kids know it."

Campus was new. When Nick was at school, the school only had *grounds*. Campuses were for colleges.

"Obviously I don't want him smoking at all," Nick put in. "I'm just saying."

"Second offense, Lucas gets thrown out of school. Expelled."

"He's a good kid. It's just been a rough time for him."

Sundquist looked at him hard. "How well do you know your son?"

"What are you saying? He's my kid."

"Nick, I don't want to overstate the situation, but I don't want to understate it, either. It's pretty serious. I spent some time this morning talking to our crisis counselor. We don't think this is just about smoking, okay? You need to appreciate that we have the right to search his locker, and we may do some surprise searches, with the police."

"The police?"

"And if drugs are found, we will let the police prosecute. That's the way we do it these days. I want to warn you about that. Lucas is a troubled kid. Our crisis counselor is very concerned about him. Lucas isn't like you, okay?"

"Not everybody has to be a jock."

"That isn't what I meant," Sundquist said, not elaborating. Another glance back at the manila folder on his desk. "Besides which, his grades are going to hell. He used to be an honor student. With the grades he's been getting, he's not going to stay in that track. You understand what that means?"

"I understand," Nick said. "I do. He needs help."

"He needs help," Sundquist agreed, tight-lipped. "And he hasn't been receiving it."

Nick felt as if he were being graded as a father, and getting an *F*. "Jerry, I just don't see how suspending him or—God forbid—expelling him is the right thing to do. How is that *helping* him?" he asked. Then he wondered how many times those words had been spoken in that office.

"We have these rules for a reason," Sundquist said smoothly, leaning back a little in his chair. "There are almost fifteen hundred kids in this high school, and we have to do what's in the best interests of all of them."

Nick took a deep breath. "It's been hard for him, what happened. I get that he's a troubled kid. Believe me, this is something that's very much on my mind. I just think that he's been hanging out with a bad crowd."

"One way to look at it." Sundquist's gaze was unwavering. "Of course, there's another way to look at it."

"How do you mean?" Nick asked blankly.

"You could say that he *is* the bad crowd."

"Luke."

"What?" He'd picked up his cell phone on the first ring. The deal was that if he failed to answer a call from his father, he'd lose the phone.

"Where are you?"

"Home. Why?"

"What the hell happened at school?"

"What do you mean?"

"What do I *mean*? Three guesses. Mr. Sundquist called me in."

"What'd he tell you?"

"Don't play this game, Luke." Nick tried to stay calm. Talking to Lucas was like dousing a fire with lighter fluid. "You were smoking, and you got caught. Forget about what *I* think about smoking—you know the rules on smoking at school. You just got a three-day suspension."

"So? It's all bullshit anyway."

"Suspension from school is bullshit?"

"Yeah." His voice shook a bit. "Because school is bullshit."

An instant message popped up on his monitor from Marge:

Compensation Committee meeting right now, remember?

"Luke, I'm furious about this," he said. "You and I are going to have a talk about this later."

Yeah, Nick thought. *That's telling him.*

"And, Luke—?"

But Lucas had hung up.

50

No sooner had Audrey returned to the squad room than Bugbee found her. He approached her desk holding a mug of coffee in one hand, a sheaf of papers in the other, looking pleased about something.

"Don't tell me," he said. "The shrink spilled it all about his looney-tunes patient."

Now she understood his self-satisfied look. He was gloating, yes, but it was something more. It was the told-you-so look she'd seen LaTonya give the boys when they got in trouble for doing something she'd told them not to.

"He gave me some useful background on schizophrenia and violence," she said.

"Stuff you could have read in a textbook, I'm figuring. But he wouldn't talk about Stadler, would he? Doctor-patient confidentiality, right?"

"There has to be a way to get access to Stadler's medical records." She couldn't bring herself to tell Bugbee he was right any more directly than that.

"What would Jesus do, Audrey? Get a search warrant."

She ignored the crack. "That won't do it. The most we can get out of a search warrant is dates of admission to the hospital and such. The medical records are still protected. Maybe a Freedom of Information request."

"How many years you got?"

"Right."

"Speaking of search warrants," Bugbee said, waving the sheaf of papers in his left hand, "when were you planning on telling me you requested the phone records of the Stratton security guy?"

"They came in already?"

"Not my point. What'd you want 'em for?"

Bugbee must have picked them up from the fax machine, or maybe he'd seen them in her in-box. "Let me see," she said.

"Why are you so interested in Edward Rinaldi's phone records?"

Audrey gave him a long cold look, the sort of look LaTonya was so skilled at. "Are you holding them back from me, Roy?"

Bugbee handed the papers right over.

Boy, she thought, I'm going to have to take LaTonya Assertiveness Training. She felt a pulse of triumph and wondered whether this was a worthy feeling. She thought not, but she enjoyed it guiltily all the same. "Thank you, Roy. Now, in answer to your question, I wanted them because I'm curious as to whether Rinaldi ever made any phone calls to Andrew Stadler."

"How come?"

"Well, now, think about it. He called our records division to find out if Stadler had any priors, right? Stadler's the *only* former Stratton employee he called about. That tells me he was suspicious of Stadler—that he must have suspected Stadler of being the stalker who kept breaking into Nicholas Conover's home."

"Yeah, and maybe he was right. There haven't been any more break-ins at Conover's house since Stadler's murder."

"None that he's reported," she conceded. "But it's only been a week or so."

"So maybe Stadler was the guy. Maybe Rinaldi was on to something."

"Maybe. Maybe not. Either way, it wouldn't surprise me if the security director called Stadler and warned him to stay away from Nicholas Conover's house. You know, said, 'We know it's you, and if you do anything again you'll regret it.'"

The computer-generated phone record faxed over by Rinaldi's cellphone provider was dense and thick, maybe ten or twenty pages long. She gave it a quick glance, saw that most of the information she'd requested was there, but not all. Dates and times of all telephone calls he'd placed and received—all those seemed to be there. But only some of the phone numbers also listed names. Some did not.

"I assume you already looked through this," Audrey said.

"Quick scan, yeah. Guy has a pretty active social life, looks like. Lot of women's names there."

"Did you come across Andrew Stadler's name?"

Bugbee shook his head.

"You looked closely at the day and night when the murder took place?"

Bugbee gave her his deadeye look. "Phone numbers don't all have names."

"I noticed that. There doesn't seem to be a logic to it."

"I figure if a number's unlisted, the name doesn't pop up automatically."

"Makes sense," she said. She hesitated, tempted to be as stingy with praise as Bugbee always was. But wasn't it written in Proverbs somewhere that a word fitly spoken is like apples of gold in settings of silver? "I think you're right. Very good point."

Bugbee shrugged, a gesture not of modesty but of dismissiveness, his way of letting her know that clever thinking was second nature to him. "That means a hell of a lot of cross-referencing," he said.

"Would you be able to take a crack at that?"

Bugbee snorted. "Yeah, like I got free time."

"Well, someone's got to."

A beat of silence: a standoff. "Did you get any more on that hydroseed stuff?"

Bugbee gave a lazy smile, pulled from his pants pocket a crumpled pink lab request sheet. "It's Penn Mulch."

"Penn mulch? What's that?"

"Penn Mulch is a proprietary formula marketed by the Lebanon Seaboard Corporation in Pennsylvania, a fertilizer and lawn products company." He was reading from notes prepared by someone else, probably a lab tech. "The distinctive characteristic is small, regular pellets half an inch long by an eighth of an inch wide. Looks kinda like hamster shit. Cellulose pellets made up of freeze-dried recycled newspaper, one-three-one starter fertilizer, and super-absorbent polymer crystals. And green dye."

"And grass seed."

"Not part of the Penn Mulch. The lawn company mixes in the grass seed with the mulch and a tackifier and makes a kind of slurry they can spray on the ground. Kind of like a pea soup, only thinner. The grass seed in this case is a mixture of Kentucky Bluegrass and Creeping Red Fescue, with a little Saturn Perennial Ryegrass and Buccaneer Perennial Ryegrass thrown in."

"Nice work," she said. "But that doesn't really mean much to me — is this a pretty common formula for hydroseed?"

"The grass seed, that varies a lot. There's like nine hundred different varieties to choose from. Some of it's cheap shit."

"The lawn companies don't all use the same mix, then?"

"Nah. The shit they use along the highway, the contractor mix, you don't want to use on your lawn. The better the mulch, the better results you get."

"The Penn Mulch—"

"Expensive. Way better than the crap they normally use — ground-up wood mulch or newspaper, comes in fifty-pound bags. This is pricey stuff. Doubt it's very common. It's what you might use on some rich guy's lawn — rich guy who knows the difference, I mean."

"So we need to find out what lawn companies in the area use Penn Mulch."

"That's a lot of phone calls."

"How many lawn companies in Fenwick? Two or three, maybe?"

"Not my point," Bugbee said. "So you find the one company that sometimes uses Penn Mulch in its hydroseed mix. Then what?"

"Then you find out whose lawns they used Penn Mulch on. If you're saying it's so expensive, there can't be all that many."

"So what do you get? Our dead guy walked over someone's lawn that had Penn Mulch on it. So?"

"I don't imagine there are too many fancy lawns down in the dog pound, Roy," she said. "Do you?"

51

During the drive from the high school back to Stratton, Nick found himself thinking about Cassie Stadler.

She was not only gorgeous—he'd had more than his share of gorgeous women over the years, especially during college, when Laura had wanted them to "take a break" and "see other people"—but she was so smart it was scary, eerily perceptive. She seemed to understand him fully, to see through him, almost. She knew him better than he knew himself.

And he couldn't deny the physical attraction: for the first time in over a year he'd had sex, and he felt like a sexual being again. This was a sensation he'd almost forgotten about. The pump had been primed. He felt horny. He thought about yesterday afternoon and got hard.

Then he remembered who she was, how he'd come to know her, and his mood collapsed. The guilt came surging back, worse than ever.

A voice in his head: *Are you kidding me? You're screwing the daughter of the man you murdered?*

What's wrong with you?

He didn't understand what he was doing. If he allowed himself to get close to her . . . Well, what if she found out, somehow? Could he keep up this crazy balancing act?

What the hell am I doing?

But he badly wanted to see her again. That was the craziest thing of all.

It was late afternoon by now, and he didn't have to return to the office.

He pulled over to the side of the road and fished a scrap of paper out of his jacket pocket. On it he'd scrawled Cassie Stadler's phone number. Impulsively—without heeding that chiding voice in his head—he called her on his cell.

"Hello," he said when she answered. His voice sounded small. "It's Nick."

A beat. "Nick," she said, and stopped.

"I just wanted to . . ." His voice actually cracked. Just wanted to—what? Turn back the clock? Reverse what happened That Night? Make everything *all better*? And since that wasn't possible, then what? He just wanted to talk to her. That was the truth. "I was just calling . . ."

"I know," she said quickly.

"You okay?"

"Are *you*?"

"I'd like to see you," he said.

"Nick," she said. "You should stay away from me. I'm trouble. Really."

Nick almost smiled. Cassie didn't know what trouble was. *You think you're trouble? You should see me when I've got a Smith & Wesson in my hands.* Acid splashed the back of his throat.

"I don't think so," Nick said.

"Don't you think you've done enough?"

He felt something like an electric jolt. Hadn't he done enough? That was one way of looking at it. "Excuse me?"

"Not that I didn't appreciate it. I did. *All* of it. But we need to leave it there. You've got a company to run. A family to hold together. I don't fit into that."

"I'm just leaving an appointment," he said. "I can be there in about five minutes."

"Hey," Cassie said, opening the dusty screen door. Carpenter-style jeans, white T-shirt, flecks of paint. Then she smiled, a smile that crinkled her eyes. She looked better, sounded better. "I didn't think you'd come back."

"Why?"

"Well, you know, buyer's remorse. Regret over what you'd done. The usual male stuff."

"Maybe I'm not your usual male."

"I'm getting that idea. Bring me anything today?"

Nick shrugged. "Sorry. There's a bottle of windshield-wiper fluid in the trunk."

"Forget it," Cassie said. "That stuff always gives me a hangover."

"Might have a can of WD-40 around, too."

"Now that's more promising. I'm really digging the idea of having the CEO of Stratton as my personal grocery boy."

"Point of pride with me. Nick Conover buys a mean turkey sandwich."

"But should I take it personally that you got me nonfat yogurt?" She brought him inside. "Let me make you some of the tea you bought."

She disappeared into the kitchen for a moment. She had a CD on, a woman singing something about, "I'm brave but I'm chicken shit."

When she came back, Nick said, "You look good."

"I'm beginning to feel more like myself again," she said. "You caught me at a low point the other day. I'm sure you know how it goes."

"Well, you look a lot better."

"And you look like shit," she said, matter of fact.

"Well," Nick said. "Long day."

She stretched herself out on the nubby brown sofa, with the gold thread woven through the upholstery like something out of the 1950s.

"Long day, or long story?"

"Trust me, you don't want to hear a grown man bitch and moan about troubles at the shop."

"Trust me, I could use the distraction."

Nick leaned back in the ancient green La-Z-Boy. After a few moments, he began to tell her about the Rumor, leaving out a few details. He didn't mention Scott by name, didn't go into Scott's disloyalty. That was too painful a subject right now.

Cassie hugged her knees, gathering herself into some tight yoga-like ball, and listened intently as he explained.

"And if that weren't enough, I get a call from Lucas's school," he went on. He stopped. He wasn't accustomed to talking about his life that way. Not since Laura's death. Somehow he'd gotten out of practice.

"Tell me," she said.

He did, telling her, too, about how he'd called Lucas at home, confronted him, and how Luke had hung up. When he finally checked his watch, he realized he'd been talking for more than five minutes.

"I never understood that," Cassie said.

"Understood what?"

"Kid gets suspended for three days, meaning what? They don't have to go to school for three days? They stay home?"

"Right."

"And get into more trouble? That's supposed to be a punishment? I mean, a baseball player gets suspended for five games for fighting with the umpire, that's a punishment. But telling a kid he can't go to school, which he hates, for three days?"

"Maybe it's like social humiliation."

"For a teenager? Isn't that more like a badge of honor?"

Nick shrugged. "Wouldn't have been for me."

"No, you were probably Mr. Perfect."

"No way. I got into the usual trouble. I was just careful about it. I didn't want to get kicked off the hockey team. Hey, where's that tea?" he asked.

"That stove takes forever. Electric, and underpowered. Dad wouldn't allow gas in the house. One of his many 'things.' But we won't go there." She craned her head, listening. "I'm sure it's ready now."

"Just that all this talking makes a man thirsty," Nick said.

Cassie came back with two steaming mugs. "English Breakfast," she said. "Though I saw that you also bought me a box of Blue Moon Kava Kava and Chamomile mix. I'm guessing that's not Nick Conover's usual cup."

"Maybe not."

"Why do I get the feeling you've got me figured for some sort of New Age nut?" She shrugged. "Possibly because I am one. How can I deny it? You make chairs, I teach *asanas*. Hey, when it comes down to it, we're both in the sitting industry, right?"

"So you're not going to tell me about my aura."

"You can take the girl out of Carnegie Mellon—and believe me, they did." A smile hovered around her lips. "But you can't take the Carnegie Mellon out of the girl. Never really got into chakras and shit. There's a lot of my dad in me. I've got an empirical streak a mile wide."

"And I took you for a nineteen waist."

"Thanks." She took a careful sip of her tea. "So you've got problems. You'll deal, because that's the kind of person you are. When life gives you lemons, you make Lemon Pledge."

"I was expecting something more Zen, somehow."

"I see you haven't touched your English Breakfast. So what kind of tea do you like?"

"Any kind. So long as it's coffee."

She found a bottle of Four Roses bourbon on a low table beside the sofa, handed it to him. "Put a slug of this in it. It'll cut the tannins."

He sloshed a little into his cup. It definitely improved the taste.

Cassie was looking at him with cat eyes. "So are you here for me or for you?"

"Both."

She nodded, amused. "You're my caseworker?"

"Come on," Nick said. "You're not exactly a charity case."

"I'm doing okay."

"Well, I want you to know that if you're ever not doing okay, you've got me here to help."

"This is starting to sound like adios."

"No. Not at all."

"Good." She got up, tugged at the cord on the venetian blinds, closing them and darkening the room. "That's a relief."

He came up to her from behind, slipped his hands under her knit top, and felt the silky warmth of her belly.

"Why don't we go upstairs?" Nick said.

"We don't go upstairs," she said at once.

"We don't, huh. Okay." Slowly he began moving his hands upward until he found her breasts, teased her nipples as he kissed and licked the back of her neck.

"Yeah," she said throatily.

Still with her back to his, she brought her hands around to his butt and squeezed each cheek, hard.

He entered her from behind this time.

"Jesus," he said, and she looked up at him, her eyes gleaming.

It took him several minutes to catch his breath.

"Wow," he said. "Thank you."

"My pleasure."

"Well, mine, I think."

She took a sip of tea, curled up next to him on the sofa. She began singing along with the CD, which must have been set on repeat mode, something about "best friend with benefits."

"You've got a nice voice."

"Sang in the church choir. Mom was a real holy roller, used to drag me there. It was the only thing that got me through. So, boss man, you can't give up the fight, you know." An odd sort of vehemence had entered Cassie's voice. "You've got to play the game balls out, with all your heart. *Everything* matters."

"That's the way I always played hockey. Gave it my all—you have to."

"Always kept your head up while you skated?"

He smiled. She obviously got hockey too. "Oh yeah. Put your head down for a second, and you're signed, sealed, and delivered. The game's fast."

"You been keeping your head up at Stratton?"

"Not enough," he admitted.

"I suspect people maybe underestimate you sometimes, because they sense you're eager to be liked. My guess is that people who push you too far live to regret it."

"Maybe." Memories swirled in Nick's head, dark ones that he didn't want to reexamine.

"You've already surprised a lot of people, is my bet. Dorothy Devries—she's cooled toward you in the past several years. Am I right?"

Nick blinked. It wasn't a conscious realization he'd had, but it was true. "Yes," he said. "How did you know?"

Cassie looked away. "Don't take this the wrong way. But when Old Man Devries's widow appoints a successor, there are a lot of things going on in her head. One thing she's *not* looking to do is to bring in someone who's going to show up her beloved Milton. A reliable hand on the tiller, sure. The kind of reliable guy about whom you could say, 'He's no Milton Devries, of course, but who is?' They could have poached some hotshot from the competition — I bet that would have been the usual thing. But it wasn't what she wanted. You were meant to be Milton's mini-me. Then you came in, and you kicked ass. You weren't Milton's protégé anymore. And even if she benefited from that financially, the whole Nick Conover show had to bother her too."

Nick just shook his head.

"You don't believe me, do you?"

"The trouble is," Nick said slowly, "I do believe you. What you say never really occurred to me before, and it's sure not doing anything for my ego, but when I listen to you talk, I'm thinking, Yeah, that's probably what went down. The old lady wasn't expecting what she got. Truth is, I wasn't either. I got in there, made three or four critical hires, let them do their thing. It could have played differently. I'm not that smart, but I know what I don't know. What I'm good at, maybe, is bringing in smarts."

"And so long as they're loyal to you, you're going to be okay. But if they aren't family-first people, you could have problems."

"Family-first?"

"The Stratton family."

"You really are the woman with X-ray eyes," Nick said. "You see right through people." Suddenly he shivered. How much *did* she see? Did she see the blood on his hands? He swallowed hard. It wasn't a good time to start losing it.

"You know what they say."

"Who?"

"They. Anaïs Nin, maybe, I forget. 'We don't see things as they are. We see things as *we* are.'"

"Not sure I get that."

"And the hardest people to see, sometimes, are the people we love. Like your son."

"A complete mystery to me these days."

"What time did you say your kids would be home?"

"Less than an hour."

"I'd like to meet them," she said.

"Uh, I'm not sure that's a good idea," Nick said.

Cassie got to her feet, ran her fingers through her hair. "Jesus, what am I saying, it's a *terrible* idea," she said. The change in her was abrupt, startling. "What was I thinking? I'm not part of your life. I don't make *sense* in your life. Listen, I'd probably be ashamed of me too." She tugged at her paint-flecked jeans. "So let's leave things here. After all, we'll always have Steeple-town. Goodbye, Nick. Have a good life."

"Cassie," Nick said. "That's not what I meant."

Cassie was silent. When Nick turned to look at her, her eyes were wells of sorrow. He felt a wave of guilt, and longing.

"Would you like to come by for dinner?" he asked.

52

Cassie was subdued as the Chevy Suburban waited in a queue in front of the Fenwicke Estates gatehouse. Nick suppressed the urge to drum his fingers on the steering wheel.

"Evening, Jorge," Nick said, as they slowly passed the gatehouse.

Cassie leaned over so she could see him. "Hi, Jorge, I'm Cassie." She smiled and gave him a little wave.

"Evening," Jorge said, more animatedly than usual.

Okay, Nick thought. Chalk one up for the girl's humanity. She noticed the guys in uniform. So long as it wasn't the start of some big worker's solidarity trip, that was probably a good sign.

He wondered how the kids would react to his bringing a woman home. More than wondered: he was, he had to admit, nervous about it. She was the first woman he'd been involved with in any way since Laura's death, and he had no idea how they'd react. Lucas, he could safely predict, would be hostile. Hostility was his default mode. Julia? Now, that was a question. There was the Freudian thing where the girl wants Daddy all to herself, and there was that powerful strain of unthinking loyalty to her mom: how dare Daddy date someone other than Mommy.

It could be ugly. But the one who'd really suffer the brunt of it was Cassie. He felt bad for her, for what she was about to experience. As he drove to the house, he began to regret his impulsive invitation. He should have introduced her to the kids more gradually.

As they approached the driveway to the house, Cassie gave a low whistle.

"Sweet," she said. "Wouldn't have guessed it was your style, I have to admit."

"Maybe it isn't," Nick admitted, but he felt self-conscious about saying it. Like he was putting the blame on Laura.

She squinted at the yellow Dumpster that was stationed underneath a basketball hoop. "Construction?"

"Always."

"*Portoncini dei morti*," she said.

"You're in America now," Nick said lightly. "About time you learned to speak English."

"I take it you've never been to Gubbio."

"If they don't manufacture casters there, I've probably never been."

"It's in Umbria. Amazing place. I spent a whole year there—painting, busking, you name it. Great place, but spooky too. You go through the old part of town, and you start to notice that a lot of the houses have these areas that look oddly bricked up. Turns out that they had this old custom, like a sacrament. They bricked up the doorway where a dead person was taken out of a house. They're called *portoncini dei morti*. Doors of the dead. Ghost doors."

"Must have kept a lot of masons busy," Nick said. *It's the front door, Nick. That's the one place you don't cheap out.* Doors of the dead.

"This was Laura's house, wasn't it?" Cassie asked.

That wasn't how Nick would have put it, but it was more or less true. It was Laura's house.

"Sort of," he said.

Marta was at the door when they came in. "I told you we'd be having company," Nick said. "Well, she's the company."

Marta didn't shake Cassie's hand, he noticed, just said, "Nice to meet you," and none too cordially. Same expression she reserved for telephone solicitors.

"Where's Julia?" Nick asked Marta.

"Watching TV in the family room. Emily just left a little while ago."

"And Luke?"

"In his room. On the computer, maybe. He said he can't stay for dinner."

"Oh, that right? Well, he's *going* to stay for dinner," Nick said, icily. Christ. The whole suspension thing—they would have to have a Very Serious Talk. Which probably meant a Perfect Storm of an argument.

Just not tonight.

Nick took Cassie over to the family room, where Julia was engrossed in *Slime Time Live* on Nickelodeon.

"Hey, baby," Nick said. "I want you to meet my friend Cassie."

"Hi," Julia said, and turned back to the show. Not rude, but not exactly friendly. A little cool, maybe.

"Cassie is going to be joining us for dinner."

Julia turned around again. "Okay," she said, warily. To Cassie, she said, "We usually don't have company for dinner."

Then she turned back to the flickering screen. Someone was getting doused with green slime.

"Don't worry," Cassie said. "I eat like a bird."

Julia nodded.

"Two and half times my body weight in earthworms," Cassie said.

Julia giggled.

"Are you a baseball fan?" Cassie asked.

"Yeah, I guess," Julia said. "You mean my jersey?"

"I *love* the Tigers," Cassie said.

Julia shrugged dismissively. "The girls in school keep calling me 'tomboy' because I wear it all the time."

"They're just jealous of your jersey," Nick put in, but Julia wasn't listening.

"You ever been to Comerica Park?" Cassie asked her.

Julia shook her head.

"Oh, it's amazing. You'd love it. We've got to go there some time."

"Really?" Julia said.

"Definitely. And listen—I got called 'tomboy' when I was a kid too," said Cassie. "Just 'cause I wasn't into Barbie."

"Really? I *hate* Barbie," Julia said.

"Barbie's kind of creepy," Cassie agreed. "I was never into dolls."

"Me neither."

"But I'll bet you have stuffed animals to keep you company, right?"

"Beanie Babies, mostly."

"Do you collect them?"

"Sort of." Julia was now looking at Cassie with interest. "They're very valuable, you know. But only if you don't use them and stuff."

"You mean like, never take the label off, and put them on the shelf?"

Julia nodded, this time more animatedly.

"I don't get that," Cassie said. "The whole point of Beanie Babies is to play with them, right? Do you have a lot, or just a couple of them?"

"I don't know. I guess a lot. You want to see my collection?"

"Really? I'd love to."

"Not now," said Nick. "Later. Right now it's suppertime, and we're having company."

"Okay," Julia said. Then she yelled, "Luke, supper! We have company."

As Nick took Cassie back to the front hall, she said, "She's a sweetie, isn't she?"

"A regular Ma Barker is what she is," Nick said. "For sweetness and light, we've got Lucas Conover." He took her upstairs, gestured toward the hallway. There was no need to specify which was Lucas's room. From beneath the closed door, thrash music pulsed, an avalanche of noise with someone shouting at the top of his lungs over a thudding bass beat. Something about *outta my mind*, something about *ashes to ashes*, something about *all pain, no gain*. A lot of incomprehensible screaming in between.

"As you can tell, he's a huge Lawrence Welk fan," Nick said. He decided against knocking on the door. Let Marta get him downstairs. Lucas responded better to her anyway.

"How do you know so much about Beanie Babies?" Nick asked.

"My knowledge of Beanie Babies is limited to what I read in *Newsweek*. Am I busted?"

"You sure got Julia believing you're a Beanie Babies expert."

"Hey, whatever works, right? Though I get a feeling your son isn't into Beanie Babies."

"He's a hard case, my son," Nick said, not wanting to dwell on it. "I'm going to change, meet you downstairs in a few."

When he came back down, Cassie and Julia were deep in conversation in the family room. "And there was blood everywhere," Julia was saying in a hushed, serious voice.

"Oh no," Cassie breathed.

"And it was Barney." Julia's eyes were moist.

"My God."

"And Daddy said he would protect us. He said he'd do whatever he had to do."

Nick cleared his throat; it wasn't a conversation he wanted to encourage. "Hey girls," he called. "Suppertime."

"I've just been hearing about what happened to Barney," Cassie said, looking up. "Sounds horrible."

"It was rough," Nick said. "For all of us." He tried to sound a little brusque, to let Cassie know he didn't want the conversation to continue.

Luckily, Marta emerged from the kitchen just then and announced that dinner was ready.

"All right," Nick said. "Let's go, girls. Marta, would you go upstairs and ask Sid Vicious to join us?"

As Marta went upstairs, Julia asked, "Who's Sid Vicious?"

"*You* know the Sex Pistols?" Cassie said to Nick, smiling.

"I think I saw part of some movie about them before I walked out," Nick said. "I'm not a total geek, you know, no matter what my son thinks."

"But who's Sid Vicious?" Julia asked again.

Lucas's heavy footsteps thundered as if a crate of bowling balls had been upended at the top of the stairs. At the landing he looked around, taking in Cassie's presence with an unblinking stare.

"Luke, I'd like you to meet my friend Cassie Stadler," Nick said.

"Cassie *Stadler*?"

The way he said it made Nick's blood run cold.

"That's right," he said quietly. "She'll be joining us for dinner."

"I have to go out," Lucas said.

"You have to stay here."

"I have a homework project I need to do with some kids in class."

Nick refrained from rolling his eyes. A science experiment, no doubt, designed to study the effect of *Cannabis sativa* on the psychophysiology of the American sixteen-year-old. "It isn't up for discussion," he said. "Sit."

"I like your music," Cassie said to him.

Lucas looked at her with something just shy of hostility. "Yeah?" His tone of voice made it short for: *Yeah, what of it?*

"If you call that music," Nick said, feeling protective of Cassie. He gave her an apologetic shrug. "And when he isn't listening to this kind of noise, it's that gangsta rap stuff."

"Gangsta rap stuff." Cassie's mimicry was perfect, and devastating.

Lucas half snorted, half chortled.

"You'd prefer it if he listened to the Mamas and the Papas?" she asked. "Like some kind of Stepford son?"

Hey, no fair, Nick wanted to say. "*I* didn't even listen to the Mamas and the Papas," he said.

Cassie wasn't paying attention. She was focused on Lucas. "I'm curious. How long have you been into Slasher?"

"A few months," Lucas said, surprised.

"Not a lot of people your age even know about Slasher. I bet you have all their albums."

"Got downloads of some stuff they haven't released yet, and some bootleg demos, too."

"Slasher would be a rock band," Nick said, feeling obscurely excluded. "Tell me if I'm warm."

"'Slasher' is what they call Dad, you know," Lucas said, pleased.

"I've heard. Anyway, Slasher's cool, but John Horrigan's kind of a jerk, I gotta tell you," Cassie said, taking a step toward Lucas.

Lucas's eyes widened. "You *know* him? No fucking way." An entirely different Lucas was making an appearance.

She nodded. "You heard about how he fell off the stage in Saratoga, during the Sudden Death tour? Well, he had some problems with his neck and back after that. Nothing helped. So I used to teach this yoga class in Chicago, where he's based. One day he shows up, and it's the first thing that really helps. Then he's asking me for extra sessions. And then . . ." She walked closer to Lucas and put her hand on his arm as she murmured the rest.

Lucas giggled, blushing.

"I can't believe it," he said. "Horrigan *rocks.* So . . ." He glanced at Nick, at Julia, and lowered his voice. "What was he like?"

"Selfish," Cassie said. "First I thought, bad technique. But then I realized it was just selfishness. Finally I just stopped returning his phone calls. Great guitar player, though."

"Horrigan rocks."

"What do you mean 'selfish'?" Julia demanded, with a ten-year-old's unerring instinct for inappropriate subjects.

"We're just talking about who gets their guitar licks in," Cassie said.

Lucas began to quake with silent laughter.

Julia started to laugh, too, for no particular reason. Then Nick, too, began to laugh, and for the life of him he couldn't say why. Except that he couldn't remember when Lucas had last laughed.

Marta brought a platter of pork chops to the table, some sort of chili and cilantro thing on top. "More in the kitchen if anyone wants," she said, sounding slightly peevish, or maybe just a little out of sorts.

"Everything smells delicious, Marta," Nick said.

"And there's salad." She pointed to two covered ceramic bowls. "And there's rice and there's ratatouille."

"That's great, Marta," said Cassie. "I think we're going to be okay."

"I didn't make a dessert, but there's ice cream," Marta added darkly. "And some fruit. Some bananas."

"I make one hell of a banana flambé," said Cassie. "Any takers?"

"Knock yourself out," Lucas said, and grinned.

Perfect white teeth, clear blue eyes, almost perfect complexion. A beautiful kid. Nick felt a surge of paternal pride. *Three-day suspension*. They'd have to have The Talk. Just not now. It hung over him like a sword.

"All you need are bananas, some butter, brown sugar, and rum."

"We've got all that," Nick said.

"Oh, and a light. For a blaze of glory." Cassie turned to Lucas. "Got a lighter, kiddo?"

53

After driving Cassie home, Nick returned to find Lucas in his room, lying back on his bed, earbuds in. Nick signaled to him to take them off. To his surprise, Lucas did without complaint, and he spoke first: "So, she's cool."

"Good. I'm glad you like her." Nick sat in the only chair in the room that wasn't piled with books and papers and discarded clothes. He took a breath, plunged in. The normal force field of hostility seemed to be down, or maybe just diminished. That was good; that would make it easier.

"Luke, buddy, you and I have to talk."

Lucas watched him, blinking, said nothing.

"I told you Mr. Sundquist called me in for a conference today."

"So?"

"You understand how serious this is, this suspension."

"It's a three-day vacation."

"That's what I was afraid I'd hear. No, Luke. It goes on your record. When you apply to colleges, they see that."

"Like you care?"

"Oh, now, come on. Of course I care."

"You don't even know what I'm studying in school, do you?"

"I didn't know you were studying anything," Nick cracked without thinking.

"That's a *big* help, Dad. You basically spend all your time at work, and now you're trying to pretend like you're interested in how I do in school?" It was amazing how Lucas could take those pure, innocent eyes and focus them like a laser beam into one cold, hard blue ray of hatred.

"Yeah, well, I'm worried about what's happening to you."

"What's happening to me," Lucas repeated mockingly.

"This is all about Mom, isn't it?" He regretted saying it as soon as it came out. That was way too blunt. But how else to say it?

"Excuse me?" Lucas said, incredulous.

"Look, ever since Mom's death, you've totally changed. I know it, and you know it."

"That's deep, Nick. Really deep. Coming from you, that's really great."

"What's that supposed to mean?"

"Well, look at you. You went right back to work, no problem."

"I have a job, Luke."

"Moving right on, huh, Nick?"

"Don't *ever* talk to me that way," Nick said.

"Get the hell out of my room. I don't need this shit from you."

"I'm not leaving until you hear me out," Nick said.

"Fine," Lucas said, getting up from the bed and walking out of his room. "Sit there and blab all you want."

Nick followed his son into the hall. "You come back here," he said.

"I don't need this shit."

"I said, get *back* here. We're not done talking."

"Hey, you've made your point, okay. I'm *sorry* I'm such a *disappointment* to you." Lucas raced down the stairs, taking them two steps at a time.

Nick ran after him. "You don't walk away from me when I'm talking to you," he shouted. He caught up with him just as Lucas reached the front door, put his hand on his son's shoulder.

Luke swiveled, swatted Nick's hand off. "Get your fucking hands off me!" he screamed, turning the big brass knob and shoving the door open.

"You get back here," Nick shouted after him, standing in the doorway. "This cannot go on!"

But Lucas was running down the stone path into the darkness. "I'm sick of this fucking house, and I'm sick of you!" came his son's voice, echoing.

"Where do you think you're going?" Nick yelled back. "You get back here right now!"

He thought about taking off after his son, but what would be the point, really? He was overcome with a sense of futility and desperation. He stood there on the threshold until the sound of Lucas's footsteps faded to silence.

Julia was there at the bottom of the stairs when he turned around. She was weeping.

He went up to her, gave her a tight squeeze, and said, "He'll be okay, baby. *We'll* be okay. Now you go to bed."

In the shower a little later, Nick cursed himself for how badly he'd handled the whole thing, how ham-handed he'd been, how emotionally obtuse. There had to be ways of reaching Lucas, even if he didn't know them. It was like a foreign country where the language sounds nothing like your own, the street signs are unreadable, you're alone and lost. As the needles of water stung his neck and back, he looked at the row of shampoos and conditioners in the tiled inset: Laura's stuff, all of it. He hadn't bothered to remove it. Couldn't *bring* himself to remove it, really.

He soaped himself up, got soap in his eyes, which made his eyes smart so that when his eyes started stinging and watering, he couldn't tell if it was the soap or the tears.

He put on a T-shirt, pajama bottoms, and got into bed just as he heard the front door open, the alert tone go off. Luke had returned.

He switched off the bedside lamp. As always, he slept on the side of the bed that had always been his, wondered when, if ever, he'd start sleeping in the middle of the bed.

His bedroom door opened, and he thought for a split second that it might be Lucas, here to apologize. But it wasn't, of course.

Julia stood there, her lanky shape and curly hair silhouetted by the night-light in the hall.

"I can't sleep," she said.

"Come here."

She ran to Nick, scrambled into the bed. "Daddy," she said very softly. "Can I sleep in your bed? Just for tonight."

He brushed back the curls, saw the tear-streaked face. "Sure, baby. But just for tonight."

54

Leon slept late, of course, so it was no problem for Audrey to be up long before him Saturday morning. She enjoyed the quiet of the morning, the solitude, being in her own head. She made herself a pot of hazelnut coffee—the kind Leon hated, but she'd make regular coffee when he got up—and read the morning papers.

The weekends used to be their little island of intimacy, before—before he lost his job, before she started working overtime hours in order to be gone as much as possible. They'd sleep late on Saturday, snuggle, make love. They'd make brunch together, read the papers together, sometimes even make love again. Take a nap together. Then go out and enjoy the weekend, shopping or going for walks. Sundays he'd sleep until she returned from church, and then they'd maybe go out for brunch or make something at home, and they'd make love too.

Those days were like ancient Mesopotamia. She'd almost forgotten what they felt like, they'd receded so into the distant shrouded past.

This Saturday morning, after she'd had her coffee, she considered getting out her case files and working. But a glimmering of ancient Mesopotamia arose in her mind.

Someone had to break the gridlock, she told herself. They were both frozen. Neither wanted to make the first move to try to change things.

She debated internally, the way she debated most things large or small. *How many times are you going to keep trying?* she asked herself. *How often are you going to butt your head against a brick wall before you realize it feels better to stop?* The other voice—the wiser, more generous voice—said: *But he's the damaged one. He's the hurt one. You need to take the lead.*

This morning—maybe it was the still beauty of the morning, maybe it was the deliciousness of the coffee, maybe it was the time alone—she decided to take the lead.

She walked quietly through the dark bedroom, careful not to wake him. She slid open her bottom dresser drawer and pulled out the pale apricot silk teddy she'd bought from the Victoria's Secret catalog, never worn.

She closed the bedroom door and went down the hall to the bathroom, where she took a nice hot shower, using the loofah. She applied lotion all over—her skin tended to get ashy if she didn't—and then put on makeup, something she never did unless she was going out. She daubed perfume on in all the right secret places—Opium, the only perfume that Leon had ever complimented her on.

Wearing just her teddy, and feeling a bit silly at first, she went into the kitchen and made brunch. French toast, bacon, even some cantaloupe balls. His favorite breakfast: he liked French toast even more than eggs Benedict. A fresh pot of coffee, the kind he liked. A white porcelain creamer, in the shape of a cow, filled with half-and-half.

Then she arranged everything carefully on a bed tray—it took her a while to find it in the overhead storage in the little pantry, and then she'd had to wash off the accumulated dust—and went in to wake up Leon.

Since he'd been in a sour mood for most of the last year, she was pleasantly surprised at his sweet smile upon seeing her and the breakfast she'd placed on the bed.

"Hey, Shorty," he rasped. "What's all this?"

"Brunch, baby."

"French toast. It's not my birthday, is it?"

She climbed into the bed and kissed him. "I just felt like it, that's all."

He took a sip of coffee, made a contented noise. "I got to go take a whiz." The breakfast tray tottered dangerously as he tried to extricate himself from the bed.

She could hear the sound of his urine splashing noisily in the toilet bowl, the toilet flushing, then she could hear him brushing his teeth, something he didn't normally do before breakfast. A good sign. Even though he was getting as big as his sister, he remained a very sexy man.

He came back into the bed; she moved the tray to allow him to get in without upsetting it. He kissed her again, to her surprise. She shifted her body, angled it toward him, a hand on his upper arm, ready—but then he pulled away and took another sip of coffee.

"You forgot the syrup," he said.

She touched the white porcelain gravy boat.

He tipped it over the stack of French toast, dousing it liberally, then took the knife and fork and cut a tall wedge. She'd even dusted it with powdered sugar, which he liked.

"Mmm-mmm. You warmed it."

Audrey smiled, pleased. Didn't they always say the way to a man's heart is through his stomach? Maybe this was all it took to break through the ice floes that had accumulated in their marriage.

After he'd wolfed down half the stack of French toast and all but two of the bacon strips, he turned to her. "How come you're not eating?"

"I ate some in the kitchen."

He nodded, devoured another piece of bacon, took another swig of coffee. "I thought you were working today."

"I'm taking the day off."

"How come?"

"Well, I thought we could spend some time together."

He turned his attention back to the French toast. "Hmph."

"You feel like going for a walk later, maybe?" she asked.

After a moment, he said, "I thought we needed the money."

"One day's not going to send us to the poorhouse. We could go for a drive out in the country."

Another silence, and then he spoke through a mouthful of cantaloupe. "Just don't be telling me about getting a job as a night watchman."

She was annoyed but didn't let on. "We don't have to talk about that stuff now, honey."

"All right."

Her cell phone rang. She hesitated. Not just that it was a flow-breaker, but it was an unwelcome reminder of the job she had and he didn't. She knew it couldn't be a personal call. It rang again.

"I'll make it quick," she said, reaching for the cell phone on her night-stand.

Leon cast her a warning look.

It was Roy Bugbee. This was unusual, a call from Bugbee on a Saturday morning. He wasn't friendly, but neither was he as rude as usual. "The phone records," he said.

"One second." She walked out of the bedroom so as not to subject Leon to her conversation. "Rinaldi's cell phone records?"

"One of the numbers kept coming up a lot, no ID, so I looked it up in Bresser's." He was referring to one of the reverse phone directories. She was impressed at Bugbee's initiative, relieved that he'd finally agreed to take this job on. Maybe he wasn't completely beyond redemption.

Bugbee had paused, waiting for her to say something, or maybe for dra-matic effect, so she said, "Great idea."

"Right. And three guesses who called Rinaldi at 2:07 in the morning, the day Stadler got plugged."

"Stadler," she ventured.

"No," Bugbee said. "Nicholas Conover."

"Two in the morning? The same morning when Stadler's body was found, you mean."

"Uh huh."

"But . . . but Conover told me he slept through the night."

"Hmph. Guess not, huh?"

"No," Audrey said, feeling a little tingle of excitement. "I guess not." An-other awkward pause. "Is that it?"

"Is that *it*?" Bugbee scoffed. "You got something better on a Saturday morning?"

"No, I mean—nice job," she said. "Well done."

She ended the call and returned to the bedroom, but Leon was no longer in bed. He was sitting in the chair, dressed, tying his sneakers.

"What are you doing?" she said.

Leon stood up, and as he walked out of the bedroom, he passed the bed

and flung out a hand at the breakfast tray, flipping it onto the floor. The cantaloupe balls went skittering across the carpet, the French toast flopping
down in a neat pile, the maple syrup puddle sitting atop the gray wool. The
coffee spill soaked right in, as did the half-and-half. Audrey couldn't keep
from letting out a squawk of surprise.

She followed him out, crying, "Leon, baby, I'm sorry—I didn't . . ." But
didn't *what*? The call was important, wasn't it?

"You'll make it quick, huh," Leon said bitterly as he clomped down the
hall. "Sure you will. You got business to do, you're gonna do it no matter
what we're doing. You got your priorities straight, don't you?"

She felt sad and almost despondent. "No, Leon, that's not fair," she said.
"I couldn't have been on the phone for more than a minute. I'm sorry—"

But the screen door slammed, and he was gone.

Audrey was alone in the house now, feeling lonely and a tad anxious. She
had no idea where Leon had stormed off to, just that he'd taken his car.

She called Bugbee back, reaching him on his cell.

He didn't sound happy to hear from her, but then he never did. "You said
Conover called Rinaldi at 2:07 on Wednesday morning. Was that the only
call that night?"

"That morning," Bugbee corrected her. She could hear traffic noise in
the background. He was probably in his car now.

"Were there any other calls that night or that morning between Conover
and Rinaldi?"

"No."

"That means Rinaldi didn't call Conover first, wake him up or something. Conover wasn't calling Rinaldi back, in other words."

"Right. Put it this way: Rinaldi didn't call Conover from either his home
phone or his cell phone. It's conceivable he called Conover from a pay-
phone, but you'd have to get Conover's phone records for that."

"Yes. I think we should talk to both of these gentlemen again."

"I'd say so. Hold on, I'm losing you." A few seconds went by, a half a
minute, and he was back on. "Yeah, put the squeeze on 'em both. I'd say we
got 'em there with an inconsistency."

"I'd like to talk to them tomorrow."

"Tomorrow's Sunday—don't you have church or something?"

"Sunday afternoon."

"I'm golfing."

"Well, I'm going to see if I can't talk to Nicholas Conover tomorrow afternoon."

"On Sunday?"

"I figure he can't be too busy at work if it's a Sunday."

"But that's family time."

"Stadler had a family too. Now the thing is, Roy, I think we should talk to these gentlemen simultaneously. And we ought to call them at the last minute before we go over. I really don't want one calling the other to get their stories straight."

"Right, but like I said, I'm golfing tomorrow."

"I'm flexible as to the time tomorrow," she said. "You tell me what works best for you. I'm usually out of church by eleven."

"Christ. Well, I'd rather do Conover. I want to take down the fucker. You can talk to Rinaldi."

"My sense, talking to Rinaldi, is that he might respond better to a male detective."

"I don't really give a shit what makes him comfortable."

"It's not a matter of comfort," Audrey said. "It's a matter of what's going to work best, what will help us extract the information we want most effectively."

Bugbee raised his voice a few decibels. "You want to get information out of Nicholas Conover, you gotta play him hard. And that calls for me. My style. Not yours. You're a pushover, and he can tell."

"Oh, I'm less of a pushover than you might think, Roy," she said.

55

Cassie was already seated at a booth when Nick arrived at the Town Grounds, Fenwick's upscale coffee house. The national craze for good coffee had even come to Fenwick, a Maxwell-House-in-the-can kind of place if ever there was one, but Starbucks had stayed clear so far. The result was this small, sort of neo-hippy joint that roasted their own coffee, did a healthy take-out business in beans, and served coffee in little glass French presses.

She was drinking a cup of herbal tea—a Celestial Seasonings Cranberry Apple Zinger packet was crumpled next to the teapot—and looked tired, gloomy. The smudges under her eyes were back.

"Am I late?" Nick asked.

A quick shake of the head. "No, why?"

"You look pissed off."

"You obviously don't know me well enough yet," she said. "You'll learn to recognize pissed off. This isn't pissed off. This is tired."

"Well, that dinner wasn't so bad, was it?"

"Your kids are great."

"You really hit it off with them. I think Julia loved having another woman around."

"It's a pretty male household, with you two Conover men exuding all that testosterone."

"The thing is, you know, Julia's at this age where—well, I don't know who's going to talk to her about periods and tampons, all that girl stuff. She doesn't want to hear it from me. Like I know anything about it anyway."

"Her nanny, maybe? Marta, right?"

"I guess. But it's not the same thing as a mom. There's Laura's sister, Aunt Abby, but we barely see her anymore since Laura's death. And Luke spends most of his time hating me. One big happy family." He told her about the big fight, Lucas storming out of the house.

"You talk about him like he's the bad seed."

"Sometimes I think he is."

"Since Laura's death."

Nick nodded.

"How'd that happen?"

Nick shook his head. "I don't want to get into that, you mind?"

"Hey, fine. What do I care?"

Nick looked at her. "Come on, don't get offended. It's just a sort of heavy topic for a Sunday morning, okay?" He took a breath. "We were driving to a swim meet and we hit an icy path and skidded." He studied the tabletop. "And blah blah blah."

"You were driving," she said softly.

"Laura was, actually."

"So you don't blame yourself for it?"

"Oh, I do. I totally do."

"But you know it's not rational."

"Who's talking rational?"

"Whose swim meet?"

"Luke's. Can we talk about something else, please?"

"So he gets to blame you and also share in the guilt, right?"

"You got it. It's a mess."

"He's a good kid, deep down. Lot of attitude, like most sixteen-year-old boys. Hard shell, but soft nougat center."

"How come I never get to see the nougat center?"

"Because you're his dad, and you're safe."

"Well, maybe you can talk to him about the evils of smoking."

"Yeah, right," she said, chuckling. She took a pack of Marlboros from her jeans jacket and tapped one out. "I think I'm not the best person to do that. Kinda like your Sid Vicious giving 'Just Say No' lectures on heroin." She took out her orange plastic Bic lighter and lit the cigarette, pulling the saucer toward her to use as an ashtray.

"I thought people who do yoga don't smoke," Nick said.

She flicked him a glare.

"Isn't yoga all about breath?"

"Come on," she said.

"Sorry."

"Can I ask you something?" she said offhandedly.

"Sure."

"Julia told me about your dog." Nick felt his guts constrict, but he said nothing. "God," she went on. "That's so incredible. I mean, how did you feel when that happened?"

"How did I feel?" He didn't know how to respond. How would anyone feel? He shook his head, faltered for a bit. "I was frightened for my kids, I guess, most of all. I was terrified they might be next."

"But you must have been furious too. I mean, God, someone who'd do something like that to your family!" She tilted her head as she peered at him, her eyes keen. "I'd want to kill him."

Why was she asking this?

He felt a wave of cold wash over him. "No," he said, "it wasn't anger so much as—as this protective instinct. That's what I felt most of all."

She nodded. "Sure. That's right. The normal dad reaction. Gotta protect the kids."

"Right. Got a new alarm system, told all the kids to be extra careful. But there's only so much you can do." His cell phone rang.

He apologized, and picked it up. "Nick Conover," he said.

"Mr. Conover, this is Detective Rhimes?"

He paused for a few seconds. "Oh, yes. Hi—"

He wondered whether Cassie could hear the police detective's voice.

Cassie smoked, idly studying a hand-lettered "THIS IS A SMOKE-FREE ZONE!" sign on a little chalkboard, pink Day-Glo chalk.

"I'm terribly sorry to bother you on a Sunday, but if there's any way you could spare a little time, I'd like to come by and talk for a little bit."

"Well, sure, I suppose. What's up?"

"There's a couple of little details I'm confused about, I thought you might be able to clear up for me. I know Sunday is family time, but if you wouldn't mind . . ."

"Sure," Nick said. "What time do you have in mind?"

"Is half an hour from now convenient for you?"

Nick hesitated. "I think that would be okay," he said.

When he ended the call, he said, "Cassie, listen—I'm sorry, but—"

"Family calls," she said.

He nodded. "Afraid so. I'll make it up to you."

She put a hand on his forearm. "Hey, don't worry about it. Family's always number one."

As soon as he'd dropped her off, he dialed Eddie's cell.

56

Driving up to the fancy iron gate with the brass plaque that said FENWICKE ESTATES, Audrey was distinctly aware that she was entering another world. She had changed out of her church clothes into something more casual, and now she felt underdressed. Her Honda Accord was definitely underdressed. The guard at the gatehouse looked her over with disapproval as he took her name and picked up his phone to call Conover. She doubted it was the color of her skin. More likely the color of the rust on her front left quarter panel.

She noticed all the security cameras. One, mounted to the gatehouse, took her picture. Another was positioned to capture her license plate at the rear of her car. There was a proximity-card reader by the guard's window too: people who lived in Fenwicke Estates probably had to wave a card at the sensor to be admitted. The security was impressive. But what must it be like to live like this, she wondered? In a place like Fenwick, where the crimes were mostly localized in the bad part of town, why would you want to live this way? Then she remembered what Conover had said about his wife's concern that the family might be threatened by employees laid off from Stratton.

When she drove up to the house, she drew breath.

This was a mansion, there was no other word for it. The place was immense, made of stone and brick, beautiful. She'd never seen a house like this in real life, outside of the movies. It sat in the middle of a huge green field of a lawn, with specimen trees and flowers everywhere. As she walked up the stone path to the house, she glanced again at the lawn and noticed that the blades of grass were small and slender and sparse. Up close she could see that the lawn had recently been seeded.

The lawn.

She pretended to trip on one of the paving stones, fell to her knees, breaking her fall with one hand. When she got back on her feet, she slipped a good healthy pinch of soil into her purse just as the front door opened and Nicholas Conover came out.

"You okay?" he said, walking down the front steps toward her.

"Just clumsy. My husband's always saying to me, 'Walk much?'"

"Well, you're not the first to trip on those stones. Gotta do something about that path."

He was wearing faded jeans, a navy blue polo shirt, white running shoes. She hadn't noticed before how tall he was and trim and powerful looking. He looked like an athlete, or a former athlete. She remembered reading that he'd been a hockey star at the high school.

"I'm so sorry to disturb you at home on a Sunday."

"Don't worry about it," Conover said. "It's probably just as well. My schedule during the week's pretty jammed. Plus, anything I can do to help you out, I want to do. You're doing important work."

"I appreciate it. This is such a beautiful home."

"Thanks. Come on in. Can I get you some coffee?"

"No, thanks."

"Lemonade? My daughter makes the best lemonade."

"That right?"

"Right from frozen concentrate. Yep."

"That sounds tempting, but I'll pass." Before they got to the front steps, she turned around and said, "That really has to be the most beautiful lawn I've ever seen."

"Now, that's what a guy likes to hear."

"Oh, right. Men and their lawns. But seriously, it looks like a putting green."

"And I don't even golf. My greatest failing as a CEO."

"Is it—do you mind if I ask, because my husband, Leon, is always complaining about the state of our lawn—did you put down sod?"

"No, just seed."

"Regular grass seed, or what's that stuff called—where you spray it?"

"Hydroseed. Yep, that's what we did."

"Well, I've got to tell Leon. He's always calling it hydro*weeding* because he says you get way too many weeds in the grass, but this looks just perfect to me."

"That Leon sounds like a real card."

"Oh, he is," Audrey said, feeling a prickle. "That he is."

The front door looked like something out of Versailles, ornately carved wood in a honey color. A quiet high-pitched tone sounded when Conover opened the door: an alarm system. He led her through an enormous foyer, high vaulted ceilings, really breathtaking. So this is how rich people live, she thought. Imagine being able to afford a house like this. She tried not to gawk, but it was hard.

She heard the sound of someone playing a piano and thought of Camille. "Is that one of yours?" she asked.

"My daughter," he said. "Believe me, it doesn't happen often, her practicing. It's like a total eclipse of the sun."

They walked by the room where a young girl was practicing, a lanky dark-haired girl around Camille's age wearing a baseball shirt. The girl was playing the first prelude from Bach's *Well-Tempered Clavier*, one of Audrey's favorite pieces. She played it haltingly, mechanically, clearly not yet grasping how fluid it had to be. Audrey caught a quick flash of a baby grand piano, a Steinway. She remembered how long LaTonya and Paul had scrimped to buy the battered old upright, which never stayed in tune. Imagine owning a Steinway, she thought.

She was briefly tempted to stop and listen, but Conover kept going down the hall, and she kept up. As they entered an elegant sitting room with Persian rugs and big comfortable-looking easy chairs, she said, "Oh, they never like practicing."

"Tell me about it," Conover said, sinking into one of the chairs. "You pretty much have to put a—" he began, then started again. "They fight you on everything at this age. You have kids, Detective?"

She sat in the chair alongside his, not the one directly opposite, preferring to avoid the body language of confrontation. "No, I'm afraid we haven't been blessed with children," she said. What was he about to say—You have to put a gun to their heads? What was interesting was not the figure of speech but that he'd caught himself.

Interesting.

She casually glanced at an arrangement of family photographs in silver frames on a low table between them, and she felt a pang of jealousy. She saw Conover and his late wife, a son, and a daughter, Conover with his two children and the family dog. An extremely handsome family.

This house, these children—she was overcome by envy, which shamed her.

Envy and wrath shorten the life, it said in Ecclesiastes. Somewhere else it said that envy is the rottenness of the bones—was it Proverbs? Who is able to stand before envy? Who indeed? *Behold, these are the ungodly, who prosper in the world; they increase in riches*. That was in Psalms, she was quite sure. *Surely thou didst set them in slippery places: thou castedst them down into destruction*.

Her entire house could fit into a couple of these rooms.

She would never have children.

She was sitting next to the man who was responsible for laying Leon off.

She took out her notebook and said, "Well, I just wanted to clear up a few things from our last conversation."

"Sure." Conover leaned back in his chair, arms folded back, stretching. "How can I help you?"

"If we can go back to last Tuesday evening, ten days ago."

Conover looked puzzled.

"The night that Andrew Stadler was murdered."

He nodded his head. "Okay. Right."

She consulted her pad, as if she had the notes from their last interview right in front of her. She'd already transcribed them and put them into a folder in one of the Stadler file boxes. "We talked about where you were that night," she prompted, "when your memory was maybe a little fresher. You said you were at home, asleep by eleven or eleven thirty. You said you slept through the night."

"Okay."

"You don't remember getting up that night."

He furrowed his brow. "I suppose it's possible I got up to pee."

"But you didn't make a phone call."

"When?"

"In the middle of the night. After you went to sleep."

"Not that I recall," he said, smiling, leaning forward. "If I'm making calls in my sleep, I've got even bigger problems than I'm aware of."

She smiled too. "Mr. Conover, at 2:07 A.M. that night you placed a call to your security director, Edward Rinaldi. Do you remember that?"

Conover didn't seem to react. He seemed to be examining the pattern on the Oriental rug. "We're talking after midnight, early on Wednesday?"

"That's right."

"Then I must have my days wrong."

"I'm sorry?"

"One of those nights I remember the alarm went off. I've got it set to make a sound in my bedroom so it doesn't wake up the whole house."

"The alarm went off," Audrey said. That was checkable, of course.

"Something set it off, and I went downstairs to check it out. It was nothing, as far as I could see, but I was a little anxious. You can understand, I'm sure, with what had just happened."

She nodded, compressed her lips, jotted a note. Didn't meet his eyes.

"Eddie, Stratton's security director, had just had one of his guys put in this fancy new alarm system, and I wasn't sure if this was a false alarm or something I should be concerned about."

"You didn't call the alarm company?"

"My first thought was to call Eddie—I asked him to come out to the house and check it out."

She looked up. "You couldn't check it out yourself?"

"Oh, I did. But I wanted to make sure there wasn't something faulty in the system. I didn't want to call the cops for what was sure to be a false alarm. I wanted Eddie to check it out."

"At two in the morning?"

"He wasn't happy about it." Conover grinned again. "But given what I've been through, we both agreed it was better safe than sorry."

"Yet you told me you slept through the night."

"Obviously I got the days mixed up. My apologies." He didn't sound at all defensive. He sounded quite casual. Matter-of-fact. "Tell you something else, I've been taking this pill to help me sleep, and it kind of makes the nights sort of blurry for me."

"Amnesia?"

"No, nothing like that. I don't think Ambien causes amnesia like some of those other sleeping pills, Halcion or whatever. It's just that when I pass out, I'm zonked."

"I see."

He'd just altered his story significantly, but in a completely believable way. Or was she being too suspicious? Maybe he really had mixed up the days. People did it all the time. If that night hadn't been unusual or remarkable for him—if, that is, he hadn't witnessed Andrew Stadler's murder that night, or been aware of it whether before or after the fact—then there was no reason for him to have any special, fixed memory of what he'd done. Or not done.

"And did Mr. Rinaldi come over?"

Conover nodded. "Maybe half an hour later. He walked around the yard, didn't find anything. Checked the system. He thought maybe a large animal had set it off, like a deer or something."

"Not an intruder."

"Not that he could see. I mean, it's possible someone was out there, walking around on my property, near the house. But I didn't see anyone when I got up, and by the time Eddie got here, he didn't see anything either."

"You said you took Ambien to go to sleep that night?"

"Right."

"So you must have been pretty groggy when the alarm went off."

"I'll say."

"So there might have been someone, or something, that you just didn't notice. Being groggy and all."

"Definitely possible."

"Did anyone else in the house wake up at the time?"

"No. The kids were asleep, and Marta—she's the nanny and housekeeper—she didn't get up either. Like I said, the alarm was set to sound in my bedroom, and not too loud. And the house is pretty soundproof."

"Mr. Conover, you said your security director had 'just' put in the new alarm system. How long ago?"

"Two weeks ago. Not even."

"After the incident with the dog?"

"You got it. If I could have had Eddie put in a moat and a drawbridge, I'd have done that too. I don't ever want my kids to be endangered."

"Certainly." She'd noticed the cameras around the house when she'd arrived. "If you'd had a system like this earlier, you might have been able to prevent the break-ins."

"Maybe," Conover said.

"But you live in this gated community. There seems to be a lot of security when you come in—the guard, the access control, the cameras in front and all around the perimeter fence."

"Which does a pretty good job of keeping out unauthorized vehicles. Problem is, there's nothing that stops someone from just climbing the fence out of sight of the guardhouse and getting in that way. The cameras'll pick them up, but there's no motion sensor around the fence—no alarm goes off."

"That's a serious security flaw."

"Tell me about it. That's why Eddie wanted to beef up the system at the house."

But now another thought appeared at the back of her thoughts, and she tugged at it like a stray thread.

The security system.

The cameras.

Nothing that stops someone from just climbing the fence.

If Stadler had climbed the fence that surrounded Fenwicke Estates and walked to Conover's house in the middle of the night, walked across the lawn, setting off the brand-new motion sensors, wouldn't that have been captured by Conover's own video cameras?

And if so, wouldn't there be a recording somewhere? Probably not videotape: no one used that anymore. Probably recorded onto a hard drive somewhere in the house, right? She wondered about that. She didn't really know much about how these newfangled security systems worked.

She'd have to take a closer look.

"You know, I've changed my mind about that coffee," Audrey said.

57

Audrey did not arrive home until a little after seven, feeling a knot in her stomach as she turned the key in the front door. She'd told him that she'd be home for dinner, though she hadn't said what time that would be. It took so little to set Leon off.

But he wasn't home.

Several nights in a row he hadn't been home until late, almost ten o'clock. What was he doing? Did he go out drinking? Yet recently he didn't seem to be drunk when he got home. She couldn't smell liquor on his breath.

She had another suspicion, though it made her sick to think about it. It explained why Leon was no longer interested in having sex with her.

He was getting it somewhere else. He was, she feared, having an affair, and lately he was being brazen about it, not even attempting to cover it up.

Leon was at home all day while she was at work, which gave him plenty of opportunity to cheat without her ever finding out. But going out, coming home at nine, ten o'clock without so much as an excuse — that was a thumb in her eye. That was blatant.

Sure enough, at a few minutes after ten she heard the jingling of the keys in the lock, and Leon walked in, went right to the kitchen, ran water into a glass. He didn't even say hello.

"Leon," she called out.

But he didn't answer.

And she knew. You didn't have to be a detective. It was that obvious. She knew, and it was like a punch to her solar plexus.

Nick sat in his study, trying to go over some paperwork. He'd been calling Eddie, at home and on his cell, but no answer. On his fourth try, Eddie answered with an annoyed "What?"

"Eddie, she was just here," Nick said.

"Fenwick's own Cleopatra Jones? She don't have no superpowers, Nick. She's just sweating you. They tried the same shit on me today—the other one came by, Bugbee, asked me a shitload of questions, but I could see they got nothing."

"She asked me about the call I made to you that night."

"What'd you tell her?"

"Well, I—see, I'd told her I slept through the night that night."

"*Shit.*"

"No, listen. That's what I said at first, but then when she said she knew I'd made a call to you on your cell phone, I told her I must have mixed up the nights. I said the alarm went off that night, so I called you to ask you to check it out." Nick waited for Eddie's response with rising dread. "My God, Eddie, did you tell the other cop something different? I mean, I figured the alarm going off, that's a matter of record—"

"No, you did the right thing. I said pretty much the same once I saw what he had. But man, I was shitting bricks you might try to wing it, say something else. Good job."

"We've got to coordinate a little more closely, Eddie. Make sure we don't say different things."

"Right."

"And something else. She was admiring the alarm system."

"She's got good taste." He lowered his voice. "And so does the superfreak who's naked in my bed. Who was just admiring my dick. Which is why I gotta go."

"Especially the cameras. Especially the *cameras*, Eddie."

"Yeah?"

"Are you *positive* there's no way to retrieve the part of the tape you erased?"

"It's not tape, it's digital," Eddie snapped. "Anyway, I told you, you have nothing to worry about. What's gone is gone. Why are we fucking *having* this conversation? I just spent ten minutes preheating the oven—now I got to stick in my French bread before it cools down, you get what I'm saying?"

"The hard drive is totally clean, right? They can't bring it back?

An exasperated sigh. "Stop being such a *girl*, okay?"

Nick felt a surge of anger he knew better than to vent. "I sure as hell hope you know what you're doing," he said stonily.

"Nick, you're doing it again. You're peeing in my pool. Oh, by the way. That work you wanted me to do on Scott McNally?"

"Yeah?"

"Remember last month when he was away for a week?"

"I remember. Some sort of dude ranch in Arizona. Grapevine Canyon, was it? He said it was like *City Slickers* without the laughs."

"*City Slickers*, he said? *Crouching* fucking *Tiger*'s more like it. He's a sneak, but a cheapskate numbers guy like him can't pass up the corporate travel rates, right? So this pencil dick puts in for a Stratton discount when he buys his ticket to Hong Kong. I got the receipts from the girls in the travel office. Unfucking*believable*."

"Hong Kong?"

Eddie nodded. "Hong Kong and then Shenzhen. Which is this huge industrial area near Hong Kong, shitload of factories, on the mainland."

"I know about Shenzhen."

"That mean anything to you?"

"It means he's lying to me," Nick replied. *It also means that all these rumors are right. Where there's smoke there's fire, as the GSA guy said.*

"Sounds to me like you got trouble everywhere you go," Eddie said. "Big trouble."

58

Audrey was surprised to find Bugbee in this early, sitting in his cubicle on the phone. She approached and heard him talking to a lawn company, asking about hydroseeding. Well, she thought, what do you know? He really is working this case.

He wore his customary sport coat, a pale green with a windowpane plaid, a pale blue shirt, red tie. In repose, he was not a bad-looking man, even if he dressed like a used-car salesman. He saw her standing nearby, kept talking without acknowledging her presence. She held up a finger. After a little while he gave her a brusque nod.

She waited until he got off the phone, then wordlessly showed him the little clear-plastic eye-cream vial.

He looked at the pinch of dirt, said suspiciously, "What's that?"

"I took it from Conover's lawn yesterday." She paused. "His lawn was recently hydroseeded."

Bugbee stared, the realization dawning. "That's not admissible," he said. "Poison fruit."

"I know. But worth taking a look at. To my eye it looks like the same stuff from under Stadler's fingernails."

"It's been, what, like two weeks since the murder. It's probably disintegrated a lot since then. The mulch pellets are supposed to break down."

"It's been a dry couple of weeks. The only water probably came from his irrigation system. More interesting, I managed to get a look at his security system while he was making coffee for me." She handed him a While You Were Out message slip on which she'd written some notes. "Pretty fancy. Sixteen cameras. Here's the name of the alarm monitoring company he uses. And the makes and models of the equipment, including the digital video recorder."

"You want me to talk to one of the techs," he said. She noticed that for the first time he didn't argue with her.

"I think we should go over there and take a look at the recorder. And while we're at it, check for blood and prints, inside and outside the house."

Bugbee nodded. "You're thinking the whole thing went down in or near Conover's house, and the surveillance cameras recorded it."

"We can't ignore the possibility."

"They'd be stupid to forget about that little detail."

"We've both seen a lot of stupidity. People forget. Also, it's not like the old days when you could just take out a videotape and get rid of it. It's got to be a lot harder to erase a digital surveillance recording. You've got to know what you're doing."

"Eddie Rinaldi knows what he's doing."

"Maybe."

"Of course he does," Bugbee said. "Are you thinking Conover did it?"

"I'm thinking Eddie did it." Now that he was a suspect, she noticed, he'd gone from Rinaldi to Eddie. "I think Conover saw or heard Stadler outside his house. Maybe the alarm went off, maybe not—"

"The alarm company would probably have a record of that."

"Okay, but either way, Conover calls Eddie, tells him this guy's trying to get into his house. Eddie comes over, confronts Stadler, then kills him."

"And gets rid of the body."

"He's an ex-cop. He's smart enough, or experienced enough, to make sure he doesn't leave any trace evidence on the body—"

"Except the fingernails."

"It's the middle of the night, two in the morning, it's late and it's dark and they're both panicking. They overlook some things. Subtleties like that."

"One of them moves the body down to Hastings."

"Eddie, I'm guessing."

Bugbee thought a moment. "The gatehouse at Fenwicke Estates probably has records of who left when. We can see if Conover drove out of there some time after Eddie drove in. Or if it was just Eddie."

"Which would tell you what?"

"If the shooting happened inside or outside Conover's house, they had to move the body down to the Dumpster on Hastings. Which they're going to do in a car. If both Conover and Rinaldi left Fenwicke Estates some time after two, then it could have been either one of them. But if only Eddie left, then it's Eddie who moved it."

"Exactly." A moment of silence passed. "There are cameras everywhere around the community."

Bugbee smiled. "If so, we got 'em."

"That's not what I'm saying. If we can get the surveillance tapes, we can confirm when Eddie entered and exited, sure."

"Or Eddie and Conover."

"Okay. But more important, we can see if *Stadler* came over. If Andrew Stadler entered. Then we've got Stadler's whereabouts pinned down."

Bugbee nodded. "Yeah." Another pause. "Which means that Eddie has an unlicensed .380."

"Why unlicensed?"

"Because I went through the safety inspection certificate files at the county sheriff's department. He's got paperwork for a Ruger, a Glock, a hunting rifle, couple of shotguns. But no .380. So if he's got one, he doesn't have any paper on it."

"I've been pushing the state crime lab," Audrey said. "I want to see if they can use their database to match the rounds we found in Stadler's body with any other no-gun case anywhere."

Bugbee looked impressed, but he just nodded.

"In any case, we're going to need a search warrant to see what weapons Rinaldi has."

"Not going to be a problem getting one."

"Fine. If we find a .380 and we get a match . . ." She was starting to enjoy the genuine back-and-forth, even if Bugbee was still prickly and defensive.

"You're dreaming. He can't be that stupid."

"We can always hope. What did he say about the phone call?"

"He was pretty slick. Said, yeah, he got a call from Conover that night, the alarm went off at Conover's house and could he check it out. Said he was a little pissed off, but he went over there to check it out. You know, the shit you do to keep your boss happy. It was like no big deal. Did Conover put his foot in it?"

"No. He—well, it felt like he sort of evolved his story."

"Evolved?"

"He didn't revise his story right away. I reminded him that he'd said he slept through the night, and then I asked him about the phone call he made at two in the morning, and he owned right up to it. He said he must have got the days mixed up."

"Happens. You believe him?"

"I don't know."

"He sound rehearsed?"

"It was hard to tell. Either he was telling the truth, or he'd done his homework."

"Usually you can tell."

"Usually. But I couldn't."

"So maybe he's a good liar."

"Or he's telling the truth. The way I see it, he's telling *part* of the truth. He called Eddie, Eddie came over—and that's where the true part ends. Did Eddie say if he found anything when he looked around Conover's yard?"

"Yeah. He said he found nothing."

"That much they got straight," Audrey said.

"Maybe too straight."

"I don't know what that means. Straight is straight. You know what? I say we ought to move quickly on this. The gun, the tape recorder—this is all stuff that they could do something about if they haven't already. Toss the gun, delete the tape, whatever. Now that we've talked to them both separately, at the same time, they're both going to be suspicious. If they're going to destroy evidence, now is the time they're going to do it."

Bugbee nodded. "Talk to Noyce, put in for the warrants anyway in case we need them. I'll make a couple of calls. Can you clear your schedule today?"

"Happy to."

"Oh, I called that Stadler chick for a follow-up."

"And?"

"She doesn't know shit about what her father did on the night he was killed. Says he never said anything about Conover."

"You think she's telling you the truth?"

"I got no reason to think otherwise. My instinct tells me, yeah, she's on the level."

Audrey nodded. "Me too."

A few minutes later, Bugbee came up to Audrey's cubicle with a cat-that-ate-the-canary smile. "Wouldn't you just know Nicholas Conover would use a company called Elite Professional Lawn Care? Sixteen days ago they hydroseeded the property around a house belonging to the CEO of the Stratton Corporation. The guy remembered it well—the architect, guy named Claflin, specified Penn Mulch. Said they had to put in a new gas line or something, tore up the old grass, and his client decided to put in a whole new lawn, replace the crappy old one. Lawn guy, he said it's a waste of money to put stuff like that in the slurry, but he's not going to argue. Not with a customer who has the big bucks, you know?"

59

Scott McNally tended to get into work around the same time as Nick did, around seven thirty. Normally, they and the other early arrivers sat at their desks working and doing e-mail, tended not to socialize, took advantage of the quiet time to get work done uninterrupted.

But this morning, Nick took a stroll across the floor to the other side and approached Scott's cubicle quietly. He felt a pulse of fury every time he thought about how Scott had lied to him about going to that dude ranch in Arizona, had instead made a secret trip to mainland China. That coupled with what he'd learned from the Atlas McKenzie and the Homeland Security guys—these goddamned rumors that Stratton was quietly negotiating to "move the company to China," whatever that meant exactly.

It was time to rattle Scott's cage, find out what he was doing.

"Got any interesting vacation ideas?" Nick asked abruptly.

Scott looked up, startled. "Me? Come on, my idea of a great vacation is a Trekkie convention." He caught the look on Nick's face and laughed nervously. "I mean, well, Eden loves Parrot Cay in the Turks and Caicos."

"Actually, I was thinking some place further east. Like Shenzhen, maybe? Where do you like to stay when you visit Shenzhen, Scott?"

Scott reddened. He looked down at his desk—it was almost a reflex, Nick noticed—and said, "I'll go anywhere for a good mu shu pork."

"Why, Scott?"

Scott didn't answer right away.

"We both know how hard Muldaur's been pushing for us to move manufacturing to Asia," Nick said. "That what you're doing for him? Checking out Chinese factories behind my back?"

Scott looked up from his desk, looking pained. "Look, Nick, right now Stratton is like a puppy with diarrhea, okay? Cute to look at, but no one wants to get too close. I'm not doing any of us any good if I don't scout out these possibilities."

"Possibilities?"

"I realize you find it upsetting. I can't blame you. But one day, when you look at the numbers and you finally say, 'Scott, what are our options here?' I've got to be able to tell you what they are."

"Let me get this straight," Nick said. "You made some sort of secret-agent trip to China to scout out factories, then *lied* about it to me?"

Scott closed his eyes and nodded, compressing his lips. "I'm sorry," he said very quietly. "It wasn't my idea. Todd insisted on it. He just felt it was too much of a sore point with you—that you'd do everything you could to block any kind of overtures to China."

"What kind of 'overtures' are you talking about? I want specifics."

"Nick, I really hate being caught in the middle like this."

"I asked you a question."

"I know. And it's really not my place to say any more than I have already. So let's just leave it right there, okay?"

Nick stared. Scott wasn't even feigning deference anymore. Nick felt his anger growing greater by the second. It was all he could do not to reach over and grab Scott by the scrawny neck, lift him up, and hurl him against the silver-mesh fabric panel.

Nick turned to leave without saying another word.

"Oh, and Nick?"

Nick turned back, looked at him blankly.

"The Nan Hai is the place."

"Huh?"

"The place to stay in Shenzhen. The Nan Hai Hotel. Great views, great restaurant—I think you'll like it."

A voice squawked out of Scott's intercom. "Scott, it's Marjorie?"

"Oh, hey, Marge. Looking for Nick? He's right here."

"Nick," Marge said. "Call for you."

Nick picked up Scott's handset to speak to her privately. "There a problem?"

"It's someone from the police."

"My burglar alarm again."

"No, it's . . . it's something else. Nothing urgent, and your kids are fine, but it sounds important."

Scott gave him a curious look as Nick hurried away.

60

"This is Nick Conover."

Audrey was astonished, actually, when Nicholas Conover picked up the phone so quickly. She was expecting the usual runaround, the game of telephone tag that powerful men so often liked to play.

"Mr. Conover, this is Detective Rhimes. I'm sorry to bother you again."

The slightest beat of silence.

"No bother at all," he said. "What can I do for you?"

"Well, now, I was wondering if we might be able to look around your house."

"Look around . . . ?"

"We were thinking it would help us a great deal in establishing Andrew Stadler's whereabouts that night. That morning." She hoped the shift to "we" was subtle enough. "If indeed it was Andrew Stadler who went to your house that night, he might have been scared off by all the new security measures. The cameras and the lights and what have you."

"It's possible." Conover's voice sounded a bit less friendly now.

"So if we're able to nail down whether he did go to your house—whether it really was him who came by and not, say, a deer—that'll be a big help in mapping his last hours. Really narrow things down for us."

She could hear Conover inhale.

"When you're talking 'look around,' what do you mean, exactly?"

"A search. You know, the usual."

"Not sure I know what that means." Was there the slightest strain in his voice? Certainly something had shifted, changed. He was no longer putting out friendly vibes. He'd gone neutral.

"We come over with our techs, collect evidence, take pictures, whatever."

They both knew what she meant. No matter how she spun it, how she dressed it up, it was still a crime-scene search, and Conover surely understood that. It was a funny sort of dance now. A performance, almost.

"You talking about searching my yard?"

"Well, yes. That and your premises as well."

"My house."

"That's right."

"But—but no one entered my house."

She was ready for that. "Well, see, if Andrew Stadler really is the stalker who's repeatedly broken into your house over the last year, we might find evidence of that inside. Am I wrong in concluding that no one from the Fenwick police ever took fingerprints after the previous incidents?"

"That's right."

She shook her head, closed her eyes. "The less said about that, the better."

"When are you talking about doing this? This week some time?"

"Actually, given how things are progressing in this investigation," she said, "we'd like to do it today."

Another pause, this one even longer.

"Tell you what," Conover said at last. "Let me call you right back. What's the best number to reach you at?"

She wondered what he was going to do now—consult an attorney? His security director? One way or the other, whether he gave permission or not, she was going to search his premises.

If he refused—if she needed to get a search warrant—she'd be able to get one in about an hour. She'd already talked to one of the prosecutors, woke him up at home this morning, in fact, which didn't endear her to him. Once the prosecutor's head cleared, he'd said that there were sufficient grounds to grant a warrant. A district court judge would sign it, no problem.

But Audrey didn't want to get a search warrant. She didn't want to play hardball. Not yet. That was escalation, and if and when she needed to step things up, she could always do it. Better to low-key things. Keep up the pretense—the *shared* pretense, she was quite sure—that Nicholas Conover was being cooperative just because he was a good citizen, wanted to see justice done, wanted to get to the bottom of this. Because the moment he shifted to opposition and antagonism, she'd be all over him.

If he refused, four patrol units would be on their way over to his house in a matter of minutes to secure the premises and the curtilage, or the surrounding area, make sure no one took anything out. Then she'd be there an hour later with a search warrant and a crime-scene team.

She didn't want to go down that road yet. But she always had to be aware of the legalities. The prosecutor had rendered his judgment that she *could* get a warrant if she wanted to, yes. Instead, Audrey wanted to conduct what they called a consent search. That meant that Conover would sign a standard Consent to Search form.

It was a little tricky, though. If Conover signed it and his signature was witnessed, that established that he'd given his knowing, intelligent, and voluntary consent to a search. But there'd been cases, she knew, where a suspect with a clever lawyer had managed to get the results of a search thrown out at trial, insisting that they'd been coerced, or they didn't totally understand, or whatever. Audrey was determined not to commit that gaffe. So she was following the prosecutor's advice: Get Conover to sign the waiver, date it, get two witnesses, and you're fine. And if he refuses, we'll get you a warrant.

Half an hour later he called back, sounding confident once again. "Sure, Detective, I have no problem with that."

"Thank you, Mr. Conover. Now, I'm going to need you to sign a consent form allowing us to search your premises. You know, cross every *T* and so on."

"No problem."

"Would you like to be there for the search? It's up to you, certainly, but I know how busy you are."

"I think it's a good idea, don't you?"

"I think it's a good idea, yes."

"Listen, Detective. One thing. I don't mind you guys searching my property, looking for whatever you want, but I really don't want the neighborhood crawling with cops, you know? There going to be a bunch of patrol cars with lights and sirens and all that?"

Audrey chuckled. "It won't be as bad as all that."

"Can you do this using whatever you call them, unmarked vehicles?"

"For the most part, yes. There will be an evidence van and such, but we'll try to be subtle about it."

"As much as a police search can be subtle, right? Subtle as a brick to the head."

They shared a polite, uneasy laugh.

"One more thing," Conover said. "This is a small town, and we both know how people talk. I really hope this is all kept discreet."

"Discreet?"

"Out of the public eye. I really can't afford to have people hearing about how the police have been talking to me and searching my house in connection with this terrible murder. You know, I'm just saying I want to make sure my name stays out of it."

"Your name stays out of it," she repeated, thinking: *What are you saying exactly?*

"Look, you know, I'm the CEO of a major corporation in a town where not everybody loves me, right? Last thing I want is for rumors to start spreading—for people to be making stuff up about how Nick Conover's being looked into. Right?"

"Sure." She felt that prickle again, like an eruption of goose bumps.

"I mean, hey, we both know I'm not a suspect. But you get rumors and all that."

"Right."

"You know, it's like they say. A lie's halfway around the world before the truth has a chance to get its pants on, right?"

"I like that," she said. Here was another thing that made her uneasy. When an innocent person is being investigated for a homicide, he almost always squawks about it to his friends, protests, gets indignant. An innocent person in the klieg lights wants the support of his friends, so he invariably tells everyone about the outrage of the police suspecting him.

Nick Conover didn't want people to know that the police were interested in him.

This was not the reaction of an innocent man.

PART FOUR
CRIME SCENE

61

Early that morning, the day after Detective Rhimes had come over to the house to talk, Nick had awakened damp with sweat.

The T-shirt he'd slept in was wet around the neck. His pillow, even, was soaked, the wet feathers and down giving off that barnyard smell. His pulse was racing the way it used to during a particularly fierce scrimmage.

He'd just been jolted out of a dream that was way too real. It was one of those movielike dreams that feel vivid and fully imagined, not like his normal fleeting fragments of scenes and images. This one had a plot to it, a terrible, inexorable story in which he felt trapped.

Everyone *knew*.

They knew what he'd done That Night. They knew about Stadler. It was common knowledge, everywhere he went, walking through the halls of Stratton, the factory floor, the supermarket, the kids' schools. Everyone knew he'd killed a man, but he continued to insist, to pretend—it made no sense, he didn't know why—that he was innocent. It was almost a ritual acted out between him and everyone else: they knew, and he knew they knew, and yet he continued to maintain his innocence.

Okay, but then the dream took a sharp left turn into the gothic, like one of those scary movies about teenagers and homicidal maniacs, but also like a story by Edgar Allan Poe he'd read in high school about a telltale heart.

He came home one day, found the house crawling with cops. Not the house he and the kids lived in now, not Laura's mansion in Fenwicke Estates, but the dark, little brown-shingled, split-level ranch in Steepletown he'd grown up in. The house was a lot bigger though. Lots of hallways and empty rooms, room for the police to spread out and search, and he was powerless to stop them.

Hey, he tried to say but he couldn't speak, you're not playing by the rules. I pretend I'm innocent, and so do you. Remember? That's how it works.

Detective Audrey Rhimes was there and a dozen other faceless police investigators, and they were fanning out across the eerily large house, searching for clues. Someone had tipped them off. He heard one of the cops say the tip came from Laura. Laura was there too, taking an afternoon nap, but he woke her up to yell at her and she looked wounded but then there was a shout and he went to find out what was up.

It was the basement. Not the basement of the Fenwicke Estates house, with its hardwood floors and all the systems, the Weil-McLain gas-fired boiler and water heater and all that, neatly enclosed behind slatted bifold doors. But the basement of his childhood house, dark and damp and musty, concrete-floored.

Someone had found a pool of bodily fluids.

Not blood, but something else. It reeked. A spill of decomposition that had somehow seeped out from the basement wall.

One of the cops summoned a bunch of the other guys, and they broke through the concrete walls, and they found it there, the curled-up, decomposed body of Andrew Stadler, and Nick saw it, an electric jolt running through his body. They'd found it, and the game of pretenses was over because they'd found the proof, a body walled up in his basement, decomposing, rotting, leaching telltale fluids. The body so carefully and artfully concealed had signaled its location by festering and decaying and putrefying, leaking the black gravy of death.

A good ten hours after he'd awakened in a puddle of his own flop sweat, Nick pulled into the driveway and saw a fleet of police vehicles, cruisers, and unmarked sedans and vans, and it was as if he'd never woken up. So much for low-key. They couldn't have been much more obvious if they'd arrived with sirens screaming. Luckily the neighbors couldn't see the cars from the road, but the police must have caused a commotion arriving at the gates.

It was just before five o'clock. He saw Detective Rhimes standing on the porch waiting for him, wearing a peach-colored business suit.

He switched off the Suburban's engine and sat there for a moment in silence. Once he got out of the car, he was sure, nothing would be the same. Before and after. The engine block ticked as it cooled off, and the late afternoon sun was the color of burnt umber, the trees casting long shadows, clouds beginning to gather.

He noticed activity on the green carpet of lawn around the side of the house where his study was. A couple of people, a man and a woman—police techs?—were grazing slowly like sheep, heads down, looking closely for something. The woman was a squat fireplug with a wide ass, wearing a denim shirt and brand-new-looking dark blue jeans. The other one was a tall gawky guy with thick glasses, a camera around his neck.

This was real now. Not a nightmare. He wondered how they knew to look in the area nearest his study.

He tried to slow his heartbeat. Breathe in, breathe out, think placid thoughts.

Think of the first time he and Laura had gone to Maui, seventeen years ago, pre-kids, a Pleistocene era of his life. That perfect crescent of white sand beach in the sheltered cove, the absurdly blue crystal-clear water, the coconut palms rustling. A time when he felt more than just relaxed; he'd felt a deep inner serenity, Laura's fingers interlaced with his, the Hawaiian sun beating down on him and warming him to his core.

Detective Rhimes cocked her head, saw him sitting in the car. Probably deciding whether to walk up to the Suburban or wait for him there.

They were looking for spent cartridges. He had a gut feeling.

But Eddie had retrieved them all, didn't he?

Nick had been such a wreck that night, so dazed and so out of it. Eddie had asked him how many shots he'd fired, and Nick had answered two. That was right, wasn't it? The thing was such a blur that it was possible it was three. But Nick had said two, and Eddie had found two shell casings on the grass close to the French doors.

Had there been a third shot?

Had Eddie stopped when he found two, leaving one there that waited to be found by the gawky man and the fireplug woman, those experts in locating spent cartridge casings?

The lawn hadn't been mowed, of course, because the grass was too new. The fast-talking guy from the lawn company had told him to wait a good three weeks before he let his gardener mow.

So a chunk of metal that might otherwise have been thrown up into the blades of Hugo's wide walk-behind Gravely could well be lying there, glinting in the late-afternoon sun, just waiting for the wide-ass chick to bend over and snatch it up in her gloved hand.

He took another breath, did his best to compose himself, and got out of the Suburban.

"I'm terribly sorry to intrude on you this way," Detective Rhimes said. She looked genuinely apologetic. "You're very kind to let us look around. It's such a big help to our investigation."

"That's all right," Nick said. Strange, he thought, that she was keeping up the pretense. They both knew he was a suspect. He heard the rattling squawk of a crow circling overhead.

"I know you're a very busy man."

"You're busy too. We're all busy. I just want to do everything I can to help." His mouth went dry, choking off his last couple of words, and he wondered if she'd picked up on that. He swallowed, wondered if she noticed that too.

"Thank you so much," she said.

"Where's your charming partner?"

"He's busy on something else," she said.

Nick noticed the gawky guy walking across the lawn to them, holding something aloft.

He went light headed.

The guy was holding a large pair of forceps, and as he drew closer Nick could see a small brown something gripped at the end of the forceps. When the tech showed it to Detective Rhimes, without saying a word, Nick saw that it was a cigarette butt.

Detective Rhimes nodded as the man dropped the cigarette butt into a paper evidence bag, then turned back to Nick. She went on speaking as if they hadn't been interrupted.

Was Stadler smoking that night? Or had that been dropped there by one of the contractor's guys, taking a cigarette break outside the house, knowing they weren't allowed to smoke inside? He'd found some discarded Marlboro butts out there not so long ago, just before the loam was hydroseeded, picked them up with annoyance, made a mental note to say something to the contractor about the guys tossing their smokes around his lawn. Back when he had the luxury to be annoyed about such trivialities.

"I hope you don't mind that we got started a little early," Detective Rhimes said. "Your housekeeper refused to let my team in until you arrived, and I wanted to respect her wishes."

Nick nodded. "That's kind of you." He noticed that the woman articulated her words too clearly, her enunciation almost exaggerated, hypercorrect. There was something formal and off-putting about her manner that contrasted jarringly with her shyness and reserve, a glimmering of uncertainty, a vein of sweetness. Nick prided himself on his ability to read people pretty well, but this woman he didn't quite get. He didn't know what to make of her. Yesterday he'd tried to charm her, but he knew that hadn't worked.

"We're going to need to get a set of your fingerprints," she said.

"Sure. Of course."

"Also, we're going to need to take prints from everyone who lives in the house—the housekeeper, your children."

"My children? Is that really necessary?"

"These are only what we call elimination prints."

"My kids will freak out."

"Oh, they might think it's fun," she said. A sweet smile. "Kids often find it a novelty."

Nick shrugged. They entered the house, the high alert tone sounding quietly. The place different now: hushed, tense, like it was bracing itself for something. He heard the sound of running feet.

Julia.

"Daddy," his daughter said, face creased with concern, "what's going on?"

62

He sat down with the kids in the family room, the two of them on the couch that faced the enormous TV, Nick in the big side chair that Lucas normally staked out, which Nick thought of as his Archie Bunker chair. The Dad chair. He couldn't remember when they'd all watched TV together last, but back when they did, Lucas always grabbed the Archie Bunker chair, to his silent annoyance.

On a trestle table next to the TV set Nick noticed the little shrine that Julia and Lucas had made to Barney: a collection of photographs of their beloved dog, his collar and tags. His favorite toys, including a bedraggled stuffed lamb—his own pet—that he slept with and carried everywhere in his slobbering mouth. There was a letter Julia had written to him in different colored markers, which began: "Barney—we miss you SO MUCH!!!" Julia had explained that the shrine was Cassie's idea.

Lucas sat on the couch in huge baggy jeans, his legs splayed wide. The waistband of his boxer shorts was showing. He wore a black T-shirt with the word AMERIKAN in white letters on the front. Nick had no idea what that referred to. The laces on his Timberland boots were untied. He was wearing that rag on his head again. My own in-house, upper-middle-class, gated-community gangsta, Nick thought.

Lucas, staring off into the distance, said, "You gonna tell us what's up with the five-oh?"

"The police, you mean."

Lucas was looking out the bay window, watching the cops on the lawn.

"The police are here because of that guy who we think kept coming by and writing things inside our house," Nick said.

" 'No Hiding Place,' " recited Julia.

"Right. All that. He was a man who had something wrong with his head."

She said in a small voice, "Is he the man who killed Barney?"

"We're not sure, but we think so."

"Cassie's dad," Lucas said. "Andrew Stadler."

"Right." Cassie's dad.

"He was fucked up," Lucas said.

"Watch your mouth around your sister."

"I've heard that word before, Dad," said Julia.

"No doubt. I just don't want either one of you using language like that."

Lucas, smirking, shook his head with amused contempt.

"So this man, Andrew Stadler, he died a couple of weeks ago," Nick went on, "and the police think he might have tried to come by our house the night he was killed, on his way to wherever he was going."

"They think you did it," Lucas said. A triumphant smile.

Nick's insides seized. Maybe he *had* heard, that night when Eddie came over. Or did he just put two and two together?

"*Hey!*" said Julia, outraged.

"Actually, Luke, what they're doing here is trying to trace his where-abouts."

"Then how come they're gathering evidence? I can see 'em out my window. They dug up some dirt from the lawn and put it in a little container thing, and they keep walking back and forth on the lawn like they're scoping for something."

Nick nodded, breathing in and out. They were gathering dirt? What did that mean? Had they found dirt on Stadler's body? He remembered that Eddie had brushed Stadler's shoes clean.

Could they have found dirt on Stadler's body that connected him with the house? Could they even do something like that? This was the awful thing: Nick had no idea of what the police were actually capable of, how advanced their forensic science was, or how backward.

"Luke," he said calmly, "they're looking for anything that can tell them whether the guy came by here that night or not." Nick knew he was treading water here. His kids were too bright. They'd watched too many TV shows and movies. They knew about cops and murders and suspects.

"Why do they care?" asked Julia.

"Simple," he said. "They need to nail down what he did that night, see if he really was here instead of somewhere else, so they can figure out where he might have gone after that, when he was killed."

"Wouldn't that be on the cameras?" Lucas asked.

"Could be," Nick said. "I don't remember when the new security system was put in and when exactly the guy was killed."

"I do," Lucas said right back. "They put the cameras in the day before Stadler was killed." How the hell did he know that, *remember* that?

"Well, if you're right, then yes, they might find something on the cameras. I have no idea. Anyway, the police want to get your fingerprints while they're here."

"Cool," said Lucas.

"How come? They don't think *we* killed the man, right?" said Julia, looking worried.

Nick laughed convincingly. "Don't worry about that. When they check for fingerprints inside and outside the house, they're going to find our fingerprints—yours and mine and Marta's—"

"And probably Emily's too," said Julia.

"Right."

"And probably that guy Digga, right, Luke?"

Luke rolled his eyes, looked away.

"Who's Digga?" Nick asked.

Lucas didn't answer, still shaking his head.

"He's this guy who wears a do-rag just like Luke and plays really loud music when you're not here and always smells like smoke. He stinks."

"When does he come over?" said Nick.

"Like once or twice," Lucas said. "Jesus Christ. This is totally wack. He's a friend of mine, all right? Am I allowed to have friends, or is this, like, a prison where you're not allowed to have visitors? You happy, Julia? Fuckin' tattletale."

"Hey!" Nick said.

Julia, so unused to being yelled at by her older brother, ran out of the room crying.

"Uh, Mr. Conover?"

Detective Rhimes, standing tentatively at the door to the family room.

"Yes?"

"Could I see you for a minute?"

63

"We found something on your lawn," she said.

"Oh?"

She'd taken him out into the hall, far enough away from the kids that they couldn't hear.

"A mangled piece of metal."

Nick shrugged, as if to say, so? Is that supposed to mean something to me?

"It may be a bullet fragment, maybe a piece of shell casing."

"From a gun?" His breath stopped. Outwardly he tried to project an image of nonchalance, but interested, as someone in his position should be. Someone who was innocent, who wanted the cops to find the killer.

"It's hard to say. I'm no expert."

"Can I take a look?" he said, and he immediately regretted saying it. Mustn't betray too much interest. Must get the balance right.

She shook her head. "The techs have it. I just wanted to ask you—it may seem a silly question—but you've said you don't own a gun, right?"

"That's right."

"So obviously you've never fired a gun on your property, I'm sure. But has anyone you know fired a gun in your yard, to your knowledge?"

He attempted a dismissive laugh, though it sounded hollow. "No target practice allowed here," he said.

"So, no one's ever fired a gun outside your house, to your knowledge."

"Nope. Not as far as I know."

"Never."

"Never." A cool trickle of sweat traced a path along the back of one ear and down his neck, where it was absorbed by the collar of his shirt.

She nodded again, slowly. "Interesting."

"The techs—are they sure it's from a bullet or whatever?"

"Well, you know, I doubt *I* could tell the difference between a bottle cap and a—a Remington Golden Saber .380 cartridge," she said. Nick couldn't stop himself from flinching, and he hoped she hadn't noticed. "But the crime scene techs, they're awfully good at what they do, and I have to defer to them on that. They tell me it sure looks like a fragment from a projectile."

"Strange," Nick said. He tried to look puzzled in a sort of neutral, disinterested way, not letting the way he was really feeling leak out—terrified and trembling and nauseated.

Eddie had assured him he'd collected everything, all the shell casings, and checked for any other trace evidence that might be on the lawn. Then again, he could easily have missed a small piece of lead or brass or whatever it was, a flying piece of metal that had lodged itself into the earth, say. That would be easy to miss.

After all, Nick had noticed the smell of liquor on Eddie's breath that night. He'd probably been sleeping it off when Nick called. Didn't have all his faculties about him. Maybe he hadn't been so thorough.

Detective Rhimes seemed about to say something more when Nick noticed someone walking by, carrying a black rectangular metal object sealed in a clear plastic bag. The fireplug woman, the evidence tech with the wide ass in the new jeans, was holding what Nick recognized at once as the digital video recorder that was hooked up to the security cameras. They must have taken it from the closet where the installer had put the alarm system.

"Hey, what's that?" Nick called out. The woman, whose nametag on her denim shirt said Trento, stopped, looked at Detective Rhimes.

The detective said, "That's the recording unit from your security system."

"I need that," Nick said.

"I understand. We'll make sure this is turned around just as quickly as possible."

Nick shook his head in apparent frustration. He hoped, prayed that the little shimmy of terror moving through his body wasn't obvious. Eddie had wiped the disk clean, he'd said. Reformatted it. Nothing was there from that night.

Nick could only imagine what the camera image would look like. The lurching of a man in a too-big flapping overcoat suddenly illuminated by the outside lights. The flailing hands. The way the man had crumpled to the ground. Or did one of the cameras capture the act itself, Nick holding the pistol, his face contorted with fear and anger, pulling the trigger? The gun bucking up and back, the smoke cloud. The murder itself.

But that was all gone.

Eddie had assured him of that. Eddie, whose breath had stunk of booze. Who was always cocky but never thoughtful and thorough, certainly not in the rink. Who'd always acted hastily, impulsively.

Who might have missed something.

Done it wrong. Failed to reformat it properly.

Might have fucked up.

"Also, Mr. Conover, we're going to need the keys to both of your cars, if you don't mind."

"My cars?"

"The Chevy Suburban that you drive, and the minivan. We'll want to dust for prints and so on."

"How come?"

"In case Stadler tried to get in, steal one of the cars, whatever."

Nick nodded, logy and dazed, reached into his pants pocket for his key ring. As he did so, he noticed a swarm of activity in his study, straight down the hall. "I'm going to need to check my e-mail," he said.

Detective Rhimes cocked her head. "I'm sorry?"

"My study. I need to get in there. I have work to do."

"I'm sorry, Mr. Conover, but this might take a while."

"How long are we talking?"

"Hard to say. The evidence techs move in mysterious ways." She smiled, her face lighting up, really lovely. "Oh, one quick question, if you don't mind?"

"Sure."

"About your security director—Mr. Rinaldi?"

"What about him?"

"Oh," she said with a quiet laugh, "I suppose it's like 'who will guard the guards' or something, but I'm sure you did a background check on him before you hired him to be your security director."

"Of course," Nick said. A background check was precisely what he hadn't done. Eddie was an old friend. Well, a buddy, maybe. Whatever that meant.

"What do you know about his police career?" she asked.

There was a yellow tape across the entrance to his study. It said, "Crime Scene—Do Not Cross."

Crime scene, he thought.

You don't know.

Two evidence techs in there, wearing rubber gloves. One was dusting the doors, door frames, light switch plates, the desk, the wood frame and glass panes of the French doors, with fluorescent orange powder. The other was vacuuming the carpet with a strange-looking handheld vacuum cleaner, a black barrel, long straight nozzle.

Nick watched for a moment, cleared his throat to get their attention, and said, "You don't need to do that. We've got a housekeeper."

A lame joke, pathetic even. Offensive, probably. *They* didn't have housekeepers.

The tech with the vacuum cleaner gave him a hard look.

Nick let it slide. They were dusting for fingerprints, but there was no way they were going to find anything incriminating. Stadler wasn't inside the house on the night of his murder. He'd dropped to the ground, easily twenty feet from the French doors.

That wasn't what bothered him.

What bothered him was why they seemed to be focusing on the study. There were lots of other rooms in the house where Stadler might plausibly have gotten in. Why the study?

Did they *know* something?

"Mr. Conover, do you have a key to this drawer?"

A confident baritone. One of the techs was pointing at the locked drawer where he'd kept the gun Eddie had given him.

He felt his entire body seize up.

"Key's right in the top middle drawer," Nick said mildly. "Real high security."

He flashed on the box of cartridges in the drawer next to the gun. A green and gold cardboard box, the words REMINGTON and GOLDEN SABER in white lettering.

Eddie had taken them away, right?

When he took the gun?

Nick didn't remember anymore. That night was such a blur.

Please God oh please God let them be gone the bullets make them gone.

He waited. Holding his breath, while the tech opened the big middle desk drawer, located the key at once, knelt down to unlock the bottom drawer.

The back of his shirt collar was seriously damp now. Downright wet.

My life is in this anonymous guy's hands right now. He has the power to lock me away forever.

There's no death penalty in Michigan, he found himself thinking. He'd never thought about it before, never had a reason to think about it. No death penalty.

Life in prison, though.

That was in the balance.

The drawer slid open, the tech bent over.

A second went by, two, then three.

The vacuum cleaner was turned off.

Nick felt like vomiting. He stood there on the other side of the yellow crime-scene tape like some casual sightseer, a tourist, and he waited.

The tech got to his feet. Nothing in his hands.

Maybe the drawer was empty.

If one stray bullet had rolled to the back of the drawer . . .

No, the tech would have taken out his camera and taken a picture if he'd found something.

The drawer had to be empty.

Nick felt relief. Temporary, maybe. Momentary.

He stood there watching the tech, the one who'd been vacuuming, take out a plastic bottle with a pistol grip and begin spraying a section of the hand-plastered walls around the light switch.

Decora rocker switch, Nick thought. Laura had replaced all the light switches in the house with Decora rocker switches, which she insisted were much more elegant. Nick had no opinion on Decora rockers. He'd never really thought much about light switches before.

The guy started spraying the bottom of the French doors, then the carpet.

He heard the two techs murmuring, heard the one with the plastic bottle say something like, "Miss my Luminol."

The other one said something in a low voice, something about a daylight search, and then the first one said, "But Christ, this LCV shit is messy."

Nick didn't know what they were talking about. He felt stupid standing there on the threshold of his own study, gawking and eavesdropping.

The first one said, "stain's gonna be degraded."

The second one said something about "DNA match."

Nick swallowed hard. "Stain" had to mean blood. They were looking for bloodstains on the door handles, on the door, on the carpet. Bloodstains that weren't visible to the naked eye, which had maybe been wiped away but not well enough.

Well, at least I'm safe on that, Nick thought. Stadler never entered the house.

But his brain was not cooperating. It kicked up a thought that made the adrenaline surge, made him break out in sweat once again.

Stadler had bled, fairly profusely.

The black puddle of blood.

Nick had walked up to him, kicked at the body with his bare feet. Maybe even stood in the blood, who knows, he couldn't remember.

Then walked back into the house.

Onto the carpet. To call Eddie.

He'd never *noticed* any bloodstains on the carpet, and neither did Eddie, but how much did it take? What scintilla of evidence, carried into the study on the soles of his bare feet from the puddle beside Stadler's body? Mere droplets perhaps, invisible to the naked eye, smeared onto the wall-to-wall carpet unseen, soaking into the woolen fibers, waiting to announce their presence?

The tech who wasn't spraying the carpet turned around to look at Nick's desk, noticed Nick still standing there.

Quickly Nick said something, just so they wouldn't think he was watching in terrified fascination, as he was. "Is that stuff gonna come off my carpet?"

The tech who was spraying shrugged.

"And what about all that powder?" Nick went on, fake-indignant. "How the hell am I going to get that out?"

The tech with the spray bottle turned around, blinked a few times, a lazy, malevolent grin on his face. "You got a housekeeper," he said.

64

"Eddie." Nick, calling from his study, scared out of his mind.

"What?" He sounded annoyed.

"They were here today."

"I know. Here too. It's bullshit. They're trying to put a scare into you."

"Yeah, well, it worked. They found something."

A pause. "Huh?"

"They found a metal fragment. They think it might be a piece of a shell casing."

"*What*? They recovered a shell casing?"

"No, a piece of one."

"I don't get it." Eddie's swaggering confidence had evaporated. "I recovered both shells, and I don't remember any fragmentation. You said you fired two rounds, right?"

"I think so."

"You *think* so? Now you *think* so?"

"I was freaked out, Eddie. Everything was a blur."

"You told me you fired two rounds, so when I found two shells, I stopped looking. I coulda spent all night on that fucking lawn walking around with the flashlight."

"You think they really might have a piece of ammunition?" Nick said, a quaver in his voice.

"The *fuck* do I know?" Eddie said. "Shit. Tell you this, I gotta start digging into this lady detective. See what skeletons she has in her closet."

"I think she's a good Christian, Eddie."

"Great. Maybe I'll find something real good."

And he hung up the phone.

"We got shit, is what we got," said Bugbee.

"The search warrant," Audrey began.

"Was as broad as I could make it. Not just .380s, but any firearms of any description. On top of the usual. No blood or fibers in Rinaldi's car anywhere."

"We didn't expect he took the body home with him."

"Obviously not."

"Any .380s?"

Bugbee shook his head. "But here's the weird thing. Guy's got a couple of those wall-mounted locking handgun racks, right? Found it in a closet behind some clothes, bolted onto the wall. Each one holds three guns, but two of them are missing."

"Missing, or not there? Maybe he only has four."

Bugbee smiled, held up a finger. "Ah, that's the thing. There's two guns in one, two in the other, and you can see from the dust patterns that there used to be two more. They've been removed."

Audrey nodded. "Two."

"I'm saying one is the murder weapon."

"And the other?"

"Just a guess. But maybe there's a reason he didn't want us to find that one too. Two unregistered handguns."

Audrey turned to go back to her cubicle when a thought occurred to her. "You didn't warn him you were doing the search?"

"Come on."

"Then how'd he know you were coming? How'd he know to remove the guns?"

"Now you get it."

"Conover knew we were coming to search his house," Audrey said. "I'm sure he told Rinaldi, and Rinaldi knew it was only a matter of time before we searched his house too."

Bugbee considered for a few seconds.

"Maybe that's all it is," he conceded.

An e-mail popped up on Audrey's computer from Kevin Lenehan in Forensic Services, asking her to come by.

The techs in the Forensic Services Unit all went to crime scenes, but some of them had their specialties, too. If you wanted to get a fingerprint off the sticky side of a piece of duct tape, you went to Koopmans. If you wanted a serial number restoration, you took it to Brian. If you wanted a court exhibit, an aerial map, a scene diagram rendered in a hurry, you went to Koopmans or Julie or Brigid.

Kevin Lenehan was the tech most often entrusted with, or perhaps saddled with, retrieving information from computers or video capture work. That meant that while his co-workers got jammed with all the street calls, he had to waste vast amounts of time watching shadowy, indistinct video images of robberies taken by store surveillance cameras. Or poring over the video from the in-car cameras that went on automatically when an officer flipped on his overheads and sirens.

He was scrawny, late twenties, had a wispy goatee and long greasy hair that was either light brown or dark blond, though it was hard to tell, because Audrey had never seen him with his hair recently washed.

The rectangular black metal box that housed the digital video recorder from Conover's security system was on his workbench, connected to a computer monitor.

"Hey, Audrey," he said. "Heard about your little bluff."

"Bluff?" Audrey said innocently.

"The bullet fragment thing. Brigid told me. Never knew you had it in you."

She smiled modestly. "You do what it takes. How's this coming?"

"I'm kinda not clear on what you wanted," Kevin said. "You're looking for a homicide, right? But nothing like that here."

It was too easy, Audrey thought. "So what is on there?"

"Like three weeks of the moon moving behind the clouds. Lights going off and on. Coupla deer. Cars going in and out of the driveway. Dad, kids, whatever. Am I looking for something in particular?"

"A murder would be nice," she said.

"Sorry to disappoint you."

"If the cameras recorded it, it's going to be on there, right?" She pointed at the box.

"Right. This bad boy's a Maxtor hundred-and-twenty gig drive connected to sixteen cameras, set to record at seven-point-five frames per second."

"Could it be missing anything?"

"Missing how?"

"I don't know, erased or something?"

"Not far's I can tell."

"Isn't three weeks a long time to record on a hard drive that size?"

Lenehan looked at her differently, with more respect. "Yeah, in fact, it is. If this baby was in a twenty-four-hour store, it would recycle after three days. But it's residential, and it's got motion technology, so it doesn't use up much disk space."

"Meaning that the camera starts when there's a movement that sets off the motion detector and gets the cameras rolling?"

"Sort of. It's all done by software here. Not external motion sensors. The software is continually sampling the picture, and whenever a certain number of pixels change, it starts the recording process."

"It recycles when the disk gets full?"

"Right. First in, first out."

"Could it have recycled over the part I'm interested in?"

"You're interested in the early morning hours of the sixteenth, you said, and that's all there."

"I'm interested in anything from the evening of the fifteenth to, say, five in the morning on the sixteenth. But the alarm went off at two in the morning, so I'm most interested in two in the morning. Well, 2:07, to be exact. An eleven-minute period."

Kevin swiveled around on his metal stool to look at the monitor. "Sorry.

Just misses it. The recording starts Wednesday the sixteenth. Three-eighteen A.M."

"You mean Tuesday the fifteenth, right? That's when it was put in. Some time on the afternoon of the fifteenth."

"Hey, whatever, but the recording starts Wednesday the sixteenth. Three-eighteen in the morning. About an hour after the time you're interested in."

"Shoot. I don't get it."

He spun back around. "Can't help you there."

"You sure the eleven-minute segment couldn't have just been erased?"

Kevin paused. "No sign of that. It just started at—"

"Could someone have recycled it?"

"Manually? Sure. Have to be someone who knows the system, knows what he's doing, of course."

Eddie Rinaldi, she thought. "Then it would have recorded over the part I'm interested in?"

"Right. Records over the oldest part first."

"Do you have the ability to bring it back?"

"Like, unerase it? Maybe someone does. That's kind of beyond what I know how to do. The State, maybe?"

"The State would mean six months at least."

"At least. And who knows if they can do it? I don't even know if it can be done."

"Kevin, do you think it's worth looking at again?"

"For what, though?"

"See if you can figure anything else about it. Such as whether you can find any traces. Anything that proves the recording was recycled over or deleted or whatever."

Kevin waggled his head from one side to the other. "Take a fair amount of time."

"But you're good. And you're fast."

"And I'm also way behind on my other work. I've got a boatload of vid-caps to do for Sergeant Noyce and Detective Johnson."

"That serial robber case."

"Yeah. Plus Noyce wants me to watch like two days worth of tape from a store robbery, looking for a guy in a black Raiders jacket with white Nike Air shoes."

"Sounds like fun."

"Eye-crossing fun. He wants it done—"

"Yesterday. Oh yes, I know Jack."

"I mean, you want to talk to Noyce, get him to move you up in the queue, go ahead. But I gotta do what they tell me to do, you know?"

65

The next morning was jam-packed with complicated, if tedious, paperwork, which Nick was actually grateful for. It kept his mind off what was happening, kept him from obsessing over what the cops might have found in the house. And that fragment of a shell casing had ruined his sleep last night. He'd tossed and turned, alternating between blank terror and a steady, pulsing anxiety.

There was a bunch of stuff from the corporate counsel's office outlining the patent lawsuit they wanted to file against one of Stratton's chief competitors, Knoll. Stephanie Alstrom's staff insisted that Knoll had basically ripped off a patented Stratton design for an ergonomic keyboard tray.

Stratton filed dozens of these complaints every year; Knoll probably did too. Kept the corporate attorneys employed. The legal department salivated at the prospect of litigation; Nick preferred arbitration, pretty much down the line. It kept the out-of-pocket costs down, and even if Stratton won the ruling, Knoll would have already figured out a workaround that would pass legal muster. Go after Knoll in a public courtroom, and you blow all confidentiality— your secrets are laid out there for every other competitor to rip off. Then there'd be subpoenas all over the place; Stratton would have to hand over all sorts of secret design documents. Forget it. Plus, in Nick's experience, the awarded damages rarely added up to much once you subtracted your legal expenses. He scrawled *ARB* on the top sheet.

After an hour of sitting at his home base, going over this sort of crap,

Nick's shoulders were already starting to ache. The truth was, home base wasn't feeling especially homey these days. His eyes settled on one of the family photographs. Laura, the kids, Barney. Two down, three to go, he thought. The curse of the House of Conover.

He remembered a line he'd seen quoted somewhere: Maybe this world is another planet's hell. There had to be a bunch of corollaries to that. He had made someone else's world a hell, and someone had made his world a hell. Supply-chain management for human suffering.

An instant-message from Marjorie popped up, even though she was sitting not ten feet away, on the other side of the panel. She didn't want to break his concentration—she knew how fragile it tended to be.

The usual for lunch today, right?

Oh, right. Nick remembered: the regular weekly lunch with Scott. Which was just about the last thing he felt like doing.

He wanted to confront Scott, tell him to get the fuck out and go back home to McKinsey. But he couldn't, not yet. Not until he got to the bottom of what exactly was going on. And the truth was, he no longer had the power to fire Scott if he wanted to. Which right now he very much did.

He typed:

OK, thanks.

He noticed that there was an e-mail in his in-box from Cassie; he could tell from the subject line.

He hadn't given her his e-mail address, hadn't gotten an e-mail from her before, and he hesitated before clicking on it:

From: ChakraGrrl@hotmail.com
To: Nconover@Strattoninc.com
Subject: From Cassie
Nick—Where's my grocery delivery boy been? Free for lunch today? Come over between 12:30 and 1? I'll supply the sandwiches.
C.

He felt his spirits lift at once, and he hit Reply:

`I'm there.`

"Marge," he said into the intercom, "change in plans. Tell Scott I'm not going to be able to make lunch today, okay?"

"Okay. Want me to give a reason?"

Nick paused. "No."

On the way to the elevator he passed Scott, who was coming out of the men's room. "Got your message," Scott said. "Everything okay?"

"Everything's fine. Just got really hectic all of a sudden."

"You'll do anything to avoid talking numbers," Scott said with a grin.

"You got me figured out," Nick said, grinning right back as he headed for the elevator bank. A couple of women from Payroll got in on the floor below, smiled shyly at him. One of them said, "Hey, Mr. Conover."

He said, "Hey, Wanda. Hey, Barb." They both seemed surprised, and pleased, that he knew their names. But Nick made it a point to know as many Stratton employees by name as possible; he knew how good it was for morale. *And there's fewer and fewer of them all the time*, he thought mordantly. *Makes it easier.*

When the elevator stopped at the third floor, Eddie got in, said, "It's the big dog."

Something awfully disrespectful about that, especially in front of other employees. "Eddie," Nick said.

"Had a feeling you were headed out to, uh, 'lunch,'" Eddie said. The way he dropped little quotation marks around the word "lunch" was unnerving. *Does he know where I'm going? How could he?* And then Nick remembered that he'd asked Eddie to start looking closely at Scott's e-mail. He wondered whether Eddie had taken that as an opportunity to look at Nick's e-mail too. If true, that would be outrageous—but how the hell could he prevent Eddie from doing it? He was the goddamned security director.

Nick just gave him a stony look, which would be missed by Wanda and Barb from Payroll.

"I'll walk you to your car," Eddie said. He was carrying an umbrella.

Nick nodded.

They walked together, silently, through the main lobby, past the water-fall that some feng shui expert had insisted they put there to repair a "blocked energy feeling" at the entrance. Nick had thought that was complete and ut-ter bullshit, but he went along with it anyway, the way he'd always avoided stepping on cracks in the sidewalk so as not to break his mother's back. Any-way, the waterfall looked good there, that was the main thing.

Nick could see through the big glass doors that it was raining. That ex-plained the umbrella, but had Eddie planned to go out for lunch, or did he "happen" to run into Nick in the elevator—by design? Nick wondered but said nothing. He considered, too, asking Eddie about what Detective Rhimes had told him—that Eddie had left the Grand Rapids police force "under a cloud of suspicion." But he didn't know why she'd told him that. Was she trying to put a wedge between the two men? If so, that was a clever way to do it. If Eddie had lied to him about why he'd left police work, what else might he have lied about?

He'd ask Eddie. Not yet, though.

Outside, Eddie opened the big golf umbrella and held it up for Nick. When they'd walked a good distance away from the building, Eddie said, "Foxy Brown better watch her ass."

"I don't know what you're talking about."

"Come on, man. Cleopatra Jones. Sheba baby."

"I'm in a hurry, Eddie. It's been fun free-associating with you."

Eddie gripped Nick's shoulder. "Your black lady detective, man. The one who's trying to roast our nuts over the fire." The rain thrummed loudly on the umbrella. "The Negro lady who's got it in for you because you fucking *laid off her husband*," he said ferociously, drawing out the words.

"You're kidding me."

"Think I'd joke about something like that? About something that should get her fucking thrown off the case?"

"Who's her husband?"

"Some fucking nobody, man, worked on the shop floor spraying paint or whatever. Point is, Stratton laid him off, and now his wife's coming to collect your scalp." He shook his head. "And I say that ain't right."

"She shouldn't be investigating us," Nick said. "That's outrageous."

"That's what I say. Bitch gets disqualified."

"How do we do that?"

"Leave it to me." His smile was almost a leer. "Meanwhile, I got some interesting stuff on your man Scott."

Nick looked at him questioningly.

"You asked me to poke into his e-mail and shit."

"What'd you get?"

"You know what Scott's been doing just about every weekend for the last two months?"

"Burning hamburgers," Nick said. "I was just over there last Saturday."

"Not last Saturday, but almost every other weekend. He's been flying to Boston. Think he's visiting his sick aunt Gertrude?"

"He's getting the corporate discount through the travel office," Nick said.

Eddie nodded. "I guess he figures you don't look at travel expenses—not your job."

"I do have a company to run. Run into the ground, some would say."

"Plus a shitload of phone calls back and forth between him and that guy Todd Muldaur at Fairfield Equity Partners. Kinda doubt it's all social chitchat, right?"

"Any idea what they're talking about?"

"Nah, that's just phone records. Voice mails I can hack into, but Scotty-boy's a good camper. Deletes all voice mails when he's done listening to them. Him and Todd-O e-mail each other, but it's all kinda generic stuff like you'd expect—you know, here's the monthly numbers, or shit like that. Scotty must know e-mails aren't safe. Maybe that's why, when he's got something he wants to keep quiet, he uses encryption."

"Encryption?"

"You got it. My techs intercepted a couple dozen encrypted documents coming and going between Scotty and Todd-O."

Nick couldn't think of any possible reason why Scott would be sending or receiving encrypted documents. Then again, he couldn't think of a reason why Scott would make a secret trip to China either.

"What are they about?"

"Don't know yet, seeing as how they're encrypted. But my guys are crackerjacks. They'll get 'em open for me. Let you know the second they do."

"Okay." They'd reached Nick's Suburban, and he pressed the remote to unlock it.

"Cool. Enjoy your"—Eddie cleared his throat—"lunch."

"You implying something, Eddie?"

"No umbrella or raincoat?" Eddie said. "Don't you have a nice view out of your office? You musta seen it was raining."

"I was too busy working."

"Well, you don't want to go out without protection," Eddie said with a wink. "Not where you're going."

And he walked off.

66

When he arrived at Cassie's, the rain had turned into a full-fledged downpour. He parked in her driveway and raced to the front door, rang the bell, stood there getting soaked. No answer; he rang again.

No answer. He rang a third time, looked at his watch. It was 12:40, so he was on time. She'd said between 12:30 and 1:00. Of course, that was ambiguous; maybe she'd wanted him to specify a time.

Drenched, shivering from the cold rain, he knocked on the door and then rang again. He'd have to change his clothes back at the office, where he kept a spare set. It wasn't exactly cool for the CEO of Stratton to walk around headquarters looking like a drowned rat.

Finally he turned the knob and was surprised when it opened. He went in, called, "Cassie?"

No answer.

He walked into the kitchen. "Cassie, it's Nick. You here?"

Nothing.

He went to the living room, but she wasn't there either. In the back of his mind he worried. She seemed a little fragile, and her father had just died, and who the hell knew what she might do to herself?

"Cassie," he shouted, louder still. She wasn't downstairs. The blinds were drawn in the living room. He opened a slat and looked out, but she wasn't out there either.

Nervous, he went upstairs, calling her name. The second floor was even

darker and dingier than the downstairs. No wonder she didn't want him going up here. Two doors on either side of a short hallway, and two at both
ends. None of the doors was closed. He started at the room at the far end of
the hall. It was a bedroom, furnished with not much more than a full-size
bed and a dresser. The bed was made. The room had the look and smell of
vacancy, as if no one had been in here for a long time. He assumed it was Andrew Stadler's room. He left and went into the room at the other end of the
hall, where a sloppily unmade bed, a discarded pair of jeans turned inside
out on the floor, and the odor of patchouli and cigarettes told him it was
Cassie's.

"Cassie," he called again as he tried another other room. It smelled
strongly of paint, and he knew even before he entered that this was the room
Cassie was using as her studio. Sure enough, there was a half-finished canvas
on an easel, a weird-looking picture, a woman surrounded by bright strokes
of orange and yellow. Other canvases leaned against the walls, and all of
them seemed to be variations on the same bizarre image of a black-haired
young woman, naked, her mouth contorted in a scream. It looked a little like
that famous painting by Edvard Munch, *The Scream.* In each one, the
woman was surrounded by concentric strokes of yellow and orange, like a
sunset, or maybe fire. They were disturbing paintings, actually, but she was
pretty good, Nick thought, even if he didn't know much about art.

Well, she wasn't here either, which meant that something really was
wrong, or they'd somehow gotten their signals crossed in the couple of hours
since he'd sent his e-mail. Maybe she'd changed her mind, or had to go out,
and had e-mailed back to tell him that, and the e-mail never arrived. That
happened.

He tried the last door, but this was a bathroom. He took a much-needed
piss, then took a bath towel and began blotting his shirt and pants. He put the
towel back on the rod, and then, before he left, he took a peek in the mirror-
fronted medicine cabinet, hating himself for snooping.

Apart from the usual cosmetics and women's products, he found a couple of brown plastic pharmacy bottles labeled Zyprexa and lithium. He knew
lithium was for manic-depressives, but he didn't know what the other one
was. He saw Andrew Stadler's name printed on the labels.

Her dad's meds, he thought. Still hasn't thrown them out.

"They're not all his, you know."

Cassie's voice made him jump. He reddened instantly.

"That lithium—that's mine," she said. "I hate it. Makes me fat and gives me acne. It's like being a teenager all over again." She waved an unopened pack of cigarettes at him, and he realized at once where she'd been.

"Cassie—Jesus, I'm sorry." He didn't even try to pretend he was looking for an Advil or something. "I feel like such a shit. I didn't mean to snoop. I mean, I *was* snooping, but I shouldn't have—"

"Would you snoop around to find out whether it's raining? It's pretty much staring you in the face. I mean, when you meet a person who was valedictorian of her high school, eight hundreds on her SATs, got into every college she applied to, and she's basically doing fuck-all in the world, well, you've got to wonder. How come she isn't pulling down six figures at Corning or working on signal-transduction pathways at Albert Einstein College of Medicine?"

"Listen, Cassie . . ."

Cassie made a circular gesture at her temple with her forefinger, the sign for crazy. "You just got to assume that this girl is a few clowns short of a circus."

"Don't talk that way."

"Would you feel better if I put on a white coat and talked about catecholamine levels in the medial forebrain of the hypothalamus? Put my science education to work? Is that less offensive? It isn't any more informative."

"I don't think you're crazy."

"Crazy is as crazy does," Cassie said in a cornpone Forrest Gump voice.

"Come on, Cassie."

"Let's go downstairs."

Sitting together on the nubby brown couch in the living room, Cassie kept talking. "Full scholarship to Carnegie Mellon. I wanted to go to MIT, but my stepdad didn't want to spend a red cent on me, and even with financial aid it was going to be a stretch. Freshman year was tough. Not the course work so much as the classmates. My sorority house burns down freshman year, and half the girls are killed. Blew me away. I mean, I came back here and didn't want to leave my room. Never went back to college."

"You were traumatized."

"I also got addicted to cocaine and Valium, you name it. I was self-medicating, of course. Took me a few years before I figured out I had 'bipolar tendencies.' Was hospitalized for six months with depression. But the meds they put me on worked pretty well."

"Better living through chemistry, I guess."

"Yeah. By then, of course, I'd wandered off the Path."

"The Path? That some religious thing?"

"The Path, Nick. The Path. You went to Michigan State, studied business, got a job at the Vatican of Office Furniture, and you were pretty much set so long as you kept working hard and kept your nose clean and didn't piss too many people off."

"I get it. And you . . . ?"

"I got off the Path. Or I lost my way. Maybe I was in the woods and a big gust of wind came and blew leaves all over the path and I just headed off in the wrong direction. Maybe birds ate the damn bread-crumb trail. I'm not saying my life lacks a purpose. It's just that maybe the purpose is to provide a cautionary tale for everyone else."

"I don't think the world is that unforgiving," Nick said.

"People like you never do," Cassie said.

"It's never too late."

Cassie stepped over to him, pressed herself against his chest. "Isn't it pretty to think so," she murmured.

67

Noyce called Audrey into his office and asked her to sit down.

"I got a call from the security director at Stratton," he said.

"He can't have been happy."

"He was ripshit, Audrey. About both him and Conover."

"I can't speak for Roy, but I know my team was as careful as can be. We didn't trash the place."

"I don't think Bugbee was as careful."

"That doesn't surprise me. Mine was a consent search. Roy had a warrant."

"And Roy is Roy. Listen." He leaned forward, rested his elbows on a bare patch of desk, rested his chin on his hands. "Rinaldi hit me with something we have to take seriously."

"They're threatening us with legal action," Audrey said, half-kidding.

"He knows about Leon."

"About Leon."

"I'm surprised, frankly, it took him this long. But he obviously did some looking into you, and Leon's name came up."

"You knew Leon was laid off from Stratton. I didn't keep that from you."

"Of course not. But I didn't really weigh that as carefully as I should have. It didn't occur to me, frankly."

"Everyone in this town's got someone in their family who's been laid off by Stratton."

"Just about."

"You start taking everyone off this case who has any connection to Stratton, and pretty soon there'd be no one left. I mean lab techs and crime scene—"

"This is always something we have to be hypersensitive about."

"Jack, I was assigned to this case randomly. My name came up on the board. I didn't request it."

"I know."

"And when I started it, there was no connection to the Stratton Corporation."

"Granted, but—"

"Let me finish. Leon's situation has nothing to do with this. I'm following the leads here. I'm not on any witch hunt. You know that."

"I know it, Aud. Of course I know that. But if and when this comes to trial, I don't want anything fucking it up. If I go to the prosecutor, he's going to say he doesn't want you involved—this has to be clean and pristine. And he'll be right. Any DA is going to worry that this'll look like payback on your part."

She sat up straight in the uncomfortable chair, looked at her boss directly. "Are you taking me off the case?"

He sighed. "I'm not taking you off the case. That's not it. I mean, maybe I should. The Stratton security guy is demanding it. But the fact is, you're one of our best."

"That's not true, and you know it. My clearance rate is pretty darned mediocre."

He laughed. "Your modesty is refreshing. I wish everyone around here had some of that. No, your clearance rate could be higher, but that's because you're still getting your chops. You tend to use a microscope when binoculars are what you want."

"Pardon me?"

"You do waste time, sometimes, looking superclose at evidence that doesn't lead anywhere. Going up blind alleys, barking up the wrong trees, all that. I think that gets better with experience. The more cases you do, the more developed your instinct gets. You learn what's worth following up and what isn't."

She nodded.

"You know I'm your biggest fan."

"I know it," she said, feeling a surge of affection toward the man that was almost love. Maybe it was love.

"I pushed you to apply for the job, and I pushed you through. You know how many hoops you had to jump through."

An abashed smile. She remembered how many interviews she'd had to do. Just when she thought she'd clinched it, someone else asked to interview her. Noyce had steered it all the way. "The race thing," she said.

"The woman thing. That was really it. But look, a lot of people are waiting for you to fail."

"I don't see it that way."

"I do, and believe me, I know. A good number of people around here are waiting for you to trip and fall flat on your face. And I don't want that to happen."

"I don't either."

"Go back to the Leon issue for a second. Whether you say it's an issue or not. We're all susceptible to being driven by unconscious biases. Protective instincts. I know you, and you have a lot of love in your heart, and you hate seeing what your husband's going through. You hate seeing him hurt in any way." Audrey started to object, but Noyce said, "Hear me out. My turn, okay?"

"Okay."

"You've got a forest of facts, of evidence and clues. You've got to find a path through that forest. I mean, the stuff about the hydroseed—that's damned good police work."

"Thank you."

"But we don't know, do we, what that means? Did Stadler walk around Nicholas Conover's premises? Sure. No one's disputing that. Did he crawl around the property on his hands and knees, get dirt under his fingernails? Sure, why not. But does that mean Conover did it?"

"It's a piece of the puzzle."

"But is the puzzle one of those easy twenty-piece wooden jigsaws that little kids do? Or is it one of those impossible thousand-piece jobs my wife likes to do? That's the thing. A hunch and some hydroseed isn't enough."

"The body was too clean," she said. "Most of the trace evidence was re-moved by someone who knew what he was doing."

"Maybe."

"Rinaldi's an ex-homicide detective."

"Don't have to be a cop to know about trace evidence."

"We caught Conover in a lie," she went on. "He said he slept through the night, the night Stadler was killed. But at two in the morning he called Rinaldi. That's in the phone records."

"They give different stories?"

"Well, when I asked Conover about it, he said maybe he got the day wrong, maybe that was the night his alarm went off and he called Rinaldi to check it out, since Rinaldi's staff put it in."

"Well, so maybe he did get the day wrong."

"The bottom line," Audrey said, exasperated, "is that they knew Stadler was stalking Conover. He butchered the family dog. Then he turns up dead. It just can't be a coincidence."

"You sound certain of it."

"It's my instinct."

"Your instinct, Aud?—don't take this the wrong way—but your instinct isn't exactly developed yet."

She nodded again, hoping her irritation didn't show in her face.

"The bullet fragments," he said. "At Conover's house. What was that all about?"

She hesitated. "We didn't find any bullet fragments."

"That's not what you told Conover. You said you found a piece of metal. You said it was a fragment from a projectile." Rinaldi must have told him this. How else could he know?

"I didn't say that."

"No, but you let him think that, didn't you?"

"Yes," she confessed.

"That was a little show you put on for Conover, wasn't it?" he said sadly. "That was all a bluff, designed to get Conover to break down and admit it. Am I right?"

She nodded, hotly embarrassed. "I hardly think I'm the first homicide detective to try a bluff."

"No, you're not. Far from it. I've done my share, believe me. But we're dealing with the CEO of the Stratton Corporation. That means we're under the klieg lights here. Everything you do, everything *we* do, is going to be scrutinized."

"I understand. But you know, if my little bluff pushes him closer to an admission, it'll be worth it."

Noyce sighed. "Audrey. Okay, so the crack on Stadler's body was really lemon drops. Whether the guy got swindled or the thing was a setup, we just don't know. But you got a schizo guy wandering around the dog pound in the middle of the night, it's not so surprising he gets shot, right?"

"None of the informants knew anything about it."

"Stuff goes on down there, our informants only know one little slice of it."

"But boss—"

"I don't want to be a backseat driver on this one, but before you go off trying to sweat the CEO and the security director of a major corporation for conspiracy to murder some crazy guy—two men who have an awful lot to lose—you want to make sure you're not being seduced by a great story. I mean, your theory is sure a heck of a lot sexier than some drug killing. But this case mustn't be about entertainment value. It's got to be about hard-nosed police work. Right?"

"Right."

"For your own sake. And ours."

"I understand."

"I can't help you if you don't keep me fully informed, okay? From now on, I want you to keep me in the loop. Help me help you. I don't want you getting burned on this."

68

Eddie lived in a small condominium complex called Pebble Creek. It had been built about half a dozen years ago, and consisted of four five-story buildings—stained wood, red brick, big windows—set on a big square of grass and gravel. Each of the condos had its own white-trellised balcony, where residents had put out things like folding chairs and trees in pots. It was a look Nick had heard described as neo-Prairie. No creek anywhere, but plenty of pebbles around the parking lot. There were homey-looking office parks that looked like this—the Conovers' pediatric dentist was located in one—and some people might have found Pebble Creek a little officey-looking for a home. Eddie wouldn't have been one of them.

"Be it ever so humble," Eddie said as he let Nick in. He was wearing black jeans and a gray knit shirt that was furred from one too many tumbles in the dryer. "Welcome to the Edward J. Rinaldi fuck pad."

Nick had never visited Eddie at his home before, but he wasn't surprised at what he saw. A lot of glass, a lot of chrome. Blue-gray carpeting. Black lacquered furniture and booze cabinet, big mirrors on the wall behind it. The biggest things in the room were two big flat Magnapan speakers, in silver, standing at either side of a black sofa like shoji screens. Everything more or less matched. In the bedroom, Eddie showed off an immense waterbed that he said got so much use he'd had to replace the liner three times already.

"So what do you know?" Eddie said, walking Nick into the area of his living room he no doubt called his "entertainment center," though maybe he had a more colorful name for it.

"Well," Nick said, "I know that 'J' was the last letter added to the alphabet."

"No shit? How did they get by without it? Jacking off. Jheri Curl. Jism. Jesus. Jock straps. You got all the basics of civilization right there." Eddie opened the drinks cabinet, twisted open a bottle of Scotch. "Not to mention J & B. And Jameson's. What'll you have?"

"I'm okay," Nick said.

"Yeah," Eddie said, settling into a chair covered in fake silver-gray suede, and putting his feet on the glass coffee table, next to a couple of books titled *Beyer on Speed* and *Play Poker Like the Pros*. "I think maybe you are."

"What makes you say that?" Nick sat on the adjoining sofa, which was covered in the same fake suede.

"'Cause, Nicky, I got something for you. Figured you wouldn't mind coming over to my place to look at a couple of e-mails our boy Scotty deleted a couple of weeks ago. I guess he figures if you delete something it's gone, poof. Doesn't realize all e-mail's archived on the server. So who's Martin Lai?"

"Martin Lai. He's our manager for Asia Pacific, out of Hong Kong. In charge of accounting. Truly the deadliest, most stultifyingly dull guy you're ever going to meet. Human ether."

"Well, check it out." He handed Nick a couple of pages.

To: SMcNally@Strattoninc.com
From: MLai@Strattoninc.com
Scott,
Can you please confirm for me that the USD $10 million that was wired out of Stratton Asia Ventures LLC this morning to a numbered account, no attached name, was done at your behest? The SWIFT code indicates that the funds went to the Seng Fung Bank-Macau. This entirely depletes the fund's assets. Please reply soonest.
Thank you,
Martin Lai

```
Managing Director, Accounting
Stratton Inc., Hong Kong.
```

And then, Scott's immediate reply:

```
To: MLai@Strattoninc.com
From: SMcNally@Strattoninc.com
This is fine — just part of the usual process of repatri-
ation of funds in order to avoid tax payments. Thanks for
keeping an eye out, but all is OK.
-Scott
```

When Nick looked up, he said, "Ten million bucks? What's it for?"

"I don't know, but it looks to me like Scotty-Boy's being a little reckless. Playing fast and loose, huh?"

"It does, doesn't it."

"Not like you."

"Huh?"

"*You're* not being reckless at all, right?"

"What's that supposed to mean?"

"What *you're* doing, man, is a fuck of a lot stupider than whatever Scott McNally's up to. You better check yourself before you wreck yourself, bro, or we're both going to the slammer. And don't think I'm going to take the rap for you."

"What the hell are you talking about?"

Eddie's gaze bore down on him relentlessly. "You want to explain what the fuck you're doing layin' pipe with Stadler's daughter?"

Nick was speechless for a moment. "Are you *spying* on me, Eddie? That's how you knew where I was going that day, in the rain, isn't it? You have no business monitoring my e-mail or my phone lines—"

"It's like we're on a road trip together, Nick. We gotta be taking the same turns. You need to be watching the speed limit, observing all traffic signs. And right here, see, there's no Merge sign. Sign says Do Not Enter. Are you hearing me? Because it's real important that you do." Eddie locked eyes with him. "Do you realize how unbelievably fucking *reckless* you're being?"

"It's totally none of your business, Eddie."

Eddie stretched, raised his arms and put his hands behind his head. Under his arms, sweat stains blackened his gray shirt. "See, that's where you're wrong, buddy. It's very much my business. Because if this keeps up, we could both be making license plates in the shithouse, and I promise you, that's not going to happen."

"This is out of bounds. You lay off her."

"I wish you'd lay off her too. You tell me you're getting rim jobs from the local Brownie troop, I could give a shit. You tell me you're setting up a crystal-meth lab in your basement, I could give a flying fuck. But this thing involves the two of us. You let that piece of ass into your life—for whatever freaky, fucked-up reasons of your own—and you are jeopardizing both of us. What the fuck do you *think* she's after?"

"I don't know what you're talking about."

"News flash," Eddie said in a low voice. "You wasted her old man."

The blood left Nick's face. He was groping for words, but none came.

"You really don't get it, do you? Cops think you might've had something to do with it. Let's say the cops talk to her, maybe let on their suspicions, let it slip, see if she knows anything, right? So this little girl figures she gets close to you— I'm just spitballing here—and maybe she finds something out. Something that could help bring you down. Who the hell knows what? Maybe her thing isn't really getting into your pants. Maybe it's about getting into your *head*."

"That's bullshit. I don't believe it," Nick said. It felt as if his guts had furled into a small hard ball.

That time at Town Grounds.

God, someone who'd do something like that to your family.

I'd want to kill him.

"Believe it," Eddie said. "Entertain the goddamn possibility." He drained his glass, exhaled with a loud alcohol wheeze. "The ass you save could be your own."

"I'm not going to sit here and listen to this," Nick said, his face burning. He stood up, went to the door, but stopped halfway there and turned back around. "You know, Eddie, I'm not so sure you're in any position to be giving lectures about recklessness."

Eddie was staring at him defiantly, an ugly grin on his face.

Nick went on, "I don't think you really leveled with me about why you left the Grand Rapids police."

Eddie's eyes narrowed to slits. "I already told you about that bullshit charge."

"You didn't tell me you were drummed out for pilfering."

"Oh, Christ. Sounds like the kinda thing Cleopatra Jones might have told you. You going to believe her, or me?"

Nick pursed his lips. "I don't know, Eddie. I'm beginning to think I believe her."

"Yeah," Eddie said acidly. "You would, wouldn't you."

"You didn't say it wasn't true."

"Did I cut corners? Sure. But that's it. You can't believe everything you hear. People talk some crazy shit."

69

Audrey's desk phone rang, and she checked the caller ID to make sure it wasn't poor Mrs. Dorsey again. But it was a 616 area code, which meant Grand Rapids, and so she picked it up.

A woman was calling from the Michigan State Police crime lab who identified herself as an IBIS technician named Susan Calloway. She was soft-spoken but authoritative-sounding, her voice arid, devoid of any warmth or personality. She gave the case number she was calling about—it was the Stadler homicide—and said, "The reason I'm calling, Detective, is that I believe you asked us to see if we could match the bullet in your case with any others, correct?"

"That's correct."

"Well, it seems we got a warm hit on IBIS."

Audrey knew a fair amount about the Integrated Ballistics Identification System. She knew it was a computerized database of archived digital images of fired bullets and cartridges that linked police and FBI crime labs across the country. It was sort of like AFIS, the fingerprint-matching network, only the fingerprints here were photographs of bullets and casings.

"A warm hit?" Audrey said. That term she hadn't heard before, though.

"I mean a possible hit," the woman said, her bland voice betraying the tiniest hint of annoyance. "To me, it looks quite similar to a bullet recovered in a no-gun case in Grand Rapids about five, six years ago. Six years ago, to be precise."

"What kind of case?"

"The file class is 0900-01."

That was the Michigan state police offense code for a homicide. So the gun used to kill Stadler had been used six years earlier in another homicide, in Grand Rapids. That could be significant—or it could mean almost nothing. Guns were bought and sold on the black market all the time.

"Really? What do we know about the case?"

"Not much, Detective, I'm sorry to say. I have only the submitting agency's case number, which won't do you much good. But I've already called over there and asked them to bring over the bullet in question so I can do the comparison."

"Thank you."

"And as to the question you're probably about to ask—how long will this take?—the answer is, as soon as I get the bullet from the GR PD."

"Well, I wasn't going to ask that," Audrey said. She thought: only because it would rankle if I *did* ask. If you had no juice with these firearms examiners, you'd better be as sweet as pie. "But I appreciate the information."

Interesting, she thought. Very interesting.

She took a stroll across the squad room and over to Forensic Services, where she found Kevin Lenehan slumped over his desk, arms folded, a dim shadowy tape playing on a TV monitor, numbers racing across the top of the screen.

She put a hand on his shoulder, and he jolted awake.

"Hey," she said, "you don't want to miss the guy in the Nike Air sneakers and the Raiders jacket."

"I hate my life," he said.

"You're too good for this kind of work," she said.

"Tell that to my manager."

"Where is she?"

"Maternity leave. Noyce's my manager these days. Aren't you tight with him?"

"I wouldn't say that. Kevin, listen. Could you take another look at my recorder? I mean, unofficially and off the books and all that?"

"When? In my voluminous spare time?"

"I'll owe you one."

"No offense, but that doesn't really work on me."

"Then how about out of the goodness of your heart?"

"Not much there," he said.

"Kevin."

He blinked. "Let's say, hypothetically now, that I had ten minutes for a coffee break that I decided to spend chasing the great white whale out of a personal obsession. What would I be looking for anyway?"

70

"I just tried Fairfield," Marge said over the intercom, "but Todd's assistant said he's out of the office for the day, so I left a message."

"Can you try his cell? You have the number, right?"

"Of course."

Of course she did. She never lost a phone number, never misplaced an address, could pull up a name from her file in a matter of seconds without fail. God, she was the best.

There was a certain etiquette to making phone calls, which she appreciated. If she called Todd's office and he was there, she'd put Nick on before Todd picked up. That was how it worked. Nick had always hated the telephone brinksmanship, where someone's assistant would call Marge, be put through to Nick, and then the assistant would say, "I have Mr. Smith," and Nick would say, "Okay, thanks," and then Mr. Smith would get on, as if he were too busy even to suffer a few seconds of being on hold. It was demeaning. Nick had devised his own way around that. He'd instructed Marge to tell the assistant, "Put Mr. Smith on, please, and I'll get Mr. Conover." That usually worked. So when Marge placed calls for him, he didn't like to play Mr. Smith's game. Todd picked up his own cell phone, of course—who didn't?—so Nick dialed the call himself.

Todd answered right away.

"Todd, it's Nick Conover."

"Oh, hey, man." No background noise. Nick wondered whether Todd actually was in his office anyway.

"Todd, we've got some funny things going on around here, and we need to talk."

"Hey, that's what I'm here for." Like he was a shrink or something.

"Two massive deals just fell through because they each, separately, heard that we're planning to shift all manufacturing to China."

"Yeah?"

"Any truth to it?"

"I can't be responsible for gossip, Nick."

"Of course. But I'm asking you now, flat out—man to man—if it's true." Man to toad, he thought. Man to weasel. "If you guys are even exploring the idea."

"Well, you know how I feel about this, and I've let you know. I think we're eroding our profit margins by continuing to operate these old factories in Michigan like it's nineteen fifty-nine or something. The world's changed. It's a global economy."

"Right," Nick said. "We've been through all that, and I've made it clear that the day Stratton stops making its own stuff is the day we're no longer Stratton. I'm not going to be the guy who shuts down our factories."

"I hear you," Todd said testily.

"I've already laid off half the company as you guys asked me to. It was the most painful thing I've ever done. But turning Stratton into some kind of virtual company, a little sales office with all the manufacturing done eight thousand miles away—that's not going to happen on *my* watch."

"I hear you," Todd said again. "What are you calling for?"

"Let me repeat the question, because I don't think I heard your answer. Is there any truth to these reports that you guys are negotiating to move our manufacturing offshore, Todd?"

"No," he said quickly.

"Not even preliminary talks?"

"No."

Nick didn't know what else to say. Either he was telling the truth, or he was lying, and if he was willing to lie so baldly, well, what the hell could

Nick do about it anyway? He thought about mentioning all the back-and-forth e-mail between Todd and Scott, the encrypted documents—but he didn't want Todd to know he was having his security director keep a close watch. He didn't want to shut one of the few windows he had into what was really going on.

"Then maybe you can explain to me why you've got Scott going to China on some secret mission, like Henry fucking *Kissinger*, without even telling me."

A few seconds of silence. "News to me," Todd finally said. "Ask him."

"Scott said he went to China to explore the options. He didn't do that for you? Because if he did, I want you to understand something. That's not the way it works around here, Todd."

"He doesn't report to me, Nick."

"Exactly. I don't want to be undermined."

"I don't want that either."

"The job's tough enough without having to worry about whether my chief financial officer's taking secret flights to the Orient on Cathay Pacific."

Todd chuckled politely. "It's a tough job, and it takes a lot out of you." The timbre of his voice suddenly changed, as if he'd just thought of something. "You know, I understand your family's been through some rough times, death of your wife, all that. If you need to spend more time with them, we're here to help. You want to take a little sabbatical, a little break, might be a good thing. You could probably *use* a vacation. Be good for you."

"I'm fine, Todd," Nick said. *Not so easy, Todd.* "Going to work every-day—that's what keeps me going."

"Good to hear it," Todd said. "Good to hear it."

71

Bugbee was gobbling Cheetos out of a small vending machine bag. His fingers—which Audrey had noticed were usually immaculate, the nails neatly clipped—were stained orange.

"Makes sense," he said through a mouthful of Cheetos. "Rinaldi picked up a piece in Grand Rapids when he was working there."

"Or here. Those guns travel."

"Maybe. So where'd he toss it?"

"Any of a million possibilities." She was hungry, and he wasn't offering her any, the jerk.

"I forget who the poor slobs were searched the Dumpster, but nothing there."

"There's probably hundreds of Dumpsters in town," Audrey pointed out. "And the dump. And sewer grates, and the lake and the ponds and the rivers. We're never going to find the gun."

"Sad but true," Bugbee said. He crumpled up the empty bag, tossed the wad at the metal trash can against the wall, but the bag unballed in the air and landed on the floor. "Shit."

"Did you have a chance to talk to the alarm company?"

He nodded. "Fenwick Alarm's just an office downtown. I don't know what the hell they do—they install, but not in this case. They don't even do the monitoring themselves. That's done by a joint called Central Michigan Monitoring, out of Lansing. They keep all the electronic records."

"And?"

"Nada. Just confirms what we already know. That Wednesday morning one of the perimeter alarms at Conover's house got triggered. Alert lasted eleven minutes. Big fucking deal. You got the hard drive—that ought to give up what the cameras recorded, right?"

She explained what she knew about Conover's digital video recording system. "I've asked Lenehan to look again. But Noyce has him doing all kinds of other things ahead of us."

"Why does that not surprise me?"

"Speaking of cameras, one of us should check out whatever they have at Fenwicke Estates security for that night."

Bugbee shook his head. "Did already. They use a central station downtown. Nothing special—Stadler climbs a perimeter fence, that's it."

"Too bad."

"I say we poly the guy. Both of those assholes."

"That's a tough one. It may be early. We may want to wait until we have more. I know that's what Noyce would say."

"Screw Noyce. This is our case, not his. You notice the way he's been breathing down our necks?"

"Some."

"He must smell something big about to pop."

She didn't know how much to say. "I think it's more that he wants to make sure we don't slip up."

"Slip up? Like we're rookies?"

Audrey shrugged. "It's a big case."

Bugbee said, with a crooked grin, "No shit."

Audrey responded with a rueful smile as she turned to go back to her cubicle.

"That thing about the shell casing or bullet fragment or whatever," Bugbee said.

She turned. "What shell casing?"

"That bluff?"

"Yes?"

"Not bad," Bugbee said.

72

Nick was beyond weary. All the shit that was going on with Todd and Scott, all the crap he didn't understand: it was draining. And that on top of Eddie and his warnings about Cassie: check yourself before you wreck yourself. And: What do you think she's after? Could there be something to what Eddie was saying?

Was it possible, he'd begun to wonder, that, on some subconscious level, he *wanted* to be found out?

And worst of all, so awful he couldn't stand to think about it, was this fragment of a shell casing the police had discovered on his lawn.

He'd always prided himself on his ability to endure pressure that would crush most other guys. Maybe it was the hockey training, the way you learned to find the serene place inside you and go there when things got tough. He never used to panic. Laura, always on the high-strung side, never got that. She thought he didn't care, didn't get it. And he'd just shrug and reply blandly, "What's the use in panicking? Not going to help."

But since the murder, everything had changed. His hard shell had cracked or turned porous. Or maybe all the stress of the last few weeks was additive, the worries heaped onto his back until his muscles trembled and spasmed. Any second now he'd collapse to the ground.

But he couldn't, not yet.

Because whatever Todd and Scott were up to—all this maneuvering, the secret trips and the phone calls and the encrypted document—it had ignited a fuse in him that crackled and sparked.

You want to take a little sabbatical, a little break, might be a good thing.

Like Todd gave a shit about his emotional well-being.

Todd wanted him to take time off. Not resign: that was interesting. If Todd and the boys at Fairfield wanted to get rid of him, they'd have fired him long ago. So why hadn't they? Was it really the huge payday, the five million bucks they'd have to pay to fire him without cause, that was stopping them? Given how many billions Fairfield had under management?

He tapped at his keyboard and pulled up the corporate directory, clicked on MARTIN LAI. A photo popped up—a fat-faced, phlegmatic-looking guy—along with his direct reports, his e-mail, his phone number.

He glanced at his watch. Thirteen-hour time difference in Hong Kong. Nine-thirty in the morning here meant ten-thirty at night there. He picked up the phone and dialed Martin Lai's home number. It rang and rang, and then a recorded message came on in Chinese, followed by a few perfunctory words in heavily accented English. "Martin," he said, "this is Nick Conover. I need to speak to you right away." He left the usual array of phone numbers.

Then he spoke into the intercom and asked Marge to locate Martin Lai's cell phone number, which wasn't on the Stratton intranet. A minute later, a long number popped up on his screen.

He called it and got a recorded voice again, and he left the same message. He checked Lai's Meeting Maker, his online corporate schedule, and the man appeared not to be away from Stratton's Hong Kong office.

Todd's words kept coming back to him: *You want to take a little sabbatical, a little break, might be a good thing.*

What the hell were Todd Muldaur and Fairfield Equity Partners up to, really? Who, he wondered, might know?

The answer came to him so swiftly that he wondered why he hadn't thought of it before. A "cousin" in the extended Fairfield family, that was who.

He opened his middle desk drawer and found a dog-eared business card that said KENDALL RESTAURANT GROUP, and underneath it, RONNIE KENDALL, CEO.

Ronnie Kendall was a sharp entrepreneur, a quick-witted bantam with an impenetrable Texan accent. He'd started the Kendall Restaurant Group with a little Tex-Mex place in Dallas and turned it into a thriving chain and eventually a prosperous restaurant holding company. It was mostly a chain of Tex-Mex restaurants popular in the Southwest, but his company also owned a cheesecake chain, a barbecued-chicken chain that wasn't doing so well, a lousy Japanese-food chain where chefs dressed like samurai sliced and flipped your food right at your table, and a "good times" bar-and-grill chain known for its baby back ribs and gargantuan frozen margaritas. Ten years ago he'd sold to Willard Osgood.

Nick had met him at some business conference in Tokyo, and they'd hit it off. Ronnie Kendall turned out to be a big hockey fan and had followed Nick's college career at Michigan State, amazingly. Nick had confessed he'd eaten at the Japanese restaurant chain that Kendall's group owned and didn't much like it, and Kendall had shot right back, "You kidding? Every time I set foot in there I get diarrhea. Never eat there, but people *love* it. Go figure."

Nick was put on hold several times before Ronnie Kendall picked up, sounding exuberant as always, speaking a mile a minute. Nick made the mistake of asking how business was, and Ronnie launched into a manic monologue about how the barbecued-chicken chain was expanding in Georgia and South Carolina, and then he somehow shifted into a rant on the low-carb craze. "Man, am I glad that fad is over, huh? That was *killing* us! The low-carb cheesecake never went over, and the low-carb diet Margaritas—*forget* it! And then just when we signed up our new celebrity endorser"—he mentioned the name of a famous football player—"and we'd even taped a bunch of fifteen- and thirty-second spots, then out of the blue he gets hit with a *rape* charge!"

"Ronnie," Nick finally broke in, "how well do you know Todd Muldaur?"

Ronnie cackled. "I *hate* the slick bastard and he loves me just the same. But I stay out of his way, and he stays out of mine. He and his MBA buddies were trying to muck around in my business, got so bad I called Willard himself and said, you put a choke collar on your little poodles or I'm gone. I quit. I'm too old and too rich, I don't need it. Willard must have taken Todd to the woodshed, because he started backing off. 'Course, he had his hands full, what with the chip meltdown."

"Chip meltdown?"

"Isn't that what you call them things? Microchips or whatever? Semi-conductors, right?"

"Yeah?"

"You read the *Journal*, right? The semiconductor industry bubble, the way all those private-equity guys overinvested in chips, then the bubble burst?" He cackled again. "Gotta love it, the way all those guys took a bath."

"Hold on, Ronnie. Fairfield Equity Partners overinvested in microchips?"

"Not the whole of Fairfield, just the funds our boy Todd runs. He made a massive bet on the chip business. Put all his chips on chips, right?"

Nick didn't join Ronnie's laughter. "I thought there's some kind of limit to how much they can invest in one particular sector."

"Todd's an arrogant guy, you know that, right? You can smell it on him. He figured when the semiconductor stocks started sinking, he'd pick up a bunch of companies cheap, turn a big fat profit. Well, he's sure gettin' his. His funds are sucking wind. Willard Osgood has got to be madder 'n a wet hen. If Todd's funds collapse, the whole mother ship goes down."

"Really?"

"I imagine Todd Muldaur should be makin' nice to you these days. I know Stratton's going through some hard times, but at least you're solvent. Compared to some of his other investments, you're a cash cow. He could take you guys public, make some real money. Of course, given how long that takes, it might be too late for him."

"That would take a year at least."

"At least. Why, they talking about spinning you guys off?"

"No. Nothing about that."

"Well, Fairfield needs what they call a liquidity event, and real soon."

"Meaning they need cash."

"You got it."

"Yeah, well, they're up to something," Nick said. "Really pushing hard to cut costs."

"Forget that. You know what I always say, when your house is on fire, you don't hold a garage sale."

"Come again?"

"I mean, Todd's so deep in the shit that he's probably desperate to make a quick buck, sell Stratton quick-and-dirty just to save his ass. I were you, I'd watch Todd's moves *real* close."

The instant he hung up, another call came in, this one from Eddie.

"The small conference room on your floor," Eddie said without preface. "Right now."

73

Ever since they'd had it out at Eddie's condo, there had been an acute chill in their already frosty relationship. Eddie no longer joked around as much. He avoided Nick's eyes. He often seemed to be seething.

But when he entered the conference room, he looked as though he had a secret he couldn't wait to share. It was a look Nick hadn't seen in a while.

Eddie closed the conference room door and said, "The piece of shell casing?"

Nick's voice caught in his throat. He was unable to speak.

"It's bullshit," Eddie said.

"*What?*"

"The cops never found any fragment of a shell casing on your lawn."

"Are you sure?"

"Positive."

"What was it, then?"

"It was bullshit. A pressure tactic. There never was any metal scrap."

"They *lied* about it?"

"I wouldn't get on my high horse if I were you, Nick."

"You're certain? How do you know this for sure?"

"I told you. I got sources. It's a fake out, dude. Don't you recognize a fake out when you see one?"

Nick shrugged. "I don't know."

"Come on, man. Remember when we were playing Hillsdale in the finals, our senior year, and you made that great deke to your backhand at the blue line before you fired a rocket behind Mallory, sent the game into overtime?"

"Yeah, I remember," Nick said. "I also remember that we lost."

74

Nick put his briefcase down in the front hall. Its antique, reclaimed pumpkin-pine flooring—the strip oak that had been there didn't make the cut, as far as Laura was concerned—glowed in the amber light that spilled from soffits overhead. Without thinking about it, he expected to hear the *click click click* of Barney's dog toenails on the wood, the jangle of his collar, and the absence of that happy sound saddened him.

It was almost eight o'clock. The marketing strategy committee meeting had run almost two hours late; he'd called home during a break and told Marta to make dinner for the kids. She'd said that Julia was over at her friend Jessica's, so it would just be Lucas.

He heard voices from upstairs. Did Lucas have a friend over? Nick walked upstairs, and the murmur resolved into conversation.

It was Cassie's voice, he realized with surprise. Cassie and Lucas. What was she doing here? The staircase was solidly mortised, no squeaks and creaks like the old house, or like the house he'd grown up in. They hadn't heard him come up. He felt a prickling sensation as he paused at the top landing and listened. Lucas's door was open for a change.

"They should have assigned this in physics class," Lucas was complaining. "Why would a poet know how the world's going to end anyway?"

"You think the poem is really about how the world is going to end?" Cassie's husky voice.

He was relieved. Cassie was helping Lucas with his homework, that was all.

"Fire or ice. That's how the world will end. It's what he's saying."

"Desire and hate," Cassie said. "The human heart can be a molten thing, and it can be sheathed in ice. Don't think outer space. Think inner space. Don't think *the* world. Think *your* world. Frost can be an incredibly dark poet, but he's also a poet of intimacy. So what's he saying here?"

"Thin line between love and hate, basically."

"But love and desire aren't the same, are they? There's the love of family, but we don't call that desire. Because desire is about an absence, right? To desire something is to want it, and you always want the thing you don't have."

"I guess."

"Think about Silas, in the last poem they gave you. He's about to die, and he comes home."

"Except it's not his home."

"In that one, Warren says 'home is the place where, when you have to go there, they have to take you in.' One of the most famous lines Frost ever wrote. Is that love or desire? How does *his* world end?"

Nick, feeling self-conscious, took a few steps down the hall toward his bedroom. Cassie's voice receded to a singsong murmur, asking something, and Lucas's adolescent baritone rose in impatience. "Some say this, some say that. You feel, like, make up your friggin' mind already."

Nick stopped again to listen.

Cassie laughed. "What's the *rhythm* telling you? The poem's lines mainly have four beats, right? But not the last lines, about hate: 'Is also great.' Two stressed syllables. 'And would suffice.' Clear and simple. Like it's funneling to a point. About the ice of hatred, how potent that is, right?"

"Mad props to my dawg Bobby Frost," Lucas said. "He could flow, no doubt. But he starts with fire."

"A lot of things start with fire, Luke. The crucial question is how they end."

Nick debated whether he should join them. He wouldn't have hesitated in the old days, but Lucas was different now. What was going on was a good thing, yet probably a fragile thing too. Lucas wouldn't let him help with his homework anymore, and now that he was in the eleventh grade, Nick wasn't much use anyway. But Cassie had somehow figured out a way to talk to him, and she knew that stuff—she was a natural. A goddamn valedictorian.

Finally, Nick walked past Lucas's bedroom, which let them know he was home, and made his way to his own room. Removed his clothes, brushed his teeth, took a quick shower. When he came out again, Lucas was alone in his room, sitting at his computer, working.

"Hey, Luke," he said.

Lucas glanced up with his usual look of annoyance.

Nick wanted to say something like, Did Cassie help? I'm glad you're focusing on work. But he held back. Any such comment might be resented, taken as intrusive. "Where's Cassie?" he said.

Lucas shrugged. "Downstairs, I guess."

He went downstairs to look for Cassie, but she wasn't in the family room or the kitchen, none of the usual places. He called her name, but there was no answer.

Well, she has the right to snoop around my house, he thought. After she caught me going through her medicine cabinet.

But she wouldn't do that, would she?

He passed through the kitchen to the back hallway, switched on the alabaster lamp, kept going to his study.

Unlikely she'd be in there.

The door to his study was open, as it almost always was, and the lights were on. Cassie was seated behind his desk.

His heart thumped. He walked faster, the carpet muffling his footsteps so his approach was silent. Not that he was intending to sneak up on her, though.

Several of the desk drawers were ajar, he saw.

All but the bottom one, which he kept locked. They were open just a bit, as if they'd been open and then shut hastily.

And he knew he hadn't done it. He rarely used the desk drawers, and when he did, he was meticulous about closing them all the way, otherwise the desk looked sloppy.

She was sitting back in his black leather Symbiosis chair, writing on a yellow legal pad.

"Cassie."

She jumped, let out a shriek. "Oh, my God! Don't ever do that!" She put a hand across her breasts.

"Sorry," he said.

"Oh—God. I was in my own world. No, I should apologize—I shouldn't be in here. I guess I'm just a low-boundaries gal."

"That's okay," he said, trying to sound as if he meant it.

She seemed instantly aware of the drawers that had been left slightly ajar and began pushing them all the way closed. "I was looking for a pad and a pen," she said. "I hope you don't mind."

"No," he said. "It's fine."

"I had this idea, and I had to write it down right away—that happens to me."

"Idea?"

"Just—just something I want to write. Someday, if I ever get my shit together."

"Fiction?"

"Oh, no. Nonfiction. Too much fiction in my life. I hope you don't mind my coming over tonight. I did call, you know, but Marta said you were at work, and Lucas and I got to talking, and he said he was busting his head over some poem. Which turns out to be one of the poems I actually know something about. So I . . ."

"Hey," Nick said. "You're doing God's work. I'm afraid my arrival broke things up."

"He's going to write the first few paragraphs of his poetry term paper. See where it's heading."

"You're good with him," Nick said. *You're amazing,* is what he thought.

Maybe that's all it was. She came over to help him figure out some Robert Frost poem.

"You ever teach?"

"I told you," Cassie said. "I've pretty much done everything." The pinpoint ceiling lights caught her hair, made it sparkle. She looked waiflike, still, but her skin wasn't so transparent. She looked healthier. The dark smudges beneath her eyes were gone. " 'He thinks if he could teach him that, he'd be / Some good perhaps to someone in the world.' "

"Come again?"

Cassie shook her head. "It's just a line from *Death of a Hired Man*. It's a poem about home. About family, really."

"And the true meaning of Christmas?"

"You Conovers," she said. "What am I going to do with you?"

"I have a few ideas," Nick said, attempting a leer. "God, you're good at everything, aren't you?"

"Coming from *you*? The alpha male? Jock of all trades?"

"I wish. I may be the most math-challenged CEO in the country."

"Is there a sport you can't do?"

He thought a moment. "Never learned to ride a horse."

"Horseshoes?"

"That's not a sport."

"Archery, I bet."

"I'm okay."

"Shooting?"

He went dead inside. After a split second, he gave a small shake of his head, looking perplexed. For a second his eyes went out of focus.

"You know," she said. "Target shooting, whatever it's called. On the range."

"Nope," he said, hearing the studied casualness in his voice as if from a distance. He lowered himself onto a rush-seated Windsor chair that invariably threatened to leave splinters in his backside. Laura had banished his favorite old leather club chair when they moved. Frat house furniture, she called it. He rubbed his eyes, trying to conceal the flush of terror. "Sorry, I'm just wiped out. Long day."

"Want to talk about it?"

"Not now. Sorry. I mean, thanks, but another time. I'd rather talk about anything else than work."

"Can I make you dinner?"

"You cook?"

"No," she admitted with a quick laugh. "You've had one of my three specialties. But I'm sure Marta left something for you in that haunted kitchen of yours."

"Haunted?"

"Oh yeah. I met your contractor right when I got here, and I got the low-down from him."

"Like why it's taking his guys forever to put in a kitchen counter?"

"Don't blame them. You're driving them crazy, is what I hear. He can't get signoffs when they need them. Things like that."

"Too many goddamn decisions. I don't really have the time for it. And I don't want to get it wrong."

" 'Wrong' defined as what?"

Nick was quiet for a moment. "Laura had very definite ideas of what she wanted."

"And you want everything to be just the way she'd planned. Like it's your memorial to her."

"Please don't do the shrink thing."

"But maybe you're afraid to finish it too, because when it's over, something else is over too."

"Cassie, can we change the subject?"

"So it's like Penelope, in the *Odyssey*. She weaves a shroud during the day, and unravels it at night. That way it's never finished. She staves off the suitors, and honors the departed Odysseus."

"I don't even know what you're talking about." Nick took a deep breath.

"I think you do."

"Except, you know, it's reached a point where I really do want the damn thing finished already. It was her big project, and, okay, maybe as long as it was underway, it was like she was still at work. Which doesn't make any sense, but still. Thing is, now I just want the plastic draft sheets out of here, and I want the Dumpster gone, and the trucks, and all that. I want this to be a goddamn *home*. Not a project. Not a thing in process. Just a place where the Conovers live." A beat. "Whatever's left of them."

"I get it," she said. "So why don't you take me out to dinner somewhere." A smile hovered around her lips. "A date."

75

They walked through the Grand Fenwick Hotel parking lot holding hands. It was a cool, cloudless night, and the stars twinkled. Cassie stopped for a moment before they reached the porte cochere and looked up.

"You know, when I was six or seven, my best friend, Marcy Stroup, told me that every star was really the soul of someone who'd died."

Nick grunted.

"I didn't believe it either. Then in school we learned that each star is actually a ball of fire, and some of them probably have solar systems of their own. I remember when they taught us in school about how stars die, how in just a few thousandths of a second a star's core would collapse and the whole star would blow up—a great supernova followed by nothingness. And I started to cry. Right there at my desk in sixth grade. Crazy, huh? That night I was talking to my Daddy about it, and he said that was just the way of the universe. That people die, and stars die too—they have to, to make room for new ones."

"Huh."

"Daddy said if no one ever died, there'd be no room on the planet for the babies being born. He said if nothing ever came to an end, nothing could ever begin. He said it was the same way in the heavens—that sometimes a world has to come to an end so that new ones can be born." She squeezed his hand. "Come on, I'm hungry."

The lobby of the Grand Fenwick was carpeted in what was meant to suggest an old-fashioned English broadloom, with lots of oversized leather furniture arranged in clubby "conversation pits," like a dozen living rooms stitched together. Velvet ropes on stanchions partitioned the restaurant from the lobby. The menu offered fifties favorites like duck à l'orange and salmon hollandaise, but mainly what it offered were steaks, for old-school types who knew the names for the different cuts: Delmonico, porterhouse, Kansas City strip. The place smelled like cigars, and not especially expensive ones; the smoke had seeped into everything like dressing on a salad.

"They have fish," Nick said, apologetically, as they were led to a corner table.

"Now why would you say that? You think girls don't eat red meat?"

"That's right, I forgot—you do. So long as it isn't actually red."

"Exactly."

Cassie ordered a rib steak well done, Nick a medium-rare sirloin. Both of them ordered salads.

After Nick ate his salad, he looked at Cassie. "Brainstorm. I always order a salad. But I just realized something: I don't particularly like salad."

"Not exactly the solution to Fermat's last theorem," Cassie said, "but we can work with this. You don't like salad. Same deal as with tea."

"Right. I drink tea. Laura would make it and I'd drink it. Same deal. I order salads. But you know, I never liked tea, and I never liked salad."

"You just realized this."

"Yeah. It was always true. I just wasn't conscious of it, somehow. Like . . . Chinese food. I don't really like it. I don't hate it. I just don't have any liking for it."

"You're on a roll, now. What else."

"What else? Okay. Eggplants. Who the hell decided that eggplants were edible? Nontoxic, I get. But is everything that's nontoxic a food? If I were some cave man, and I weren't starving, and I bit into an eggplant, cooked or not, I wouldn't say, wow, a new taste sensation—I've discovered a foodstuff. I'd say, well, this definitely won't kill you. Don't bother to dip your arrowhead in it. It's like—I don't know—maple leaves. You could probably eat them, but why would you?"

Cassie looked at him.

"You're the one who was complaining I was a stranger to myself," Nick said, tugging on the table linen absently.

"That wasn't really what I meant."

"Gotta start somewhere."

She laughed. He felt her hand stroking his thigh under the tablecloth. Affectionately, not sexually. "Forget eggplant. Give yourself credit—you know what's most precious to you. Not everyone does. Your kids. Your family. They're everything to you, aren't they?"

Nick nodded. There was a lump of sadness in his throat. "When I was playing hockey, I could convince myself that the harder I worked, the harder I trained, the harder I *played*, the better I'd do. It was true, or true enough. True of a lot of things. You work harder, and you do better. In hockey, they talk about playing with a lot of 'heart'—giving it your all. Not true of family, though. Not true of being a father. The harder I try to get through to Lucas, the harder he fights me. You got through the force field. I can't."

"That's because you always argue with him, Nick. You're always trying to make a case, and he doesn't want to hear it."

"The way he looks at me, I think he couldn't care less whether I lived or died."

"That's not what's going on here. Has Lucas ever talked to you about Laura's death?"

"Never. The Conover men don't really do *feelings*, okay?" Nick looked around the darkened room, and was surprised to see Scott McNally being seated a few tables away. Their eyes met, and Scott waved a hand. He was with a tall, gangly man with a narrow face and a prominent chin. Nick saw Scott talking to his dinner companion hurriedly, gesturing toward him. It looked like Scott was deciding whether to do the dessert visit, or to get it over with, and had decided that it would be better to get it over with. The two men stood up and came over to Nick's table.

"Fancy seeing you here," Scott said, patting Nick's shoulder. "I had no idea this was one of your hangouts."

"It's not," Nick said. "Scott, I'd like you to meet my friend Cassie."

"Pleasure to meet you, Cassie," Scott said. "And this is Randall Enright." He paused. "Randall's just helping me understand some of the legal aspects of financial restructuring. Boring technical stuff. Unless you're me, of course, in which case it's like *Conan the Barbarian* with spreadsheets."

"Nice to meet you, Randall," said Nick.

"Pleased to meet you," the tall man said pleasantly. His suit jacket was unbuttoned, and he put his glasses in his breast pocket before shaking hands.

"We get that contract with the Fisher Group analyzed?" Nick said.

"Not sure that's something we want to rush into, actually," said Scott.

"Sooner the better, I'd say."

"Well," said Scott, fidgeting with a lock of hair above his left ear, glancing away. "You're the boss."

"Enjoy Fenwick," Cassie said to the lawyer. "When are you heading back to Chicago?"

The tall man exchanged a glance with Scott. "Not until tomorrow," he said.

"Enjoy your dinner," Nick said, with a hint of dismissal.

Soon, heavy white plates arrived with their steaks, each accompanied by a scoop of pureed spinach and a potato. Nick looked at Cassie. "How did you know he was heading back to Chicago?"

"The Hart, Schaffner & Marx label inside his jacket. The obvious fact that he's got to be some sort of hot-shot lawyer if he's having a working dinner with your CFO." She saw the question in his eyes and said, "He put his glasses away because they were reading glasses. And they hadn't been given their menus yet. We're definitely looking at a working dinner."

"I see."

"And Scott wasn't happy about introducing him. He did it strategically, but the fact is, he chose to have dinner here for the same reason you did. Because it's a perfectly okay place where you don't expect to see anyone you know."

Nick grinned, unable to deny it.

"And then there's the 'you're the boss' stuff. Resent-o-rama. A line like that always comes with an asterisk. 'You're the boss.' Asterisk says, 'For now.'"

"You're being a little melodramatic. Don't you think you might be overinterpreting?"

"Don't you think you might not be seeing what's right in front of your face?"

"You may have a point," Nick admitted. He told her about Scott's secret trip to China, the way he tried to cover it up with a lie about going to a dude ranch in Arizona.

"There you go," she said with a shrug. "He's fucking with you."

"Sure seems that way."

"But you like him, don't you?"

"Yeah. Or maybe it's more accurate to say, I did. He's funny, he's a whiz with numbers. We're friends."

"That's your problem—it's blinding you. Your alleged 'friendship' with Scott didn't exactly keep him from stabbing you in the back, did it?"

"True."

"He's not scared of you."

"Should he be?"

"Most definitely. Scared of you, not of what's-his-name, the Yale guy from Boston."

"Todd Muldaur. Todd's really calling the shots, and Scott knows it. Truth is, I'm surprised by him. I brought him in here, I would have expected a modicum of loyalty."

"You're a problem for Scott. A speed bump. An impediment. He's decided you're part of the problem, not part of the solution. His deal is all about Scott Incorporated."

"I'm not sure you're right, there—there's actually nothing greedy or materialistic about him."

"People like Scott McNally—it's not about making a life, or attaining a certain level of comfort. You told me he wears the same shirts he's probably worn since he was a student, right?"

"So whatever he's about, it's not exactly money. I get it."

"Wrong. You *don't* get it. He's a type. People like him don't care about enjoying the things money can buy. They're not into rare Bordeaux or Lamborghini muscle cars. At the same time, they're incredibly competitive. And here's the thing. *Money is how they keep score.*"

Nick thought about Michael Milken, Sam Walton, those other billionaire-next-door types. They lived in little split-level ranch houses and were completely fixated on adding to their Scrooge McDuck vaults, day after day. He remembered hearing about how Warren Buffett lived like a miser in the same little suburban house in Omaha he bought for thirty thousand bucks in 1958. He thought about Scott's nothing-special house and how much money he had. Maybe she was right.

"Scott McNally has his mind on winning this round, so he can play in the big-stakes games," Cassie went on.

"They teach this after the lotus position or before?"

"Okay, then let me just ask you this. What do you think Scott McNally wants to be when he grows up?"

"What do you mean?"

"Does he want to be selling chairs and filing cabinets, or does he want to be a financial engineer at Fairfield Partners? Which is more his style?"

"Point taken."

"In which case, it's fair to ask yourself, who's he really working for?"

Nick gave a crooked smile.

She stood up. "I'll be right back."

Nick watched as she made her way to the ladies room, admiring the curve of her butt. She wasn't there long. On her way back, she walked past Scott's table, and stopped there briefly. She said something to the lawyer, then sat down next to him for a moment. She was laughing, as if he'd said something witty. A few moments later, he saw the lawyer hand her something. Cassie was laughing again as she stood up and returned to her seat.

"What was that about?" Nick asked.

Cassie handed him the lawyer's business card. "Just check him out, okay?"

"That was quick work." Nick glanced at the card and read, "Abbotsford Gruendig."

"Just being neighborly," Cassie said.

"By the way, I *can* see what's in front of my face," Nick said. "You're in front of my face. I see you quite well, and I like what I see."

"But as I said, we don't see things as they are. We see things as we are."

"Does the same go for you?"

"Goes for all of us. We lie to ourselves because it's the only way we can get through the day. Time comes, though, when the lies get tired and quit."

"What's that supposed to mean?"

Cassie looked at him steadily, searchingly. "Tell me the truth, Nick. What's the real reason the police were at your house?"

76

For a moment, he was at a loss for words.

He hadn't told her about the police searching the house and yard, which was a pretty damn huge thing not to have told her about. Especially given the connection to her father. Both Lucas and Julia knew the police had been searching for traces of Andrew Stadler. They just didn't know the real reason.

"Lucas told you," Nick said neutrally. He tried to keep his pulse steady, his breathing regular. He took a forkful of steak for which he had no appetite.

"It freaked him out."

"Yeah, well, he seemed to think it was a hoot. Cassie, I should have said something to you about it, but I knew how it would upset you. I didn't want to bring up your dad—"

"I understand," she said. "I understand. And I appreciate it." She was toying with a spoon. "They actually think my *father* was the stalker?"

"It's just one possibility," Nick said. "I think they're really groping." He swallowed hard. "Hell, they probably even wonder if I had something to do with it." The last words came out in a rush, not the way he had heard himself say it in his mind.

"With his death," Cassie said carefully.

Nick grunted.

"And is it possible that you did?"

Nick couldn't speak right away. He didn't look at her, couldn't. "What do you mean?"

She set down the spoon, placed it carefully alongside the knife. "If you thought he might have been the one doing all that crazy stuff, maybe you could have intervened, somehow. Helped him to get help." She broke off. "But then, these are the questions I ask myself. Why didn't I *make* him get help? Why didn't I intervene? I keep asking myself whether there was something I could have done that would have changed things. Stratton's supposed to have all these great mental health programs, but suddenly he wasn't eligible for them anymore—that's a real Catch-22, isn't it? Because of a mental illness, you quit and lose your right to treatment for your mental illness. That isn't right."

Warily: "It's not right."

"And because of these decisions—decisions you and I and God knows how many other people made—my daddy's dead." Cassie was weeping now, tears spilling down both cheeks.

"Cassie," Nick said. He took her hand in his, and fell silent. Her hand looked pale and small in his. Then a thought came to him, and he felt as if he had swallowed ice. His hand, the hand with which he tried to comfort her, was the hand that had held the gun.

"But you want to know something?" Cassie said haltingly. "When I got the news about—you know—"

"I know."

"I felt like I'd run into a brick wall. But, Nick, I felt something else too. I felt *relieved*. Do you understand?"

"Relieved." He repeated the word numbly.

"All the hospitalizations, all the relapses, all the agony he'd endured. Pain that's not physical but every bit as real. He didn't like the place he was in—the world that, more and more, he *had* to live in. It wasn't your world or my world, it was his world, Nick, and it was a cold and scary place."

"It had to have been hell, for both of you."

"And then one day he disappears. Then he's dead. *Killed*—shot dead, God knows why. But it was almost like an act of mercy. Do you ever think that things happen for a reason?"

"I think some things happen for a reason," Nick said slowly. "But not everything. I don't think Laura died for any particular reason. It just happened. To her. To us. Like a piano that just falls out of the sky and flattens you."

"Shit happens, you're saying." Cassie palmed away the tears on her face. "But that's never the whole story. Shit happens, and it changes your life, and then what do you do? Do you just go on as if nothing happened? Or do you face it?"

"I choose option A."

"Yeah. I see that." Cassie rumpled her spiky hair with a hand. "There's a parable of Schopenhauer's, it's called *'Die Stachelschweine'*—the porcupines. You've got these porcupines, and it's winter, and so they huddle together for warmth—but when they get too close, of course, they hurt each other."

"Allegory alert," Nick said.

"You got it. Too far, and they freeze to death. Too near, and they bleed. We're all like that. Same with you and Lucas."

"Yeah, well, he's a porcupine, all right."

"Got to hand it to you Conover men," Cassie said. "You're as well defended as a medieval castle. Got your moat, got your boiling oil over the gate, got your castle keep. 'Bring it on,' right? Hope you got plenty of provisions in the larder."

"All right, babe. Since you see so much more clearly than I do, let me ask you something. How much do you think I have to worry about my son?"

"Well, some. He's a stoner, as you know. Probably gets high a couple of times a day. Which can do a number on your ability to concentrate."

"A *couple* of times a day? You sure?"

"Oh please. He's got two bottles of Visine on his dresser. He's got Febreze fabric spray in his closet."

Nick looked blank.

"Fabric freshener. You spritz it on your clothing to remove the smell of the herb. Then he's got these Dutch Master leavings in his wastebasket. For making a blunt, okay? This is all Pothead 101 stuff."

"Christ," said Nick. "He's sixteen years old."

"And he's going to be seventeen. And then eighteen. And that's going to be rough too."

"A year ago you wouldn't have recognized him. He was this totally straight, popular athlete."

"Just like his dad."

"Yeah, well. My mom didn't die when I was fifteen."

"What makes it worse is if you can't talk about it."

"He's a kid. It's hard for him to talk about stuff like that."

Cassie looked at him.

"What?"

"I wasn't just talking about Lucas," she said quietly. "I was talking about you."

A deep breath. "You like metaphors? Here's one. You know the cartoon coyote that's always racing off the edge of the cliff?"

"Yes, Nick. Wile E. Coyote. An odd role model for the CEO of Acme Industries, I'd have thought."

"And he's in midair, but his legs are still pumping and he's moving along fine. But then—he looks down, and he sinks like a stone. Moral of the story? *Never fucking look down.*"

"Beautiful," Cassie said, her voice as astringent as witch hazel. "Just beautiful." Her eyes flashed. "Have you noticed that Lucas can't even *look* at you? And you can barely look at him. Now why is that?"

"If you bring up those Black Forest porcupines again, I'm out of here."

"He's lost his mom, and he desperately needs to bond with his father. But you're not around, and when you are, you're not *there*. You're not exactly verbally expressive, right? He needs you to be the healer, but you can't do it— you don't know how. And the more isolated he feels, the more he turns on you, and the angrier you get."

"The armchair psychologist," Nick said. "Another one of your imaginative 'readings.' Nice guess, though."

"No," she said. "Not a guess. He pretty much told me."

"He *told* you? I can't even imagine that."

"He was stoned, Nick. He was stoned, and he started to cry, and it came out."

"He was *stoned*? In your presence?"

"Lit up a nice fat doobie," Cassie said, with a half-smile. "We shared it. And we had a long talk. I wish you could have heard him. He has a lot on his mind. A lot he hasn't been able to say to you. A lot you need to hear."

"You smoked marijuana with my *son*?"

"Yes."

"That is *incredibly* irresponsible. How could you do that?"

"Whoa, Daddy, you're missing the big picture here."

"Lucas has a problem with this shit. You were supposed to help him. Not encourage him, goddammit. He looks up to you!"

"I told him to lay off the weed, at least on school nights. I think he's going to."

"Goddammit! You haven't got a clue, have you? I don't care what kind of a fucked-up childhood you had. This is my *son* you're dealing with. A sixteen-year-old boy with a drug problem. What part of this isn't registering?"

"Nick, be careful," she said, in a low, husky voice. Her face was turning a deep red, but her expression remained oddly fixed, a stone mask. "We had a very open and honest conversation, Luke and I. He told me all kinds of things." Now she turned to look at him with hooded eyes.

Nick was torn between fury and fear, wanting to lay into her for what she'd done, getting high with Lucas—and yet frightened of what she might have found out from Lucas.

Lucas, who might—or might not—have heard shots one night.

Who might—or might not—have overheard his father and Eddie discussing what had really happened that night.

"Like what?" he managed to say.

"All *kinds* of things," she whispered darkly.

Nick closed his eyes, waited for his heart to stop hammering. When he opened them again, she was gone.

77

Audrey's e-mail icon was bouncing, and she saw it was Kevin Lenehan, the electronics tech.

She walked right over there, almost ran.

"What's the best restaurant in town, would you say?" Kevin said.

"I don't know. Terra, maybe? I've never been there."

"How about Taco Gordito?"

"Why do you ask?"

"Because you owe me dinner. I told you the recording on this baby started at three-eighteen in the morning on Wednesday the sixteenth, right? After the sequence you're so interested in?"

"What'd you find?"

"The hard drive's partitioned into two sections, right? One for the digital images, the other for the software that drives the thing." He turned to his computer monitor, moved the mouse around and clicked on something. "Very cool system, by the way. Internet-based."

"Meaning?"

"Your guy had the ability to monitor his cameras from his office."

"What does that tell you?"

"Nothing. I'm just saying. Anyway, look at this."

"That doesn't mean anything to me. It's a long list of numbers."

"Not a techie, huh? Your husband has to program the VCR for you?"

"He can't either."

"Same with me. No one can. So, look. This is the log of all recorded content."

"Is that the fifteenth?"

"You got it. This log says that the recording actually started on Tuesday the fifteenth at four minutes after noon, right? Not like fifteen hours later."

"So you found more video?"

"I wish. No, you're not following me. Someone must have gone in and reformatted the section of the hard drive where the recordings are made, then started the whole machine over, recycled it, so it just *looked* like it started from scratch at three-whatever in the morning on Wednesday. But the log here tells us that the system was initiated fifteen hours earlier. I mean, it's saying there's recorded content going back to like noon that day. Only, when you click on the files, it says 'file not found.'"

"Deleted?"

"You got it."

Audrey stared at the screen. "You're sure of this."

"Am I sure the box started recording at noon the day before? Yeah, sure as shit."

"No. Sure you can't retrieve the recording."

"It's, like, so gone."

"That's too bad."

"Hey, you look, like, disappointed. I thought you'd be thrilled. You want proof part of the video was erased, you got it right here."

"You ever read the book *Fortunately* when you were a kid?"

"My mom plopped me down in front of *One Life to Live* and *General Hospital*. Everything I learned about life I learned from soap operas. That's why I'm single."

"I must have read it a thousand times. There's a boy named Ned, and he's invited to a surprise party, but unfortunately the party's a thousand miles away. Fortunately a friend lends him an airplane, but unfortunately the motor explodes."

"Ouch. I hate when that happens."

"Fortunately there's a parachute in the airplane."

"But unfortunately he's horribly burned over ninety percent of his body and he's unable to open the chute? See how my mind works."

"This case is like that. Fortunately, unfortunately."

"That pretty much describes my sex life," Kevin said. "Fortunately the girl goes home with Kevin. Unfortunately she turns out to be a radical feminist lesbian who only wants him to teach her how to use Photoshop."

"Thanks, Kevin," Audrey got up from the stool. "Lunch at Taco Gordito's on me."

"Dinner," Kevin said firmly. "That's the deal."

78

Nick's cell phone rang just as he was pulling into the parking lot, almost half an hour later than usual this morning.

It was Victoria Zander, the Senior Vice President for Workplace Research, calling from Milan. "Nick," she said, "I'm at the *Salone Internazionale del Mobile* in Milan, and I'm so upset I can barely speak."

"Okay, Victoria, take a deep breath and tell me what's up."

"Will you please explain to me what's going on with Dashboard?"

Dashboard was one of the big new projects Victoria was developing, a portfolio of flexible, modular glass walls and partitions—very cool, beautifully designed, and something Victoria was really high on. Nick was high on it for business reasons: there was nothing else like it out there, and it was sure to hit a sweet spot.

"What do you mean, 'What's going on'?"

"After all the time and money we've put in on this, and—it just makes no *sense*! 'All major capital expenditures on hold'—what do you *mean* by that? And not even giving me the courtesy of advance notice?"

"Victoria—"

"I don't see how I can continue working for Stratton. I really don't. You know, Herman Miller has been after me for two years, and frankly I think that's a far better home for—"

"Victoria, hold on. Cool your jets, will you? Now, who told you we're shelving Dashboard?"

"You guys did! I just got the e-mail from Scott."

What e-mail? Nick almost asked, but instead he said, "Victoria, there's some kind of glitch. I'll call you right back."

He clicked off, slammed the car door, and went to look for Scott.

"He's not here, Nick," Gloria said. "He had an appointment."

"An appointment where?" Nick demanded.

She hesitated. "He didn't say."

"Get him on his cell, please. Right now."

Gloria hesitated again. "I'm sorry, Nick, but his cell phone doesn't work inside the plant. That's where he is."

"The *plant?* Which one?"

"The chair factory. He's—well, he's giving someone a tour."

As far as Nick knew, Scott had been inside the factories maybe twice before. "Who?"

"Nick, I—please."

"He asked you not to say anything."

Gloria closed her eyes, nodded. "I'm really sorry. It's a difficult position."

Difficult position? I'm the goddamned CEO, he thought.

"Don't worry about it," he said kindly.

Nick hadn't visited the chair plant in almost three months. There was a time when he'd visit monthly, sometimes more, just to check out how things were running, ask questions, listen to complaints, see how much inventory backlog was on hand. He'd check the quality boards at each station too, mostly to set an example, figuring that if he paid attention to the quality charts, the plant manager would too, and so would everyone below him.

He visited the plant just like Old Man Devries used to do, only when the old man did it, they weren't called Gemba walks, as they were now. That term had been introduced by Scott, along with Kaizen and a bunch of other Japanese words that Nick didn't remember, and that sounded to him like types of sushi.

It was the layoffs that made walking the plants an unpleasant chore. He could sense the hostility when he came through. It wasn't lost on him, or anybody else, that Old Man Devries's job had been to build plants, and his was to tear them down.

But he knew it was something he should probably start doing again, both here and in the other manufacturing complex about ten miles down the road. He'd go back to the monthly walks, he vowed.

If he had the chance.

If the factories were still here.

He noticed the big white sign on the front of the red brick building that said DAYS SINCE LAST ACCIDENT, and next to it a black LED panel with the red digital numerals 322. Someone had crossed out ACCIDENT and scrawled over it, with a heavy black marker, LAYOFFS.

He went in the visitors' entrance and caught the old familiar smell of welding and soldering, of hot metal. It took him back to visits to his father at work, of dog-day summers in high school and college spent working on the line.

The plump girl who sat at the battered old desk and handed out safety glasses, greeted visitors, and answered the phone, did a double take. "Good *morning*, Mr. Conover."

"Morning, Beth." Beth-something-Italian. He signed the log, noticed Scott had signed in about twenty minutes earlier along with someone else whose signature was illegible.

"Boy, both you *and* Mr. McNally in the space of an hour. Something going on I should know about?"

"No, in fact, I'm looking for Mr. McNally—any idea where he is?"

"No, sir. He had a visitor with him, though."

"Catch the other guy's name?"

"No, sir." She looked ashamed, as if she hadn't been doing her job. But Nick couldn't blame her for not checking the ID of the CFO's guest too carefully.

"Did Scott say where they were going?"

"No, sir. Sounded like Mr. McNally was giving a tour."

"Brad take them around?" Brad Kennedy was the plant manager, who gave tours only to the VIPs.

"No, sir. Want me to call Brad for you?"

"That's okay, Beth." He put on a pair of dorky-looking safety glasses.

He'd forgotten how deafening the place was. A million square feet of clattering, pounding, thudding metal. As he entered the main floor, keeping to the "green mile," as it was called—the green-painted border where you'd be safe from the Hi-Lo electric lift trucks that barreled down the aisles at heedless speeds—he could feel the floor shake. That meant the thousand-ton press, which stamped out the bases of the Symbiosis Chair control panel, was operating. The amazing thing was that the thousand-ton press was all the way across the factory floor, clear on the other end, and you could still feel it go.

The place filled him with pride. This was the real heart of Stratton—not the glitzy headquarters building with its silver-fabric cubicles and flat-panel monitors and all the backstabbing. The company's heartbeat was the regular thud of the thousand-ton behemoth, which sent vibrations up your spine as you passed through. It was here, where you still found some of those antique, dangerous, hydraulic-powered machines that could bend steel three-quarters of an inch thick, the exact same one on which his father had worked, bending steel, a seething monster that could take your hand off if you weren't careful. His dad had in fact lost the tip of his ring finger to the old green workhorse once, which caused him more embarrassment than anger, because he knew it was his fault. He must have felt that the brake machine, after all those years of a close working relationship, had been disappointed in him.

As he walked, he looked for Scott, and the more he looked, the angrier he got. The idea that Scott, who worked for him, a guy he'd hired, would dare shelve projects, block funding, change vendors without consulting him—that was insubordination of the most egregious sort.

Four hundred hourly workers in this plant, and another hundred or so salaried employees, all turning out chairs for the Armani-clad butts of investment bankers and hedge-fund managers, the Prada-clad rumps of art directors.

He was always impressed by how clean the factory floor was kept, free of oil spills, each area clearly marked with hanging signs. Each section had its own safety board, marked green for a safe day, yellow for a day with a minor injury, red for an injury requiring hospitalization. Good thing, he thought grimly, he didn't have one of those hanging in his house. What was the color for death?

He was looking for two men in business suits. They shouldn't be hard to find here, among the guys (and a few women) in jeans and T-shirts and hard hats.

Periodic messages flashed on the TV monitors, a steady stream of propaganda and morale-building. THE STRATTON FAMILY CARES ABOUT YOUR FAMILY—TALK TO YOUR BENEFITS ADVISER. And: THE NEXT INSPECTOR IS OUR CUSTOMER. And then: STRATTON SALUTES JIM VEENSTRA—FENWICK PLANT—25 YEARS OF SERVICE.

A radio was blasting out Fleetwood Mac's "Shadows" from the progressive-build station where the Symbiosis chairs were assembled. Nick had borrowed the process from Ford and pretty much forced it on the workers, who resisted any further dumbing-down of their jobs. They liked building the whole chair themselves, and who could blame them? They liked the old piecework incentives. Now, one chair was assembled every fifty-four seconds as a light cycled from green to amber to red, signaling the workers to finish up. This plant turned out ten thousand Symbiosis chairs a week.

He jogged past the in-line washer that cleaned the oil off the chair-control covers and then sent them clattering down into an orange supply tub. He couldn't help slowing a bit to admire the robotic machine, a recent acquisition, that took sized and straightened wire stock, made five perfect bends, and then cut it, all in twelve seconds. In front of a press that made tubes out of eight-foot steel coils for the stacking chairs, a guy wearing green earplugs was asleep, obviously on break.

The floor supervisor, Tommy Pratt, saw him, threw him a wave, came hurrying up. Nick couldn't politely avoid the guy.

"Hey! Mr. Conover!" Tommy Pratt was a small man who looked like he'd been compacted from a larger man: everything about him seemed *dense*. Even his hair was dense, a helmet of tight brown curls. "Haven't seen you down here in a while."

"Couldn't stay away," Nick said, raising his voice to be heard above the din. "You seen Scott McNally?"

Pratt nodded, pointed toward the far end of the floor.

"Thanks," Nick shouted back. He gestured with his chin at an orange tub stacked high with black chair casters. An unusual sight—Scott's new inventory-control system made sure there was never a backlog. Keeping too much inventory on hand was a cardinal sin against the religion of Lean Manufacturing. "What's this?" he said.

"Yeah, Mr. Conover—we've been having a problem with, like, every other lot of those casters. You know, they're vended parts—"

"Seriously? That's a first. I'll have someone call Lenny at Peerless—no, in fact, I'll call Lenny myself." Peerless, in St. Joseph, Michigan, had been manufacturing chair casters for Stratton since forever. Nick vaguely remembered getting a couple of phone messages from Lenny Bloch, the CEO of Peerless. "Uh, no, sir," Pratt said. "We switched to another vendor last month. Chinese company, I think."

"Huh?"

"The bitch of it is, sir, with Peerless, if we ever got a bad batch, which hardly ever happened by the way, he'd just truck us a new lot overnight. Now we gotta deal with container ships, you know, takes forever."

"Who switched vendors?"

"Well, I think Brad said it was Ted Hollander who insisted on it. Brad put up a fight, but you know, the word came down, we're cutting costs and all that."

Ted Hollander was vice president for control and procurement, and one of Scott McNally's direct reports. Nick clenched his jaw.

"I'll get back to you on that," he said in a voice of corporate cordiality. "When I tell the guys to look at cost containment, some of them go a little overboard." Nick turned to go, but Pratt touched his elbow. "Uh, Mr. Conover, one more thing. I hope I'm not driving you away here—I don't want you to think all we're ever gonna do is bitch at you, you know?"

"What is it?"

"The damned Slear Line. We had to shut it down twice since the shift started this morning. It's really bottlenecking things."

"It's older than I am."

"That's just it. The service guy keeps telling us we gotta replace it. I know that's a load of dough, but I don't think we have a choice."

"I trust your judgment," Nick said blandly.

Pratt gave him a quizzical look; he'd been expecting an argument. "I'm not complaining. I'm just saying, we can't put it off that much longer."

"I'm sure you know what you're doing."

"Because we couldn't get the requisition approved," Pratt said. "Your people said it wasn't a good time right now. Something about putting major capital expenditures on hold."

"What do you mean, 'my people'?"

"We put the request through last month. Word came down from Hollander a couple of weeks ago."

"There's no freeze on major expenditures, okay? We're in this for the long haul." Nick shook his head. "Some people do tend to get a little overzealous. Excuse me."

Two men in suits and safety glasses were walking through the "supermarket," the area where parts were stored in aisles. They were walking quickly, and one of them—Scott—was waving a hand at something as they left the floor. Nick wondered what he was saying to the other man, whom he recognized from last night.

The attorney from Chicago who was supposedly advising Scott on structuring deals. The man whom Scott, who hadn't been on the shop floor in more than a year, was showing around in such a low-profile, almost secretive way.

There was, of course, no reason in the world for a financial engineer to tour one of Stratton's factories. Nick thought about trying to catch up with them, but he decided not to bother.

No need to be lied to again.

79

There wasn't any e-mail from Cassie. Not that he expected any, but he was sort of hoping there'd be something. He realized he owed her an apology, so he typed:

```
Where'd my little porcupine go?
—N
```

Then he adjusted the angle on the flat-panel monitor, opened his browser and went to Google. He typed in Randall Enright's name, and the name of his law firm, from the card Cassie had gotten from him last night.

Abbotsford Gruendig had offices in London, Chicago, Los Angeles, Tokyo, and Hong Kong, among other places. "With over two thousand lawyers in 25 offices around the world, Abbotsford Gruendig provides worldwide service to national and multinational corporations, institutions and governments," the firm's home page boasted.

He typed in Randall Enright's name. It appeared, as part of a list of names, on a page headed with the rubric MERGERS & ACQUISITIONS and then more boilerplate:

Our corporate lawyers are leaders in M&A, focusing on multi-jurisdictional transactions. They can advise on licence requirements and regulatory compliance and provide local legal services in over twenty jurisdictions. Our clients include many larger corporations in the telecommunications, defence and manufacturing sectors.

Blah blah blah. More legal gobbledygook.

But it told him that Scott sure as hell wasn't getting up to speed on new accounting regulations.

He was up to something completely different.

Stephanie Alstrom, Stratton's corporate counsel, wore a navy blue suit with a white blouse and a big heavy gold chain necklace that was probably intended to make her look more authoritative. Instead, the necklace and matching earrings diminished her, made her look tiny. Her gray hair was close-cropped, her mouth heavily lined, the bags under her eyes pronounced. She was in her fifties but looked twenty years older. Maybe that was what decades of practicing corporate law could do to you.

"Sit down," Nick said. "Thanks for dropping by."

"Sure." She looked worried, but then again, she always looked worried. "You wanted to know about Abbotsford Gruendig?"

Nick nodded.

"I'm not sure what you wanted to know, exactly, but it's a big international law firm, offices all over the world. A merger of an old-line British firm and a German one."

"And that guy Randall Enright?"

"M and A lawyer, speaks fluent Mandarin. A real hotshot. China law specialist, spent years in their Hong Kong office until his wife forced them to move back to the States. Mind if I ask why the sudden interest?"

"The name came up, that's all. Now, what do you know about Stratton Asia Ventures?"

She wrinkled her brow. "Not much. A subsidiary corporation Scott set up. He never ran it by my office."

"Is that unusual?"

"We review all sorts of contracts, but we don't go after people and insist on it. I assumed he was using local counsel in Hong Kong."

"Check this out, would you?" Nick handed her the e-mail from Scott to Martin Lai in Hong Kong, which Scott had tried to delete.

"Ten million dollars wired to an account in Macau," Nick said as she looked it over. "What does that tell you?"

She looked at Nick, looked down quickly. "I don't know what you're asking me."

"Can you think of a circumstance in which ten million dollars would be wired to a numbered account in Macau?"

She flushed. "I don't want to be casting aspersions. I really don't want to guess."

"I'm asking you to, Steph."

"Between you and me?"

"Please. Not to be repeated to anyone."

After a moment's hesitation, she said, "One of two things. Macau is one of those money-laundering havens. The banks there are used for hidden accounts by the Chinese leaders, same way deposed third-world dictators use the Caymans."

"Interesting. Are you thinking what I'm thinking?"

She was clearly uncomfortable. "Embezzlement—or a bribe. But this is only speculation on my part, Nick."

"I understand."

"And not to be repeated."

"You're afraid of Scott, aren't you?"

Stephanie looked down at the table, her eyes darting back and forth, and she said nothing.

"He works for me," Nick said.

"On paper, I guess," she said.

"Excuse me?" Her remark felt to Nick like a blow to his solar plexus. It felt like the wind had been knocked out of him.

"The org chart says he's under you, Nick," she said hastily. "That's all I mean."

80

"Got something for you," Eddie said over the phone.

"I'll meet you in the small conference room on my floor in ten minutes," Nick said.

Eddie hesitated. "Actually, why don't you come down to my office?"

"How come?"

"Maybe I'm tired of taking the elevator up there."

The only thing worse than this kind of idiotic, petty game, Nick thought, was responding to it. "Fine," he said curtly, and hung up.

"You know how much e-mail Scotty blasts out?" Eddie said, leaning back in his chair. It was a new chair, Nick noticed, one of a premium, super-limited run of Symbiosis chairs upholstered in butter-soft Gucci leather. "He's like a one-man spam generator or something."

"Sorry to put you out," Nick said. He also noticed that Eddie had a new computer with the largest flat-panel monitor he'd ever seen.

"Guy's a Levitra addict, first off. Gets it over the Internet. I guess he doesn't want his doc to know—small town and all that."

"I really don't care."

"He also buys sex tapes. Like *How to Be a Better Lover. Enhance Your Performance. Sex for Life.*"

"Goddammit," Nick said, "that's his business, and I don't want to hear about it. I'm only interested in *our* business."

"Our business," Eddie said. He sat upright, reached over for a thick manila folder, and set it down in front of Nick with a thud. "Here's something that's very much our business. Do you even know the first fucking thing about Cassie Stadler?"

"We're back to that?" Nick snapped. "You stay out of my goddamned e-mails, or—"

Eddie looked up suddenly, his eyes locked with Nick's. "Or what?"

Nick shook his head, didn't reply.

"That's right. We're joined at the hip now, big guy. I got job security, you understand?"

Nick's heart thrummed, and he bit his lower lip.

"Now," Eddie said, a lilt to his voice. "I'm not reading your fucking e-mails. I don't need to. You forget I can watch your house on my computer."

"Watch my *house*?" Nick shook his head. "Huh?"

Eddie shrugged. "Your security cameras transmit over the Internet to the company server, you know that. I can see who's coming and going. And I can see this babe coming and going a *lot*."

"You do not have permission to spy on me, you hear me?"

"Couple of weeks ago you were begging for my help. Someday soon you'll thank me. You know this chick spent eight months in a psycho ward?"

"Yeah," Nick said. "Only it was six months, and it wasn't a 'psycho ward.' She was hospitalized for depression after a bunch of college friends of hers were killed in an accident. So what?"

"You know that for the last six years, there's no record of any FICA payments on this broad? Meaning that she didn't have a job? Don't you think that's strange?"

"I'm not hiring her to be vice president of human resources. In fact, I'm not hiring her at all. She's been a yoga teacher. How many yoga teachers make regular social-security payments, anyway?"

"I'm not done yet. Get this: 'Cassie' isn't even her real name."

Nick furrowed his brow.

Eddie smiled. "Helen. Her name is Helen Stadler. Cassie—that's not on her birth certificate. Not a legal name change. Totally made up."

"So what? What's your point?"

"I got a feeling about her," Eddie said. "Something about her ain't correct. We talked about this already, but let me say it again: I don't care how sweet the snatch. It ain't worth the risk."

"All I asked you to do was to find out what Scott McNally was up to."

After a few seconds of sullen silence, Eddie handed Nick another folder.

"So, those encrypted documents my guys found?"

"Yeah?"

"My guys cracked 'em all. It's really just one document, bunch of different drafts, went back and forth between Scotty and some lawyer in Chicago."

"Randall Enright."

Eddie cocked his head. "That's right."

"What is it?"

"Fuck if I know. Legal bullshit."

Nick started to page through the documents. Many of them were labeled DRAFT ONLY and REDLINE. The sheets were dense with legal jargon and stippled with numbers, the demon spawn of a lawyer and an accountant.

"Maybe he's selling company secrets," Eddie said.

Nick shook his head. "Not our Scott. Huh-uh. He's not selling company secrets."

"No?"

"No," Nick said, once again short of breath. "He's selling the company."

81

"Why do you trust me?" said Stephanie Alstrom. They met in one of the smaller conference rooms on her floor. There was just no damned privacy in this company, Nick realized. Everyone knew who was meeting with whom; everyone could listen in.

"What do you mean?"

"Scott's stabbing you in the back, and you hired him too."

"Instinct, I guess. Why, are you working against me too?"

"No," she smiled. Nick had never seen her smile before, and it wrinkled her face strangely. "I just guess I should feel flattered."

"Well," Nick said, "my instinct has failed me before. But you can't be distrustful of everyone."

"Good point," she said, putting on a pair of half-glasses. "So, you know what you've got here, right?"

"A Definitive Purchase Agreement," Nick said. He'd looked over hundreds of contracts like this in his career, and even though the legalese froze his brain, he'd learned to hack his way through the dense underbrush to uncover the key points. "Fairfield Equity Partners is selling us to some Hong Kong–based firm called Pacific Rim Investors."

Stephanie shook her head slowly. "That's not what I pick up from this. It's strange. For one thing, there's not a single mention in the list of assets of any factories or plants or employees. Which, if they were planning to keep any of it, they'd have to list. And then, in the Representations and Warranties section, it says the buyer's on the hook for any costs, liabilities, et cetera, associated with shutting down U.S. facilities or firing all employees. So, it's pretty clear. Pacific Rim is buying only Stratton's name. And getting rid of everything else."

Nick stared. "They don't need our factories. They've got plenty in Shenzhen. But all this money for a *name*?"

"Stratton means class. An old reliable American name that's synonymous with elegance and solidity. Plus, they get our distribution channels. Think about it—they can make everything over there at a fraction of the price, slap a Stratton nameplate on it, sell it for a premium. No American firm would have made a deal like this."

"Who are they, this Pacific Rim Investors?"

"No idea, but I'll find out for you. Looks like Randall Enright wasn't working for Fairfield after all—he represents the buyer. Pacific Rim."

Nick nodded. Now he understood why Scott had given Enright the factory tour. Enright was in Fenwick to do due diligence on behalf of a Hong Kong–based firm that couldn't come to visit because they wanted to keep everything very quiet.

She said, "The least they could do is tell you."

"They knew I'd go ballistic."

"That must be why they put Scott on the board. Asians always demand to meet with the top brass. If Todd Muldaur thought firing you would help, he'd have done it already."

"Exactly."

"It freaks potential buyers out if a CEO gets fired right before a sale. Everyone's antennae go up. Plus, a lot of the key relationships are yours. The smarter move was to hermetically seal you off. As they did."

"I used to think Todd Muldaur was an idiot, but now I know better. He's just a prick. Can you explain this side agreement to me?"

Her pruned mouth turned down in a scowl. "I've never seen anything like it. It looks like some kind of deal-sweetener. From what I can tell, it's a way to speed up the deal, make it happen fast. But that's just a guess. You might want to talk to someone who knows."

"Like who? Scott's the only one I know who understands the really devious stuff."

"He's good, but he's not the only one," Stephanie said. "Does Hutch still speak to you?"

82

Nick had begun to dread going out in public.

Not "public" as in going to work, though that still took a fair amount of effort, putting on his Nick Conover, CEO act, confident and friendly and outgoing, when a toxic spill of anxiety threatened to ooze out through his pores. But whether it was school functions or shopping or taking clients out to restaurants, it was getting harder and harder to keep the mask fastened securely.

What was once just uncomfortable, even painful—seeing people the company had laid off, exchanging polite if tense words with them, or just generally feeling like a pariah in this town—was now close to intolerable. Everywhere he went, everyone he ran into, he felt as if a neon sign was hanging around his neck, its gaudy orange tubes flashing the word MURDERER.

Even tonight, when he was just another spectator at Julia's piano recital. Her long-dreaded, long-awaited piano recital. It was being held in one of the old town performance theaters, Aftermath Hall, a mildew-smelling old place that had been built in the nineteen thirties, a Steinway grand on a yellow wooden stage, red velvet curtain, matching red velvet upholstered seats with uncomfortable wooden backs.

The kids in their little coats and ties or their dresses streaked across the lobby, propelled by nervous energy. A couple of little African-American boys in jackets and ties with their older sister, in a white dress with a bow: unusual in Fenwick, given how few blacks there were.

He was startled to find Laura's sister there. Abby was a couple of years older than Laura, had two kids as well, married a guy with a trust fund and no personality. He claimed to be a novelist, but mostly he played tennis and golf. Abby had the same clear blue eyes as Laura, had the same swan neck. Instead of Laura's corkscrew brown curls, though, her brown hair was straight and glossy and fell to her shoulders. She was more reserved, had a more regal bearing, was less approachable. Nick didn't especially like her. The feeling was probably mutual.

"Hey," he said, touching her elbow. "Nice of you to come. Julia's going to be thrilled."

"It was sweet of Julia to call me."

"She did?"

"You seem surprised. You didn't tell her to?"

"I can't tell her to do anything, you know that. How's the family?"

"We're fine. Kids doing okay?"

He shrugged. "Sometimes yes, sometimes no. They miss you a lot."

"Do they. Not you, though." Then she softened it a bit with a smile that didn't look very sincere.

"Come on. We all do. How come we haven't seen you?"

"Oh," she breathed, "it's been crazy."

"Crazy how?"

She blinked, looked uncomfortable. Finally she said, "Look, Nick, it's hard for me. Since . . ."

"Hey, it's okay," Nick put in hastily. "I'm just saying, don't be a stranger."

"No, Nick," Abby said, inclining her head, lowering her voice, her eyes gleaming with something bad. "It's just that—every time I look at you." She looked down, then back up at him. "Every time I look at you it makes me sick."

Nick felt as if he'd just been kicked in the throat.

Little kids, big kids running past, dressed up, taut with the pre-performance jitters. Someone playing a swatch of complicated music on the Steinway, sounding like a professional you might hear at Carnegie Hall.

Laura's nude body on the folding wheeled table after the embalming, Nick weeping and slobbering as he dressed her, his request, honored by the funeral director with some reluctance. Nick unable to look at her waxen face, a plausible imitation of her once glowing skin, the neck and cheek he'd nuzzled against so many times.

"You think the accident was my fault, that it?"

"I really see no sense in talking about it," she said, looking at the floor. "Where's Julia?"

"Probably waiting her turn at the piano." Nick felt a hand on his shoulder, turned, and was stunned to see Cassie. His heart lifted.

She stood on her tiptoes, gave him a quick peck on the lips.

"Cass—Jesus, I had no idea—"

"Wouldn't miss it for the world."

"Did Julia order you to show up too?"

"She *told* me about it, which is a different thing. I'd say a daughter's piano recital falls in the category of a family obligation, don't you think?"

"I'm—wow."

"Come on, I'm practically family. Plus, I'm a big classical piano fan, don't you know that about me?"

"Why do I doubt that?"

She put her lips to his ear and whispered, her hot breath getting him excited: "I owe you an apology."

Then she was gone, before Nick had a chance to introduce her.

"Who's the new girlfriend?" Abby's voice, abrupt and harsh and brittle, an undertone of ridicule.

Nick froze. "Her name's . . . Cassie. I mean, she's—"

I mean, she's what? Not a girlfriend? Just a fuck? Oh, she's the daughter of the guy I murdered, ain't that a funny coincidence? Tell that to Craig, your alleged-writer husband. Give him something to write about.

"She's beautiful." Abby's arched brows, lowered lids, glimmering with contempt.

He nodded, supremely uncomfortable.

"She doesn't exactly seem like the Nick Conover type, though. Is she an . . . artist or something?"

"She does some painting. Teaches yoga."

"Glad you're dating again." Abby could not have sounded more inauthentic.

"Yeah, well . . ."

"Hey, it's been a year, right?" she said brightly, something cold and hard and lilting in her voice. "You're allowed to date." She smiled, victorious, not even bothering to hide it.

Nick couldn't think of anything to say.

LaTonya was lecturing some poor soul as Audrey approached, wagging her forefinger, her long coral-colored nails—a self-adhesive French manicure kit she'd been hounding Audrey to try—looking like dangerous instruments. She was dressed in an avocado muumuu with big jangly earrings. "That's right," she was saying. "I can make a hundred and fifty dollars an hour easy, taking these online surveys. Sitting at home in my pajamas. I get paid for expressing my *opinions*!"

When she saw Audrey, she lit up. "And I figured you'd be working," she said, enfolding Audrey in an immense bosomy hug.

"Don't tell me Leon's here too." LaTonya seemed to have forgotten about her sales pitch, freeing the victim to drift off.

"I don't know where Leon is," Audrey confessed. "He wasn't at home when I stopped in."

"Mmm *hmm*," LaTonya hummed significantly. "The one thing I *know* he's not doing is working."

"Do you know something you're not telling me?" Audrey said, embarrassed by the desperation she'd let show.

"About Leon? You think he tells me anything?"

"LaTonya, sister," Audrey said, moving in close, "I'm worried about him."

"You do too much worrying about that man. He don't deserve it."

"That's not what I mean. He's—well, he's gone too much."

"Thank your lucky stars for that."

"We—we haven't had much of a private life in a very long time," Audrey forced herself to say.

LaTonya waggled her head. "I don't think I want to know the gory details about my brother, you know?"

"No, I'm . . . Something's going on, LaTonya, you understand what I'm saying, don't you?"

"His drinking getting even worse?"

"It isn't that, I don't think. He's just been disappearing a lot."

"Think that bastard is cheating on you, that it?"

Tears sprang to Audrey's eyes. She compressed her lips, nodded.

"You want me to have a talk with him? I'll slice his fucking balls off."

"I'll handle it, LaTonya."

"You don't hesitate to call me in, hear? Lazy bastard don't know what a good thing he has in you."

83

Audrey's heart broke when Nicholas Conover's daughter played the first prelude from the *Well-Tempered Clavier*. It wasn't just that the girl hadn't played all that well—a number of note fumbles, her technique not very polished, her performance mechanical. Camille had all but stolen the show with the Brahms waltz, had played perfectly and with heart, making Audrey burst with pride. It was what was about to happen to Julia Conover. This little girl, awkward in her dress, had lost her mother, something that should never happen to a child. And now she was about to lose her father.

In just a couple of days her father would be arrested, charged with murder. The only time she'd ever see her remaining parent would be during supervised jail visits, her daddy wearing an orange jumpsuit, behind a bulletproof window. Her life would be upended by a public murder trial; she'd never stop hearing the vicious gossip, she'd cry herself to sleep, and who would tuck her in at night? A paid babysitter? It was too awful to think about.

And then her daddy would be sent away to prison. This beautiful little girl, who wasn't much of a pianist but radiated sweetness and naïveté: her life was about to change forever. Andrew Stadler may have been the murder victim, but this little girl was a victim too, and it filled Audrey with sorrow and foreboding.

As the teacher, Mrs. Guarini, thanked the audience for coming and invited everyone to stay for refreshments, Audrey turned around and saw Nicholas Conover.

He was holding up a video camera. Next to him sat a beautiful young woman, and next to her Conover's handsome son, Lucas. Audrey did a double take, recognizing the woman, who just then put her hand on Conover's neck, stroking it familiarly.

It was Cassie Stadler.

Andrew Stadler's daughter.

Her mind spun crazily. She didn't know what to think, what to make of it.

Nicholas Conover, having an affair with the daughter of the man he'd murdered.

She felt as if a whole row of doors had just been flung open.

84

It had to happen, since the two of them got into work at about the same time.

Nick and Scott had been avoiding each other studiously. Even at meetings where both of them were present, they were publicly cordial yet no longer exchanged small talk, before or after.

But they could hardly avoid each other right now. Nick stood at the elevator bank, waiting, just as Scott approached.

Nick was the first to speak: " 'Morning, Scott."

" 'Morning, Nick."

A long stretch of silence.

Fortunately, someone else came up to them, a woman who worked in Accounts Receivable. She greeted Scott, who was her boss, then shyly said, "Hi" in Nick's general direction.

The three of them rode up in silence, everyone watching the numbers change. The woman got off on three.

Nick turned to Scott. "So you've been busy," he said. It came out more fiercely than he intended.

Scott shrugged. "Just the usual."

"The usual include killing new projects like Dashboard?"

A beat, and then: "I tabled it, actually."

"I didn't know new product development was in your job description."

Scott looked momentarily uncertain, as if he were considering ducking

the question, but then he said, "Any expenditures of that magnitude concern me."

The elevator dinged as it reached the executive floor.

"Well," Scott said with visible relief, "to be continued, I'm sure."

Nick reached over to the elevator control panel and pressed the emergency stop button, which immediately stopped the doors from opening and
also set off an alarm bell that sounded distantly in the elevator shaft.

"What the hell are you—"

"Whose side are you on, Scott?" Nick asked with ferocious calm, crowding
Scott into the corner of the elevator. "You think I don't know what's going on?"

Nick braced himself for the usual wisecracking evasions. Scott's face
went a deep plum color, his eyes growing, but Nick saw anger in his face, not
fear.

He's not scared of you, Cassie had observed.

"There aren't any sides here, Nick. It's not like shirts versus skins."

"I want you to listen to me closely. You are not to kill or 'table' projects,
change vendors, or in fact make any changes whatsoever without consulting
me, are we clear?"

"Not that simple," Scott replied levelly, a tic starting in his left eye. "I
make decisions all day long—"

The elevator emergency alarm kept ringing.

Nick dropped his voice to a near-whisper. "Who do you think you're
working for? Any decision you make, any order you give, that's not in your
designated area of responsibility will be countermanded—by me. Publicly, if
need be. You see, Scott, like it or not, you work for me," Nick said. "Not for
Todd Muldaur, not for Willard Osgood, but for me. Understand?"

Scott stared, his left eye wincing madly. Finally he said, "The real question is, who do you think *you're* working for? We both work for our stake-
holders. It's pretty simple. Your problem is that you've never really understood
that. You talk about managing this company as if you own the place. But I've
got news for you. You don't own the place, and neither do I. You think you're
a better man than me because you got all teary-eyed when the layoffs came?
You talk about the 'Stratton Family,' but guess what, Nick. It's not a family.
It's a business. You're a great face to parade in front of the Wall Street analysts. But just because you look good in tights doesn't make you a superhero."

"That's enough, Scott."

"Fairfield gave you the car keys, Nick. They didn't give you the car."

Nick took a deep breath. "There's only one driver."

The tic in Scott's eye was coming more rapidly now. Nick could see a vein pulsing at his temple. "In case you haven't figured it out," Scott said, "things have changed around here. You can't fire me." He tried to reach around for the emergency stop button to get the elevator doors open. But Nick swiveled his body in one quick motion to block Scott's hand.

"You're right," he said. "I can't fire you. But let me be really clear: so long as I'm here, you are not to conduct any discussions regarding the sale of this company."

A thin smile crept across Scott's face as he kept staring. Several seconds ticked by. The only sound was the ring of the elevator alarm. "Fine," he said freezingly. "You're the boss." But his tone called to mind Cassie's interpretation of Scott's refrain: those unspoken words *for now*.

85

He returned to his desk shaken and began to go through his e-mail. More Nigerians who sought to share their plundered millions. More offers to add inches, or borrow money, or acquire painkillers.

He called Henry Hutchens and made an appointment for coffee or an early lunch tomorrow. Then he tried Martin Lai in Hong Kong, at home, where it was around nine in the evening.

This time, Martin Lai answered. "Oh—Mr. Conover, yes, thank you, thank you," he said, a cataract of nerves. "I'm very sorry I didn't call you back—I was on a trip, sir."

Nick knew that wasn't true. Had Lai, surprised to get a call from the CEO, checked in with Scott, who told him not to reply? "Martin, I need your help with something important."

"Yes, sir. Of course, sir."

"What can you tell me about a ten-million-dollar transfer of funds out of Stratton Asia Ventures to a numbered account in Macau?"

"Sir, I don't know anything about that," Lai answered, too quickly.

"Meaning you don't know why the transfer was made?"

"No, sir, this is the first I hear of it."

He was covering up. Scott must have gotten to him.

"Martin, this financial irregularity has been called to my attention, and it's something I'm quite concerned about. I thought I'd see if you know anything before the formal investigation is launched by Compliance."

"No, sir," Lai said. "I never heard of it before."

As he stared at the computer screen, Marjorie's voice came over the intercom, and at the same instant, an instant message popped up.

"Nick," she said, "it's the high school again."

Nick groaned.

The message was from Stephanie Alstrom:

```
Nick—info for you—talk soon?
```

"Is it Sundquist again?" he said to Marjorie, as he typed:

```
come by my office now.
```

"I'm afraid it is," Marjorie said. "And this time—well, it sounds awfully serious."

"Oh, God," he said. "Can you put me through?"

Stephanie Alstrom was getting out of the elevator just as Nick was about to get in. He gestured for her to stay in the cabin, and once the doors closed, he said, "I'm in a rush. Personal business. What do you have, Steph?"

"Pacific Rim Investors," she said. "Apparently it's a consortium whose silent partner—their anonymous sugar daddy—is an arm of the P.L.A.—the People's Liberation Army of China."

"Why the hell would the Chinese *army* want to buy Stratton?"

"Capitalism, pure and simple. They've bought up thousands of foreign corporations, usually through shell companies to avoid the political backlash. I wonder if Willard Osgood knows it. He's somewhere to the right of Attila the Hun."

"I wonder," Nick said. "But no one's a bigger archconservative than Dorothy Devries. And you can bet *she* has no idea."

86

"Nick, I know you're an extremely busy man," Jerome Sundquist said, leading him past the framed photos of multicultural tennis champs, "but if anyone owes you an apology, it's your son." He spoke loudly so Lucas could hear.

Lucas sat in one of the camel-upholstered side chairs, looking small, shoulders hunched, furled into himself. He was wearing a gray T-shirt under a plaid shirt and track pants that were zippered above the knee so you could turn them into shorts, not that Lucas ever did.

He didn't look up when Nick entered.

Nick stood there in his raincoat—this time he was prepared for the lousy weather, even brought an umbrella—and said, "You did it again, didn't you."

Lucas didn't reply.

"Tell your father, Lucas," Sundquist said as he took a seat behind his overly large desk. Nick wondered, fleetingly, why it was that people with the biggest desks and the biggest offices were often not all that powerful, in the scheme of things.

Then he reminded himself that Jerry Sundquist might only run a high school in a small town in Michigan, but right now he was as powerful in the lives of the Conovers as Willard Osgood.

Lucas cast the principal a bloodshot glare and looked back down at his feet. Had he been crying?

"Well, if he doesn't have the courage to tell you, I will," Sundquist said, leaning back in his chair. He actually seemed to be enjoying this moment,

Nick thought. "I told you that the second time he was caught smoking he'd be expelled."

"Understood," Nick said.

"And I think I also told you that if we found drugs, we'd let the police prosecute."

"Drugs?"

"The school board voted unanimously a few years ago that any student using, distributing, or even possessing marijuana on school property will be suspended, arrested, and face an expulsion hearing."

"Arrested," Nick said, suddenly feeling a chill, as if he'd just stepped into a meat locker. Lucas wasn't crying. He was high.

"We notify the police and let them prosecute. And I have to tell you, Michigan tends to be tough on minors in possession of marijuana. The two-thousand-dollar fine is probably insignificant to you, Nick, but I've seen judges give minors anything from probation to forty-five days in prison, as much as a year."

"Jerry—"

"Under Michigan law, we're required to notify the local police, do you know that? MCL three-eighty, thirteen oh eight. We don't have a choice about it."

Nick nodded, put a hand on his forehead and began massaging away the headache. My God, he thought. Expulsion? There wasn't another high school for forty miles. And what private school would take Lucas, given his record? How would Laura have handled this? She was so much better at difficult situations than he was. "Jerry, I'd like us to talk. You and me. Without Luke."

Sundquist didn't have to do anything more than raise his chin at Lucas, who quickly got up, as if shot from a cannon. "Wait in the faculty lounge," he said to Lucas's back.

"I'm sorry, Nick. I hate to do this to you."

"Jerry," Nick said, leaning forward in his chair. For a moment, he lost his train of thought. Suddenly he wasn't a prominent parent, the president and chief executive officer of the biggest company in town. He was a high school kid pleading with the principal. "I'm as angry about this as you are. More so, probably. And we've got to let him know it's totally unacceptable. But it's his first time."

"Somehow I doubt it's his first time using marijuana," Sundquist said with a sidelong glance. "But in any case, we have a zero-tolerance policy. Our options are severely limited here."

"It's not a gun, and he's not exactly a dealer. We're talking about one marijuana cigarette, right?"

Sundquist nodded. "That's all it takes these days."

"Jerry, you've got to consider what the kid has been going through in the last year, with Laura's death." There was a note of pleading in his voice that embarrassed Nick.

The principal looked unmoved. In fact, he looked almost pleased. Nick felt the anger in him rise, but he knew anger would be the worst response in this situation.

Nick took a deep breath. "Jerry, I'm asking for your mercy. If there's anything I can do for the high school, the school system. Anything Stratton can do."

"Are you offering a *payoff*?" Sundquist said, biting off the words.

"Of course not," Nick said, although both men knew that was exactly what he was talking about. An extra deep discount on furniture could save the high school hundreds of thousands of dollars a year.

Sundquist closed his eyes, shook his head sadly. "That's beneath you, Nick. What kind of lesson do you think it's going to teach your son if he gets special treatment because of who his dad is?"

"What we talk about stays between us," Nick said. He couldn't believe that he'd just offered the high school principal a bribe. Was anything lower? Bribes—that was the coin of Scott McNally's realm, Todd Muldaur's realm. Not his.

Jerome Sundquist was looking at him with a new expression now, one of disappointment and maybe even contempt. "I'm going to pretend I didn't hear it, Nick. But I'm willing to show some leniency on the grounds of his mother's death. I do have to notify the police that we're willing to handle the incident ourselves, and generally they leave it to our discretion. I'm giving Lucas a five-day suspension and assigning him to crisis counseling during that time and for the rest of the school year. But the next time, I go right to the police."

Nick stood up, walked up to Sundquist's desk and put out his hand to

shake. "Thanks, Jerry," he said. "I think it's the right decision, and I appreciate it."

But Sundquist wouldn't shake his hand.

Ten minutes later Nick and Lucas walked out together through the glass doors
of the high school. The rain was really coming down now—it was monsoon
season, had to be—and Nick held up his umbrella for Lucas, who shunned it,
striding ahead through the rain, head up as if he wanted to get soaked.

Lucas seemed to hesitate before getting into the front seat, as if contem-
plating making a run for it. As the car nosed through the parking lot and onto
Grandview Avenue, the silence was electric with tension.

Lucas wasn't high anymore. He was low, and he was silent, but it wasn't
a neutral silence. It was a defiant silence, like that of a prisoner of war determined to reveal nothing more than his name, rank, and serial number.

Nick's own silence was the silence of someone who had plenty to say but
was afraid of what would happen if he began to speak.

Lucas's hand snaked around to the radio dial and turned on some alter-
native rock station, blasting it.

Nick immediately switched it off. "You proud of yourself?"

Lucas said nothing, just stared fixedly ahead as the windshield wipers
flipped back and forth in a lulling rhythm.

"You know something? This would have broken your mother's heart.
You should be relieved she isn't around to see this."

More silence. This time Nick waited for a reply. He was about to go on
when Lucas said, in a hollow voice, "I guess you made sure of that."

"And what's that supposed to mean?"

Lucas didn't respond.

"What the *fuck* is that supposed to mean?" Nick realized he was shouting. He could see a spray of his own spittle on the windshield. He pulled the
car over, braked to an abrupt stop, and turned to face Lucas.

"What do *you* think?" Lucas said in a low, wobbly voice, not meeting his
eyes.

Nick stared, disbelieving. "What are you trying to say?" he whispered,
summoning all the calm he could muster.

"Forget it," Lucas said, making a little buzz-off gesture with his left hand. "What are you trying to say?"

"I wouldn't know, Dad. I wasn't there."

"What's gotten into you, Lucas?" The windshield wipers ticked back and forth, back and forth, and he could hear the regular clicking of the turn signal that hadn't gone off. He reached over, switched off the signal. The rain sheeted the car's windows, making it feel like the two of them were inside a cabin in a terrible storm, but it wasn't a safe place. "Look, Luke, you don't have Mom anymore. You just have me. You wish it were otherwise. So do I. But we've got to make the best of a bad situation."

"It wasn't me who made that situation."

"No one 'made' that situation," Nick said.

"You killed Mom," he said, so quietly that for a moment Nick wasn't sure Lucas had actually spoken the words.

Nick felt like someone had grabbed his heart and squeezed. "I can't deal with this right now. I can't deal with *you*."

You Conover men. Better defended than a medieval castle.

"Fine with me."

"No," Nick said. "No. Scratch that." He was breathing hard, as if he had just done an eight-hundred-meter sprint. "Okay, listen to me. What happened to your mother that night—God knows we've talked about it . . ."

"No, Dad." Lucas's voice was shaky but resolute. "We've never talked about it. You *refer* to it. You don't talk about it. That's the house rule. We don't talk about it. *You* don't. You talk about what a fuck-up I am. *That's* what you talk about."

The windows had begun to fog up. Nick closed his eyes. "About your mother. There isn't a day that goes by when I don't wonder whether there was anything I could have done—anything at all—that might have made a difference."

"You never said . . ." Lucas's eyes were wet and his voice was thick, muffled.

"The truck came out of nowhere," Nick began, but then he stopped. It was too painful. "Luke, what happened happened. And it wasn't about me and it wasn't about you."

Lucas was quiet for a moment. "Fucking swim meet."

"Lucas, don't try to make sense of it. Don't try to connect the dots, as if there was some kind of logic to it all. It just *happened*."

"I didn't visit her." Lucas's words were slurred, whether from the pot or from emotion, Nick couldn't tell, and didn't care. "In the hospital. Afterward."

"She was in a coma. She was already gone, Luke."

"Maybe she could have heard me." His voice had gotten thin and reedy.

"She knew you loved her, Luke. She didn't need reminding. I don't think she wanted you to remember her like that, anyway. She wouldn't have been sore that you weren't there. She would have been glad. I really believe that. You were always attuned to her feelings. Like there was some radio frequency only the two of you could hear. You know something, Luke? I think maybe you were the only one of us who did what she would have wanted."

Lucas buried his face in his hands. When he spoke again, his voice sounded as if it were coming from a long way off. "Why do you hate me so much? Is it 'cause I look like her, and you can't deal with that?"

"Lucas," Nick said. He was determined to hold it together. "I want you to listen to me. I need you to hear this." He squeezed his eyes shut. "There is nothing in my life more precious to me than you are." His voice was hoarse, and he got the words out with difficulty, but he got them out. "I love you more than my life."

He put his arms around his son, who at first stiffened and squirmed, and then, suddenly, put his own arms around Nick and clasped him tightly, the way he did when Lucas was a little boy.

Nick felt the rhythmic convulsions of grief, the staccato expulsions of breath, and it took him a moment before he realized that Lucas wasn't the only one who was weeping.

87

The phone rang, and Audrey picked it up without thinking.

"Is this Detective Rhimes?" A sweet, female voice, the words slow and careful.

Her heart sank. "Yes it is," Audrey said, although she was sorely tempted to say, No, I'm afraid Detective Rhimes is on vacation.

"Detective, this is Ethel Dorsey."

"Yes, Mrs. Dorsey," she said, softening her voice. "How are you doing?"

"I'm doing as well as could be expected with my Tyrone gone and all. But I thank the good Lord I still have my three wonderful sons."

"There's so much we can't understand, Mrs. Dorsey," Audrey said. "But the Scriptures tell us that those who sow in tears will reap with songs of joy."

"I know he records our tears and collects them all in his bottle."

"He does. That he does."

"God is good."

"All the time," Audrey said, her response a reflex.

"Detective, I'm so sorry to disturb you, but I was wondering if you've made any progress on my Tyrone's case."

"No, I'm sorry. Nothing yet. We keep plugging away, though." The lie made her ashamed.

"Please don't give up, Detective."

"Of course not, Mrs. Dorsey." She hadn't given the case more than a fleeting thought in the last several weeks. She was thankful that Mrs. Dorsey worshipped in another church, the next town over.

"I know you're doing your best."

"Yes, I am."

"May the Lord keep you strong, Detective."

"You too, Mrs. Dorsey. You too."

She hung up filled with sorrow, ashamed beyond ashamed, and the phone rang again immediately.

It was Susan Calloway, the bland-voiced woman from the state police lab in Grand Rapids. The firearms examiner in charge of the IBIS database. She sounded a little different, and Audrey realized that what she was hearing was excitement, in the woman's tamped-down, squelched way.

"Well, I do think we have something for you," the woman said.

"You have a match."

"I'm sorry this has taken so long—"

"Oh, not at all—"

"But the Grand Rapids PD certainly took their time. I mean, all I was asking them to do was to check the bullets out of Property and drive them all of seventeen blocks over to Fuller. You'd think I'd asked for a human sacrifice or something."

Audrey chuckled politely. "But you got a match," she prompted. The technician sounded positively giddy.

"Of course, the real problem was that it wasn't anyone's case anymore. I mean, it was from six years ago, and both detectives are gone, they tell me. There's always an excuse."

"Tell me about it," Audrey laughed.

"In any case, the bullets they brought over matched the ones in your case. They're copper-jacketed Rainiers, so the ammunition is different. But the striation markings are identical."

"So it's a positive match."

"It's a positive match, yes."

"The weapon—?"

"I can't tell you that for absolute certain. But I'd say it's a safe guess it's a

Smith and Wesson .380. That's not legally admissible, though." The woman read off the Grand Rapids PD report number for the bullet.

"So Grand Rapids should have all the information I need," Audrey said.

"Well, I don't know how much more they'll have than I already told you. "Both detectives on the case are off the force, as I say."

"Even so, those names would be a help."

"Oh, well, if that's all you want, I have *that*. The submitting detective, anyway. Right here in the comments box." The technician went silent, and Audrey was about to prompt her for the name, when the woman spoke again, and Audrey went cold.

"Says here it was submitted by a Detective Edward J. Rinaldi," the technician said. "But they say he's retired from the force, so that's probably not going to be much use to you. Sorry about that."

PART FIVE
NO HIDING PLACE

88

Mulligans—never an apostrophe—was a diner on Bainbridge Road in Fenwick famous for its Bolognese sauce, the subject of a yellowed framed article from the *Fenwick Free Press* on the wall as you entered. The headline was typical of the paper's dopey, punning style: "A Meaty Subject." This was the place Nick used to go at three in the morning, after the junior and senior proms. Frank Mulligan was long gone. It was now owned by a guy who'd been a few years ahead of Nick and Eddie in high school, Johnny Frechette, who'd done three years in Ionia for drug trafficking.

Nick hadn't been here in years, and he noticed that the place had a staleness to it. The Formica tables had a faint cloth pattern, faded to white in the areas where mugs and plates had banged and scraped against it. They were serving breakfast now, and the place smelled of coffee and maple syrup and bacon, all blended into a single aroma: Eau du Diner.

Eddie seemed to know the waitresses here. Probably he came here for breakfast a lot. They were seated in a corner, away from the window. Aside from a few people eating at the counter, the place was empty.

"You look like shit," Eddie said.

"Thanks," Nick said irritably. "You too."

"Well, you're not going to want to hear this."

Nick held his breath. "What is it?"

"They ID'd the gun."

The blood drained from Nick's face. "You said you tossed it."

"I did."

"Then how could that be?"

The two fell silent as an overperfumed waitress arrived with a Silex carafe, and sloshed coffee into their thick white mugs.

"They got all kinds of tricky ballistics shit these days," Eddie said.

"I don't get what you're telling me." Nick took a hurried sip of his black coffee, scalding his tongue. Maybe he didn't *want* to understand what Eddie seemed to be getting at.

"They matched the bullets with the gun."

"They matched the bullets with *what?*" Nick was aware that his voice was a bit too loud, and he lowered it at once. "There's *no gun*, right? You said it's *gone!*"

"Yeah, well, apparently they don't need a gun anymore." Eddie popped open a couple of little half-and-half containers and tipped them into his mug, stirring until it turned an unappealing gray. "All's they need is bullets, 'cause of the big new computer database, I forget what it's called. They must have matched up the bullets in Stadler's body with the ones from the scene years ago where I got the piece—how the hell do I know? My source didn't get into details."

"Who's your source?"

Eddie ducked his head to the side. "Forget it."

"You know this for a fact? You're one-hundred-percent certain?"

"It's a fact. Suck it up."

"Jesus Christ, Eddie, you said everything was cool!" Nick's voice cracked. "You said the gun wasn't registered to you. You—you said you picked it up at a crime scene, and there was no record of it anywhere."

Eddie's normally confident expression had given way, disconcertingly, to a pallid, sweaty discomfort. "That's what I thought. Sometimes shit gets out of your control, buddy boy."

"I don't believe this," Nick said, his voice hoarse. "I don't fucking believe it. What the hell do we do now?"

Eddie set down his coffee mug and gave Nick a stone-cold look. "We do absolutely nothing. We say nothing, admit nothing, we don't say a fucking word. Are you getting this?"

"But if they—they know the gun I used was one you took—"

"They're going to try to connect the dots, but they don't have it nailed down. Maybe they can prove the ammo that killed Stadler came from that gun, but they can't prove I took it. Everything they got is circumstantial. They got *nada* when they searched your house—that whole thing was a scare tactic. They got no witnesses, and they got a lot of little forensic shit, and now they got this gun, but in the end it's all circumstantial. So all they can do now is scare you into talking, see. This is why I'm telling you about it. I want you to be prepared. I don't want those jokers springing this on you and having you crumble, okay? You got to be a rock." Eddie took a sip of coffee without moving his eyes from Nick's.

"They can't just arrest us? Maybe they don't need us to talk."

"No. If neither one of us says a damned thing, they're not going to arrest."

"*You* wouldn't say anything, would you?" Nick whispered. "*You're* not going to say anything, right?"

Eddie smiled a slow smile, and Nick got a shivery feeling. There was something almost sociopathic about Eddie, something dead in his eyes. "Now you're starting to understand," he said. "See, at the end of the day, Nick, they don't give a shit about me. I'm just some small-time corporate security guy, a nobody. You're the CEO everyone in this town despises. They're not interested in putting my puny antlers on the wall. You're the monster buck they're hunting. You're the fucking *twelve-point rack*, okay?"

Nick nodded slowly. The room was turning slowly around him.

"The only way this thing unravels," Eddie said, "is if you talk. Maybe you decide to play 'Let's Make a Deal' with the cops. Try to strike your own separate deal—good for you, bad for me. This would be a huge, *huge* fucking mistake, Nick. Because I will hear about it. You have even the most preliminary, exploratory conversation with those jokers, and I will hear about it in a matter of *seconds*, Nick—count on it. Believe me, I'm wired into that place. And my lawyer will be in the DA's office so fast it'll make your head spin, with an offer they will fucking jump at."

"Your . . . *lawyer?*" Nick croaked.

"See, Nick, let's be clear what they got me for. It's called 'obstruction,' and it's no big deal. First offenders get maybe six months, if any time at all, but not me. Not when I agree to tell the whole story, testify truthfully in the grand jury and at the trial. They get a *murderer*, see. And what do *I* get out of it? A walk. Not even probation. It's a sure thing, Nick."

"But you wouldn't do that, would you?" Nick said. He heard his own voice, and it seemed to be coming from very far away. "You'd never do that, right?"

"Only if you change the rules of the game, bud. Only if you talk. Though I gotta tell you, I shoulda done this on day one. Why I ever came over to help you that night, I don't know. Goodness of my heart, I guess. Help an old buddy who's in deep shit. I shoulda said, sorry, not me, amigo, and just stayed in bed. Look what I get for being a nice guy. Very least, I should have shopped you long ago. Rolled over, made a deal. I don't know why I didn't. Anyway, what's done is done, but let's be crystal clear, I am *not* going down for this. You try to make a deal, you talk, and at that point I'm gonna do what's in my own best interests."

Nick couldn't catch his breath. "I'm not going to talk," he said.

Eddie gave him a sidelong glance, and he smiled as if he were enjoying this. "All you gotta do, Nicky, is hold it together, and we're going to be just fine, you and me. Keep your fucking mouth shut, don't panic, and we'll ride this out."

The waitress was back, wielding her glass carafe. "Freshen your coffee?" she said.

Neither Eddie nor Nick responded at first, and then Nick said slowly, not looking at her, "I think we're okay."

"That's right," Eddie said. "We're okay. We're just fine."

89

The Fenwick Racquet Club wasn't a place where much tennis was played, as far as Nick could tell. But for Henry Hutchens—Hutch, as he was always known—it had evidently become a home away from home. Hutch had been Stratton's chief financial officer back when the position was called, less grandly, controller. He had served Old Man Devries for a quarter of a century, and when Nick took over, he helped prepare the financial statements for the sale to Fairfield. Did a good job of it too. His manner was unfailingly courtly, maybe a little formal. And when Nick had come to his office—that's how he did it, in Hutch's office, not his own—and told him that Fairfield wanted to replace him with one of their own, he didn't utter a word of protest.

Nick had told him the truth about Fairfield. Still, they both knew that if Nick had seriously objected, Fairfield would have backed down. Nick hadn't. Hutch was a highly competent old-school controller. But Fairfield was loaded up with high-powered financial engineers, ready to lecture you on the advantages of activity-based costing and economic-value-added accounting systems. They viewed Hutch as a green-eyeshades guy; he didn't use words like "strategic." Scott McNally was someone the people at Fairfield were comfortable with, and he was someone who could help Nick take Stratton to the next level. *The next level*—there was a time when Nick couldn't get enough of that phrase; now the cliché had the stink of yesterday's breakfast.

"Long time between drinks, Nick," Hutch said as Nick joined him at a table inside the clubhouse. He lifted a martini glass, and smiled crookedly, but didn't stand. "Join me?"

Hutch had the kind of ruddy complexion that looked like good health from a distance. Up close, Nick could see the alcohol-inflamed capillaries. Even his sweat seemed juniper-scented.

"It's a little early for me," Nick said. Christ, it wasn't even noon yet.

"Well, of *course*," Hutch said, with his Thurston Howell III purr. "You're a working man. With an *office* to go to. And lots of employees who *depend* on you." He drained the last drops of his drink, and signaled to the waiter for another.

"For the moment, anyway."

Hutch clasped his hands together. "You must be riding high, though. Layoffs—everyone talks about the layoffs! They must be *ecstatic* in Boston. To think that my own humble self was to be the first of so many on the gallows. It's kind of an honor, really."

Nick blanched. "The company owes you a lot, Hutch. I've always been grateful to you, personally."

"Oh please. Not everyone has the privilege of selling the rope to one's own hangman." Another drink was placed before him. "Thank you, Vinnie," Hutch murmured. The waiter, a sixtyish man whose neck strained against the club-required red bowtie, nodded pleasantly.

"A tomato juice would be great," Nick told him.

"You surprised a great many people, you know," Hutch went on. He popped the cocktail olive into his mouth and chewed thoughtfully. "Have to keep my strength up," he added with a wink.

"What happened has been hard for everyone. A lot of good people have been hurt. I'm very aware of that."

"You misunderstand," Hutch said. "I didn't mean about the layoffs. I just meant that not everyone took you to be CEO material. A solid company man, absolutely. But not quite cut out for the corner office."

"Well." Nick looked around, taking in the fieldstone fireplace, the white tablecloths, the red patterned wall-to-wall carpet. "I guess Old Man Devries—"

"It had nothing to do with Milton," Hutch said sharply. "If he'd wanted to, Milton could have named you president, or chief operating officer. One of those next-in-line positions. That's the custom with a corporate heir apparent. He did not choose to do so."

"Fair enough," Nick said, trying not to bridle.

"He was *fond* of you. We all were. But when the issue came up, well . . ." Hutch peered into the watery depths of his cocktail. "Milton considered you a little callow. Too much of a big-man-on-campus type. Someone too concerned with being popular to be a real leader." He looked up. "Thought you didn't have the killer instinct. Now *there's* one heck of an irony."

Nick's face was hot. "Being that you're such a connoisseur of irony, you might enjoy this one." He unzipped his black leather portfolio and presented Hutch with the contract that Eddie had taken from Scott's e-mail.

"What is this?"

"You tell me." *If you're not too drunk to make sense of it,* Nick thought.

Hutch reached for his reading glasses, convex lenses with wire frames, and started paging through the document. A few times he tapped on the pages and gave a dry chuckle. "My, my," he finally said. "I take it this isn't your masterwork."

"Not mine."

"Milton! Thou shouldst be living at this hour: Stratton hath need of thee." Hutch put his reading glasses away, and made tsk-tsking sounds. "Pacific Rim Investors," he said, and then: "I can't even pronounce this name— is it Malaysian? Good Lord." He looked up, bleary-eyed. "So much for the match made in Heaven. Looks like your white knights came riding in from Boston only to sell Stratton down the Yangtze River."

Nick explained what Stephanie Alstrom had told him about the real owner being the Chinese P.L.A.

"Oh, that's rich," Hutch said happily. "That's really a thing of beauty. Though it's not exactly sporting to put one over on the Communists like that these days, is it?"

"Put one over?"

"If these balance sheets are authentic, then Stratton's doing marvelously well. But I have a suspicion they're as phony as a glass apple."

Lipstick on a pig, Nick thought.

"If I had access to your most recent P and L statements, *and* if I weren't three sheets to the wind, *and* if I actually *cared,* I could give you a breakdown of this document that was so clear even *you* could understand it." He took a swallow of his drink. "But even in my current condition, I can tell you that somebody's been coloring outside the lines. For one thing, you're taking your reserves against losses from your last profitable year and using it to cover over the new tide of red ink. That's 'cookie jar' accounting, and we both know about that company that got caught doing it not so long ago and had to pay three billion dollars in damages to make it all better. It's not nice to fool with your accrued liability."

"What good is that?" Nick said. "Once the new owners find out the truth, they'll hit Fairfield with a huge lawsuit."

"Ah, but you see, that's the beauty part, my boy. They can't sue."

"Why not?"

"There's a clever non-litigation clause here," Hutch said, tapping the paper. "Once the deal goes through, no lawsuits are permitted over any representations and warranties made herein, ya de ya de ya."

"Why in the world would the buyers agree to that?"

"I think the answer is manifest," Hutch said, looking up again. "It's in the side agreement. Guaranteeing a seven-figure payout to someone, no doubt a Chinese government official with the ability to speed through the acquisition."

"A bribe."

"You put it so *harshly*, son. The Chinese have a wonderful tradition of giving red envelopes of *hong bao*—good-luck money—to start off the lunar new year right."

"Ten million dollars is a lot of good-luck money for one man."

"Indeed. But to grease a deal like this through the Chinese bureaucracy without endless quibbling—well, that's quite a bargain, isn't it?"

"It's early for Chinese New Year, isn't it?"

"Now you're catching on. Unless you can think of some other reason why Stratton would be routing him his money to a numbered account in Macau. From where, I'll wager, it was immediately transferred to another account at the Bank of Commerce of Labuan."

"Labuan?"

"Labuan is an island off the coast of Malaysia. A speck of sand, and a great big offshore financial services industry. The bankers of Labuan make the Swiss seem *gabby*. Basically, it's where Chinese kleptocrats like to sock away their ill-gotten gains."

"I had no idea."

"I'm sure they were *counting* on that. Good boys and girls don't know about Labuan. And they certainly don't wire money there."

"Christ," Nick said. "How many people are in on this thing?"

"Impossible to say, though it only takes two countersigners to execute it. One corporate officer—that would be your charming young CFO—and a managing partner from Fairfield. It does seem a little low-rent, the whole thing, but I suppose these are two young men in a hurry. There are a *lot* of people in a hurry these days. Sure you won't join me in a drink?"

"Still waiting for my tomato juice," Nick said. "Seems to be taking an awfully long time."

"Oh dear," Hutch said in a low voice. "I should have realized. Doubt it's ever going to come, Vinnie being your waiter and all. I guess you must be used to this sort of thing."

"What are you saying?"

Hutch glanced at the waiter and shrugged elaborately. "It's just that you laid off his brother."

90

Audrey tracked down Bugbee on his cell phone at the Burger Shack, the place he liked to go for lunch. He could barely hear her. In the background was a cacophony of laughter and clinking plates and bad rock music.

"When are you coming back?" she said several times.

"I'm on lunch."

"I can tell that. But this is important."

"What?"

"You'd better get over here."

"I said it can wait."

"No, it can't," she said.

"I'm at the Burger Shack for the next—"

"See you there," she said, and she hung up before he could object.

Bugbee quickly got over his pique at having his lunch with the guys—three uniformed officers, all around his age—interrupted.

He excused himself, and he and Audrey found an empty booth.

"That's it," he said when Audrey told him about the weapon match. "We got 'em."

"It's still tenuous," she said. "It's circumstantial."

He glared. There was a large splotch of ketchup on his hideous tie, which only improved its appearance. "The *fuck* are you waiting for—Nick

Conover's diary with a special entry for that night saying I plugged the guy, me and Eddie?"

"We're connecting dots that I don't know if the prosecutor's going to let us connect."

"Connecting *what* fucking dots?" he spat out.

She briefly considered asking him to cut out the potty-mouth stuff, but now was not the time. "We know this suggests that Eddie Rinaldi and Nick Conover were behind it."

"Tell me something I don't know—"

"Will you shut up for a second, please?" It was worth saying just to see Bugbee's stunned expression. "The gun that was used to kill Stadler was also used on a no-gun case that Eddie Rinaldi worked six years ago. But does that prove Rinaldi pocketed the gun back in Grand Rapids? The case is still full of holes."

"Yeah? I don't think so, and neither do you."

"Our opinion isn't the same thing as what's going to convince the DA to prosecute. Especially in a capital case involving the CEO of a huge corporation and one of his top officers."

"Tell you something—once we hook our boy Eddie up to a polygraph, he'll crack."

"He doesn't have to submit to a polygraph."

"If he's facing a first-degree murder charge and life without parole, believe me, he'll take it." He leaned back in the booth, savoring the moment. "This is beautiful. Shit, this is beautiful." He smiled, and she realized that this was the first time she'd seen him give a genuine smile of pleasure. It looked wrong on his face, didn't come naturally, looked like a disturbance in the natural order of things. His cheeks creased deeply like heavily starched fabric.

"Conover won't take a polygraph," Audrey said. "Let's face it, we still don't know which one of them the shooter is," Audrey said.

"Fuck it. Charge 'em both with first-degree murder, and sort it out later. Whoever comes to the window first gets the deal, that's how it works."

"I don't know if we're even going to get to that point, if we'll get a prosecutor to write out a warrant."

"So you go prosecutor-shopping. Come on. You know how the game works."

"Noyce really frowns on that."

"Screw Noyce. This is our case, I told you. Not his."

"Still," she said. "I don't know. I don't want to mess this up."

Bugbee started counting on his left hand, starting with his thumb. "We got the soil match, we got the fucking erased surveillance tape, we got Conover's alarm going off at two A.M., followed by the desperate cell phone call, we got Schizo Man with a history of attacks on the suspect, and now we got a gun match." He held up five fingers triumphantly. "The fuck else you want? I say we run with it."

"I want to pass this by Noyce first."

"You want to run to Daddy?" He shook his head. "Haven't you figured out that Noyce isn't our friend?"

"Why do you say that?"

"Take a look. The closer we get to Stratton's CEO, the harder Noyce's been fighting us, right? He doesn't want us taking on the big kahuna. Wouldn't surprise me if he's in Stratton's pocket."

"Come on."

"I'm fucking serious. Something's off about the way that guy's taking their side."

"He's got to be cautious on a case this big."

"This is way beyond cautious. You notice how when I searched Rinaldi's condo, total surprise, and all of a sudden a couple of guns are missing from his rack, like someone gave him a heads-up?"

"Or maybe he dumped them after he or Conover murdered Stadler," Audrey said. "Or Conover called him, told him a team was coming to search Conover's house, and Eddie races home and disposes of the evidence."

"Yeah, any of those are possible. Theoretically. Then you notice how Noyce is trying to make life difficult for you, jam up your schedule with other shit so you don't have time to do this right? Look, Audrey, I don't trust the guy."

"He's my friend, Roy," she said softly.

"Oh, is he?" Bugbee said. "I wouldn't be so sure of that."

She didn't reply.

91

Dorothy Devries's mansion on Michigan Avenue in East Fenwick didn't seem quite as big as Nick remembered it, but was possibly even darker. Outside, the gables and peaked eaves stopped just shy of Addams Family gothic. Inside, wooden floors were stained to a chocolate hue and partly covered with blood red Orientals. The furniture was either a dark mahogany or covered in a dark damask. She kept the curtains drawn, and he remembered her once saying something about how sunlight could bleach the fabrics. The moon glow of her pale skin was the brightest thing in the house.

"Did you say you wanted tea?" she asked, squinting at him. She sat almost motionless in a burgundy-clad Queen Anne's chair. There was a chandelier above them, which she kept pointedly unlit.

"No thanks," he said.

"But I've interrupted you," she said. "Please go on."

"Well, the basic situation is what I've described. You and I worked hard on the sale to Fairfield, and we did that because we wanted to preserve your father's legacy. And your husband's."

"Legacy," she repeated. In the gloom, he wasn't sure whether her dress was charcoal gray or navy. "That's a pretty word."

"And a pretty big accomplishment," he said. She seemed to brighten. "Harold Stratton created a company that did what it did as well as—or better than—any other, and he did it right here in Fenwick. And then your husband put Fenwick on the map, as far as corporate America was concerned."

Dorothy had had a glossy vanity biography of her husband, Milton, privately printed, copies distributed widely. Nick knew she always responded to the most unctuous praise of her father's historical significance. "So the prospect of seeing Stratton bundled in brown paper and shipped to the Far East— well, I think he'd be appalled. I know I am. It isn't right. It's not right for Fenwick, and it's not right for Stratton."

Mrs. Devries blinked. "But you're telling me all this for a reason."

"Well, sure."

"I'm all ears, Nicholas." She used his full name as if he were a grade student, and a little small for all three syllables.

"You're part owner of the company. You sit on the board. I thought if I could enlist your support, we might be able to present the case together to the others. That way, they'd see it wasn't just about a manager trying to save his job. Because this deal—well, frankly, it would be a disaster. The Chinese aren't interested in our manufacturing facilities. They've got their own. They're going to gut Stratton, run a fire sale of the shop machines, and pass out walking papers to the remaining employees."

"That puts things rather starkly."

"It's a stark situation."

"Well, you do have a flair for the dramatic. That isn't a criticism. But then you haven't come here to consult, have you?"

"Sure I have."

"Because I didn't hear you ask me my opinion. I heard you telling me yours."

"I just thought I should fill you in," Nick said, perplexed. "See what you thought." A pause. "I'm interested in getting your . . . help and guidance."

A watery smile. "Is that right," she said.

Nick looked at her, and his face started to prickle. *Had she already known before I came here?*

"I must say I'm a little taken aback to hear you make an argument that's based on sentiment, as opposed to dollars and sense. Because, you see, I don't recall your seeking my help or guidance when you decided to discontinue the Stratton Ultra line. Which was, of course, one of my husband's proudest *legacies*." In a quiet voice, she added, "Pretty word."

Nick said nothing.

"And I don't recall your seeking my help or guidance when you decided to lay off five thousand workers, dragging the Stratton name through the mud," she went on. "And after Milton worked *so* hard to make it a byword for what was *best* about Fenwick. That was part of his legacy, too, Nicholas."

"Dorothy, you voted to approve the layoffs."

"Oh, as if I could stop that train in its tracks! But please don't misunderstand me. I'm not complaining. We sold the firm. Almost all of it belongs to Fairfield Partners. And so we must be *very* businesslike about the whole thing."

"With all respect, Dorothy, aren't you bothered by the idea of Stratton being owned by—by the Chinese government? The Communist Chinese?"

Dorothy Devries shot him a wintry look. "Please. Coming from *you*? Business is business. My family made good money when we sold to Fairfield, and we stand to make quite a bit more when they sell it to this consortium."

"But for God's sake—?" He saw something in her face. "You knew all about it, didn't you?"

She refused to reply. "Nicholas, I didn't give you Milton's job in order for you to dismantle his company, believe it or not. But you did. You cheesed it up with all that Office of the Future eyewash. You got rid of what was real, what was solid, and replaced it with gilt and papier mâché. Milton would have been appalled. Though I suppose I really can't judge you without judging myself, can I? *I'm* the one who gave you the keys to the corner office."

"Yes," Nick said, finally. "And why did you?"

Dorothy sat silent for a while. "As you might imagine," she said with a drawn smile, "I've often asked myself the same thing."

92

Audrey had promised to keep Noyce in the loop, that was the thing. Strictly speaking, she knew she had the right to go right to the prosecutor's office and request an arrest warrant for Conover and Rinaldi without even telling Noyce. She knew that. But it wasn't right to exclude him. It was a matter of courtesy to keep Noyce updated. She'd told him about the gun match as soon as she found out, and there was no reason to start keeping him in the dark now. It would infuriate him, but worse, it would hurt his feelings, and she wasn't about to do that.

Music was playing softly in Noyce's office as she entered. Audrey recognized Duke Ellington's "Mood Indigo," a trumpet solo.

"Is that Louis?" she asked.

Noyce nodded, absorbed. "Ellington and Armstrong recorded this in one take. Unbelievable."

"Sure is."

"The Duke was great at composing under deadline pressure, you know. The night before a recording date, he's waiting for his mother to finish cooking dinner, and he goes to his piano, and in fifteen minutes he knocks off a piece he calls 'Dreamy Blues.' Next night his band plays it over the radio, broadcasting from the Cotton Club. Later he renames it 'Mood Indigo.'" Noyce shook his head, waited for the song to end, and then clicked off the CD player. "What can I do you for?"

"I think we've got enough to arrest Conover and Rinaldi."

Noyce's eyes widened as she explained, then just as quickly narrowed. "Audrey, let me take you out for ice cream."

"I'm trying not to eat—"

"Well, you can watch. I've been thinking about one of those chocolate-dipped strawberry sundaes at the Dairy Queen."

Noyce tucked into a boat-sized dish of soft-serve vanilla ice cream smothered in syrupy strawberries, while Audrey tried to avert her eyes, because it looked too good, and her will was weak when it came to desserts, especially in the midafternoon.

"You don't want your butt out there for false arrest, Aud," he said, a strawberry smear at the side of his mouth. "You realizing who you're dealing with, don't you?"

"You think Nicholas Conover's all that powerful?"

"He's a wealthy and powerful guy, but more to the point, he now works for a holding company in Boston that's going to be intent on protecting their investment. And if that means suing the police department in the town of Fenwick, Michigan, they've got the resources to do it. That means they sue you. And us."

"That could work the other way too," she pointed out. Her stomach was growling, and her mouth kept filling with saliva. "The holding company could get nervous about having a CEO charged with first-degree murder and jettison him."

Noyce didn't look up from his ice cream. "You willing to take that chance?"

"If I have a genuine belief that Conover and Rinaldi were involved in a homicide, and I got a prosecutor to back me up on it, how is that false arrest?"

"It just means more of us in the soup. Plus, I can tell you, you're not going to get a prosecutor to write a warrant unless he's sure he can win the case. And I worry that we're still thin on the ground here."

"But look at what we've got, Jack—"

He looked up. "Well, let's take a look at it, Aud. What's your most damaging lead? The gun? So you've got Rinaldi on some case in Grand Rapids, and the same gun in that one turns up here."

"Which is no coincidence. Rinaldi had a reputation as a bad cop."

"Now, you've got to be careful there. That's hearsay. Cops are always gossiping, stabbing each other in the back, you know that better than anyone." He sighed. "No one's going to let you run with that. If you want to say he took the gun, fine—but you don't have any proof of that."

"No, but—"

"Look at it through the eyes of a defense attorney. The same gun used in Grand Rapids turned up here? Well, you think that's the first time a gun was used in Grand Rapids and here? Where do you think our drug dealers get their guns? Flint, Lansing, Detroit, Grand Rapids. They've got to come from somewhere."

Audrey fell silent, watching him spoon the soft-serve, careful to catch a dollop of strawberry goo in each spoonful.

"Far more likely, in fact," Noyce went on, "is that some shitbird in Fenwick bought a piece from some other shitbird in GR. Pardon my French, Audrey."

"But the hydroseed stuff—the soil match—"

"That's an awfully slender reed to hang a first-degree murder on, don't you think?"

She felt increasingly desperate. "The cell phone call Conover lied about—"

"Again, maybe he really did get the day wrong. Audrey, I'm just being devil's advocate here, okay?"

"But Conover's own security system—the video for that night was erased, and we can *prove* it."

"You can prove it was erased, or you can prove the tape recycled? There's quite a difference."

Noyce had clearly been talking to Kevin Lenehan. "You have a point," she conceded.

"Then there's the fact that both you and Bugbee canvassed Conover's neighbors, and not one of them heard a shot that night."

"Jack, you know how far apart the houses are in Fenwicke Estates? Plus, a three-eighty isn't all that loud."

"Audrey. You've got no blood, no weapon, no footprints, no witnesses. What *do* you have?"

"Motive and opportunity. A stalker with a history of violence and a hand-gun who was stalking the CEO of Stratton—"

"Unarmed, as far as we know."

"Even worse for Conover if Stadler was unarmed."

"And you yourself told me the guy had no prior history of violence. 'Gentle as a lamb,' wasn't that the phrase you used? Audrey, listen. If you had a solid case against these guys, no one would be happier than me. I'd love to take 'em down for this murder, you kidding me? But I don't want us to fuck it up. I don't want us to go off half-cocked."

"I *know* we have a case here," she said.

"You know what you are? You're an optimist, down deep."

"I don't know about that."

"Anyone who loves God the way you do's got to be an optimist. But you see, here's the sad truth. The longer you stay in this job, the harder it is to stay an optimist. Witnesses recant and the guilty go free and cases don't get solved. Pessimism, cynicism—that's the natural order. Audrey, did I ever tell you about the case I had when I was just starting out? Woman shot in the head standing in her front parlor, shifty cheating husband, we kept catching him lying about his alibis, which kept changing. The more we looked at him, the more we were convinced he was the shooter."

"He wasn't," she said, impatient.

"You know why he kept lying about his alibi? Turned out he was in the sack with his sister-in-law at the time. This guy wouldn't own up to the fact that he was cheating on his wife even when he was faced with a first-degree murder charge. He didn't crack until just before the trial was scheduled, the bastard. And you know what it was killed the wife? Just a random, stray bullet through her open window, a street shooting gone bad. Wasn't her lucky day. Or maybe that's what you get for living in a bad neighborhood. What seemed so obvious to us turned out not to be true when we really dug into it."

"I get it, Jack," she said, watching him scrape the boat clean, pleased to see that his last spoonful contained equal portions of ice cream and strawberry. "But we've dug into it."

"A crazy guy's found in a Dumpster in the dog pound, with fake crack on him—I'm sorry, but you've got to go with a crack murder as your central hypothesis. Not some white-collar CEO with so much to lose. You know the old saying—in Texas, when you hear approaching hoofbeats, you don't think zebra. You gotta think horses. And I think you're going after a zebra here."

"That's not—"

"Oh, I know it would be a hell of a lot more intriguing to spot a zebra than a horse, but you've always got to consider the likelihoods. Because ultimately your time is limited. Who's that woman who calls you every week?"

"Ethel Dorsey?"

"Tyrone's her son, probably killed in a drug deal, right? How much time have you been putting in on that case?"

"I haven't really had much time recently."

"No, you haven't. And if I know you, I'll bet you feel that you're letting Ethel Dorsey down."

"I—" she faltered.

"You're good, and you have the potential to be great. You can make a real difference. But think of how many other cases are clamoring for your attention. There's only so many hours in the day, right?"

"I understand." She was shaken; what he said made sense.

"There's another case I want you to get involved in. Not instead of this one, but in addition to it. One that will really, I think, give you an opportunity to shine. Instead of just getting bogged down in this dog-pound murder. Now, Jensen's got the Hernandez robbery trial on Monday, but he's going on vacation, so I'd like you to handle it."

"Isn't Phelps the secondary on that? I only did one follow-up interview."

"Phelps is on personal leave. I need you on this. And the prosecutor wants a pretrial conference on Friday."

"Friday? That's—that's in two days!"

"You can do it. I know you can."

She was befuddled and most of all depressed now. "You know," she said in a small voice, "that looks good, what you had. What do I ask for?"

93

Marta came to the front hall, holding a dish towel in wet hands. No doubt she'd heard the little double beep of the alarm system when he opened the door. Somewhere in the background were peals of girlish laughter.

"Something wrong?" Nick asked her.

Marta shook her head. "Everything's fine," she said huffily, her tone implying the exact opposite.

"Is it Luke?"

Marta stiffened. "Miss Stadler invited herself over."

"Oh," Nick said. "That's fine."

Marta shrugged unhappily. It wasn't fine with *her*.

"Is there a problem, then?" Nick asked. What was with this Mrs. Danvers act, anyway?

"It's just getting hard to keep track of who's in the family and who isn't, these days."

It was an invitation to a heavy conversation; Nick silently declined.

In the family room he found Cassie, in an oversized Stratton T-shirt and black jeans, sitting with Julia, who was wearing an outfit Nick hadn't seen before, a turquoise velour tracksuit. Very J. Lo. The word "Juicy" ran across her butt.

He stood at the threshold and watched, unnoticed.

"There's nothing dirty about it," Cassie was saying.

"Dirty pillows!" Julia said, in silly mode. "Dirty pillows!"

"You get older, your body changes. Boys seem less yucky. You start to feel more private about your body. Everyone goes through it. It's as natural as granola."

Julia giggled at that, somehow anxious and pleased at the same time. "I hate granola," she said.

"The main thing is, don't feel it's something you can't talk about. Don't feel it's some weird, shameful thing, okay? Tits aren't the end of the world. Zits, on the other hand . . ."

Another burst of giggles, less nervous and more high-spirited.

They were having The Talk. Relief washed over him, mixed with a little jealousy over the intimacy Cassie and Julia seemed to have developed. He'd mentioned to Cassie how much he was dreading the prospect of having the girl-stuff talk with his daughter: in his hands, it would probably have ended in some grisly level of mutual embarrassment. Marta, despite her tight jeans, was prim and embarrassed about talking about sex and had let Nick know that she most emphatically didn't consider it her place to tell Julia about things like periods.

Cassie, though, was talking about it as if it were no big deal, and somehow *making* it no big deal. Something about her low, commonsensical voice was keeping everything real, down-to-earth, and comfortable. Or at least as comfortable as it could be for a giddy, giggly ten-year-old.

"Lot of things change, lot of things don't," Cassie told Julia. "Just remember, whatever happens to you, you're always going to be your daddy's little girl."

Nick cleared his throat, then said to Julia, "Hey, baby."

"Daddy!" She got up and received his hug.

"Where's your brother?"

"He's upstairs working."

"Good to hear. And where'd you get this outfit?"

"Cassie bought it for me."

"She did, huh?" A velour tracksuit? It even exposed her tummy. She was ten years old, for Christ's sake.

Cassie looked up, shrugged sheepishly. "*All* the fifth-graders consider me their fashion guru," she said.

———

When Julia had left to go to her room, Nick looked at Cassie and shrugged. "Thanks, by the way. I gather you were talking about girl stuff with her. Not easy for her old man to do."

"She's a sweet pea, Nick. The main thing is that she knows you're always going to be her daddy, and you're always going to love her."

"Stay for dinner?"

"I can't," she said.

"Plans?"

"No. I just—you know, what's that they say about guests and fish? They start stinking after—I forget how many days."

"You think Julia considers you a guest? Or Luke?"

She couldn't hide her smile. "You understand, don't you?"

"Stay. Plus, I could use your take on what's going on at work."

"You've come to the right place," she said. "The wisdom tooth of Fenwick, Michigan."

He told her about his meeting with Dorothy Devries.

"Well, she's not calling the shots anymore," Cassie said. "You said Todd Muldaur is."

"That's the problem."

"The question I always like to ask is: Who's your daddy?"

"Yeah. You and Shaft."

"So who's Todd Muldaur's daddy?"

A shrug. "Willard Osgood is the chairman of Fairfield Partners. But it sounds like he's become an absentee father."

"Willard Osgood—the guy with the thick glasses and all that folksy investment advice, right? I read that profile in *Fortune* you showed me. He's the one you've got to go to."

"For what? I don't see the upside."

"Correct me if I'm wrong, but doesn't Osgood really think of himself as a father figure? What you're describing doesn't sound like his style."

"True," Nick said. "But times change. The face of the future is probably Todd Muldaur."

"See, that doesn't add up to me. The way it's all been kept under wraps—that's not just about keeping the details away from you. Is it possible they're trying to keep the details away from Daddy too?"

"Hmph. I hadn't thought of that."

"But it's possible, right?"

"It's possible, yes."

"So maybe you should go right to Osgood."

"And what if you're wrong? What if he knows everything that's going on?"

"Consider your options right now. The real question is, What if I'm right?"

94

Audrey's e-mail icon was bouncing. It was a message from Kevin Lenehan in Forensic Services. She opened it immediately, then practically ran to Forensic Services.

"Guess what?" he said.

"You got it. The video."

"No fucking way. I told you, that's so gone."

"Then what?"

"This is cool. I noticed this code on here. It backs up to an FTP server on a preset schedule."

"Can you explain that?"

"Sure. Certain archivable events, ranging from alarm inputs to motion-detector inputs, get automatically sent to an FTP server using the IP address that's preprogrammed in here."

"Kevin," she said, mildly exasperated, "that really wasn't much of an explanation, now, was it?"

"The eleven minutes of video you're looking for? That we thought got totally erased? Well, it got erased on the box, here. But it also got sent over the Internet to Stratton's LAN—sorry, the company's computers. There's a backup copy at Stratton. That clear enough?"

Audrey smiled. "Can you get into the Stratton computers from here—on the Internet or something?"

"If I was that good, do you think I'd have a job like this?"

She shrugged.

"But get me into Stratton and I'll know where to look."

95

It was an hour drive to the Gerald R. Ford International Airport, then a five-hour flight to Logan Airport, a bustling place that seemed as populous as all of Fenwick. Nick made his way past a Legal Seafoods restaurant, a W. H. Smith bookstore, and a Brookstone gadget center before he reached the escalator to Ground Transportation. Among a flock of livery drivers, he caught the eye of an olive-skinned man in a blue blazer and gray slacks who was holding a card that read NICHOLAS CONVER. Close enough.

Fairfield Partners was the anchor tenant of a vast glass- and granite-faced building on Federal Street, in the heart of downtown Boston. Willard Osgood's offices were on the thirty-seventh and thirty-eighth floors. The reception area was all dove-gray velvet and tropical woods, and Nick expected he'd be given plenty of time to study its details, cooling his heels in preparation for his audience with the Great Man. To his surprise, though, the strawberry blond receptionist told him to go right in. Nick wondered whether he was late. His watch told him that he was a few minutes early if anything.

As he walked through the glass door, Nick was immediately met by another blond woman, this one with red plastic-framed glasses. "Mr. Conover," she said. "Your flight okay?"

"It was," Nick said.

"Can I get you anything? Water, a soda, coffee?"

"I'm fine," Nick said, striding to keep up with her power walk.

"I'm sorry Todd's on the road. I'm sure he would have loved to say hi if he knew you were coming in."

I'm sure he would have, Nick thought. "Well, you might want to check with Mr. Osgood before you tell Todd or anyone else that I was here."

"Yes, sir," she said quickly. "Of course."

The offices of Fairfield Equity Partners were soaring and glass-walled, two floors combined into one. Along the walls, he noticed framed magazine covers featuring Willard Osgood—holding a fishing reel on the cover of *Field & Stream*, wearing a blue suit and yellow tie on *Forbes*. Osgood's square, bespectacled face and pleased-yet-concerned expression were always identical, as if the head had been Photoshopped onto different models.

Finally, she gestured toward a tan leather sofa in what looked like a vast waiting area, and said, "Have a seat. I'll leave you here."

Nick craned his head around, took in the large glass desk and various fishing trophies on the wall. It took a moment before he figured out he was in Willard Osgood's own office. He looked out of the windows on two sides and could see the Boston harbor in the distance, then some scrubby little islands beyond that.

Moments later, Willard Osgood himself strode in: the square, weathered face, the Coke-bottle glasses—he could have been peeled off one of those magazine covers. Nick stood up and realized that Osgood probably had an inch or two on him.

"Nick Conover," Osgood said in a booming voice, giving him a friendly bump on the shoulder. "I hope you noticed what kind of chair I've got at my desk." He pointed to the Stratton Symbiosis chair.

Nick grinned. "You liked it so much you bought the company."

Osgood raised a shaggy eyebrow. "Did I make the right decision?"

"Hope you still like the chair. It's still a good company."

"Then what the hell are you doing here in Beantown?"

"I'm here to ask your help solving a problem."

Osgood's expression vacillated between amusement and perplexity. "Let me put that Stratton chair into service," he said after a moment, walking over to his desk. Nick took a chair in front of it. "I always think better on my butt."

Nick started right in. "As I recall, when you came to Fenwick, you told us that your favorite holding period is forever."

"Ah," Osgood said, seeming to understand. He blinked a few times, folded his hands on the desk, and then cleared his throat. "Nick, I think I also told you that my rule number one is, never lose money."

Osgood knew Todd was selling the company, Nick now realized. So maybe Cassie was wrong. Did he know *everything*, though? "Which is a lesson that Todd Muldaur seems to have forgotten, if he ever learned it," Nick said.

"Todd's had a rough year," Osgood came right back, sounding a little annoyed. "There are some mighty good explanations for that, though."

"Yeah, well, 'explanations aren't excuses,' as you also like to say."

Osgood smiled, exposing a blinding row of porcelain veneers. "I see the gospel spreads."

"But I can't help but wonder whether one of the explanations is that no one's watching the shop. That's what Todd seems to indicate, anyway. He says you've taken to spending a lot of time away from the office. That maybe you've gotten more interested in fly-fishing than in profit margins."

Osgood's smile almost reached his eyes. "I hope you don't believe that."

"I don't know what to think."

"What my lieutenants really mean by that, of course, is that my day has passed. They like to think that, because it means their day has arrived." Osgood leaned back in his chair, but of course the Stratton Symbiosis chair, being ergonomic, wouldn't let him tip all the way back like the older chairs would. "Tell you a story, but don't repeat it, okay?"

Nick nodded.

"Couple years ago I took Todd down to Islamorada, Florida, for the annual migration of the tarpon. 'Course, he showed up with his brand-new Sage rod and his Abel reel, and he's got a leather belt on, with a bonefish on the buckle." He gave a hearty guffaw. "He's a confident fellow—told me he'd done a lot of fly-fishing at some fancy lodge in Alaska, kind of place with gourmet meals and a sauna and the guide does everything for you except wipe your ass. So I graciously allowed him the bow and watched him flail for hours. Poor guy missed shot after shot, got more and more frustrated, his line kept getting wrapped, the flies hitting him on the backside." He blinked a few times. "Finally I decided I'd had enough fun. I stood up, stripped out ninety feet of line. Soon as I spotted a school of fish approaching, I delivered the fly.

The fish ate, and six and a half feet of silver king went airborne. You with me? One school of fish—one shot—one cast—and one fish brought to the side of the boat."

"Okay," Nick said, enjoying the tale but wondering what the point was.

"See, I don't think Todd realized that the secret isn't how pricey your equipment or how nice your Ex Officio slacks are. All that counts is *bow time*—just doing it over and over and over again. Takes years of practice. No substitute for it."

"How do you cook tarpon?"

"Oh, heavens, no, you don't eat it. That's the beauty part. You release it. It's all about the fight."

"Huh," Nick said. "Doesn't sound like my kind of sport."

"From what I understand, hockey's all about the fight too. And you don't even get a fish to show for it."

"I guess that's one way of looking at it."

"But anyway, you're right. Todd's made some mistakes. A couple of bold gambles."

"I believe the phrase 'sucking wind' might be more accurate."

Osgood wasn't amused. "I'm well aware of what's happening," he said brittlely.

"Are you? I wonder." Nick leaned over and removed a file folder from his briefcase, then slid the folder across the desk. Osgood opened it, tipped his glasses up onto his forehead, and examined the documents. Nick noticed that the horizontal creases on Osgood's forehead were equally spaced and straight, almost as if drawn with a ruler.

Osgood looked up for a moment. "I wish he hadn't done things this way."

"What way?"

"Keeping you out of the loop. It's not the way I prefer. I like to be a straight shooter. Now I see why you've come to talk to me. I understand why you're upset."

"Oh, no," Nick said quickly. "I totally understand why he didn't want me to know. Hell, he knew how opposed I was—am—to a sale like this. Even though I don't have the power to stop it, he was probably afraid I'd kick up a fuss, maybe even take it public. Better to just do the deal without me knowing, he figured, so that by the time I figured it out, it would be a fait accompli. It would be too late."

"Something like that. But as I say, that's not my way."

"Todd needed a quick infusion of cash to help bail out the firm, after all his bad bets on semiconductors. And an IPO takes forever. I get it."

"I told Todd you're a reasonable man, Nick. He should have just leveled with you."

"Maybe he should have leveled with *you*. Like telling you who the fairy godmother behind 'Pacific Rim Investors' really is. Though he probably figured that you, with your political beliefs, wouldn't want to hear where the money comes from." Nick paused. "The P.L.A."

Osgood blinked owlishly.

"That's the People's Liberation Army," Nick explained. "The Communist Chinese army."

"I know who they are," Osgood said curtly. "Wouldn't have gotten to where I am without doing my homework."

"You knew this?" Nick said.

"Good Lord, of *course* I knew it. There's nothing illegal about it, my friend."

"The Communist Chinese," Nick persisted, hoping the incantation might jangle the old right-winger.

"Oh, for heaven's sake, this is *office furniture*. Not Patriot missiles or nuclear weapons or something. Desks and chairs and file cabinets. I hardly call that selling our enemy the rope they're going to hang us with."

"But have you actually looked at the numbers on Stratton that Todd provided Pacific Rim Investors?"

Osgood pushed the folder away from him. "I don't micromanage. I don't look over my partners' shoulders. Nick, we're both busy men—"

"You might want to. See, the balance sheet Todd gave them is a fraud. Prepared by my CFO, Scott McNally, who knows a thing or two about how to put lipstick on a pig."

Another flash of the porcelain Chiclets. "Nick, maybe you've been in the Midwest a bit too long, but that Jimmy Stewart, *Mr. Smith Goes to Washington* bit's not going to play here."

"I'm not talking morality, Willard. I'm talking illegality."

Osgood waved Nick away with an impatient hand. "There's all kinds of ways of doing the books. Anyway, we've got a no-litigate clause, even if they do get buyer's remorse."

"You know about that too," Nick said dully.

Osgood's stare seemed to drill right through him. "Conover, you're wasting your time and mine, trying to backtrack over everything. Horse is out of the barn. Gripe session's over. Now, this it? We done here?" Osgood rose, pressing a button on his intercom. "Rosemary, could you show Mr. Conover out, please?"

But Nick remained in his seat. "I'm not done yet," he said.

96

The Information Technology Director at the Stratton Corporation didn't look like the computer type, Audrey thought. She was a tall, matronly woman named Carly Lindgren, who wore her beautiful and very long auburn hair knotted on top of her head. She wore a navy suit over an olive silk shell, a braided gold necklace and matching earrings.

Audrey had gotten an appointment with Mrs. Lindgren with a single phone call, telling her only it was "police business." But once Audrey had presented the search warrant, she could see Mrs. Lindgren rear up like a cornered tigress. She examined it as if searching for flaws, though very few people knew what to look for, and in any case the warrant had been written carefully. It was as broad as Audrey could get the prosecutor to sign off on, even though all she really wanted was any archived video images on the Stratton network that came from Nicholas Conover's home security system.

Mrs. Lindgren kept Audrey and Kevin Lenehan waiting in an outer office while she placed a flurry of panicked calls all the way up her reporting chain—the Chief Information Officer and the Chief Technology Officer, and Audrey lost track of who all, but there really was nothing Mrs. Lindgren could do.

After twenty minutes or so, Kevin was given a chair and a computer in an empty office. Audrey had nothing to do but watch. She looked around, saw a blue poster with white letters that said something about "The Stratton Family," sort of a mission statement. The chairs they sat in were particularly comfortable; she noticed they were Stratton chairs. Nothing like this in Major Cases. Kevin put a CD in the computer and installed a program. He explained to her that it was viewer software he'd downloaded from the Web site of the company that made the digital video recorder in Conover's home. This would allow them to view, and capture, the video images.

"You know where to look?" Audrey asked, worried.

"It was in the settings in the DVR," replied Kevin. "The folder it was written to, the date and time and everything. No *problema*."

Audrey felt a little tremble of anticipation, which she tried to tamp down, tried to reason herself out of. She was sure that the murder of Andrew Stadler would be on this eleven minutes of camera footage. If indeed there was a backup here.

How often in any homicide detective's career could one hope to come across a piece of evidence like that? A digital image of a murder being committed? It was almost too much to hope for. She didn't want to allow herself to hope for it, because the disappointment would be crushing.

"Anything I can do to help, Detective?"

She looked up, saw Eddie Rinaldi standing in the doorway, felt her heart do a flip-flop. From where she sat, that angle, Rinaldi seemed tall and broad and powerful. He wore a dark blazer and a black collarless shirt. He was smiling, and his eyes glittered malevolently.

"Mr. Rinaldi," she said. Even when talking to murder suspects, she tended to be polite, but she refused to be cordial with this man. Something about him she really couldn't stand. Maybe it was his air of knowingness, his cockiness, the feeling she got that he was enjoying the games he was playing with her.

"So you have a search warrant for the company's network, that it?"

"You're welcome to examine it."

"No, no, no. I don't doubt you dotted every *I* and crossed every *T*. You're one thorough lady, I can tell."

"Thank you."

"Maybe thorough's a polite way to say it. Obsessed, maybe? Looks like you're still after my boss's home security tape."

"Oh, we have the recorder in our custody." She considered telling him they knew the tape had been erased, just to see his reaction, but that would be giving him information he shouldn't have.

Kevin muttered, "Almost there."

Rinaldi glanced at Kevin curiously, as if he'd only just noticed him. Then he looked back at Audrey. He couldn't have been more blasé.

"I still don't get what you're hoping to find," Rinaldi said.

"I have a feeling you know," Audrey said.

"You're right. I do."

"Oh?"

"Right. Couple of frames of some crazy old coot hobbling across my boss's lawn in the middle of the night. But what's that going to tell you, come right down to it?"

Audrey leaned over to the computer where Kevin was working. He tilted the monitor toward Audrey, who squinted, didn't see any picture, and then saw the words "ERASED HERE TOO" on a document on the screen.

"Excellent," Audrey said, nodding. "Good work." She reached for the keyboard and typed out the words, "PLAY ALONG WITH ME." Then she said, "Beautiful, Kevin. Can you improve the resolution just a bit?"

"Oh yeah," he said. "Sure. I've got some great digital-imaging firmware that'll eliminate the motion artifacts and reduce the dot crawl. A comb filter oughta separate the chrominance from the luminance. A little line doubling and some deinterlacing, and we got a nice clean image. No problem at all on this guy."

Kevin tapped some more, and the document disappeared before Rinaldi had a chance to look for himself.

But that was the peculiar thing. Eddie Rinaldi never moved from where he stood, never bothered to peer at the monitor. He seemed utterly uninterested.

No, that wasn't it, Audrey realized.

He was utterly confident. He knew what Kevin had just discovered, that the backup video had been deleted on the Stratton LAN, just as it had been deleted from Conover's home security recorder.

And his confidence had just given him away.

97

Nick felt a tiny tremble in his hands. He put them in his lap so Osgood wouldn't see. "Willard, don't get me wrong. I have no interest in taking you on. I'd much rather work together with you on this. You want to save the funds Todd's running, and I want to save the company. We both want to make money."

Osgood slid his glasses back into place and gave Nick a steely stare as he stood behind his desk. He grunted.

"Now, I don't know you," Nick said, "but I can tell you're not a gambler." Nick noticed that the blond woman with the red glasses had slipped into the office to usher him out and was hovering in the background, waiting for her cue. He lowered his voice so that the woman couldn't hear. "So when Scott McNally and Todd Muldaur funnel a ten-million-dollar bribe to a Chinese government official to make sure this deal happens, that's where I think they're crossing a line you don't want to cross."

"What the hell are you talking about?" Osgood put his hands flat on the glass of his desk and leaned forward, intimidatingly.

"They're putting your company at risk, doing that. Word always leaks out. And then your entire firm will be jeopardized." Nick opened his arms wide. "All of this. Everything you've worked your whole life building. And I wonder whether you think it's really worth taking such an enormous risk, when there's another way to get what you want."

"Rosemary," Osgood barked. "Excuse us, please. We'll be another few minutes." When his secretary had left, he sat down again. "What the hell are you talking about, bribe?"

"Stratton Asia Ventures," Nick said.

"I don't know anything about that."

Was he being straight? Or was he being careful? "It's all right there in front of you—the last couple of pages in that pile. How do you think Todd was able to get this deal done in a month instead of a year? Call it a deal-sweetener or a kickback or a bribe—whatever you call it, it's a clear-cut violation of the Foreign Corrupt Practices Act. And it's the kind of legal exposure that you can't afford."

The way Osgood yanked the folder back toward him, Nick realized that this really was news to the man. Osgood shoved his glasses back up on his forehead and hunched over the papers.

A few minutes later, he looked back up. His leathery face seemed to color. He looked thunderstruck. "Jesus," he said. "Looks like you weren't the only one kept out of the loop."

"I had a feeling Todd wasn't telling you everything," Nick said.

"This is *stupid*, is what it is."

"Desperate men sometimes do stupid things. Frankly, on some level I resent it. My company's worth a hell of a lot more than what Pacific Rim Investors is paying for it. There's no need to pay anyone off."

"God*damn* it," Osgood said.

"You may be great with tarpons, Willard, but I think what we're dealing with here is a snakehead."

Osgood seemed to be doing a slow burn. "I think my Yale boy just got hisself in over his head."

"I guess he figured no one was watching the shop . . ."

Osgood's pearly Chiclets looked more like a snarl than a smile. "From time to time, someone thinks they can pull one over on the old man. Maybe they've been reading too many *Parade* magazine profiles of me. But they always realize the error of their ways."

Nick realized then how terrifying Willard Osgood could be once the cornpone mask fell away, a truly formidable opponent.

"A lot of people have been underestimating you too," Osgood said. "I think I may be one of them. So tell me: What do you have in mind?"

98

"Daddy!" Julia ran up to Nick as he entered the house. "You're back!"

"I'm back." He set down his garment bag, lifted her up, felt a slight twinge in his lower back around the lumbar. Yikes. Can't be picking her up anymore like she's an infant. "How's my baby?"

"Good." Julia never said anything else. She was always good. School was always good. Everything was good.

"Where's your brother?"

She shrugged. "Probably in his room? Do you know Marta just left a couple of hours ago for Barbados? She said she's going to visit her family."

"I know. I thought she needed some time off. Her trip to Barbados is a present from all of us. Where's Cassie?" Cassie had happily agreed to come over to watch the kids.

"She's here. She was just teaching me yoga."

"Where is she?"

"In your study, maybe?"

Nick hesitated a moment. That again. But there was nothing to find there. He had to stop being so suspicious.

"She has a surprise for you," Julia said with a mischievous smile, her big brown eyes wide. "But I can't tell you what it is."

"Can I guess?"

"No."

"Not even one guess?"

"No!" she scolded. "It's a *surprise!*"

"Okay. Don't tell me. But I have a surprise for *you.*"

"What is it?"

"How would you like to go to Hawaii?"

"*What?* No *way!*"

"Way. We're leaving tomorrow night."

"But what about school?"

"I'm taking you and Luke out of school for a few days, that's all."

"Hawaii! I don't believe it! Maui?"

"Maui."

"The same place as last time?"

"Same place. I even got us the exact same villa on the beach."

Julia threw her arms around him, squeezing hard. "I want to do snorkeling again," she said, "and take those hula lessons, and I want to make a lei, and this time I want to learn how to windsurf. Aren't I old enough?"

"You're old enough, sure." Laura had been afraid to let her try, last time.

"Luke said he'd show me how. Are you going to scuba dive again?"

"I think I might have forgotten how."

"What about surfing? Can I learn how to surf too?"

Nick laughed. "Are you going to have time for all these lessons?"

"Remember when I found that gecko in our room, and its tail broke off? Oh, wow, this is so *awesome.*"

Nick went to the kitchen to take the shortcut to his study, but he stopped at the threshold.

In place of the usual plastic draft sheets hanging down was some kind of paper barrier. He looked closer. Wrapping paper had been taped across the entrance, floor to ceiling and jamb to jamb. A wide blue ribbon crisscrossed it like a gift. The paper, he noticed, had little pictures of Superman all over it, cape flying.

"Even though you look more like Clark Kent right now." Cassie's voice. Her arms slid around his waist; she kissed the back of his neck.

"What's this?"

He turned, gave her a hug and planted a big kiss on her mouth.

"You'll see. How was Boston?"

"Let's just say your instincts were right."

Cassie nodded. The dark smudges were visible beneath her eyes again. She looked drawn, exhausted. "Well, you'll get things back on track. You'll see. It's not too late."

"We'll see. Can I open my gift?"

She bowed her head, turned up an "after you" palm.

Nick punched a fist through the gift wrap. The kitchen was all lit up, every light on, dazzling. The granite-topped kitchen island was perfect, just as Laura had once sketched it for him.

"Jesus," Nick said. He went in slowly, taking it all in, awed. He ran a hand over the island top. There was an overhang, enabling the whole family to sit around it. Exactly what Laura had wanted.

He felt its edge. "Bullnose?"

"Half bullnose."

He turned to look at Cassie, saw the little pleased smile. "How the hell did you do this?"

"I didn't do it myself, Nick. I mean, I may have inherited my dad's mechanical ability, but I'm not *that* good. What I'm good at is getting what I want." She shrugged modestly. "It really only took them one full day of work. But it took me a lot of begging and pleading to get them here to do it and finish it by the end of the day."

"My God, you're a miracle worker," Nick said.

"Just like to finish what I start, that's all. Or what your wife started." She paused and then said in a small voice, "Nick, are you ever going to be able to talk about her death?"

He closed his eyes for a while before he spoke. He opened his eyes, took a breath. "I can try. Lucas had a swim meet. It was half past seven, but dark, you know? First week of December. It gets dark early. We were driving to Stratford, because the meet was in the high school there. We're on Stratford-Hillsdale Road, which is what truckers sometimes use to connect to the interstate."

Nick closed his eyes again. He was back in the car on that dark night, a nightmare he had relived only in dreams, and then in shards and fragments of time. He spoke in a low, expressionless monotone. "So there's a tractor trailer heading the opposite way, and the guy driving it had had a couple of beers, and the road surface was icy. Laura was driving—she hated to drive at night, but I asked her to, because I had some calls to make on the cell phone. That was me—company man, always working. We were bickering over something, and Laura was upset, and she wasn't paying attention to the road, see. She didn't see the truck drifting into our lane, across those double yellow lines, until it was too late. She—she tried to turn the wheel, but she didn't do it in time. The truck rammed into us."

He opened his eyes. "Funny thing is, it didn't seem like we were hit all that hard," Nick went on. "It wasn't like some horrible collision in the movies where everything goes black. It was a hard bump, like you might feel if you were playing bumper cars. Kind of a hollow crunch. I didn't get whiplash. Never blacked out. Nothing like that. I turn to Laura and I'm yelling, 'Can you believe that guy?' And she doesn't say anything. And I notice how the windshield is all spiderwebbed on her side. And there's some pebbles of glass on her forehead. Something glistening in her hair. But there's no blood, or hardly any. A fleck or two, maybe. She looked fine. Like she'd nodded off."

"There was nothing you could have done," Cassie breathed.

Nick only knew that his eyes were wet because his vision was blurred. "Except there were *hundreds* of things I could have done. Any one of them, and Laura would still be alive. You know, when we were leaving the house that night, Laura was about to make a phone call, and I made her hang up. I told her she was making us late. I told her it was ridiculous that she'd spent fifteen minutes putting on makeup and perfume for a goddamn *swim meet*. I told her that, for once, we weren't going to be late. I told her I wanted to get a good seat in the stands so I could see what the hell was going on. Now, thing is, if she had made that phone call, we wouldn't have been in an accident. If I hadn't been in such a hurry, we would actually have arrived. And I didn't have to make those goddamned phone calls in the car that night, for Christ's sake. Like they couldn't wait till the morning. I could have driven the car—I mean, look, I was the better driver, we both knew that, she *hated* driving. I shouldn't have been arguing with her while she was behind the wheel. Oh, and here's a sweet one. She wanted to take the Suburban. I said it would just be a pain to park. I insisted that we take the sedan. If we'd taken the Suburban, she might have survived the impact. And I'm just starting a long, long list. All kinds of things I could have done differently. The weeks after she died, I became the world's leading expert on this subject. Had 'em all cross-tabulated in my mind. Should have been on *Jeopardy!* Thanks, Alex, I'll take Vehicular Fatalities for a hundred."

Cassie looked wan, ran her fingers through her hair. Nick wondered whether she was even listening to him. "Intracerebral hemorrhage," he went on. "She died in the hospital the next day."

"You're a good person."

"No," Nick said. "But I wish I were."

"You give so much."

"You don't know, Cassie. All right? You don't know what I've *taken*, what I've done. You don't know . . ."

"You've given me a family."

And I've taken yours away. He looked at her for a long time. He felt foolish about how he'd suspected her secret intentions and worried that she'd been trying to dig up the truth about what had happened to her father.

Then again, he obviously wasn't so good at sizing people up, he realized. He'd gotten Osgood wrong in all sorts of ways, and he'd gotten Scott wrong. Todd Muldaur—well, he had Todd's number from the start, so no surprise there. Eddie? He wasn't really surprised, when it came right down to it, that Eddie wouldn't hesitate to kick the skates out from under him.

But Cassie. He hadn't known just what to make of her, and maybe he still didn't know her all that well. Maybe his overpowering guilt and her overpowering seductiveness made it hard for him to see her clearly. She was a little emotionally unstable, that was obvious. Bipolar and having your dad murdered—that was a fairly lethal combination.

And he wondered how she'd react when he came clean.

It made no difference to him whether Eddie would strike some kind of deal with the police or not. He'd leave Eddie to his own smarmy fate.

When he and the kids came back from Hawaii, he was going to tell her the truth. And then he'd tell Detective Rhimes the truth.

And there would be an arrest, he knew that. Because whether a DA decided it was self-defense or not, he had killed a man.

Back in Boston, after his meeting with Willard Osgood, he'd taken a cab over to Ropes & Gray, a big law firm where a friend of his worked as a crimi-

nal defense attorney. A really smart guy he knew from Michigan State. Nick
had told him what had happened, the whole story.

The lawyer had blanched, of course. He told Nick he was in deep shit,
there was no way around it. He said the best Nick could hope for was criminally negligent homicide, that if he were very lucky he might get only a couple of years in prison. But it might well be more—five, seven, even ten years,
because there was also the matter of having moved the body—tampering
with physical evidence. The lawyer said that if Nick wanted to go through
with it, he'd get a local counsel and petition to try the case in Michigan *pro
hoc vici*, whatever that meant. He'd arrange for Nick to surrender, and he'd
try to negotiate a plea agreement with the DA in Fenwick. And he said he'd
ask for a lot of money up front.

Whatever would happen to him, though, was the least of it. What was
going to happen to his kids? Would Aunt Abby be willing to take care of
them?

This was the worst thing of all, the thing that truly terrified him.

But he knew it was the right thing to do, at long last, however long it
had taken him to come to his senses. It was like that dream he'd had recently, the one about the body in the basement wall that gave away its hiding place by oozing the fluids of decay. He couldn't hold the horrible secret
inside anymore.

So in a week or so, after his last vacation with the kids, he was going to
tell Cassie the truth. He'd already begun to rehearse, in his head, how he'd
tell her.

"What is it?" she said.

"I've been doing a lot of thinking, and I've made some decisions."

"Decisions about the company?"

"Not that, no. My life is about other things."

An anxious look came over her. "Is this bad?"

"No," he said, shaking his head.

"Is it bad for us?"

"No. It's not about us, exactly."

"'Not about us, exactly'—what's that supposed to mean?"

"We'll talk when the time is right. Just not yet."

She placed her hand on his. He took it in his hand, holding it gently. Hers was small and trembling; his was big and steady.

The hand that killed her father.

"Cass, we're off tomorrow," he said. "We're going to Hawaii for a few days. I already got the tickets."

"Hawaii?"

"Maui. Laura loved that place most of all. There's this great resort Laura and I discovered before we had kids. We had our own villa, right on the beach, with its own pool—not that you needed it—and all you could see from it was the Pacific Ocean."

"Sounds amazing."

"Until Laura died, we used to take the family there every year. Our big splurge. Same villa every time, Laura made sure of it. I think of it as a time when we were completely happy, all of us. I remember last time we were there, Laura and I were in bed and she turned to me and she said she wanted to spray a fixative on the whole day and keep it forever."

"God, it sounds beautiful, Nick." A light seemed to flicker in her eyes. She looked almost serene.

"I called the travel agency we'd used, and—it felt like a miracle—they said that exact same villa's available."

"Are you sure you want to return to a place they associate so closely with Laura? It might be better to go somewhere new—you know, create new memories."

"You may be right. I know it won't be the same. It'll be sad in some ways. But it'll be a new start. A good thing—just going there as a family, being to-gether again. And there isn't going to be any pressure to talk, or work through 'issues,' or anything else. We're just going to play on the beach and do stuff and eat pineapple and just *be*. It won't be the same, but it'll be *something*. And it'll be something we can all remember when things change, because they're going to change."

"The kids can miss school, right? No big deal."

"I already called the school, told them I'd be taking Julia and Lucas out of classes for a few days. Hell, I even picked up the tickets at the airport when I got in." He pulled an envelope from his breast pocket, took out the tickets and held them up, fanning them like a winning hand of cards.

Cassie's smile vanished. "Three tickets." She pulled her hand away.

"Just family. Me and the kids. I don't think we've ever done this. Just us three, heading off for a few days somewhere."

"Just family," Cassie repeated in a harsh whisper.

"I think it's important for me to try to reconnect with the kids. I mean, you get along with them better than I do, which is great. But I've let my part in it slip—I've sort of delegated that to you, like I'm CEO of the family or something, and that's not right. I'm their dad, whether I'm any good at it or not, and it's my job to work on making us a family again."

Cassie's face was transfigured, weirdly tight as if every muscle in her face were clenched.

"Oh God, Cassie, I'm sorry," Nick said, flushing, embarrassed by his own obliviousness. "You know how much you mean to us."

Cassie's eyelids fluttered oddly, and he could see the veins in her neck pulsing. It was as if she were struggling to contain herself—or maybe to contain something larger than herself.

He smiled ruefully. "Luke and Julia—they're my direct reports, you know. And I don't know when I'll have the chance again."

"Just family." The sound of one heavy stone scraping against another.

"I think it'll be really good for us, don't you?"

"You want to get away."

"Exactly."

"You want to escape." Her voice was an incantation.

"Pretty much."

"From me."

"What? Jesus, no! You're taking this the wrong way. It isn't about—"

"No." She shook her head slowly. "No. No hiding place. There's no hiding place down there."

Adrenaline surged through Nick's veins. "What did you say?"

An odd smile appeared on her face. "Isn't that what the stalker spray-painted in the house? That's what Julia told me."

"Yeah," Nick said. "Those very words."

"I can read the writing on the wall, Nick."

"Come on, Cassie, don't be silly."

"It's like the book of Daniel, isn't it? The king of Babylon throws a big drunken party and all of a sudden he sees a mysterious hand appear and start writing something strange and cryptic on the plaster wall, right? And the king's scared out of his mind and he calls in the prophet Daniel who tells him the message means the king's days are over, Babylon's history, he's going to be killed." Her expression was glassy.

"Okay, you're starting to creep me out."

Suddenly her eyes focused, and she met his gaze. "Maybe I should be grateful. I was wrong, wrong about so many things. It's *humbling*. Humbling to be put right. Just like with the Stroups. But so necessary. Listen, you do what you think is best. You do what's best for family. There's nothing more important than that."

Nick held out his arms. "Cassie, come here."

"I think I'd better go," she said. "I think I've done enough, don't you think?"

"Cassie, please," Nick protested. "I don't get it."

"Because I can do a lot more." Noiselessly, she walked out of the kitchen, her steps so fluid she could have been gliding. "I can do a lot more."

"We'll talk, Cassie," said Nick. "When we get back."

A final glance over her shoulders. "A *lot* more."

99

Early Sunday morning, before church. Audrey sat in the kitchen with her coffee and her buttered toast while Leon slept. She was poring over the bills, wondering how they'd be able to keep up, now that Leon's unemployment benefits were running out. Usually she paid off the entire credit-card balance each month, but she was going to have to start paying only the minimum balance due. She wondered too, whether they should drop to basic cable. She thought they should, though Leon would not be happy about losing the sports channels.

Her cell phone rang. A 616 number: Grand Rapids.

It was a Lieutenant Lawrence Pettigrew of the Grand Rapids police. The man who'd first talked to her about Edward Rinaldi. She'd placed several calls to him over the last few days and had all but given up on him. Noyce had made it clear that he didn't want her asking around in GR about Rinaldi, but she had no choice in the matter.

"How can I help you, Detective?" Pettigrew said. "The kids are waiting for me to take them out for pancakes, so can we make this quick?"

The guy was no fan of Edward Rinaldi, so she knew that asking about Rinaldi again would be like pushing a button and watching the vitriol spew out. But she had no reason to expect that he'd know the specifics of a long-forgotten and, in fact, quite minor, drug case.

He didn't. "Far as I'm concerned, Rinaldi's gone and good riddance," he said. "He wasn't exactly a credit to the uniform."

"Was he fired?"

"Squeezed out might be more accurate. But I were you, I wouldn't be bad-mouthing Eddie Rinaldi over there in Fenwick."

"He's the security director of Stratton, is that what you mean?"

"Yeah, yeah, but that's not what I'm talking about. Didn't you say you're in Major Cases?"

"That's right."

"Hell, you want to know chapter and verse on Eddie Rinaldi, you could ask Jack Noyce. But then again, maybe you shouldn't."

"I don't think Sergeant Noyce knows all that much about Rinaldi."

Pettigrew's laugh was abrupt and percussive. "Noyce knows him like a book, sweetheart. Guarantee it. Jack was Eddie's partner."

Audrey's scalp tightened.

"Sergeant Noyce?" she said, disbelieving.

"Partner in crime, I like to say. Don't take this the wrong way, Detective—what's your name again?"

"Rhimes." Audrey shuddered.

"Like LeAnn Rimes, the singer?" He warbled, off-key, 'How do I *live* . . . without you?'"

"Spelled differently, I believe."

"Quite the babe, though, no matter how you spell it."

"So I hear, yes. Noyce . . . Noyce was known to be dirty, is that what you're telling me?"

"Hell, there's a reason Jack got sent to Siberia, right?"

"Siberia?"

"No offense, sweetheart. But from where I sit, Fenwick is Siberia."

"Noyce was . . . squeezed out too?"

"Peas in a pod, those guys. I got no idea who did more pilfering, but I'd say they both did pretty good. Works better in a team, so they're each willing to look away. Eddie was more into the guns, and Jack was more into the home electronics and the stereo components and what have you, but they both loved the cash."

"They both . . ." she started to say, but she lost the heart to go on.

"Oh, and Detective LeAnn?"

"Audrey." She wanted to vomit, wanted to end the call and throw up and then wrap herself in a blanket and go back to sleep.

"Sweetheart, I were you, I wouldn't use my name with Noyce. Guy's a survivor, and he'll wanna let bygones be bygones, know what I'm saying?"

She thanked him, pushed End, and then did exactly what she knew she would. She rushed to the bathroom and heaved the contents of her stomach, the acid from the coffee scalding her throat. Then she washed her face. All she wanted to do right now was to enrobe herself in the old blue blanket on the living room couch, but it was time for church.

100

The First Abyssinian Church of the New Covenant was a once-grand stone building that had slowly, over the years, gone to seed. The velvet pew cushions, badly in need of replacing, had been repaired in far too many places with duct tape. The place was always cold, summer or winter: something about the stone walls and floor, that plus the fact that the building fund was suffering, and it cost a fortune to heat the cavernous interior adequately.

Attendance was sparse this morning, as it was on most Sundays except Easter and Christmas. There were even a few white faces: a couple of regulars who seemed to find the sustenance here they didn't get in the white congregations. LaTonya's family wasn't here, which was no surprise, since they came only a few times a year. Early in their marriage, Leon used to accompany Audrey here, until he announced it wasn't for him. She didn't even know whether he was sleeping late this morning or doing something else, whatever else he'd been doing.

Leon was only one of the reasons why her heart was heavy today. There was also Noyce. That news had punctured her. She felt betrayed by this man who'd been her friend and supporter and who hid from her his true nature. It sickened her.

But this discovery, as much as it shook her to the core, liberated her at the same time. She no longer had to agonize about betraying him, going behind his back, end-running him. She knew there was no choice, really. Whether Jack Noyce was in the Stratton Corporation's pocket, had been leaking to his old partner details of the investigation—or was simply compromised, trapped, by what Rinaldi knew about him—he had been working to defeat her investigation. She thought back to the many talks she'd had with him about this case, the advice he'd dispensed so freely. The way he'd cautioned her to proceed carefully, telling her she didn't have enough to arrest Conover and Rinaldi. And who would ever know what else he'd done to slow things up, block her progress? What resources had he quietly blocked? Whatever the truth was, she couldn't tell Noyce that she and Bugbee were about to get an arrest warrant for the CEO and the security director of Stratton. Noyce had to be kept in the dark, or he'd surely notify Rinaldi and do everything in his power to halt the arrest.

But here, at least, here she felt at peace and welcome and loved. Everyone said good morning, even people whose names she didn't know, courtly gentlemen and polite young men and lovely young women and hovering mothers and sweet old white-haired women. Maxine Blake was dressed all in white, wearing an ornate hat that looked a little like an upside-down bucket with white tendrils coming out of it and encircling it like rings around a planet. She threw her arms around Audrey, pressing Audrey to her enormous bosom, bringing her into a cloud of perfume and warmth and love. "God is good," Maxine said.

"All the time," Audrey responded.

The service started a good twenty minutes late. "Colored people's time," the joke went. The choir, dressed in their magnificent red-and-white robes, marched down the aisle clapping and singing "It's a Highway to Heaven," and then they were joined by the electric organ and then the trumpet and drum and then Audrey joined in along with most everybody else. She'd always wanted to sing in the choir, but her voice was nothing special—though, as she'd noticed, some of the women in the choir had thin voices and tended to sing out of tune. Some had spectacular voices, it was true. The men mostly sang in a rumbling bass, but the tenor was more off-key than on.

Reverend Jamison started his sermon as he always did, by calling out, "God is good," to which everyone responded: "All the time." He said it again, and everyone responded again. His sermons were always heartfelt, usually inspired, and never went on too long. They weren't particularly original, though. Audrey had heard he got them off the Internet from Baptist Web sites that posted sample sermons and notes. Once, confronted on his lack of originality, Reverend Jamison had said, "I milk a lot of cows, but I churn my own butter." Audrey liked that.

Today he told the story of Joshua and the armies of Israel fighting the good fight, battling five of the kings of Canaan for the conquest of the promised land. About how the kings played right into Joshua's hands by joining the battle together. About how it wasn't the Lord who fought the battle, it was Israel. The five kings tried to hide in a cave, but Joshua ordered the cave sealed up. And after the battle had been won, Joshua brought the kings out of their cave, out of their hiding place, and humiliated them by ordering his princes to place their feet on the kings' necks. Reverend Jamison talked about how there's no hiding place. "We can't hide from God," he declared. "The only hiding place from God is Hell."

That made her think, as it had so many times, about Nicholas Conover and the graffiti that had been repeatedly spray-painted on the interior walls of his house. No hiding place.

That could be frightening, as no doubt Conover found it to be. No hiding place: from what? From a faceless adversary, from a stalker? From his guilt, his sins?

But here in church, "no hiding place" was meant to be a stern yet hopeful admonition.

In his most orotund voice the reverend recited from Proverbs 28: "He that covereth his sins shall not prosper: but whoso confesseth and forsaketh them shall have mercy."

And she thought, because every single one of Reverend Jamison's sermons was devised to mean something to each and everyone in the congregation, about Nicholas Conover. The king hiding in his cave.

But no hiding place. Andrew Stadler had been right, hadn't he?

Reverend Jamison cued the choir, which went right into a lively rendition of "No Hiding Place Down Here." The soloist was Mabel Darnell, a large woman who sang and swayed like Aretha Franklin and Mahalia Jackson put together. The organist, Ike Robinson, was right up front, on display, not hidden the way the organist usually was in the other churches she'd seen. He was a white-haired, dark-skinned man of near eighty with expressive eyes and an endearing smile. He wore a white suit and looked like Count Basie, Audrey had always thought.

"I went to the rock to hide my face," Mabel sang, clapping her hands, "but the rock cried out, 'No hiding place!'"

Count Basie's pudgy fingers ran up and down the keys, syncopating, making swinging jazz out of it, and the rest of the choir joined in at *the rock* and *my face* and *cried out* and *no hiding place no hiding place no hiding place.*

Audrey felt a thrill coursing through her body, a shiver that moved along her spine like an electric current.

And the instant the choir had finished, while the organ chords still resounded, Reverend Jamison's voice boomed out, "My friends, none of us can hide from the Lord. 'And the kings of the earth, and the great men, and the rich men, and the chief captains, and the mighty men, and every bondman, and every free man'"—his voice rose steadily until the sound system squealed with feedback—"'hid themselves in the dens and in the rocks of the mountains.'" Now he dropped to a stage whisper: "'And said to the mountains and rocks, fall on us, and hide us from the face of him that sitteth on the throne, and from the wrath of the Lamb. For the great day of his wrath is come; and who shall be able to stand?'"

He paused to let the congregation know that his sermon had concluded. Then he invited anyone in the congregation who wished to come up to the altar for a moment of personal prayer. Ike Robinson, no longer Count Basie, played softly as a dozen or so people got up from their pews and knelt at the altar rail, and all of a sudden Audrey felt moved to do it too, something she hadn't done since her mother's death. She went up there and knelt between Maxine Blake and her enormous rings-of-Saturn hat and another woman, Sylvia-something, whose husband had just died of complications from liver transplant surgery, leaving her with four small children.

Sylvia-something was going through a terrible, terrible time, and what did Audrey have to complain about, really? Her problems were small ones, but they filled her up, as small problems will until the big ones move in and elbow them aside.

She knew she had allowed her anger at Leon to fester inside her, and she recalled the words from Ephesians 4:26: "Do not let the sun go down while you are still angry, and do not give the devil a foothold." And she knew it was time to let go of that anger and confront him once and for all.

She knew that her hurt and disappointment over Jack Noyce might never heal, but it would not get in the way of her doing the right thing.

She thought of that poor little daughter of Nicholas Conover, fumbling at the piano, that beautiful needy face. That little girl who had just lost her mother and was about to lose her father too.

And that was the most wrenching thing of all, knowing that she was about to orphan that little girl.

She began weeping, her shoulders heaving, the hot tears running down her cheeks, and someone was rubbing her shoulder and consoling her, and she felt loved.

Outside the church, in the gloomy daylight, she took her cell phone out of her purse and called Roy Bugbee.

101

The throaty growl of a car coming up the driveway.

Leon? No, Leon's car didn't sound that way. Out catting, Leon was. And on a Sunday. She felt a swell of resentment, of resolve.

She parted the sheer curtains in the front parlor. Bugbee.

His leering grin. "Finally decided to do it, eh?"

She invited him into the front parlor, where he took Leon's chair and Audrey sat facing him on the couch. Bugbee's foot jostled something, and a couple of brown glass bottles clattered.

He glanced down. "Hitting the sauce, Aud? Pressure getting too much for you?"

"I don't even like the taste of beer," she said, embarrassed. "So what's up?"

"One complication."

"Oh no."

"A good complication. Our friend Eddie's rolling over on Conover."

"What does that mean, exactly?"

"He wants to deal."

"How much did he tell you?"

"Not a fucking thing. Just that he might have some information of interest to us."

"He's got to show us the wares."

"He wants a deal first. I'm betting he's the coconspirator."

She thought a moment. "What if he's the shooter, not Conover?"

"Them's the breaks. If he gives up Conover for aiding and abetting, we got 'em both."

"He knows about the gun match." Another car engine, had to be Leon.

"You tell him? I sure as hell didn't."

She shook her head and told him about the call from Grand Rapids.

"Fucking Noyce," said Bugbee. "What'd I tell you?"

"What did you tell me?"

"I never liked him."

"That's because he doesn't like you."

"Touché. But not my point. Him and Eddie Rinaldi both have something on each other. Now looks like we have something on Noyce."

"I don't play that game," Audrey said firmly.

"Christ," said Bugbee. "The fuck is the point of being a church lady, time like this?"

"How about I put it in terms you might understand? You want to be up front and open with Noyce, I have no problem with that. But I'll bet you he knows that we know."

"You think?"

"He knows I've been talking to Grand Rapids. He knows I dig deep. Anyway, you want to play games with him later, I really don't care. My heart breaks for him, but right now I'm just thinking about this case and how we make it work. My way is to ignore him, work around him, put through this arrest paperwork on the down low so he doesn't have a chance to tell Rinaldi."

Bugbee shrugged, accepting defeat.

"And I'll tell you something else. I don't want to make a deal with Rinaldi."

"That's fucked up," Bugbee protested. "He's our way in."

"You're the one who kept saying we have this case nailed, right? Why do you want to give up so easily?"

"It's not giving up," Bugbee said.

"It's not, huh? I want to charge them both with open murder. That way we have maximum bargaining room. We sort it out later."

"So now *you* think we've got it nailed, that it?"

"Just about. Tomorrow morning first thing, I'm going to talk to Stadler's psychiatrist again."

"A little late for that, don't you think?"

"Not at all. It'll strengthen our hand considerably with the prosecutor's office if he'll agree to testify that Stadler could be deranged, even dangerous. If we get that, we'll get the arrest warrants for sure."

"I thought he already refused to talk to you."

"I'm not giving up."

"You can't force him."

"No, but I can persuade him. Or try, at least."

"You believe it?"

"Believe what?"

"Believe that Stadler was dangerous."

"I don't know what to believe. I think Conover and Rinaldi believed it. If we have the psychiatrist on board, we have motive. The slickest lawyer Nick Conover can find's going to have a steep hill to climb on that one. And then we sure don't need any deal with Eddie, understand?"

"Roll the dice, you mean?"

"Sometimes you have to," she said.

"You don't want to roast Noyce's balls over a campfire like I do, huh?"

She shook her head. "I'm not angry. I'm . . ." She thought. "I'm disappointed. I'm sad."

"You know something, I always thought you Jesus freaks were kidding, on some level. But I think you're serious about all that do-the-right-thing stuff. About being good. Aren't you?"

She laughed. "It's not about being good, Roy. It's about trying to be good. You think Jesus is some . . ." She searched for the word. "Some wimp? No. He was a real hard ass. He had to be."

Bugbee smiled, his eyes crinkling. She tried to read his expression, wasn't sure if she detected the tiniest glint of admiration. "Jesus the hard ass. I like that."

"So when was the last time *you* went to church, Roy?"

"Oh, no. Don't fucking start on me. Let's get one thing clear. That's not going to happen." He paused. "Besides, sounds to me like Jesus's got some work to do in your own household."

Stung, Audrey didn't reply.

"Sorry," Bugbee said after a few seconds. "That was out of bounds."

"That's okay," she said. "You may be right."

102

A chill was in the air, the fall days tinged with the coming winter. The sky was steel gray and ominous, threatening to rain at any moment.

In the living room, however, where Audrey sat reading, it was warm almost to the point of stifling. After Bugbee left, she'd made a fire in the fireplace, the first of the season. The fatwood had caught right away, which pleased her, and now the logs crackled loudly, making her jump from time to time as she lingered over a passage that wouldn't let go.

She opened the Bible to the book of Matthew and wept for the man who'd been her friend. She thought, too, about Leon, about how she'd have it out with him. Now she was all the more determined to somehow rise above anger and recrimination.

Noyce and Leon: they were nothing alike, but both were men with feet of clay. Leon was a lost man, but he was a man she loved. She knew how quick she was to judge others. Maybe it was time to learn forgiveness. That seemed to be the whole point of the parable of the unmerciful servant in the book of Matthew.

A king was owed a great sum of money by one of his servants and was about to sell the servant and his family in order to raise the money. But when the servant pleaded, his master took pity and forgave him his debt. Not long afterward, the servant met a fellow servant of the king's who owed *him* some money, and what did he do? He grabbed the man by the throat and demanded payment. The king summoned the ingrate and said, "You wicked servant! I forgave you all that debt because you besought me; and should not you have had mercy on your fellow servant, as I had mercy on you?"

A key jangled in the front door lock.

Leon. Back from wherever he went without telling her.

"Oh, hey, Shorty," he said as he entered. "You made a fire. That's nice."

She nodded. "You're out and about early."

"Looks like it's about to pour out there."

"Where'd you go, Leon?"

He immediately looked away. "Gotta get out of the house sometimes. Good for me."

"Come sit down in here. We need to talk."

"Uh oh," he said. "Those are words no guy ever wants to hear." But he sat down anyway, in his favorite chair, looking supremely uncomfortable.

"This is not going to continue," she said.

He nodded.

"Well?"

"Well what?" he said.

"I've been doing some reading in the Bible."

"I see that. Old Testament or New?"

"Hmm?"

"As I recall from my churchgoing days, the Old Testament God's a pretty judgmental sort."

"None of us is perfect, baby. And the Bible tells us about when Jesus refused to condemn an adulterer who was about to be stoned to death."

"Where's this going?" Leon said.

"You going to tell me what you're up to?"

"Ah," he said with a low chuckle that began to grow. "Oh, yeah," he said and his chuckle grew into an unrestrained guffaw. "My sister been putting crazy ideas in your head?"

"You going to explain yourself? Or is this going to be the last talk we ever have?"

"Oh, Shorty," Leon said. He got up from his chair and sat down on the couch next to her, snuggling close. She was astonished, but she didn't hug him back, just sat there, stiff and angry and confused. A bottle rolled around under the couch. She reached a hand down and grabbed it. A brown beer bottle. She held it up.

"Is it this, or is it a woman?" she said.

He was laughing, enjoying himself, and she grew steadily more furious. "It's funny to you?"

"You're some detective," he finally said. "That's root beer."

"Oh, so it is," she said, embarrassed.

"I haven't had a drink in seventeen days. You haven't noticed?"

"Is that true?"

"Forgiveness is step nine. I'm nowhere near that."

"Step nine?"

"The eighth step is to make a list of everyone I ever harmed and be willing to make amends to them. I should do that too. You know I was never good about lists."

"You—how come you didn't tell me you're doing AA?"

Now it was his turn to look sheepish. "Maybe I wanted to make sure it would take."

"Oh, baby," she said, tears springing to her eyes. "I'm so proud of you."

"Hey, Shorty, don't go getting all proud yet. I still haven't gotten past step three."

"Which is what?"

"Hell if I know," Leon said. He put a big callused hand on her face, brushed away her tears, and leaned in to kiss her, and this time she kissed him back. She'd almost forgotten what it was like, kissing her husband, but she was remembering now, and it was nice.

The two of them got up and went to the bedroom.

Outside it began to rain, but it was warm in their bed.

In the morning she would get up early and arrange the arrest warrants for Eddie Rinaldi and Nicholas Conover.

103

On her way to the prosecutor's office, Audrey heard Noyce's voice calling to her.

He was standing in the door to his office, waving her in.

She stopped for just a moment.

"Audrey," he said, something different in his voice. "We need to talk."

"I'm in a rush, Jack. I'm sorry."

"What's up?"

"I—I'd rather not say."

His eyebrows shot up. "Audrey?"

"Excuse me, Jack. I'm sorry."

He put out a hand, touched her shoulder. "Audrey," he said, "I don't know exactly what they told you about me, but . . ."

He knew. Of course he knew. She fixed him with a level gaze. "I'm listening," she said.

Noyce took a breath, colored, and then said, "Fuck it. I don't want your pity." He turned and went into his office, and she hurried on.

Dr. Aaron Landis's habitual sneer had become an incredulous scowl. "We've been over this, Detective. You've already asked me to breach Mr. Stadler's confidentiality. If you somehow imagine that your persistence is going to make me reconsider—"

"I'm sure you're aware what the *Principles of Medical Ethics*, published by the American Psychiatric Association, says about confidentiality."

"Oh, please."

"You're permitted to release relevant confidential information about a patient under legal compulsion."

"As I recall, it says 'proper' legal compulsion. Do you have a court order?"

"If that'll make a difference to you, I'll get one. But I'm appealing to you not as a law enforcement officer, but as a human being."

"Not the same thing, I take it."

She ignored this. "Ethically you have the right to testify about Andrew Stadler's history, especially if you have any interest in helping bring his killer to justice."

Landis's eyelids drooped as if he were deep in thought. "What does one have to do with the other?"

"Well, you see, Dr. Landis, we've found Andrew Stadler's killer."

"And who might that be?" His phlegmatic tone, carefully calibrated, didn't quite mask his natural curiosity.

"That I can't tell you until he's charged. But I'm going to ask you to take the stand and testify to the fact that Andrew Stadler was, at times, violent."

"I won't."

"Don't you understand what's at stake, Dr. Landis?"

"I will not testify to that," Landis said.

"If you refuse to speak for this man," Audrey said, "his killer may not find justice. Doesn't that make a difference to you?"

"You want me to testify that he had violent tendencies, and I'm not going to do that. I can't. I can't say what you want me to say—because it's not true."

"What do you mean?"

"I saw no violent inclinations whatever."

"What makes you say that?"

"I didn't tell you a thing."

"Pardon me?"

"You didn't hear any of this from me." He scratched his chin. "Andrew Stadler was a sad, desperately afflicted man. A tormented man. But not a violent man."

"Dr. Landis, the man who killed him held him responsible for a particularly sadistic attack, an evisceration of a dog, a family pet. In fact, a whole series of attacks on the suspect's home. It's the reason, we're convinced, this man killed Stadler."

Landis nodded, a glint of recognition in his eyes. "Yes," he said. "That would make a certain sense."

"It would?"

"If it were true, yes. But I can tell you with a high degree of certainty that Andrew Stadler never did these things."

"Hold on a second. Last time we spoke, you talked about a pattern of sudden rages, brief psychotic episodes—"

"Indeed. I was describing a syndrome we call Borderline Personality Disorder."

"All right, but you said a schizophrenic like Stadler could have this borderline disorder."

"I've seen it, sure. But I wasn't talking about Andrew Stadler."

"Then who *were* you talking about, Doctor?"

He hesitated.

"Doctor, please!"

Ten minutes later, short of breath, Audrey raced out of County Medical, cell phone to her ear.

104

The special board meeting was set to start at 2 P.M., and by a quarter to, most of the invited participants had arrived in the narrow anteroom. Scott had come first, and he didn't dance around the subject. Nick had a stack of unanswered phone messages from him, all from this morning. Marjorie had been instructed to keep him away from Nick's home base.

"Don't leave me in the dark here, Nick," Scott said. Nick noticed he was wearing a brand-new shirt: white, narrow-point collar, looked like Armani, completely different from the frayed Oxford-cloth button-downs he usually wore. "Come on, Nick, I can't read my lines if I don't have a script, okay?"

"I thought we'd be spontaneous."

"Spontaneous," Scott repeated. "Spontaneous combustion. Spontaneous abortion. Spontaneous aortic aneurysm." He shook his head. "I don't like that word 'spontaneous.'"

Nick cocked his head. "We're trying something new, here," he said, deliberately cryptic.

"I just want to help, Nick." There was a sullen look in his lilac-rimmed eyes.

"I'm counting on it," Nick said. "In fact, could you get me a Diet Coke? No ice if it's already cold."

Scott looked like he was about to say something when Davis Eilers—khakis and a white polo shirt beneath a blue blazer—slung an arm around Scott's shoulder and took him away.

"So where's the agenda?" Todd Muldaur asked Nick, as the anteroom started to grow crowded. "Dan, Davis, and I flew here on the Fairfield corporate jet together, and guess what—none of us got an agenda."

"Oh, there's an agenda," Nick said with a smile. "It's just not printed."

"I never heard of that. Special board meeting but no written agenda?" He exchanged glances with Dan Finegold. "Hope this isn't one of those panic moves," he said to Nick with what was meant to be a look of kindly concern in his too-blue eyes.

Finegold gave Nick an upper-bicep squeeze. "Slow and steady, right?"

"How's the brewery?" Nick asked him.

"Couldn't be better," Finegold said. "On the brewing end, at least. Micro's a crowded category right now."

Nick dropped his voice confidingly. "Truth is, Rolling Rock's more my speed. I like a beer I can see through." He scanned the room until he saw Scott McNally, huddled in a corner with Davis Eilers. Nick didn't need to hear them talk to work out that Eilers was trying to get the lowdown from Scott. Scott's response was evident from series of nervous shrugs and headshakes.

Now Todd took Nick by the elbow, and spoke to him in a low, tense voice. "Pretty short notice, don't you think?"

"The chairman of the board has the power to convene an extraordinary session of the board," Nick said blandly.

"But what's the goddamned *agenda?*"

Nick grinned, didn't answer. "Funny, I was remembering what you said about turtles and turtle soup."

Todd shrugged. "Dan and I didn't mind canceling our other appointments, but, hey, there's a Yankees–Red Sox game tonight. We both had to give away our tickets. So I hope it's going to be worth our while, huh?"

"Definitely. Count on it. We weren't able to rustle up that good coffee, though. You'll have to overlook a few things."

"We're getting used to that," said Todd with a grin that snapped shut an instant later. "Just hope you know what you're doing." He craned his head and exchanged a long glance with Scott.

Nick noticed Dorothy Devries making her entrance. She was wearing a royal blue skirt suit, with big clown-suit buttons. Her mouth was pursed and she was fingering her silver brooch with a clawlike hand. Nick waved to her from across the room, a big hearty gesture that she returned with a refrigerator smile.

Nick continued to shake hands, and make welcoming noises, until he noticed that Eddie Rinaldi had entered the room. Eddie sidled up to him with a look of impatience. "Guess what? Your fucking alarm went off again."

Nick groaned. "I can't—can you handle it?"

Eddie nodded. "Gas leak."

"*Gas* leak?"

"Alarm company called, then they called back, said a 'Mrs. Conover' told them she's handling it, but I think I should check it out. Unless you got married without telling me."

Nick, distracted, shook his head. "And Marta's out of the country."

"Your girlfriend?"

"She's not there. The kids should be home by now, though."

Eddie put a hand on Nick's shoulder. "I'll head over there. You don't fuck around with a gas leak." He took an amused look around the room before sidling off.

"Well, why don't we go sit down?" Nick said. His words were addressed to Todd but were loud enough to count as instructions to the room.

A couple of minutes later, everyone had taken a seat around the oversized mahogany table in the boardroom. Scott was playing with his plasma screen, raising it and lowering it nervously, like a kid with a Transformer action figure.

Nick didn't sit at his usual spot at the head of the table. He left that chair empty and took the seat next to it. He nodded at Stephanie Alstrom, who wore her usual look of arid unease. She rested her hands on a thick file folder.

"I want to start with some very good news," Nick said. "Atlas McKenzie is in. They signed this morning."

"Why, that's *tremendous*, Nick," Todd said. "Good going! You talk them off the ledge yourself?"

"Wish I could take the credit," Nick said. "Willard Osgood had to get on the horn himself."

"Really," Todd said, coolly. "That's an unusual tactic."

"He volunteered," Nick said. "I didn't twist his arm."

"Did he? I guess he likes to show that he can land a big one from time to time." Todd's expression hovered between amusement and condescension. "They don't make 'em like that anymore."

"I'll say." Nick pressed an intercom button and spoke to Marjorie. "Marjorie, I think we're all ready here. Could you let our visitor know?" Looking up, he went on, "Now, I didn't convene this extraordinary session to crow about good news. There are some serious issues we've got in front of us, which have to do with the future of this company." He paused for a moment. "A number of you have urged me to take a hard look at manufacturing costs. I've been resistant, and maybe I've been too resistant. Looking forward, now, we have decided to start diversifying our manufacturing base. Stratton is going to contract out the manufacturing for our low-cost Stratton/Basics lines. We're currently in negotiation with a number of overseas manufacturers, including some strong candidates in China. It's a move that will ensure we'll continue to be competitive in the most price-sensitive part of our market."

Dorothy Devries's expression was almost a smirk. Todd and Scott both looked confused, as if they were on a train that had gone one stop past their destination.

"We've reached a different decision about the higher-end lines, which are at the core of our brand identity," Nick went on. "These we'll continue to manufacture right here in Fenwick."

"I'm sorry to step in," Todd said, clearing his throat. "But you're referring to 'we,' and I don't know who you mean by that. Are you talking about your full management team? Because a lot of us are inclined to think that it's too late in the day for half measures."

"I'm aware of this." In a louder voice, he said, "As some of you here know and some of you don't know—and until recently, I was among those who didn't know—certain parties representing Fairfield have been negotiating to sell the Stratton brand to a consortium called Pacific Rim Investors, which controls a large Shenzhen-based manufacturer of office furniture, Shenyang Industries."

Nick didn't know whether he had been expecting gasps or cries of astonishment, but there weren't any. Just the sound of shuffling papers and cleared throats.

Todd looked smug. "May I say a few words?"

"Absolutely," Nick said.

Todd turned slightly, addressing the other members of the board. "First, I want to apologize to the CEO of this company for keeping him out of the loop on the deal. We at Fairfield have been taking a long, hard look at the numbers, and, frankly, we see an opportunity here, one we cannot afford to pass up. Stratton has entered into a crisis phase. Nick Conover—and I want to commend him for his candor—has made it very clear, every step of the way, that there are certain options he just can't accept. Well, we respect his views. And we certainly respect his excellent work on behalf of the company. But this is a case where management cannot be given the final word." A beat. "The greatest praise I can give any manager is to say that he does his work with passion." He turned to face Nick. "That's certainly true of you, Nick. But when a firm reaches a critical inflection point, there are hard choices to be made—and they need to be made with *dis*passion."

He leaned back in his black Stratton chair, looking sleeker by the moment. "That's the thing about being in a crisis zone," he said, hardly bothering to conceal his self-satisfaction. "It's what everyone at McKinsey gets drummed into their heads from day one. The Chinese word for 'crisis' combines the characters for 'danger' and 'opportunity.'"

"No doubt," Nick said breezily. "And the Chinese word for 'outsourcing' combines the characters for 'lost' and 'jobs.'"

"We owe you a lot," Todd said in a lordly tone. "Don't think we're not grateful. I'm sure I speak for *everyone* when I say that we appreciate all you've given to Stratton. It's just that the time has come to move on."

"I know you'd *like* to speak for everyone. But maybe some of us prefer to speak for themselves." Nick stood up, nodding at the tall bespectacled man who had just let himself into the room.

Willard Osgood.

105

The central monitoring station for Fenwicke Estates also serviced three other gated communities in and around Fenwick, including Safe Harbor, White-wood Farms, and Catamount Acres. It was a low-slung windowless building located in an anonymous area of strip malls and fast-food restaurants. It could have been a warehouse. It was surrounded by chain-link fencing and was unmarked except for a street number. Audrey knew this was for security reasons. Out back were two hulking emergency diesel generators.

When in doubt, get a warrant. You couldn't count on people to be coop-erative, even in an emergency, so she'd called in for a search warrant, had it faxed over to the central monitoring station, to the attention of the facility's general manager. Police headquarters had all that information on file.

The assistant operations manager, Bryan Mundy, was a man in a wheelchair who was as cooperative as could be, as it turned out. He was also extremely voluble, which was annoying, but she nodded and smiled pleasantly, silently urging him to hurry. She pretended to be interested, but not too interested.

As he led her through a maze of cubicles where women, mostly, sat in front of computers wearing headsets, he maneuvered his chair deftly and boasted about how they also monitored fire alarms for quite a few businesses and residences in the area. He talked about how they were connected via se-cure Internet protocol to the many cameras and guard booths they moni-tored. About how they did live remote viewing of all cameras via a Web browser. Rolling through another area where other people, mostly men, were watching video feed on computer monitors, he talked proudly, and in endless detail, about the digital watermark on the video files that provided authentication using something called an MD5 algorithm that ensured the image had not been altered.

Audrey didn't understand but stored away the fact that Bryan Mundy would be a good resource when the case went to trial.

He told her that he'd considered a job in law enforcement too, but preferred the pay of the private sector.

"Events up to thirty days ago are stored right here," he said as they entered another area, which was crowded with large racks of computer servers and storage media. "You're in luck. Anything older than that gets sent off to secure storage."

She gave him the date she was interested in viewing, and he hooked up the black disk-array box, inside of which were several hard drives containing digital video backups. He located for her the video file from between noon and 6 P.M. on the day that Nicholas Conover's family dog had been killed. She'd gotten the date and time from the uniform division. He showed her how to identify the files by camera number, but she told him she didn't know what camera it was she was looking for. Any camera located along Fenwicke Estates' perimeter fencing whose motion sensing might have been triggered during that time period.

Anyone, she thought, who had slipped into, or out of, Fenwicke Estates in the time surrounding the slaughter of Conover's dog.

"Lot of interest in this disk, huh?" Bryan Mundy said. "Log says that the security director of the Stratton Corporation came in here a while back and made some video caps off of it."

"Do you have a record of which video frames he copied?"

Mundy shook his head and poked at his teeth absently with an orange wooden plaque stick. "He said he worked for Nicholas Conover, the CEO of Stratton. Wanted to know if we had any perimeter video near the Conover house, but no dice. Conover's house is apparently a good ways from the fence."

It didn't take her long to find a tall, gawky figure in a flapping coat, wearing heavy-framed glasses, approaching the fence, captured on camera 17.

"That's what he wanted too, the security director."

Yes. That's how he and Conover came to believe it was Stadler who had eviscerated the dog.

But she could see from the way Stadler was craning his neck and squinting, his body language, that he was following someone. He wasn't looking behind, not afraid that he might have been followed. He was definitely *following* someone.

She knew who he was following. Dr. Landis's speculations made a terrible and clear sense.

"Can this rewind slowly?" she asked.

"Doesn't really rewind per se," he said, smacking his lips around the plaque stick.

"How do I view earlier images, then?"

"Like this," he said, and he pointed and double-clicked the mouse.

"Let's go back, I don't know, fifteen minutes and go from there."

"You know which cameras you want?"

"No, unfortunately. Any one of them for fifteen minutes before this guy appears."

He set it up for her and sat back as she moved through the images. His curiosity had gotten the better of his politeness; he sat there and watched as if he had nothing better to do.

Fortunately there weren't too many images to go through, since the recording was triggered by motion.

Seven minutes before Andrew Stadler had climbed the fence around Fenwicke Estates, scrambling like he was in hot pursuit, she found another figure. This one was smaller, wearing a leather jacket, moving nimbly and with great purpose.

Dr. Landis's words: *Stadler would go off his meds periodically. His wife was unable to stay married to the man, understandably, and she abandoned her child, then took her away from her father a few years later—a psychic wound from which the child might have recovered had she not had an inherited genetic predisposition.*

As the leather-jacketed figure approached the wrought-iron fence, it turned its face to the camera, almost as if posing. A smile.

The figure's face was now distinct.

Cassie Stadler.

Helen Stadler, Dr. Landis had corrected Audrey.

She changed her name to Cassie some time in adolescence. She thought it was a more interesting name. Maybe she liked the association with Cassandra, the Greek heroine endowed with the gift of prophecy whom no one heeded.

She had been the one who had repeatedly broken into Nicholas Conover's house to spray ominous and threatening graffiti. The timing now made it clear that Cassie had been the one who had killed the Conovers' dog.

Not her father, who had followed her to Conover's house, just as he'd probably followed her many times before.

Knowing that his daughter was disturbed.

Andrew Stadler knew Cassie was afflicted with this disorder, talked about it with Dr. Landis obsessively, blamed himself.

With unsteady hands she picked up her cell phone and called Dr. Landis. His answering machine came on. After the beep, she began speaking.

"Dr. Landis, it's Detective Rhimes, and it's urgent that I speak with you at once."

Dr. Landis picked up the phone.

"You told me Helen Stadler was obsessed with the notion of the family she never had," Audrey said without giving her name. "Families she could never be a part of, families that excluded her."

"Yes, yes," the psychiatrist cut in, "what of it?"

"Dr. Landis, you mentioned a family that lived across the street from the Stadlers where Cass—Helen used to play all the time when she was growing up. A little girl she considered her best friend—she used to spend all of her time over there until they became annoyed and asked her to leave?"

"Yes." Dr. Landis's voice was grave.

"Andrew Stadler was questioned years ago in connection with a tragic house fire across the street in which an entire family, the Stroups, died. He apparently did some repair work for them. Was this—?"

"Yes. Andrew said his daughter had his mechanical ability, and he'd taught her how to fix all sorts of things, and one night after they'd asked her to stop coming over she slipped into their house through the bulkhead doors, opened the gas line, and lit a match on her way out."

"Dear God. She was never charged."

"I was quite sure this was simply a fantasy of Andrew's, a manifestation of his paranoid fixation on his daughter. In any case, who would suspect a twelve-year-old girl? The authorities thought it was Andrew, but his alibi apparently held up under questioning. Something similar happened, you know, at Carnegie Mellon University during Helen's freshman year there. Andrew told me that his daughter belonged to a sorority, and she was quite obsessed with them as a surrogate family of sorts. Much later, he said, he heard about the terrible gas explosion in the sorority house in which eighteen women perished. This was the same night that Helen drove home from Pittsburgh, quite upset that one of her sorority sisters had said something to make her feel rejected."

"I—I have to go, Doctor," she said, ending the call.

Bryan Mundy had rolled up to her in his wheelchair and was signaling to her. "Talk about coincidences," he said. "We were talking about Conover's house, and what do you know? We just got an alert on that system, maybe ten, fifteen minutes ago."

"An alert?"

"No, not a burglar alarm or anything. Combustible gas detector. Probably a gas leak. But the homeowner said she's got it under control."

"She?"

"Mrs. Conover."

"There is no Mrs. Conover," Audrey said, heart knocking.

Mundy shrugged. "That's how she identified herself," he said, but Audrey was already running toward the door.

106

Todd immediately sprang to his feet, followed by Eilers and Finegold. Their faces were wreathed in anxious cordiality.

"Mind if I join you?" Osgood asked gruffly.

"Willard," Todd said, "I had no idea you were coming." He turned to Nick. "You see? The personal touch—some people never lose it."

Osgood ignored him as he took the empty seat at the head of the board table.

"There isn't going to be any sale," Nick said. "The sale is wrong for Stratton, and wrong for Fairfield. We too have looked at the numbers—and by 'we,' I mean Willard and I—and that's our considered assessment."

"May I speak?" Todd said.

"We're talking about an opportunity here," Scott said. "Not something that's going to knock twice."

"An opportunity?" Nick asked. "Or a danger?" He paused, and turned to Stephanie Alstrom. "Stephanie, a few words? I know I haven't given you enough time to prepare a PowerPoint presentation, but maybe you can do it the old-fashioned way."

Stephanie Alstrom started sorting through the stapled sheaths in her file, making three separate stacks next to her. "Here's the principal tort and criminal case law governing the salient issues, starting with federal statutes," she began in her most juiceless tone. "There's the Bribery of Foreign Officials Act of 1999, part No. 43, and the International Anti-Bribery and Fair Compe-

tition Act of 1998, and—oh heavens—the antifraud provisions of the securities laws, Section 10(b) of the Securities Exchange Act of 1934 and Rule 10b-
5. And, though I haven't read through the case law properly yet, there's
Section 13(b)(5) of the Exchange Act and Rule 13b2-1, to deal with." She was
sounding increasingly flustered. "And, of course, Sections 13(a) and
13(b)(2)(A) of the Exchange Act, and Rules 12b-20 and 13a too. But also
there's—"

"I think we get the picture," Nick said smoothly.

"Pretty much what Dino Panetta told me back in Boston," Osgood
rumbled.

"That is ridiculous," Todd said. Blood was returning to his face. Too
much blood. "These are completely unfounded allegations that I dispute—"

"Todd?" Osgood's craggy face formed a scowl. "It's one thing if *you* want
to go fly-fishing with your private parts for bait, but you do *not* put the partnership at risk. Question I was asking myself last night was, Where did I go
wrong? Then this morning, I had the answer. I didn't go wrong. You went
wrong. You ignored company policy and made a huge bet on microchips,
way more than you should have, and the entire firm almost went belly-up as
a result. Then you figured you could save your ass, and ours, by doing a
quick-and-dirty sale. A nice big pile of dough, and who cares how you got it.
Well, not like this." He struck the table, stressing each word. "Not. Like.
This." His eyes flashed behind his Coke-bottle glasses. "Because you've put
Fairfield Equity Partners in a potentially ruinous legal situation. We could
have brown-suited lawyers from the SEC camped out on Federal Street for
the next five years, combing through our files with a jeweler's loupe. You
wanted to land a big fish—and you didn't care if you rammed the boat
through a goddamned barrier reef to do it."

"I think you're blowing this out of proportion," Todd said, wheedling.
"Fairfield is in no danger."

"Damned right," Osgood replied. "Fairfield Equity Partners is completely in the clear."

"Good," Todd said uncertainly.

"That's right," Osgood said. "Because the partnership did the responsible
thing. Demonstrated it wasn't party to the misdeeds. As soon as the errant be-

havior came to our attention, we severed our relations with the principals—*former* principals, not to put too fine a point on it, and took all possible measures to separate ourselves from the malefactors. Including the commencement of legal action against Todd Erickson Muldaur. You violated the gross misconduct clause of your agreement with the Partnership, which means, as I'm sure you know, that your share reverts to the general equity fund."

"You're joking," Todd said, blinking as if there was a bit of grit lodged behind one of his blue contact lenses. "I've got all my money invested in Fairfield. You can't just declare—"

"You signed the same agreement we all did. Now we're activating the provision. Only way to show the feds we're serious. You can contest it—I'm sure you will. But I think you'll find most high-powered lawyers are going to want to see a hefty chunk of their fee up front. And we've already filed for a separate tort claim against you and your coconspirator, Mr. McNally, for a hundred and ten million dollars. We've requested that the judge place the funds we're trying to recover in escrow, pending legal resolution, and we've received indications that he intends to do so."

Scott's face looked like a plaster death mask. He tugged robotically at a lock of hair at his temple. As Nick listened to Osgood, he found himself staring out the window at the charred buffalo grass. It no longer looked like a lifeless black carpet anymore, he noticed. The new grass had begun to grow back. Tiny green blades were now peeking through the black.

"That's insane!" Todd spoke with a squeaky groan, a crowbar pulling out a long nail. "You can't do that. I will *not* be treated this way, Willard. I'm owed some basic respect. I am a full-fledged partner at Fairfield, of eight years standing. I'm not some . . . some goddamn *catfish* you can play catch-and-release with."

Osgood turned to Nick. "He's got a point. You wouldn't want to mix him up with a catfish. You see, one's a bottom-feeding, scum-sucking scavenger . . ."

"And the other's a fish," Nick said. "Got it. And one more bit of business." He looked around the table. "Now that Stratton's future is secure, I'm hereby submitting my resignation."

Osgood turned to face him, stunned. "*What?* Oh, Christ."

"I'm about to face a legal . . . situation . . . which I don't want to drag my company through."

The men and women around the boardroom table seemed as astonished as Osgood was. Stephanie Alstrom began shaking her head.

But Nick stood up and shook Osgood's hand firmly. "Stratton's been through enough. When we make the announcement, we'll just say that Mr. Conover resigned 'in order to spend more time with his family.'" He gave a little wink. "Which has the added virtue of being true. Now, if you'll excuse me."

He got up and strode confidently out of the room, and for the first time in a long while he felt a palpable sense of relief.

Marjorie was crying as she watched him gather up his framed family pictures. Her phone was ringing nonstop, but she was ignoring it.

"I don't understand," she said. "I think you owe me an explanation."

"You're right. I do." He reached down to the bottom drawer of his desk and pulled out the rubber-banded stack of Post-it notes in Laura's handwriting. "But first, could you find me a box?"

She turned and, as she passed her desk, she picked up the phone. A few seconds later, Marge looked around the partition, looking grim. "Nick, there's some kind of emergency at your house."

"Eddie's handling it."

"Well, the thing is—that was a woman named Cathy or Cassie, calling from your house. I didn't get the name—she was speaking fast, sounding panicked. She said you've got to get over there as fast as you can. I don't have a good feeling about this."

Nick dropped the picture frames onto his desk and broke into a run.

107

On his way to the parking lot he called home, let it ring.

No answer, which was strange. Cassie had just called from there—and what the hell was she doing there anyway? Plus, both kids should have gotten home from school by now to do their last-minute packing, both of them excited about the trip. Even, in his grudging way, Lucas, or so Nick thought.

But the phone rang and rang and the voice mail kept coming on.

Okay, so Lucas often didn't answer the home phone, let the voice mail get it, but Julia always answered. She loved the phone. And Cassie—she'd just called. Weird.

No answer.

Lucas's cell? He didn't remember the number, too many numbers in his head and this one he didn't call all that often. He hit the green call button on his phone, which pulled up the last ten or whatever calls he'd dialed.

There it was, LUCAS CELL. Had Marjorie programmed that in? Probably. He hit SEND as he ran through the parking lot, a couple of employees waving hello but he didn't have time for niceties.

Come on, damn it, answer the fucking phone. Told you if you don't answer the cell, I take it away, that's the deal.

A couple of rings and then his son's recorded voice, adolescent-buzzy in timbre, curt and full of attitude in just a few words.

Hey, it's Luke, what up? Leave a message.

A beep, then a female voice: *Please leave your message after the tone. Press One to send a numeric page—*

Nick ended the call, heart drumming and not from the run. He fumbled for the Suburban's key-fob thing, pressed it to unlock just as he reached the car door.

Roaring out of the parking lot, he tried Eddie's cell.

No answer.

"She's not here," Bugbee said. The cellular signal began to fade . . . "Patrol units, but no Cassie Stadler at her house."

"She's at Conover's," Audrey said. "Gas leak."

"Huh?"

"I'm heading over there now. You too. Right away. Notify the fire department."

"You know she's there?"

"She answered the phone when the alarm monitoring service called. Get over there, Roy. Right now."

"Why?" Bugbee said.

"Just do it. And bring backup." She ended the call so he didn't have a chance to argue.

Gas leak. The Stroups, her neighbors when she was twelve.

She lit a match on the way out.

Her sorority house at Carnegie Mellon when she was a freshman.

Eighteen young women perished.

The families she desperately wanted to be part of. Who all rejected her.

Then Audrey called Nicholas Conover's office at the Stratton Corporation, but she was told he wasn't there.

Tell him it's urgent, she said. It's a matter of safety. His house.

The secretary's voice lost its hard edge. "He's on his way over there, officer."

The alarm company?

Nick didn't even remember the name.

A gas leak? He tried to imagine what that was all about—something goes wrong in the house, the kids smell gas, maybe they're smart about it and get the hell out of the house, that's why the house phone line went unanswered—but what about Lucas's cell?

Say he left it inside in the rush to get out. Sure, that was all.

But Eddie?

Guy lived with a cell phone planted to his ear. Why the hell would he not answer either?

Twelve minutes he could be at the gates of Fenwicke Estates. Assuming he caught the lights right. He gunned it, then slowed just a bit, keeping it no more then ten miles an hour over the speed limit. An overzealous cop could pull him over, slow things way down even if Nick told him it was an emergency. Ask for my license and registration, maybe decide to take his fucking time about it once he caught the name.

He drove the whole way in a mental tunnel of concentration, barely aware of the traffic around him, thinking only of getting to the house. Kept hitting REDIAL for Eddie's cell, but no answer.

A moment of relief as he pulled up to the gatehouse. No emergency vehicles here, no fire trucks or whatever, probably no big deal.

A gas leak is not the same thing as a fire, of course.

Could the kids and Eddie and Cassie all have been overcome by gas fumes, maybe that's why they couldn't answer? He had no idea if natural gas did that.

"Hi, Mr. Conover," said Jorge, behind the bulletproof glass in the booth.

"Emergency, Jorge," Nick called out.

"Your security director, Mr. Rinaldi, he came through here already."

"How long ago?"

"Let me check the log—"

"Forget it. Open the gate, Jorge."

"It's opening, Mr. Conover."

And so it was, glacially slow. Inching open.

"Can you speed it up?" Nick said.

Jorge smiled apologetically, shrugged. "You know this gate, I'm sorry. Also your friend came by."

"My friend?"

"Miss Stadler? She came by too. Hour ago, I think."

Did the kids call Cassie to come over? he wondered. Why didn't they call me? They know how to reach me. More comfortable calling Cassie, that it?

"Goddammit," Nick shouted in frustration. "Speed this fucking thing up."

"I can't do that, Mr. Conover, I'm sorry."

Nick floored it, the Suburban lurching forward, hitting the solid iron bars of the gate, a crunch of metal that he knew wasn't the gate. Even the goddamned Suburban is a fucking tin can, crumples like a wad of aluminum foil. Front-end work. Fuck it.

It didn't budge the gate, which continued its stately pace, oblivious, arrogant, taking its goddamned fucking time.

Jorge's eyes widened. Finally the gate was open just enough, Nick calculated, to get through. He gunned it again, the squeal of metal against metal as the car scraped against the gate but got through, just barely.

SPEED LIMIT 20, the sign said.

Fuck it.

No fire trucks on the street or along the driveway. No police cars either.

Maybe this was nothing. He was overreacting, no emergency at all, no gas leak at all, a false alarm.

No. A false alarm, there would have been an answer, one of the calls he'd made.

Gas leak for real. Eddie came by, got the kids out of there and Cassie too, saved them all, thank God for that traitorous bastard, a bastard but *my* bastard, maybe turned out to be a real friend after all, maybe I owe him an apology.

Eddie's GTO in the driveway, parked behind the van. Cassie's red VW convertible too. It didn't compute. Cassie came over, Eddie too, both of their cars here, the van here too. That meant no one drove the kids away, thus the kids are still here and Eddie and Cassie too, so what the hell, then?

He raced up the stone path to the house, noticed all the windows were closed, the house sealed tight as if they were already out of there, on vacation, and as he approached the front door he smelled rotten eggs.

The gas smell.

It was for real. It was strong too, if he could smell it out here. Very strong. That odorant they add to natural gas so you know if there's a leak.

Front door was locked, which was a little strange if everyone had just run out of there, but he didn't linger on that, totally single-minded. He grabbed his key ring, got the door open.

Dark in here.

He yelled out, "Hello? Anyone here?"

No answer.

The rotten-egg smell was overpowering. More like skunk, maybe. A wall of odor, sharp as a knife, nauseating.

"Hello?"

Faint noises now. Thumping? From upstairs? He couldn't tell, the house was so solid. He entered the kitchen, but no one there either.

Distant bumping sounds, but then footsteps nearby, and Cassie appeared, walking slowly, looking worn out, a wreck.

"Cass," he said. "Thank God you're here. Where are the kids?"

She kept approaching, one hand behind her back, slowly, almost hesitant. Her eyes sleepy, not looking at him, her stare distant.

"Cass?"

"Yeah," she said at last. "Thank God I'm here." Flat, almost affectless.

He heard a high-pitched mechanical beeping coming from somewhere. What the hell was that?

"Where is everyone?"

"They're safe," she said, but something in her tone seemed off, as if she wasn't sure.

"Where's Eddie?"

A beat. "He's . . . safe too." She drew out the words.

He stepped toward her to give her a hug, but she stepped backward, shook her head.

"No," she said.

"Cassie?"

He felt the twang of fear even before his brain could make sense of it.

"You've got to get out of here. We've got to open some windows, call the fire department. Jesus, this is incredibly dangerous, this stuff is unbelievably combustible. Where are Luke and Julia?"

The high beeping was getting faster, higher in pitch, and Nick realized the source was a device on the kitchen counter he'd seen before, a small yellow box with flexible metal tubing coming out of it. What was it, and what was it doing there?

"I'm glad you came home, Nick." Her eyes were smudged, looking like black holes. They darted from side to side. "I knew you would, though. Daddy protects his family. You're a good daddy. Not like my daddy. He never protected me."

"Cassie," he said, "what *is* it? You look so frightened."

She nodded. "I'm terrified."

He felt his skin go cold and goosefleshy. He saw it in her eyes, that same absent look he'd seen before, as if she'd gone somewhere else where no one could reach her. "Cassie," he said in a gentle and firm tone, hollow inside, "where are my children?"

"I'm terrified of *me*, Nick. And you should be too."

With her left hand she reached into the pocket of her denim shirt and pulled out an object that he recognized as Lucas's Zippo lighter. The lighter decorated with a skull crawling with spiders and surrounded by spider webs, a real stoner lighter. She flipped the top off, one-handed, and her thumb touched the flint wheel.

"No!" Nick shouted. "What are you doing, are you *crazy*?"

"Come on, Nick, you *know* I am. Can't you read the writing on the wall?" She began singing softly, "Oh, I ran to the rock to hide my face, the rock cried out 'No hiding place.'"

"Where *are* they, Cassie?"

The electronic beeping, rising all the while in pitch, had now become a steady high squeal, almost ear-piercing. He realized where he'd seen that yellow box before: in the basement, placed there by the gas company serviceman. A combustible gas detector. Supposed to warn you about gas leaks. Beeping got higher and faster as the concentration of gas in the air increased. A steady squeal meant dangerous amounts of gas. Combustible levels. Someone had taken the device upstairs from the basement, and he now knew who.

"I told you, they're safe," she said in a flat voice, and her other hand, the one she'd been keeping behind her back, came around to the front now, gripping the huge carbon-steel Henckels carving knife from the kitchen knife rack.

Heart thumping a million miles a minute now. Oh sweet Jesus, she's out of her mind. Dear God, help me.

"Cassie," he said, moving closer, his arms outspread to give her a hug, but she raised the knife and pointed it at him, and with her left hand she held up the lighter, thumb on the wheel, and said, "Not another step, Nick."

The guard's face appeared behind the tempered glass of the security booth at the entrance to the Fenwicke Estates.

His voice squawked through the intercom. "Yes?"

She flashed her police badge. "Police emergency," she said.

The guard looked at it through the glass and immediately activated the security gate.

"Jesus, Cassie, please *don't*—"

"Oh, I really don't like this part," she said, and at that instant he noticed the red slick on the knife blade, still wet.

108

The high wrought-iron gate began to open, but so slowly, so agonizingly slowly. She drummed her fingers on the steering wheel and finally she said, "Please, speed this up. There's no time to waste."

"Sorry, I can't make it go any faster," the guard said. "That's as fast as it goes. I'm sorry."

"Put the knife down, Cassie," Nick said, all forced calm, voice soft and wheedling.

"When I'm done with my work, Nick. I'm very tired. I just want to finish. It has to end."

"Your work," Nick said numbly. "Please, Cassie. What have you done with them?" Fear rose in him like a flood tide.

Please God no not the kids no oh Jesus Christ no.

"Who?" she said.

No please not that dear God not the kids.

"My . . . family."

"Oh, they're safe, Nick. Like a family should be. Safe. Protected."

"Please, Cassie," he whispered, a catch in his throat, hot tears in his eyes. "Where are my kids?"

"Safe, Nick."

"Cassie, please tell me they're . . ." He stopped, couldn't say *alive*, couldn't allow himself to think the word, even, because its opposite was unendurable.

She cocked her head. "You can't hear them? Banging away? They're locked up nice and safe in the basement. You can hear it, I know you can."

And he could, now that she pointed it out, hear a distant thumping. The basement door? He almost gasped in relief, his knees buckling. She'd locked them in the basement. They were alive down there.

Where the gas was coming from.

"Where's Eddie?" he managed to say.

Oh God please if Eddie's down there he'll get them out, he'll figure out a way, he can bust through a locked door, pick it. Fucking windowless basement. Vent grates are too small to climb out of. But he'll figure it out.

She shook her head. "He's not down there. I never trusted him either." She waggled the lighter, the skull leering at him.

"Don't do it, Cassie. You'll kill us all. Please don't do it, Cassie."

She kept waggling the lighter back and forth, back and forth, her thumb at the flint wheel. "I didn't ask him to come. I told *you* to come. Eddie's not family."

His eyes frantically scanned the kitchen, then stopped when he saw a shape on the lawn outside the kitchen doors. Through the glass of the French doors he recognized Eddie's body.

He saw the blood-darkened front of Eddie's pale shirt.

The contorted position. The unnatural splay of the limbs.

He knew, and it was all he could do to keep from screaming.

Audrey couldn't stand how slowly the gate was opening, almost deliberately so, as if the residents of the Fenwicke Estates were never in a hurry, because haste was unseemly.

Move it! she screamed in her mind.

She gripped the steering wheel, tapping at the gas pedal.

Faster!

She knew what was going to happen, what the poor demented soul was doing, as she'd done before. Somehow Cassie Stadler had gotten into the

Conover house—well, that couldn't have been too hard, right? She and Conover had become intimate; maybe she had a key—and something had happened to set her off, make her feel rejected. Cassie Stadler was a border-line personality, Dr. Landis had said, with a dangerous psychotic component. An obsession with family, with inclusion, and rejection always propelled her into a towering irrational rage.

Cassie Stadler was going to incinerate the Conover home.

Audrey prayed that the children weren't home. It was early in the after-noon—maybe they were still in school. Maybe the house was empty. The worst that could happen, then, was that the house would be destroyed.

Maybe no one was home. She prayed that was so.

"Put down the lighter, baby," Nick said, voice silky, all the fake affection he could summon. "Is this about Maui? Because I didn't invite you?"

Fuck the knife. He'd lunge at her, grab it.

The lighter? All that took was a flick of her Bic. Could happen by acci-dent. That he'd have to be careful of.

"Why should you invite me on a family trip, Nick? I mean, it's just for family, right? I'm not family."

He understood. He realized that he didn't know her, had never known her, that he'd seen in her only what he wanted to see.

She'd said as much, hadn't she? "We don't see things as they are," she'd said once, quoting someone. "We see things as *we* are."

But he knew enough about her to understand what she was saying now.

Audrey could smell the natural gas as soon as she got out of the car.

She saw all the other vehicles in the driveway, two of them belonging to Nicholas Conover, the other she didn't recognize. Not Bugbee's. He was all the way across town. It would take him a while. She hoped he knew to get here fast, sirens and lights on.

Her instinct told her not to go in the front door. She had to obey her in-stinct, times like this.

She took out the pistol from her shoulder holster under her jacket and began walking across the wide expanse of lawn, so very green, heading toward the back of the house where she could enter unnoticed.

She chose the right side of the house, where she remembered the kitchen was. As she rounded the house she noticed a figure standing in the kitchen, a small slender figure, and she knew it was Cassie Stadler.

And then she saw the body sprawled on the lawn.

Running now, low to the ground, she approached the body.

A terrible bloody mess. Sweet Jesus. It was Edward Rinaldi, and it looked as if he'd been disemboweled.

His eyes open, staring, one hand curled by his abdomen, the other outstretched toward the kitchen. Blood-soaked beige knit shirt crisscrossed with slashes as if from a knife.

Most of his shirt front dark with blood, which pooled on the green lawn.

She dropped to her knees to feel for a pulse.

She wasn't sure.

If there was a pulse, it was so slow she couldn't detect it. Maybe there was a pulse. Maybe not.

She touched his jugular vein and felt nothing, and she knew for certain the man was dead.

Nothing she could do for him. She set down her pistol, took out her cell phone, got Bugbee on the first ring.

"Alert the ME," she said. "And body conveyance."

She was frightened as she'd never been frightened before, and she'd been through some horrific crime scenes. She got up and ran around to the back of the house.

"God, I wasn't even thinking," Nick said, shaking his head. "I was in such a rush to just get the kids out of town, get us on a vacation, I really fucked that up. I mean, I really blew it."

"Don't, Nick," she said, but he saw something flicker in her eyes, as if maybe she wanted to believe.

"No, seriously, I mean, how could it be a true family vacation without you? You've become such an important part of the family, babe, you know that? If I hadn't been so distracted with everything that's been going on at work, I—"

"*Don't*, Nick," she said a little louder, her voice still petulant. "Please."

"We can still be a family, Cass. I'd like that. Wouldn't you like that?"

Her eyes glistened with tears. "Oh, Nick, I've been through this before, you know. I recognize the pattern."

"The pattern?" Heart thwacking, because he saw that faint glint of hopefulness in her eyes go dark like the last winking of a dying fire.

"The first signs. It's always the same. They take you in and make you feel like a part of everything and then something always happens. There's like a line you can never cross. A brick wall. It's like the Stroups."

"The Stroups?"

"One day, no reason, they say I can't keep coming over, I'm spending too much time over there. Lines are drawn. They're family, you're not. Maybe that's the way it has to be. But I know I can't go through it again. It's too much."

"That's where you're wrong, baby," Nick said. "It's not too late. We can still be a family."

"Sometimes a world has to come to an end. So new ones can come into being."

The electronic squeal, steady, earsplitting.

Audrey considered, then rejected, entering through the French doors that led into the kitchen. No. She'd have to approach with some stealth. She raced to the next set of French doors, but they were locked too. Was there no basement entrance, bulkhead doors or whatever?

There didn't seem to be.

A hissing sound drew her to the far side of the house near the pool fence. She saw pipes—gas pipes, she realized. Some kind of metal objects were lying on the ground next to the pipe stand, and a crescent wrench. Valves or something. They'd been removed, and maybe that was why the hissing was so loud, like the flow had been turned up full, maybe.

The gas pipes had to lead into the basement, she knew, because that was always where they went.

Over the hissing she could hear a shout. It was coming from a grate about twenty feet away.

She ran to the grate, put her face against it, the skunky, metallic smell of gas nauseating her. "Hello?" she called out.

"Down here! We're down here!" An adolescent male voice. Conover's son?

"Who is it?" Audrey said.

"Lucas. And my sister. She's got us locked in here."

"Who does?"

"That crazy bitch. Cassie."

"Where's your dad?"

"I don't know—just, shit, will you *help* us? We're going to fucking *die* down here!"

"Stay calm," Audrey said, though calm was the one thing she didn't feel. "Listen, Lucas. Help me out. You can help me, okay?"

"Who're *you*?"

"I'm Detective Rhimes. Listen to me. How's your sister doing?"

"She's—she's scared, what the fuck do you think?"

"Julia, right? Julia, can you hear me?"

A small, frightened voice. "Yes."

"Are you getting enough oxygen?"

"What?"

"Stand over here by this grate, sweetheart. Make sure you get enough air from the outside. You'll be okay."

"Okay," the girl said.

"Now, Lucas, is there a pilot light down there?"

"A pilot light?"

"Are you near the water heater? There's usually a pilot light going on the water heater, and if that ignites the cloud of gas, the whole house is going to blow. You've got to turn it off."

"There's no pilot light." His voice was faint, distant, as if he'd gone to check. "No pilot light. She must have put it out so the gas wouldn't ignite too early."

Smart kid, she thought. "All right. Is there a shutoff for the gas line? It would be on the wall where the gas pipes enter."

"I see it."

"You see the shutoff?"

Footsteps. "No. I don't see a shutoff."

She sighed, tried to think. "Are any of the doors to the house open?"

"I—I don't know, how would I know?" the boy replied.

"I think they're all locked. Is there a key hidden somewhere outside, like under a rock or something?"

She heard a jingling, and a small steel key ring poked up through the slats in the grate. "Use mine," the boy said.

Thumping from the basement, frantic, the noises reassuring because they were alive. Now in the few seconds of stillness Nick could faintly hear Lucas's voice yelling. They were alive. And desperate to get out of there.

"I'm going to call United right now," Nick said. "I'll get you on our flight no matter what it costs. First class if you want it, but you probably want to sit with us in business class." He thought, *Don't pick up the phone, even as a pretense. The phone could ignite the gas.* He remembered reading somewhere about a woman who had a gas leak and she picked up the phone and called 911, and an electric arc from the phone circuit sparked and the house exploded. "The kids would love that. You know they would, baby."

"Please, Nick." She toyed with the lighter, and in her other hand the knife dangled at her side.

He could leap at her, hurl her to the ground, if he did it carefully, chose the right moment.

"I know you now," she said in a monotone. "I can see right through you."

Quietly, quietly, Audrey turned the key in the back-door lock, and then pushed the door open.

A tone sounded. The alarm system's entry alert.

It had just announced her arrival.

The skunk stench was overpowering in here.

———

She walked slowly, orienting herself. She didn't remember the layout of the house well, but then she could hear voices, female and male, and she knew which way to go.

Was the unhinged woman holding Conover hostage? If she was, then the sound of Audrey entering might attract her attention, unnerve her, maybe make her do something rash. The wrench, the gas pipes—it told Audrey that Cassie Stadler, it had to be her, had opened the pipes in order to fill the house with gas just as she'd done in other houses before.

All she'd have to do would be to strike a match and the house would explode, killing herself and the children in the basement and Audrey too. But why hadn't she done it yet?

Audrey had an idea now.

Cassie Stadler was filling the house with gas, had been for a while. Maybe she was just waiting for the entire house to fill up. So she could get the biggest bang possible.

Yes. That's what she was waiting for.

The children. That was the first thing. She had to free them.

A pounding on a door somewhere nearby told her where to go. A door in the hall. She heard the kids, or maybe it was just Lucas, pounding and pounding.

Swiftly she turned the dead bolt with a loud, satisfying click, and she pulled the door open. The boy tumbled out, sprawled to the floor.

"Hush," Audrey whispered. "Where's your sister?"

"Right here," said Lucas, and the girl came streaking out, weeping, her face red.

"Go!" Audrey whispered. "Both of you." She pointed to the open door. "Run!"

"Where's Dad?" Julia cried. "Where is he?"

"He's all right," Audrey said, not knowing what else to say. She had to get them out of here. "Go!"

Julia took right off, pushed open the screen door and began running across the lawn, but Lucas didn't move. He looked at her.

"Don't fire that gun," he said. "That'll set it off."

"I know," she said.

———

"What was that?" said Cassie.

"What?"

"That sound. The alarm. Someone just came in the house."

"I didn't hear it."

Cassie turned slowly, looked from one entrance to the other, all the while flicking her eyes back to Nick, making sure he didn't advance toward her.

"You know," she said, her eyes trained on him, "it's funny, the way I went through stages of thinking about you. First I saw you as the destroyer of families. You sure destroyed my dad's life when you fired him, so I had to let you know you weren't any safer than anyone else."

"The graffiti," Nick said, realizing. " 'No hiding place.' "

"But then I got to know you a little better, and I thought I'd been wrong, I decided you were a good man. But I know better now. Sometimes you gotta trust your first impressions."

"Put the lighter down, Cassie. You don't want to do this. Let's talk, let's figure things out."

"You know what fooled me? When I saw what a good daddy you were."

"Please, Cassie."

Behind her was the entrance that led to the back hallway. He became aware of a slight change in the light, a shadow. A movement.

A figure slowly approaching.

Nick knew enough not to break eye contact with Cassie. He looked into her red-rimmed eyes, while in his peripheral vision he could make out a woman moving stealthily along the wall, advancing toward the kitchen.

It was the police detective, Audrey Rhimes.

Don't break eye contact. He forced himself to look into Cassie's desperate heavy-lidded eyes, bottomless pools of anguish and madness.

"Not like my daddy. He was scared of me, he followed me everywhere, wouldn't leave me alone, but he'd never do for me what you did for your kids."

"He loved you, Cass, you know that." His voice was shaking a little.

Keep your eyes on Cassie.

Detective Rhimes was advancing ever so slowly.

"You were so scared that night. I could see it from where I was standing, in the woods. I could hear it. The way you told him, 'Freeze,' and, 'One more step, and I shoot!'" She shook her head. "I don't know what they told you about him, but I can just imagine. Schizophrenic, right? You thought *he* was the one who killed your dog. You didn't know he was just trying to hand you a note saying he was innocent, right? You thought he was pulling out a gun. So you did the right thing, the brave thing. You protected your family. You protected your kids. You squeezed the trigger and you shot him down, and you did what a dad should do. You protected your family."

Oh, Christ. I took her father away from her and she knew it all along. Before we met she knew it.

I took her family, and now she's going to take mine.

A terrible chill ran through his body.

She nodded, raised her left hand, the lighter hand, and Nick flinched, but she only rubbed her left forearm against her nose, sniffling. "Yeah, I was there that night, Nick. I was there first. He was following me, always following me. He knew I was paying another visit to your house. I *saw* you, Nick."

Out of the corner of his eye he saw Detective Rhimes inch ahead, closer, closer, but he didn't dare shift his eyes even a millimeter.

"He just kept coming at you and coming at you, didn't he? And no matter how much you told him to stop he kept coming because he really didn't understand." Her voice deepened, in an eerie imitation of her father's voice: "Never—safe! Never—safe!" She shook her head. "I'll never forget the look on your face afterward. I've never seen a man look so frightened. And so sad."

"Cassie, I—God, I'm so, *so* sorry, I don't know what else to say. I'm going to face up to what I've done. I'm going to answer for it."

"Sorry? Oh, don't get me wrong, I'm not *mad*. Don't apologize. It was beautiful, what you did. You were protecting your family."

"Cassie, please . . ."

"Of course you had to do it. Oh, don't I know it. Don't get me wrong, I'm grateful. It was a liberation, you know. It freed me. My daddy was in a prison of his own mind, but I was a prisoner, too, until you freed me. And then I met you and I saw what a strong man you were. A good man, I thought. You needed a wife, and your kids needed a mommy, and we could all be a family."

"We can still be a family."

She shook her head, knife dangling at one side, toying with the lighter in the other. A rueful smile. "No, Nick. I know how these things work. I've been through it time and time again, and I just"—her voice cracked, her face got small and wrinkled, and she began to really cry now—"I just can't go through it again. I'm tired. I can't do it again. Once the door slams shut you can't open it again. It's never the same. Do you understand?"

"I understand," Nick said, moving closer, wearing an expression of gentle empathy.

"Stop, Nick," she said, holding up the lighter warningly as she stepped back. "No closer."

"Things can change, Cassie. In a good way."

Tears were streaming down her face now from her smudged eyes. "No," she said. "It's time," and Nick could hear the rasp of her thumb on the flint wheel.

109

Audrey listened closely as she advanced toward the kitchen. She could hear everything the two said, and it was strange how insignificant, all of a sudden, it was to have Nicholas Conover's guilt confirmed from his own mouth.

She thought of that passage from Matthew, the parable of the unmerciful servant. She thought of the sign taped to her computer monitor that said, "Remember: We work for God."

She understood what she had to do about Nicholas Conover. The weapon that had killed Andrew Stadler had been stolen years earlier by Eddie Rinaldi, who now lay dead on the lawn.

You can't convict a dead man.

Things would be sorted out later.

But for now she had to stop Cassie Stadler.

The problem was that this situation fit no pattern she had ever trained for. She slid along the wall, felt it cold against her cheek. Gripped the smooth paint of the doorframe molding.

Did Conover know she was there?

She thought he did.

She could hear the steady high-pitched tone, and she saw where it was coming from. It was a combustible gas detector, which measured the concentration of gas in the air. The steady tone meant that the gas in the air had reached optimal combustibility—she forgot the exact percentages, but she knew it was a range on either side of ten percent. Cassie Stadler was waiting until the air up here had reached the most dangerous concentration of propane gas, no less and no more.

You must always think several steps ahead, she told herself. What if, as she stole up on Cassie, relying on the element of surprise to take her down barehanded, she startled the woman, causing her to strike the lighter?

That had to be avoided at all costs.

She slid past the hall table, careful not to jar it and thus knock the alabaster lamp to the floor. Finally, she entered the room, and she didn't know what she was going to do next.

She listened hard, and she thought.

The flint didn't spark on her first try. Cassie frowned, tears coursing down her cheeks.

The gas detector shrilled, and meanwhile she sang softly in her lovely, lilting voice: "Oh, the rock cried out, I'm burning too—I want to go to Heaven the same as you."

"Cassie, don't do it."

"This was your decision. You made this happen."

"I made a mistake."

She looked above Nick's shoulder, saw something. "Luke?" she said.

"Cassie," Lucas said, walking across the kitchen straight toward her.

"Luke," Nick said. "Get out of here."

"What are you doing here, Luke?" Cassie said. "I told you and Julia to stay in the basement."

Audrey Rhimes had somehow gotten into the house through the back door; that was the alert tone sounding, she knew to unlock the basement, let the kids out. But where was Julia?

Lucas must have taken the back corridor around, through the family room to the kitchen's other entrance.

"You locked us in," Lucas said, coming right up to her, standing to one side of her. "I know you didn't mean to. But I found the spare key."

What the hell was he doing? "Luke, please," Nick said.

But Lucas was ignoring his father. "Cassie," he said, touching her shoulder, "remember that poem you helped me with—that guy Robert Frost?" He smiled, warm and winning and appealing. "'Hired Hand' or 'Hired Man' or whatever it was called."

Cassie didn't move Lucas's hand off her shoulder, Nick noticed. She turned to look at him, her expression seeming to soften just a bit, he thought.

"Home is the place where, when you have to go there, they have to take you in," Cassie said, her voice hollow.

Lucas nodded.

His eyes slid toward Nick's for just a fraction of a second.

Nick saw it.

Lucas wasn't ignoring him at all. He was *signaling* to his father.

"Remember what you told me?" Lucas said. His luminous blue eyes held hers. "There's nothing more important than family. You said that's what it's all about, finally, in the end. That's what makes us human."

"Lucas," Cassie said, and there was a slight shift in her tone, and at that instant Nick dove at her to knock her to the ground—

—but Cassie spun, snakelike, off to one side, the speed of a jungle animal, all lithe arms and legs. He slammed against her, knocking the knife out of her hand, but she managed to sidestep him. The knife went clattering across the tile.

She sprang to her feet and held the lighter aloft, displaying it for both men to admire, and she said, "You Conover men. What am I going to do with you?" She made a strange grimace. "I think it's time. We have to go now. A world must come to an end."

A sudden movement from behind Cassie.

Must hold her attention.

"Cassie," Nick said. "Look at me."

Her opaque eyes locked with his.

"I'm not hiding anymore, Cass. Look in my eyes and you can see it. I'm not hiding."

Her face was radiant, flushed and gleaming, more beautiful at that moment than Nick had ever seen her before. She was transfigured. A remarkable serenity had settled over her features as she thumbed the flint wheel.

And something flew out of the background and smashed down upon her head, the white alabaster lamp, and as the stone cracked into her skull,

Cassie crumpled to the floor with an *Unnnnh* sound as the lighter skittered under the refrigerator.

An eerie burbling sound escaped her lips.

Audrey Rhimes's face was streaked with sweat. She looked down at the lamp still in her hand, apparently stunned by what she'd just done.

Nick stared in shock. Mixed with the powerful gas smell he could detect the faint scent of Cassie's patchouli perfume.

"*Run!*" she shouted. "Get out of here *now!*"

"Where's Julia?" Nick said as he started toward the exit.

"She's outside somewhere," Lucas said.

"*Go!*" Audrey screamed. "Anything—the slightest spark—can set this gas off. We've all got to get out of here immediately and let the fire department clear the house. *Now!*"

Lucas vaulted ahead of Nick, crashing against the front screen door before he managed to get it open, then held it open for Audrey and his father.

Julia was standing on the front lawn alongside the driveway, a good distance away.

Nick raced to her, grabbed her and hoisted her up to his shoulder, and kept on running, Lucas and Audrey close behind. They all stopped at the edge of the property just as Nick heard the loud wail of sirens.

"Look!" said Lucas, pointing back toward the house, and Nick immediately saw what he was indicating. It was Cassie, standing unsteadily at the window, watching them, a cigarette dangling out of her mouth.

"*No!*" Nick shouted, but he knew she couldn't hear him and wasn't listening anyway.

There was a blinding flash, and in the next instant, the house erupted in a massive brilliant fireball.

The ground shook, and fire engulfed the house almost instantly, entirely, throwing up a great column of sparks and billowing gray smoke, and seconds later the windows popped and the glass in the French doors shattered as the door frames and the window frames flew into the air, and then the flames began to plume out of every orifice, blackening the stone walls and chimneys, lighting up the clouded sky a terrible orange, and waves of heat came after them, searing their faces as they ran. Julia shrieked, and Nick held her tight, as they all ran down the long driveway.

Nick didn't stop until they had reached the road, when, winded by carrying his daughter, he had to stop. He turned back to look at the house, but all he could see now were the plumes of fire and smoke. The sirens of the fire trucks had gotten no louder, no closer. Nick knew they'd been halted at the security gate.

There would be very little left for the fire department to salvage.

He squeezed Julia harder as he said to Audrey Rhimes, "Before I come in to . . . face charges . . . I'd like to take a little vacation with my kids. Just a few days together. Is that possible, you think?"

Detective Rhimes stared at him. Their eyes locked. Her face was impassive, unreadable.

After what seemed an endless pause, she nodded. "That should be okay."

Nick looked at the blaze for a moment, and then turned to thank her, but she had already started walking down the driveway toward the police car that was just pulling in ahead of a convoy of fire trucks. The blond detective was behind the wheel.

He felt something clutch his elbow, a trembling needy grip, and he saw it was Lucas. Together, dazed and speechless, they watched the inferno for another few minutes. Though the afternoon was overcast and gray, the fire blazed so brightly that it illuminated the sky a dusky orange, the color of sunrise.

EPILOGUE

·

The first couple of days, Nick did little besides sleep. He went to bed early, got up late, took naps on the beach.

Their "villa," as the resort called it, was right on Ka'anapali Beach. You stepped out the door and onto the sand. At night you could hear the lulling sound of the waves lapping against the shore. Lucas, normally the late sleeper, got up early with Julia to swim or snorkel. He even taught her to surf. By the time the kids returned to the bungalow in the late morning, Nick would just be getting up, drinking his coffee on the lanai. They'd all share a meal, a late breakfast or early lunch, and then the kids would go snorkeling at Pu'u Keka'a, a volcanic reef that the ancient Hawaiians revered as a sacred place where the spirits of the dead leaped from this world to the next.

He and the kids talked some, but rarely about anything serious. They'd lost just about all of their earthly possessions, which seemed not to have sunk in yet. It was funny how they never mentioned it.

Several times he tried to bring himself to talk with them about the legal nightmare he'd face when he got home: the likelihood of a trial and the near-certainty of his going to prison. But he couldn't do it, maybe for the same reason nobody wanted to talk about the day the house burned down. He didn't want to spoil what was sure to be their last vacation together for many years.

It was as if they were all surfing, riding the perfect wave, and for the moment it didn't matter that deep in the water beneath them were big, scary creatures with big, sharp teeth. Because the Conovers were up here, in the sun, and they all seemed to know without articulating it that the key to staying afloat was not thinking about what might lurk down below.

So they swam and snorkeled, surfed and ate. Nick fell asleep on the beach too long on the second day and got a painful sunburn on his ears and forehead.

Nick brought no work—he had no work—and he left his cell phone on his bedside table, switched off. He lay on the beach reading and thinking and dozing, wriggling his toes in the powdery gray sand and watching the sun shimmer over the water.

On the third day, he finally turned his cell phone back on, only to find dozens of messages from friends and Stratton colleagues who'd heard or read about what had happened to their house and wanted to make sure Nick and the kids were okay. Nick listened but answered none of them.

One was from his former assistant, Marge Dykstra, who reported that the Fenwick newspaper had run several front-page stories about how Fairfield Equity Partners had been on the verge of selling the Stratton Corporation to China, shutting down all U.S. operations, and laying off all employees— until the deal had been blocked by "ex-CEO Nicholas Conover," who'd just announced his resignation "in order to spend more time with his family."

It was the first good press he, and Stratton, had gotten in a long time. Marge pointed out that it was the first time in almost three years that his name had appeared in a headline without the word "slash" next to it.

On the fourth day, Nick was lying on a lounge chair on the lanai, reading a book about D-day that he'd been trying to read for months and was determined to finish now, when he heard the distant ring tone of his cell phone. He didn't get up.

A minute later, Lucas came out from the bungalow holding the phone and brought it over to him. "It's for you, Dad."

Nick looked up, marked a place in his book with his forefinger, reluctantly took the phone.

"Mr. Conover?"

He recognized the voice immediately, and he felt the old tension clutch his abdomen again. "Detective Rhimes," he said.

"I'm sorry to interrupt your family vacation."

"That's quite all right."

"Mr. Conover, this call is completely off the record, okay?"

"Okay."

"I think you should have your attorney contact the district attorney's office and arrange a plea bargain."

"Excuse me?"

"If you're willing to plead guilty to criminally negligent homicide—or maybe even just attempted tampering with evidence—the DA's willing to recommend probation with no time served."

"*What?* I don't get it."

"I don't imagine you've been reading the *Fenwick Free Press*."

"Delivery out here's kind of spotty."

"Well, Mr. Conover, we both know that the DA is a very political animal—again, this is purely between you and me, you understand?"

"Yes, of course."

"And it seems the climate around here has changed. The news about what you did for your company—well, the DA's just not optimistic that a jury will convict. Then there's the death of one of our chief suspects, Mr. Rinaldi. The district attorney's reluctant to go to trial." She paused. "Hello? Hello?"

"I'm here."

"And—well, there was another article in the paper, this morning. Raising questions about how the police handled the Andrew Stadler case."

"Such as?"

"Oh, I'm sure you know some of it. How nothing was done to stop the stalker at your house or follow up on . . . her. I think it's become obvious that if the police hadn't been so negligent, the situation wouldn't have escalated the way it did. I had to let the DA know that my testimony would inevitably make even more of this negligence public. Which no one in this department wants."

For a long time, Nick was unable to speak. Finally, he said: "I—and how do *you* feel about this?"

"That's not for me to say. You mean, do I feel justice is being served?"

"Something like that, yeah."

"I think we both recognize that the DA's decision to drop most of the charges is motivated by political expedience. But as for justice?" Audrey

Rhimes sighed. "I don't know that there's any justice to be done here, Mr. Conover. I certainly don't think it would serve justice to cause your children to suffer anymore. But that's just my personal opinion."

"Am I allowed to thank you?"

"There's nothing to thank me for, Mr. Conover. I'm just trying to do the right thing." She was silent for a moment. "But maybe there *is* no right thing to do here. Maybe it's not so much a matter of doing the right thing as trying not to do the wrong thing."

Nick set down the cell phone and for a long while watched the sunlight dance on the blue water.

He watched the seagulls caw and swoop, the waves surge and recede, the froth dissolve into the sand.

A few minutes later, Lucas and Julia emerged from the bungalow together and announced that they wanted to go for a hike, explore the nearby tropical forest and waterfalls.

"All right," Nick said, "but listen, Luke—I want you to keep a close watch on your sister."

"Dad, she's almost eleven," Lucas said. His voice seemed to be getting even deeper.

"Dad, I'm not a baby," said Julia.

"I don't want you doing anything crazy like jumping off the waterfalls," Nick said.

"Don't give me any ideas," Lucas said.

"And stay on the trail. It's supposed to be muddy and slippery in some places, so be careful."

"Dad." Lucas rolled his eyes as the two of them started down the palm-lined path. A few seconds later he turned around. "Hey, can you give me twenty bucks?"

"What for?"

"In case we stop to get something to eat on the way."

"All right." Nick pulled a couple of twenties out of his wallet and handed them to Lucas.

He watched them walking away. They were both bronzed already. Julia's curly hair was flying wildly in the breeze. Her legs were lanky, coltish; she was neither a girl nor a woman. Lucas, taller and broader all the time, wore long surfer shorts and a white T-shirt, dazzling in the sun, that was still creased from the suitcase.

As Nick stared after his kids, Lucas suddenly turned around. "Dad?"

"What?"

A gull cawed as it spotted a fish, then dove to the water.

Lucas looked at him for a moment. "You come too."

ACKNOWLEDGMENTS

No, the Stratton Corporation is *not* a thinly disguised fictional version of Steelcase or Herman Miller—as anyone who works there knows. But I'm grateful to several key people at those great companies who understood the difference between fiction and reality and were willing to let me poke around, tour their offices and factories, and ask rude, provocative, and irrelevant-seeming questions. At Steelcase, Inc., in Grand Rapids, Michigan, I was helped immeasurably by Debra Bailey, director of corporate communications, and Jeanine Hill, public relations manager. I've visited a lot of corporations by now, but I've never encountered a PR staff as open and honest and welcoming and just damned *friendly*. Deb Bailey also gave me the consummate insider's tour of Grand Rapids that made me want to move there . . . almost. I was particularly impressed by the president and CEO of Steelcase, Jim Hackett, who was generous with his time and insights into the challenges (personal and professional) of running a major corporation, modernizing it, and getting it through some really tough times. Frank Merlotti Jr., president of Steelcase North America, told me about being a hometown kid who makes it to the top of the biggest company in town. At Herman Miller in Zeeland, Michigan, Bruce Buursma gave me a fascinating introduction to that company's very cool headquarters. Rob Kirkbride of the *Grand Rapids Press* gave me an interesting journalistic perspective on those companies. Unfortunately, in neither place did I meet anyone who remotely resembled Scott McNally.

Most of the CEOs and CFOs I talked to during the research for *Company Man* prefer to remain anonymous. They know who they are, and I thank them for setting aside precious time for this fictional enterprise. My friend Bill Teuber, chief financial officer of the EMC Corporation, contributed in innumerable ways, including explaining what the hell a CFO does. My Yale classmate Scott Schoen, senior managing director of Thomas H. Lee Partners in Boston, kindly took time away from some very high-powered deal-making to help me flesh out the fictional Fairfield Partners and its machinations. No Todd Muldaurs there either, by the way.

Once again, my old buddy Giles McNamee, managing director of McNamee Lawrence & Co., was a key unindicted coconspirator in devising creatively evil financial plots; I appreciate his complicity and generosity. Mike Bingle of Silver Lake Partners was an immense help in solving all sorts of tricky plot problems. (Thanks to Roger McNamee of Elevation Partners for introducing us.) Nell Minow, founder of the Corporate Library, clarified how corporate boards of directors work (or don't).

Many thanks to my corporate security experts, none of whom bore any resemblance to Eddie Rinaldi, including George Campbell, former chief security officer at Fidelity Investments; and the brilliant Jon Chorey, chief engineer, Fidelity Security Services, Inc. Bob McCarthy of Dedicated Micros illuminated the intricacies of digital video surveillance systems, as did Jason Lefort of Skyway Security, and particularly Tom Brigham of Brigham Scully. Thanks, too, to Rick Boucher of Seaside Alarms in South Yarmouth, Massachusetts. Skip Brandon, formerly deputy assistant director of the FBI and founding partner of the international security consulting firm Smith Brandon—a valued source, and friend, since *The Zero Hour*—provided some intriguing background on money laundering and shell corporations. And again, the attorney Jay Shapiro, of Katten Muchin Zavis Rosenman, was my main man on criminal law. If I got in trouble like Nick, I'd hire Jay in a second.

Even an ordinary homicide investigation can be complicated, but in trying to make Audrey Rhimes's job as hard as possible, I surely drove my two homicide experts half-crazy. My deepest thanks to Dean Garrison of the Grand Rapids Police Department's Forensic Services Unit—writer, firearms specialist, and mordantly funny observer of the foibles of police work—and

Detective Kenneth Kooistra, legendary homicide investigator recently retired from the GRPD Major Case Unit, whose war stories are spellbinding and whose generosity was boundless. Trooper Ryan Larrison, firearms examiner with the Michigan State Police, patiently took me through the intricacies of the Integrated Bullet Identification System. I thank, also, Gene Gietzen of Forensic Consulting in Springfield, Missouri; George Schiro of Acadiana Criminalistics Laboratory in New Iberia, Louisiana; Sergeant Kathy Murphy of the Cambridge Police Department; and Detective Lisa Holmes of the Boston Police Department. Stanton Kessler, M.D., was again my chief source on autopsy procedures and pathology. Mike Hanzlick was quite instructive on the perils of natural gas.

It's been a while since I've been a sixteen-year-old—I seem to have repressed all memories—so when it came to Lucas, I was fortunate to draw upon the trenchant observations of Eric Beam and Stefan Pappius-Lefebvre, who are both charismatic and articulate (though, alas, nowhere *near* as angry and alienated as I wanted them to be, for my purposes). Nick's family life, and particularly his relationship with Luke, owes much to Michael Gurian, therapist and bestselling author of *The Wonder of Boys*.

On the esoterica of fly-fishing, my friend Allen Smith was a great source; on hockey, I'm indebted to Steve Counihan, tennis pro and hockey star. Thanks again to my gifted researcher on this and several other of my books, Kevin Biehl, and to my wonderful former assistant, Rachel Pomerantz. And to a few good friends for chipping in, too: Joe Teig and Rick Weissbourd. My brother Dr. Jonathan Finder, contributed medical advice; my younger sister, Lisa Finder, a research librarian at Hunter College, assisted with research; and my older sister, Susan Finder, an attorney in Hong Kong, fact-checked the China stuff. I'm grateful, as always, to my terrific agent, Molly Friedrich, and her assistant, Paul Cirone, of the Aaron Priest Agency for their constant support as well as some very useful editorial contributions.

Now, as to my publisher, St. Martin's Press—man, am I lucky to have joined such an excellent and enthusiastic publishing team, and I thank them all, particularly CEO John Sargent, publisher Sally Richardson, Matthew Shear, John Cunningham, George Witte, Matt Baldacci, Christina Harcar, Nancy Trypuc, Jim DiMiero, Alison Lazarus, Jeff Capshew, Brian Heller, Ken Holland, Andy LeCount, Tom Siino, Rob Renzler, John Murphy,

Gregg Sullivan, Peter Nasaw, Steve Eichinger, and at Audio Renaissance, Mary Beth Roche, Joe McNeely, and Laura Wilson.

And to my amazing editor, Keith Kahla—well, you're the best.

My daughter, Emma, was my chief source on the lives of ten-year-old girls, from baseball to The Sims. In the frenzied last months of my work on *Company Man*, she had to suffer my long absences; but she cheerfully brought lemonade down the hill to my writing studio in Truro and always kept my spirits up. She and my wife, Michele Souda, were my great sources of support during the writing of this book.

And once again I thank, above all, my brother Henry Finder, editorial director at *The New Yorker*: perpetual-motion idea generator, tireless brainstormer, peerless editor of first and last resort. I could not have done it without you.